Iris & Lily
Book One

Angela & Julie Scipioni

ACKNOWLEDGMENTS

Cover art by Pietro Spica
Used with permission
www.pietrospica.it

Lyrics from
"Lift Me Up," "The Path," and "Halfway Round the Moon"
© Rick McKown
Used with permission
www.RickMcKown.com

Iris & Lily: Book One is the first in a three-volume series.

To all our sisters, wherever they may be,
and to the little girls who live on in their memories

Book One

From: Iris Capotosti <iris.capotosti@gmail.com>
To: Lily Capotosti <lilycapotosti@gmail.com>
Sent: Sat, December 12, 2009 9:31 AM
Subject: Windows

Hi, Lily!

I hope all is well with you. This time of year is pretty crazy for me with all the reports that have to go out before the holidays, but I've been promising myself I'd take a break and get caught up with my emails, so here I am!

It's hard to believe Christmas is only two weeks away, with no snow (or shopping lists!) to remind me. All I can see from my window is a bright sun in a cloudless blue sky, and a green hillside spattered with olive trees. A far cry from the snowy scenes framed by the winter windows of our childhood, isn't it? Remember getting up on those freezing cold mornings, and hurrying to scratch our names on the frosty panes before the boys could? And the way those ice crystals glittered like diamonds in the sun?

We did have an olive tree of sorts outside one of those windows, though. Remember that Russian olive Mom planted by the lilac bushes, right in front of the kitchen window? Whenever I tackled a stack of dirty dishes, I would stare out at that tree and daydream as I plopped plate after plate into the tired suds. I didn't know it wasn't really an olive tree, but that didn't matter. What mattered was that its branches were full of birds, and its name exotic enough to spark fantasies of faraway places. Mom was always pretty enigmatic, but I like to think that tree was her way of letting us know there was another world out there, beyond the realm of the kitchen sink. Then again, maybe she just liked having a tree to look at when she washed the dishes. And maybe it inspired her daydreams, too.

1

Sometimes I wish I could look out my window and see that Russian olive again, and just for a moment, find myself standing at that kitchen sink. I'd like to take a look around, and see whether I may have left anything behind. Do you ever get that feeling? Like when you're all ready to go out, and your hand is on the doorknob, but some vague feeling of having forgotten something prevents you from shutting the door?

I might peek upstairs, too, and steal one more look at that bed we shared for so many years. I'm pretty sure I would be able to hear the hushed voices of two little girls huddled in the dark. Do you remember those fairy stories we used to spin as we drifted off to sleep? All I remember about them is that Iris and Lily were always quite beautiful, and very well-loved. Sometimes I find myself wishing we had written them down.

Listen to me ramble on, would you? I guess that's just Christmas, making me a little homesick for the old days. Enough about me, though. What are you up to?

Love,
Iris

Dear Iris:

All you need to do is say the words "Russian Olive" and I'm there, standing in front of the sink, washing dishes, or soaking a totally frozen hunk of ground beef in hot water, trying to thaw it in time to make meatloaf for dinner. (God help the child who forgets to take the meat out of the freezer before going to school.)

We were a study in incongruence, weren't we? Little girls playing house for real. Poor, but cultured. Unconsciously beautiful - even though we had holes in our socks and underwear and often washed our hair with dishwashing detergent. I don't even remember washing my face in the mornings. I only remember sitting over the heating grate, with my knees pulled to my chest, and my nightie pulled all the way over them, down to my feet, creating a little tent of warmth, just for me. And bobbing puffed rice cereal in a bowl of milk with my spoon. They never put any prizes in a bag of puffed rice. It was just cereal, totally utilitarian.

But you know, you're making me crazy with your talk about bright sun and blue sky. Being stuck here in middle-of-nowhere, Wisconsin - in a blizzard no less - is about as far away as I can be from you and your Mediterranean bliss.

All I can see is white and barren and people scurrying about, clutching their parka hoods tightly to their collars. Maybe that's the fundamental difference between us – the mere idea of snow and ice makes me feel desolate, while it inspires you to wax sentimental about our childhood.
I suppose the worst part about the way we grew up was that it created the sense that things – good or bad - just happened randomly, and

there was nothing we could do about it. (Or maybe that's just the worst thing I am brave enough to talk about.)

To this day, one of the most challenging questions anyone can ever ask me is, "What do you want?" Damned if I know. But not this. Not to be stuck on this tundra with a boss who is always overcompensating for his small penis (don't ask me how I know *that*) and a colleague who would push me under a bus for a corporate pat on the head. In this snow that just won't stop.

Funny that you remember the icy window panes and I remember the stifling summer heat, with the sound of the night train crossing Coldwater Road. And "Dream Weaver" playing on the radio. And the rickety old fan we had would sweep the room, blessing each of us with a touch of breeze in turn, and it would hum, and the train would wail, and the radio would play, and your voice would trail off as you drifted to sleep, telling me unfinished stories of fairies who would come and bring magic into my life.

The only thing I remember about those little fairies was that they soothed me enough to help me fall asleep, despite my childhood woes. I wonder how they would fare against the grown up monsters I entertain?

They've just finished deicing. Looks like it's time to board. I'll scratch your name into the window pane somewhere over Lake Michigan.

Love,
Lily

From: Iris Capotosti <iris.capotosti@gmail.com>
To: Lily Capotosti <lilycapotosti@gmail.com>
Sent: Sun, December 13, 2009 9:47 AM
Subject: Fairy tales

Dear Lily,

I hope you had a safe trip home. I couldn't stop thinking about you after I got your email, and you were still on my mind when I went to bed last night. You really sounded like you could use another one of those fairy stories, and before I knew it, I was whispering to you in the dark, just like when we were small. Except instead of lying in bed next to me, you were sitting in a plane.

I started out by describing the host of sparkling fairies pirouetting joyfully in the swirling snow of Wisconsin, and how with a grand jeté, they soared into the sky alongside you as your plane took off. And how as you flew east, they cradled the plane in their arms to keep you safe, and hushed the wind so your journey would be smooth. A simple gesture of a graceful hand was all it took for them to part the clouds, so that you might admire the infinite blue sky above you, and the storybook countryside below, nestled beneath a glittering blanket of freshly fallen snow.

And throughout the entire trip, one very beautiful, very kind fairy with gossamer wings hovered just outside your window. If you looked closely enough, you might have seen her smile in the ice crystals on your window, and you might have seen her loveliness in your own reflection.

Love,
Iris

Hi, Iris:

Finally home, thank God.

Your note from the other day got me thinking about the old days, so I've been lost in thought, too, but not in a way that could be described as reverie. It's more like a haunting.

Thanks for the story, although I have to say that the idea of ballet-dancing fairies that used to seem so comforting when we were children now seems ridiculous and even a bit cruel. Back then, I was innocent (or should I say ignorant) enough to believe that it might really happen, that a benevolent magical force might surround me, scoop me up, deliver me from the helplessness I felt during most of my childhood. Though I am no longer a child, I can't say that I feel that much less helpless. Only now, it's worse because I'm old enough to know that there's no such thing as magic.

It might have been better if we hadn't found a way to escape into our imaginations back then. Seems that all we accomplished was to delay the inevitable: that we would eventually have to face the reality of what our life was. Trying to escape now seems at least as ill advised. It would make more sense to me not to try and slip away from the truth but rather chase it down, subdue it, wrest it until it yields that forgotten something that lingers in the back of our minds (yes, I feel it too). If we could go back there and find that thing, could we put it in our pockets and bring it back here with us? Would it change anything at all?

I suppose the only way to find what you've forgotten is to recognize what you've remembered. Then, like a jigsaw puzzle, you would at least see the shape and color of the missing pieces so you could begin to look for them in the scattered pile of images, thoughts, and feelings.

What else do you remember, Iris?

Love,
Lily

1. IRIS

Dawn broke, streaking the sky over Rugby Road with innocent pinks and optimistic reds, soon to be gobbled up by the prevailing overtones of grey. Iris slid down from her bunk above Lily's and wriggled out of the flannel nightgown Auntie Rosa had given her the previous Christmas, anxious for the new day to begin. Grabbing the garb she had piled in a neat heap at the foot of her bed, she slipped into her clothes in exactly the opposite order of how she had slipped out of them the night before. Socks were the last to come off and the first to go on, as she hopped between the bed and the chilly linoleum floor; next came the thin cotton undershirt she tucked into the frayed waistband of her panties (those she kept on at night); finally, there were the pants and pullover that had paused upon one growing girl's body after another before coming to rest temporarily on her own.

Iris was never as happy to climb into bed as she was to rise to a new day. The night was dark, and she couldn't even see Lily in the bunk below her, and if she tried to talk to her, their other sisters would tell her to shut up. The only thing good about sleeping was that you couldn't do it wrong (except if you had an accident), unlike all the other activities she muddled through in a cloud of confusion, fretting over how to please, at best, or how to go unnoticed, at worst. Being noticed was never good, because that only happened if you made Trouble. The Big Kids, especially the Big Boys, were always making Trouble. As Number Eight in the Capotosti sibling hierarchy, following two boys, three girls then two more boys who were also twins, but not the kind that looked or even acted alike, Iris was considered the oldest of the Little Kids, coming before Lily and the three Little Boys. It was not a role she relished, especially as she began to understand that the Big Kids jealously guarded the privileges that came with age, (and strength) like getting to sit on the sofa instead of the floor when they watched TV, or sitting by the window in the station wagon instead of being crammed into the cargo bed (which always made Iris puke), yet they were pretty clever when it came to shirking any duties that might be borne by those too young or weak to rebel. One time, Iris had made the mistake of telling Marguerite she was bored. Marguerite, who was the youngest of the Big Kids, had taken Iris by the hand, led her to the dining room, and introduced her to the towering pile of laundered diapers on the table waiting to be folded. Marguerite was supposed to be helping Violet, who was two sisters and two brothers older than Iris. Instead, Marguerite set about teaching Iris how to fold, and Iris tried really hard to line up the corners just right, and she must have succeeded, because Violet patted her on the head and said she was a really fast learner and was doing such a good job that she could take over. Iris smiled proudly as she concentrated on smoothing and folding the soft fabric into neat rectangles, while Marguerite and Violet sneaked down to the basement to listen to one of Alexander's LPs. Lily soon came looking for Iris, who had in turn tried to teach her how to fold, but Lily was either too little to learn, or just plain didn't want to, and giggled as she dashed away with a diaper on her head. That had been the last time Iris complained of being bored.

After dressing, Iris peered out the window of the upstairs bedroom of which she occupied a corner. Yawning, she ground her fists into bleary eyes, then picked at the crusts of sleep that clung to her lashes. She vaguely recalled the reassuring feeling of someone passing by to tuck her in as she drifted off to sleep the night before. Had it been her father? Probably not. She couldn't remember smelling that cologne he wore, or feeling his bristles scratch her cheek. Maybe it had been her mother, or her oldest sister Jasmine; they were the only ones besides Auntie Rosa who knew Iris loved her sheets tucked in so tightly she could barely move her legs. It made her feel so warm and safe, and helped melt away the goosebumps she got while reciting the bedtime prayer that reminded her she might fall asleep, never to wake again.

Now I lay me down to sleep,
I pray to God my soul to keep.
And if I die before I wake,
I pray to God my soul to take.
Please bless Mommy and Daddy,
Auntie Rosa and Uncle Alfred,
Alexander and John,
Jasmine and Violet and Marguerite,
Louis and Henry,
Me and Lily,
and William and Charles and Richard

...and all the cats and dogs, gerbils and rabbits and living creatures encompassed in her sphere of affection, and of course Grandma Whitacre, who lived far away, and Grandma and Grandpa Capotosti, who lived near but were old and crippled and really needed it. To think that God could whisk away the souls of any or all of them, even Lily's, while Iris lay sleeping on her pancake mattress always made her shiver with loneliness.

It was remarkable that Iris could ever feel alone in that crowded bedroom, as she waited for dreams to come and quell her fears. The air in the room pulsed with the sounds and smells of youth and humanity: the coughing and sneezing, the giggling and farting, the clanging of the puke pan as it was passed from one moaning sibling to another if a bug was going around, the jumble of odors emanating from the communal body of childhood in constant metamorphosis. Yet she did feel alone. Lots of times.

Golden brown locks bounced behind Iris as she skipped down the sidewalk; her hair flowed long and wild, unrestrained by the little-girl hairdos that crowned the prim heads of her classmates at

St. Augustine's grammar school. Pigtails and ponytails, braids and bows required time and attention, precious commodities in the economics of morning minutes in the Capotosti household, where chaos reigned over the routine of feeding, clothing, and consigning to parochial school a squad of squirming subjects by eight o'clock sharp. By the end of the school day, Iris's triangular face was framed by tangled tresses that looked as frazzled as she was from the effort of following the lessons imparted by the dour nun who commanded her classroom. Iris fancied her hair was endowed with special powers, like the trigger hairs of the Venus flytrap her mother had shown her in the encyclopedia. She imagined her locks sensing and rejecting the things that were distasteful or useless, while gobbling up everything that would nourish her, and breaking it down for transmission straight to the brain. Iris felt a peculiar attachment to her hair, and was constantly being reprimanded for twirling her locks between her fingers, and stuffing them in her mouth. Earlier, absorbed in a reading exercise, she had unconsciously slipped a strand between her lips and curled her tongue around it. There was something about the way the sucking and gnawing engaged the tip of her tongue and her teeth that seemed to help her concentrate, overcome her shyness, and placate her fear of making mistakes. Squinting at the words on the page while chewing on the hair in her mouth, a sense of serenity had settled over her, only to be shattered moments later.

"Young lady!" Sister Josephine had scolded, towering over her, tall and straight as a tree – no, more like a telephone pole; she was not nearly as shapely or friendly as a tree. Iris had felt her cheeks burn with embarrassment, and she felt the flush rising again as she recalled how the other twenty-three pairs of eyes in the classroom had turned on her at once, as Sister Josephine continued. "Do you know what happens to little girls who chew on their hair? Do you?" The nun went on to predict a grim future for Iris if she could not overcome her habit; a painful and premature demise would be her lot, owing to the massive hair balls that were at that moment growing and festering in her belly, clogging her gut, strangling her stomach, entangling her bowels. "And pay attention when I speak to you. You look like you're a thousand miles away."

Iris couldn't help that look in her eyes any more than she could help her habit. Each time Sister Josephine reprimanded her, she was both mortified and terrified, yet as soon as she got distracted, the hair somehow wound up back in her mouth again. One positive effect of Sister's tirades was that Iris started spitting out her gum instead of swallowing it when she entered the classroom, because she feared it would make the hairball problem even more fatal. The gum she chewed never tasted very good anyway, since it came from the neighborhood driveways and sidewalks Iris scoured on her way to and from school in search of the more appealing wads that had not yet been flattened by tires, and didn't have too much grit ground into them.

As she loped back home down Rugby Road, with a fresh pink wad of used gum in her mouth (scraped off the driveway of that weird family with only one little girl named Rosemary whose parents probably bought her all the new Bazooka bubblegum she wanted), the unpleasant episode of Sister Josephine was soon behind her. Her bottled-up energy bubbled to the surface, yearning for release after the constraints of the classroom. Long, lean legs sent her pinafore flapping as she ran, her gait slowing only when her knee socks dropped to her ankles, and she stopped to roll back into place the rubber bands that held them up. As she bent over her knobby knees, she admired the fresh set of scabs, her trophies from yesterday's bicycle practice, when her brother John, running behind her, had released his grip on the fender, and sent her off solo, for the first time without training wheels. Thrilled and terrified at her own audacity, she had careened down the road in daring spurts, slamming into the trunks of the oaks and elms that jumped out from between the modest homes on the modest city street. Somehow she never saw the trees until it was too late, and hurting them made Iris feel worse than hurting herself, until she remembered that the trees were not as innocent as they looked. They played tricks on her all the time, with those gnarled roots that burst through the sidewalks to trip her whenever she played hopscotch.

Iris always watched for cracks when she ran, but sometimes she didn't see those, either, though she heard over and over again in her mind the warning of every little girl who played sidewalk games: "Step on a crack, break your mother's back!" Iris visualized her quiet, fair-skinned mother, doling out Spanish rice to her brood from a cracked ceramic platter while jostling a cranky infant on her hip. She thought of the graceful way her mother tossed her head to rearrange her auburn tresses when they fell in front of her clear blue eyes. The thought of breaking her back made Iris so sick to her stomach she thought she would puke. Or maybe it was the balls of hair. Iris slowed to a walk, and breathed a sigh of relief when she reached the Capotosti driveway, remembering to spit out the gum before Lily could ask her if she could have some.

2. LILY

"Step on a crack, break your mother's back."

Lily considered the path before her. The neglected sidewalk was riddled with cracks and holes, punctuated by an occasional old maple tree root, threatening to erupt through the concrete and fulfill its destiny of wreaking havoc on skaters, bicyclists, and children trying to get to school without rendering their mothers crippled.

"I don't want to play that," said Lily.

"It's not really real," said Mary Beth. "It's just pretend."

But all Lily could think about was coming home from school at lunchtime to find her mother in the basement doing laundry, doubled over in pain, back broken. Then there would be no one to make Lily's bologna sandwich with mayonnaise or take care of the babies, or cook her father's coffee tonight.

Auntie Rosa would come over with her white stockings and her shot needle and she would say, "Betty – what in heaven's name happened to you?" and Auntie Rosa would take Lily's mother back to the clinic and Dr. Johnson would put one of those big Popsicle sticks in her mouth and then bang on her knee with his hammer. Then, they would make her stand in front of that big machine and take pictures of her insides and they would all gasp and cover their mouths and Auntie Rosa's bottom lip would start to tremble a little and they would all see that Lily's mother's back was all broken– it would look like that wishbone on Thanksgiving after Jasmine and John pulled on it. Then Dr. Johnson would say, "Betty, your back is broke; did you fall down the stairs or something?" and Lily's mother would say, "Why no – I was just in the basement waiting for Lily to get home from school so I could make her bologna sandwich with mayonnaise, and I suddenly fell over and I haven't been able to get up again since."

Then Dr. Johnson would turn to look at Lily and then Auntie Rosa would turn to look at Lily, and then finally, Lily's mother would turn and they would all know that it was because Lily stepped on a sidewalk crack and now Lily's mother would have to walk around bent over all the time and Auntie Rosa would yelp like she does when someone is apprehended on TV. And probably on the way out of the clinic, Kay at the front desk wouldn't even give Lily a butterscotch hard candy, and the babies would cry all the time and Lily's father wouldn't have his coffee and it would be all Lily's fault.

"Well, I say we play," said Mary Beth, skipping ahead. She chanted her mantra of doom and torture, stepping on almost all of the cracks, with no thought at all to the pain and misery she could be causing. It seemed to Lily if she were going to play such a game, she should at least do so with some level of compassion and care.

Lily and Mary Beth lived four houses apart on Rugby Road. Lily's house was loud and messy, but Mary Beth's house was magical. It had a 7 and a 2 on it and it was green on the bottom and white on the top. Every morning in the summer Lily would skip down to Mary Beth's, stand outside the side door, and call, "Ma-ry Be-e-e-eth!"

If Mary Beth could play, she would soon appear at the door and let Lily inside where all sorts of pleasures awaited. There were Fluffernutter sandwiches, and Big Shot chocolate syrup for their milk, and an endless supply of Beefaroni. Lunch at Mary Beth's was better than going to a birthday party with cake.

Once, Mrs. Barone - Mary Beth's mother - took Lily down into the basement with her and off in the corner was a shelf that was bigger even than Mrs. Barone was. There was a curtain hanging there so you couldn't see what was on the shelf. Mrs. Barone pulled the curtain back and there were hundreds of cans of Beefaroni – probably more than they have at the store – or even at President Kennedy's old house. It wasn't likely that the Barones ever ran out of food.

One of the strangest things about Mary Beth's house was that there were no brothers or sisters, so Mr. Barone used to play with them all the time. He taught them how to skip down the driveway, how to ride a two-wheeler with training wheels, and how to swing upside down on the monkey bars – which were right in the backyard. Lily tried to imagine her own father skipping rope or roller skating, but she just couldn't see it. No matter how tightly she closed her eyes, all she could see was her father stepping off the city bus in his brown suit or standing at his workbench, bending over to mend the latest broken toaster, fan, or radio. The only things in Lily's backyard were a rusty old chair, a rusty old swing set, Princess's poop, and a bunch of rabbit cages full of rabbits that Lily wasn't allowed to pet unless she was with Jasmine. Anyway, her father definitely did not have time to play. Jeepers Cripes, there was always so much work to do around here.

So mostly, when Lily came over to play, Mary Beth would open the door and they would laugh and eat Beefaroni and drink chocolate milk and skip and play until Lily was summoned home by the *clang-clang!* of the cowbell that her father rang at dinner time. That's how all the children – and the entire neighborhood – knew it was dinnertime at the Capotosti house. And you definitely did not want to be late for dinner.

On some summer mornings, Mary Beth was not allowed to play. Once, Mrs. Barone came to the door and she said to Lily, "I'm afraid Mary Beth can't play today, Lily. She was sassing back and so today as her punishment she is going to stay in her room and think about that."

Lily considered asking whether she might have some Beefaroni or perhaps a Fluffernutter sandwich anyway, but before she could

16

get her courage up, Mrs. Barone closed the door and that was that.

Lily tried to imagine what it would be like to sit in your room all afternoon, thinking about sassing back, and wondered why it was punishment. Thinking doesn't even hurt.

Beginning on the first Wednesday in September, Mary Beth had come to Lily's house every morning and they walked together, sometimes ahead of Lily's brothers and sisters and sometimes behind them. As they'd headed down the street, doors would fly open and children would pour out in groups of fours and fives, all headed for St. Augustine's school. The Smiths, Dr. Schwartz's family, the Silipinis, the Farruggias, the Cullens, and Bobby Rose, the only colored boy on the block.

But this morning, Lily stood paralyzed. If she didn't agree to play, maybe Mary Beth wouldn't answer the door the next time she went over. Torn between a desire to protect her mother and an unending appetite for Fluffernutter, Lily crossed herself InthenameofaFatherandofaSonandofaHolyGhostAmen, and silently asked God to help her not step on any cracks. Lily approached the task with the balance and agility developed over a long summer of playing hopscotch. She quickly caught up to Mary Beth again, proud of her poise, and relieved at having avoided all cracks.

"I made it!" Lily cried out. "I didn't step on any."

Mary Beth looked at Lily, looked down at the ground, and then with a giggle, she gave Lily a swift and definitive nudge, causing her to lose her balance, landing her foot directly over an unmistakable crack in the concrete.

"No fair!" shouted Lily, and in her rage, she gave Mary Beth a shove, sending her against a chain link fence with such force that she bounced off and landed face down on the ground.

"Lily Capotosti!"

Lily turned to find Mrs. Linden marching toward her, waving the Stop sign paddle that she used to halt traffic so the children could cross the street. She helped a now sobbing Mary Beth to her feet, brushed the dirt from her knees, and kissed her forehead. She then turned to Lily, and leaned in so close that Lily could see the tiny holes in the shiny skin of her nose. Lily wondered if there were any bugs small enough to fit inside there and what it would feel like to have a teeny tiny bug curled up inside one of the holes in your skin. It would probably tickle a bit. The thought made Lily giggle.

"Young lady, what is so funny? Do you know the rules for safety on the way to school? Can you tell me what they are?"

"No running?" said Lily, trying unsuccessfully to squelch a grin. She knew she was supposed to take the questioning seriously, but all she could think about was the little bug. She would call him Jack, like that exercise man on television.

"And what else?"

"No pushing, no shoving, and no crossing the street without a crossing guard." Lily quickly added, "But she pushed me first."

Self-defense was one of the few arguments that had any effectiveness when attempting to escape The Belt at home. Hurting others was never allowed, but if someone was beating you up, or pounding on you, no one expected you to sit there and take it.

Mrs. Linden was the one who didn't seem to understand the rules. "It's OK, sweetheart," she said, taking Mary Beth's hand. With her other hand, she grabbed Lily's left upper arm.

"Wait until your mother hears about this," said Mrs. Linden. "Pushing your little friend, making her cry and then laughing about it."

Lily considered explaining to Mrs. Linden that she wasn't laughing at Mary Beth, but then she would have to explain about Jack the bug and how she imagined him all curled up inside one of the holes on Mrs. Linden's nose, and Lily was pretty sure that would just get her into more trouble than she was already in.

"Now come along, both of you. The bell is about to ring."

Lily imagined her mother at home, hobbling up to answer the door when Mrs. Linden knocked.

"Why hello, Irma," her mother would say.

"I'm afraid I have some bad news, Betty," Mrs. Linden would say. "Your daughter Lily was apprehended shoving a classmate on the sidewalk today, which – as you know – is breaking the rules. I'm sorry to say that your daughter Lily is a rule-breaker."

Lily's mother would look up at Mrs. Linden, unable to stand up straight - because of the broken back - and she would say, "I know Irma, I know – just look at me. We don't know what we're going to do about her. She's definitely a rule breaker."

As Lily and Mary Beth entered the school, the bell rang and the children all scurried to take their places on the red carpet for circle time.

Miss Swift stood before them and said, "Now class, you are no longer babies in nursery school – you are all big boys and girls, and it's time for you to begin taking care of yourselves and behaving as young ladies and gentlemen."

Miss Swift continued. "First, by the end of the week, I want each of you to demonstrate to me that you can tie your own shoes." This made Lily smile. They had been practicing tying in class all week, and every night, Lily would tie her shoes and untie them over and over again, even putting them on in bed and running the drill until she fell fast asleep.

"Second," continued Miss Swift, "when you need to use the bathroom, please raise your hand, and when I call upon you, you say, 'May I please use the lavatory?' Once I grant you permission to do so, you may proceed to the lavatory in an orderly fashion."

Anxious to get started with this business of arriving home with a gold star on her forehead, Lily mentally practiced her line: *May I use the labatory? May I please use the labatory?* even though it seemed quite ridiculous to ask permission to do something that you didn't really have a choice about. And in the back of her mind, Lily worried about what might happen if she should ask permission, and if Miss Swift should say "no."

"No, Lily – you may not use the labatory. You may sit there and you may think about how you broke your poor mother's back on the way to school today."

Lily shot her right hand into the air, but Miss Swift kept talking. Lily wriggled her fingers, reaching her hand as high as she could.

"Third, I want everyone to have a tissue on hand at all times. When ladies and gentlemen have a sniffle, or have the need to cough or sneeze, a handy tissue is quite necessary." Miss Swift then pulled a white tissue out from under the cuff of her pink satin blouse, dabbed delicately at the end of her nose in demonstration, and then tucked it away again. "When you have demonstrated to me that you have mastered each task, you will receive a shiny gold star on your forehead, so that everyone knows that you are well on your way to becoming a fine young lady or gentleman."

It occurred to Lily that they didn't use tissues at her house. If they needed to blow their noses, they used toilet paper. What would she do? She wondered if Mrs. Barone had any tissues behind a curtain in the basement.

With a sigh of irritation, Miss Swift finally turned to Lily and said, "Miss Capotosti, when an adult is speaking it is quite rude to thrust one's hand into the air, and wave it about like a confederate flag of surrender. What is it that is so urgent that you felt it was necessary to interrupt?"

But by then, Lily was worried about the tissue, completely forgot all about the proper phrasing, and in a moment of panic, she blurted out, "I have to go pee-pee."

The other children burst into laughter, and realizing her *faux pas*, Lily slowly lowered her hand, feeling the cool rush of blood back into her arm and the warm flush of it into her face.

"Miss Capotosti, you have disrupted this class, which is something I will not tolerate. You may go into the cloakroom, and stand quietly until I give further notice. The rest of you, please take your seats."

It was late summer – the time of year when it was cool enough to wear pajamas to bed, but not so cool as to need a coat during the day. Except for Lily and her shame, the cloakroom was empty. The space itself was nothing more than a wall with hooks on it, separated from the rest of the room by a stationary room screen that was open by about two feet at the top and at the bottom. The side that faced the inside of the cloakroom was of rough

20

unfinished particleboard. The side of the screen that faced the classroom was a chalkboard. From where she stood in the cloakroom, Lily could see the feet of the desks and chairs in the classroom, as well as those of the children who sat at them. She could see Miss Swift's feet moving about the room, and when she wrote on the chalkboard, the whole wall would shake – especially when she dotted her "i"s or crossed her "t"s.

After counting the hooks on the wall (Lily counted twelve of them, two times), there wasn't much else to do. All she wanted was that gold star. Then she could go home and show everyone how lovely she was, what a fine young lady or gentleman she was becoming. And then her mother and Auntie Rosa and her father and Uncle Alfred would hug her and kiss her and maybe Auntie Rosa would even let her play with the bric-a-brac on the shelf in the back room where Lily was never allowed to go alone. After all, children with gold stars don't break fine things. They know how to be quiet and gentle like Iris. In fact, she could be quiet and gentle, starting right now. And she could prove it. She would stand still, and not make a fuss, and Miss Swift would see that she is a fine young lady who knows her place and doesn't cry or whine too much.

So Lily stood in the cloakroom, watching feet. Miss Swift's were easy to spot because they were the largest. And those over there in the back must be Patrick Cullen's – he never ties his shoes. Probably doesn't even know how. Mary Beth's were easy, too, since Lily saw them every day. And those shiny black shoes must be Tricia Cortellini's because she always has fancy white socks with the lace and the little pink bows. Now there's a lady.

Having flubbed her lavatory lines, and with no proper tissues at home, Lily's best bet was to demonstrate her ability to tie her shoes – it was her only hope now. Until her chance came to get her shoe-tying star, Lily was intent on practicing being still and quiet in the cloakroom. She followed along with the class by participating in the lessons in her head. They recited the days of the week, counted past twenty and practiced printing the letters of their names. Since Lily had no paper or pencil, she scratched her letters into the particleboard with her fingernail. Lily could already print all the letters of her first name. She was glad it was so simple – just mostly a bunch of straight lines. She guessed that if she was sitting out there with the other children, she might very well be the only one who could do it – surely Alexandria Hawthorne wouldn't have such an easy time of it, what with all of those loops and everything. After scratching L-i-l-y into the board a few times, it occurred to her that you could scratch at the wall and draw on it - almost like an Etch-a-Sketch - except you couldn't erase it. What would happen when Miss Swift found those letters there? She surely would not give Lily a gold star for learning to print her name, even though she had mastered the task. And there would be no way to claim self-defense, or to deny having done it. She would surely be apprehended.

Her fear of future shame was overcome by a more pressing and immediate problem – after standing in the corner all during letters and writing, Lily really did need to go to the bathroom. But there was no way to ask proper permission without leaving the cloakroom before further notice was given, or without speaking out of turn.

Just then, Miss Swift clapped her hands twice with such force, that it startled Lily, and a little bit of pee came out before she could clutch herself and stop the flow.

"OK class, one by one, I want each of you to first visit the lavatory, and then come back to your desks and tidy up before going home."

Lily watched as each set of shoes disappeared out into the hallway. Tricia Cortellini's shoes tapped against the tile, like one of those dancers on *The Lawrence Welk Show*, and the ends of Patrick Cullen's shoe laces whipped from side to side, hitting the floor with a *click-click*. Once the last of the children returned from the lavatory, Lily was certain that Miss Swift would come and give her further notice, but she didn't. Lily stood still and quiet as the children collected their pencils, discarded their scraps, and finally joined in the closing prayer.

IntheNameoftheFatherandoftheSonandoftheHolyGhostamen
God in heaven hear my prayer,
Keep me in thy loving care.
Be my guide in all I do,
Bless all those who love me too.
IntheNameoftheFatherandoftheSonandoftheHolyGhostamen

Shoe by shoe, the other children filed out of the classroom. Surely interrupting the class was not so bad as to not be allowed to go home, was it? Lily imagined her father ringing the bell for dinner. All of her brothers and sisters would come running home from every direction, the side door swinging open and banging closed again and again, her father shouting, "Jeepers Cripes! Don't let the door slam!" The boys would just laugh and the girls would try to stay out of the way, and they would all take their places at the dinner table. Then Lily's father would count, just as he does every night.

"One, two, three," and so on. Then he would say, "Wait a minute – is someone missing?" he would ask, and then he would look around the table and point and call out each name – and finally Iris would shout out, "It's Lily! Lily is missing!"

Then they would look all over the house for her – up in the girl's bedroom, in the boy's bedroom, maybe even up in the attic where Alexander and John sleep. They would look in the linen closet, thinking she was in there playing pretend, but they wouldn't be able to find her. Finally, her mother would start to cry, and she would call out, "I don't care if Lily did break my back – I want my baby to come home!" and Iris would go get her some toilet paper to blow her nose, and she would say, "Now I wish I would have bought some tissues so Lily could get her gold star."

Just the image of seeing her mother so sad, and of her brothers and sisters frantically running about the house looking for her made Lily's eyes well up with tears, and her body lurched with the force of a squelched cry, at which time she lost control of her bladder, and stood crying as the warm fluid ran down her legs, soaking her tights, and collecting as small puddles in her shoes.

"Who's there?" called out Miss Swift.

Lily watched as the large shoes moved closer. When Miss Swift appeared in the cloakroom, she gasped and covered her mouth with her hand; Lily was amazed to see a grownup with such a look on her face.

"Lily," she said, walking over to Lily. There was softness and sweetness in her voice that Lily had never before heard. "I am so sorry… you were so quiet, I forgot you were in here. Why didn't you say something?"

The tenderness in her voice broke Lily's resolve and she burst into tears.

"I was standing quietly until further notice," said Lily, forcing each word out in between sharp breaths. "Can I please go home now?"

"Are you alright? Are you allowed to walk home alone?" said Miss Swift. She seemed unaware of Lily's accident, and Lily hoped to get out of there before she noticed.

"I'm fine. I just want to go home, OK?" Lily pleaded.

"Of course, dear, of course."

Lily ran from the cloakroom, bolted down the hallway, the urine squishing in her shoes with every step. Out the door she ran, down Chili Avenue, past the bakery where they sell half-moon cookies, past Case's Diner, past the big house on the corner with all the flat stones across the front of it. When she turned the corner, she ran smack-dab into Bobby Rose, who caught her by the shoulders, and said, "Slow down, little cracker! Watch where you're going!"

But Lily didn't stop. She didn't slow down, she didn't pay any attention to the cracks in the sidewalk or to the fact that she just touched a colored boy. She spotted the front porch of her house peeking out from behind the profiles of the ones before it, and as she cut across the front lawn and threw the side door open, all she cared about was that was she home, a place where she could be loud and stick up for herself – a place where at least she understood the rules, and could tolerate the punishments.

3. IRIS

Iris's eyes popped open. It was Saturday! Not that she really minded school. In fact, she rather liked the structure and discipline of the classroom, and could have done with a bit more of both in the chaotic Capotosti household, where she relied upon her own internal set of rules to bring a measure of order to her life. Iris always rose with a smile on her face, got dressed and ate her cereal without anyone prompting her, relishing the clean, unblemished feeling of a new day before her as she set off for school. She enjoyed the walk, listening to the chitchat of her other siblings as she tagged along, stopping occasionally to check out the best driveways for freshly spit-out wads of gum. However, just minutes after arriving at school, her enthusiasm was flattened by the monotonous sound of Sister Josephine's voice hammering the class with Morning Prayers and the Pledge of Allegiance.

Instead of filling her with inspiration to pursue the ideals of the church and country into which she had been born, the morning ritual made Iris feel trapped in a system from which she sensed there would be no escape for many years to come. By the time the words, "with liberty and justice for all," left her lips, and her right hand dropped from its place over her heart, Iris felt the same stabbing awareness that each day spent in that classroom was one day less she could devote to something else. She saw her days as blocks of time, like bricks. They might pave the way to someplace magical, like the yellow brick road of *The Wizard of Oz*, or block her vision of what lay beyond, if they were stacked really high like the wall that penned in the school playground. When Sister Josephine taught them about free will in Catechism, Iris was struck by the sinking sensation that no matter how she decided to lay her bricks, she might find a wall obstructing her road, and there would be nothing she could do about it. The notion that God was all-powerful and all-knowing, while pretending to let her decide, puzzled her, and when she tried to voice her doubts to Sister Josephine, she was told that the good thing about faith was that you did not need to understand, you just needed to memorize the answers in the book, and pray for God's grace.

As for the rest of her lessons, Iris was often left unsatisfied. She imagined how lovely it would be if all the knowledge school had to offer could be spread out before her, like an all-you-can-eat-buffet, the kind her ravenous Uncle Alfred favored when he treated Auntie Rosa, and sometimes Iris, to Sunday dinner at Case's Diner. (Iris had just recently discovered that Uncle Alfred and Auntie Rosa were not even married, but were her father's brother and sister, and she wondered how a brother could ever be so nice to take a sister to dinner, let alone never threaten to pound her.) Iris would pile her plate high with enticing things to learn, and take it to a quiet corner where she could savor the delicacies without interference, then go back for more, sampling the taste of new notions, scooping up the subjects she liked best, like spelling and reading, until her appetite was sated. Instead, she was forced to sit at school's formal banquet table, where miserly portions of information were doled out according to the needs of those with the least appetite by the mean nuns who were so preoccupied with the rituals of serving and conserving that they paid no heed to how the victuals would be received by unseasoned palates, or that Iris was literally starving in the meantime.

This Saturday morning Iris had risen early and helped herself to a breakfast of puffed rice, drowning the cereal in milk (even though you couldn't really drown puffed rice, no matter how much milk you poured over it, because it always floated). The milk came from one of the glass quart bottles she found in the milk box, just delivered by Lipman's Dairy. Oceans of milk were consumed at the Capotosti household, and even though Roy the milkman brought it every day except on Sundays, it still ran out sometimes. When it did, one of the Big Kids was supposed to go fetch more, but that was another one of the jobs like folding diapers that someone figured Iris would be good at, so she was often the one sent off to the dairy if someone had to go, an aluminum carrier rattling with six empty bottles hanging from her arm. Instead of trying to get out of the job by saying she was too little or too weak, Iris fretted over doing it well. Even though milk was milk, before setting off, Iris always asked her big brother Louis, who always knew the exact names of things, to test her to see if she remembered what to ask for. Iris concentrated so hard on remembering the right words as she walked to the dairy, that she didn't even scout for gum wads along the way. When she got there, she kept repeating the words over and over in her head as she waited for Mr. Anderson, the man with the rubber face and the rubber apron and the rubber boots, to emerge from behind the shiny vats of milk. (She was too shy to call out for him, even though she disliked waiting there, in that dank damp dairy smell.) Mr. Anderson always smiled and said good morning miss when he saw her.

"May I please have six quarts of pasteurized, homogenized, vitamin D milk, please?" Iris would say, and Mr. Anderson would chuckle as he took the empties and replied, "Coming right up!" She wasn't sure what made him laugh, maybe he just liked his job, but anyway she liked the kind look in his eyes as she turned and wobbled away with the bottles that still rattled, but made a dull thumping noise now that they were full, instead of the bright tinkling noise they made when they were empty, kind of like the way her stomach growled one way when she was hungry, and another way when she ate too many apples. The warmth of Mr. Anderson's rubber smile on her back when she walked away made her want to look stronger, even though it felt like her arm would pop out of its socket. She wondered whether carrying all those heavy bottles would stretch her arms out until they were as long as her legs, and she looked like one of those chimps with the pink fannies she had seen at the Seneca Park Zoo. Maybe that was why the Big Kids never wanted to go get the milk.

Yes, Iris definitely enjoyed Saturdays. Saturday was the only day with no morning obligations: no school, and no church. Iris so looked forward to this time that she always tried to get up before everybody else, and slipped down from her bunk and out of the bedroom without even waking Lily. She turned on the television, and watched it come slowly alive with a dot in the center of the screen, which miraculously blossomed into the image of a guy holding a finger in front of his lips. *The Shhh! Show* host spoke in a hushed tone as he invited his young audience to keep the volume down low, so as not to disturb sleeping parents. Iris loved it when people spoke softly, like her mother, instead of shouting like her father and her big brothers. Between the man's quiet voice and the volume set at the minimum, Iris could hardly hear, as she sat cross-legged on the floor with her bowl of cereal, balancing it on the trampoline she fashioned with the nightgown she hooked over her knees. After she had skimmed off all the puffed rice (which she swallowed without chewing because the noise echoing inside her ears drowned out the man's voice), and tipped the bowl to her mouth to drink the milk, she inched closer to the set, until her nose nearly touched the screen. Iris could only see things up close, but she refused to wear her glasses. They didn't even work; all they did was make her feel like puking, and sharpen all the fuzziness out of people's faces, which usually made them look worse instead of better. That was why Iris hid them in her last resort drawer, the one with the underwear with no elastic and the socks with holes in the heels (she didn't mind holes in the toes too much because no one could see them), which she used when she ran out of the good underwear and socks, which was almost every day. What was the worst thing that could happen if she get caught not wearing her glasses? She would say she forgot, and then go put them on. It only happened every once in a while, especially when she first got them, but mostly no one noticed. The whole thing with the glasses was Sister Josephine's fault. She was the one who told Iris's mother that Iris always looked distracted and kept wandering to the front of the classroom to squint at the chalkboard. Iris's mother said that she had always had that faraway look in her eyes, ever since she was born, but Iris's mother told her father about the chalkboard anyway, and Iris's father told her mother to take her for an eye exam. That was how Iris ended up with her mother and the three Little Boys in the waiting room of Julius Corvo, the eye doctor from Yonkers who was married to Iris's father's first cousin Dolores. Iris's mother attempted to read "Good Housekeeping" magazine to William and Charles, who of course were too little to understand, but squirmed with joy at the opportunity to sit in their mother's lap where they could tear and tug at the glossy pages of the magazine, while Ricci, being the baby, got the softest spot, cradled at his mother's breast.

Dr. Julius (that was how everyone in the family called him) took Iris by the hand and led her to the examining room. "Up you go," he said, as he placed his big hands around her bony hips and lifted her to the seat of the tall chair. His hands were still squeezing her hips when he looked straight into her eyes, and said, "I'll just turn off the lights, and we'll see what we have here." His voice was almost as hushed, but not nearly as reassuring, as the voice of the mustachioed man on *The Shhh! Show*. His thin lips twitched and curved up at the corners, but his smile wasn't nearly as friendly as Mr. Anderson's as he sent her home with her bottles of milk, and it disappeared altogether when the room was plunged into darkness. Dr. Julius stabbed the beam of a tiny flashlight straight into one eye, then the other. He leaned in very close to her as he observed her and told her to look up and down and at his finger here, and at his other finger there. She could see nothing but the finger, and the halo of frizzy hair that surrounded his head, and the tiny droplets of sweat glistening on his shiny brow as he peered into her eyes, wavering slightly on his feet as he inhaled and exhaled. She didn't like the feel of his warm breath on her face, and it stank like cigarette butts mixed with stale coffee, like the smell of the cups her father sometimes left on his workbench out back in the garage.

"Just relax," Dr. Julius whispered so close to her ear it tickled, but not in a way that made her laugh. She sank lower in the chair. "Look straight ahead, now, like a good girl. Don't look at me." Iris tried very hard to stay focused, but the smell of his rotten breath made her eyes water and her stomach lurch.

"Perfect. That's a good girl," Dr. Julius cooed as he snapped off the flashlight, patted her head with his free hand and moved behind the chair. He placed a hand on her shoulder and pointed to the opposite wall. "You see that chart over there, honey?" he said. "Now read the letters you see in the third row from the top, starting from the left."

Iris grasped the armrests with both hands and scooted herself up in the chair, preparing to concentrate on her new task. The backs of her bare legs were glued to the vinyl upholstery of the chair, and she reached behind her to pull down the back of her dress, in the way Auntie Rosa and Sister Josephine said a young lady should.

"Here, let me help you, sweetheart," said Dr. Julius, his voice as sticky as the vinyl. His offer required no answer, but before she could say anything, one of Dr. Julius's hands slid beneath her and cupped her buttocks (that's what Auntie Rosa said was the proper way to call your fanny), while the other tugged at the thin cotton fabric. Iris didn't like the feeling of his hand underneath her, but she knew she couldn't say that out loud to him. He was a grown-up, and cousin Dolores's husband, and a doctor to boot.

"There you go, isn't that better?" he said, as he smoothed the hem of her dress over her legs, then covered her right eye with a small plastic paddle. "Can you read those letters for me, honey?" he said, his left hand lingering on her thigh. Iris tried to decipher the letters her mother and her big sisters and the nuns at St. Augustine's had taught her to recognize, but her already blurry vision was clouded further by the uneasy feeling that she was doing something wrong. She tried harder to focus on the chart. "F, O, or maybe Q?" she began to read. "Z, V, R or P? I dunno … I don't feel so good. Can I go?" It was true, she really did think she was going to puke. Without waiting for an answer, she jumped down from the chair, twisting her ankle as she landed, and hobbled out the door as fast as her legs could carry her. Her mother, struggling to prevent her toddlers from shredding all the outdated magazines in the waiting room, did not notice the flush in her cheeks as Iris blurted out, "Can we go now, Mom?"

Dr. Julius was close behind. "Our Iris is an impatient little one, Betty!" he said with a chuckle. "No real problem here, she's just a tad nearsighted. I would have run some more tests, but she's not one for sitting still, is she? Anyway, I've seen enough to fit her for her first pair of specs. Would you like to pick out some frames, Iris?"

Dr. Julius stood in the doorway in his long white coat, with his tiny flashlight and gold pen stuck in his pocket, his thin smile stuck on his face, his Adam's apple stuck in his throat. "I don't feel good," Iris said. "I wanna go home."

Her mother, flustered and anxious to be on her way, gathered up her baby boys and said, "You take care of it, Julius. Nothing fancy, of course, just affordable. We trust you. Give Dolores my regards." Dr. Julius nodded and kept smiling that horrible thin smile of his.

Iris hated thinking about the day when her mother brought her to see Dr. Julius. She hated the way the world looked to her in those glasses, and she hated the way she looked in them. She hated the way the glasses slid down her nose when she ran and fogged up when she came in from the cold. She would rather sit close to the TV, like she did that Saturday morning, at least until the scraggly bunch of barefooted brothers and sisters in crooked pajamas and tousled hair tumbled down the stairs, looking like the stunned survivors of an predawn earthquake. Iris's brief moment of solitude was shattered, as they fought over cereal bowls, fought over who was to blame for the spilt milk, fought over seats on the sofa. Already Marguerite and Louis were complaining that Iris was blocking their view of the TV, and that *The Shhh! Show* was for babies. Iris relinquished her spot without a word, and slipped from the room. She had grown tired of being silenced by that man without a voice when she wasn't even making any noise, anyway.

She wanted to find a place to be alone, but it was too early to go outside. She cracked open the door to the basement, and stood at the top of the stairs, squinting into the darkness, trying to summon up the courage to go down. She flipped a switch on the wall, and a feeble light illuminated the steps. She placed a bare foot tentatively on the first one, pausing to speculate as to what dangers might be lurking in the fuzzy shadows down below. She took a deep breath, and forced her second foot to follow the first, then both feet to take her all the way to the bottom. As she stood trembling on the last step, she was tempted to turn on her heels and scurry back up to safety, but with a rush of bravery she leaped into the air, and yanked on the chain dangling from the ceiling light. An arc of light from the naked bulb dispelled the first cluster of sinister shadows, revealing the lumpy leftovers that furnished the "rec room." Dark places (especially dark places with lots of stuff in them, like attics and basements, more than dark empty places, like the night sky), scared Iris even more since that time when her parents had gone out, and Violet had let Iris stay up to watch a movie with her. Mostly, Iris liked the idea of curling up with Violet on the sofa, even though she couldn't see much that far from the TV. But what she did see was that scene where the woman stabs a man in the back with scissors, after he jumps out of from behind a curtain and tries to strangle her with a stocking. Iris was terrified, but wouldn't look away until she was sure the man was dead, and at least Violet hugged her until she stopped shaking, though probably it was mostly because she was worried about getting in Trouble for letting Iris watch the movie, but Iris wasn't one to snitch, especially if it meant getting Violet or one of her sisters in Trouble.

Iris was proud of her bravery coming down here this morning, and a sigh of relief deflated her lungs as she searched for her reward. Her heartbeat slowed, then instantly sped up again as she spotted the object of her desire: the record player. She knew she risked a pounding from Alexander if she was discovered, but she simply couldn't resist. She slipped the vinyl LP from its jacket and dropped the Beatles album onto the turntable. A scraping sound came over the speaker as she picked a clump of fuzz from the needle and eased the arm down into the groove, being extra careful not to make any scratches, like she had seen Violet and Marguerite do the previous afternoon, when they had granted her temporary permission to stay in the basement with them because she had folded all the diapers and even brought them glasses of orange juice. Iris had stayed out of their way, like they made her promise, sitting silently on the lumpy couch, wiggling her bare foot to the beat as she watched them twist and turn, but after a while she couldn't stand it anymore, kind of like when she had to pee real bad and someone else was taking a real long time doing number two in the bathroom. When it was just too much for her and she jumped up and started dancing, they told her she didn't know how to keep promises and kicked her back upstairs.

This morning, there was no one to stop her from dancing all she wanted, at least not until someone sniffed her out. She turned the volume down lower than she would have liked, to avoid attracting unwanted attention, and as the music began to play, she started imitating the moves she had seen her sisters make when they danced. It was Iris's favorite tune, the wanna hold your hand song, which she used to call the Hawaii song, because of the part that went "and I held her hand in Hawaiii-iii." That was until Marguerite had heard her singing, and started laughing at her, and told her she was too young to listen to the Beatles if she couldn't even get the words right, and then embarrassed her to death at supper when she told all the Big Kids how Iris had mistaken the word "mine" for "Hawaii" and then they all had a good laugh at her, except Alexander, who just gave her a mean look, and said he better not catch her with her sticky paws on his album, or he would pound her. As if she didn't already know that.

But the more she danced, and the more she sang, the less she thought about the risk of Alexander catching her with her sticky paws on his record. She played the song over and over again, dancing from beginning to end, then rushing to raise the needle, and lower it carefully in just the right spot without scratching, which was getting harder to do as the dancing made her hands all shaky and sweaty. She finally collapsed on the couch, her nightgown soaked with perspiration, her ribcage rising and falling as she sucked in gulps of musty basement air. Just as the next tune started playing, she heard a loud squeak groan over the sound of the music. Someone was opening the door at the top of the stairs! Images of Alexander coming down to pound her instantly materialized with such frightening clarity that she could hear the thump his fist of knuckles would make against her back. Cringing, she ran to turn off the record player, lifted off the album while the turntable was still spinning, and shoved it into its jacket.

"Anyone down there?" her father's voice bellowed from the top of the stairs.

"I am!" Iris called out with the scraps of voice left after all the singing and dancing, shaking with relief that it was not her brother, though everyone must be up by now, judging by the sounds of Saturday morning bedlam tumbling down to the basement through the open door.

"Jeepers Cripes!" her father shouted. "How many times do I have to tell you kids to turn the lights off?!" He must not have heard Iris over the ruckus, because if he had, he never would have flicked the switch and slammed the door and left her stranded there with all the creepy shadows and leftover furniture in a tiny island of light, with no way out but through the darkness.

Clouds played in the spring sky, somersaulting in from Lake Ontario, then scuttling off capriciously every which way. Like Iris, they didn't seem to have a clear idea of what they should do this Saturday afternoon. After her unnerving experience in the basement (she was finally liberated when her mother switched on the light and came down to get started on the Saturday washing), Iris set off for a walk down Rugby Road. As usual, she found that walking was too slow a means of locomotion, unless she was on

34

the prowl for gum wads, and soon broke into a skip. She enjoyed the hopping rhythm she set for herself, and the sense of freedom she felt when she let her arms swing back and forth, gaining momentum with each carefree, sweeping motion. Heading in the direction of Rita Esposito's house, she spotted Rosemary, the girl who lived alone in the corner house with her parents, presumably on her way home from the corner drugstore, judging from the little paper bag in her hand, which was probably filled with Bazookas, each soft pink square of bubblegum still ensconced in its miniature comic strip, and wrapped up in its waxy wrapper. Each piece had a little line down the middle, so it was easy to break in half if you had to share it, but Iris doubted Rosemary would be interested in sharing with anyone, let alone her. Iris waved to her, and Rosemary waved back, blowing bubbles and clutching her bag even more tightly. Iris wondered whether she might even have some Juicy Fruit in there. Her mouth watered at the thought; she hardly ever found Juicy Fruit on the ground because its neutral color made it harder to spot than pink bubblegum, and when she did, it never tasted very juicy or very fruity. Iris felt a certain sense of awe mixed with pity for Rosemary, ever since that day when Sister Josephine had made each of them stand in class and state their dates of birth. When Rosemary said hers was February 29th, Sister Josephine got all excited and told the class that meant she only had a birthday every four years, which seemed like a pretty awful thing to have happen to you, especially if you were supposed to have a free will, because no one with a free will would ever give up their birthday, and there was no amount of gum that could change that.

In the Capotosti family, your birthday was even better than Christmas. It was the one day of the year when people actually noticed you, in a good way, though, not like when you got in Trouble. You got to pick out which kind of cake and frosting you wanted, and your mother made it, just like that, the very exact one you asked for! Your brothers and sisters were all real nice to you, at least part of the day, and put cards they made specially for you by your plate at supper. Auntie Rosa came over straight from work, wearing her nurse's uniform and white stockings, unpinning the cap from her hair as she sighed over the emergency that had held her up, but then got in a happy mood when she saw the whole family gathered together, and started pinching everybody's cheeks and saying *"Bella della mamma!"* Then she set down a prettily wrapped box which always made everyone curious, even though underneath the tissue paper there was never anything but a new pair of pajamas for the boys or a nightgown for the girls. After dinner Uncle Alfred always sneaked out of the room, then the lights suddenly went out, and Uncle Alfred returned with his guitar, and started leading the Capotosti chorus in "Happy Birthday." Her mother brought in the cake, ablaze with just the right number of candles that meant you really were one year older, and the frosting with your name written on it in colored gel, which meant the cake really was for you, and your face felt all warm when you bent to blow out the candles and everyone clapped, and you felt all warm inside, too, because of the way nobody tried to butt in and blow out your candles, or tried to rip up your cards, or steal the box with your new nightie, or threatened to pound you or make you fold diapers or send you to the dairy, all because it was your birthday. Maybe, since Rosemary didn't have any brothers or sisters, she didn't really need a birthday every year.

Bright yellow shingles clung to the sides of Rita Esposito's house, dressing it like a spring frock. The house was separated from the cracked and buckled tree-lined sidewalk by a lush lawn of emerald grass that beckoned Iris to take her shoes off and wade through it, even though it wasn't summer yet, and even though she knew Mr. Esposito detested people walking on his grass, which was the one thing that made him yell even louder than Iris's father, though it was hard to imagine anyone yelling on such a lovely day. Iris sensed the arrival of spring in her bones; she loved the way it made her feel all fluttery inside, and hopeful that she had seen the last of the cold and grey and dark and ice and wind that pummeled her hometown in upstate New York during the long winter months. It was funny how seasons changed, how one day you suddenly noticed that it was already light out when you got up in the morning, and still light out when you went to bed. And how suddenly the last traces of dingy snow and icy slush were washed away by the rain and sucked up by the sun. She hoped Rita could come out to share the sunshine while it lasted.

Hopping up the steps to the front porch, Iris peered through the curtained windows but saw no sign of life. She went around to the side of the house, and stopped below Rita's bedroom window. Iris liked playing in Rita's room when it was too cold to play outside; the only girl and the youngest of four kids, Rita had the room all to herself and slept on a neatly made bed covered with a frilly pink bedspread and piled with stuffed animals that Rita called by name. Toys and games were kept in a wooden chest in one corner of the room, from which they were taken and into which they were returned with meticulous care. Iris shared Rita's penchant for neatness, but doubted whether Rita would ever understand how Iris felt upon discovering strewn about the living room floor the Crayola crayons her parents had given her for her birthday which she had hidden in her last resort drawer together with her glasses that didn't work and the underwear with frayed elastic and socks with holes in the heels, where she was sure no one would ever look. So although Iris admired Rita's toys, sometimes she felt like a part of her got locked out when they played together in her room. Outdoors, they were more on Iris's turf; Rita was afraid of dogs, and cars, and colored kids. She was afraid of getting dirty, and of getting caught in the rain. Rita made Iris seem much more courageous than she actually was when they played outside, and after surviving her experience in the basement, Iris felt primed for the role of fearless leader. Standing beneath the window, she cupped her hands around her mouth, mustered up her strongest voice and sang, *"Ri-ta-aaa!! Ri-ta-aaa!!"* No answer. She inflated her lungs and tried again. *"Ri-ta-aaa!! Ri-ta-aaa!!"* Still no answer. After a few more tries, Iris felt lightheaded and her throat was all scratchy. She finally gave up and walked back down the street with no destination in mind, and ended up in her own backyard. Half disappointed, half surprised to find no one else there, she spent her courage climbing to the very top rung of the Jungle Gym to have a look around. She loved the feeling of being able to observe without being seen. From her perch, she could see the backyard of the house next door where, when the weather was fine, two old ladies sat for hours on end, draped in crocheted shawls, mumbling and moaning and rocking back and forth in their chairs. Iris and Lily sometimes crouched near the fence to spy on them and try to decipher the lyrics of their laments, until they got bored by the total lack of action, or scrambled away in fear when the ladies made gurgling animal noises that made the hairs on their arms stand up straight.

Today was still too chilly for the old ladies, and the neighbors on the other side didn't have anything interesting in their backyard, at least nothing she could see without her glasses, so Iris took stock of her own yard. There were a couple of boys' bicycles propped against the side of the garage, while the one she had been learning on, which had a banged up fender and a flat front tire, slouched dejectedly next to the rabbit hutch, waiting to be fixed by her father. The rabbits belonged to her sister Jasmine. Jasmine loved animals of every kind, and her father loved making Jasmine happy. Probably because she was so sweet and pretty with her curly hair and dimples and was the first girl to be born, after Alexander and John. Jasmine was even nice to Iris, the way she stopped by her bunk bed to tucked her in and stuff, even when no one asked her to. After a while, the original hutch their father had built for the half-dozen rabbits Jasmine had started out with wasn't big enough, so her father built another hutch next to the garage, but Iris heard him yelling the other day that those gosh darn rabbits kept having baby bunnies and now even that hutch wasn't enough. Iris wondered if he would build another house for their family, too, if her mother had more babies.

A cool wind came up, chilling Iris and reminding her she was all the way on the top rung of the Jungle Gym. Feeling a little jittery, she climbed down cautiously, thinking it would be safer to go pet the rabbits instead, even though she couldn't hold them, but would have to be content with sticking her fingers through the mesh. She was not allowed to pick up the rabbits unless Jasmine or her parents were there, since she had gotten into big Trouble one time when she opened the door, and the rabbits started jumping right out, and Jasmine's French poodle started yelping and chasing them all over the place.

As Iris approached the hutch, she heard a noise coming from the garage. The garage door was closed, and she didn't see anyone around, which was pretty strange for a Saturday afternoon. Iris crept closer, then stood on her tiptoes, hoping to peek in the side window. Though she stretched her toes and her legs and her neck as much as she could, the tip of her nose barely made it to the window frame. She dragged over a rusty lawn chair and climbed up on the seat, grasping the window frame to steady herself. Pressing her face against the glass, she squinted her eyes and tried to focus on what she saw.

The man bent over the work table was definitely her father, that she could see, even if his back was turned to the window. He spent hours in the garage, that was where he kept all his tools and hardware, all lined up in perfect order, hanging from hooks above his bench, and all kinds of screws and bolts and nails inside stacks of cigar boxes, even though he did not smoke cigars, just cigarettes and of course he also drank coffee and sometimes dropped the butts in the used cup which for a minute almost made her lose her balance and want to puke as she was reminded of Dr. Julius and that sickening smell that came from his breath, even though her father did not have that breath, nothing like it; it was the coffee cup with floating cigarette butts that smelled so foul. Dr. Julius couldn't even give her a pair of glasses that worked, but her father knew how to fix just about anything, even people. During the day, his job was to attach brand new arms and legs to veterans and teach them how to use them. He said if a man gave an arm or leg to his country, Jeepers Cripes, they deserved to have a replacement. Her father was a nurse, too, but not the same kind as Auntie Rosa.

Whenever anyone got hurt (which was mostly her brothers) he was the one who rushed to the rescue faster than you could believe. He scooped his patient up in his arms and set him or her on the kitchen table. If they were crying, he knew how to make them stop by asking questions about where it hurt and how it hurt instead of yelling. Then he sent her mother to the medicine cabinet for disinfectants and ointments and gauze and bandages. The liquid in some of the bottles burned when he poured it on you, even though he always said it wouldn't. "You were lucky this time," he would say. "You don't need stitches. I think what we really need here is a nice Band-Aid." At the mention of a Band-Aid, which was always a great trophy to show off, because Band-Aids were not just handed out to everyone, his patient would nod his or her head, and that was usually the end of it. It wasn't always as easy as that, though.

One time Alexander clobbered his thumb with a hammer, and a huge purple bubble swelled up under his nail. Alexander was already too old to blubber like a baby, but he couldn't stop hopping around the kitchen screaming. Her father took one look at the thumb, and hurried out the door, returning a few minutes later with his drill. He sat Alexander down at the table, hand flat in front of him. Louis screeched with excitement and clapped his hands at the sight of the power tool, while his twin Henry just stared silently, with the same sort of expectant smile he wore when he was in line for an ice cream cone. Iris and Lily stood off to a side, hugging the legs of their mother, who cupped a hand over her mouth.

"Everyone quiet now, or leave!" her father had ordered, revving up the drill. A hush fell, then the silence was broken by the whine of the drill as it hovered over Alexander's hand. Before anyone could chicken out, her father drilled a hole in the nail, and a geyser of blood spurt into the air and Alexander dropped his head to the table in relief. Everyone cheered at the heroic show of bravery of father and son and the boys laughed at the sight of the blood trickling down the door of the Frigidaire and the cabinets all the way across the room.

Iris saw more than a trickle of something red there in the garage, it was more like a little stream, dripping from the work table and into a rusty bucket. She wiped off the glass that was all fogged up from her breath, then pressed her face against it again, squinting her eyes to see, while trying not to fall off the chair that wobbled beneath her feet. Iris saw her father turn, then raise a hand holding some sort of knife, a big one, then lower it down, a lot faster and harder than that day he cured Alexander with the drill. She saw something fall to the floor, bounce once, roll away, then come to a stop just below the window. At first, Iris thought she was seeing things, but even after she blinked real hard and pushed her face into the glass until her nose was flat and her forehead hurt, it still looked like a pair of bunny ears pointed at her from a furry head. Iris opened her mouth to yell for him to stop, but her throat was blocked so tight no words could make it past. She raised her hand to bang on the window, but lost her balance and toppled from the chair. She scrambled to her feet in a panic, tripped as she ran to the house, and burst through the back door into the kitchen, where she found her mother humming as she worked at the sink.

"*Moommmmy!!*" Iris cried, throwing her arms around her mother's legs, burying her head between the folds of her house dress and apron, seeking comfort between her warm thighs.

"What is it, honey? What's the matter?" her mother said as she set down her knife and wiped her hands on her apron.

"It's… it's …" Iris sobbed, her eyes darting from her mother's face to the sink, which Iris was just tall enough to see into without having to climb up on a chair. And what she saw was the bloodied blade of the knife her mother had been using.

"What's that?" Iris asked, pointing to the chunks of raw meat on a cutting board.

"We're trying something new for dinner, honey," her mother said. "Wait till you taste how good it is!"

That meat sure didn't look like the kind her mother usually put in Spanish rice or Sloppy Joes. Iris knew what it was, she had seen it all. She didn't care what it tasted like, and didn't plan on finding out. There was no way she would eat Jasmine's rabbits, and there was no way she could keep on living in that house! She bolted from the kitchen, tore up the stairs and burst into her bedroom. Lily was sitting cross-legged on her bottom bunk, looking at the pictures in the Sears catalogue. She looked up at Iris.

"Hey, Iris. Whatsa matter?" she asked, the smile vanishing from her face when she saw her tears. When a sister cried, you always asked why, and tried to figure out a way to make her stop.

Iris sniffed the snot back up her nose, but didn't answer. She was too upset to talk about what she had seen, even to Lily. She reached under the bed and pulled out the little blue valise Auntie Rosa had surprised her with on her last birthday, for her to use when she went on overnight stays at her house. Iris had fallen in love with the valise immediately, though she was a teeny weeny sorry at first because she had been counting on the new nightie, but when she opened it, and found that Auntie Rosa had hidden one inside, her disappointment gave way to delight. Iris had learned to like disappointments for that very reason, for that way they had of multiplying every unexpected good thing that happened. By then, Iris was all quivery with joy, and filled with wonder about where she might travel one day besides Auntie Rosa's, but when she saw Lily staring at the valise with a blank look on her face, a chord of sadness vibrated deep inside her.

Iris brushed away the dust mice slumbering on the valise and flipped the locks open, then stomped over to the dresser she shared with Lily. She pulled open the underwear drawer, found it empty, and slammed it shut again. She opened her last resort drawer, grabbed a handful of ragged underclothes, then took her now not-so-new nightie from under her pillow, threw everything into the valise, and snapped it shut. Wiping the tears from her eyes, she paused to look at the design in the lower left-hand corner of the little valise, which always made her feel better. Sometimes she pulled the valise out just to stare at it, even when she wasn't going anywhere (which was most of the time), but only when Lily wasn't around. She adored that sketch of a woman and a man, smiling and holding hands by something that looked like the world's tallest Jungle Gym. Auntie Rosa said it was called the Eiffel Tower and that it was in Paris, which was in France, and that France was not too far from Italy, where Grandma and Grandpa Capotosti had come from. But it was very far from Rugby Road.

Paris! That was where she would go. She opened her last resort drawer again and took out her glasses. Even if they didn't work, she might need them to get to Paris. She looked around the room one last time, fresh tears welling in her eyes. "Whatsa matter, Iris?" Lily asked again, her eyes glued to the valise. Iris just shook her head and hugged Lily, then hurried down the stairs and out the front door, trying not think of the little sister she was leaving alone in her room with the Sears catalogue, or the mother she was leaving in the kitchen with the dead rabbit parts, or the father she was leaving in the garage with bloodied hands. She ran down the street as fast as her legs would carry her.

4. LILY

The air was cool and dank, steeped in must. There was something about the way the basement smelled and felt that both attracted and repelled Lily. The rough concrete floor was mottled from the incontinence of the rusted washing machine, the air heavy with the story of life that transpired there. The stark odors of chlorine bleach, sweat, urine, and sour milk emanating from the laundry basket, the earthy smells of hand degreaser, WD-40, and sawdust – all testament to a life and a culture built on dedication to hard work and its inherent suffering.

Going into the basement wasn't like going into the kitchen or the living room. Each time Lily was forced to go down, to grab a pair of snow pants off a hook, or retrieve still dirty socks from the laundry pile (which were better than no socks, after all), she did so with an acute awareness that she was not just going into a different room, but that she was going into a different part of herself. Going into the basement required that she become different, as well. Braver. Older, somehow.

Lily sat in the tiny basement bathroom, which was little more than an old white toilet situated in an alcove that may have originally been intended as a fruit cellar, or maybe a dungeon. The space was separated from the machines that kept life going in the house – the washing machine, the furnace, the sump pump – by a tattered sheet hung from a bent curtain rod that Lily's father had mounted across the doorway. With the sheet pushed aside, Lily watched her mother move with precision and grace as she went through the motions of laundering dirty clothes, a constant and continual chore at the Capotosti household. Reaching, stooping, turning, and humming, she was like one of those ballerinas on TV.

First, the clothes would go into the tub of water, where a giant mixer arm would lurch and grind, rocking the entire machine back and forth, beating the dirt out of those soiled clothes the way the Holy Ghost beats sins out of your soul.

Once the machine stopped, Lily's mother took a dark blue T-shirt, and fed one end of it between two large white rubber rollers, which she put into motion by cranking an aluminum handle on the side. The rollers grabbed the shirt, and squeezed all the excess water out of it, depositing it into the stationary tub. And that was the beginning of a new pile of wet but clean clothes – ready to be hung out on the line. Lily peeled her urine-soaked tights, underpants, and skirt from her skin, and added them to the never-ending pile of childhood that camped at the bottom of the basement stairs.

"It looks like you had a little accident there," said her mother.

"I'm sorry, Mommy," said Lily. "I didn't mean to. I just couldn't hold it." No need to tell her about the incident at school, about interrupting Miss Swift's class, or about being forgotten in the cloakroom.

"That's OK," said her mother. "It happens." She leaned down, gently took Lily's chin between her thumb and index finger, tilted Lily's face upwards and kissed the tip of her nose. Lily felt the frustrations of the day melt away, safe in the knowledge that her mother still loved her no matter what - even when she did wet her pants, and even if she had lost her balance and stepped on a crack on the way to school that morning.

"Now," she continued, patting Lily's bare bottom. "Go on upstairs and get some pants on, and then send the rest of your dirty things down the chute."

The laundry chute ran up the center of the house, making a stop on each floor – in the kitchen, and then again in the hallway upstairs where the bedrooms were. The chute was marked by a small wooden door with a round knob. It looked just like a regular door, but made for a teeny tiny person – someone smaller even than Lily. If you opened the chute door, stuck your head inside and looked down, you could see the pile of clothes in the basement. Lily peered down the chute as her mother grabbed a few things, placed them into the washer, and then moved out of view. Lily was often tempted to climb inside the laundry chute, to see what it would be like to plummet down and land in the basement, her fall cushioned by plaid skirts and white blouses, black trousers and blue jeans, countless towels and strange underpants with a pocket in front.

The laundry chute often taunted Lily with its silent, lingering call for daring and disaster. The closed, dark space could be a place to escape, or hide. But what if no one noticed her there, atop that sweat-soaked, urine-soaked, tear-soaked pile? What if her mother reached out, thinking she was grabbing a towel or a tablecloth and then took Lily and fed her through the wringer? Her mother would be so upset when she discovered she had sent her youngest daughter through the laundry rollers. She would probably just stand there, overcome with sadness just like the Virgin Mother in that statue where she is holding Jesus in her lap. She looked so sad, and Jesus was there, wearing only his underpants, and Lily wondered what Jesus was like when he was little, and where he went to kindergarten. Did he ever interrupt the entire class or wet his pants, or get forgotten in the cloakroom? If they made a statue about Lily, her mother could hold her, except Lily would be almost completely flat, from being sent through the wringer and all. Her mother would be wearing her special blue dress with the white polka dots, and maybe even her pearl necklace. And there would be tears rolling down her face, and her eyes would be turned toward Heaven, as if to say, "Our Father, why didn't I pay better attention? Why didn't I notice Lily there? Now she is gone and I will never be able to kiss her little nose again, or pat her naked bottom." Lily slammed the laundry chute door closed again and tried to block the image from her mind.

And then there was the milk door – Lily's favorite place to play. The milk door was located next to the side entry of the house and was discernible from the laundry chute because it was painted white, but also because if you opened it, you would see another door that led to the outside. Every morning, Roy from Lipman's Dairy drove his big white milk truck up the driveway. He hopped out, clad in his white pants and white cap. His white shirt had "Roy" embroidered on the left breast pocket. He would open the back doors of his truck, reach inside, and pull out two small rectangular aluminum crates that had handles like Easter baskets. Each crate held six glass bottles of milk. Roy was always whistling, and Lily figured it was because he was so happy – after all, he had milk all the time, every day, no matter what.

Roy would open the outside milk door, put the baskets inside, and close the door again. All the Capotosti children knew the sound of that little door opening and closing. On cue, Lily's mother or one of the Big Kids would retrieve the baskets, and place the bottles into the Frigidaire. At the end of the day, Lily's mother would place the baskets with the empty bottles back into the milk box so Roy could get them again the next morning. Roy went to each house in the entire neighborhood, left milk in each box, and then disappeared. The only time anyone ever even saw Roy up close was if Lily's mother forgot to leave money in the baskets for him on Friday. Then he would come back later and knock on the door.

"Why hello, there, half-pint!" Roy said to Lily when she answered the door one Friday afternoon.

"Hi, Roy!" Lily greeted him with the exuberance usually reserved for Santa Claus sightings or for when Uncle Alfred brought over maple walnut ice cream. Lily didn't really like maple walnut, but any kind of ice cream was better than no ice cream at all.

"Is your Mommy home?" asked Roy.

"Mo-o-o-m-m-y!" shouted Lily. "Roy the milkman is here!" Lily stood, a wide grin on her face, beaming at Roy.

After standing and grinning back at her for about fifteen seconds, Roy looked past her into the house and said with a wink, "Maybe you should go find her."

"OK!" Lily slammed the door in Roy's face and ran to find her mother.

"Mommy, Mommy," she called, reeling from room to room, finally finding her mother in the bedroom which was situated on the first floor, at the front of the house, facing the street. She was sorting through the coins in a small change purse of worn brown leather. She swiped at her right eye with the back of her right hand. She sniffed.

"Mommy – what's wrong?" asked Lily.

"Why nothing, baby," replied her mother, looking up at Lily and forcing a smile.

"Roy is at the door and he wants to see you."

"I know, I know," her mother replied. With a sigh, she poured the contents of the change purse into the palm of her hand, and then shook it, as if some small hole in the cosmos might open up and more coins would pour out. Convinced that the purse was empty, she tossed it onto the bed. She stood up and used her free hand to straighten out her dress. Walking over to the mirror, she vigorously pinched each cheek, which instantly turned them from milky white to rosy red, making it look like she had applied some of Grandma Whitacre's rouge. She adjusted the auburn curls that lay across her brow, and said to Lily, "Now, you stay here, and keep an eye on Ricci. I'll be right back."

Lily peeked into the bassinet that sat next to her parent's bed. With his pink cheeks and auburn curls, Lily figured Ricci looked exactly as her mother must have when she was a baby. She tried to imagine Grandma Whitacre changing her mother's diapers and feeding her a bottle, but Grandma was so fancy and sparkly that it was hard to picture her performing such mundane tasks – after all, Grandma Whitacre was practically a movie star.

"I'm sorry you came out a boy, Ricci," Lily whispered to the baby. "If you were a girl like me and Iris, you would have a beautiful flower name - on account of Grandpa used to be a gardener but now he can't do it anymore cuz he's a cripple. Maybe your name woulda been Dandelion, or Lilac." Little Ricci drew long, deep sucks on his thumb. "But Ricci is a pretty good name for a boy, I guess."

The baby had been dubbed "Ricci" by Grandma Capotosti, not because it was short for Richard, but because of his curly hair. *Bel bambino, col ricciolino.* Beautiful baby, with tiny curls. He was the only one in the whole family who had a shortened name, by strict orders from their father. "If I'd wanted you to call her 'Margie,'" he'd say, "I would have named her 'Margie.' It's Marguerite - like the daisy." Allowing everyone to call the baby "Ricci" was a concession he made out of obedience to Irene Capostosti. She wasn't a woman with whom you argued and won.

Watching Ricci quickly proved to be a boring chore, so Lily tiptoed out into the hallway where she could glimpse her mother and Roy, and hear their muffled voices.

"If I give you a partial payment, could you leave me just one crate today?" asked Lily's mother.

"Mrs. Capotosti, I have to answer for each crate that leaves my truck, and I have to balance my books at the end of each day. I'd love to help you, but ..."

"Roy -" said her mother, shifting her weight to her right foot, and placing a clenched fist at her hip. Lily noticed a slight rise in the pitch and volume of her mother's voice. It was her angry voice, and it was as close to shouting as she ever came.

"I have twelve children. In just a few hours, they will be pouring in from all directions, and will take their places around the dinner table and will ask me for milk. What will I tell them? Do you want me to tell them they can't have any, or do you want to take this payment – and I know it's not nearly enough – and figure out a way to give me another day or two to catch up?"

After a few seconds of silence, Lily tiptoed into the kitchen and peeked around the corner so she could see her mother's back, and Roy standing in the doorway. Roy shot Lily a glance, and then his gaze trailed down the length of Lily's body, resting on her foot, complete with big toe poking through her white sock. He looked back up at Lily. She giggled, and then quickly retreated back around the corner.

Lily's mother tousled her curls, flashed a smile and said, "Honestly Roy, where do you think I'm going? There is no other dairy within ten miles of here. You'll get your money. I give you my word."

When Lily heard the door close, she ran back to her mother's bedroom and watched out the window as Roy backed his truck down the driveway. She pushed the ivory sheers aside and furiously waved to him. Just before he reached the end of the driveway, he stopped, tipped his cap to Lily, and then disappeared down the street.

Lily took her post beside Ricci, sitting on the edge of the bed, her hands folded in her lap. Her mother glided into the room, put the change purse back into the top drawer of her dresser, and scooped a now stirring baby out of his bassinet. She held the baby up at eye level and said, "We shall overcome, little Richard. We shall overcome." She drew his small body close, and unbuttoned the front of her dress. Instinctively, the baby turned his head toward her breast, opened his mouth, and captured her nipple with hungry lips. Ricci was the only one in the house who never had to worry about running out of milk. Being a baby was the next best thing to being Roy.

"Oh, Mommy, the little hand is on the five. Is it time for the city bus?"

Lily's mother glanced at her watch. "Why yes – I believe it is."

"I'm gonna go meet Daddy!" The side door slammed behind Lily as she disappeared down the driveway in her stocking feet.

Each morning, Lily's father would make a bologna sandwich, wrap it in wax paper like it was a birthday present, slip it into a small brown paper bag, and walk to the corner to catch the city bus. Some afternoons – when Lily remembered to ask if it was time – she would go down to the corner and wait for the bus to bring him home again, its magical doors opening with a loud whoosh, depositing her father onto the sidewalk. The walk back home was the only time he wasn't working at the office or fixing something in the garage, or watching the news. And Lily could have him all to herself.

"Hey, Lily of the Valley!" he called that Friday afternoon, stepping off the bus.

"Daddy!" she cried, jumping up into his arms.

"What did you do today?" He kissed her forehead and placed her back on the ground. Reaching into his breast pocket, he pulled out a Parliament, tapped it three times on the back of his left hand, and placed the filtered end into his mouth. He reached into his pocket again, to retrieve a pack of matches, and without slowing down or breaking stride, he plucked a match, struck it against the pack, and held it to the tip of the cigarette, puffing and dragging until it glowed like a light on a Christmas tree.

Lily craned her neck, trying to catch a whiff of the smoke as it swirled around her father's head. The only smells she loved more than a newly lit cigarette were gasoline, and fresh ground coffee. They were the smells of her father.

"Were you a good girl today?"

"I think so." Lily replied.

"You think so?"

"Well, I didn't cause Mommy any trouble, and no one pounded me."

He chuckled. "All good signs, I'd say." He tilted his face toward the sky, took a long draw on his cigarette and then exhaled the smoke overhead with a broad, deep sigh. Lily marched alongside her father, straining to keep in step with his long, heavy strides. Lily's father was slightly bowlegged and had a hitch in his step, so that when he walked, he rocked back and forth a bit, almost as though he were thinking about dancing.

"Guess what I did today?" he asked.

"What Daddy?" Lily knew what was coming, but playing the game was part of the fun.

"I went to the White Tower at lunchtime and ordered a cup of soup to have with my bologna sandwich."

"You did?" Lily giggled.

"I did," said her father. "And they gave me a pack of saltine crackers to go with my soup, but I was so full, I couldn't even eat them." He reached his hand into the pocket of his suit coat, and pulled out a worn paper bag and two saltine crackers in a plastic wrapper. "So, I brought them home for you."

Lily snatched the crackers from her father's calloused palm, ripped the package open and took an enthusiastic bite. There were plenty of saltines at home, but none of them tasted this good; none of those other crackers were intended especially for Lily.

"Daddy, today when I was coming home from school, I ran into that colored boy and he called me 'little cracker.'"

"He did?" Lily's father flicked an ash from his cigarette. "Was he harsh about it?"

"Nope. He just said, 'Hey, little cracker.'" Lily's father laughed at her impression of Bobby Rose, with her bottom lip thrust out and her brow furrowed, looking more like Shirley Temple scolding a kitten.

"Hmmm," he said, dropping his cigarette to the ground and crushing it with the toe of his battered black leather shoe. "The next time he says that, just tell him, 'Nothing goes better with crackers than a nice glass of chocolate milk.'"

Lily finished the second cracker and shoved the empty wrapper into her front pants pocket. Her father's advice made no sense to her, but she made a note of it, in the unlikely event that a colored boy should ever call her a cracker again.

By the time Lily's father rang the dinner bell, the house was filled again with the twelve lively children, over-stimulated and hyperactive from having spent the last two hours running around the neighborhood on bicycles, tricycles, jump ropes, and pogo sticks - children who hadn't eaten anything since the solitary bologna or peanut butter and jelly sandwich at lunch. Sweating, red-faced, and famished, they collected around the dinner table with the determination and order of pigs at the trough. Lily's mother moved about the chaos with an aura of acceptance, or resignation. The sun descends, the children descend, the kitchen becomes a circus of hands battling for peas and rice and bottles of milk. Forks and plastic drinking cups and melamine dishes with faded floral patterns are whisked from the cupboards to the table, and then shuttled back to the sink, where they constitute yet another pile.

Lily sat in the corner in her special chair, observing more than participating. She was almost too big for the chair now, but there was no room for her at the Big Kids' table, and anyway, she would just get underfoot. So she sat and watched. Watched the flurry, watched the whirl of people and activity, and there would be her mother, moving quietly and unruffled, doling out bread, sopping up spills, breaking up spats about whose elbow was in whose face. The rest of the world was traveling at warp speed, and she was at the center of it all, like the conductor of an orchestra of untrained musicians, trying to at least keep everyone playing in time.

The following day was Saturday, also known as Confession Day. Lily and Iris sat in the pew at St. Augustine's church, waiting for Jasmine and Violet and Marguerite to get their souls cleaned. From what Lily could tell, her soul was a small white pillow that fit inside of her, somewhere between her stomach and her heart. If she committed a sin, like killing someone or having an impure thought, her soul would get little black splotches on it, and only Father Connor could get them out. He calls up the Holy Ghost, and then the Holy Ghost comes and beats the splotches out with grace. Lily figured that there were an awful lot of people having impure thoughts, because whenever she went with the Big Kids to confession, there was always a long waiting line, and since she never did see anyone get killed, the sinners must have all come by for some other reason.

Alexander, John, and Louis went to confession, too. Henry usually walked to church with the others, pretending to be on his way to confess, but then slipped into the record store, making Louis promise to come by and get him before they all headed home again. Even for the older boys who did go, it just didn't seem that they really understood about the suffering of Our Lord and Savior and the importance of getting your soul cleaned. They just didn't understand it at all.

Jasmine was usually the fastest at confessing. Violet didn't put her heart into it, by her own admission. "I just tell him the same thing each time: I disobeyed my parents three times, I had one impure thought, and I called Marguerite a bad name. He doesn't even notice that I say the same thing every week – and he gives me a different penance every time. One week, he'll tell me, 'Say five Hail Marys and an Our Father,' and the next week he'll tell me to say the whole damned rosary!" Violet popped a piece of Bazooka bubble gum into her mouth. "I mean c'mon, Father – which one is it?"

"You know, Violet," said Marguerite, "lying in confession is just another sin. So not only aren't you getting absolution for your real sins, but the ones you're making up are just more lies. You're getting deeper into a hole each time you come here. You'd be better off if you didn't even confess."

"Believe me," said Violet, using her front teeth to pull the pink gum over the tip of her tongue, "I wouldn't come here at all if I thought I could get away with it."

"I just hope you change your tune before you die, or you'll be spending a very long time in Purgatory. I'd rather spend five minutes in confession every week and then go straight to heaven when I die."

"Purgatory," spat Violet, "I bet there isn't even such a place." She read the comic from her gum wrapper, and chuckled. "See?" she added. "My fortune says, 'You will soon embark on a pleasant voyage.'"

"You're also not supposed to chew gum in church," added Marguerite. Violet responded by blowing as big a bubble as she could manage, and then delivering a sharp slap to her lips. The loud pop echoed off the cavernous walls of the church, drawing looks and "tsk, tsk"s from parishioners who just wanted to finish their prayers in peace and get home for dinner.

"Both of you, just stop it!" Jasmine spoke with as much force as she could muster without breaking a whisper. "Marguerite, it's your turn." Jasmine motioned to the confessional as a crooked white-haired woman emerged and hobbled to the front pew.

Of the five Capotosti sisters, Marguerite and Violet looked the most alike. They both had Carlo Capotosti's deep-set dark brown eyes, heavy eyebrows, stately Roman nose, olive complexion, and thick, coarse, black hair. But the similarities ended there. Except that they both loved Jasmine, which was the one thing that motivated them to at least try to get along.

Marguerite was always in the confessional the longest. "Geez Louise, Marguerite," Violet said when she finally emerged, "What did you do – rob a bank?" To which Marguerite simply stuck out her tongue and then slipped into position to say her penance.

On the back of each pew were mounted a metal clip and a rectangular wooden box. The clip was for the men to hang their hats, and the box had little pencils and envelopes in it. The envelopes and pencils were probably so you could send a letter to Jesus, or God. You definitely wouldn't want to write to the Holy Ghost, though. Besides the fact that he could send you to Purgatory, he didn't even have a face, and how can you write a letter to someone without a face?

Lily planned to send a note to Jesus as soon as she was able to make more letters, and could write something else besides her name. She took an envelope and pencil from the box. "Dear Beloved Savior," she pretended to write. "My Auntie Rosa says that some bad men apprehended you and killed you. And Auntie Rosa also says that they killed you because of the bad things we do. I don't really understand that, because that definitely is not fair. I hope you did not have to go to Purgatory, and if you did have to go to Purgatory, I hope you are in Heaven by now. Your friend, Lily."

Lily wasn't sure what Purgatory was like, but it didn't sound like anywhere anyone wanted to go. When she was older, she would be able to say penance for her sins, but what if she died before the Holy Ghost could beat the sins out of her soul? Maybe if she just did penance all the time the Holy Ghost would go ahead and dissolve her sins and let her get into Heaven anyway. So that's what she would do.

Lily knelt down, looked up at the altar, and folded her hands. The far wall of the church was hand-painted in a geometric floral pattern of orange, blue, green, yellow, and red. Lily imagined that if she walked up to it and licked it, it would taste like the taffy that comes wrapped in wax paper that they have at Pop's store at the corner of Arnett Boulevard and Post Avenue. Lily would stay in church all day, if she could lick those taffy walls. She wouldn't even have to stop praying, since you only use your mind to pray, and not your tongue. It would start to get dark, and at long last someone would come looking for her – probably Jasmine – and she would say, "Lily – have you been in church all day? My, but you will certainly skip right past Purgatory and go straight to Heaven when you die."

Suspended over the altar was a life-sized statue of Christ crucified. Jesus' eyelids were halfway closed, heavy with agony and exhaustion. Drops of blood trailed from his crown of thorns down to his jawbone. He looked down at Lily with sorrow, as if to say, "Why did you do this to me?" Lily's eyes stung with her own sense of helplessness and with the guilt of thinking about candy while Jesus was suffering so much, when he didn't even do anything wrong at all.

Getting your sins dissolved must hurt, too, because each person had to go through that little door, and when they came out again, they went directly to a pew, knelt down and started praying, some of them crying, even, but definitely none of them looked very happy at all. Except sometimes John and Alexander. Sometimes they came out of the box making faces and giggling.

"What did you tell him?" John asked Alexander as they slipped into the pew in front of where Lily sat holding the envelope between her folded hands.

"I told him I whacked off six times this week," said Alexander.

"You did not," replied John incredulously.

"You bet your ass I did."

It seemed to Lily that if Alexander just got out of the box, and the Holy Ghost just got done dissolving his splotches, he shouldn't come out here and make more of them by saying the "a" word – especially right in front of Jesus, who had already suffered enough.

"What did you say?" asked John.

"I walked right in there, I knelt down and I said, 'Bless me Father for I have sinned, it has been one week since my last confession. These are my sins: I had lustful thoughts and then whacked off every day."

John let out a yelp, and then he crouched down behind the pew, his body shaking with stifled laughter.

"Oh, man – what did the old man say?"

"He said, 'Masturbated. I had lustful thoughts and I masturbated every day.'"

"So I said to him, 'Wow - you too, Father?'"

By that point, John was on the floor between the pew and the kneeler, fat tears rolling down his red cheeks.

"So he said to me, 'No, young man, I am instructing you to use the term 'masturbate' rather than saying 'whacked off.' Then he said something about character and humility - who knows what the hell he was saying?"

"I can't believe you got him to say 'whacked off,'" John said, sitting up. John noticed Lily watching them, and he reached over and snatched the collection envelope from her hand.

"Whatcha got there, Lily of the Valley?"

"John-" protested Lily. "Give it back."

"You're not supposed to write on these, you know – you're supposed to put money in them. You could get in big trouble for this."

Lily's eyes widened and she looked to Jesus, as if hoping for a revelation that writing a message to him on a collection envelope wasn't causing Him more suffering.

"You better cut it out or when you have your first confession, you're never gonna get outta there." John flipped the envelope toward Lily like a losing blackjack dealer. It landed under the pew so Lily had to climb under to retrieve it. She shoved the envelope into the back pocket of her pedal pushers, with plans to place it in the public garbage can on the way home so no one would ever be able to connect her to the crime.

John turned to Alexander, "So what's your penance?"

"I have to say one Our Father and one Hail Mary for each time, but I'm going to say at least ten, 'cause I'm saving up for next week."

At that, both boys burst into laughter and one of the little doors opened. Father Connor's white head emerged. He scowled and put a "shhh" finger to his mouth. John and Alexander snapped to Catholic attention with their knees to the kneeler pad, their folded hands at their chests, and their heads bowed. As soon as the little door closed again, they sidled down the pew, stopping quickly to genuflect before turning and running down the aisle. They pushed the door open and burst out into the sunshine.

Every once in a while on Saturday nights, Lily's mother and father would go to Auntie Rosa's for pie and coffee. When they did, Jasmine was in charge, and if the kids were lucky, she would make a pan of fudge, or pop up a big bowl of popcorn. Lily loved just about anything made out of chocolate, so when she heard that Jasmine was babysitting, she rushed to get her order in.

"Jasmine, can you make fudge tonight?" Lily jumped up and down in place, shaking her hands like they were on fire. "Can-you-can-you-can-you-can-you *plllleeeassse?*" In a contest between fudge and popcorn, fudge was the easy winner, even though it took longer. In fact, you had to wait so darn long for the fudge to cool and get hard, that Lily found it practically unbearable. And the creamy chocolaty yumminess was all the sweeter for the waiting.

"Have you been a good girl?" Jasmine teased Lily. "Have you been helping Mommy with the three little boys?"

"Yes, yes – I have!" spurted Lily. "Just yesterday, I watched Ricci while Mommy paid Roy for the milk."

"And have you been saying your prayers?"

"Oh, yes, Jasmine – every night. And sometimes even in the daytime, too!" Lily didn't tell her she was saying extra prayers, just in case she should die before being old enough for confession.

"Well," said Jasmine, placing her index finger to her chin and looking up as if she were thinking about it. "OK – I guess you deserve fudge."

With that, Lily threw her body against Jasmine's, wrapping both arms around Jasmine's leg.

"Thank you, thank you, thank you!" Jasmine reached down and tickled Lily's ribs until she laughed so hard that she had to let go. Getting tickled by Jasmine was fun. It was much better than when Alexander played his tickle torture game. Even though Lily laughed every time, it just didn't feel like being tickled. Every time, she would try not to laugh. She would try to hold it in, or think of the suffering of Our Beloved Savior to try and get sad, but she just couldn't stop the laughing. And even though she would tell her brother to stop, he wouldn't. You could say "no" all you wanted during tickle torture, but if you didn't like it, you wouldn't laugh.

But with Alexander and John heading over to Bony Murphy's house for a boy-girl party, there would be no tickle torture tonight. Lawrence Welk would be on TV and Lily may even get two pieces of fudge.

As soon as her parents pulled out of the driveway, Lily headed for the stairs, to make the prerequisite change into her pajamas. Fourteen steps. One for each Capotosti. She always recited their names as she climbed: *Mommy, Daddy, Alexander, John, Jasmine, Violet, Marguerite, Henry, Louis, Iris, Lily, William, Charles, Richard*.

Lily shared a bedroom with her sisters. Jasmine had a single bed in the corner, Violet and Marguerite slept in the double by the window, and Lily and Iris slept in the bunk bed, with Lily on the bottom. She didn't mind being on the bottom bunk. Having Iris hanging over her made her feel safe. The underside of the upper bed frame was a grid of rectangular springs and Lily would poke at them with her fingers when she needed to get Iris' attention. Iris was like that princess in the story who couldn't fall asleep because there was a pea under her mattress – unlike Lily who could fall asleep under almost any conditions – crying babies, teenage brothers chasing each other up and down the stairs, teenage sisters giggling into the wee hours.

It was also fun to lie in bed on her back, place the soles of her feet on the bottom of Iris' mattress, and bounce Iris up and down. Sometimes Iris got angry, but mostly she laughed. Once in a while, Lily would think about what it might be like if Iris' mattress broke through and fell on top of her. One minute, laughing and having fun, the next minute mashed like a potato. If it did happen, Lily hoped all the sisters would be there. Between the four of them, they would be able to save her. They would lift Iris' bed off of her and she would have little rectangle marks all over her body, but they would go away in time. Such an accident might even earn Lily an extra piece of fudge, but she wasn't sure if it was worth it or not. It would depend on how much having the mattress fall on her would hurt.

Lily crossed her arms at her waist, grabbed the tail of her shirt with both hands, and in one smooth motion whisked it off, turning it inside out and dropping it on the floor next to her bed. She lowered her pants to the floor and pulled her feet out one by one, using each foot to free the other. Just as she was reaching under her pillow for her nightie, the bedroom door closed. Lily jumped.

"Lily of the Valley," said Violet. "You should keep the door closed whenever any of us is in here getting undressed, OK?"

"OK, Violet," said Lily, pulling her nightgown over her head. "I'm sorry." It was difficult for Lily to keep track of the rules she knew but forgot to obey, as opposed to the things that she just didn't know. So she simply apologized for everything, just in case.

"Don't apologize, silly goose," chided Violet. "Just remember it."

Lily watched as Violet crossed over to the dresser, opened the bottom drawer, and pulled out her nightgown. Violet studied her own face in the mirror as she unbuttoned her white cotton blouse. Pausing, she placed her index finger at the end of her nose, making various faces into the mirror as she pressed against her nose, making it wider, pushing the tip of it up, or down. Lily was still fumbling with her nightgown, working to bring the side with the label round back, the side with the ribbons round front, and get her hands into the arm holes.

"What are you grinning at?" asked Violet, looking at Lily in the mirror.

"You're making funny faces!" Lily giggled as her nightgown fell into place. She pattered across the room and out the door.

"Lily!" Violet called after her. "The door!"

"Sorry!" called Lily from halfway down the stairs.

The kitchen counter was staged for fudge: Baker's chocolate, corn syrup, sugar, and evaporated milk, which – even though it came in a little can with a picture of a cow on it - was store-bought and did not come from Roy's truck. Lily's father put evaporated milk in his coffee, and Jasmine used it to make fudge. Lily once took a sip from a can that she found in the Frigidaire. After all, life would be a lot easier if she could drink evaporated milk instead of regular milk – but she ran to the sink and spit it out. She then added evaporated milk to her list of things that sounded good, but tasted awful. Like baker's chocolate. She once scaled the counter and broke off a square to nibble on. It tasted like dirt, or poop. How could something so vile be part of something so delicious as fudge?

Lily climbed the kitchen stepladder and sat on the top so she could get a good view of Jasmine putting the ingredients into the bowl and mixing it all up. When it was time to grease the pan, Jasmine wrapped Lily's hand in wax paper, and placed a glob of butter at her fingertips. With the care of an artist, Lily coated the bottom and sides of the pan with the butter, making sure to get into the corners and to not leave any clumps.

"Now, we wait," announced Jasmine.

Bobby and Cissy had to be the two most beautiful people in the whole world. Cissy looked a lot like Jasmine, except she had sparkly dresses, and a perfect little bow in her blond hair. Dancing and singing on *The Lawrence Welk Show* was just about the greatest thing you could do – you got to wear beautiful things every Saturday, and you would just be smiling all the time.

"Take Sominex tonight and sleep... safe and restful sleep, sleep, sleep." As soon as the commercial came on, Lily jumped up and ran into the kitchen to check on the fudge. Jasmine and Violet were playing cards at the table.

"War!" shouted Violet.

Each of the girls placed two more cards face down, and one face up. Jasmine's facing card was a three of spades. Violet's was a Jack of Hearts.

"Take that!" Violet jumped up from the table, and did a little victory dance before capturing Jasmine's cards into her pile.

"Geez, Louise," said Jasmine. "You act like you just won a million dollars or something. And no, little one," she added, turning to Lily, "the fudge is not ready yet. You've been in here three times already!"

"Holy crap!" shouted Louis from the living room. "It's a bat!"

Jasmine, Violet and Lily ran into the living room to find Iris and Marguerite huddled together on the floor, forming a sister tent over William, who was startled and crying. Henry sat in his favorite chair in the corner, his attention trained on the chords he strummed out on his guitar. Louis was running around the living room, flailing a small couch pillow overhead, throwing his entire body into the task as if he believed he had a chance first of making contact with the creature and second of immobilizing it. But Louis was no match for the bat as it darted about bashing itself from wall to wall.

Jasmine ran around the living room, turning on all the lights, which flushed the bat into the dining room. Louis ran ahead, pillow in motion, and Jasmine followed, turning on all the lights, followed by Lily, Iris, Violet, and Marguerite with a wailing William in her arms. Louis landed a firm blow to the brass floor lamp in the corner, causing it to teeter. Jasmine caught it before it fell. She shouted, "Louis, stop! You're going to break something."

"I can catch it!" he cried.

"There it is – over there!" shouted Violet.

Jasmine flicked on the lamp, and the bat fled into the kitchen.

"Not the fudge!" screamed Lily, and all the children ran into the kitchen, screaming, shouting, and turning on lights. They circled back around toward the living room, and the bat headed up to the darkened second floor, which set off a new wave of screaming as the girls were terrified to think that this diminutive Dracula would seek refuge in their bedroom, or closet.

The children climbed the stairs *en masse*, with Lily bringing up the rear. *Mommy, Daddy, Alexander, John, Jasmine, Violet, Marguerite, Henry, Louis, Iris, Lily, William, Charles, Richard.*

"Cover your head!" cried Violet. "Bats like to make nests in your hair," which, of course, made everyone scream all the more loudly and frantically.

Jasmine ran around turning on all the hallway lights, but the bat went directly up to the third floor, one half of which was Alexander and John's room, and the other half an attic crammed full of boxes of Christmas decorations, baby photos, yellowed linens, and musty textbooks. Up went the children.

"Jasmine? Violet?" their mother called from the bottom of the stairs.

"Jeepers Cripes," shouted their father. "Why the heck are all the lights on?"

Lily ran down the stairs to the second floor, anxious to deliver the news.

"There's a bat up there!" she shouted. "And Louis is trying to get him with a pillow and Jasmine is turning on all the lights, and Violet said he is going to get stuck in my hair, and -"

"A bat?!" Lily's mother threw her purse against her husband's chest, opened the linen closet, grabbed a broom, took up her skirt with her free hand, and mounted the attic stairs two at a time, with Lily at her heels. She found the children standing in a circle, looking up, the bat hanging upside down from a rafter in the ceiling. Without hesitation, Elizabeth Whitacre Capotosti charged over and delivered one sure, swift, fatal blow. Her children watched as the bat released its grip and fell with a tiny thud to the floor. Lily walked over to get a closer look. She expected it to look like a bird, but jumped back with a gasp, suddenly afraid and disgusted when she caught sight of its gnarled, brutish face.

Everyone stood speechless. Lily's father, holding the purse, and her mother, breathless, broom in hand like a victorious Highland warrior - the same mother who pounded the dirt out of clothes, who cleaned up pee and vomit, who constantly had a baby to her breast, who cajoled and convinced the milkman. There was Louis with his pillow, and Jasmine, Violet, and Iris clinging to each other, and Marguerite wiping the tears from William's cheeks. Then, as if on cue, the children broke into applause, cheering for their mother, the bat slayer.

5. IRIS

There were not many things Iris would rather do on a Saturday evening than sit cross-legged at the foot of Grandma Capotosti's rocker, watching her favorite variety show, with no one to make her move or complain that she was blocking their view. There may not be any popcorn, like there sometimes was at home, but if Iris was lucky, Auntie Rosa would make floats with the creamiest vanilla ice cream in the world and root beer that fizzed like crazy, which Iris got to drink with a straw. Besides drinking root beer floats, her favorite part of the evening was watching the plumed and costumed June Taylor Dancers filmed from above as they clustered and scattered like the multicolored chips in a kaleidoscope. She also liked seeing Grandma Capotosti smile, which she didn't do very often, when the jolly man in a suit said to the audience "And *awaaay* we go!" and "How sweet it is!"

During the show, Auntie Rosa got caught up with the ironing, and Grandpa Capotosti sat in his easy chair in the back corner of the living room, where Grandma couldn't see him, but he could see both her and Iris. Grandpa Capotosti had a mustache and a cane, and a little container he sometimes spit into, but he hardly ever talked. When Iris came to visit, the first thing he did when he saw her was smile and point his cane in the direction of the windows, and Iris knew exactly what that meant, even without words. It meant that when she reached her hand behind the heavy green drapes, and ran her fingers over the polished wood of the window sill, they would find what they were looking for: a hidden chocolate Kiss wrapped in silver foil, just for her! His eyes would twinkle when she hugged him, the way they twinkled when he placed a finger over his lips, and gestured for Iris to help him out the back door and down the stairs so he could go across the street to the tavern, and they would be so quiet Grandma Capotosti wouldn't even notice.

Iris was always sorry when the show ended, and it was time to rub lotion on her grandmother's feet, nice and gentle, like Auntie Rosa had taught her. Grandma's feet were cracked and blue, and sometimes she winced before Iris even touched her, which made her dread the task even more. When Iris asked Auntie Rosa why her feet never got better, Auntie Rosa told her the only thing to do was pray, and keep rubbing in the lotion. "*Ricordati le preghiere*, Iris," Grandma Capotosti would tell her when she finished, then Iris would kiss her parchment cheek, and scuttle off to bed, where she would say an extra prayer just for her grandmother, before she could forget, and wait for Auntie Rosa. Sometimes, if it took Auntie Rosa a long time to help her grandmother to bed, Iris would pretend she was already asleep, counting on the fact that Auntie Rosa would never wake her up to make her say the rosary together. Auntie Rosa liked to recite five whole decades on the glow-in-the-dark beads that hung from her bedpost, but repeating all those Hail Marys and Our Fathers and Glory Bes, on top of rubbing lotion on her grandmother's blue feet, made the memory of the dancers on TV fade away too fast, when all Iris wanted was to fall asleep with the root beer float in her tummy and the visions of the dancers in her eyes. Sometimes Auntie Rosa was so tired herself that she settled for "Now I Lay Me Down To Sleep" which Iris recited every night anyway, except with Auntie Rosa, it always took a lot longer to name all the people they had to ask God to bless. When it was Auntie Rosa's turn to list her names, she repeated the same ones as Iris, except for some minor changes, like calling Iris's grandmother Mamma, and Iris's father Carlo and her mother Betty, which was kind of a waste of time, and then she added a bunch of her own names, which was only fair, but then she got all strange and quivery when she mentioned her "little sister Teresa."

Although it made Iris feel guilty, it gave her the jitters when Auntie Rosa asked her whether she had ever told Iris about her little sister Teresa, and even though Iris replied yes, she had already told her about her little sister Teresa, Auntie Rosa went ahead anyway and told her the story all over again. One day, when Auntie Rosa was a little girl, not much older than Iris, she and her little sister Teresa took a shortcut home from school, and her little sister Teresa slipped down the embankment and into the Barge Canal, and drowned right in front of Auntie Rosa's eyes. Hearing that story made Iris's mind go berserk imagining her and Lily walking home from school, and Lily drowning in the canal, and when that happened, the visions of the dancers she was saving up for when she went to sleep scattered all over the place like the mirrors and beads of a smashed kaleidoscope. During prayers, Iris silently thanked God that there were no canals between Rugby Road and St. Augustine's and that the worst thing that could happen was to step on a crack in the sidewalk or not find any good bubblegum wads.

When the prayers were over, Auntie Rosa would press Iris's head to the soft flannel stretched over her enormous breasts, and wrap her arms and legs around Iris so tightly that she thought her ribs would crack. For the first few minutes, Iris didn't mind, because feeling so loved and protected was even better than seeing dancers in her eyes. But then Auntie Rosa fell asleep instantly, just like that, and began snoring right in Iris's ear, with her mountainous breasts shoved right in Iris's face, and her arms and legs pinning down Iris's skinny body. Unable to move, unable to breathe, Iris sometimes wished for a minute she were in her own bunk above Lily's, with no one loving her quite so much.

Pink feathers of daylight flitted around the edges of the bedroom shades, tickling Iris awake. Sunday mornings at Auntie Rosa's were nothing like weekdays on Rugby Road, with the chorus of bells and buzzes and voices resounding throughout the house, priming Iris for the first of the day's battles with her brothers and sisters as they squabbled over turns in the bathroom. This morning, the blissful silence and the comforting thought of a clean, sweet-smelling bathroom at her leisurely disposal afforded Iris the opportunity to savor the fresh linen sheets tucked snugly around her legs, and the cushion of feathers cradling her head. Iris rubbed her eyes, and ran a hand over her face, feeling the impression left there by the embroidered pillowcase. Sometimes, she slept so soundly in this bed she didn't budge all night, and in the morning when she looked in the mirror, she could see the initials *RC* imprinted on her cheek. Auntie Rosa said she had started sewing and crocheting and cross-stitching initials on all her linens when she was only slightly older than Iris, then stashed them away in her hope chest. Iris wondered what kind of hope was attached to sheets and towels, and then got to thinking that if they didn't have such nice linens in her house, maybe her mother hadn't been hopeful enough when she was a young girl. Or maybe that girls who grew up in Independence, Missouri had different hopes from the girls who grew up in Medina, New York.

Just enough light filtered in from the window for her to make out the shape of Auntie Rosa bent over at the foot of the bed, herding the pendulous breasts that had nearly suffocated Iris the night before into the capacious cups of a brassiere with a long row of hooks up the back. Making all that flesh fit inside the contraption and clasping all the right eyes together with all those hooks seemed an immensely annoying task to Iris. Not to mention the inconvenience of having those protuberances bouncing around on your chest when you ran or skipped or danced, which was probably why she never saw Auntie Rosa do any of those things. Terrified at the prospect of such an incapacitating development preventing her from engaging in the activities she liked best, Iris slipped a hand under her nightgown, and was greatly reassured to find her two tiny nipples still sitting atop her bony chest like two lonely pebbles on a tundra.

Once Iris was awake, she did not want to miss a minute of

Sunday morning with Auntie Rosa. She adored driving around with her aunt in her cream-colored Ford Fairlane 500, with the Blessed Virgin Mary magnet stuck to the dashboard. When the two of them drove across the rickety old five-ton bridge, there was no one to laugh at Iris for frantically trying to sum up the weight of everyone in the car, certain the rusty iron trusses would collapse, sending them all to a horrific death by drowning in the Barge Canal. It was just her and Auntie Rosa, and when she got afraid, she just buried her face in Auntie Rosa's lap and prayed to the Blessed Virgin Mary magnet until the reassuring hum of the tires on the asphalt and Auntie Rosa's declaration, "It's over, Lover-dover!" confirmed they had made it safely to the other side.

Iris felt all cozy and comfy inside Auntie Rosa's car, whose interiors were the same pretty shade of powder blue as Iris's valise, and smelled of Estée Lauder (she knew that was Auntie Rosa's favorite perfume, because there was always a bottle sitting on a lace doily on her dresser), which was a zillion times better than the stink of stale cigarette smoke and her brothers' B.O. that made surges of hot saliva flow to her mouth when she rode in the back of her father's station wagon. That flowery feminine fragrance, coupled with the privilege of sitting in the front seat next to her aunt, meant that Iris could ride in the car for more than ten minutes without wanting to puke. Sometimes, she did puke in her father's car, but that was only when she couldn't help it, just like she couldn't help spraying with vomit whoever got stuck riding in the back with her. Her brothers always got grossed out and call her stupid names, then took revenge by laying bombs in her face, which made her want to puke again. Her sisters weren't so mean about it, they just whined and looked at her in disgust, making Iris wish she could just disappear, together with the acrid taste in her mouth and the puke stains on her shirt.

"Lover-dover," Auntie Rosa whispered when she saw Iris sit up in bed. "It's early, go back to sleep." Iris detected her aunt's usual halfhearted attempt at injecting a tone of command into her suggestion, but knew she would have her way, because Auntie Rosa wanted to bring her along almost as much as Iris wanted to go with her.

"But can't I come, Auntie Rosa?" she pleaded. "I'm awake now, and I'll get ready real fast!" Not waiting for an answer, she hopped out of bed and swiftly exchanged her nightgown for the underclothes she had folded and placed neatly inside the blue valise that sat on a chair in the corner. A wide smile crossed her aunt's face, as with an upward sweep of her arm she passed a silver brush gently over the short, thinning curls streaked with grey that had flattened against the back of her head during the night. Seeing her aunt's smile reflected in the mirror as she dabbed perfume behind her ears, Iris noticed how unfamiliar and lopsided she appeared, with everything reversed, except for the nose that anchored her features in place. She wondered if her aunt saw herself the way she looked in the mirror, or the way Iris saw her.

"Skedaddle, then, Lover-dover! But don't wake up Grandma!" Her warning was superfluous; the last thing Iris wanted to do was wake up her grandmother. Grandma Capotosti suffered from lots of pains, besides the ones in her blue feet. She slept in the room next to Auntie Rosa's and had a little silver bell on her nightstand she was supposed to ring if she needed help. She usually started moaning when she heard Auntie Rosa get up, but it was hard to tell whether that meant she needed help, because that was what the little silver bell was for, and she never rang it. Iris supposed moaning was just another of Grandma's ways of communicating, a notch or two more basic than the words of broken English she spoke to everybody except Auntie Rosa, because she spoke to her in Italian. Iris tried to imagine Grandma Capotosti running around like Auntie Rosa, or even walking, but she couldn't, and figured it was probably the weight of all those hardships she suffered immigrating to America that crippled her. Auntie Rosa said Grandma had grown up in a little hilltop village in Abruzzo, just like those other Italian ladies with fat ankles that sometimes came calling on Sunday afternoons, and even though Iris didn't understand what they said to her, she loved those visits because they brought the very best cookies Iris had ever tasted. Auntie

Rosa told her everyone in that old village was hungry all the time, which maybe explained why they baked so many cookies in America, and that Grandma's parents had wanted her to be a nun, but she wanted to marry Grandpa Capotosti, and that was why they had to run away. But even when they got to America and had Auntie Rosa and poor little Teresa (she couldn't really call her "Auntie" if poor little Teresa died before Iris was born, could she?), and Uncle Bartolomeo and Uncle Alfred and her father, they were going hungry again, because they got the Depression, and then little Teresa ended up in the Barge Canal, to top it all off.

All those things happened a very long time ago, and Grandma Capotosti was old now, and spent her days in a rocking chair by the window, where she controlled the TV, the radio, Auntie Rosa, Uncle Alfred, Grandpa Capotosti (except when he snuck out the back door), and the sympathy of anyone who had any respect for sick, old people. Iris felt sorry for her Grandma, with all her pains and sorrows, and tried to think of all she had been through when it came time to rub lotion on her blue feet or comb her thin hair when really she would rather not. Grandma Capotosti may not have been real lucky, but Iris figured it must be better than being stuck in that little hilltop village. Good thing she left when she did, because she would never be able to get down from that hilltop now, in her condition. She couldn't even get to the bathroom alone.

Whenever Auntie Rosa heard Grandma Capotosti moaning in her bed or groaning in her rocker, she dropped what she was doing and rushed to see what she needed, even if she didn't ring the bell. Iris thought maybe she didn't ring the bell because she didn't like coming right out and asking for things, that she wanted Auntie Rosa to catch on by herself, or otherwise she would rather suffer in silence. But Auntie Rosa always heard, even without the bell, even without the words, and then when she got there, Grandma Capotosti would look at her with her watery old lady eyes and stitched white eyebrows, shake her head, and say *"Perchè corri sempre, figlia mia? Lasciami stare."* Once Iris asked Auntie Rosa why she said the same thing all the time, and Auntie Rosa said it meant, "Why do you run all the time, my daughter? Let me be." Iris thought it strange that it was Grandma Capotosti's moans that made Auntie Rosa run, but then when Auntie Rosa got there, Grandma Capotosti told her to leave her alone. It seemed like it would be easier if she just talked in words instead of moans and groans, even in Italian words, because Auntie Rosa could understand those perfectly well.

St. John the Baptist's church was just a few blocks closer to downtown Rochester than St. Augustine's; Iris was not quite sure why Auntie Rosa sometimes preferred to attend Sunday Mass there rather than in her own parish. Maybe it was because the stained glass windows were more colorful, or there were more statues of the Blessed Virgin Mary to light candles for, or maybe she liked the priest's voice better than Father Connor's. But it was Iris's hunch that maybe once a week Auntie Rosa just wanted to go someplace where everyone did not know her and stop to say how is your poor crippled mother, and your poor old father and my, how big Iris is getting, and are there any new additions to the family? Because as soon as they rushed through all those questions, they grabbed Auntie Rosa's hand tight and wouldn't let it go until they told her all about their problems, and asked her how to cure their ailments, and informed her so-and-so was in the hospital and had she heard about so-and-so dropping dead just like that, and all that talking made the big smile Auntie Rosa started out with whenever she ran into someone she knew flicker, then fade altogether. By the time they went on their way, all that was left was a whole slew of other people's problems to pray about, and sick people to call on and funerals to attend. That must be because Auntie Rosa was a gifted listener, that was what everyone said. Auntie Rosa said Iris was just like her, that way, but Iris wasn't sure if she was happy about that. Iris thought in her case maybe she was just quiet, and only talked when she had something to say, leaving all the space for other people to talk, so they figured she was listening, but maybe she was just thinking about root beer floats or the June Taylor Dancers.

It was a treat for Iris to attend a different church, too. She was all too familiar with every piece of stained glass at St. Augustine's, where every Friday and Holy Day of Obligation she filed into the pews with the rest of her class and all the other classes, her head covered with a lace mantilla, and of course on Saturdays there was Confession and on Sundays Mass with her family. Iris had made her First Confession and her First Holy Communion at an early age, the year the bishop said children should make the Sacraments as soon as they were spiritually prepared. Iris did not know how she would know when she was ready, but since she was next in line, her father decided they should get it over with as soon as possible, so every evening after dinner she sat with him as he smoked cigarettes and drank coffee and tutored her on her Catechism lessons and tested her on the Act of Contrition and the Credo and all the other prayers that must be committed to memory before she could be committed to Christ. The day of her First Holy Communion came and went without much ado, though Iris got to dress up in the same frilly dress that Marguerite and maybe even her older sisters had worn for their First Holy Communion, which was still pretty white, except for a few stains her mother said wouldn't come out. They also drove to church that day instead of walking, and Iris did get to ride in a window seat so she wouldn't puke all over her dress and make more stains. Mass was the same as usual except that she, too, rose at Communion time and knelt at the rail with her parents and the Big Kids. She was elated when her very first Communion wafer was placed upon her tongue, and surprised to find it tasted like the top layer of the torrone candy sold in tiny cardboard boxes decorated with scenes from the Old Country at the Italian import store. The only problem was, the wafer got stuck to the roof of her mouth and to the back of her front teeth. When that happened on the rare occasions she got to eat torrone, she just scraped it off with her fingernail, but one of the things her father had taught her was that it was forbidden for a lay person to touch the consecrated host, which was why you had to stick out your tongue at the priest. Iris breathed a sigh of relief when the wafer finally dissolved on its own, just in time for her to join the congregation in the closing hymn.

Outside, a snapshot was taken by the shrine of the Blessed Virgin Mary that graced the side lawn of the church, and everyone, including Auntie Rosa and Uncle Alfred, went home for a dinner of spaghetti and meatballs, which was Iris's favorite, but Iris knew that was not the reason why her mother made it, that was just what the Capotostis always ate on Sundays. Then there was a cake, although it was not like birthday cake because Iris didn't get to pick what kind she wanted, and there were no candles or anything to make it seem like it was really her cake rather than everyone's cake. While the adults were drinking coffee, Alexander and John made Iris follow them to the basement, where she hoped they would play the album with the wanna hold your hand song, maybe even let her dance to it, since it was, after all, a special occasion in her honor, even if her name was not written on the cake. Instead, John took a slice of Wonder bread from his pocket, and tore off the crusts, and Alexander flattened bits of the soft doughy part into little flat rounds. Under threat of tickle torture, Iris was forced to stick out her tongue and when Alexander raised the bread in the air and said, "Body of Christ," she had to respond by saying "Amen," then eat the bread, even though she knew it was wrong because if anyone, even her brothers, could turn Wonder bread into Communion and hand it out like that, what was the point of going to church? She certainly didn't think her brothers would make very good priests, either, and apparently her father thought the same thing, because when he came down to the basement to get the plunger for the kitchen sink which always got clogged when they had spaghetti, he screamed and yelled like crazy, mostly at Alexander and John, though. Just the same, Iris crumbled into a mortified heap on the floor, her frilly dress puddled around her legs, her anger at her brothers for ruining her day bursting from her in tears. Iris cried at thought of a fresh stain already marring her soul which, until her stupid brothers made her sin, she was envisioning pure and white after its first official cleansing. At that moment, she was struck with the realization that remaining in a state of grace was going to be more complicated now that she had crossed the line of First Holy Communion. Now she would have to take Communion every time she went to church, or everyone would think she was in a state of sin. And in order to take Communion every Sunday, she would have to make sure she remembered all her sins when she went to Confession on Saturday. To make matters worse, she would have to be especially careful not to shatter her state of grace by committing new sins on Saturday night or Sunday morning before church, which was easier if she slept over at Auntie Rosa's because no one tricked you into sinning over there.

Having already received Holy Communion dozens of times by now, Iris was feeling pretty smug and smart sitting beside Auntie Rosa at St. John the Baptist's, as she reflected upon the progress she had made. She worried less about her state of grace ever since she had stipulated a sort of insurance policy that covered the risks in the post-Confession-pre-Communion time span. She simply added extra prayers to the penance assigned by the priest on Saturday, and deposited them in an emergency account God could dip into directly as needed without using Father Connor as a middleman. Once Iris figured out the system, and settled the matter of how to reconcile the states of sin and grace, she was able to put the dilemma out of her mind, and enjoy all the good parts of going to church, like the quiet tones of voice, and the way the priest and congregation always knew whose turn it was to talk, without interrupting each other. Sometimes words were not even necessary: all it took was a nod of Father's head, and the altar boys knew exactly what to do, just as parishioners knew when to stand, when to kneel, when to beat their chests, when to cross themselves. Iris took pleasure in reciting the responses and prayers she had memorized, and enjoyed the sound of hearing her own voice, as it chimed in chorus with the others, instead of being drowned out like at home. She decided she liked ceremony: Once you learned what to do, how to do it, when to do it, you would always fit in just fine.

Mouth-watering visions of crispy Italian toast and bubbles of butter floating on the milky surface of dunking coffee sent Iris bounding up the stairs two at a time, chasing the aromas that wafted down from the upstairs kitchen. "Slow down, *Bella della mamma!*" Auntie Rosa called after her, as Iris flew over the green vinyl runner that carpeted the flight of stairs, and burst into the kitchen, just as Grandma Capotosti moaned, "*E' bruciato!*" Those two foreign yet familiar words made Uncle Alfred rush to the toaster, and pop out two smoking slices of bread. Irene Capotosti's frown of disapproval somersaulted and landed in a smile when she spotted her granddaughter, and she extended her arms for a hug. Her grandmother and Uncle Alfred were in the middle of their morning ritual of breakfast, consisting of half-burnt Italian toast, soft-boiled eggs, freshly squeezed orange juice, Postum for Uncle Alfred and coffee for Grandma, all of which were enjoyed at an even more leisurely pace on Sunday morning, after Grandma had watched the Mass for shut-ins on TV. Uncle Alfred always took care of fixing Grandma's breakfast, since he didn't have to rush off to work in the morning like most men, or like Auntie Rosa. Uncle Alfred had one of the best jobs in the world: He was a guitar player.

During the week, Uncle Alfred taught private guitar lessons in his studio (it was down in the basement of the double house, but it was not a scary basement like the one at Rugby Road, because there were lights everywhere, and lots of guitars). Sometimes, if Iris came over on Saturday afternoons, she was allowed to sit at the desk in the little waiting room and pass out candy to the guitar students and their mothers, and of course to be polite and encourage them to take a butterscotch or a peppermint, Iris had to have a piece herself. Uncle Alfred called her his "very private secretary" when she sat at the desk, and Iris thought it wouldn't be so bad if she got a job as a secretary one day if all she had to do was smile and pass out candy.

On weekends Uncle Alfred's Hawaiian Trio played at The Luau, a restaurant where they served strange-sounding food like

Pu-Pu Platters and drinks with chunks of pineapple and maraschino cherries in them. She heard all about it from the adults, who sometimes went there on special occasions, like when Grandma Whitacre came up from Independence for a visit. Iris longed for the day when she would be old enough to tag along and have one of those drinks and hear Uncle Alfred play on the stage. She loved hearing him rehearse, and when she closed her eyes to listen it seemed like the notes were surfing along on the foamy waves she saw in the posters that decorated the walls of his studio. Uncle Alfred was always so elegant when he went to The Luau, dressed in a tuxedo with a ruffled shirt and cuff links and a bow tie, more handsome even than Jackie Gleason. Way more, because he was so nice and trim.

Although Iris didn't really remember much about it, she heard plenty of stories from the days when she and her family had lived on the floor between the basement and the upstairs floor where Grandma Capotosti and Auntie Rosa and Uncle Alfred lived, before there were so many babies and they had been forced to move, since you certainly couldn't just build another hutch for babies in the backyard, or serve them up for dinner, like you could when you had too many rabbits. Iris sometimes regretted that her parents had preferred to move to another house rather than stop making babies, but then she wouldn't have Lily for a little sister, and that would be much worse.

After Iris hugged her Grandma, she went to hug Uncle Alfred, although he was never as grabby as the other people in the family. Sometimes, when there were all kinds of relatives around and everybody started hugging and kissing and Auntie Rosa was pinching cheeks and saying *"Bella della mamma!"* to all the kids, Iris would notice Uncle Alfred sneaking away to wash his hands. Uncle Alfred did lots of other things to make up for not being a great hugger; for example, not doing a good job squeezing the oranges when he knew Iris would be there for breakfast, like today. Iris could already taste the burst of tartness on her tongue when she spotted a pile of orange halves on the counter by the sink where he was scraping the burnt edges of the toast, and when

Uncle Alfred nodded it was all right for her to have them, she went through the whole stack, first sucking on the flattened pulp that still clung to the skins, then ripping it off with her teeth and eating it. She probably could have had orange juice too, if she had asked for it, but she never liked asking for things. Plus, juice was over way too fast, while she could suck on skins forever if they would let her.

"*Vieni qui*," Grandma Capotosti urged, calling her away from the oranges, and over to an empty place at the table, where she was delighted to see a dainty blue porcelain cup sitting on a saucer, just like the ones the grown-ups were drinking coffee from.

"How about pouring a little drop for Iris, Alfred?" Auntie Rosa said. "Add a little warm water, though, it's too strong for her."

"No, please! No water!" Iris begged. Her mother sometimes had to water down milk or juice to make it go around, and Iris hated the way it made the taste and texture turn all weak and flat.

"Well, then you'll have to be content with half a cup," replied Uncle Alfred as he poured, then set down a fresh round of buttered toast, browned to perfection.

"Thank you!" Iris said, pouring in cream, scooping in sugar, and stirring eagerly. Grandma smiled as she watched, then reached for a little bottle standing on the table, and said, "*E' domenica!*" Unscrewing the cap, she poured a few drops of clear, syrupy liquid into Iris's cup, under the reproving glance of Auntie Rosa. Iris raised the cup to her lips, and sniffed. Her eyelids fluttered and she swooned with pleasure at the mixed aromas of coffee and anisette. She sipped the hot drink ever so slowly, remembering to extend her pinkie, like Auntie Rosa did. Raising her eyes over the rim of her coffee cup, she saw Uncle Alfred to her left, Auntie Rosa to her right, Grandma kitty-corner across the table, and from the corner of her eye, Grandpa, sitting in his easy chair in the living room. As she dunked her first piece of toast, Iris doubted she could ever be more content. Biting into the crispy, buttery slice dipped in the most heavenly coffee on earth, she listened blissfully as the adults chatted about friends and relatives and neighbors, about the doctors and patients where Auntie Rosa worked, about the turnout at The Luau the night before.

Whenever her big brothers wanted to make Iris cry for no good reason, they called her "spoiled brat" because of the special treatment they imagined she received here, though Iris avoided talking about it. She was especially careful about not bragging to Lily about privileges her sister could not share, but sometimes a detail or two leaked out about a particularly delicious ice cream float Auntie Rosa had made her, or how much she would rather have buttered Italian toast dunked in coffee for breakfast instead of puffed rice. Iris had asked Auntie Rosa whether Lily might come one weekend, and she had replied possibly, when she was older, but for now, that little rascal Lily was a tad rambunctious and her presence would undoubtedly have an unsettling effect on Grandma. Iris felt so bad about the rejection of her request, and of Lily, that she never told her, but at the same time, she knew there was some truth to what Auntie Rosa said.

In the end, her desire to spend time at Auntie Rosa's always outweighed her uneasiness, so she went on accepting the special treatment she was offered, and went on feeling guilty about it. Iris knew she would never fight for attention. She knew she did not possess faults so atrocious or qualities so remarkable they would earn her special standing in her own home. All she had to offer was a smile and a sunny disposition. At Auntie Rosa's, it was enough to earn her unlimited affection and like a stray cat presented with a brimming bowl of sweet milk, Iris lapped it up.

6. LILY

It was Sunday, and Lily awakened with the unfulfilled desire for fudge in her belly. The children had received stern orders from their father to go directly to bed after the bat incident. Lily tossed and turned with frustration for what seemed like hours before she succumbed to sleep, finally lulled by her sisters' recounting of all that had happened that night, talking and teasing about who had screamed like a baby, who had acted the most afraid, and who the bravest. But all the sisters were silent now, except for wispy breaths and rolling snores, all in varied cadences, yet each in perfect measure unto itself. Lily moved across the floor in time, adding her own tiptoe rhythm to the daybreak symphony. Once out into the hallway, she hitched up her nightgown, tied the ends between her legs, swung her left leg over the banister, and carefully balanced her torso against the smooth, dark wood. Letting go of the railing, she slid down to the first floor with such speed that she flew off the end of the banister and landed on the white marble tiled foyer with a thud.

"Ouch!"

"Shhh…" her younger brothers admonished in unison from the living room, without taking their eyes from the television screen.

There was only one thing that Lily cared about more this morning than watching *The Shhh! Show*, and that was getting her hands on some fudge. Her stomach growled and her mouth watered as she made plans to sneak a piece before church. She slipped into the kitchen and opened the door of the Frigidaire, but the pan of fudge was not inside. She quietly dragged the step stool over from the corner, and climbed atop it. There in the sink was the aluminum pan, scraped clean, no doubt by Alexander and John who must have come in late, and had themselves a fudge feast. They had probably sat around, laughing and saying the "a" word without giving Lily a thought at all.

Lily reached into the sink, and scraped off the remnants left behind – hardly enough to even discern the taste of chocolate from the taste of aluminum, or from the dirt packed under her fingernail. She climbed down from the step stool, and with a grunt, she pushed it and sent it clamoring across the linoleum floor. She didn't even care if she woke up the whole house.

Lumbering into the living room, Lily plopped herself onto the floor in front of the television. She slipped her right thumb into her mouth, and ran the tip of her right index finger up and down the gentle slope of her nose.

The Whitacre nose was thin and delicate, turning up slightly at the tip, just enough to be perky, yet not enough to be pug. It was a sharp contrast to the Capotosti nose, which was fleshier, and seemed better suited to things like smelling cheese and getting angry. All of the children had either the typical Whitacre nose or the typical Capotosti nose – except for Iris. Iris' nose was a tad longer and straighter than the Whitacre nose, as stately as the Capotosti, but not as overpowering. Iris' nose offered the best of both worlds, and it was unlike any other in the whole family, which is probably how they could all tell she was so special.

Iris could also make her nostrils flare on command, a skill Lily had desperately tried to master repeatedly. If only she could learn to do that, she could really seem scary. Then the next time one of the boys tried anything with her, she could just puff out her nostrils and those boys would evaporate like the smoke from a blown out birthday candle, stretching out longer and thinner and finally drifting away into nothingness, like they had never even been there in the first place.

"Show me again," Lily had pleaded with Iris, the first time she had revealed her talent. Iris faced Lily, taking an official demonstration stance with her shoulders squared, her eyes closed, and her chin thrust forward, and flared both nostrils out and in, out and in. Lily craned her neck and peered straight up into Iris' nose, as though she expected to discover a lever, a switch, or maybe a button.

"But what do you do to make it happen?" Lily demanded, stomping her foot.

"I don't know," said Iris. "You just do it, and then it happens."

"OK – let me try one more time. You watch and tell me if it works, OK?" Lily closed her eyes and furrowed her brow, as if she could flare her nostrils just by thinking about it intently. Iris stood close, staring at Lily's nose, squinting at it, with the hopes of discerning even just the slightest quiver.

"Lily!" shouted Iris.

"Did I do it? Did I do it?"

"No – but you did something else. Your nose - it moved!"

"My whole nose?" asked Lily, grabbing the end of her nose with her hand.

"No, just the tip of it. You wriggled it back and forth. It was far-out!"

So while Lily never mastered the nostril flare, she did discover her own unique talent of nose wriggling. It wasn't exactly scary, and it didn't come in handy much, but it would be good to be able to perform it sometimes, like whenever Mary Beth came over to show off her latest new dress or sock monkey.

Sunday morning was usually Lily's favorite time of the week. She and William and Charles would often be awake before anyone else and they could watch whatever they wanted on TV. But if you were loud, and if you woke up one of the Big Kids, they might come down and change the channel and they wouldn't even ask. (And if you woke up Henry, you'd better run faster than him.) You could object, of course – for all the good it would do you. Challenging a Big Kid only ended in frustration at best, and with a pounding at worst. It was a lesson Lily knew well, but one to which she never quite learned to submit.

So the unspoken agreement on Sunday morning was to watch and whisper, united under the common cause of maintaining control of the TV at least until Sylvester the Cat was kicked out of the house by Granny, or until it was time to get ready for church. Tilting her head slightly, Lily reached up with her left hand and selected a section of golden brown hair, which she would twist and twirl, often until it became knotted – even sometimes with her finger still stuck inside.

"Where did you get all these rats in your hair?" her mother would say with a huff. And Lily would cover her face with her hands, partly to keep from crying as her mother tugged and pulled at the knots with a comb, but also partly to banish the image of little rat faces peeking out from behind her bangs, nibbling on her lobes, pooping in her ear.

Slowly, the rest of the Capotosti clan awakened and the house began to beat with the life of a new day. Lily's mother entered the living room with the baby in her arms, and placed him in the path of a sunbeam on the worn wooden floor. Lily called to him, "C'mon Ricci – wanna play rolly?" He squealed and scrambled over to Lily, his shiny curls flopping about like long, loose springs, and then he lay down on the floor in front of her. She placed one hand at his shoulder and one at his hip, and she rolled him first away from her and then toward her – as though she were using his chubby little body to roll out dough for biscuits - building both momentum and suspense with each roll. With a final "Whee!" she gave him a push that sent him rolling across the room. He laughed so heartily that it made Lily laugh, too. When he came to a stop against the ottoman he thoughtfully and carefully raised himself onto all fours, teetered for a moment or two, then crawled back toward Lily in a crooked dizzy line. With his mouth still agape in pleasure, he lay down on the floor in front of her again, his little face bright with anticipation and excitement.

Lily loved playing with Ricci. William and Charles were only one and two years younger than she, and there wasn't much that they needed from her. But playing rolly was something special that Lily and Ricci shared. It made him happy, and when they played she was a big sister, too.

St. Augustine's church was connected directly to the grammar school where Lily attended kindergarten. By now, the route was second nature to her, but it was different walking with the family. Everyone would be in their Sunday clothes, looking spiffy from their clip-on ties right down to their patent leather shoes. All of the Capotosti girls were crowned with thick waist-length hair, and on Sunday they would take extra time to make a braid for one another, or tie ribbons on ponytails for each other. Lily admired her sisters' beauty, and she knew that the dresses they wore today would one day be hers. She would not shun them as hand-me-downs, but welcome them as little pieces of Jasmine, Violet, Marguerite and Iris. And when she wore their clothes, then maybe she would be beautiful, too.

As the family marched down the aisle toward the altar, various frilly bonnets, white lace chapel veils, and shiny black heads matted down with Brylcreem would turn up from their prayers to look. Some people would whisper and softly laugh, others would make a face like something smelled bad. But Lily didn't mind. She knew they weren't looking at her; they were looking at them. All of them. God gave her mother and father more children than He gave to anyone else, and that meant He loved them the most.

One by one, the family filed into the fifth pew from the front. Lily's mother and Ricci moved down to the far right end. Then came William, Charles, Lily, and Jasmine. It was Jasmine's job to help watch the Little Kids during Mass to make sure they didn't slam the kneeler on the floor or get their fingers pinched in the hat clips – which someone invariably did every week, regardless. Lily wondered why God would put kneelers and hat clips right there in front of you that He knew you really really wanted to touch and play with, and then tell you that you couldn't. It must have been some kind of a test to see if you knew your rules. That must have been what it was like for Adam and Eve in the Garden of Eden.

After Jasmine came Iris, Violet, and Marguerite. Lily's father led the three oldest boys to fill up the left end of the pew, seating them on the aisle where Father Connor would be able to see them, which was almost the same as having God watch you.

The family stacked up like the bars of a xylophone, with the older boys gaining on their father's height. Soon he would be dwarfed by their burgeoning adolescence. Soon, they would be the ones capable of overpowering him. And soon, the booming, bellowing voice he employed in his attempts to rule them by fear would sound like little more than an impotent whine.

Once everyone was in place, Jasmine gently lowered the kneeler to the floor. She crossed herself as she knelt, and placed her folded hands in front of her face, with the tips of her index fingers touching her mouth. She closed her eyes, bowed her head, and moved her lips in silent prayer.

The walls that flanked the church hosted a series of stained glass windows, each one depicting scenes of saints, angels, even cute little lambs, which Lily figured must be the lambs of God that Father Connor was always praying about. She didn't know what was wrong with the lambs, or why the whole church needed to pray for them every Sunday, but it was nice that God cared so much about them, since Miss Swift said that animals didn't have souls, and didn't go to Heaven. She must not be paying very good attention to the prayers.

When the sun shone in through the windows, it captured the purples, reds, greens, and yellows of the glass and splashed them all over everyone, with no regard for such rules as coloring in the lines or being quiet in church. This morning, gold light painted Jasmine. Her bronze hair gleamed, and her rosary beads sparkled like tiny blue stars in her hands. She looked just like one of the angels from the glass, but only more beautiful, because she was real. As if sensing Lily's gaze (a talent the Capotosti girls seemed to have been born with, or perhaps learned to develop early in life), Jasmine opened her right eye slightly and peeked over at Lily. "Boo!" she whispered, making Lily giggle. Their father passed a warning glare down the pew and it landed directly in

Lily's lap.

"Jasmine," Lily whispered. "You're getting me in trouble."

"Then kneel down and say your prayers," Jasmine answered.

"I already did," whispered Lily.

"Well then, say more."

"I don't know any more."

"You don't have to say memorized prayers. You can just talk to God."

Lily considered this for a moment, then replied, "What should I talk about?"

"Well, you can talk to Him about anything that you care about. You know, school, or your friends."

Lily scrunched up her nose. "I can talk about anything?"

"Yep. As long as you're sincere, He'll hear you."

"What's 'sincere'?" Lily asked.

"It's like when you really mean something. Think of God as your father, and then just talk to Him from your heart."

Lily pictured God stepping off of the city bus with a Parliament clenched between his front teeth. He had a long white beard and a white robe, but no feet, and he floated down Rugby Road, with Lily walking beside him, wondering what He might have in His pocket for her. She closed her eyes and bowed her head.

"In the name-a the Father and-a the Son, and-a the Holy Ghost, Amen." Lily wasn't quite sure how to talk from her heart, but it was probably like when she said, "Night-night, nut-nut" to Iris as they drifted off to sleep, a ritual they kept each night, and which made them laugh, but which also made Lily feel warm inside, somewhere near her soul. Maybe that was her heart. Lily bowed her head.

"Dear God. Last night we had a bat in our house, and it was really scary and Mommy killed it, but then we all had to go to bed right this instant and Alexander and John ate all the fudge. I was very good all day, and when Uncle Alfred teaches me to play the guitar, he says, 'Every Good Boy Deserves Fudge.' I'm pretty sure it counts for girls too. I was just wondering if maybe we could get more fudge or something. Oh - and bless your lambs. Amen."

Sunday morning yielded to a buzz of afternoon activity as the entire family prepared for a rare event: company for dinner. It was Auntie Rosa's birthday, and she and Uncle Alfred were coming over for Sunday supper, also known simply as "spaghetti". Pasta was served every Sunday all year 'round, and it could come in any shape or size, but it was always referred to as spaghetti. During Lent, they had spaghetti every Friday too, except the tomato sauce was made with tuna fish instead of being simmered with pork butt and Italian sausage.

Auntie Rosa and Uncle Alfred weren't like most aunts and uncles. They weren't married; they were brother and sister, sharing a house and taking care of Lily's grandparents, Irene and Anselmo Capotosti from Scurcola, Italy. Grandma Capotosti had the arthritis and she had to sit in a rocking chair all the time. If she needed to go to the bathroom or into the kitchen to fix pastina and butter for lunch, she had a special walker to help her stand up, but she couldn't change her own clothes, and she definitely could not come over for dinner.

While the older girls were scurrying about cleaning and baking, Lily busied herself making a card for Auntie Rosa. Violet gave her a sheet of paper from one of her school notebooks, and she rummaged through the splintered Tinker Toys, Lincoln Logs, assorted Legos, and the smell of stale cat urine of the toy box to gather enough crayons to color a rainbow. First she drew a yellow sun up in the left hand corner of the paper, then an arch of blue across the page, followed by an arch of red, then one of green, orange, and purple. At the bottom of the paper, she painstakingly penned the letters of her name. Holding her creation in both hands as if she were presenting a king with his crown, Lily brought the card into her parent's room to show them. Her mother was sitting on the edge of the bed with a white cotton shirt in her lap. She was holding a needle up to the light of the window, and running the end of a white thread through her lips. There, on the bed, right next to the open sewing kit, sat an entire box of Russell Stover's chocolates.

"Oh, Mommy!" cried Lily, reaching for the box. "Can I have a chocolate?"

"No, Lily," replied her mother, pushing the box beyond Lily's reach. "That's for Auntie Rosa – it's her birthday present."

"Do you think she will give me one?" Lily asked.

"I can't really say," said her mother, pulling the thread through the eye of the needle and tying the ends together in a triple knot. "A person can do whatever they like with a gift."

"How's that button coming, Betty?" Lily's father called from the kitchen. "They're going to be here any minute now!"

"It's coming!" Lily's mother called back, adding, "Carlo, can you please ask Jasmine to check on the cake?"

"Will she open it after dinner?" Lily asked her mother.

"Mom!" called Jasmine. "Is this one of those 'spring back when you push on it in the middle' cakes, or do I need to prick it with a toothpick?"

"It should spring back when you touch it in the middle, and the cake should be pulling away from the sides – is it pulling away?"

Lily repeated the question, with a sense of irritation at having been ignored the first time she asked. "Will – she - open it - after - dinner?"

"For goodness sake, Lily - " her mother replied, biting the loose end of the thread off with her teeth. "How in the world should I know?"

"I don't know, Mom," Jasmine called. "I can't really tell."

Lily considered her options, and her best chance at a piece of that chocolate was to be close by Auntie Rosa when it was time for presents. "Well if I can't have a chocolate now," Lily asked, "then can I be the one to give the present to Auntie Rosa? I could put it with my card. Isn't it lovely?" Lily proudly held up her rainbow card.

Louis popped his head into the bedroom. "Mom – Henry won't stop looking at me."

"Can I, Mommy?' Lily repeated, still holding her rainbow card overhead.

"Mom – I can't tell if this cake is done!" called Jasmine.

"For the love of God, Louis," said Lily's mother. "Don't pay any attention to Henry; he's just trying to get your goat. Jasmine – I'll be right there!"

"Mommy - " whined Lily.

"Yes, Lily, yes. It's very nice. Carlo, your shirt is ready!" Lily's mother draped the shirt over the highboy and walked out of the room.

Lily was alone with the chocolates. She reached out and pulled the box closer.

"Whatcha got there, little one?" Lily's father blew into the room, a gust of cigarette smoke trailing close behind.

"Well, I have my card that I made for Auntie Rosa," said Lily, holding up the card. "And Mommy said I could put it with this box of chocolates and give them to Auntie Rosa when we sing 'Happy Birthday'."

"She did?" Lily's father watched himself in the mirror as he buttoned up his newly mended shirt.

"Oh, Carlo – they're here," Lily's mother called from the kitchen. "Can you please get the door?!"

Lily's father crushed his cigarette out in the ashtray on the dresser, thrust his shirttails into his pants, and blew back out of the room.

Lily placed the card on the bed, and picked up the box of chocolates with both hands. She turned the box over, and there on the bottom was a small tear in the cellophane. She picked at the loose edge, then picked at it again, and again, until the wrapper fell away.

Auntie Rosa might open the chocolates right away and pass them around for everyone to share. Lily lifted the lid off of the box, just to get a better look, and to decide which chocolate she would choose. Carefully, she pulled back the white tissue paper cover to reveal a gorgeous display of candies – some were square, some were shaped like little cupcakes, and some were like tiny igloos with a curlicue on top, all gloriously chocolate.

Lily placed her index finger at the end of the first row, and touched each piece of candy, leaving her fingerprint on every one as she counted: Mommy, Daddy, Alexander, John, Jasmine, Violet, Marguerite, Henry, Louis, Iris, Lily, William, Charles, and Ricci. She stopped and considered for a moment before continuing, Auntie Rosa, Uncle Alfred. There might be enough if everyone only had one.

"Mom!" Louis shouted from the dining room. "John took my fork and he won't give it back."

Lily leaned over slightly to the left, gaining a view of the hallway outside her parent's room, beyond the kitchen and into the dining room where she could see a sliver of activity as everyone scurried about, placing various items on the table, selecting their seats for dinner.

"Well, I'm really hungry," said John. "I need two forks."

"John – behave yourself," scolded Lily's mother. "Honestly, I don't understand some of the things you boys do to each other." She snatched the fork out of John's hand and gave it back to Louis.

Lily raised the box to her face and inhaled deeply. The scrumptious scent of chocolate wafted up and wrapped itself around her like a thick, soft, brown scarf. She put her index finger to her mouth, and licked it, savoring the hint of gratification on her skin.

Of course, Auntie Rosa might put the box right into her pocketbook and bring it home with her. Or she might open it right there, and Henry might take two or three pieces before Lily could even get close enough to choose one. And Auntie Rosa is always saying how much she loves the children, and she tells Lily, "Give me a big hug," and she squeezes Lily so tight that it hurts, and she can't even breathe. Then Auntie Rosa shakes her and says, "Ooooh – I felt that in my big toe!" Lily lets her do it every time, even though she doesn't like it all and it's a little bit scary. Plus, her prayer to God in church that morning was sincere, and she had been a very good girl.

With that, Lily took a truffle from the box, placed it into her mouth, closed her eyes, and bit down. Oh! the sweetness - the long-awaited pleasure as the soft chocolate exploded in her mouth, enveloped her tongue, squelched the nagging longing at the back of her throat.

"Do Mom and Dad know that you're eating that?" Lily was startled from her reverie by Alexander, who was standing in the doorway. Lily looked up at him, feeling stunned.

"Dad – Hey Dad!" he shouted over his shoulder toward the dining room. "Did you know that Lily is in your bedroom eating a whole box of chocolates?" Alexander didn't turn around; he just stepped aside in anticipation of what he knew to be the inevitable and just kept right on staring at Lily, with the hint of a grin on his face.

A rush of panic filled Lily's small body as she caught sight of her father charging toward the bedroom. She froze. Her father entered the room, pushing Alexander aside. He looked at the opened box of chocolates, minus one truffle, and then at Lily, paralyzed, with a rivulet of brown saliva trailing from the corner of her mouth to her chin.

"Lily Elizabeth Capotosti!" The room fell away. Gone were the chocolates, gone was her beautiful rainbow card, gone was the cigarette smoke and the sunshine. There was only her father's rage and his booming voice, which seemed to shake the window pane, shake the bed, shake Lily's small body. And for the second time in three days, Lily wet her pants.

"What in the name of God do you think you're doing?" he screamed.

By now a small sibling crowd had gathered in the doorway to get a glimpse of this latest drama. At one time or another, every one of the children had borne the brunt of their father's rage, and while it was usually just one or two of them at a time upon whom he would wail his hand - or The Belt - punishment was a group activity. If you were a Capotosti, and one of your brothers or sisters was in trouble, you were there to watch. There was a certain fascination with witnessing a different version of you experiencing something that you yourself had experienced, but which you never quite understood. Or it could be that you were just thrilled that you were not the one being punished right then and there, and this incident made you feel grateful – an emotion that was as scarce at the Capotosti household as were time, attention, and milk. Or maybe you looked on, knowing that sooner or later, by design or by accident, you would be sitting where Lily sat at that moment, and like a death-row cellmate, even though you were horrified at what was coming next, you were helpless to turn away from a glimpse at your own fate.

With one humongous hairy hand, Lily's father grabbed Lily by the arm and in a single motion flipped her over onto her stomach and laid her across his lap. He pulled down her pants, exposing her bare behind, and delivered several blows to her buttocks with his open hand, a grunt escaping from his throat with each one. Each blow sent a stab of both physical pain and humiliation through Lily and she cried out, until she broke down sobbing, looking down at the small brown truffle pool forming on the floor.

"Carlo – Carlo!" Auntie Rosa was shouting, pushing her way past the children and into the bedroom. "Carlo, stop it! That's enough!"

Lily's father looked up at his sister, distracted from his fit of rage, and ceased his punishment in mid-spank. Auntie Rosa bent over and took Lily into her arms, turning her backside away from the spectators at the door and pulling her damp pants back up over her reddened buttocks.

Perhaps because Louis still had the taste of being bullied in his own mouth, he stepped forward, and held his arms out to Lily. "C'mon Lily of the Valley," he said with a smile. "Wanna go watch Fred Flintstone?"

Her mind still clouded and confused over what had just happened, Lily was glad for this, her first offer of post-punishment sibling compassion. It was a commodity she would learn to treasure. Even though Louis was a Big Kid, and someone whom she usually went out of her way to avoid, Lily sensed that what had just transpired changed the rules, and at least for now, he was her comrade, her comforter. She reached her arms out to him.

Louis took a seat on the floor in the living room and placed Lily in his lap. She slipped her thumb into her mouth, and grabbed a section of hair to twirl, still gasping to catch her breath, searching for solace in her brother's embrace.

Lily loved the mysterious doors that marked her life at Rugby Road. The milk door, the laundry chute, the city bus, the confessional; she found them all fascinating. You just never knew for sure what was behind a closed door. She relished that single delicious moment, with her hand on the knob, that final fleeting instant of ignorance, when she had her last chance to imagine what wonderful or horrible thing lay in wait. That day, Lily opened a different kind of a door, a door inside herself, a door where she took charge of her own desires, where a sense of her personal power lay undiscovered, a door where crime and punishment were stored and through which innocence was lost.

With the lingering taste of chocolate truffle on her tongue, and the sting of rage on her behind, she knew the true cost of pleasure. That day, Lily accepted that the limits of tenderness and love and prayer were defined by rules that she didn't know and couldn't understand. And one thing she had learned from all the doors of her childhood suddenly had new meaning: Once a door is opened, you can never again be blind to what's on the other side.

From: Iris Capotosti <iris.capotosti@gmail.com>
To: Lily Capotosti <lilycapotosti@gmail. com>
Sent: Wed, January 19, 2010 5:31 PM
Subject: Going home

Dear Lily,

Finally, a place to rest my weary bones! Just let me slip the backs of my high heels down before my feet burst. Ah, better! I lucked out and got one of the good trains with power sockets in all the first class compartments, so at least I can use my laptop.

Rome is something else, besides being tough on your feet. Every time I go there, I experience two miracles: the fact that I am there in the first place, and the fact that I made it out alive. The older I get, the more I am impressed by the latter. Take today. I just got out of a meeting in a hotel near Piazza di Spagna, which did not go well, for the record. But it was worth coming, if only to get an early taste of spring (yes, that can happen in January, in Rome), and smell the *caldarroste* on the street corners. Those vendors probably make more than I do (which isn't all that much, but that's another story). Imagine, a little paper cone with a dozen roasted chestnuts costs 5 euros! So I was walking, or at least trying to walk, with traffic the way it is in Rome. I don't know what's worse, the cars or the people. They're both all over the place, piled on top of each other, cars and people, people and cars, cars parked on the sidewalks, people walking in the streets. Not to mention the motorcycles and scooters and mopeds. I skipped window shopping in Via dei Condotti, that's where all the designer boutiques are (the only people with enough money to shop there are probably the chestnut vendors!), and cut through a little side street. I started checking my messages on my Smartphone while I was walking (not actually so smart, I know) and thank God some guardian angel made me look up just in time to see a Land Rover careening straight toward the intersection I'm crossing. Why would anyone need a Land Rover in Rome? In the shopping district, no less? That was the second time today I almost got run over. This morning, when I walked out of my hotel, in a pedestrian area, mind you, I was just crossing the square in front of the Temple of Hadrian to grab a taxi. The sign says it was built in 145 A.D. and I got thinking about time, as in thousand-year chunks, when there I was, worrying about being five minutes late. Something about looking up at a 2000-year-old monument made me wonder why I bother to rush. Out of the blue, a dozen Moto Guzzis with flashing lights cut me off at the corner. They were blazing the trail for this official looking sedan with tinted windows, no doubt with some sleazy politician who decided to put in an appearance in Montecitorio today, just in case there's a photo op.

But as you and I know, it takes more than a crazy driver, or even a whole motorcade to take down a Capotosti, doesn't it? Reading through some of the things we remember from our childhood makes me realize it is nothing short of a miracle that we are still around to talk about it. I suppose you get good at learning how to survive, when you start as young as we did.

You know, to me, exploring those memories from way back is a little like opening that box of Russell Stover's and choosing which piece of candy to take. You don't know what you're getting until you bite into it, and you don't know whether you'll be sorry you did until it's too late. One thing I've been noticing is how the good things stand out in my mind more than the bad, kind of like remembering when I hit on a caramel-filled chocolate and forgetting when I got a maple cream.

Let's write more soon.

Love,
Iris

From: Lily Capotosti <lilycapotosti@gmail.com>
To: Iris Capotosti <iris.capotosti@gmail. com>
Sent: Thur, January 20, 2010 6:04 PM
Subject: Who's home?

Dear Iris:

Your timing couldn't be worse. Seriously.

I had an absolutely horrendous day – I don't even want to talk about it. The only saving grace was that I had a dentist appointment at 3:00 this afternoon so I was able to escape early. Imagine a situation in which going to the dentist is a relief... and the dentist gives me two shots of Novocain, but I *still* don't care because it's *still* an improvement over being at work - even though he never gets my name right. He'll call me everything but Lily - Lulu, Lila, Frank (OK, maybe not Frank) and I want to say to him, "Hey – why don't you just check the chart?" But even then, even though he's stabbing me and drilling me and he has no idea what my name is, it's still better. (Anyway, there's some truth to it too, and maybe he knows that I don't have a clue about who I am either.) But really, I don't want to talk about it.

By the time I got out of there, half of my face was numb, and I was still all wound up so I decided I was going pamper myself a little bit. I had bought this anti-aging facial mask from Dr. Lee, so I came home, brewed up some tea, applied the facial, and sat down to catch up on some personal email. So here I am.

(Oh, I swear, this mask smells like alpaca shit. I can't wait to wash it off. I am trying to drink this tea, but since half of my face is paralyzed from the Novacain, the tea keeps dribbling all down the front of me. I feel like a total stroke victim - who just fell down face-first in a steaming pile of alpaca shit. Really – I just can't even stand it anymore. I'll be right back; I have to go wash this off before I vomit.)

OK, I'm back now, but get this: Dr. Lee sold me some moisturizer, too, and after I put it on and rubbed it all in, I looked at the label it says, "Ingredients: Vitamin E, Bee embryo, Finely crushed pearl powder." Bee embryo? Really? Isn't that something you would tell someone ahead of time? Like, "So Dr. Lee, do you have any moisturizer to go with that facial mask?" and she'd say, "Sure – but it has bee embryo in it." I mean, doesn't that sound like something you'd warn someone about?

Of course then I found myself wondering what the hell *that* factory is like, and how many pregnant bees were forced to terminate so that I could have younger looking skin. I don't even know if I can use it again now. Anyway, what's the use of looking younger if you smell like alpaca shit, right?

Then there's this lovely letter from you, talking about train rides and ancient Roman buildings and car chases and politician motorcades and ROASTED CHESTNUTS ON THE STREET CORNER?? – Jesus Christ – your life sounds like a scene from a movie. (I should have auditioned.)

It must be really strange, though, to be able to walk past and touch a building that is almost 2000 years old. The oldest thing here besides the land is only about 250. Still, that does get you thinking, you know? It makes me think about Mom's forbears who fought in the Civil War (the fact that they were fighting a lost cause even back then should have given us all a clue), and about Grandma and Grandpa Capotosti who traveled here twice – probably under unthinkable conditions - until they found a way to make it work. How funny to realize that if they had stayed in Italy, you wouldn't be there now. Maybe no matter what we want or wish for, we are compelled to take the same trip over and over until it sticks. And maybe we are all destined to end up where we started.

One thing's for sure: You and I come from a long line of scrappy, which is probably why we survived our childhood. Well, I survived mine, anyway. I think.

Love,
Frank

7. IRIS

"Up you go!" said Alexander, squatting so Iris could step into the stirrup formed by her brother's clasped hands. With a swift thrust and a grunt, he consigned her to the back of the moving van.

"Ouch!" Iris cried, landing with a thump on the cargo bed, her blue valise clutched tightly in her hands as she peered into the windowless space in front of her.

"Just sit over there, and don't move, you hear me?" ordered Alexander, his voice booming with the authority temporarily conferred upon him.

"Ouch!" complained another little girl's voice, followed by another little girl's body landing with another dull thump in the semi-darkness.

"Hey, I'm over here!" Iris cried to Lily, who was sprawled face-down. Lily pulled herself up and crawled over to Iris on her hands and knees. "Come on, sit here," Iris said, patting the grimy floor next to her. Lily wriggled close to Iris, resting her back against the side of the van, and drawing her legs to her chest.

"Are you scared?" Iris asked, draping an arm around her sister's shoulder. Lily hesitated a second before responding.

"Kinda. All our stuff is gone, and our house is empty. I opened all the doors, and there's nothing on the other side of any of 'em."

"It's not really, gone, Lily. It's all here. And it's all coming to our new house with us."

"But what about our bunk bed?" Lily asked.

"That's it over there, see?" Iris said, pointing to the bed springs and slats of wood stowed in the corner across from them.

"But it's all broken! It must be in a million pieces!" Lily said. "Where are we s'posed to sleep tonight?"

"Don't worry," Iris said. "I'm sure Dad will fix it. He knows how to fix everything."

"I sure hope so," Lily said. "When are we gonna get there, Iris?"

"How the heck should I know? I don't even know where we're going! Besides, we haven't even left yet."

A jumble of approaching voices made the girls turn to look at the open van doors. The late summer sun framed a female silhouette as it hoisted itself into the van, followed by another, taller silhouette, and then a third, which sprung inside with an athletic jump. They belonged to Jasmine, Violet, and Marguerite: all five Capotosti sisters were present and accounted for.

"Well, ain't this just the cat's meow!" Violet said, standing with her arms akimbo, while Jasmine and Marguerite took seats on the floor across from Iris and Lily. "First, Mom decides to have Ricci right on my birthday. And now, what day does Dad pick to move? My birthday! Again! So much for even getting a cake this year."

"Shut up and sit down!" ordered Alexander, wagging his finger at Violet. From her spot on the floor, Iris could only see the puffed-out chest and head of her brother standing in the street below. Seen like that, with no bottom half, he looked less menacing, even a little ridiculous.

"Who died and made you pope?" Violet snapped back, as she plopped down next to Iris. Iris and Lily stared at her, their eyes wide and their mouths agape at Violet's show of wit and courage. As soon as they looked at each other, the two little girls burst into laughter, but they had to cover their mouths and pinch their noses which made their ears pop and their bodies shake, but that was nothing compared to the punishment that would be inflicted upon them if Alexander heard.

"Everybody in?" their father shouted, approaching the van. He looked inside, pausing to tug off his work gloves and mop the sweat from his brow with his rolled-up shirtsleeve. His eyes surveyed the last heaping load of furniture and grocery store boxes stuffed with fourteen people's worth of belongings, flanked by helter-skelter piles of the sundry items which were indispensable to such a family up till the last minute: pots and pans, spatulas and spoons, grocery bags brimming with open packages of sugar, flour, rice and cereal, a wicker laundry basket stuffed with the sheets just stripped from beds, two bicycles, a tricycle, a toolbox, Jasmine, Violet, Marguerite, Iris and Lily. "Now for cryin' out loud, don't touch anything, girls!" their father warned. "The big pieces are all lashed down and that net and all those ropes will hold everything else in place."

"Maybe I'd better ride with them, Dad," Alexander suggested. "Just in case, you never know!"

"Nooooooo!!" the girls cried out, their voices of various ages and timbres joining forces to communicate their unconditional disapproval of such an idea. Iris cringed at the thought of Alexander presiding over them in the dark van, with all those ropes and utensils at his disposal.

"We're perfectly able to take care of ourselves, thank you," Jasmine said. "And since I'm the oldest girl, I'll watch out for my sisters."

"Sure you don't need a big brother to look out for you and keep you safe?"

"Noooooooooooo!!" sang the girls.

"All right then, Alexander, you'll ride with your mother in the station wagon, together with Henry and Louis and the three little boys. I want you to look out for that stuff strapped on top of the car, we can't have it slipping off in the middle of the road. John can ride in the truck with me."

"But Dad…"

"Jeepers Cripes, Alexander! Can't you just do as you're told? For once? Let's move! Grab that door there, and I'll get this other one."

Alexander's eyes narrowed to nasty slits as he grasped the metal handle of the van door and, putting all the weight of his teenage body behind it, slammed the door shut with a bang, making the girls jump and the bicycles slide to the floor. "Have a nice ride!" he called out. Iris felt goosebumps rise on her skin at the sound of his sinister laughter.

She looked at her father, who was lighting a cigarette and shaking his head as Alexander swaggered away. He looked pretty tired, Iris noticed; she worried that he might not have the strength to fix her and Lily's bunk bed before night after all. He reached for the open door, and pulled it slowly shut.

"It's not a long ride," he said, giving them one last look through the narrow slit of light. "You'll be fine. And just wait till you see your new house." Iris searched her sisters' faces, but no flickers of enthusiasm illuminated the gloomy shadows.

"I can't wait, Dad!" Jasmine piped up after a few seconds. She was always good at making their father happy. "I actually saw the place, you guys," she said. "There's room for all kinds of animals there!"

"Tell the girls all about it on the way, sweetheart. We'll be there in a jiffy." A plume of cigarette smoke snaked its way into the van just before he closed the door, plunging them into total darkness. There was a groan from the hinges, and a thud from the latch as they were locked in. Iris was glad for that familiar whiff of her father's cigarette that had sneaked in to accompany them on the trip, even if it did make her stomach do a little flip.

Car doors slammed. Engines coughed. The van lurched forward. Iris made the sign of the cross, just like Auntie Rosa always did when they drove past a church or a cemetery. Rugby Road was a bit of both.

Each time the van made a turn, Iris was thrown either against Lily or Violet. As their bodies swayed in one direction and then the other, Iris tried to picture where they were, but couldn't. It was a strange feeling, knowing where you had come from, but not knowing where you were, or where you were going. But what was the worst thing that could happen?

Iris had been sitting on the stoop for nearly an hour, putting out feelers. She was intent on observing her surroundings, and training her nose to the new smells in the air as she gazed at the large lot of unkempt land on which her new home stood. Swaying in a light breeze, the last Queen Ann's lace and Black-Eyed Susans of the season waved farewell to the summer, their heads hanging in wilted acquiescence to their imminent end. Like the other wildflowers in the field, they would soon be beheaded, and tossed onto the fire smoldering in the backyard of 75 Chestnut Crest, ignited by the new owner, Carlo Capotosti, to burn the mountains of greenery produced by his mowing and chopping.

Iris was thinking about Jasmine, who knew all kinds of things about animals. She said that cats adapted more easily to a new environment if their whiskers were trimmed after a move; Jasmine didn't have a cat, not yet at least, but she did have a poodle, and had already clipped its whiskers, just in case the trick worked for dogs, too. Iris wondered whether getting her own hair cut would help her grow accustomed to her new surroundings, too. There was one way to find out.

"Mom!" Iris called out, as the screen door slammed behind her, and she entered the kitchen.

Her mother looked up from the stack of cardboard boxes she was unpacking in the kitchen, with the help of Violet and Marguerite. Maybe coming inside wasn't such a good idea after all, Iris thought, when she spotted her sisters. They would probably find some way to rope her into taking over so they could go explore the neighborhood.

"What is it, Iris?" Her mother looked up, as she unpacked the large ceramic platter from which she always served Spanish rice. Iris must have seen the platter hundreds of times, but it somehow seemed different now, as if it were out of place. She felt sorry for it, in a way, moving to a new house all cracked and chipped like that. Though the house itself was far from new; in the van, Jasmine had said it was a hundred years old. But the impression you got from old houses was different from the one you got from

103

old platters. Looking at her mother gripping the platter in her hands, Iris wondered whether she wished she could have a new one, or maybe even wished she could quit serving Spanish rice altogether. But that was not why Iris had come into the kitchen.

"Can you cut my hair?" she asked her mother.

"For heaven's sake, Iris, does this look like a good time to you?"

Iris felt sorry for her mother, with all those old household items to put away, but that did not prevent her from rolling her eyes at her reply. It exasperated Iris to no end when her mother answered her questions with another question or with some reply she couldn't figure out. It was almost as if she didn't feel convinced enough to come right out and say either "yes" or "no." By now, Iris knew that the response, "Aren't you flying high lately?" when she asked for permission to do something or go somewhere was close to a "no," but left some possible room for negotiation. "We'll cross that bridge when we come to it" meant neither "yes," nor "no," but simply that her mother was not inclined to make any kind of decision at that time, and that Iris would just have to be patient. Iris hated guessing or waiting for an answer, especially when she could already see the bridge in question, and it worried her, like the problem of what she was supposed to wear for the first day at public school, where she wouldn't be given a uniform. That wasn't going to happen next year, or next Christmas, but next week.

"But, Mom ..." Iris wanted to explain the theory that having to insert herself in the unfamiliar environments of a new house and school made this a perfect time for a haircut.

"Buzz off, Iris," Marguerite said, cutting her off. "Or pitch in."

Iris knew when it was time to give up; she hurried back out the door before another word could be said, and headed toward the road, counting her steps, as always, whenever she walked anywhere. She was impressed on discovering that their new driveway was thirty-six paces longer than their old one, and disconcerted to see there were no sidewalks to walk on once she made it to the end. She figured she would be doing an awful lot of counting to very high numbers before she could get her bearings in this new neighborhood where the houses were all spread out and set way back from the road. Good thing she had outgrown her taste for used gum wads, because the pickings would certainly be pretty slim out here. Shielding her eyes from the glare with a hand, Iris gazed down the ribbon of road that rolled passed the house. She wondered which direction it was to Auntie Rosa's, and how long it would take to walk there. Probably a whole day, provided she would even be allowed. She had asked her mother about it before the move, but that was another one of those bridges she said they would cross when they got to it. Her musings were interrupted by frantic yelling coming from the back yard. She ran back up the driveway to see what was going on.

"*Yiiiiiikes!*" Louis screamed, blazing a zigzagged trail through the knee-high grass that separated the house from a dilapidated shack out back. Jasmine said it was a chicken coop, but Iris still hadn't seen any chickens in the vicinity. Louis was running like crazy, dragging little Ricci behind him, a cloud of insects circling around their heads. "Wasps! Wasps!" Louis cried. "*Heeeelp!*" Ricci screamed, as his brother bounced him across the grass.

"For cryin' out loud!" Iris heard her father yell from out back, where he was trying to fan enthusiasm into both the fire and the sons whose help he had enlisted. John was raking grass into a pile as tall as he was, while Alexander stood at the edge of the fire, disappearing and reappearing as the smoke shifted according to the wind's whims. Seeing Louis and Ricci engulfed in the swarm of wasps, their father grabbed the nozzle of the garden hose he kept handy by the fire and ran toward the boys, turning the water on full blast. He trained the spray on his sons, dousing them from head to toe as they screamed and stomped and flailed their arms, until the wasps retreated in reluctant surrender.

The sound of an approaching siren pierced the air, joining the concert of Ricci's wailing, Louis's shouting, Alexander's laughing, John's exclaiming, Iris's gasping, their father's yelling. Iris ran toward a stunned and soaking wet Ricci who was weaving his way in her direction like a drunken sailor. His bottom lip was trembling, his head of curls dripping. "Come here, honey!" Iris said, extending her arms to draw him close in a comforting hug, but abruptly blocked him when he was still inches away. She cried out in horror at the sight of one – no, two – no, five – no! - there must have been at least a dozen drowning wasps writhing in his soggy crown of curls.

While a crying Ricci clung to Iris and an excited Louis pointed out the location of the wasp nest to their father, Alexander darted to the garage and back to the smoldering fire, carrying a shiny red tank. He unscrewed the top, swung back his arm as if preparing to pitch a softball, and sprayed a shower of gasoline over the pile of branches and grass. After a few seconds' hesitation, the stunned pyre belched, sending a burst of flame into the air. Alexander was knocked flat on his butt, but sprang back to his feet immediately. "I got it going, Dad!" he cried out excitedly. "Look!"

"Jeepers Cripes!" their father yelled, rushing, hose in hand, back to the blaze. A bawling Ricci and a stupefied Iris were riveted in place by the sight of flames leaping in the air, and the shrill sound of the siren screaming louder and louder. The screen door slapped in rapid fire as Capostostis of various shapes and sizes came tumbling out of the house to see what all the commotion was about. Their eyes widened in collective awe as a gleaming red fire engine cornered the driveway and a crew of men outfitted in yellow slickers and hardhats hopped down from the truck even before it came to a halt. The firemen shouted orders to each other as they manned a huge hose and raced over to the blaze in the back yard. Amid shouts and cries and screams, the fire Alexander had forced to life was extinguished in a matter of seconds. The firemen stood in a semicircle, nodding their heads and patting each other on the back as they stared at the defeated heap of soaked greenery as if it were a slain dragon. Across from the firemen stood Alexander, the empty gas can on the ground beside him, a satisfied grin branded on the face topped by a mop of singed hair.

Iris gathered in close with her brothers and sisters, as one of the firemen marched over to their father. "I'm Fire Chief Maloney. And would you be the man of the house here?" he said in the scariest voice Iris had ever had the misfortune to hear.

"Yes," her father replied, running a hand across his sweaty brow.

"Well, Mister... what's the name, please?"

"Capotosti," Iris's father muttered. "Carlo Capotosti."

"Listen up, Mister Capotosti," the chief continued, "I don't know where you folks come from, but out here, we have respect for safety and property. We get a call from your neighbors complainin' about all this smoke comin' from your yard, and what do we find when we get here? A blazing inferno, for cryin' out loud, and a kid playin' with gasoline. Right under his father's nose. Gosh, with a little more wind this coulda turned into a three-alarm fire! You coulda burnt the whole neighborhood down!"

Even if he was a chief, Iris did not like that man talking to her father that way. He would never let Alexander play with gasoline, and he would certainly never burn down their brand new neighborhood. Blood rose to her indignant cheeks, but no words came from her paralyzed lips, despite her desire to speak up in her father's defense. Her father just stood there panting, his sleeveless undershirt clinging to his muscular torso. All eyes were on him. He released his grip on the garden hose, dropping it to the ground in defeat, then reached into the back pocket of his trousers, extracted a pack of cigarettes, and flipped it open. Iris thought she had never seen him look so tired, except for maybe when her mother was in the hospital giving birth to Ricci and he came home to cook fried bologna for the family's dinner. He offered a cigarette to the chief, and the deep furrows in his brow seemed to soften when he accepted. "You got a light, Chief?" he asked him. "Looks like I lost mine." The chief reached under his slicker, pulled out lighter, and lit both cigarettes.

"Look, Chief," her father said. "I have to clear this land somehow. Everything was under control. We just had a little emergency that called for my attention, and then, well, accidents can happen. Do you have kids, Chief?"

The chief looked around at the rapt audience encircling them. "They all yours?" he asked, waving a hand the way Father Connor did before giving his blessing to the congregation.

"Darn right. A whole dozen, that's what God gave me and the little woman." Iris had never heard her father call her mother "the little woman" before. Maybe it had something to do with being in a new neighborhood.

The chief shook his head and sighed. "Let's just say you come down to the station with Lucifer over there, and we'll explain a few things to ya' both. Firehouse number twelve. Be there at four o'clock. Sharp." The chief flicked his cigarette butt into the soggy cinders and turned away, gesturing for his men to follow. "C'mon men. Let's move on out." The crew pranced back to the truck behind their chief, looking proud as peaches.

"You should see your hair, Alexander!" John yelled, standing on his rake.

All faces turned to Alexander, who ran a hand over his head, then looked with disgust at the singed clump of hair that came off in his hands. He made a dash for the house before his father could react. They all knew as well as Iris that their father's temper exploded instantly when it came to the small stuff, which might be resolved simply and swiftly by The Belt, but when someone caused serious Trouble, they might be forced to wait for their punishment, and the anticipation made it even worse.

"OK, everyone. The show's over. Get back to your chores," he said, disbanding the group of onlookers. Sisters and brothers spun off from the nucleus into clusters of two or three, reluctant to leave the scene of such excitement. Iris walked toward the house, a sniffling Ricci in tow. She stopped outside the screen door to take another look at Ricci's hair. She could still see the wasps trapped in his curls, but they appeared to be dead now. As she was trying to muster up the courage to pick them out, she heard her mother's voice coming from the kitchen.

"Well, the only solution is a haircut, Alexander," she said. "You're in luck. I just unpacked the barber kit a few minutes ago."

Iris raised her head and pushed her forehead against the screen door to peer inside.

"I love the burnt chicken smell, Mom. Can't I just keep it like this? At least until I start school?"

"No son of mine is going to go to school looking or smelling like that!" Iris watched her mother set a chair in the middle of the room. "Now sit down, and let me cut that hair."

As soon as the razor began whirring, Ricci wriggled from Iris and pushed open the screen door. "Mommy! Mommy!" he cried. "Wasps!"

"What on earth are you talking about, Richard? What wasps?" she asked, her voice as calm as holy water in the font. Iris followed Ricci into the kitchen and stood immobile as she watched her mother plow the razor through the charred remains of Alexander's hair.

"He and Louis found a wasps' nest," Alexander said to his chest, as his mother tilted his head forward. "And they headed straight for his curls. You're gonna have to buzz him, too! He looks like a girl, anyway, with that hair. You don't want to look like a Miss Curly-head Cutie-Pie, do you, Ricci?"

"I'm not Miss Cutie-Pie!" Ricci cried, hitting Alexander ineffectually on the knee with his hand. "Mommy!"

"That's enough, boys," intervened their mother. "You just stay put, Richard, and I'll tend to your hair next."

Iris stood with her mouth agape, a sense of injustice stirring deep inside her, sending blood to her cheeks, and, finally, words to her lips. "Thanks a lot, Mom!" she cried, joining the group in the kitchen. "I could have sworn you said you didn't have time for haircuts! I guess what you meant was that you didn't have time for me! Why's that, I wonder? Is it because I'm not a troublemaker, or just because I'm not a boy?"

"For Pete's sake, Iris, whatever has gotten into you?" her mother said, looking up from the task at hand while Alexander snickered. "You got a bee in your bonnet, too, Iris?" he said.

Without answering, Iris snatched a pair of shears from the box on the table and hurried off into the bathroom, slamming the door behind her. Her hands were shaking as she grabbed a fistful of hair with one hand and chopped it off with the other. There was no mirror on the bathroom wall as yet, or Iris might have been stopped by the twisted expression on her face, or by the sight of what she was doing to her hair. She snipped away furiously, then with trembling hands she swept up her severed locks, and flushed them down the toilet. She stormed out of the bathroom, out of the house, and down the driveway.

Tears of resentment stung her eyes as she ran down Chestnut Crest, so upset she neglected to count her steps, not stopping until she came upon the duck pond Jasmine had spoken about. She stumbled down the grassy bank, her sudden intrusion sending ducks flapping and geese waddling away amid quacks and honks. She spotted a weeping willow tree close to the shore of the pond, and parted the fronds of its shady dome to slip inside. Her chest rose and fell rapidly as she leaned against the tree trunk, taking comfort in its solidity. She let her knees buckle, and the bark scratch her back through her thin shirt, as she slid lower, until her butt rested on the soft, spongy ground. As its cool dampness seeped into the fabric of her shorts, Iris wondered vaguely if she were sitting in duck poop, but decided she didn't care if she was, just like she didn't care if anyone ever came looking for her. They probably wouldn't even notice she was gone. The weeping willow's slender branches fluttered around her, concealing her from the world, its long, narrow leaves whispering their welcome in the soft breeze. Iris settled in for a cry, thankful that she had found her first new friend.

8. LILY

Space. That was the most striking thing about Chestnut Crest. Space to run and play, space to get lost in your own backyard or in your own imagination. All the Capotosti sisters had been piled into the back of the windowless moving van on Rugby Road, and came back out on the other side of the world. The trip to this mystical place known as Chili was dark and bumpy and scary. It was only ten miles, but it took them from the tidy city blocks, street lamps, and closely knit community of the nineteenth ward neighborhood to this sprawling anonymous place known as the suburbs. When the van finally came to a stop and the back door was thrown open, the excited but anxious gaggle of girls poured out into the sunshine and erupted into exploration.

"It's got an acre-and-a-quarter of land," Lily's father had boasted. They were just words to Lily, but to be here, to kick off your lace-less sneakers and run on the grass was something she understood fully, and it filled her with such a sense of exhilaration that she kept running and running, beyond the freshly mowed lawn and into the field of milkweed and goldenrod whose tips tickled her armpits and brushed against her chin. In her wake a dozen monarch butterflies rose into the air and flitted away. She kept running, deeper and deeper into the wild undergrowth, past the dilapidated chicken coop where Queen Anne's lace yielded to young cottonwoods, maples, and chestnut trees. They were all vying to establish territory in this neglected expanse of what was once someone's farm, but had been parceled off into split-levels and center entrance colonials, all of which made the Capotosti house - with its peeling white paint and crooked dark green shutters - stand out as the throw-back of the neighborhood.

Once into the small woods of the far back yard, Lily stopped, awash in the sense of being at home, but slightly frightened by the unfamiliarity of her surroundings. The birds twittered among themselves, as if conferring with each other about the newcomer and what they should make of her. Twigs snapped under the tiny feet of critters who scurried away, just in case, and cicadas sang their love song as Lily's quickened breath and heartbeat slowed down to meet the unhurried rhythms of this enchanted place.

Quietly, Lily sang the first line from the song Iris had taught her.

"There is a little man in the deep, dark woods." She stopped and listened, but there was no response. No echo, no ridicule. The woods absorbed her voice, absorbed her.

She continued, a little louder. "He wears a purple cloak and a small black hood." A chipmunk chirped and scuttled past, which delighted Lily and made her giggle.

Emboldened by the safety and comfort of the shade of trees above and the soft cushion of moss beneath her feet, Lily sang out in full voice, "Do you know him standing there, silently without a care, can you see him standing in the deep, dark, woods?"

Just ten minutes off the truck and Lily had already discovered the best part about her new backyard: She could sing – as loud as she wanted – and no one could hear her. And if no one could hear her, no one could make fun of her, or tell her to shut up.

Lily ventured further into the small woods, finally coming upon a chain link fence, which marked the end of her exploration, the edge of her new world. She was glad for the fence; it was a sign that there were limits to her new freedom; and while her world had been thrown open, she could never get so lost that she wouldn't be able to find her way back.

The distant clang of the dinner bell was both an intrusion and a comfort; a tether back to things and people she knew. For as intriguing as Lily found the anonymity of the woods, it was good to hear that the breeze carried the sounds of her family, which in turn, carried her home.

"Daddy says we have to leave our shoes in here." Iris was crouched over, lining up assorted sneakers on a mat in the back porch. "And we can hang our coats on these hooks in the winter time," she added with glee.

Iris had a passion for keeping things in order, a skill that Lily didn't possess and couldn't understand. Auntie Rosa always said, "A place for everything and everything in its place," but you could put something exactly right where it belongs and the next day it would be gone anyway. What good would it do to save things and clean things if someone else might just come along and take them or break them? Furthermore, tasks such as making the bed simply didn't make any sense at all, given that you would just be getting back in later on. There were too many other things to do, too much else to explore to waste time being tidy.

Having made fast friends with the yard, Lily was anxious to get inside and see the rest of the house. She dropped her sneakers and climbed over Iris, into the kitchen. The massive rectangular table was of solid maple, and had been acquired from the cafeteria of Rochester Jesuit, the high school that Alexander and John attended. Rather than chairs, backless wooden benches surrounded it. One long bench was up against the wall opposite the stove and refrigerator – both appliances were in "avocado," as Lily had heard her mother describing with delight to Auntie Rosa. But really, they just looked green.

What was once Lily's special chair was positioned over to the side, with Ricci comfortably nestled in it.

"Mommy – where do I sit?" Lily asked.

Her mother pointed to a spot on the wall. "You'll be sitting there, right next to Iris."

Lily took her place, looking about her and surveying the places where all of her brothers and sisters would sit, proud to finally recognize herself as one of them. Lily would happily sit in that spot next to Iris forever, learning to jostle and maneuver and negotiate meals with the rest of the family.

As the other children filed into the kitchen, Lily's mother assigned each one a seat that had been strategically selected to maximize efficiency and minimize fuss. All of the girls sat on the same bench as Lily, because they were smaller and it was easier for them to slide in and out, just like in church, with Henry sitting on the end because he was claustrophobic and refused to get wedged between two of his brothers like smelly sardines in a can.

Directly opposite from the bench that Lily sat on was a second long one, and upon it sat the three eldest boys, plus Jasmine and Lily's mother. This enabled Alexander, John, and Louis to get up and down from the table just by swinging a leg over the bench, and it also gave Jasmine and her mother access to the stove, refrigerator, and cupboards during meals, making it easier for them to retrieve another fork, more butter, and of course to put the water on for coffee – which had to be timed perfectly so as to coincide with their father's final bite of food.

At the foot of the table and within arm's reach of Lily's mother was a short bench for William and Charles. And of course, the short bench at the head of the table was for their father, the only person in the family for whom dinner ever waited, and who was the only one who could signal its beginning with the recitation of "Grace Before Meals." Lily wondered why they never said "Grace Before Meals" at breakfast or lunch, but maybe that was because no one really felt that grateful for puffed rice or bologna.

"Grace Before Meals" was no doubt the title of an entry in a long since discarded book of rhyming prayers, intended to cajole God and invoke His favor by saying just the right things at just the right time. There were prayers for mealtime, prayers for waking, prayers for bedtime, prayers to St. Anthony for lost items and to St. Jude for lost causes. Perhaps as a child, Auntie Rosa – being the eldest English-speaking Capotosti in her family – was charged with teaching these essentials to her four siblings, as well as to her parents. And quite possibly, as she read the prayer from

114

the book, its title was mistaken as part of the prayer itself. This is how they learned it, how they taught it, and how they said it every night, starting and ending with the sign of the cross:

"InthenameoftheFatherandoftheSonandoftheHolyGhostAmen. Grace before meals bless us O, Lord and these Thy gifts which we are about to receive from Thy bounty through Christ our Lord, AmenInthenameoftheFatherandoftheSonandoftheHolyGhost-Amen."

It seemed like way too many Amens, but nonetheless no morsel of food was eaten, no glass of milk was raised until the final "Amen" was uttered, and when it was, all pretense of decorum was hastily discarded.

Lily sat, fork in hand, watching as dishes whizzed past, grateful that a glass bowl of applesauce had at last come to rest next to her plate. She could barely reach the serving spoon, and getting a full scoop from the bowl to her plate took concentration and time – something she would learn you could not afford when the food was circulating. By the time she successfully managed to give herself a serving of applesauce, the mashed potatoes had passed her by, and the corn had settled at the far end of the table, separated from her plate by three hungry brothers and a distant father. Lily made a note to herself not to waste time on applesauce in the future; her mother always bought those big jars and they never ran out. Go for your favorite stuff first, and then look into the applesauce situation. The same thing applied to canned fruit cocktail, boiled cauliflower, and pickled beets.

Lily pulled herself to a standing position on the bench in order to reach the platter upon which a pile of ham had been heaped, but which had been quickly depleted to a few small remaining scraps. She stretched out to the full length of her body, grabbed the serving fork and speared the two slices she wanted.

"Lily," said her father. "Eat a piece of bread before you take seconds on meat."

"But this is my firsts," said Lily.

"Well then, sit down and ask someone to pass the platter to you next time. We don't stand up on the bench and reach for our food."

"We do if we want some ham," said Lily under her breath, pulling the meat from the serving fork and placing it next to her applesauce.

"What was that?" her father asked.

"Nothing," Lily answered quickly, sliding back into her seat and smacking the salty drippings from her fingers. She was fully aware of her father's intolerance for talking back, and firmly dedicated to avoiding the wrath of his hand. His poor hearing was a saving grace; if some sass slipped out before you could catch it, chances are that he didn't understand it, which came in very handy, especially for Lily, Marguerite, and Alexander – who grew to become the most outspoken of the clan.

"Me and Marguerite went exploring," said Violet in between enthusiastic chomps of corn-on-the-cob. "And we found a pond with all these ducks just walking around with no fence or anything."

"Marguerite and I," corrected Lily's mother.

"Marguerite and I." Violet wiped bits of corn from the corners of her mouth with the back of her hand. "Then, we kept going past the school and there's this little store called The Bungalow where they sell milk and eggs and bread and stuff, Mom."

"A loaf of bread in there probably costs an arm and leg," said Lily's mother, while slicing the ham on William's plate into bite-sized pieces. "You pay extra for that kind of convenience." It worried Lily that convenience was so expensive, which would probably explain why her mother looked so tired all the time. Saving money was hard; it required the making of everything "from scratch," and traveling great distances for cheap baked goods. On Saturday mornings, they would drive past three grocery stores to go to the Millbrook outlet where you could buy day-old bread for half-price.

"But it is good to know there's a place nearby," she added, "in case of an emergency." Lily wondered what might constitute a bread emergency and decided that any night when they had meat and no bread was a bad situation, since no one would be allowed to have seconds that night.

Violet continued. "And they have two huge racks of candies. Candy lipsticks, jawbreakers, Tootsie Rolls… all for a penny! Right, Marguerite?"

"Uh-huh," Marguerite mumbled, enthusiastically nodding in assent as she shoved a slice of buttered bread into her mouth.

"That stuff will pull the fillings right out of your teeth," said their father. "That's all we need – more dentist bills."

"They sell Parliaments in there too, Dad – but I didn't see any Thunderbird."

Their father kept a gallon jug of Thunderbird wine in the refrigerator to have with Sunday spaghetti. It had a screw top and a sketch of a bird with huge wings on the label, which read, "Alcohol: 17.5% by volume."

Their father chuckled. "Well, no, I don't suppose you would find Thunderbird at The Bungalow. I'll have to see if there's a liquor store around here somewhere."

"Thunderbird is what the winos down on Broad Street drink," said Alexander. "'Cuz you can get plastered for about two bucks."

"Young man," said Lily's father, straightening his back and placing the palms of his hands on the table, one on each side of his dinner plate, "I'll have you know that your grandfather – Anselmo Carlo Capotosti - has enjoyed Thunderbird every day practically since the day he arrived in this country."

Their father stared at Alexander, and Alexander stared back, each of them convinced that his point had been made.

"OK," said their father, turning to the rest of the family. "I want to make sure you all know the dinner rules here. Most of them are the same as our old house, but because it takes me longer to get home from work now, we will be eating dinner at five forty-five sharp. Just as a reminder: Rule number one – Jasmine, what is it?"

"Being late will not be tolerated." Jasmine recited.

"Marguerite – what's Rule number two?"

Marguerite looked down into her lap. "No getting up from the table unless you're excused." Everyone knew that this rule was inspired by Marguerite, since she couldn't wait to get up from dinner each night to wash her hands. She liked to wash her hands. A lot. She washed her hands before dinner, after dinner, during dinner, first thing in the morning, just before bed, and sometimes even in the middle of the night. Marguerite washed her hands so much that they were all red and cracked, which made Lily's father very angry. But the more he yelled at her to stop washing her hands, the more she washed her hands. Whenever they came back from seeing the special hand-washing doctor, Marguerite was either crying or very quiet and would go into the bedroom and not come out – sometimes for the whole rest of the day. When Lily asked her mother what kind of medicine they give you for washing your hands too much, she simply said, "Never you mind about that."

"And Rule number three, Henry?" continued Lily's father.

"No phone calls during dinner," replied Henry dispassionately. Henry didn't seem to have any friends – at least none that ever called or came over. He simply disappeared after dinner each night, and no one would see him again until the next night – but as long as you went to school every day and showed up on time for supper, no one seemed to really care where you were or what you were doing in-between.

One of many other rules governing the use of the telephone was that it could not be answered unless it had completed two full rings. Uncle Alfred operated his guitar studio out of their home on Winston Road, so they had a business line, which meant that Uncle Alfred and Auntie Rosa had to pay a dime each time they made a phone call. In order to avoid the fee, whenever they wanted to call the Capotosti house (which accounted for nearly all of the calls they made), they would let it ring once and then hang up. A one-ring call was the secret signal to call them back. It was almost as cool as having a special red phone, like on the *Batman* show. So, under threat of the blame for costing Auntie Rosa an extra dime, no one was allowed to answer the phone until it rang twice. And if it rang twice during dinner, you had better hope that it wasn't one of your friends on the other end.

At the new house, the telephone sat on the wall directly behind Lily's father, like the tabernacle behind the priest at the altar. Across from him was the back door. He was the sentinel of both during dinner. He could reach the phone from where he sat at the table, and when it rang that evening, he extended his right arm up and over and placed it on the receiver. It rang a second time. Forks froze and glasses halted in mid-sip as all eyes turned to the head of the table for a clue about who was ignorant or stupid or forgetful enough to call during dinner.

Their father raised the receiver from the cradle and, with a grand motion, brought it to his ear.

"Mmmm....yell-oohhh," he answered melodically. "Alex? I'm sorry, dear, but there's no one here by the name of Alex."

Alexander dropped his fork onto his plate. "Dad, cut it out!"

"No, dear, I'm sure. I do have a son named 'Alexander' however. Is that whom you are looking for?"

Alexander put his elbows on the table and placed his face in his hands.

"Yes, as a matter of fact he is here, but we're having dinner, and we don't take phone calls during dinner. May I take a message? Umm-mmm. OK, yes I will tell him. Good-bye." He hung up the phone and turned back to his plate. The children all watched as he sliced a pat of butter from the stick and smeared it over his corn.

"Well....?" Alexander asked.

"Christine would like you to call her back after dinner."

"Christine? Christine who?"

"Christine – I don't know. She didn't give me her last name."

"I don't know any Christine, Dad."

"Maybe it was Kathy, or Karen – do you know a Karen?"

"Jesus Christ, Dad –"

Their father pounded his fists on the table with such force that all of the flatware hopped in place, jingling like the bells in church during the Eucharistic prayer. Lily instinctively closed her eyes and bowed her head. *My Lord and my God.*

"We do not use the Lord's name in vain in this house, young

man," shouted their father.

"Yeah? Well at least I got his name right." Alexander mopped up the last of the food from his plate with the crust of white bread and shoved it into his mouth. He swung his leg over the bench and stood up.

"You have not been excused," said their father.

"I have to take a crap," said Alexander, walking out the back door.

After dinner, the older girls were given unpacking chores, and Lily and Iris were sent outside to play. The swing set in the backyard hosted two white plastic swings hanging on rusted chains. As Lily and Iris swung to and fro, the chains creaked and moaned, each one singing its melancholy song, perhaps of days gone by and of children long since grown and moved on. The wails echoed throughout the neighborhood so loud that maybe even Auntie Rosa could hear it from her house. Even though it wasn't a pretty sound, it made Lily happy – it was the sound of playing in your own big yard with your own favorite sister.

When they tired of swinging, they wandered, exploring, climbing the apple tree, playing tag, peering into the windows of the chicken coop (which was even creepier than the basement), and as the sun settled lower into the sky, they settled onto a spot on the grass amid a patch of clover and dandelions, sitting cross-legged, facing each other. Together they picked pink and white cloverleaf flowers from the ground, making them into chains by tying the stem of one flower into a knot around the bloom of another. They fashioned tiaras, necklaces, and bracelets, adorning each other with them. Iris made one extra chain, and set it aside for Auntie Rosa.

"Close your eyes and make a wish," said Iris, handing Lily a fluffy white dandelion.

There was so much to wish for; Lily couldn't decide. She wished for a Barbie Doll, she wished to see the duck pond and go to The Bungalow and buy some penny candies, and she wished that their father would figure out how to fix the bunk bed in time.

"OK – now open your eyes and blow on this, and if you can get all of the little fluffies to come off in one breath, your wish will come true."

Lily blew as hard as she could, spraying the dandelion more with spit than with her breath.

"Ewww!" Iris giggled, wiping the spittle of Lily's effort from her face with the palms of her hands. "Just blow on it, Lily – like you do with your birthday candles. Like this – watch."

Iris picked another dandelion and sat up high and straight as she filled her lungs with air, and then blew on the flower, spinning it as she rotated the stem between her thumb and forefinger, sending the tiny white fuzz into the air.

"Oh, man!" she cried, pretending to collapse from the effort. "Here, let's try again." She handed Lily another dandelion and took another one for herself. Over and over again, they blew and blew, exhausting the supply of flowers within reach, as the bright orange sun faded into pink, cloaking wispy clouds in purple twilight.

"I'm getting dizzy!" said Lily. She crossed her eyes, hung her tongue out of her open mouth, and rolled her head.

"You look like Crazy Guggenheim," said Iris laughing. "OK - but we have to try one more time, OK? This is our last chance. On the count of three – ready? One… two… three!"

With a loud wheeze, they each drew in a deep breath and then blew with the entire force of their small bodies. With the effort of her exhalation, Lily farted, and they both fell over onto their backs, laughing uncontrollably. When their laughter finally subsided, they watched overhead as the hundreds of white seed heads they had set free drifted away, swirling and dancing in the slanted sunshine of the waning day.

"Where do you think they'll go?" asked Lily.

"I dunno," Iris replied. "Prob'ly far, far away from here."

9. IRIS

"But you said Daddy would fix our bed, Iris!" Lily cried, standing in the middle of the new bedroom she was to share with Iris. The new bedroom that contained a bunch of cardboard boxes and Iris's blue valise, but not their bunk bed.

"Well, he did fix it, Lily," Iris said, "just not for us." She still couldn't believe their bunk bed had been assigned to William and Charles, with plans to add a third tier to accommodate Ricci, without anyone telling them so, let alone asking for their consent. But there was no use complaining about it now. "This bed's not so bad, though. You'll see." Iris spread a once white sheet over the worn mattress of the double bed, making sure the edges were even on top and bottom, and on both sides, then proceeded to tuck it all around, and secure it in place with neat hospital corners, just like Auntie Rosa had taught her.

"But I won't be able to bounce you with my feet anymore!" Lily whined.

"It's just as well," Iris said, unfolding the top sheet and tucking it nice and tight along the sides and bottom, just the way she liked it.

"But I'll never be able to sleep without you above me. What if something falls on top of me and crushes me?"

"If it does, it will crush us both."

"But it's not fair! That bed was ours!" Lily wailed. She was right. Your bed was all you had, in their family; it was not simply the place you went to sleep, it was the only place you could go and finally be alone. To think, to cry, to pray, to read, to study, to dream. And now she would be sharing hers with Lily. A hot ball of anger rose in her throat, but she swallowed it back down, just like when she almost puked but stopped herself in time.

"Stop crying and hop in," Iris said, wishing her mother could have at least found some pillows for them. Maybe tomorrow.

"I don't wanna!" Lily sniveled.

"It won't be so bad, Lily. You'll see." Maybe it wouldn't. "You take that side, by the window. I'll sleep by the door." Lily obeyed, and Iris climbed in next to her. They both lay on their backs, side by side, staring at the unfamiliar ceiling. Lily's body trembled as she whimpered, making the bed shake and shiver. "Come here," Iris said, opening her arm. Lily snuggled close, and said, "It's not fair!"

"No, Lily, it's not. But that's the way it is. I have an idea, though."

"What idea?"

"How about I tell you a story?"

"What kind of a story?"

"A story about two sisters who live in a fairyland."

"A fairyland?"

"Yes, a fairyland, where everyone says things like, 'May I please?' or 'Would you mind?' before they do anything at all that might bother the sisters, and no one takes things from them just because they're older or stronger and no one can stop them."

"OK," Lily said, slipping her thumb into her mouth, and parking her index finger alongside the slope of her runny nose.

"Once upon a time …" Iris began the journey, those first four words paving the way for many others that would lead her, hand-in-hand with her little sister, to a place where she wanted to be. At least for the night.

"Hey, Iris, I think I hear voices!" Lily said, sitting up in bed some nights later. A cool breeze fluttered in the open window, a train wailed in the distance. When the sound of the whistle subsided, Iris nodded. "Let's go!" she said. "But keep quiet."

The girls scrambled noiselessly out of the bed they had learned to share, together with their nightly fairy stories. They tiptoed to the wall, and crouched on their haunches, facing each other, nightgowns hitched up around their knees. Iris tipped the lever of the heating vent built into the wall between their room and the room shared by Jasmine and Violet and Marguerite.

"Ouch, not so tight!" Jasmine's voice filtered through the vent.

"Well, you said you wanted it straight, and the tighter the straighter." Marguerite was the sister Jasmine appointed to roll her curly hair up in orange juice cans at night. Iris figured she must really hate her hair to go to bed with a head full of orange juice cans.

"You're not even listening are you?" Violet asked. Lily smiled, and Iris held an index finger to her lips. She sniffed a prelude to some juicy conversation, and didn't want Lily to spoil it all by giggling.

"Yes, I am. You said his name is Todd, right? Now go on. I'm all ears," Jasmine said.

"Isn't that a nice name? Anyway, Todd comes over to the Ichbergs' twice a week to clean the pool."

"Those people pay you to clean the house and watch their daughter, and someone else to clean the pool? What are they, millionaires?" Marguerite said.

Iris leaned in closer in the hopes of hearing more about the Ichbergs. Violet had encouraged Iris to come over and meet the girl, Alba, and since then they had played together occasionally. She wasn't nearly as nice as Rita Esposito, but at least she lived in the neighborhood. And maybe they were rich, judging from the clothes and toys Iris saw in Alba's room.

"If they were millionaires, they'd at least have a built-in pool. But as long as they cough up the moolah they owe me every week, I don't care how rich they are," Violet said. "What I care about is Todd. He's *sooo* cute, and *sooo* nice."

Iris and Lily stared at each other, eyes widening. Iris had

caught a glimpse of Todd once, skimming the pool in his trunks and T-shirt. He was very tan, and muscular. If ever Alba invited Iris over to swim, she wouldn't be afraid to jump in with Todd there.

"What does he say to you?" Jasmine asked.

"He doesn't really *say* much," Violet said. "What he does is *listen*. Like, he actually lets me finish my sentences, and even laughs when I crack a joke."

Iris figured those were pretty good qualities for a boyfriend.

"This afternoon, I went out back and just talked to him while he was working, and then when he was about to leave we started holding hands."

Lily's eyes bulged, as the giggles bubbled and bounced inside her with nowhere to go. Iris wondered how it would feel to hold the hand of a boy who wasn't related to her.

"You held hands?" Marguerite exclaimed. "Far out!" An orange juice can crashed to the floor.

"Well, sort of. Todd's a little shy. So his hand was just there, resting on the edge of the pool, and just looking at it was blowing my mind. So I put my hand on top of it. And he didn't freak out or anything. We just stood there a minute, like that, touching, you know?"

"So what's next? Are you just gonna keep seeing him at the Ichbergs'?" Jasmine asked.

"Well, here comes the good part. He lives right behind us, in that new tract. And we're gonna meet some night, after dusk, in the playground back there."

"And then what are you gonna do?" Marguerite asked.

"Then, whether he's ready or not, I'm gonna kiss him!"

Iris and Lily muffled snorts and squeals as they raced back to their bed, dived between the sheets, buried their faces in the pancake pillows their mother had dug out from a box, and giggled until they were so exhausted they fell asleep. Sometimes real life was almost as entertaining as fairy stories.

Iris's tendency to worry prompted her to set off much earlier

125

than necessary on the first day of school. There was no crowd of older Capotostis to tag along with: Alexander and John were in one school, Jasmine and Violet and Marguerite in another, Henry and Louis in another. There had been no room for the two youngest Capotosti sisters at the Sacred Family parish school, where Henry and Louis were now enrolled, but there was hope for an opening the following year. Until then, Iris and Lily were on their own, and Iris was responsible for getting them both to school.

After a lifetime of warnings that she must never stray from the sidewalk under threat of spankings at best, or getting hit by a car at worst, Iris found herself leading Lily along the undefined shoulder of dirt and gravel that ran between the drainage ditches of front lawns and the asphalt road. She wondered how many of the other rules that had been drilled into her head might reveal themselves temporary, and just die off like mosquitoes in autumn when circumstances changed.

Iris hardly ever spotted anyone walking anywhere in the new neighborhood, and as they marched to school that morning, the girls encountered no other children, only men in cars heading across town to work at one of the companies Iris heard the grownups talk about. When her father or Auntie Rosa mentioned that so-and-so worked at Kodak or Xerox (her mother was not much impressed by such talk), there was something in their tone of voice, a sort of admiration bordering on awe, that gave rise in Iris to the notion that no more desirable job could be had, unless maybe you were one of the doctors Auntie Rosa worked for. It was strange, though, because from what she could see, the men driving by in their cars did not look very happy. Iris wondered whether her father would rather drive a car to one of those fancy jobs than take the bus downtown to fix veterans' limbs, but she didn't really think so. Besides, her mother needed the car because the only place she could go without one was the duck pond, which didn't really interest her, and The Bungalow, which was only good for penny candy and an emergency quart of milk or dozen eggs.

Iris's stomach was all in knots, as she commanded her legs to take her to her new school as quickly as possible, while fighting against her inclination to not go there at all. She wasn't even enjoying the walk down the desolate road, or being responsible for her little sister. When Lily pointed out a more adventurous path through the trees, Iris was tempted to make a detour, and might have, except for the fact that she had overheard Alexander tell John a very creepy story about a girl who had been seen taking that same shortcut through the woods and never came out on the other side. They said her fish-nibbled body was found several days later in Red Creek, by a group of teenagers who were skinny-dipping in the company of Jenny Cream. When Iris asked who this Jenny was, Alexander laughed, and said Genny with a "G" was a beer, not a girl. She couldn't tell whether Alexander was joking about Genny, or the entire story for that matter, but she didn't want to take any chances, considering what had happened to Auntie Rosa when she was around her age and took the shortcut by the canal with her little sister, and never saw her alive again.

As a rule, Iris preferred the safety of obedience, and insisted they follow their mother's instructions, taking the long way up the hill, and turning left at the intersection. In the end, the walk wasn't so bad, once she and Lily both confessed to feeling a little nervous, as well as a bit odd, outfitted as they were in faded dungarees that mumbled something about older sisters, and spanking white Keds that screamed of newness. Iris would have loved a pair of navy blue sneakers, and Lily red, but their mother had found a bargain on the white remainders at the Westgate Plaza Sidewalk Sale. Iris had just managed to convince herself and Lily that white wasn't so bad, when Marguerite spotted their shoes and started teasing them, saying she wouldn't be caught dead wearing white after Labor Day. Iris didn't know how anyone's life could depend on the color of their sneakers, and besides, Auntie Rosa wore white shoes and a white nurse's uniform all year round, and she was very much alive. Just the same, maybe the Labor Day rule was important out here in the

127

suburbs, so to be on the safe side, during their walk, she and Lily kicked up clouds of dirt and took turns trampling each other's feet, until they parted ways once inside their school.

Iris never liked looking out of place, and apart from the sneakers, which might not have bothered her if it hadn't been for the seed of doubt planted by Marguerite, she had fretted excessively over the necessity of having to pick out clothes for school instead of wearing a uniform. That was when Iris decided that having the freedom to choose was an unwelcome complication, when you had so little to choose from. With a little luck, maybe no one would notice if she wore white sneakers, or the same clothes every day. And with a little bit more luck, maybe no one would notice her at all.

The only sound in the deserted classroom was the ticking of the clock hanging over the doorway, as the second hand nudged the minute hand toward the official end of summer vacation and the beginning of Iris's first day at her new school. She searched in vain for a crucifix to which she could pray, in hopes of being granted the courage to face her first lay teacher and a classroom full of children who were not only unfamiliar to Iris, but were foreign to her. They were public school children. "Help me, Holy Jesus," she whispered, her head bowed over clasped hands, "wherever you are."

There were six rows, each six desks across, in the classroom; Iris had counted them before sitting in a front seat, chosen for its proximity to the chalkboard (she continued to make do without glasses, rather than submit to another exam by Dr. Julius). On the polished desktop sat a speckled composition book with the name "Iris Capotosti" written in careful penmanship on the cover, a moderately masticated ballpoint pen, a twelve-inch ruler and a freshly sharpened number two pencil crowned by a spongy pink eraser.

Iris flipped open the composition book and ran her slender fingers over the lined pages, wondering what combinations of words and sentences and paragraphs might soon take up residence there. She visualized the teacher's red marks that would inevitably spatter the pages like droplets of blood, and hoped they would offer more praise than criticism of her work. The idea of being forced to disclose her thoughts and demonstrate her capabilities to a perfect stranger, who wasn't even a nun, made her cringe. Iris was instinctively protective of her intimate space and wary of intrusions, and though she knew she must crack open the window to her mind wide enough to allow the feeding of her intellect, what really went on in her head remained protected behind closed shutters. Despite her reluctance, she felt a flutter of excitement at the prospect of knowing more tomorrow, or next week, or next month than she knew now, and she was starting to grow curious about, and already grateful toward, the person who would guide her to that knowledge.

Iris ran her fingers nervously through her hair as she waited for the other children and the teacher to arrive; now her locks were too short to suck on, but she was older, and thankful to have survived all those hair balls in her stomach. She didn't miss the habit much anymore, except in tense situations like this one. Her mother had done a handsome job adjusting her hair after Iris had butchered it, declaring that her new style, clipped flush with her chin, was called a French bob. French, like the couple on her blue valise. Iris had felt prettier when she heard that.

From where she sat, Iris was afforded a strategic view of the corridor, which had started to fill as the procession of school buses circled to the entrance and discharged their cargo of fresh fodder for the public school system. The silence was broken by the excited voices of friends greeting each other after summer vacation; girls giggled their way into the classroom, chased by boys surfing through the door on waves of amicable pushes and shoves. Iris observed them surreptitiously, averting her eyes when anyone glanced her way. Not being allowed to talk was different from not having anyone to talk to, and Iris found herself missing the sight of a stern nun in her reassuring black and white habit at the front of the room, demanding silence and order as students took their seats.

Claaaang! The chaotic buzz was drowned out by the bell

announcing that the school year had officially commenced. The teacher walked in the door, a stack of books and folders tucked under one arm. *Holy Moley!* Not only was the teacher not a nun, he was a man. Just what Iris needed: another guy telling her what to do.

"C'mon, Lily, don't be afraid," Iris said, holding the door halfway open, taking care not to let the three yapping cocker spaniels escape. "They won't bite." Though Iris had been to Alba Ichberg's house on many occasions, this was the first time she had brought Lily along. The two sisters stepped gingerly into the breezeway that connected the house to the garage, latching the door behind them. Like each time Iris first walked in, the initial impact made her want to turn on her heels and *am-scray*, as Louis would say.

"Gross! It stinks in here, Iris!" Lily blurted out, as they tiptoed over yellowed newspapers glued to the linoleum floor by dog pee in varying stages of evaporation. Iris shot Lily a look to remind her of her promise that she would not embarrass Iris by making impolite comments, or asking for things before they were offered to her.

Iris had assembled quite a bit of information about the goings-on at the Ichberg home, between the tidbits gleaned through the heating vent, and the stories Violet told at the supper table about the family's quirky behavior and questionable hygiene, including but not limited to the disgusting habit of letting the spaniels lick scraps right from their dishes and poop on the fake grass of the miniature golf game down in their basement. It took someone as courageous as Violet to brave the constant interruptions of the Capotosti clan during feeding time, even if she was armed with a spicy topic of conversation. Iris was occasionally tempted to interject an anecdote of her own, but demurred, partly out of fear that if her parents knew certain things, they might not let her go there anymore, but mostly because she knew her voice would be trampled under the clanging of forks and shouts to pass this or that, and her words diced by the slices of bread being frisbeed from one end of the long wooden table to the other.

It was Violet who greeted them at the kitchen door. "C'mon in, girls," she said, tossing her long mane of dark hair over her shoulders as she tilted her head back to drain a can of Tab. The sight of a whole can of soda pop in her sister's hand would have been enough to confirm the Ichbergs' wealth, had the idea of paying a person to vacuum their house and clean their pool left any doubt. "Alba's downstairs," she said.

"Can we have some pop, too?" Lily said.

"Lily!" Iris said. "You know what I told you."

"But it's Violet!" Lily said, then averted her eyes, almost managing to look contrite, before saying, "Why is it so dark and stuffy in here?"

"Tell me about it!" Violet wiped her brow with the sleeve of her shirt. "Mr. Hooper, that's Mrs. Ichberg's second husband," she continued in a confidential tone of voice, "hates the fresh air. Mrs. Ichberg says he's allergic or something. And the dogs get all randy when they see the sunshine. So we have to keep the windows closed and the curtains drawn all the time."

"Why do Mr. Hooper and Mrs. Ichberg have different names?" Iris whispered. That was one detail she still had not figured out.

"I heard it's because they're not really married, like in the church and all. But you don't go around asking those things. Remember that, both of you. And remember about the windows, OK?"

"Sure." Iris was already familiar with the rule about the windows.

"Do you have to wash all those?" Lily asked, her eyes wide as she pointed to the towering pile of food-encrusted dishes in the sink.

"You bet," Violet answered.

"Why can't Alba wash the dishes?" Lily asked. "Is she allergic to soap or something?"

"She's allergic to doing anything she doesn't want to do," Violet whispered. "But allthe better for me. That's how I make my do-re-mi. Which I use to buy this," she said, fluttering her lids to show off her dark eyes and long lashes accentuated by the eyeliner and mascara their father always told her to scrub off her face. "And this," she said, puckering lips coated in white lipstick, which her father said made her look like a cadaver. "And these!" she said, extracting a cigarette from a pack of Virginia Slims sitting on the counter and lighting it, which her father would kill her for, if he knew.

"But Violet!" Iris said. "What if you get caught?"

"Who's gonna say anything? Can't you smell the air in here? Everyone smokes. Except Alba. For now, anyway. At least it covers up the stench of dog pee." Violet picked up the receiver of the wall phone. "Go right on down. I'm taking a break. And don't you dare fink on me!" Iris would never tell on Violet, or any of her sisters. In fact, the complicity thrilled her. She would rather hang around and enjoy the feeling of being in on something, maybe listen in on Violet's conversation, even help her with the dishes. One of the things Iris liked about going to Alba's was seeing Violet in another setting; she looked happier here, despite the stink and the gloom. Iris sort of wondered why, but she sort of knew.

"Oh my God, it's Todd!" Violet gasped into the phone, peeking into the backyard from behind the kitchen curtains. "I gotta go!" She slammed down the receiver, and rushed from the room.

Iris elbowed Lily, who rushed to the window and pushed back the curtain. As the girls pressed their faces to the dirty pane in the hopes of glimpsing Violet and Todd kissing, Alba emerged from the basement, which made the three spaniels go berserk. "Let's go to my room!" Alba shouted to make herself heard over the yapping of the dogs who ran excited circles around the girls' legs. She turned and led the way through the living room, swinging her hips like an older woman, but not like any of the ones Iris knew, such as her mother or Auntie Rosa, or even her older sisters. It was more like the way one of those women who worked in saloons on TV westerns would walk. In the living room the smell of dog urine receded to the background, succumbing to a more complex bouquet of odors emanating from the wall-to-wall shag carpeting and crushed velvet sofa set covered with dog hairs. The stench of stale cigarettes added an almost pleasant touch, like the way those sickly sweet air fresheners smelled a different kind of bad from the odors they were supposed to eliminate.

"You girls go in," Alba said, opening the door to her room. "And you guys stay there!" she yelled at the pups, but as soon as she kicked one out, another one sneaked in.

"Didn't I tell you it was pretty?" Iris whispered, as she scanned the amenities of the preteen sanctuary. Iris watched Lily's eyes widen in admiration as they roamed over the canopy bed draped in lilac linens with flounces and frills, purple bookshelves stacked with a collection of hardcover books Alba could read whenever she wanted without going to the library, a vanity that lit up like the kind you would see in a movie star's dressing room, a white chair and matching desk where crumpled copies of *16* magazine and half-used bottles of nail polish were scattered among discarded penny-candy wrappers and a glass jar full of Tootsie Rolls and Mary Janes. Lily licked her lips. "Can we have one, Alba?" Lily asked, as soon as Alba shut the door on the dogs. Iris looked at Lily and sighed.

"I guess so, just one each though."

"Thank you, Alba," Iris said loudly, hoping Lily would get the hint.

"Thank you, Alba," Lily parroted.

Iris always felt torn when she spent time in Alba's room; she loved it, but it frustrated her. She had everything a girl could possibly need to be happy in there, yet Alba didn't even seem to care. Why, if Iris had a room like that, she would smooth every last wrinkle from the pretty bedspread, and puff the pillows up just so, the way she had learned to do at Auntie Rosa's. The spines of the books would all face the same direction, with the mysteries arranged neatly on one shelf, and the horse stories on another. She would be so happy to sit at that pretty white desk and write in her composition book, she might never get up. Sometimes, when Alba wasn't looking, Iris couldn't stop herself from tidying up, just a bit.

"Mmm ... I love Mary Janes," Lily said, rolling her eyes in delight as her jaws worked over the chewy nougat.

"Me too," Iris said, slowly unwrapping her piece of candy and placing it in her mouth.

"They're OK," Alba said, "but sometimes I get kinda sick of them." Alba's cow eyes stared at Iris and Lily from between the two sheets of greasy hair hanging at either side of her pasty moon face. Her fashionable halter top and hip-hugger bell-bottoms exposed a pudgy midriff that reminded Iris of the Pillsbury Doughboy. She wondered whether Alba would chuckle if Iris poked her belly with a finger, like in the TV commercial. Alba hardly ever laughed, despite the privilege of having her own room, and a Barbie and a Ken and a Skipper, each with a complete series of outfits. Not to mention a swimming pool in her backyard, and frozen dinners with individual portions of everything, which she got to eat on a tray in front of the TV if her mother didn't feel like cooking when she got home from her job at the trucking company down by the railroad tracks, which was practically every night, according to Violet.

Sometimes Alba got to stay home alone without a babysitter if her half-brother Andy was around, even though he stayed in a room over the garage. Iris did not know exactly what a half-brother was, but she did know he was much older than Alba and had a different last name from hers and from Mr. Hooper's. Andy was creepy; he had long hair tied back in a skinny ponytail and green teeth. Iris thought that maybe that was because there was no place for him to brush them, out there in the garage. She did not like going to Alba's when Andy or the grownups were around, so before ringing the bell she always sprinted past the house first, to check whether there were any cars in the driveway or she could hear Andy's electric guitar cranked way up, playing that song Alba said was called "Purple Haze" though it didn't really sound like a song at all to Iris, at least not anything like Uncle Alfred would play on his guitar.

"Here Iris, you have to read me chapter ten," ordered Alba, as she sat on the bed, and stuck a book under Iris's nose. Iris accepted the book with a mixture of joy and irritation. It had been her favorite story for a long time; Jasmine used to read it to her every time she checked it out of the library, so Iris practically knew it by heart. She especially loved the drawing of the horse on the cover and the illustrations at the beginning of each chapter. She wished it were hers so she could read it to Lily in bed for once instead of making up a fairy story, but the new library didn't have a copy. She had asked Alba if she could borrow the book, but Alba had refused. Instead, she forced her to read her favorite chapters to her, over and over again, every time she came to visit, but never let her read from start to finish.

"Let's all sit on the bed," Alba said. Iris nearly choked on her Mary Jane when Alba crossed her ankles, allowing the soles of her blue sneakers to come in contact with the lilac bedspread. She debated whether to say something to her, but couldn't think of any words that wouldn't risk making Alba mad. Iris kicked off her shoes, and Lily followed her example. The girls climbed on the bed and sat next to Alba as ordered.

"*Misty of Chincoteague*. By Marguerite Henry" Iris began by stating title and author, as she always did when she read aloud. Her teacher often praised Iris for her advanced reading skills, and sometimes asked her to read in front of the whole class.

"Hey, Iris! Like our sister Marguerite and our brother Henry!"

"That's right, Lily. Funny, isn't it?" Iris smiled at her sister, then turned back to the open book on her lap.

"Chapter Ten. 'Colts Have Got To Grow Up.'"

She was soon lost in the story of Phantom and her filly, the wild pinto pony with which she had grown to identify to such an extent she insisted that Lily call her Misty whenever they played horse in their backyard. Iris loved to gallop, flanked by Lily, until she got pangs in her side. Then they would trot over to the apple tree by the swing set and fall down in the grass, stretching out on their bellies as they picked through the dropped apples to see whether there were any without wormholes. When they found good apples and bit into them, they were crisp and tart, the kind horses loved so much they foamed at the mouth when they chomped on them.

As Iris read, Lily snuggled in closer to her and slipped her thumb in her mouth, something she hardly did anymore, except to fall asleep at night.

"Chapter Eleven. 'Storm Shy,'" continued Iris, flipping the page to the next chapter as she elbowed Lily so she would stop sucking her thumb before Alba could call her a baby.

"OK, that's enough," pronounced Alba, ripping the book out of Iris's hands, pushing a startled Lily off the bed and onto her feet.

"But Alba, we just started!" Iris protested.

"Books are boring, let's go down in the basement. We can play with the slot machine," said Alba, not waiting for an answer. She pushed the girls out of the room, and headed for the basement door, kicking the spaniels out of her way as she walked.

It was pleasant enough reading in Alba's room, but the thought of spending a delightful Indian summer afternoon down in her damp, dark basement did not appeal to Iris at all. Granted, there was a slot machine, and Iris felt a rush of excitement when she pulled a row of cherries or bars. Even though the machine just jingled and jangled like crazy instead of spitting out coins like in the movies, Alba always got mad when Iris hit a jackpot. There was a pinball machine down there, too, but Alba hardly ever let her have a turn. Violet had told Iris that Mr. Hooper had brought the games home from the job he had before becoming an editor. Alba boasted that Mr. Hooper ran his own weekly newspaper now, which must be true, because his name was printed, plain as day, in the upper left hand corner on the front page of *Them*. Sometimes, while Alba played pinball, if she didn't make Iris stand there and watch, she would flip through the musty stacks of back issues piled up in the basement. *Them* was a different kind of paper from the one the paperboy delivered every morning. In Mr. Hooper's paper, she had seen pictures of a little boy who had grey hair and wrinkled skin like an old man, and a woman with legs as thick and wrinkled as an elephant's, and a pair of Siamese twins joined at the head. Iris both hoped and feared she would find a picture of the girl whose fish-nibbled body had been found in Red

Creek, but still hadn't come across it.

The thought of all the abnormalities lurking down in that basement were suddenly too much for Iris to bear on a sunny autumn day. "We're going across to the duck pond!" she called down the stairs to Alba, who had gone ahead, followed by the dogs.

"We are?" Iris was sorry to see Lily's face wilt with disappointment. She had described the games in the basement to her in detail, and now she was depriving her of the chance to play them.

"Whaddaya mean?" Alba yelled from below. "You can't just leave!"

"Well, you could come too, if you want," Iris offered, to appease the angry moon face staring up at her from the bottom of the stairs.

"Oh, all right, I guess so!" came the response from below, followed by the thumping of the feet that conveyed Alba and her irritation back up the stairs.

"Do you have any stale bread, Alba?" Lily asked. "We always bring the heels 'cuz no one in our family likes them. Only Dad sometimes has them toasted for breakfast with orange marmalade. No one else likes that, either. I think that's why he likes it, just 'cuz we don't eat it all up on him."

Alba shuffled over to the counter and opened the breadbox. She took out a plastic bag and held it up to examine its contents. "There's only a few slices left, but we can take it," she said. "Let's take these, too," she added, grabbing a wax paper cylinder of Ritz crackers and a handful of Oreo cookies, and tossing everything into the bread bag.

"Good idea!" Lily concurred, clapping her hands. "Those ducks are gonna be happy!"

The trio headed out the door and into the golden afternoon light. Iris paused a moment where the green grass of the front lawn met the gravelly shoulder, drinking in the fresh air until her eyes could adjust, then dashed across the street to the duck pond, holding Lily's hand. The best spot to sit and feed the ducks was the concrete ledge near the road, under which ran a drainage gully that fed the pond several feet below. When she didn't come in search of solitary refuge among the fronds of willow trees, Iris always sat on that ledge, her feet dangling below her, as she watched the ducks and geese paddling around, occasionally standing on their heads to fish something out of the murky water, where catfish with long whiskers could also be spotted. As the girls took their places, Alba in the middle clutching the bread bag, flanked by Iris to her left and Lily to her right, the ducks quacked their greeting, paddling furiously in their direction in the hopes of an afternoon snack.

Alba tossed an entire slice of bread into the water, which landed with a soft splash, cushioned by a layer of green scum. There had been little rain lately, and the water was low and malodorous.

"Why'd you throw a whole piece like that, Alba?" asked Iris.

"That's why! Look!" Alba said with a smirk, pointing to a group of five ducks that had outraced the others to the bread and were attacking it, and each other, in a quacking flurry of flapping wings and pecking beaks.

"I like to throw the bread in little bits, and try to make sure all the ducks get a piece," Iris said.

"Me, too," Lily said. "I feel sorry for the ones who can't swim so fast or don't want to fight just for a piece of food."

"That's dumb!" Alba said. "But just take some, and do whatever you want with it." She held the bag out to Iris, who took some bread, and then handed it over to Lily, who reached deep inside and grabbed a fistful of food. Iris and Lily tore off little pieces of bread and tossed them in, which made the ducks quack contentedly, while Alba kept trying to hit them in the head with the Ritz crackers. Each time she succeeded, she erupted in a tight burst of laughter. Iris was disturbed by its sound.

"Hey, I saw you!" Alba cried suddenly, pushing a finger into Lily's chest.

"Sawr wrhat?" asked Lily between pursed lips.

"You ate an Oreo!" Alba cried. "They were for the ducks!"

"Bb..bb... but...," Lily stammered, her stuffed mouth torn between the options of spitting or swallowing, her hand swiping incriminatory crumbs of chocolate cookie from her lips. Lily's grey-green eyes were wide as she looked at Iris, and Iris knew it was true. Oreos were her sister's favorite cookies, but they rarely had any at their house, and when they did, they were gone before they could make it to the cupboard. Iris liked them too, and when she got her hands on one, she always tried to make it last as long as possible. First, she separated the sandwich of cookies and cream, taking care not to break it, then she licked all the sweet white filling with her tongue, then she dunked the chocolate wafers in a glass of cold milk and nibbled on them slowly. She could make an Oreo last five, sometimes ten minutes, not counting the time spent sipping the milk which ended up tasting almost as delicious as the cookies. When Lily got her hands on an Oreo, she liked to shove it in her mouth all at once, which was apparently what she had done now.

"Admit it, you little brat!" insisted Alba, this time pushing at Lily's chest with her whole hand.

"And so what if she did?" Iris cried, indignant that Alba would think a duck had more right to enjoy an Oreo than her little sister.

"So what if she did? *So what if she did??*" mimicked Alba, as anger crept up her neck, finding its way to her pasty face, and painting it a bright shade of pink.

"*Here's what!*" she yelled, pushing Lily from behind, and flinging her over the ledge, and into the pond.

Splooash! The ducks scattered, quacking madly as Lily made her landing, face down in the stagnant green water.

"*Lily!!*" Iris cried, jumping to her feet, "Are you all right?" Lily pulled herself to a kneeling position, her lovely blond hair dripping with slime as she looked up at Iris, speechless, her features contorted by shock and disgust.

"You pig!" screamed Iris, grabbing Alba by her halter top. "You can keep your stupid Oreos! You may have your very own swimming pool, but let's see how you like this one!" With one swift shove, Iris sent Alba flying into the pond with an even louder *splooash!*.

Iris ran to Lily, who kept slipping in the mud and grass at the edge of the pond, and reached out to pull her to safety. Holding hands, the girls scrambled up the embankment to the road, pausing briefly to look back at the water and the ledge where just a few minutes earlier their legs had been kicking the air as they fed the ducks. Iris felt angry and confused, as shaken by her reaction as she was by Alba's outburst of violence.

"She'll live," Iris said, thinking she should feel proud of herself, but she wasn't. What she had done wasn't right, it just needed doing. She stood there until Alba pulled herself to her feet, covered in the same green slime that dripped from her trembling sister. Then Iris and Lily turned away and broke into a run, and didn't stop until they reached home.

10. LILY

The remaining days of summer passed quickly, as Lily was surrounded by Capotosti playmates – most of whom had lost their neighborhood friends as she had. A troupe of brothers and sisters was ever available for jumping rope, and for playing tag, kickball, baseball, and games of "Mother May I", and "Red Light Green Light."

Lily retreated to the back woods behind the chicken coop whenever she was overwhelmed by the endless activity of endless days, or whenever she felt the need simply to be alone. In the woods, trees were just trees; they never got mad at you, pushed you around, or insisted on playing games you didn't like - and Lily could just be who she was, too – telling made-up stories out loud, singing, or just lying on her back, looking through the branches of trees as clouds passed leisurely overhead. But mostly, she loved the woods because it was quiet – it was the only quiet place. No one was talking or yelling or crying or screaming. There was no TV, no record player, no fighting – just birds chirping, and even they never talked unless they had to, or unless they were really, really happy.

Daily life was radically different at Chestnut Crest. Lily's mother was completely consumed with getting all the boxes unpacked and getting settled in, and then by registering all the children for school, and finding a new dentist, library, and grocery store. She was rarely available to read books, and when Lily tried to help her around the house, she would say, "Lily, what will help me the most is if you go outside and play."

For the most part, Lily's days were defined by playing with Iris and by walking with her to the duck pond and to The Bungalow, the former of which occurred whenever there were old crusts in the bread box, and the latter on Pay Day, when allowances were distributed in increments of nickels.

In exchange for a meager supply of spending money, each child was assigned a set of duties. The older girls did the more complicated work, such as the laundry and cooking. Most of the other chores were rotated, with each child taking a turn to set the table for supper, "doing" the dishes (which meant clearing the table, sweeping the kitchen floor, wiping down the counters, washing out the sink, and loading and running the dishwasher), and, once the fruit started falling from the trees, picking up the apples.

The apple tree in the side yard was prolific, but half of its bounty was wormy or rotten, and fell to the ground, littering it with mushy brown fruit.

"Iris," Lily called one evening after dinner. "It's our turn to pick up the apples!"

"Yuck," replied Iris from the top of the stairs. Wooden railings flanked the stairway and Iris placed one hand on each railing like a gymnast on the parallel bars, her weight on her hands and her long legs swinging to and fro as she gracefully floated down to the kitchen. The hem of her faded red cotton pants fell just above her ankles, and the cuffs of her blouse flapped, unbuttoned. Already it was obvious that Iris would be tall like her mother, and she outgrew her clothes faster than the older girls could pass theirs down to her. Often, they would be too small before she even had the chance to wear them.

Like eating, wearing clothes was mostly a question of necessity; it didn't matter if you liked a particular blouse or pair of pants. What mattered was whether or not it was your turn to wear them. Lily was slightly small for her age, shorter in stature like her father's side of the family. As soon as Iris grew out of an article of clothing, it found its way to Lily. Except for items that became permanently soiled or damaged beyond repair, every piece of girls clothing eventually became Lily's, but rarely at a time when her size could adequately accommodate it, and usually years after it had gone out of style. If only they had been born in a different order – maybe then things would have fit better. With her shirtsleeves hanging down over her hands, and the baggy legs of her corduroy pants making a *zip-zip* sound as they brushed back and forth against each other, Lily followed Iris out to the garage.

"Let's skedaddle and get this over with," said Iris, using an Auntie Rosa word. "Daddy has to cut the grass first thing in the morning." She handed Lily a bushel basket.

The fallen apples were always crawling with ants and other such detestable and creepy critters. Lily hated bugs, and she gagged at the slime and ooze that rotten apples became. The thick stench of rotting fruit flesh made her queasy. It was hard to imagine that these apples had ever been shiny, red, and firm – full of life and flavor. The only way Lily could manage to pick them up without getting disgusted was to never look directly at them – the way they were told not to look directly at the sun during the eclipse. Admittedly, this was difficult to do, if only because of the temptation to explore and challenge what was taboo. However, in both cases Lily managed to resist. A peek at the eclipse just wasn't worth going blind over. And once you got the image of a worm-infested apple in your mind, it could take days before you would forget, and even then, you could be enjoying yourself on the swings, or watching TV before dinner, and that image could just barge right in and take over your whole brain. So Lily learned to pick up the apples using her peripheral vision. They were easy to spot in the green grass, and when you saw one out of the corner of your eye, you could stoop down and scoop it up, without ever having to look right at it, thereby avoiding all of the gross possibilities that entailed.

Bolstered by the knowledge that tomorrow was Pay Day, and fueled by her desire for her very own penny candies, Lily trailed around the yard behind Iris, scanning the edges of her scope of vision and retrieving apples from their grassy graves, all the while looking up at the sky or into the neighbor's yard.

"Lily – you missed one, over there." Iris warned, pointing. "And another one over there. You know what will happen if Daddy runs them over."

"I'm getting them," said Lily, not entirely sure if she was or not. As they roamed, Lily's pant cuffs became unfurled and dragged along in the dewy grass. They worked in silence for several minutes, with Lily unconsciously following a route that kept her within a few feet of her sister at all times.

"Iris," Lily asked, "you know that song about 'the worms crawl in, the worms crawl out?'"

"The worms play pea-knuckles up your snout!" Iris sang in reply.

"Is that really true? When you die, do you have worms go up your nose like that?"

"No, silly – they put you inside a special big box. How can worms get in a box?"

Lily was relieved about the worms, but now concerned about the box.

"What kind of a box? Like one of those big refrigerator boxes?" Those were fun – good for playing fort or house.

"Well," explained Iris, "Auntie Rosa has a picture of her little sister Teresa who died, and she is lying in this big box that looks like a fancy bed, and she has on a brand new beautiful dress that Grandma made, with a big bow in her hair."

Lily hiked up her right pant leg to pull it out from underfoot, and bent down to grab another apple. She liked the idea of wearing a pretty dress, but it seemed a shame to put a new dress in a box and bury it in the ground.

"How did she die?

"They were taking a shortcut home from school and she fell into the canal and drownded." Iris tossed an apple into her basket, then ran the palm of her hand up and down along her thigh.

"Why didn't she hang onto the side, like we have to do when

we go to family swim?" Lily asked.

"Auntie Rosa says her shoes got stuck in the mud at the bottom, and she couldn't get out."

Lily stopped, and with irritation she said, "Well why didn't Daddy jump in and save her?"

"Silly, Daddy was still a little boy. He wasn't even there because he was too little to even go to school." Iris checked the sole of her bare foot, then wiped it on the cool wet grass. She added, "He was even smaller than you!"

Lily couldn't imagine her father as a child – she pictured him with the same hairy forearms, running around the house in his white boxer shorts and sleeveless ribbed white undershirt, with a Parliament hanging out of the corner of his mouth, only he was very short. The image made her laugh.

"C'mon, lazybones," Iris teased. "Get moving – we gotta finish this before it gets dark."

The sun had set, September had cooled the evening air, and the smell of rotted apples rose up from the basket and filled Lily's head. She bent over and scooped up a round red object off to her right, but as soon as she got it into her hand, she knew from its weight and texture that it was not an apple. Instinctively, she looked down and was horrified to discover she was holding a dead robin, whose head was almost completely severed and covered with squirming white maggots. Lily screamed and threw the dead bird up into the air, dropping her basket, and spilling all of the collected apples back onto the ground. Frantically, she danced around the yard, shouting out, "It's a birdie – it's a dead birdie!"

"Where?" asked Iris, surveying the area.

"I don't know – I threw it," Lily cried, jumping up and down. "But I picked it up in my hand and his head was coming off!" The gruesome image now firmly planted in her mind, and the rotted apples spread all around her, a wave of nausea came over Lily, and she vomited in the grass.

Lily's mother opened the door to the back porch, and stuck her head out. "What in heaven's name is going on out there?"

"Lily puked," said Iris, matter-of-factly.

"Come on inside, Lily. Iris, you too – it's nearly dark." Lily's mother disappeared from the doorway.

"I'm almost done, Mom," called Iris. Turning to Lily she said, "You go inside, Lily. I'll be right there. If we don't finish, we might not get allowance."

"OK," said Lily. "But I'm gonna wait for you, OK?" She walked over to the back door, slipped into the porch, and stood looking out the window. Iris continued to scan the yard, looking just like the ballerina inside Jasmine's wind-up jewelry box. When she bent forward, she would raise one leg up behind her and Lily imagined her wearing one of those pink cotton candy skirts, leaping across the yard, spinning and twirling as she collected apples and placed them gently into the bushel. She was graceful; that's what Auntie Rosa called it.

Iris disappeared into the garage, emerging a minute later with a garden shovel in one hand and a flap torn from a cardboard box in the other. She walked to a spot on the ground, and using the shovel, she pushed the dead bird onto the cardboard. She squatted under the apple tree, dug a hole in the dirt, placed the bird into it, and then covered it up again, patting the loose dirt back into place. Lily's nose was pressed against the porch window, and her breath steamed up the glass. She used her shirtsleeve to wipe a spot clean and saw Iris on her knees, making the sign of the cross.

Lily whispered along, "In the name of the Father and of the Son, and of the Holy Ghost Amen."

As Iris hauled the bushels to the garage, Lily arranged all the shoes neatly on the mat, and then held the back door open for her sister.

"It's late, girls." Lily's mother was bent over the dishwasher, her head enveloped in a cloud of steam that filled the kitchen with the smell of melted plastic. "Better get in the tub."

"OK, Mom," said Iris, taking Lily's hand. Together they sneaked around behind their mother, and Iris snatched the dishwashing liquid from the kitchen sink as they passed by. She shot Lily a smile. "Bubble bath," she whispered.

The girls climbed the stairs, hand in hand. "I'll run the water, Lily. You go get two towels."

Lily retrieved two towels from the hall closet, and then knocked on the bathroom door, using the secret code they had devised. *Knock. Knock-knock. Knock.*

"Who is it?" asked Iris.

"I-r-i-i-is…" said Lily. "It's me."

Iris unlocked the bathroom door and let Lily inside.

"I used the secret code – why didn't you let me in?"

"You did it wrong. It's like this." Iris demonstrated the code. *Knock. Knock-knock-knock. Knock.*

"Oh, man," said Lily, stomping her foot. "I always get it wrong!"

Iris reached over Lily's head and re-locked the door. Taking the towels, she draped them over the rack and said, "OK – let's get in before the water gets cold."

Iris and Lily shed their clothes, Iris stacking hers neatly in the corner. Lily let hers drop to the floor and simply stepped out of them, leaving them in a pile. They climbed in, exclaiming "ooohs" and "ows" as they lowered their small bodies down into the tub brimming with hot water and mounds of dishwashing soap bubbles. Disappearing into all that white foam was Lily's favorite part of the bath. She gathered piles of it around her like a soft fluffy blanket, then scooped it up into her hands, examining the way the bubbles sparkled blue and pink, like each tiny dome might burst and reveal a precious gem. Of course, when bubbles popped, there was nothing there; they were just gone - which is why bubble baths sometimes made Lily sad. She couldn't understand why something so magical had to fade so quickly.

Within moments, the girls' cheeks were flushed and their faces were beaded with perspiration. Iris scooped up a mound of bubbles with both hands and placed them along her jaw line.

"Look at me, Lily. I'm an old man."

"Look at me, look at me," said Lily with a giggle. "I'm a princess!" She placed a pile of bubbles atop her head.

"That's not a princess, silly. That's a snowman!"

"Ho, ho, ho!" Lily bellowed heartily.

"You're a snowman, not Santa Claus!" Iris laughed.

"Ho, ho ho – I'm Santa-man!" Lily thrust a clenched fist into the air.

Iris placed a generous handful of bubbles over each nipple. "Look - I'm Auntie Rosa!"

They played and laughed and splashed until the bubbles dissipated and the water turned cold and dingy.

"I'm fr-fr-freezing!" chattered Lily, standing up. Iris stepped out of the tub, grabbed a towel from the rack, and draped it around her little sister's shoulders.

"Here, dry off," said Iris, wrapping herself in the other towel. "And let's go put our pajamas on."

The girls cinched their towels around their chests, gathered up their dirty clothes, and padded down the hallway, leaving a puddle on the bathroom floor, and a ring in the tub.

The cool breeze that came in through the bedroom window carried the distant moan of the Coldwater Road train. Lily and Iris nestled up against each other under the threadbare white cotton bedspread. The muffled voices from the television in the living room below lulled Lily, but just as she was drifting off to sleep, the image of the dead robin assaulted her imagination, and she startled.

"Whatsa matter?" Iris whispered.

"I keep thinking about that birdie," said Lily. "How did his head come off?"

"I bet Skipper did it."

"I hate that Skipper! Why did Jasmine get a kitty that kills birdies?"

"That's just what cats do - they like to catch birds and play with them."

"Do you think that birdie will go straight to Heaven right away, Iris?"

"Prob'ly," said Iris. "He can fly right up there."

"Not if he's dead, though. And not if you buried him in the ground."

"Well," said Iris, "Maybe a fairy will come, and fly him away. She will wave her magic wand, and flap her golden wings, and that little birdie will just come right up out of the ground."

Lily smiled. "Will he be singing?"

"Oh, yes," Iris answered. "He will be singing that val-da-ri song: 'I love to go a-wandering, along the mountain track…' "

Lily closed her eyes and slipped her thumb into her mouth. Iris pulled it back out again, and continued. "… and as I go, I love to sing, my knapsack on my back."

With a sleepy voice, Lily joined in and they sang quietly together. "Val-de-ri, val-der-a, val-de-ri, val-der-ah-ha-ha-ha-ha-ha…." Iris' eyelids lowered as her voice trailed off. Lily slipped her thumb back into her mouth, and began to snore, and the sisters drifted off to sleep in each other's arms.

The late summer sun blared in through the bedroom window, and the girls were shaken awake by the unmistakable cha-chung of the lawnmower blades hitting and spewing apples, followed by a resounding, "Jeepers Crrr-ipes!"

"Oh, no!" said Lily, covering her head with the bedspread.

"I told you you missed some," said Iris, pulling on a pair of jeans under her nightgown.

"I hope he doesn't run over the puke!"

The lawnmower engine ceased, and Lily's father called out, "Whose turn was it to pick up the apples last night?"

Any question in the Capotosti house that started with "Whose turn was it…." usually ended with someone getting into some serious trouble either for neglecting their duties, or for executing them improperly. "Whose turn was it…" was never followed with a compliment or a reward. It was a phrase that rendered all of the children deaf, mute, and entirely ignorant of whose turn it actually was. If you could hold out from confessing – in spite of the propaganda that doing so provided a measure of virtue - it was possible to avoid the issue altogether because when it came to the chores, an unspoken code of silence among the children all but guaranteed that you would not be tattled on.

Lily looked out the bedroom window into the front yard to see her mother come into view and hand her father a glass of water.

"What does it matter now, Carlo?"

"These kids need to understand how to do a job properly, Betty. If I was going to just run over all the apples, making this God-awful mess all over the place, I wouldn't even bother having them pick up in the first place." With several deep, long gulps, he drained the glass and gave it back to his wife.

"I'm sure they do their best, Carlo – they're just children, after all."

"Well what good does it do to give them a chore if they only cause me more work in the long run?" Without waiting for an answer, Carlo pulled the cord to restart the mower; without attempting to provide an answer, Lily's mother turned and walked away.

"Ask him," Lily prodded Iris.

"No – you ask him," Iris replied.

The girls sat on the forest green loveseat in the living room, anxious for their father to emerge from the bedroom and pass out allowances. They had waited, squirming, as he finished cutting the grass, and then sat watching as he walked back and forth through the living room, which separated his bedroom from the first-floor bathroom where he showered. The first time through, he walked into the bedroom and emerged in his boxer shorts and sweaty ribbed white undershirt, soiled grass-cutting clothes in hand. The next time they saw him, he was fresh out of the shower, wearing nothing but a white towel about his waist. When he emerged from the bedroom again, he had on fresh white boxers and a clean undershirt, and was carrying his wet towel. As though he were the ball in a ping-pong tournament, Iris and Lily followed his every move, anticipating how many bounces it would take before he landed.

They sat and listened to the buzz of his electric razor, the repeated sliding and slamming of the mirrored doors of the medicine chest, the clinking of nail clippers, nail file, and combs as he retrieved them from the cabinet and then tossed them back in again. The girls knew the routine; their father got ready for work every morning while they sat and had their cereal, watching him in the bathroom from the kitchen table. Soon the ritual would be complete.

Each time their father passed by, he glanced at his daughters sitting there waiting, swinging their legs nervously, kicking the loveseat with the backs of their heels. He never gave a hint as to whether he knew what they were waiting for, and if he knew, he made no attempt whatsoever at easing their anxieties. As it grew closer to allowance time, more children gathered around. Like soldiers in the rations line hungry for their allotment, they awaited the nickels they'd earned, which each would convert to some form of freedom, pleasure, or power.

"No – you ask him; he likes you better," Lily insisted.

Iris didn't argue. "Daddy –" she quietly called.

"Yes," he sang from inside the bedroom.

"Are we getting allowance today?"

Their father didn't reply, and the children sat and stared at each other, shrugging, leaning forward to try and gain a view into the next room, to get a hint of what was going on in there, the most mysterious and fearsome room in the house. Going into their parents' bedroom was a mission for the intrepid – one that you did not undertake unless you absolutely had to, such as if you were deathly ill in the night, or if you needed milk money for school in the morning.

Part of the danger of entering the bedroom was that their father slept in nothing but a pajama top, and he was not the sort of a man who liked to nestle beneath the covers. If you had to go into the room, and if he happened to be in bed, regardless of whether he was facing the door or facing away from it, you were sure to get an eyeful of exposed body parts in all their glory, covered with a thick coat of black hair. Even if you knew he wasn't in there sleeping, since every child had the experience at some point of walking in and seeing their father *al fresco*, the emotional experience stayed with you, and accompanied you every subsequent time you approached the door – the way even a huge and fierce dog will cower at the sight of a rolled up newspaper if you intimidate it enough with one when it is a puppy.

And so the children and their father entered a sort of showdown on allowance day, whereby he would pretend he didn't know what they were waiting for - all convened as they were out in the living room – and they would speculate whether he had remembered or forgotten that it was Pay Day, and negotiate among themselves for a spokesperson to approach his room to remind him, and to get an estimated time on the nickel distribution.

Lily placed her open hand on Iris' back, and giving her an encouraging push she said, "Go see if he's coming. He never gets mad at you."

Iris rose from the loveseat and timidly headed for the bedroom door. At that moment, Marguerite breezed into the living room, assessed the situation, and asked, "Waiting for allowance?" The younger children nodded collectively, and Marguerite strode over to the bedroom, nudging Iris aside, and delivered three strong raps to the partly closed door.

"Hey, Dad," she said. "Can we please have our allowance now?"

Their father opened the door, holding a small rectangular plastic case containing two rolls of nickels. Ceremoniously, he removed the lid, and the children immediately formed a line behind Marguerite, in order of age.

Marguerite held out her hand. Her father counted nickels into her palm, "Five, ten, fifteen, twenty, twenty-five, thirty, thirty-five."

"Thanks, Dadd-i-o!" sang Marguerite, shaking the nickels in her loosely held fist the way a gambler shakes dice before a throw.

Iris stepped up next, hand out, with the deference and reverence usually reserved for receiving Holy Communion.

"Five, ten, fifteen, twenty, twenty-five, thirty" counted her father.

"Thanks, Daddy!" Iris gave her father a peck on the cheek.

Lily stepped up, hand held out, mouth watering for candy lipstick and Sugar Daddy nuggets.

Her father held the nickels out, as though he were going to count them into her hand, but he stopped and said, "Was it your turn to pick up the apples last night, young lady?"

Lily glanced over at Iris, and then back at her father. "Yes, Daddy," said Lily, her body growing hot.

"I ran over quite a few with my new lawnmower this morning."

Lily considered telling him about the bird and how she got sick, and how scary it was, but she just didn't see the point. "I'm sorry, Daddy."

"Don't let it happen again," he replied, placing the nickels into Lily's palm. Lily stepped out of line and counted.

"How much did he give you?" Iris asked.

"Twenty-five cents, " replied Lily. And even though she received her prescribed number of nickels, Lily felt cheated and guilty.

The book banks were filed on a shelf among many books, and to a casual observer they could as easily have been another copy of Dickens or Shakespeare – which was probably why they were so disguised. Lily had deduced that disguising a bank so that it looked like a book on the shelf was probably to get you to open more books, in the hopes that you might find money inside.

Iris retrieved her bank from among the books, and slipped a nickel into the slot at the top. She held the bank up to her ear and shook it, as if she could judge the amount of money she'd saved by the jingling it made. Satisfied, Iris returned the bank to its place.

"Aren't you going to save some of your allowance?" Iris asked Lily.

"What for?"

"A rainy day. Or for Christmas, maybe."

"Well," said Lily, thinking about which items from The

Bungalow she might have to sacrifice if she were to save one of her nickels. "You're older and you get more. I only have five. If I put a nickel in the bank, you'll be able to buy more candy than me." She laid her palm open, showing her allowance to Iris.

"OK," said Iris. "Then how about if I put another one in my bank? That way we'll both have four – it'll be even-Steven!"

Before Lily could figure out what about this arrangement still didn't seem quite right, Iris had slipped a second nickel through the slot. Reluctantly, Lily pulled her bank out from among the books and dropped a nickel in. It made a lonely plunk as it hit bottom.

11. IRIS

Sacred Family had some things in common with St. Augustine's, some with Fairview Elementary, and some that were totally new. To start with, the teachers were all women, but not all were nuns. The principal was a nun, too, but didn't seem like a woman, not even in a nunnish way. Even her name, Sister Mary Benedict, was a cross between a man's and a woman's, and she was heftier than most men Iris knew, including her father and Uncle Alfred. She was even bigger than Father Delaney, although Father Delaney ruled over everything and everyone, because he was the pastor of the whole Sacred Family parish. Father Delaney was one of the bad things about Sacred Family. He didn't talk, he yelled. Every time he made surprise inspection visits to the classroom, he yelled at the students, and he yelled at the teachers. He didn't even care if they were nuns, although everyone knew you did not yell at nuns. He yelled at Iris in the confessional, and he yelled at the entire congregation at Mass. Iris figured he probably yelled at God, too.

There were some good things about Sacred Family, though. Like the fact that the students had to wear uniforms, and Iris got a brand new one, since none of her older sisters had attended the school before her. The girls' jumpers had pleated skirts, and were green, like Ireland, because Father Delaney loved everything Irish as much as he loathed everything that wasn't. There was only one thing Fairview had that Iris missed: Lily, who still had not been enrolled at Sacred Family for lack of space. Iris got a shaky feeling deep in the pit of her stomach every morning when she walked to the end of the driveway with Lily, silently counting her paces, until the time when Lily had to turn right, and Iris left. Sometimes, after she kissed Lily goodbye, she only pretended to start off in the other direction, and instead stayed put and watched her sister climb the hill until she was out of view, to make sure she stayed on the shoulder like she was supposed to, and walked past the shortcut Iris had made her promise never to take.

At this desolate time of year, there was no shoulder. There was nothing except snow and ice the same blank non-color of the sky. Iris hated walking to school during winter, slipping and sliding in whatever leaky leftover boots fit her at the time, which she customized with a plastic bread bag lining that helped keep her feet dry, but not warm. By the time she got to school, she couldn't feel her toes at all, or her bright pink thighs either, and she was exhausted from traipsing up and down the snow banks that instead of melting kept getting taller and taller each time the plow passed. Iris never tried to keep up with Henry or Louis; the twins would only laugh at her when she slipped, and throw snowballs at her instead of helping her up.

Some days, Iris felt so cold after walking to school, that it was lunchtime before she warmed up. That was virtually the only time of day she didn't feel frozen, because after cafeteria, the students were all shooed outdoors for recreation, which to Iris meant finding a place near the trees that might shield her from the biting wind, where she would stand and shiver uncontrollably as she played the balmy strains of Uncle Alfred's Hawaiian music over in her head, until one of the nuns opened the door and let them back inside.

As Iris took her bologna and cheese sandwich from a wrinkled brown bag, she sighed at the prospect, and wished with all her might that she could go to the library and read instead of going to recreation, but you had to be almost dead before they would let you do that. She stared at the sandwich in her hand which, to make matters worse, had been rolled flat by the apple, which somehow always ended up on top, despite the care she took to pack her lunch properly. She unwrapped the sandwich and nibbled on it slowly, concentrating on chewing each bite before washing it down with cold milk from a carton. But the smell of hot cafeteria food was more effective at making Iris hungry than her bologna sandwich was at satiating her. She sat alone, without raising her eyes, her mind wandering as she chewed and sipped, imagining the components of her lunch on their descent to her stomach: the spongy white bread coated with a thin layer of mayonnaise, the dry brown crusts that stuck in her throat, the slippery round slice of pink lunch meat, the orange square of American cheese she had lopped off the brick in the refrigerator, the creamy white milk. Each morsel of each element would soon lose its individual identity, as the separate colors and textures were lumped together in a masticated mush. The thought of the food sitting in her stomach disgusted Iris so much that if she hadn't been so starving, she might have stopped eating altogether.

When her sandwich and milk were gone, she refolded her lunch bag and rose, brushing the crumbs from the table and chair. Glancing around quickly as she left, she caught the eye of Mrs. Fish, the hunchbacked, white-haired lady who tended to the cafeteria. They smiled at each other: Mrs. Fish in silent approval, Iris in polite pity. She left, apple in hand, and spotted another student heading up the stairs as she approached. Not feeling equipped to face Don O'Donnell, Iris slowed her pace, since it was too late for her to turn around without looking dumber than she probably already did. Everyone said Don was the coolest kid in class; no matter what kind of trouble he got himself into, he never stopped smirking, even when he was being reprimanded by the formidable Sister Mary Benedict, whom he referred to as "Big Ben" behind her back, which made everybody laugh, though Iris did not think it was particularly funny. Sister always found plenty of reasons to scold Don, like catching him with an unbuttoned button, or a spot on his green tie, or with his hair so long in the back it touched his collar. Though Iris didn't approve of his behavior, and was often irritated because of the time it made them waste in class, she was fascinated by the way Don flirted with danger. He had never spoken to Iris directly before, or even acknowledged her existence in any way, and she was taken aback when he halted abruptly on the stairs, then backtracked a few steps, causing her to bump into him. As soon as she did, Don stuck a hand into his left pocket, and pulled out a rectangular object wrapped in foil. Without turning around, he mumbled over his shoulder.

"You can have as much of it as you want, you know?"

Iris looked around, thinking his words were directed at someone behind her, but she saw that they were standing alone on the stairs; he in front, she a step behind.

"What?" she asked, as her heartbeat accelerated, squirting her cheeks and neck with enough blood to ensure her embarrassment would be complete should he pivot to face her.

Don snapped the foil-wrapped object in two. "Here," he said, furtively passing a piece to Iris. She looked down, and found herself holding a chunk of chocolate that looked suspiciously like the bars the students were selling for the school fund-raiser. Iris hadn't tried to sell any yet because she abhorred the idea of ringing the doorbells of strangers to try and peddle them anything, let alone chocolate she hadn't even tasted. And no one she knew would buy that fancy chocolate, when you could get twice as much candy for the same money at The Bungalow. Just the same, Iris had read the mouth-watering descriptions in the handout several times a day, and was sure it must be delicious.

"Try it," Don said.

As Iris raised the chocolate to her mouth, her nostrils flared, titillated by the scent of pure cocoa, forcing the banal aftertaste of bologna and cheese still lingering on her palate to scamper away in shame. After glancing up and down the stairs to make sure no one was watching, she bit off a piece of chocolate and placed it on her tongue, her eyelids instinctively dropping in pleasure. The candy was softened from being in Don's pocket and began melting instantly, infusing Iris with its exquisitely sweet taste and velvety texture, punctuated by crunchy slivers of roasted almonds. The thought of Don's thigh warming the chocolate as it lay hidden in his pocket, and that same chocolate now sending waves of pleasure to her mouth, was almost too much to bear.

"Holy cow … this really is divine!" Iris whispered, "Nothing like the stuff they sell at The Bungalow. Did you buy it yourself?"

"Yes and no," replied Don.

"What do you mean?"

"Well, what I mean is, I bought it, but I didn't pay for it."

"So who paid for it?"

"No one."

"But someone had to pay for it."

"That's what I thought, too," replied Don, still talking over his shoulder. "But no one ever asked."

"What do you mean, no one ever asked? Can I have another piece?" Iris asked from behind him.

"Sure. I told you. Have all you want. What I mean is, they just let me have it."

"You mean, you just asked, and they gave it to you?" Iris asked, incredulous. "Will they give some to me, too?" A group of kids rushed passed them, their giggles propelling them up the stairs.

"Follow me, and I'll explain," Don said, as he started climbing again. Iris followed him up the steps and down the hallway, to the empty library. He glanced around surreptitiously, then slipped between the stacks, nodding for Iris to join him. Iris spotted the book entitled *St. Thérèse, the Little Flower*, which she had returned that very morning, sitting on a cart, waiting to be placed in its proper place on the shelf. She felt uneasy about engaging in a clandestine conversation with Don in front of the heaven-cast gaze of the saint on the cover. She flipped the book over.

"What I'm gonna tell you is top secret, dig?" Don began.

"Sure thing." Iris was dying of curiosity, but uneasy about being sworn to secrecy before the nature of the confidence was revealed.

"You know those order forms they give us?" Don asked. "You have to write down how many bars of each kind people order, right?"

"Right," Iris nodded.

"Then you add the numbers of each row across, and the grand total at the bottom. You line up at the cafeteria, show Mrs. Fish the form, and she gives you the number of bars on the order." Iris nodded again; that was easy enough to understand.

"But," he said, raising his index finger, and lowering his voice another notch, "you don't have to turn in the money until after you deliver the candy, right?"

"And so?" Even if she hadn't sold any candy yet herself, she knew that was how the system worked. She wondered what he was getting at.

"So, I just figured I'd add a few extra bars to my order, fill out the form in pencil, then erase the number and change it to the right amount when I bring the money in. How's that for smart?" Don grinned.

"I guess," Iris said. "But isn't that stealing?"

"Nah, not really. Everyone gets what they paid for. And we get a little bonus for doing such a good job. Me and two other guys in our class have already pulled it off a few times, and it works like a charm. We could use a new partner for the pick-ups before Big Ben gets suspicious. You're smart, you never get in trouble, and you never talk to anyone. You'd be perfect. Plus, you have to start placing orders soon if you don't want to be last in the class." His trademark smirk left little room for discussion, and the index finger he touched to the tip of her nose electrocuted any remaining doubts. "So? Can we call it a deal, or are you as much a Miss Goodie Two Shoes as you look?"

The hairs on her neck bristled, just like when Alexander or John called her "Spoiled Brat" because she got to spend weekends with Auntie Rosa. She was not a Goodie Two Shoes, and she was not a Spoiled Brat. Suddenly, she was inundated with a desire even greater than the longing for some more of that heavenly chocolate. At that moment, more than anything, she yearned to be included. She was intrigued, and knew how to keep a secret. And maybe Don might touch her on the nose again. What was the worse thing that could happen?

"Count me in," she said.

"Cool! Wait here for a minute after I leave. Then meet me in the cloakroom after recreation, and I'll slip you one of my order forms." Don squeezed her left arm above the elbow so hard it hurt. The skin of her uneaten apple stuck to the palm of her hand as she watched him walk away, then rushed to join her class for recreation. Maybe getting some fresh air wasn't such a bad idea.

Second thoughts assailed Iris as she waited in line to place her order the next morning, her mind searching for justifications for the act of deception she was about to commit. Don said they deserved the chocolate, but Iris couldn't quite see why. There were many things Iris wanted, but didn't feel she deserved. The closer she came to the front of the line, the more jittery she felt. She probably would have chickened out, if Mrs. Fish's hunchback hadn't prevented her from looking Iris in the eye when it was her turn to hand in the order form. When she walked away with five bars in excess of the bona fide order she had squeezed out of neighborhood clients, she trembled with fear of getting caught, and with excitement at how easily she had pulled it off.

She sighed with relief when she sat in her seat and raised her desktop to drop the goods inside. She caught Don's eye as she pulled out her Ancient History textbook, and nodded. He winked at her. She blushed. When they met in the cloakroom again at the end of class, Iris handed over three of the five extra bars she had procured; three were for the team, two she got to keep for herself. She couldn't wait for school to be over so she could go home and give one to Lily, and they could eat them together while they hid out in the sun room and listened to music, even if there was no sun.

Iris had just opened her book for the day's English lesson, when the door snapped open, and its frame was filled by the ominous form of Sister Mary Benedict.

Sister Agnes stopped writing on the chalkboard in mid-sentence, swiveled around to face the students, and said, "Class?"

"Good afternoon, Sister Mary Benedict," the class stood, responding to the prompt, then fell silent.

Without returning the greeting, Sister Mary Benedict pointed a finger at Don. "Young man!" she said. Iris felt a sinking sensation in her gut, as Sister's beady eyes scanned the room. "And you!" she said, singling out one of Don's buddies. "And you!" Iris gasped audibly, as the crooked finger pointed to the third member of the band. When she puffed out her massive chest, it looked as though it would burst the seams of her habit, and when she pointed her finger at her, Iris felt all the blood drain from her head, then her heart, and possibly even her body, and imagined it pooling on the floor beneath her desk in a dark red puddle. "And you, young lady!" Sister said to Iris. "You four follow me to the library. Immediately!"

Thirty-two heads turned in Iris' direction, sixty-four eyes bored holes in her flesh, sucking out any remaining drops of blood from her body, which had turned limp and cold. Steadying herself on the edge of her desk, she broke rank and took her place in the shamed procession that filed out the door and silently down the corridor to the library. Sister Mary Benedict pronounced her Accusations, while the Accused stood before their one-nun jury and judge. Confessions were dictated. Iris's head was spinning with confusion and fear and a sense of injustice. It wasn't fair, she thought. Don had been running his racket for days, whereas this was her very first time. She hadn't even eaten any of the chocolate yet, or underpaid her fudged order, so technically she hadn't really taken anything that couldn't be put back. She would return the chocolate, and go to Confession, and promise to never steal again. If only Sister would let her talk, she could explain. But one did not question Sister's orders. Not if one did not want to dig oneself into an even deeper grave.

Iris was handed a blank piece of paper on which she was instructed to write, "I, Iris Capotosti, stole $7.50 (seven dollars and fifty cents) worth of chocolate from Sacred Family." Her hands trembled as she wrote, especially when it came to the word "stole." She signed her name at the bottom of the page in quivering penmanship that looked like her grandmother's.

"These confessions will be filed with your permanent records," said Sister Mary Benedict. "Those records will follow you to your future high schools, and will be viewed by the admissions boards of colleges you may hope to attend, and by any employers for whom you may wish to work."

A lump larger than the apple she wished she had eaten instead of following Don to the library formed in Iris's throat, as she saw a desolate future stretch out before her. Hadn't she always obeyed the rules and done her best to avoid sinning? How had one boy and one bite of chocolate convinced her to become so evil, so quickly? Who would ever want to have anything to do with her again?

"You have until Monday to return the stolen money. Report to me, in my office, before the morning bell. That will be all. Go, now. Go in shame."

Weak-kneed, Iris retraced her steps back down the corridor. She fought back tears as she glanced at Don, who was already smirking again, followed by his two buddies, whose grins were only slightly sheepish. Visions of college rejections and a life on the dole mercifully receded to the wasteland of the distant future, as she braced herself for the more immediate consequences of her actions. First, she must endure the gawking of the other students as she reentered the classroom with the boys. She would manage somehow, she thought, suddenly buoyed by a wave of gratitude that no mention was made of involving parents in this scandal. Just as swiftly, she was knocked over by the undertow, and dragged to the depths of despair by the impossible task of raising seven dollars and fifty cents in three days.

No matter how many times Iris added up her financial resources, the result never varied, even by one cent. The six nickels that constituted the allowance she would receive on Friday night only amounted to thirty cents. She could kick herself for having cracked open her book bank to buy some green wool knee socks that didn't have any holes in the toes and would hug her calves tightly in the cold instead of slipping to her ankles; as a result, the only money left in there was the special two-dollar bill she had received from Auntie Rosa for her First Holy

Communion. That rare bill would still only be worth two dollars to someone as mean as Big Ben, though Iris was told if she saved it, one day it might be worth much more. She couldn't bring herself to approach Lily, even in the unlikely event she had continued dropping part of her allowance in her own bank and resisted the urge to crack it open. What would Lily think, having a thief for a big sister? What kind of example was she setting for her? What path was she paving for the day when Lily would also be enrolled at Sacred Family?

At least Iris would be going to Auntie Rosa's for the weekend, and Saturday she would earn a dollar by helping out Uncle Alfred at his guitar studio. That would bring her total up to three dollars and thirty cents. Which was still nowhere near seven dollars and fifty cents. Maybe an idea would come to her; Monday was still a few days away. She'd cross that bridge when she came to it.

Saturday morning saw Iris standing guard by the kitchen door at a quarter to eight, her blue valise by her feet. She had been debating about whether to ride the bus to Auntie Rosa's, but one look out the frosty windows at the swirling snow resolved the matter. She would surely freeze before the bus passed by on one of its infrequent runs. Besides, she needed every penny in her pocket. Her only option was to bum a ride from Alexander, if he would have her. He went to the guitar studio on Saturday mornings, too, because Uncle Alfred had set him up with a few beginner students so he could earn some cash. Everyone in the family got free guitar lessons, and Alexander was real good by now. Iris thought Henry was even better, but he was still too young to teach. And anyway, he didn't really like to play with other people around.

Although Iris knew Alexander would be driving to the studio alone, and there would be plenty of room for her and her blue valise in his rusty blue Volkswagen Beetle, she was terrified to ask him. Maybe it had something to do with her memories of his favorite game back in their days on Rugby Road, when he was charged with supervising his younger siblings. As soon as her parents were out of view, Alexander would announce playtime. "OK kids, it's time for Prison Camp!" he would say with a smile that made Iris's blood freeze. From that moment, any wrong answer, any unauthorized move, would result in the swift execution of the punishments he devised, ranging from tickle torture to being forced to drink hot water and pepper.

One thing Iris could do to grease her request was to be ready to run out the door when he did. She pulled on her coat and boots, never budging from the door as the minutes passed. The thought of the drive with Alexander made her uncomfortably warm in her coat, the dilemma of how she would get to Auntie Rosa's if he said no made her perspire, and the predicament of the debt hanging over her head made the sweat flow freely. She was tempted to rip her coat open, when she heard feet thundering down the stairs. Alexander appeared, and headed straight for the door.

"CanIgettaride?" Iris blurted out before her courage, fragile as thin ice, could crack. Alexander's only response was to stick a foot out behind him as he rushed through the door, so it wouldn't slam in Iris's face. Iris hurried out after him and into the fresh snow, sliding into the back seat of the Beetle so he would not even have to see her during the drive. She hated cars in the winter, and she hated the vinyl seats that sucked body heat from her legs and buttocks. Alexander turned the key in the ignition, and after a few attempts the engine sputtered to life. He hopped out to scrape two peepholes through the snow and ice glazing the windshield, then took some bricks from a pile beside the garage and loaded them into the trunk, like he did when it snowed a lot. Behind the wheel, Alexander blew into his bare hands, lit a cigarette and rolled down the window. He shifted the car into reverse and accelerated, slipping and sliding backwards down the driveway and onto the road, while Iris squeezed her eyes tight, shutting out the numbing coldness of both the winter and her brother, wondering whether it was a sin to hate either.

"Good morning, Alfred's Guitar Studio!" Iris said, thawed and seated at the desk. Sometimes she slipped up, and said "Uncle Alfred's Guitar Studio," which made people laugh, and made her embarrassed, but today she got it right, and thought her voice sounded rather grown-up. As she waited to hear who was on the other end of the line and what they wanted, her fingers toyed with the adhesive label stuck in the center of the rotary dial, imprinted with the number Fairview 8-5210. Later, she would spray the phone and everything else in the waiting room with Lysol. Uncle Alfred didn't like germs.

"Hello, miss," a woman on the other end answered. "My son Paul has a three o'clock lesson today, but we're not gonna be able to make it." Iris ran through the day's schedule in her mind, trying to place Paul and the owner of the voice, who spoke over the sounds of a blaring television, a child whining, and a boy shouting. The medley caused a series of images to flash through Iris's mind: a sink full of breakfast dishes smeared with congealed egg yolk, bowls with remnants of cereal clinging to their sides scattered about the table, spilled orange juice being tracked across linoleum tiles by the bare feet and knees of snotty-nosed toddlers in dirty diapers.

Iris scrunched up her shoulder to cradle the receiver, flipped open the appointment book, and fished a red pen from the pencil-holder. Cancellations were not good; they took a bite out of Uncle Alfred's earnings and left a hole in Iris's day, but she did relish the sense of grown-up power she felt when wielding a red pen. Her eyes scrolled down the page marked Saturday to the 3:00 slot. As soon as she spotted the name "Lewes," Iris recalled the stocky woman who always asked for a second piece of candy while leafing through the *Daily News* in the waiting room. She and Mrs. Lewes shared the same taste in candy: her favorites were Brach's caramels (even though they were to blame for pulling out one of Iris's fillings), with butterscotch hard candy coming in a close second. Like answering the phone and dusting, passing out candy to the students and parents who transited the small waiting room was just one of Iris's duties as Uncle Alfred's "very private secretary." The role came with privileges, like skimming a piece or two of candy off the top each time she passed around the tin canister, which was stenciled with musical notes, like everything else in the studio. She always felt a little guilty when she dipped into the candy jar more than usual, but that was nothing like how she felt now.

Iris sighed, and tried to muster up a tone of authority. "You know our cancellation policy, Mrs. Lewes. You are supposed to notify us twenty-four hours in advance, otherwise you could be charged."

"I know that, honey," replied Mrs. Lewes, politely but impatiently, "but try tellin' that to my other little one who waited till a hour ago to come down with an intestinal bug, and to Mr. Lewes who got called to put in some overtime at the plant. We can't afford to turn down that time-and-a-half pay so he can babysit. Especially if we want to pay off that guitar."

"I'll tell Mr. Capotosti." Iris uncapped the red Bic with her teeth and drew two parallel lines diagonally across the three o'clock slot, printing the letters CXL in the space between them. She wished she could do the same with the last few days of her life. "We'll see you next Saturday, then. Tell Paul to keep practicing." He needed it; he was still working on "Bonanza." The song was one of the standards Uncle Alfred used to teach his students to read music because of its simple notes on open strings, its peppy tempo, and the catchy tune that was readily recognizable from the television series.

As Iris hung up, a lanky colored boy emerged from the studio, guitar in tow. He dug a hand into the pocket of his dungarees and extracted a skimpy wad of crumpled dollar bills which he proffered to Iris on a amazingly pink palm crisscrossed with numerous lines. She heard that all kinds of information, like how long someone would live or how many children they would have could be read in those lines. Iris wished someone would read hers, and tell her where she could find the four dollars and twenty cents she still needed.

"Let's see," she said, as she glanced at the appointment book. "You owe for last week's lesson, and today's, plus two weeks of

T.P., right?" Her uncle had devised a Trial Plan for students whose families could not afford to buy them a guitar. They were allowed to rent the instrument for a dollar and twenty-five cents a week and if they decided to proceed to its purchase, the sum of rental fees paid would be deducted from the price. Uncle Alfred had learned to play the guitar on his own, using borrowed instruments, and got all wistful looking when he talked about the joy of owning his first guitar. Iris knew he sometimes let the T.P. payments slide for families that didn't have much money, and she had proof that more than once he had let ownership of a guitar shift nonchalantly to the hands of a promising but needy student after a few months. There was no ceremony to his actions, but Iris was always touched by the proud look on a student's face when at the end of a lesson Uncle Alfred stepped out of his studio, leaned over the desk where Iris sat and in a tone of confidentiality instructed her to remove the (T.P.) designation that followed his name on the appointment roster. Those students always carried their guitars differently after that happened.

"Music keeps boys out of trouble!" Uncle Alfred would say, when Auntie Rosa suggested he might pursue a more lucrative profession. "All these boys need is a guitar in their hands, and once they learn to play a few chords, they can start up a little rock and roll band." Her uncle was extremely soft spoken, as opposed to her vociferous father, and exuberant Auntie Rosa. When he talked about guitars and the power of music, his jaw quivered even more than when he sat down to a plate of steaming spaghetti.

The guitars came and went in Uncle Alfred's basement studio, stopping briefly in the bathroom that doubled as a storage room. Once in a while Iris was lucky, and was granted the privilege of unpacking a shipment of guitars that arrived from New York City, or even all the way from California. She loved running her fingertips over the instruments before anyone had played them, and as she caressed the smooth curves of the bodies and the long, slender necks of the guitars, she fantasized about whose hands would hold them, and whether they would succeed in coaxing harmonious notes and chords from their strings. Iris was learning to play, too, and hoped she would have her own instrument one day. For now, Alexander and Henry were the only ones in the family who had their own guitars, which no one was allowed to touch, but there were a couple more lying around in the house for general use. Iris didn't really like things for general use, whether they be guitars, bicycles, or roller skates, because no matter how diligent she was about tuning the strings, or filling the tires, or replacing the key, someone else more careless always came along and mistreated everything.

Iris thought that besides being a famous night club performer and the world's best guitar teacher, Uncle Alfred must be one of the most sought after bachelors in the neighborhood. His manners were impeccable, his appearance dapper, and ladies were quick to accept his invitations to Sunday dinner at the Ponderosa steak house or, on a fine day, perhaps an outing to Canandaigua Lake. On such occasions, Uncle Alfred did not drive the battered station wagon he used to transport instruments, but sat at the wheel of Auntie Rosa's gleaming Ford Fairlane 500. Regardless of whether any lady friends were invited, the Sunday drives included not only Auntie Rosa's automobile, but Auntie Rosa herself, and also Iris, if she happened to be around and very lucky. At Uncle Alfred's insistence, Auntie Rosa always sat next to him in the front seat, ensconced in her force field of Estée Lauder Youth Dew, and the ladies who sat in the back seat with Iris were always very kind, although Iris would have preferred to just look at the countryside rather than keep repeating the same polite answers to the same boring questions. Iris supposed Uncle Alfred didn't care to have male friends, except for the men in the Hawaiian trio, and he seemed quite content to spend his free time with family, especially Auntie Rosa and Grandma, and the ladies who fluttered in and out of the Ford Fairlane 500. But, of course, he never looked happier than when he was playing the guitar.

Iris loved many things about those Sundays when Grandma and Grandpa were well enough to be left alone for an outing to be arranged. She loved the way Uncle Alfred held open doors and pulled out chairs for the ladies, herself included. She loved the grown-up way she felt when the waiter placed a menu in her hand, and the grand feeling when Uncle Alfred chuckled and said, "The sky's the limit!" Iris never ordered more than she could eat, and always kept an eye on the prices, but sometimes she simply could not resist ordering the steak, even if the cheapest one did cost a couple of dollars more than the chicken Auntie Rosa invariably ordered. To Iris, it was easily worth a million bucks more to be served her own sizzling steak, with a colored flag on a toothpick sticking out of the juicy meat, as proof it had been cooked specifically to her preference, as if what she preferred actually mattered to someone. She loved dining in a place where people conversed instead of yelling, and having a cloth napkin in her lap, which she could use to dab daintily at the corners of her mouth, and sipping water from a sparkling tumbler filled with clinking ice, instead of having to drink milk from a plastic glass.

When dinner was over, Uncle Alfred always paid with the bills that filled his wallet on Sundays after a weekend of teaching and playing at The Luau, and he always placed the tip right in the waiter's hand when they left, as he waved away Auntie Rosa, who always wanted to know how much he was leaving, and even if Uncle Alfred didn't answer, which he never did, she always said it was too much.

Leisurely Sunday drives to Canandaigua would not be happening for a long time yet, if ever, Iris thought, as she sat in the studio that Saturday, smack dab in the middle of the frigid Rochester winter that blocked the basement windows with drifting snow, and made Iris wish she could be somewhere far away from the cold, and far away from the bridge she would eventually have to cross on Monday morning, and Sister Mary Benedict who would be waiting for her on the other side.

Despite the nasty weather, all of Uncle Alfred's students except for Paul Lewes had shown up that day, and the plastic money pouch with the bank emblem on it was chubby with the loose change and bills Iris stashed away after each payment, with all the

170

heads of Washington and Lincoln facing the front. Uncle Alfred didn't like taking money from people; he said it was filthy, and Iris figured he certainly wouldn't want to contaminate his guitar with all those germs. Uncle Alfred washed his hands a lot, even without soap and water, like when he was standing around talking and rubbing one hand over the other, instead of toying with coins in his pocket like some men did.

Iris wasn't crazy about touching the money either, especially if the coins were sweaty or the currency crumpled, but sometimes she did like to hold the pouch to her nose and smell the money. Today, she was particularly attracted to the pouch, and had taken several sniffs. She had also counted the money obsessively before each student, and after each student. Between Trial Plan proceeds and lesson money, there was a total of forty-five dollars and fifty cents. She was just sticking her nose in the pouch when Alexander left, making her jump in her seat and shove the pouch back in the drawer as he breezed past her without a word, his shoulder-length hair billowing behind him. Iris had fished all the caramels out of the canister and sucked so much butterscotch candy that the roof of her mouth was raw. By now, the waiting room was devoid of waiters, and the phone had fallen silent. Uncle Alfred's last student was playing "Crocodile Rock" on the bass and kept falling behind tempo. The guitar-shaped wall clock ticked like a time bomb. Her cheeks grew hot, her heartbeat accelerated, and an unfamiliar tension in her loins made her legs shake.

Iris slid the desk drawer open again, unable to resist checking the pouch one more time. Feeling its weight in her hands, she was proud of herself for cashing in all the Trial Plan money today. Uncle Alfred would be surprised when she told him. If she told him. She was thinking about how Uncle Alfred never bothered asking who had paid the T.P. fee and who hadn't, though he always knew exactly how much money to expect from his lessons. If she erased the (T.P.) designation next to four of the students' names, and took that money, all her problems would be solved. But that would be stealing, wouldn't it? Maybe not; maybe she deserved it, maybe she could consider it a bonus for doing such a good job collecting the money. Iris zipped opened the pouch. She'd just take one more sniff. The grubby smell of the cash made that weird feeling between her legs get worse. There was another aspect she hadn't considered before, but now that she thought about it, she realized Uncle Alfred was more than happy to let the students use his guitars. Whether or not they paid the T.P., he had already purchased the instruments, and they would just be sitting there in the bathroom gathering dust if no one were renting them.

Aaay-aya-yaya-yaay, aya-yaya-yaay, aya-yaya-yaay. Iris heard the beat pick up for the final chorus of "Crocodile Rock." The kid had finally gotten the hang of it. His lesson would be over soon.

Iris jiggled in her chair, and tapped her feet with the music, watching a hand slip into the pouch and come back out with five one-dollar bills clutched between its fingers.

12. LILY

"OK class," said Miss Dalton. "Put your books away and let's line up by the door for recess." It was a command she never had to repeat. The children had been squirming in their seats all morning, tormented by the blue skies and sunshine dangling on the other side of thick transom windows, just out of reach. On the heels of another treacherous New York winter, they were anxious to swing on the monkey bars and fly down the slide, parched to taste these first luscious drops of spring.

"Billy Armstrong, you are leader today. Please stop by the water fountain so everyone can get a drink before we leave the building – and remember class, no one will be permitted to reenter the building until recess is over, so drink up!"

Lily couldn't slam her book closed fast enough. She didn't have any specific plans for recess, but anything was better than sitting in class. Anything. Whenever a classmate came down with the latest cold or flu bug, Lily secretly hoped she would catch it, so she could stay home and avoid this whole business of school altogether. And if she didn't catch whatever was going around, she would sometimes invent an illness and get excused to go sit in the nurse's office. Complaining of a stomachache was usually a good bet. After all, no one could prove that you didn't have a stomachache, and the last thing anyone wanted was to have a student puking in class. Except maybe for Mr. Schuler, the janitor. He probably liked it because then he could come down with his bag of sawdust and sprinkle it all over the puke, and all the children and teachers would really appreciate him for scooping it up and taking it away.

"Hello, Mrs. Capotosti?" the nurse would say. "This is Nurse Bickley from Fairview Elementary school." Nurse Bickley would look over at Lily. "Yes, I'm afraid she is – she's right here in the office, lying down on the cot."

That would be Lily's cue to come up with a simple groan, perhaps rolling to her side, drawing her knees up, and placing her hands over her belly.

"Yes, it seems to be a bad one this time," Nurse Bickley would say, with the hint of a grin on her lips. "All right then, Mrs. Capotosti, we'll see how it goes, and I'll call you back and let you know... You're very welcome... You too. Bye-bye now."

"Well, Miss Lily, what do you think? Do you want to stay here for a bit and see if you think you might feel better in a little while?"

"OK," Lily would mumble.

Then the nurse would take Lily's temperature, and invariably she would announce, "Ninety-eight point six!"

Lily knew the drill. Once the phone call was made and the temperature taken, she would have about half an hour on the cot and then she would have to decide if she wanted to go back to class, or if she wanted the nurse to call her mother to come and pick her up. This decision was predicated on several factors, including what time of day it was (the later in the day, the more likely she would be willing to go back to class, saving a "go home" for a more dire situation), whether she had remembered to pack an extra apple or graham cracker so she would have something to eat at snack time, and which classes were scheduled - with art, recess, and music all reasons to consider sticking it out for the day.

But it wasn't as though she was "faking it" as her brothers would accuse her of when they arrived home to find her in her pajamas watching *The Andy Griffith Show* in the middle of the day. School really did give her a stomachache, and some days she simply could not bear to sit in that chair one moment longer. It was especially hard now that Iris had gotten off the waiting list and was going to Sacred Family. Lily had to walk to school alone, eat lunch alone, and there wasn't one person she trusted to sit on the other end of the teeter-totter at recess.

Lily couldn't understand why school was so easy for the other children, all of whom happily got up, sat down, came in and went out on command. She learned very early on in her elementary career that phrases such as "Why do I have to?" and "But I don't want to" were not acceptable responses to the requests of teachers, bus drivers, and lunch ladies. In fact, there were no acceptable responses except to just obey. It made her feel trapped not to have choices. Sometimes she didn't like sitting in a circle and sometimes she didn't feel like practicing her penmanship, but at school what she wanted was even less important than it was at home. Getting bossed around all the time really did give her a stomachache, even if it wasn't the kind that made you throw up all over the place.

A request to line up for recess was always welcome, however, if only because it meant freedom from sitting in a chair, in a row of desks, in a room of rows, in a school of rooms, and where your success in passing to the next grade landed you in another seat just the like the one you already hated, for yet another dreadfully interminable year. So Lily eagerly took a place in the line. Once all the children were single-filed by the door, Miss Dalton gave the word, and Billy Armstrong led them down the hallway.

The children all stood against the wall, which was comprised of concrete blocks painted with a thick coat of beige that had been slapped on with such nonchalance that drips of paint were still frozen in place, like permanent latex-based tears of all the children who had ever been confined there. The line inched along as each child took his or her turn at the drinking fountain. Lily surveyed the faces behind her and spotted Claudia Johnson. She hadn't gotten Claudia yet, so when Lily's turn came to drink, she let the other children go ahead of her, one by one, until Claudia ended up right behind her.

Lily stepped up to the fountain, and turned the handle with her right hand, placing the fingers of her left directly into the spouting water. Then she turned to Claudia and flicked her fingertips, spraying Claudia's face with water.

"Lily!" shouted Claudia. "What did you do that for?! Ow, ow, ow! You got it in my eye!" Claudia started to cry.

Miss Dalton bolted into the hallway. "Claudia, what's the matter?" she called.

"It's Lily!" said Claudia. "She splashed water in my eyes!"

Lily stood, covering her face with her hands.

"Again, Lily?" said Miss Dalton. She pulled Lily out of line. "Stop mumbling and take your hands away from your face. We've talked about this antisocial behavior of yours before. I'm afraid we need to take a little visit to Mr. Davenport's office. Billy – you wait until everyone has had a drink, and then you lead the class out to the playground. I will be along presently." She turned to Lily. "You, young lady – come with me." She wriggled her bent forefinger at Lily. It was like a tiny hook – a miniature version of the one they used on *The Ed Sullivan Show* when your act was so bad they didn't even want you to finish.

The walk to the Principal's office seemed to go on forever, with Miss Dalton not saying even one word. She didn't hold Lily's hand the way she always did when she walked her to the nurse's office, and she didn't ask Lily, "How is your mother?" or "What do you want for Christmas?" or any of the other nice questions that friends ask one another. Miss Dalton wore her shiny brown hair in a flip, and she always had on white frosted lipstick – she was almost as pretty as Violet – and while she was usually very nice, Lily knew that she was really angry this time. But it didn't matter; it wouldn't have mattered. What mattered most was that she got Claudia Johnson. Getting in trouble with the Principal was the least of her worries; there were still at least ten more children left to get.

Mrs. Basso was a stout, quiet woman with short gray hair and pink diamonds in her eyeglass frames. She always kept a box of black licorice Smith Brothers cough drops on her desk, and sometimes if you coughed enough, she would offer you one. Lily liked the cherry flavored Smith Brothers much more, but even a black one was better than no cough drop at all. She coughed once, twice, three times, but Mrs. Basso never even looked up from her typewriter. *Clickety-clickety-click.* So Lily coughed louder. Nothing. *Clickety-clickety-click-ding!* Lily supposed that being brought to Mr. Davenport's office for actual antisocial behavior disqualified her from the kind of compassionate treatment she received when she had a stomachache. Being sick was definitely better than getting in trouble.

Miss Dalton emerged from Mr. Davenport's office, leaving the door open behind her.

"Come on in and have a seat, Miss Capotosti," called Mr. Davenport. "And close the door behind you." Mr. Davenport sat behind a mammoth wooden desk, the surface of which was littered with individual sheets of notepaper, a stapler, a cup filled with a dozen sharpened yellow pencils, a Rolodex, and one manila folder marked "Capotosti, Lily."

Lily sat in the chair directly across from Mr. Davenport with her feet dangling several inches from the floor. The chair was upholstered in a deep burgundy leather, adorned with a row of brass tacks along the edges. Lily counted the tacks as she ran her fingers along each arm of the chair. There were sixteen. You never did know when that kind of information might come in handy. Like on *Truth or Consequences,* or *Let's Make a Deal* - people won money and cars and trips to Bermuda for knowing things all the time. Lily's concentration was broken only by the sounds of recess in the yard outside the window. She craned her neck to see who was chasing whom, and whether the puddle at the bottom of the slide had dried up yet.

"All eyes forward, please," announced Mr. Davenport. "I would think that you would be more interested in what is going in here, Miss Capotosti. Do you remember what I told you the last time we had this problem?'

"Yes sir," said Lily.

"What did I tell you?"

"You said that the next time there was a incident you were going to call my parents."

"And now here we are," he said, folding his hands on the desktop in front of him. "So what do you suggest I do?"

"I dunno," said Lily. "Call my parents?"

"If that is an attempt at humor, Miss Capotosti, then I strongly advise you against further attempts at this point in time."

Lily couldn't understand why grownups asked such obvious questions and then got mad at you when you answered them. Like that one day when Lily was writing a secret note to Charlot in class. Miss Dalton stopped in the middle of her reading aloud and asked, "Lily, do you have something you want to share with the class?" To which Lily answered, "No thank you - this is a secret note to Charlot." Answering that question earned Lily fifteen minutes in the corner.

Mr. Davenport continued, "What I don't understand is that you are always such a nice young lady, except that you seem to have this propensity."

Lily shrugged her shoulders and looked down at the floor. In addition to all of her other problems, now she had a propensity to deal with. She wondered who was the patron saint of propensities and if there was a special prayer she could say.

"Do you have an explanation to offer?"

"No sir," said Lily. Lily wondered if she would have the courage to get Mr. Davenport if he ever happened to be in line behind her at the drinking fountain.

Every week in catechism class, Sister Jerome told stories about the days when the courage of the faithful was tested all the time, when it was against the law to be Catholic and the people had to hide down in the catacombs to keep from being burned alive, or from having their skin peeled from their bodies, or being sent to the lion's den. Sister cradled a large book in her left hand, balancing its spine in her palm. She gesticulated fiercely with her right arm, passionately recounting the agony of it all like a mad one-armed conductor alone in an empty concert hall.

"Believers were considered criminals," Sister had said breathlessly. "They were not allowed to read the Bible, or hold a Rosary, or wear a crucifix around their necks. Soldiers would burst into homes and if they found any evidence that you believed in Our Lord Jesus Christ or the Blessed Virgin Mother, they would throw you in jail - or worse."

Lily raised her hand. "But you don't really need to hold a rosary to say the rosary," she said. "After all," she added, "No one can see what you're doing inside your own mind. Those persecuted believers should have just prayed in their minds, and not made such a big deal out of it. That way, they could be safe, and still say their prayers and everything."

At first, Sister Jerome just stared, with an expression that Lily interpreted as amazement, as though no one had ever considered such an elegant solution to this age-old problem that had threatened to cause the extinction of Catholics everywhere.

In a single motion, Sister Jerome slammed the book closed and tucked it under her left arm. She addressed Lily in a low, somber voice as though even the act of Lily's having the thought revealed the presence of an evil spirit that must immediately be exorcised.

"Because, Miss Capotosti," she spat, "We don't hide our faith to save ourselves. It is our suffering for our convictions that leads us to everlasting hope." As she accentuated the final "p" on hope, her mouth blossomed into a wide ghoulish grin - one whose sole purpose seemed to be to reveal the presence of teeth and not to express any sense of joy at the ideas of undying conviction and eternal bliss.

It didn't make much sense to Lily that safely praying without a rosary was in some way an offense to God, while flaunting a rosary and getting killed or locked up led to heavenly rewards. After all, you could have a rosary in your hand and not say even one Hail Mary. This basic lack of logic frightened Lily, especially because if God loved us, wouldn't He rather we hide the rosary and save ourselves? It was clear that if Lily had been an early believer, she would have been a rosary hider, and would probably still be in purgatory, paying for her lack of conviction.

Even now, if God asked her to get Mr. Davenport at the fountain she wasn't sure she could do it, and she dreaded the thought. In her heart she secretly wished she would never have to face such an awful choice, because surely she would be too afraid and her lack of devotion would be revealed. *Dear God,* she thought, *I'm sorry I'm so weak.* She made a note to say an extra five Our Fathers the next time she said her penance - just in case.

"Well, then," said Mr. Davenport, "I'm afraid you leave me no choice." He opened the manila folder, picked up the receiver and dialed the phone.

Lily's mother entered the school office briskly, the faint scent of cleanser and vanilla extract in her wake. Lily was placed back into the waiting room while Mr. Davenport and Lily's mother talked. Between Mrs. Basso's *clickety-clicking* and the other children now on their way down to the cafeteria for lunch, Lily could only hear muffled conversation until the door opened and her mother's voice spilled out.

"Thank you very much, Mr. Davenport. I appreciate the call. We certainly will have a talk with her." Lily's mother shook the Principal's hand, which she then extended toward Lily. "Come along, Lily," she said curtly. "You're being sent home for the day."

It was all Lily could do to contain her excitement, until she realized that "we certainly will have a talk with her" meant that Lily's mother might be planning to tell her father. Suddenly, the whole water fountain plan seemed like a really bad idea, even if it was doing God's work.

"So," said Lily's mother as they drove home. "What in the world is this all about, anyway?"

"Nothing," said Lily, cranking the window open. She had never had to explain it to anyone before. It was a secret between her and Jesus.

"Lily Elizabeth," said her mother. "You know that splashing other children isn't allowed, don't you?

"Yes."

"But you're doing it anyway. You must have a reason. I'm just asking you what the reason is."

"Well," said Lily. She looked over at her mother, who

momentarily took her eyes from the road. Lily could see that she was genuinely curious, and since she used to be a Protestant, maybe she would understand. "The reason is... limbo." Lily looked up at her mother, searching for signs of understanding on her face.

"Limbo?" her mother asked.

"Yeah, Limbo."

"I'm lost, Lily. What does any of this have to do with Limbo?"

"In catechism class Sister Jerome says that children who die before they get baptized Catholic don't get to go to Heaven – even if they don't do anything wrong. They go to Limbo instead. She says it's not good there and it's not bad there, but it's not Heaven and they don't have any angels or Jesus in Limbo. Are you going to tell Daddy?"

"Tell him what? Lily, I still don't understand. Why did you splash Claudia Johnson in the face? Honestly, her mother is in my sewing circle, and I'm sure I'll have to hear all about it on Thursday."

"I'm sorry," said Lily. "But I had to do it - Claudia is a public - they're all publics, Mommy," Lily tried to erase the image of Claudia Johnson and Charlot Heinz and Ruthie Goldman banished to the desolation of Limbo for all eternity, with no flying horses, or cotton candy clouds, or rainbow to slide down, or any of the other treats Heaven was sure to hold. "None of the children in my class go to Sacred Family. And Sister Jerome says that if you are with a baby who is about to die and you don't know if he has been baptized, then you should do it – even if you're not a priest – and that will help the baby get into Heaven instead of Limbo. You just have to pour water on their head and say 'I baptize thee in the name of the Father and of the Son and of the Holy Ghost.' I figured if it works for babies, it works for third-graders, too."

"Are you telling me that you've been secretly baptizing your classmates by splashing them with water from the fountain?" Lily's mother squelched a smile, and then cleared her throat.

"I had to do it, Mommy," Lily began to cry. "They don't even know they're going to Limbo, and their mothers and fathers don't know any better and it's just not fair. They didn't do anything wrong at all and they should all get to go to Heaven."

"Calm down, now. Calm down. No need to get all worked up about it."

Really? Lily thought. *All those children all alone in Limbo – and I shouldn't be worried?* "Are you going to tell Daddy?"

"We'll see" she replied. Lily knew that "we'll see" was her mother's way of being noncommittal. Any time she didn't know or didn't have time to make a decision, she just said "we'll see" which meant to drop the matter entirely, and that pushing her for an answer was quite likely to produce the one you didn't want to hear.

The evening couldn't pass quickly enough for Lily. The agony of not knowing whether her mother was going to tell her father, and the fear of what he would do if he found out that she was called to the Principal's office tied her stomach up in knots, so much that she was barely able to finish her Sloppy Joe at dinner. All she could think about was getting yelled at, or getting The Belt, and she hoped that Jesus or the Holy Ghost would come in time, like in the Bible when Issac was on the altar and Abraham was about to kill him. The Holy Ghost did come just in time, but as far as Lily was concerned, he cut it way too close, and she worried that he might not make it in time to save her. It scared her that God would take such a chance, but when she told Sister Jerome that she didn't think it was right for God to wait until the last minute that way, she said it wasn't our place to judge God and then informed Lily that she had broken the first commandment to "Love the Lord thy God with all thy Heart, all thy Mind, and all thy Soul." So if you have to obey even though obeying might get you in trouble, and if you're supposed to call upon God when you are in need but you can't rely upon him to show up on time and if you can't even complain about that without committing a sin, Lily wondered how people were ever supposed to manage.

After dinner, she sat in front of the television with Iris, Charles, and Ricci, pretending to watch *I Dream of Jeannie*. It was one of her favorite TV shows, but she couldn't stay focused on it tonight. She kept one watchful eye on the kitchen, where her mother was wiping the table down with one of the tattered and faded kitchen washcloths (which always felt slightly slimy and smelled slightly moldy, leaving their stink upon your hands long after the dishes were done), while her father was having his after dinner coffee and cigarette. The kitchen light went out, and Lily heard the scraping of the wooden benches against the linoleum floor as they were being pushed back into their places at the table. Her father emerged from the kitchen and passed through the living room, followed by her mother. They both went into their bedroom and closed the door. If she was going to tell him, it was going to be now.

Lily slowly got up from the couch, without giving any thought to losing her spot or asking anyone to save it for her, even though it was a very big deal to have a good seat for watching TV. Most of the time, there were several children watching, and only a couple of places to sit besides the floor. If you got hungry, or had to go to the bathroom, and you had a good seat, it was sure to be gone when you returned to it - unless you could get someone to save it for you. There was an unspoken code about saving seats. If you agreed to do it, it was law. No one else could come along and claim that place if it was being saved, especially if it was being saved in exchange for a favor. And it always was. If you got up and left someone else in charge of saving your seat, you would have to bring him back an orange, or a slice of toast with butter. But tonight, Lily didn't care about much except for what was going on in her parent's bedroom.

The sun room was separated from the living room by a set of French doors, a fact that Lily loved to share whenever a new friend came to visit for the first time. It added an air of sophistication to the old farmhouse, which almost made up for the fact that there was a chicken coop in the backyard. "This is the sun room," Lily would announce, "and these are French doors."

The sun room faced south toward the street and had windows

all across the front and along the eastern wall. It was the room that was home to all the things that didn't or couldn't fit or didn't belong elsewhere in the house: a writing desk, Jasmine's record player, and often, Lily. She felt most at home among the Capotosti odds and ends. Her mother had placed a collection of classical music there in the seductive sunshine. Lily learned her Roman numerals as she filed them volume-by-issue, in the old wooden record cabinet, listening to Tchaikovsky and Beethoven while warming herself on wintry Sunday afternoons.

The sun room also shared a wall with Lily's parent's bedroom. She gently pulled the French doors closed and crouched down, pressing her ear against the adjacent wall, hoping to hear the conversation that would reveal her fate.

"... so I said 'Limbo?' and she said, 'Yes, they're all publics Mommy,' and then she went on to tell me how worried she was about them being sent to Limbo. Carlo – she was baptizing them."

"Baptizing them?"

"Yes – she would wait until they were at the drinking fountain, and then she would get her fingers wet, and splash one of the other children while saying some blessing they taught her in catechism class, because she wants to make sure they get into Heaven."

"You've got to be kidding me..." said Lily's father.

As Lily's mother told her father all about the talk she'd had with Mr. Davenport and the conversation Lily and her mother had on the way home, Lily kept trying to imagine her punishment, hoping that her father would come and get her now and just get it over with. Thinking about getting The Belt was almost as bad as actually getting it, and it seemed like Lily had already been thinking about it all day.

"Baptizing them?" repeated Lily's father. "In the drinking fountain at school?"

"Yes – well, sort of, I guess," said Lily's mother. "Except none of them actually knew they were being baptized."

The room fell silent, and Lily imagined her father walking over to the highboy and retrieving The Belt, and then opening the bedroom door and calling her name. His footfall would shake the room and the wail of The Belt would sting Lily's behind as she fought off brave tears, knowing in her heart that she was suffering for Our Lord and Savior. Instead, both of her parents burst into laughter. They laughed for what seemed like hours, and Lily went from feeling confused about what was so funny, to feeling relieved, to experiencing indignity that neither one of them realized the importance of what she was doing: she was saving souls.

"Shhhh …" Lily's mother said. "Seriously, Carlo – what should we do about it? She's obviously acting on a personal conviction – and she's got one school telling her to do one thing and the other one punishing her for it."

"Just let it go," Carlo said. "The year is almost over, she'll be in Sacred Family next year full-time, and then she won't have to worry about the eternal destiny of her classmates anymore. I'll talk to her just to reinforce the Principal's efforts, but the less we do at this point, the better. We certainly can't punish her for saving her friends from Limbo, can we? By the way, how many children did she baptize?"

"I don't know," said Lily's mother. "At least two or three, I suppose. By the end of the year, she'll be personally responsible for populating the Protestant section of Heaven. Claudia's mother is going to just die when I tell her not to worry - her daughter's soul has been saved, thanks to Saint Lily." Her parents laughed as they opened the bedroom door.

Lily quickly and quietly slipped out of the sun room and found a place on the floor in the living room. She acted as though she was engrossed in the show, sitting with her arms folded across her body - the way Jeannie did when she was about to blink Major Healey to the Antarctic - and refused to acknowledge her parents' glances as they passed back through the living room. The only thing worse than getting The Belt for doing the Lord's work was getting laughed at. Except at least with The Belt, you knew when it was over, and you could be pretty sure that when Thursday rolled around, the ladies wouldn't be sitting in a circle, laughing at you when they should just be quiet and do their sewing.

13. IRIS

It seemed curious to Iris that she never remembered anything good about winter. Maybe it was because except for Christmas, which both excited and disappointed her, winter offered nothing to look forward to and nothing worth remembering. Not unless for some unfathomable reason she wished to dwell on how she would rather die than crawl out of her warm bed on those cold, dark mornings, or how she could hardly move by the time she waddled from the house bundled up in coat and scarf and hat and mittens and boots, or how raw her face and chapped her lips felt after a pummeling by the biting wind and stinging snow, or how stiff and numb her toes and fingers became, she feared they might snap right off like the icicles she and Lily sometimes broke from the roof of the chicken coop to suck on when they got thirsty playing outdoors and were sick of eating snow.

Summer thoughts were another story altogether; they were worth hanging onto, like a sweet dream. Summer was sitting cross-legged in the grass with Lily, feeling the tall, cool blades tickle her feet and stick to the skin of her bare legs, while singing songs and stringing necklaces of clover, and shooing off the bumble bees that buzzed possessively over the flowers.

Summer was not really minding the splinters when she straddled the split wood fence to hop on Jasmine's pony, Jiffy, as he grazed placidly with swishing tail and twitching ears in the shade of the cherry tree, then prodding him with calloused heels and thrusts of the pelvis to take her for a walk, but being content to just sit astride him, even if he refused to budge. It was wrapping her thighs around Jiffy's back and feeling their sweat mingle, and resting her chest on his neck, and burying her face in the coarse hairs of his mane, inhaling his horsey scent as he chomped on the sweet summer grass.

Summer was blue dragonflies flitting past her as she sat on the bank of the duck pond, the dampness seeping through her shorts, her back resting against the trunk of her favorite willow tree, ensconced in a wispy cupola of feathery fronds. Some days, when it was too hot to stay outside, summer was hiding out with Lily to play house in the cool, dark basement, where she saw boyfriends to flirt with and husbands to marry lined up in place of the steel poles that stood tall and strong, stoically holding up the house, even when she pressed her puckered lips against them to practice kissing, until their impassivity drove her mad with frustration. It was unfurling musty curtains from a steamer trunk and seeing a wedding gown so lovely it made her clap her hands with joy; it was fluffing up an old pillow, and welcoming it into her arms as a newborn baby to cradle to her breast.

Summer was hurdling over the lawn sprinkler to cool off, yelping as the cold spray shocked her body in unexpected places, rather than waiting for invitations that didn't come from neighborhood kids with pools. It was the bell of the ice cream truck jangling as it rounded the corner, and dashing off in search of leftover allowance nickels to pacify the parched tongue screaming for the icy sweetness of a cherry Popsicle.

Summer was stripping the husks and picking the silk from mountains of freshly picked corn piled on the kitchen table, and jamming her teeth as she typewritered them across the rows of sweet, buttery kernels until her tummy felt like it would burst. Corn on the cob was her very favorite dinner, and always made Iris happy, but on one particular summer evening, her spirits hovered close to the ground, pestered by the mosquitoes that feasted on her ankles as she sat under the apple tree, feet dangling from the glider, and watched the light being sucked from the sky. It disturbed her to think that only a few months earlier, it had seemed she would be trudging through the slushy snow to Sacred Family forever and then, before she knew it, school was over and there she was, flying home to free her sweaty feet of their penniless penny loafers and darned to death knee socks.

Iris knew that it was precisely then, when she had kicked off those loafers, tossed her socks in the garbage bin, and stood barefoot on the cusp of an endless summer, that she had lived the season's most sublime moment. Not that summer was over yet; there was another whole month of vacation ahead of her. Yet she couldn't stop thinking about how perfect that moment had been, as delicious and tender as the kernels as they tumbled from cob to tongue, and how the memory of the summer's first half was already fading, like the sweetness from her tastebuds, even as the corn sat in her bloated belly. Iris was conscious of each minute slipping by and receding into the past, their memories lasting no longer than the echo of their tick on the clock. She wondered what she would reminisce about when she was old, as she often heard the adults do, if each season of her life were to pass in an unremarkable blur of nothingness. She thought of Grandma Capotosti, and one of those ladies with thick ankles who wore hairnets over their buns and carried rosary beads in their pockets, the one Grandma called Comare Giuseppina. Comare was born up in that Scurcola place, just like Grandma, and when she visited, the two of them spent hours swapping stories about things that had happened forty or even fifty years ago as if it were yesterday. Iris had witnessed so many of their emotionally charged conversations spoken in a hodgepodge of what little they had learned of English and retained of Italian that she could predict when they would cross themselves, or roll their eyes to heaven, or suddenly start wailing, right there in the middle of coffee and cookies. You would probably never run out of things to talk about if you did stuff like elope to another country, or cross the Atlantic in a steamer ship, or survive two world wars, a Depression, a death of a daughter, a string of illnesses. Iris wondered, when the

189

day would come for her to glance over her own bent, arthritic shoulder, whether the portrait of her past would be etched in such dramatic strokes, or instead appear as an insignificant smudge on a vast blank canvas.

Such thoughts made her sigh as she lounged on the glider, digging her bare heels into the grass to make it swing back and forth in the muggy air. Not a leaf stirred on the low, laden branches of the apple tree which were appreciated for the shade they provided by day, but were constantly cursed for their nasty habit of dropping defective fruit on whomever sat beneath them.

"Gosh darn apples," her father muttered from his lawn chair, as one bounced off his shoulder and landed at his feet with a dull thud, distracting him from his pleasurable pastime of blowing smoke rings and sipping coffee. Each year, her father threatened to spray the trees, and each year her mother convinced him not to, saying the kids liked to eat fruit straight from the branches when they played outdoors, and she did not want them munching on chemicals. The apples weren't so bad, if you liked them tart, and didn't mind spitting out the bad parts. And looking ugly didn't stop them from tasting delicious when they ended up in her mother's homemade pies and crisps.

Iris watched the perfectly formed smoke rings float up into the air above her father's head like tiny halos, then slowly lose their shape and dissipate. She wondered whether God would judge her ungrateful if He heard her complain about summer, after praying so hard for winter to please be over. The things that annoyed her were mostly small things, like the way sweat made her shirt cling to her back, and her thighs stick to the nylon seat of the glider. And mosquitoes; those she really hated. She swiped at one, but missed, as it attempted a landing on her arm.

Silence, a rare commodity at the Capotosti residence in any season, was broken that moment, when the screen door slammed behind Henry, who hurried past, guitar slung over his shoulder, followed by Louis. "See you later," Henry said with a quick wave, without even glancing at Iris or her father. He had a habit of looking down when he walked, instead of at what was ahead or around him. Iris wondered how he didn't get run over when he walked down the street.

"Where are you going, young man?" A half-formed smoke ring followed her father's words out of his mouth.

"Over to the Grange," Henry hardly ever went anywhere, except down in the basement, or out in the chicken coop, where he played his guitar for hours on end. The Grange was a glorified name for an abandoned shed down behind the playground where neighborhood kids sometimes hung out.

"I'm coming, too!" Louis said.

"No, you're not," Henry said. "It's musicians only tonight."

"So it'll just be you and Bob Dylan?" Louis said.

"I don't like you wandering the streets until all hours, Henry," their father said, though Henry was already halfway down the driveway. "Be back in an hour." *Plunk!* This time the apple landed right in his lap. "Jeepers Cripes!" he said, tossing the pocked green fruit to the ground. He lit another cigarette, and shook his head. "All we need in this family is another Uncle Alfred."

"Hey, Iris, want me to show you how to get revenge on those gals?" Louis asked. Louis wasn't the meanest of her brothers, so she didn't really mind when he sat down next to her on the glider. In fact, though he wasn't aware of it, Louis had actually done her a big favor. He was nearsighted like her, so when he had gone to get his vision checked by creepy Dr. Julius, she had tagged along. Louis was curious about everything, and he had been the one to suggest that they go into the examining room together so he could watch up close how Dr. Julius checked her eyes with that machine with all the lenses. Iris still hated wearing her glasses, but had to get used to it, since reading and sleeping were the only things she could do without them.

"What gals?" Iris waved a hand in front of her face. It maddened her that those pesky insects could ruin one of the most pleasant times of day.

"The mosquitoes," Louis replied. "It's the females that feed on human blood."

"Says who?"

"Says me. And my science teacher. They need human blood to make their eggs."

"Gross!" Louis may not share his twin's talent for playing the guitar, but he sure knew about lots of other things.

"Watch this!" Louis said, grabbing her wrist. "Let one of them land on you, and tell me as soon as you feel the prick."

"Now!" Iris said a few seconds later, followed by, "Ouch!" as her brother pinched the flesh of her forearm between his thumb and index finger, gorging the mosquito until it burst, staining her skin with her own freshly sucked blood.

"Gross!" Iris said again, as Louis squealed with laughter and ran back inside the house.

"Hey, Dad!" Louis ran out the door again a minute later.

"What is it now, Louis?"

"Mom said to tell you Auntie Rosa called. She can't come over because Dolores is there."

"Dolores is there?"

"Yes. Mom said to tell you there is a situation."

"Another situation? Oh, for cryin' out loud," her father said, shaking his head, and draining his coffee cup.

Iris knew "situations" were not a good thing. Last time there had been a "situation" was at Easter, when Dolores had stayed at Auntie Rosa's for a whole week, without Dr. Julius, and wore these big sunglasses all the time, even though she never left the house, and even though the sun had barely shown its face since Groundhog Day. Uncle Alfred kept trying to cheer Dolores up by saying, "Who's behind those Foster Grants?" as if she were a movie star, but instead of laughing, Dolores dabbed at the corners of her shaded eyes with one of the hankies she always clutched in her hand.

Iris swatted at another mosquito as it landed on her arm. If Auntie Rosa wasn't coming over, there was no sense hanging around doing nothing except letting swarms of pesky mosquitoes feed on her blood so they could make more swarms of pesky mosquitoes, when she could go to her room and read. She hopped off the glider and went over to her father. "Good night, Dad," she said, feeling reassured by his evening stubble as she brushed her cheek against his.

"Get a good night's sleep, honey. Tomorrow's the big day."

"I know," But it wasn't tomorrow yet, was it? Tonight, she could still look forward to *Little Women*.

Once inside, Iris climbed the stairs, the temperature rising with each step of her ascent into the breathless air of the upper floor. She was sweating and irritated, but relieved to find the bathroom free; she went in and locked the door. She sighed as she leaned over the sink she had scrubbed clean that very morning. The basin was coated by a grey film, sprinkled and spattered with bits and pieces of Capotostis and their grooming habits: whiskers in shaving cream scum, shed armpit hairs, gobs of toothpaste and wads of saliva, granules of acne scrub, plucked eyebrows, nail clippings, boogers and mucus in various shapes and shades of green. She turned on the hot water full blast, and chased it all down the drain.

When the goop and gunk were gone, Iris plugged the drain, filled the sink with cold water, and submerged her head to cool off. She stayed that way, blowing bubbles out of her nostrils until she had squeezed all the air out of her lungs, then came up for air, and dunked her head again. When she ran out of air again, she stood up straight, tossing her hair back with a jerk of her head, enjoying the feel of the cool drops trickling down her neck and back. She felt better for a moment, as she watched the water swirl down the drain, but her irritation resurfaced when she fished her toothbrush out of a glass, and found the bristles wet, a sure sign that someone else had used it. She brushed her teeth anyway, knowing she could not sleep with corn wedged between them. She lowered the seat on the toilet, which was always in boy position, and sat; while peeing, she looked down at her feet, which were covered in dirt and grass stains, and contemplated washing them, but decided she did not feel like it. The sheets on the bed were never clean, anyway. She reached for the toilet paper, and her irritation grew when she found there was only one square of tissue clinging to the roll. She sat to air dry until someone started banging on the door.

"it's about time!" John pushed past her as soon as she unlocked the door. Iris went to her room and flopped down on the mattress next to Lily who lay on her back with her eyes closed, the vestiges of light from the window throwing a soft blanket of grey over her motionless form. The bed bounced under Iris's weight, its tired springs groaning.

Iris reached down to pick up her book from the floor; there was still enough light to read for a bit without disturbing Lily. She couldn't wait to find out whether Jo would marry the German professor she had met in New York.

"Iris?" Lily said.

"What?" Iris replied, flipping to the page she had marked with a clover necklace.

"I can't sleep."

"It's pretty hot, isn't it?" Iris said. Though the sun had gone down, the temperature and humidity had barely budged. Iris might have wished for a thunderstorm to clear the air, but lightning scared her at night. She heard all kinds of stories about lightning striking houses and setting them on fire while everyone was sleeping.

"It's not because I'm hot," Lily said.

Iris rested the open book against her chest. "Is it because you are excited about tomorrow?" she asked.

"I dunno." Lily rubbed her eyes and yawned.

"Are you all packed?"

"Yep. Look over there," she replied, pointing to a brown grocery bag slouched against the dresser. Iris could spot Lily's favorite outfit sitting atop the jumble of familiar fabrics peeking out from the bag. Like most of Lily's clothes, the flowered top and turquoise shorts had once been worn by Iris, and by one or more sisters before her. No one had ever gotten around to replacing the top button that had gone missing from the shorts, which were still a size too big for Lily, and when she ran, they tended to slide down her narrow hips. One look at those shorts made Iris picture Lily running behind her, in that lopsided way of hers, with one hand clutching the waistband, and the other churning the air as she tried to keep up. Sometimes it was faster to grow into an article of clothing than to get it fixed, but Iris was thinking maybe she would find a button and sew it on for her one of these days.

"Good girl. Me too." Iris pointed to another brown grocery bag standing tall and straight next to her blue valise, its posture expressing confidence that it could do the job as well as a proper suitcase, even if it only had a Star Market logo on its side instead of a sketch of the Eiffel Tower.

"Did you pack enough socks and underpants?" Iris asked.

"I guess. I took what was in the drawer. That's all there is."

"How about your bathing suit? Maybe we'll get to go swimming. Wouldn't that be nice?" Iris wasn't crazy enough to think she would ever make it to any of the Hawaiian beaches depicted in Uncle Alfred's posters, but maybe it wasn't too much to wish for a swim in one of those crystal clear lakes she admired in the glossy magazines in the waiting room of the guitar studio.

"Remember where they took us last year, Iris? To that swimming hole that stank like pigs? And we floated around on those tractor trailer tire tubes? And you had to wear sneakers in the water or the mud would grab your toes and suck you in, just like it did to Auntie Teresa?" Lily didn't look at Iris, but at the ceiling, as she spoke.

"It was kinda gross," Iris had to admit, picking her memory for some other feature that would make her look forward to two weeks on the farm. Two weeks in which her parents would have two less mouths to feed, and two weeks in which her cousins would have two extra pairs of free farmhands. It sounded like everyone would be getting a break; everyone but Iris and Lily.

"Can't you remember anything good? Try harder." Iris wished that Lily, just for once, would recognize her need to see the positive side of things, and try to support Iris, instead of always pointing out the negative side. Anyone could do that, and all it did was make you feel worse.

"Like what, Iris? Like when you got out of the water and I pulled that big fat leech off your back?" It was no use; Lily

195

obviously relished her role as saboteur of memories.

"Oh, yeah. I forgot about that!" Iris cringed at the recollection. "I give up!" She closed her book and rolled on her side to face Lily. "Good thing you saw that thing, before it sucked out all my blood." She scratched at the constellation of mosquito bites on her left ankle. What was so good about her darn blood that they all wanted a taste?

By unspoken accord, the girls fell silent, as a distant freight train wailed of worries of its own. Iris and Lily loved to listen to that sound on summer nights, with the window thrown wide open. Sometimes, when they had trouble falling asleep, they would lie in bed and fantasize about where the trains were headed, and Iris would hang upside down over the side of the bed, and reach underneath to pull out the dusty atlas she kept hidden there. She had discovered the atlas in the garage, under her father's workbench, where it had been abandoned together with the plan to drive the family all the way down to Independence to visit Grandma Whitacre. Iris and Lily liked to snuggle close together under the sheet with a flashlight (that, too, came from the workbench, and was even more top secret than the atlas); after studying the maps of all the states, they would each pick out a city they would like the train to take them to. Iris loved the French-sounding Boca Raton; Lily's favorite was Kalamazoo.

As the last faraway whistle grew faint then faded altogether, and the only sound sticking to the thick night air was the chirping of the crickets, Iris felt herself sinking more deeply into the mood of sadness that had pervaded her earlier. Summer was pressing on, just like the train, leaving her and her expectations behind. Though she could live without going to Boca Raton, she still wished she could go swimming in one of those silvery blue lakes. But there was no sense thinking about that now, if there was no way she could make it happen. "Have you counted them tonight?" she said.

"What? The trains?" Lily asked.

"No, silly. The cricket chirps. Remember how Louis taught us about figuring out the temperature? You start by counting the number of chirps per minute."

"No. I mean, yes, I remember. But I don't feel like counting anything tonight."

Because Iris had always liked to count things, sometimes she got Lily to play a game where one of them closed their eyes, and asked the other questions about the room they were in, such as how many linoleum tiles ran across the floor each way, or how many butterflies there were on a certain section of wallpaper. Numbers helped Iris define her surroundings, and she felt a sense of security in knowing how many steps were in each staircase, how many toothbrushes in the bathroom glass, how many pews ahead and behind her in church, how many rows of how many seats in her classroom.

"Why not?" Iris asked.

"I'm just thinking about tomorrow. About the farm."

"We'll have fun. You'll see. You're Nancy's favorite, that's why she picked you to be her flower girl when she got married. You were so pretty in that yellow gown with the hoop skirt. And we can play with her baby."

"Big deal!" Lily replied. "We have plenty of kids around here."

"But Nancy has a little girl," Iris said. "And you're the only Capotosti girl that doesn't have a little sister. Just little brothers.

"I don't care. I don't want a little sister. And anyway, why should I pretend she's a sister when she's only a cousin? And I really don't want to help milk the cows. They make me sick to my stomach."

"Well, if it makes you feel any better, they scare me!"

"I hate cows!" Lily said.

"Lily, don't say that! It's not nice," Iris reprimanded her, wondering what would happen if she blurted that out to their cousin's husband. He was a real farmer, and cows were his life. Bill Jablinski had the blondest hair and pinkest skin Iris had ever seen. Their father said that was because his grandparents came from Poland, and not from that Scurcola place, or anywhere else in Italy. When cousin Nancy was out of earshot, Bill always called Iris and Lily "guinea" and "wop" and a bunch of other names that made him laugh, and when his tractor wouldn't start, he blamed it on them, saying the engine got all clogged up on account of them being greasy Italians.

"Well, it's true!" Lily said. "I do hate cows! And you do, too. Admit it!"

Iris tried to remember more about their time on the farm the previous summer. When she squeezed her eyes shut, her skin flinched at the sting of horseflies, and her stomach turned at the stink of the knee-deep manure she had to wade through in the barnyard to herd the cows into their milking stalls. Anxiety gripped her chest, and fatigue seeped into her limbs at the recollection of the endless rows of cows with their bulging, swaying udders, and of how she had to squeeze in between their dirty, hulking frames, terrified that they would shift their weight and crush her like a fly when she tossed the milking strap over their backs and crept below them to hook it under their bellies. Her nose wrinkled at the pungent smell of hot urine as it cascaded freely from bovine backsides, showering her arms and legs as she tried to dodge the stream. Her belly churned with nausea at the image of cow poop plopping into the trench behind the animals, and the cruddy pail of foul water everyone used to rinse excrement from their arms. It was amazing how many memories she had of those cows, if she really thought about it.

"Who ever decided we had to like cows, anyway? Iris said. "You're right, Lily! I hate cows, too!" She knew it wasn't holy to think, let alone say, the word "hate" but it sure felt good. A sense of liberation rippled through her, making her giggle. "Everyone expects us to be all thrilled about going out to that farm, but we both hate cows!"

"We hate cows!" Lily said, jumping to her knees on the bed, the squeaking of the springs as she bounced making them both laugh harder. "We hate cows!" they chanted together. "WE HATE COWS!"

"In case you guys don't understand it in English, BOOO MOOO!" Iris tackled Lily, and tickled her under the armpits. The girls laughed and rolled on the bed until their stomachs hurt and

Marguerite yelled from their big sisters' room for them to shut up. Clamping their hands over their mouths until they regained control of themselves, they fell on their backs, sweaty and panting.

"I ... don't .... wannagothere ... Iris," Lily said, between breaths. Neither did Iris, but that was what they had to do.

"I only know one way out," Iris said. "How about a fairy tale? One set in a very special place, in a fairyland where there are no cows to milk. But everyone can have all the creamy white milk they want, because it gushes from a waterfall – a giant one, like Niagara Falls. And the swimming holes are filled with chocolate milk instead of mud."

"Please, Iris?" Lily whined. "Couldn't we go there for vacation instead of Miltonville?"

The girls lay on their backs, their rib cages rising and falling rapidly, then slowly settling into an even rhythm. The chirps of crickets were drowned out by the roll of thunder, followed by a loud clap that made them jump into each other's arms.

"Don't worry, Iris," Lily said. "We're going to that fairyland now. Houses can't get struck by lightning there."

Iris sucked in a deep breath, then sighed. A long, loud sigh, that ended with a *hmmpf.*

"You sounded like Mom," Lily remarked.

"What do you mean?"

"Just now, when you made that weird sound."

She was right. It did sound like that sigh her mother made sometimes. Like a tea kettle just before it whistled, when all the steam built up inside.

"Go ahead, Iris. Start."

"How do you want it to begin?"

"Like it always does in fairy stories. You know."

"OK." Iris took her storytelling seriously; she cleared the crumbs of laughter from her throat, paused a moment, then began.

"Once upon a time," she said, her voice soft and low, as she set aside the considerations about present and future that had been worrying her, and tumbled freely back into the childhood that was quickly slipping into the past. She took hold of Lily's hand, and held on tight as her imagination whisked them both away; out the open windows into the summer night they were carried, floating toward the world they alone shared. Iris was pretty sure she heard Lily sucking her thumb, but didn't say anything. She figured it couldn't hurt, just for tonight.

14. LILY

Even though all the children at Sacred Family wore the exact same uniform, you could still tell the rich kids from the poor ones. Mary McDonough's father was a doctor, which was just about as rich as you could get. The pleats in Mary's skirt were always razor sharp, and her dark green knee socks never slid down her shins. Hannah Cullen's father worked at Kodak and they lived in Golden Oaks, which was all new houses with thick wall-to-wall shag carpeting and push-button telephones. Hannah wore a diamond pendant that her parents had given her for her First Holy Communion, and every day she came into school with her hair all done up fancy with shiny clips or ribbons, just like in the *Professional Hair Salon* magazines in the waiting room at Uncle Alfred's guitar studio.

Like Lily, the girls from the poorer families wore standard issue forest green jumpers that had been shortened and lengthened many times as they were passed on from sister to sister. Since Father Delaney might burst onto the scene at any moment and conduct an inspection, lowering a hem was one of the first domestic tasks mastered by the poor girls at Sacred Family. They passed this skill along to one another the way a family might pass a secret recipe down from one generation to the next. When Iris taught Lily how to lower her hem, she was doing more than teaching a little sister how to sew. She was providing her protection from the humiliation of being chastised in front of the entire class for having her jumper too short.

One day a few months after Lily had arrived at Sacred Family, Father Delaney popped in to speak to the class, and to look for such infractions as short skirts on the girls, and boys' hairlines touching shirt collars.

"Miss Capotosti," he announced. "Get up here and let me look at that skirt of yours."

Lily surveyed the faces of her classmates as she tentatively rose from her seat, leaving her pencil unattended rather than placing it in the pencil reservoir that was molded into the desktop. Lily's gaze met first with Mary McDonough's, who looked down at Lily's hemline and back up to her face and, finding nothing of interest to hold her attention, casually turned back to her doodling. Lily's eyes locked with those of Maureen Bevilacqua - who, like Lily, was named after an Irish grandmother, but because of her surname would be forever branded as a half-breed Irishman, her heritage contaminated with Italian blood, which was the same as not being Irish at all. Maureen wasn't a carrot top like Elizabeth Kelly; her hair was a deep, dark red and she had bright blue eyes, but it didn't help one bit. She looked from Lily to Father Delaney, back to Lily, and then quickly returned to her schoolwork without making a show of sympathy. The poor Italian children couldn't afford to stick up for each other; they each had enough trouble of their own.

Father Delaney stood at the front of the room, staring, with his arms folded across his chest. His eyes were hidden behind lenses that reflected the fluorescent panels in the ceiling, making it look as though the light was coming straight out of his eyes like the very judgment of God, beaming condemnation directly onto Lily's thighs. The room was completely silent except for the *tick-tock* of the wall clock and the rolling of Lily's runaway pencil along the surface of the desk, followed by the sounds of it hitting her chair, and then landing on the floor - right at William Nolan's feet. Lily crouched down to retrieve it and just as she touched the pencil with her fingertips, William nudged it, sending it further out of reach. He offered Lily his trademark smirk, a troublemaker's pleasure at watching someone else walk into the fire. Lily lowered herself further, stretching and twisting her body to reach the pencil.

"Miss Capo-tosti!"

A shock of fear zipped through Lily's body and she bolted up, hitting her head on the underside of the desk, producing the definitive clang of skull against metal, and provoking a round of laughter. Lily quickly slapped the pencil into its holding place on the desk, and as she turned to walk to the front of the room she heard it as it again rolled off and onto the floor. Rubbing her head and straightening her jumper, she approached her accuser.

"I can see what you're doing there," said Father Delaney, impatiently gesturing for Lily to come forward more quickly. "Shimmying your skirt down to make the hemline appear lower. You Capotostis are all the same."

Lily's face grew hot, and her heart quickened with her gait. She finally stood facing Father Delancy, who took her by the shoulders and spun her around so that she faced her classmates. He then extracted a small ruler from his breast pocket and lowered his body into a crouch. He placed the ruler against Lily's skin, and moving his hand from the front, to the side, and around to the back, tugged at her hem, measuring. The feel of his warm breath and his ruler against her skin made Lily flinch, despite her determination to remain still. She became momentarily distracted from her predicament, intrigued at this opportunity to see Father Delaney's bald head close up, and from above. Tiny beads of sweat were bursting onto his shiny skin, which was stretched over the bumps and creases of his calvarium, as Auntie Rosa would call it. (Lily liked knowing the words that doctors and nurses used for parts of the body, with ischial tuberosities being her very favorite for sounding impressive, and coccyx number one for making someone laugh, although she couldn't understand what was so funny about *that*.) When Lily leaned in slightly to get a better look, her long silky hair fell forward, brushing against Father Delaney's cheek. He inhaled sharply and dropped his ruler. Rising to stand, he extracted a white cotton handkerchief from his pants pocket and dabbed at his brow.

"This is at least half an inch too short. The next time I see you, I expect it to be corrected." He waved Lily away. "Sit down."

The problem with the one-inch rule was that you could go home and rip out your hem, lower it, re-hem it, and then in a few months, the skirt would be too short again. Lily meant to keep track of it, to maybe borrow the tape measure from her mother's sewing kit and check every once in awhile. But the length of her hem was something she only really thought about when Father Delaney came by, and by then it was too late.

"Boys and girls," Father addressed the class. "Today I want to talk to you about something called accountability." Lily was excited to be part of a discussion about such a big and impressive word. She could not wait to find out what it meant, so that she could look for an opportunity to use it at the supper table, or perhaps on her next essay assignment.

"Accountability means being responsible for the things that you say and do. Now, the little kindergarten babies we see in the hallway are accountable for very little, because they don't know any better. But all of you here have already made your First Holy Communion, and so you have reached what we call the age of accountability - you must pay the consequences of your actions."

Father Delaney picked up a stick of white chalk from the aluminum tray. He held his long arms up in front of him, bent at the elbows and at the wrists, like the praying mantis Lily had found in the garden that summer. Even though it was said to be praying, the odd creature with its waving antennae and spindly appendages was made more repulsive to Lily after Louis told her that the females bit the heads off of the males after mating, in order to keep the males from eating the praying mantis babies. While Lily fully supported a praying mantis mother protecting her young, she felt that there surely must be a better way. Such an ugly and violent existence made her cringe, and filled her with dread.

Father Delaney turned toward the green chalkboard. "We have two kinds of sins, and when you commit these acts, you are held accountable by God. First, we have your mortal sins." He wrote in large block letters on the board. "M-O-R-T-A-L. Mortal." He underlined the word.

"Next, we have your venial sins. V-E-N-I-A-L." He set the chalk back into the tray and brushed the palms of his hands back and forth against each other, sending a cloud of chalk dust into the air. Turning toward the class, he continued. "Now, a mortal sin is quite serious. These are willful acts against God, such as murdering someone or engaging in homosexual behavior. A mortal sin destroys the grace of God in your heart and cuts you off from His Love. So to put it in layman's terms, if you have a mortal sin on your soul, God can't even stand the sight of you. If you die with an unconfessed mortal sin, you cannot join our Lord and Savior in Heaven."

A wave of panic rushed through Lily's body. She knew she had never murdered anyone, but perhaps she was engaging in homosexual behavior. Terrified at the thought of dying with a mortal sin on her soul, she shot her hand up into the air.

"Do you have a question, Miss Capotosti?"

"Yes, Father."

Lily stood up next to her desk, as was the requirement when addressing an adult in class. "What's homosexual behavior?"

Father Delaney removed his black framed glasses, and pinched the bridge of his nose with the thumb and forefinger of his left hand. Eyes squeezed tightly shut, he paced back and forth across the front of the room. "Homosexual behavior is when two men engage in acts that men are supposed to engage in with women, or when two women do things together that they are only supposed to do with men." He replaced his glasses. "In other words, there are some things that are good and right when a man and a woman do them together, but that cause damnation and eternal suffering if two men or two women do them together."

Absentmindedly sliding her body back into her chair, Lily could only think of a few things that her parents did together: They had coffee after dinner every night, and then they took turns reading the *Times-Union* in the living room. But sometimes Auntie

Rosa and Lily's mother had coffee together, too, so that couldn't be right because Auntie Rosa would never commit a mortal sin. She probably didn't have any sins at all, just like Our Blessed Virgin Mother.

"Now venial sins are bad, but they are minor in comparison to mortal sins. They include acts such as disobeying your parents, lying to Sister Mary Ellen here about why your homework isn't done, and of course touching yourself with lust."

Lily looked around the room to see if any hands were going up, but all she saw were the blank stares and confused faces of her classmates. Again, she shot her hand into the air.

With a sigh, Father Delaney said, "Yes, Miss Capotosti? No doubt you have another question."

"Yes, Father," said Lily, standing. "What's lust?"

"Lust is wanton pleasure. Touching yourself with lust is touching yourself with wanton pleasure. You may sit down."

Unsatisfied and confused, Lily obeyed. Yet she still needed to know whether she was touching herself with wanting pleasure, so she could be sure to stop right away. Only her fear of further angering Father Delaney kept her from raising her hand yet again. Her mother sometimes said she was an "instigator" and she did not want to instigate Father Delaney - surely making him angry would be at least a venial sin. It might even be a mortal one, seeing how he was so close to God.

An entire school year had passed since then, and the subject of touching oneself with wanting pleasure never came up again in any of Father Delaney's talks. Lily decided to just be careful, and whenever she had to touch herself - as in drying off from a bath or putting her socks on in the morning - she made sure it didn't feel too good - and if it did, she would distract herself by pulling a hair out of her head or by thinking of the suffering of starving children in Biafra, or of all the lost souls in Purgatory and Limbo.

On her first day in the fourth grade, Lily felt excited about finally making the passage from the primary grades, and thrilled to be wearing her new school shoes. She had placed them on the dresser the night before and she could barely sleep, thinking of how wonderful it would feel to slip them on her feet for the very first time. Of all the shoes at the Buster Brown store, they were her favorites – even including the shoes that weren't on the clearance rack. They were slip-ons, but not penny loafers like most of Lily's classmates wore. Mary Hannah and some of the other rich kids wore penny loafers, but they put dimes in the slots where the pennies were supposed to go. What a waste of twenty cents. That was equal to a Three Musketeers bar, a Sugar Mama, and a handful of penny candies. If Lily had an extra twenty cents just laying around, she sure wouldn't waste it by wearing it in her shoes.

The best part about Lily's new shoes was that they had a little flap of fringe that laid across the toe like a tiny leather fan, and no one else in the whole class had a pair just exactly like them. At the same time, however, she felt sad because she knew that in a month or two, they would be scuffed and dull, and she would have to wait until school started next year before she would have another new pair. It seemed inevitable; she knew that soon she would be sitting there, looking down at a pair of worn out, lackluster shoes. She vowed to herself to treat these shoes carefully. She wouldn't wear them for play, she would gently place them under the bed at the end of each day instead of hurriedly kicking them off, and she would never ever wear them outside in the rain or snow. She just had to take care of them this year. They were so pretty. She could sit there and look at them all day.

She didn't hear her name the first time, or even the second time.

"Lily Capotosti," Sister Elaine repeated loudly. Whenever any of the nuns or priests at Sacred Family said her last name, they did so as though they were spitting it out it, like Grandma Capotosti did with the pasta whenever it was overcooked.

Lily looked up from her shoes to see Sister Elaine glaring at her from the front of the room, rapidly tapping the eraser end of a yellow number two pencil on her desk.

"Here!" blurted Lily.

A spattering of laughter erupted among Lily's classmates.

"Miss Capotosti," said Sister Elaine. "We took roll call an hour ago. At this time, I would like you to stand up and read us your summer essay assignment on what you did during your break from school. That is, if you're not too busy staring at the floor."

Lily stood up and opened her black and white composition book to page one, where she had penned her first and usually most dreaded assignment of the year. Her family never took vacation, and it embarrassed her to talk about their Fourth of July family reunion and their annual summer excursion to the drive-in movies, when the other children had stories about vacations to Disneyland, Yellowstone Park, and camping in the Adirondack Mountains. But this year, Lily was sure she had something special to share, and she was almost as excited about reading her essay as she was about her new shoes. She was certain that no one else in her class had such a story to tell; it would surely set her apart.

"What I did on my summer vacation," Lily began. "It all started when my whole family came over for my Grandma's birthday on the Fourth of July. I used to think it would be just awful to have your birthday on the Fourth of July, but every year my Grandma gets sparklers on her cake instead of candles, which I think would be really fun.

"Everyone comes for Grandma Capotosti's birthday – my cousins Bill and Nancy, Ed and Gloria, and of course Auntie Rosa and Uncle Alfred. Aunt Selma and Uncle B. come, too. I don't really like Uncle B. because he smells like Genesee Cream Ale and he always makes me sit on his lap and if I try to get up he tells me, 'Where are you going, Miss Lily of the Valley? What's your rush?'"

Sister Elaine cleared her throat. Lily looked over to see her scribbling on a pad of paper. Lily looked up at her classmates before continuing. Neil Schickler was picking his nose, and Mary Dunne passed Margaret Callahan a note.

"Out of a clear blue sky," Lily continued dramatically, borrowing one of Auntie Rosa's signature phrases, "my cousin Nancy said to my mother, 'Betty, we would love to have the girls come and stay with us for a couple weeks.'" Lily addressed her classmates. "'The girls' – that's my sister Iris and I – 'They would have a blast!' said Nancy."

Lily didn't exactly lie about Uncle B. in her essay, but she didn't exactly tell the whole truth, either. Uncle B. (his given name was Bartolomeo, but since everyone had such a hard time pronouncing it, they just called him "B") had a big round belly and most of his teeth were missing so that when he talked, tiny fountains of saliva shot up out of his mouth, and if you were sitting on his lap while he was engaged in a conversation, then you just had to hope and pray that you wouldn't get nailed. Shielding your face with your hand or wiping spittle off your cheeks was not acceptable, and would be met with The Look - a form of non-verbal communication adults used to discreetly let the children know that they were behaving badly. Anyone could give you The Look, but it was most fearsome coming from Lily's father. His nostrils would flare and he would get the Crazy Eyes, probably due to the fact that he wanted to yell, but wasn't able to, on account of that The Look was used mostly out in public where things like nose-picking, expelling flatus, and yelling at children were unacceptable. So while The Look itself could be quite intimidating, if you were feeling lucky or brave, you could actually pretend you didn't notice it at all, as it was just too hard to prove that you did.

The thing about Uncle B. was that he could bombard you with his spit bombs and you had to sit there and take it, just like you had to sit on his lap if he asked you to, even though he made you stay there much longer than you could stand it. In fact, he seemed to like it if you wriggled around, laughing as you tried to work yourself free. Sometimes, getting The Look just wasn't enough to make you stay.

The last time Uncle B. had visited, Lily offered her obligatory greeting kiss to him quickly, hoping to escape before he finished swigging on his can of beer.

"Hey - c'mere!" he caught Lily by the hand as she turned to walk away. "You call that a greeting?" With Lily's face squished between his hands he planted a wet sloppy kiss smack dab on her mouth. Lily wiped her mouth with the back of her hand. Uncle B. just laughed, pulled her onto his lap, and jostled her around on his knee.

Lily continued reading. "'There is so much for the girls to do out there'," said Nancy. "'And now that I have the little ones and all, they would be a great help, too. In fact, the Orleans County Fair is just around the corner - if we brought them back with us tonight, they would have enough time to train a show cow.'

"The next thing I knew, me and Iris were each packing our clothes and a toothbrush into a Star Market bag. 'Be good,' said my mother. And then we were in Nancy and Bill's truck, headed for the country."

Lily tried to infuse her voice with a sense of enthusiasm hoping to make it sound as if going to the farm was the best vacation ever, filled with adventure, and as if she and Iris were dying to go. As if they had a choice. After all, no one wants to hear an essay about being forced to spend the summer on a stinky messy farm.

Their first morning at the farm, they were awakened by Nancy shouting from the bottom of the stairs. "Rise and shine! Those eggs aren't going to collect themselves!"

Lily and Iris dutifully got up, and together they made the bed, stuffed their pajamas under their pillows, and got dressed. There was no breeze coming in through the window, just the stifling promise of another scorching summer day on the farm. The daily chores took the girls out to open fields of hay, where the sun bore down with unrelenting insistence. Lily felt choked by the afternoon as she rode on the back of the baler, stacking up bales of hay and dreaming about getting back to the house where there were shade trees and frosty aluminum pitchers of sweet iced tea in the refrigerator.

The stairs creaked and moaned the way farmhouse stairs do, and when Lily and Iris arrived in the kitchen, they were greeted by cousin Nancy holding out two banged up aluminum buckets. Farmers seemed to have a thing for aluminum.

"Watch out where you step," warned Nancy. "And you may have to nudge a hen with your foot to get her to move. You won't want to be reaching under her with your hand while she's sittin' on an egg. Then just put the eggs in the bucket and bring them here when you're done. Your shoes are out on the back porch."

When Lily stepped out onto the porch, a fleet of fleas immediately attached themselves to her bare legs and started gnawing on her exposed suburban skin.

"Grab your sneaks!" shouted Iris, frantically slapping at the fleas that had jumped onto her. "We can put them on outside."

The yard was constantly patrolled by a troop of dogs, but the dogs that hung around Bill Jablinski's farm were not like Jasmine's gray French poodle, Princess. Nancy called them "working dogs." They were not pets; they were there to do a job. The animals weren't allowed in the house – they stayed outside all day, had their meals outside, pooped and peed wherever they wanted, and then settled onto the back porch to sleep at night, making their hearty deposit of fleas into the musty straw floor mats and ragged curtains.

Misty was a pointer, bred for hunting. Sometimes, for no reason at all, she would freeze in a pose, just like the dummies that Lily saw at Sibley's downtown once, when she was allowed to accompany Auntie Rosa and Iris on one of their shopping trips. It was Misty's job to guard the hen house to keep the foxes and raccoons out. The problem was that Misty couldn't really tell the difference between hungry intruders and young girls who were sent out to collect eggs. As Iris and Lily approached the hen house, Misty positioned herself in front of the entrance, bared her teeth, and growled. The girls took a step forward and Misty barked ferociously.

"What do we do?" asked Lily.

"How am I s'posed to know?" said Iris. "Get away!" she called to the dog. Lily had never heard Iris scream that loud before, but the volume of her voice remained slight and fragile, barely perceptible over Misty's warnings. Misty snarled again and took a small but emphatic leap forward, kicking up the dirt into an ominous cloud around her.

Lily set her bucket down and picked up two rocks from the ground. She pitched one, shouting, "Let us by, you stupid dog!"

"Hey, Ernie!" shouted Bill, snatching the remaining rock out of Lily's hand. Bill was a huge man with strawberry blond hair and pink cheeks - like a giant Campbell's soup boy in suspenders and blue jeans. He had dubbed Iris and Lily "Bert and Ernie", after the Muppet characters from *Sesame Street*. "What in God's name do you think you're doing?"

"That dog is mean!" said Lily. "Nancy told us to come out and get the eggs and she won't let us by."

"She's just doin' her job, same as you're doin' yours," said Bill. "Misty! Git!"

Misty immediately backed up, tucking her tail between her legs, which made Lily want to go and give her a hug and apologize for throwing the rock. The dog watched cautiously as the girls walked past her into the hen house.

As it turned out, collecting eggs wasn't that much different than picking up apples, except the hen house smelled about a jillion times worse. Bill and Nancy's farm was marked by odors that you couldn't wash off – not even after a bubble bath. They got into your skin and they coated the hairs on the inside of your nostrils: cow urine that splashed you as it hit the concrete floor of the milking house with the force of water from a fire hose, manure that was gathered up as though it were gold and then loaded into a truck, hen feed and the resulting poop that seemed to follow you no matter where you went, and of course, hay dust.

Lily couldn't wait to get to the part of her essay that she was sure would impress her classmates the most: playing in the hay loft. Every day – once all the chores were done and before the afternoon milking - Lily and Iris would go up into the hay loft to swing on the ropes. The ceiling in the loft was higher even than the ceiling at church, and it felt more like God was there, too - lolling about in the sunshine, hanging around with the countless swallows and tabby kittens who called this place home. The sun poured in through the single window at the top and millions of tiny bits of hay dust danced in the golden light.

You could stand in the middle of the barn and look straight up and out through a door in the roof. Bales of hay were stacked into graduated towers on both sides, forming steps that could be climbed to the top. A thick burly rope hung down from the center rafter, and was anchored off to the side about halfway up the tower. It took both girls to hold the rope as they climbed all the way up, where they would take turns jumping off of the tower on one side and swinging across the loft to the tower on the opposite side. It didn't even matter if you fell – that was actually the most fun part – because you would just land in the thick pile of loose hay that padded the floor.

The worst injury you could sustain swinging in the loft was a rope burn on your thighs, which didn't hurt that much worse than the Indian sunburns John and Alexander gave them, for no reason at all. For this particular torture, the boys would place their hands next to each other on your forearm, palms flat against your skin. Before you even had a chance to cry for help, they would turn the grip of one hand in one direction, while turning the other one in the opposite direction. The result was to twist your skin, causing a tremendous pain akin to a severe sunburn. It only took a second or two for them to give you an Indian sunburn, so by the time you knew what was happening, they were already gone; it was a crime that it was nearly impossible to get caught at. The Indian sunburn wasn't even the worst of the big brother tortures. There was Dodge Lego, where they stood you against the wall and pitched tiny plastic blocks at you, and there was also the famed game dubbed, "Prison Camp" that the children would be required to play whenever Alexander and John were babysitting. But there were no brothers on the farm to torment you, and by comparison a little rope burn was a small price to pay for the thrill of soaring through the air in the hay-filled sunshine.

After supper each evening, the girls went out to work with the cows that had been selected for showing at the Orleans County fair. Since all cows looked pretty much the same, and since everyone at the fair was a farmer with cows of their own, Lily couldn't quite figure out what the point was. But Bill and Nancy seemed really excited to teach them how to lead the cows around in a circle with a rope - and no one asked them if they wanted to anyway - so the girls obliged.

Even though Iris said she hated cows - just like Lily - she still practiced and smiled, and of course the judges gave her a blue ribbon. Lily tried to care - she even pretended that her cow Masie was actually a beautiful white horse with wings, like the kind she imagined they had in Heaven. After all, who wouldn't love to show off such a magnificent creature - one who may have been ridden by angels, or even by Jesus Himself? But no matter what, every time she looked behind her, all Lily could see was fat ugly Masie, and all she got was a white ribbon, which they gave to everyone who showed up with a cow in tow. Lily tossed the ribbon into her brown paper bag of clothes and threw it into her underwear drawer when they got back to Chestnut Crest.

Lily told her classmates all about the way countless kittens show up at milking time, about how baby bulls are kept in a separate pen and fed through a bucket with a huge nipple on it. For one week, it was Lily's job to feed a bull calf each afternoon. Even though the udders of all the cows in the barn were bursting and dripping with fresh warm milk, the little bull was not allowed near any of them. He was kept in a dedicated stall, in a separate room all by himself. Lily was glad to take care of him and be his friend. Bill showed Lily how to measure out the formula powder, how much water to add, and how to mix it all up real good.

Carrying the bucket of formula to the calf's pen was the most difficult task Lily had that summer. The weight of the filled bucket wrenched Lily's shoulder and elbow, the thin aluminum handle cutting into the flesh of her fingers and palm. During the short trip from the sink to the pen, she would need to stop several times to change hands and rest. But it was worth it, because Lily was taking care of the baby bull and he was depending on her for his dinner.

Although cows were sweet and kind, they weren't the most attractive animals in the world. They always had thick streams of mucus which would hang from their mouths, and swing back and forth with each languid chomp. They always peed or pooped right where they stood - they didn't even stop eating - and their backsides were constantly encrusted with manure. But Lily decided that there were fewer things in this world cuter than her baby bull. She named him Toro, and when she came by each day he would stick his head out from between the slats of his pen. Lily loved to stroke and kiss his smooth soft snout.

Lily hoisted the bucket up with both hands, bringing the long rubber nipple up to Toro's hungry mouth. Wriggling his fleshy lips, he found and grabbed hold of it, sucking and chewing on it voraciously. As the calf drank, the bucket became lighter, and Lily was able to free one of her hands to pet his head.

"You're such a sweet baby, Toro" Lily cooed. Toro stopped suckling and looked up at Lily with his big brown eyes. He shook his head and snorted, sending splatters of formula all over the front of Lily's shirt and shorts. She laughed so hard that she had to set the bucket down, as she lowered herself to the concrete floor, face to face with her charge. Leaning forward, Lily nuzzled Toro's nose with her own and said. "I love you, little Toro."

"Now don't be gettin' all attached to that bull calf there, Ernie," said Bill, wiping his hands with a red handkerchief. "You shouldn't be givin' him names and kissin' on him and what not."

"But he's my friend," said Lily.

"No," said Bill. "He's not your friend. And in about another two weeks, he's going to make some folks a fine dinner. So don't go gettin' too attached."

"What do you mean?" Lily rose to her feet.

"Now Ernie, you know this is a farm. We're in the business of raisin' animals, and sellin' animals and the things that they produce. We sell milk and eggs to the grocer's, we sell manure to other farmers, and sometimes we sell bull calves to the butcher."

A rush of heat zipped through Lily's body, shooting out from her gut, radiating down to her feet and up through her chest and arms. Her knees weakened, and she put her hand out to grasp the rough wooden railing of the pen. She looked down at Toro, who was vigorously contorting his mouth, trying in vain to reach the nipple of the bucket which had been abandoned on the ground. He bleated in frustration.

"What do you MEAN?! What are you going to do to him?!" Lily repeated the question, furiously hoping that she misunderstood, or that Bill was playing a cruel joke. Her eyes stung with tears.

"Now don't go gettin' all hysterical there, Ernie. This is just the way it is." Bill shoved the handkerchief into the pocket of his overalls and crouched down to meet Lily's eye level. "Let me ask you a question, Ernie. Do you like cheeseburgers?"

"Yes."

"And exactly where do you think those cheeseburgers come from?"

"I dunno."

"Yes, you do. They come from cows. Some cows we keep for milkin' and some we sell for beef. And we send 'em off to the butcher and the butcher slaughters 'em, and grinds 'em up and puts that meat into little packages."

Though Lily tried to steel herself, to will herself not to cry, a single tear escaped down her cheek, which she quickly swiped away, hoping Bill did not notice.

"And those little packages," he continued, "are sent to Star Market grocery out there in Chili Center where your mama shops. She puts them into her basket and she brings 'em home and she fries 'em up in a pan so you can have your dinner, and that's the way of the world. I don't send creatures out to slaughter because I'm mean; I do it because people like to eat meat."

Lily stood, dumbfounded. Toro was on his way to the slaughterhouse, and she was partly to blame.

"Finish feeding that calf and then come up to the house for dinner."

As soon as Bill disappeared from view, Lily picked up the bucket, placed the nipple into Toro's mouth, and watched as he sucked down the last of the formula, oblivious to the sprinkling of Lily's tears on his snout.

"In conclusion," Lily looked back up at her classmates, hoping to impress upon them that such was the proper way to end an essay, "farms are good places that give us lots of food." Raising her index finger, she added, "But remember when you eat a cheeseburger that you are eating a cow that has been slaughtered and ground up into little bits."

Most of the children just stared at Lily, with the exception of William Nolan, who cupped his hands around his mouth and called, "Moooooo."

Sister Elaine told Lily to take her seat and then announced that it was time for lunch. Lily checked her jumper pocket to make sure she still had her lunch slip. Today was pizza day - not only was it her favorite, but last pizza day Mike Dylan traded her his chocolate peanut butter square for her pepperoni. If she could convince him to do that again, she wouldn't have to worry about eating any cows. And anyway, what if the butcher got confused and put Toro in the pepperoni line instead of the cheeseburger line? Lily couldn't bear the thought of eating even a tiny slice, no matter how good it tasted.

As the class filed into the cashier's line in the cafeteria, Lily looked around to see if anyone was watching, and then placed the crumpled green lunch slip into Mrs. Fish's palm. She tried to be nonchalant, which was what Auntie Rosa called it that time when she had invited Lily to come along with her and Iris to the East Avenue Inn. They had finished breakfast, but there were still a few small muffins left in the wicker basket on the table.

"We're going to take these home so they don't go to waste," Auntie Rosa said. It seemed like stealing to Lily. She was sure that Auntie Rosa would never steal, but if it wasn't wrong to take the muffins, why would she try to hide it?

"Now watch. This is how we do it," Auntie Rosa smoothed a paper napkin over her lap. "Very nonchalant..." she selected one muffin from the basket, and then with a smile planted on her lips, pretending to admire the surroundings of the restaurant she placed the muffin into the napkin. She repeated this, one muffin at a time, until all the leftovers were safely nestled in her lap. Lily bent over and lifted up the corner of the white tablecloth, so she could watch as Auntie Rosa gently folded in the four corners of the napkin, then slipped the small package into her purse. Iris kicked Lily in the shin, causing her to drop the tablecloth and bolt upright, to find Iris and Auntie Rosa both giving her The Look.

Auntie Rosa must have felt the same way Lily did when she passed the lunch slip to Mrs. Fish. It wasn't wrong, but you didn't necessarily want anyone to see you doing it, either. Mrs. Fish seemed to know even less about being nonchalant than Lily did; she took the slip, laid it on the counter, flattened it out next to the cash register, and then taking it in both hands, she sawed it back and forth over the edge of the counter, smoothing out the creases. Lily stood frozen in place, staring down at her slice of pizza and fruit cocktail, not wanting to know who was watching. Mrs. Fish might as well have stood on the table and announced, "Lily Capotosti is on the free lunch program!"

At a cost of thirty cents, buying lunch at school had been a rare treat - and pizza was Lily's favorite. It was almost as good as the East Avenue Inn. But now with the lunch slips that the school gave to her family, Lily could buy lunch every day - all for the bargain price of a little embarrassment, which could have been spared if Mrs. Fish knew anything at all about being nonchalant.

Lunch in the school cafeteria was a noisy, risky affair - especially if you were not one of the "cool kids," who enjoyed the social status that afforded them their own table. It wasn't that you couldn't sit there; it was more like when they reserved the front pews in church for a wedding - seats were saved for the people who mattered most, and for the girls who wore ribbons in their hair and dimes in their penny loafers. You knew if you belonged, and Lily knew she didn't. But perhaps today they would invite her to sit with them. Now that they knew what an interesting summer Lily had spent, they would probably want to hear more. And once they got to know Lily better, it wouldn't matter so much that she was poor; maybe she could even invite Mary or Midge to come along to the farm next summer. In a year or two, getting

218

invited down to the farm for the Orleans County Fair would be cooler than getting invited to Peggy Donnelly's boy-girl party.

Lily stood with her tray, giving the rich girls enough time to notice her. But they just kept talking among themselves and didn't even acknowledge Lily's presence. She could just walk over there and sit down. It wasn't like there was a rule or a law or anything that said she couldn't sit with them if she wanted to. Why not? She could just walk over there and sit down.

"So how is everyone doing today?" she could say.

"Hi, Lily," they would say. "We loved your essay about the farm, but it was so sad about that baby bull. Come sit with us and tell us more about what it's like to swim in a real pond. By the way," they would add, "LOVE your new shoes!"

"Take a seat, little missy." The lunch lady placed her arm around Lily's shoulder and directed her to her usual table. "Keep the aisle clear, now."

Safely planted in a seat next to Barbie Hooke - a girl who had almost as many sisters as Lily had - Lily devoured her lunch, all the while torn between the desires to fill her belly and to savor the delight of a mouthful of soft dough, sweet tomato sauce, and chewy mozzarella cheese that you can only get from pizza. That was the bad part about having something really delicious to eat: before you knew it, it was gone and you didn't have it anymore.

Lily got up from her seat to deposit her used but very clean tray, which now held only an empty milk carton, a paper straw wrapper, several tomato sauce-stained paper napkins, a plastic plate, and a set of stainless steel flatware. As she passed by one of the boys' tables, she heard, "Moooooooo....." She turned just in time to see William Nolan drawing a straw out from his milk carton, his index finger sealing the end of it to keep the milk inside.

"Hey, Farmer Lily!" William called. "Here's your milk!" With that, William placed the straw into his mouth, pointed it at Lily, and blew, spewing milk all over her shoes.

As Lily bent over to wipe the milk up from in between the beautiful leather fringe, all of the items from her lunch tray slid off and fell to the floor with a resounding clatter. The children all erupted into applause. Refusing to look up, Lily collected her things, placed them back onto the tray and walked away.

"Moooo...." William repeated, to a chorus of adolescent boy laughter.

Lily watched her lunch tray as it was carried away on the conveyor belt, which was spattered and streaked with remnants of spilled pudding, applesauce, and creamed corn. At the other end, the tray disappeared past a rubber curtain behind which the secret inner workings of the school kitchen took place. She imagined putting William on the belt, and sending him through the curtain, where the kitchen ladies would take off all of his clothes and spray him with their dishwasher hoses. William's screams would disappear into a cloud of steam and hot water, as the ladies scrubbed him with their steel brushes. Scrub that smirk right off of his face.

From: Iris Capotosti <iris.capotosti@gmail.com>
To: Lily Capotosti <lilycapotosti@gmail.com>
Sent: Wed, May 5, 2010 at 7:47 PM
Subject: The Farm

Dear Lily,

Where did you come up with that stuff? I know this is just supposed to be a story about our story, but we should probably try to get some basic facts straight.

First of all, I think you're a little confused about how the whole farm "vacation" happened. The year Nancy and Bill came for a slice of Grandma's birthday cake and left with two child slaves was the first time we went out to the farm. We got off easy with just a week that time, even though Mom and Dad probably would have been just as happy to ship us off for the whole summer. The year we were set up with those cows to show at the County Fair was the second time we went. And the last.

I don't know where you were when you drank from those frosty pitchers of sweet iced tea you mention. The only thing I remember drinking was thick milk poured out from those aluminum jugs (you're right about farmers and aluminum), and it was way too fresh for my suburban palate. It tasted exactly the way the barn smelled, and it was never cold enough. Now that I think about it, I don't remember even opening the refrigerator in Nancy's kitchen. Maybe we weren't allowed. But I do remember coming home starving from afternoon chores, and asking Nancy what was for dinner. She always gave the same answer: "Shit on a stick."

As for the cows, they made a heck of a first impression on us, thanks to the way they stood and stared belligerently when we tried to get them to budge, the way they looked as though they would trample us when they finally did move, the way they nonchalantly defecated on us whenever we were within range. It wasn't until you fell in love with little Toro the following year that you had any sympathy at all for the beasts. Which brings me to the next point. As soon as "Campbell Soup Bill" clued you in as to the untimely fate that awaited Toro (funny how you remember the Muppet monikers he bestowed upon us, and I the derogatory ethnic terms of endearment), you came down with one of those stomachaches that so conveniently got you out of situations you didn't want to be in.

You weren't being of any help moaning and groaning all day, and Nancy sure as heck didn't want to be stuck nursing a sick child, so she called Mom and told her to come and pick you up. When she caught me packing my blue valise, she went and called Bill, and he summoned me out back for a walk. I remember him towering over me, and chewing on a stalk of grass while he lectured me on the meaning of responsibility, the importance of duty, and basically doing his darnedest to make me feel guilty about all that time he and Nancy had invested teaching us how to prance our heifers around the ring. Needless to say, I got stuck staying until after the fair, while you got to go back home. For the record, I really worked hard with Betsy and Masie for that show, and that's why I came away with a red ribbon (not a blue one). Still, I felt bad you didn't get one, so when I spotted the box where they kept them, up by the judge's stand, I decided to sneak into the arena while everyone else was over watching the greased pig contest. I fished a ribbon out of the box to bring home to you, but you didn't even seem to care. That's how it ended up in your underwear drawer.

By the way, the day after you left, I was so upset I started crying out there in the hen house while I was gathering the morning's eggs dipped in poop and plastered with feathers, that I must not have latched the door properly when I left, because Misty broke in afterwards and massacred at least a dozen hens. Bill said once a pointer tastes chicken blood, it keeps going back for more. So he took out his shotgun and killed him, right then and there.

The thing that still really irks me was that after they finally let me go home, I looked up Miltonville in that atlas I kept under the bed, and I realized it was within spitting distance of Lake Silver. And the only place they let me swim was that stinking mud hole.

C'est la vie, I guess.

Love,
Iris

P.S. What was a priest doing talking to a class of fourth graders about homosexuality??

From: Lily Capotosti <lilycapotosti@gmail.com>
To: Iris Capotosti <iris.capotosti@gmail.com>
Sent: Thu, May 6, 2010 at 9:38 AM
Subject: Re: The Farm

Iris:

Honestly, I know there are holes in my memory, but at least I admit them. The simple fact that you even remember so much in such great detail and are so completely sure of how things transpired is a little suspect, don't you think? Who remembers the events of 40 years ago with such precision and clarity?

Anyway, I am sure of the main points that I do remember. I remember getting sick, but it was because I had a stomach bug, not because of what Bill told me about Toro. I threw up all afternoon once I got home, and I felt terrible that they made you stay - I never even would have let Mom come and get me if I thought for one second they wouldn't let you come, too. Why did you let Bill make you stay? Did Mom know he was making you stay against your will? I thought I was providing the perfect excuse for both of us to get the hell out of there. In your vast record of the facts, do you happen to remember why you didn't say anything?

"For the record" - I do remember "shit on a stick" and that awful warm milk with brown streaks in it, and how Nancy poured us a full glass at dinner and wouldn't let us up from the table until we drank it all.

HE SHOT THE DOG?! Did that really happen? How can it be that I never heard about this until now? I can no more believe that you would make it up than I can believe that I would forget hearing about it.

I know I shouldn't insist that I "won" that pathetic white ribbon, but believing that I did is still more appealing than the idea that you put it in my dresser drawer. Seriously, if you were going to steal a ribbon for me, why the hell would you steal me a third place one? All during my childhood, it was one more reminder to me that I wasn't as good as you were. I can convince myself of that all on my own, but thanks anyway.

Lily

PS: Father Delaney was a pervert. I still remember his lectures on masturbation before I even knew what it was - let alone that it never even occurred to me to try it until he gave me the idea.

15. IRIS

Iris's chin was tilted to the sky, her right arm raised and elbow bent in military fashion, her hand sliced across her forehead to shield her bespectacled eyes against the glare of the midsummer sun. The lower the plane descended, the higher her excitement soared, until at last, through squinting eyes she was able to discern the lettering on the fuselage of the orange aircraft as it approached for landing.

"That's it, Mom!" she cried. The crescendo of emotion, now uncontainable, jettisoned her several inches off the concrete floor of the open air observation deck. "I saw the letters!" she said, hopping in place. "A capital B and a capital I, just like you told me!" As the Braniff International flight from St. Louis touched down in a high-pitched whir of speed-arresting maneuvers, she cupped her hands over her ears, until it slowed to a roll, then finally screeched to a halt.

"Yay! Grandma's here! Grandma's here!" Lily cried. She and Iris joined hands, encircling their mother, as they jumped up and down, giggling with joy.

"Girls! Girls!" their mother said, as Iris and Lily skipped in circles around her as if she were a maypole, chanting "Grandma Whitacre! Grandma Whitacre!" It wasn't clear to Iris whether their mother's softly pronounced words were intended to scold or encourage them, but the smile on her lips told her she was happy, too.

Although Grandma Whitacre's visit meant that the two youngest Capotosti girls were forced to relinquish the meager claim to privacy their bedroom afforded, remove all their clothes from their closet, and sleep on a mattress on the sunroom floor, Iris and Lily had been counting the days until her arrival. Just between themselves, the girls confessed to rather liking the idea of camping out in the sunroom, which was their favorite spot in the whole house, with its uninterrupted row of windows, its record player, and its separate exit complete with stoop for sitting and talking while watching the comings and goings of life on Chestnut Crest. To sweeten the deal, their parents had ruled that access to the sunroom would be restricted exclusively to Iris and Lily for the duration of Grandma Whitacre's stay. Sacrificing their room also gave the girls more bargaining power to obtain special privileges, like being the only ones allowed to come to the airport. Who could say what other benefits they might reap, if they played their cards right, as Auntie Rosa would say.

The only contact they had with their maternal grandmother between visits was on their birthdays, when she mailed them one of those fancy store-bought cards. The cards she sent the boys always had pictures of dogs or cars or horses on them, but the cards she sent the girls always had pictures of the flowers they were named after on the front, and wishes that rhymed like poetry on the inside. It was already a huge treat for Iris to receive an envelope addressed to her personally, but when she saw those all the extra postage stamps, and weighed the card in her hand, a thrill always shot through her. It was hard not to be excited, knowing that behind the pretty picture of a purple iris, the real Iris would find four quarters taped to the inside of the card. Even if it only came once a year, birthday money was better than weekly allowance, because the amount never varied, no matter how old you were, or how well you performed your chores, which Grandma would never be able to keep track of anyway, way down there in Independence.

Grandma Whitacre entered their lives with a flair again at Christmas, when she sent the Capotostis the biggest box of Russell

Stover chocolates Iris ever saw. When their mother ceremoniously lifted the lid and removed the white sheet of padding, unveiling the neat rows of chocolates, some dark, some light, sitting in their fluted brown cups, the divine smell was almost too much for a body to bear. As Iris's eyes lingered over the tantalizing assortment of goodies in the box, she was inundated with mouth-watering expectations of crispy, nutty, and caramel fillings, yet always a bit wary when she recalled how easily those expectations might be crushed, when the one chocolate you were allowed to pick out each day turned out to be filled with maple cream or jelly. Sometimes, when her mother opened that box, Iris wished time would stand still, and the chocolates could remain untouched forever, allowing her to remain suspended in a state of blissful anticipation and non-disappointment.

Iris always wrote to Grandma Whitacre to thank her when the gifts arrived, and sometimes at other times of the year, too. She thought there was something quite exotic about having a grandmother in Missouri, and the idea of corresponding with someone so far away stirred a sense of adventure in Iris. She found letter-writing especially satisfying when her mother allowed her to use a sheet of her boxed stationery and a matching envelope, instead of the ruled paper Iris used for school and one of the long white envelopes her father used for paying bills. The joy she felt weeks later upon opening the latch of the mailbox at the end of the driveway, and finding a reply, with the name "Miss Iris Capotosti" in her grandmother's spidery scrawl on the envelope was every bit worth the money she used to buy the postage stamp.

And now she would get to see Grandma again in person! A stair was wheeled to the side of the jet, the door hatch was opened, and even before she could spot her grandmother, Iris could smell the sweet cloud of White Shoulders perfume that trailed her everywhere she went. Iris strained her neck to catch a glimpse of the stewardess standing at the top of the stairs, looking sharp and sophisticated in her trim blue dress and matching pumps. Iris was fascinated that a woman could pursue such a career instead of being a teacher or nurse, a nun or a mother. Though Iris hoped one day she might fly on a plane herself, she was pretty sure she wouldn't want to be a stewardess, unless maybe Lily was one, too, and they could travel together to some of those places they saw in the atlas.

Until recently, Iris had thought she would be too terrified to ever fly, but after the school's spring field trip to the county airport, she had started thinking it might not be so scary, after all. The day before the outing, the students had been informed that they would be simulating a real departure on a plane. Iris could hardly sleep that night, and when she got off the bus at the airport with the rest of the class and followed Sister Brigida to the departures wing, her heart was thumping so hard she was sure everyone could hear it. By the time she presented herself at the check-in desk with her blue valise and was assigned a seat, she was flushed and sweaty, but before she could chicken out, she had boarded the plane, and a smiling stewardess with bobbed blond hair greeted her saying, "Right this way, Miss Capotosti," and showed her to her seat. She was just starting to feel at ease, when the stewardess came by and showed them how to fasten their seat belts, like the announcement instructed them. Iris felt butterflies in her stomach and a sweaty itch in the palms of her hands, even though she knew no one was going to take them anywhere in that plane, not even across the street to the frozen custard stand. The stewardess must have picked up on Iris's state of agitation, because when she came by with a tray full of individually wrapped pieces of gum, she winked at Iris and told her she could take two sticks, one for takeoff, and one for landing.

The taste of a fresh piece of Juicy Fruit exploding in her mouth worked wonders to chase away her anxiety, and by the time the pilot came sauntering down the aisle, Iris wished she could stay on the plane all day. She would certainly trust such a nice man in such a nifty uniform to pilot the plane safely, she thought, as she observed him stopping now and then to exchange a few words with the students. He was a bit taller and slightly younger than her father, but not much, with eyes as blue as the sky. His white shirt with pilot's stripes on the sleeves set off the deep tan of his muscular arms and square-jawed face, making Iris wonder where he had spent his winter. Maybe he had flown to Florida or California, or even as far away as Hawaii. She was dying to ask him, but wasn't sure whether questions like that were allowed, or even polite. Besides, when he approached Iris and smiled one of the brightest smiles Iris had ever seen, and touched the rim of his cap and nodded as if she were a grownup lady, and to top it all off said, "Good morning, Miss!" right to her face, her tongue got all wrapped up in the Juicy Fruit, and all she could do was stare back at him like a nincompoop.

As Iris kept her eyes on the open door of her grandmother's plane, she wondered whether that same handsome pilot might appear at any moment, tipping his hat at Grandma Whitacre, perhaps commenting on her exquisite scent, and lending her an arm as they descended the stairs together. Meanwhile, as the other passengers ducked their heads to step through the door and walk down the to the tarmac, Iris played a little game with herself, trying to imagine who the people were, where they had been, and why they were coming to Rochester. She could not always make out the expressions on their faces, but she searched for telltale signs in the way they walked down the stairs, some of them pausing to look around, others rushing ahead purposefully, that might indicate whether someone would be waiting there, ready to greet them with a hug or a handshake, the thought of which made Iris happy, or whether they had left behind everyone they knew, and would find themselves among total strangers, which made her sad.

At last, Iris spotted a coiffed blond head atop a soft-shouldered figure in an orange dress emerging from the open door with the countenance of a glamour queen. "There she is! I saw her!" she exclaimed, waving her hands wildly in the air as she jumped up and down, hoping to be seen.

"It *is* her! Let's go!" Lily said, tugging at her sister's elbow.

"Hold your horses, girls!" their mother said in a voice that was as close to a shout as it ever came. "We'll all go down together.

Iris, go call your father, please. Lily, you stay here with me."

Iris approached her father, who leaned against the railing, his eyes fixed on the shiny fuselage of a Pan Am aircraft standing on the runway. Iris tapped him on the arm. "Grandma's here, Dad!" she said, raising her voice to be heard over the increasing engine noise of the plane preparing for takeoff. Her father placed a hand on Iris's head, but said nothing. He stood immobile, watching and smoking as the plane accelerated, then raised its nose as if to sniff the air. As it lifted off and disappeared from view, he took one last puff from his cigarette, then let it fall from his fingers. He ground the smoldering butt into the concrete with the toe of his shoe, then silently took Iris's hand. Iris led him over to where her mother and Lily were waiting, and they went down the stairs to the arrivals gate together, accompanied by the sound of loose change and car keys jangling in his pockets.

Half an hour later, her father was hefting into the station wagon the set of three matching suitcases he had lugged across the parking lot. "When are you leaving, Grandma?" Iris asked, sliding into the backseat of the car next to her.

"Iris!" her father said, in a stern voice. "That's not polite. Your grandmother just got here, after a thousand-mile trip!"

Iris's cheeks burned at the reprimand. She always had misgivings about whether she was saying the right thing, or the wrong thing, and certainly hadn't meant to sound rude; she just wanted to know precisely how many days she could bank on. She was already aware that time and money came in limited quantities, and she applied the same thriftiness to both. She knew that a day was not really twenty-four hours, because she had to sleep away at least eight of them, which left just sixteen at best, or a mere nine hundred and sixty minutes. And that was in the summertime, when you were not forced to waste any of those precious hours at school. This summer, she was determined to hold each day tightly in her fist, and squeeze every last drop of life from every single second. All she wanted to know now was how much time she had to work with during this visit.

"You sweet thang," Grandma Whitacre said with a smile, as

she placed a spotted, bejeweled hand on Iris's bare knee. "I know y'all didn't mean it that way, dahlin'."

One of the things that fascinated Iris most about her grandmother was her drawl; the only other accent she had ever heard was Italian, and it amazed her to think that there were Americans born in other parts of the country that could sound so different, even if they had not immigrated from anywhere. Sometimes she even misunderstood her grandmother, like once when she had asked Iris for a pen and Iris had brought her a pin. It wasn't only the accent that was different, but the slow, honey-like manner in which she spoke, as if her soft words stuck together to cushion her from any loud tones or vulgar expressions that might be tossed around in her proximity. To Iris, her pronunciation and mannerisms seemed like a fancy accessory, like her Zsa Zsa Gabor wig or the hairpins that fastened it to her head, which were encrusted with glittering jewels her big sisters said were rhinestones, but to Iris were every bit as beautiful as diamonds.

Her grandmother's affectionate response softened the effect of her father's scolding (even though she still did not reveal how long she would be staying), especially after her mother surprised her by speaking up, too, and saying of course everyone knew Iris didn't mean anything rude by asking how long her grandmother would stay. From her seat, Iris could see little more than the back of her mother's head as they drove home, with her wavy auburn hair blowing in the breeze from the open window, and snatches of her profile when she turned halfway around to follow the comments being volleyed between the front and back seats. Iris admired the delicate shape of her mother's nose, her high brow and bright eyes, the smooth, translucent skin that blushed pink in the sun but never tanned, the perfectly pursed lips glistening with a light coat of pearly coral lipstick, the only makeup she ever wore. It seemed odd to hear her mother call her grandmother "Mother," and Iris realized consciously for the first time, that Betty Capotosti had not always been a mother, but had also been a little girl named Elizabeth Whitacre, with a mother of her own.

"Can I have first turn at brushing your hair tomorrow, Grandma?" Lily asked, speaking up for the first time. Iris couldn't blame Lily for wanting to take advantage of the fact that Iris, and not she, had been scolded, but she also knew that had it been a more serious infraction, Lily would have taken a stance in her defense, even if she was younger.

"It's 'may I,' and of course you may, my l'il Lily of the Valley," came the reply; though slow, it was quicker than the time it took a tongue-tied Iris to lodge her own request. She knew Grandma Whitacre had a soft spot for Lily, the same way Grandma Capotosti had a soft spot for her, and felt slightly disloyal for thinking how much more pleasant it was to brush Grandma Whitacre's long blond hair, than Grandma Capotosti's thin white wisps that barely covered her balding head. Iris was rarely the one to suggest combing Grandma Capotosti's hair, but never refused to comply when asked, her fingers nimbly dodging contact with the warm, pink skin of the scaly scalp that smelled like the old chunks of Parmesan Auntie Rosa said could be used for grating after you trimmed away the mold, even though Iris thought it made the spaghetti taste musty. Ritual dictated that after twisting the hair into a little bun that she fixed in place with hairpins, Iris would pass her grandmother a mirror, holding another at the back of her head so that she could inspect her bun while remaining seated in her rocking chair.

It was at that moment when Iris always thought of the faded portrait of a young Irene Capotosti taken back in Italy, which she had found one day tucked away in the bureau drawer when her grandmother had asked Iris to fetch her a pair of nylons. In the photograph, her grandmother was young and handsome, dressed in an high-collared blouse with puffy sleeves and a row of tiny buttons peeking out from embroidered eyelets that ran down its front to meet her dainty waist, where it was tucked into a full-length skirt. A mass of thick, black hair was swept into a curly crown that sat atop her head as she posed with her index finger resting in the indentation of her chin, her lush eyebrows lending her dark eyes a sultry look. Iris wondered which head her grandmother saw in the reflection when she handed her back the mirror, nodded, and complimented her on her work with a "*Brava.*"

In the end, Iris always felt better for having groomed Grandma Capotosti, but never as good as she felt those mornings when she sat cross-legged on the bed as she and her sisters took turns brushing Grandma Whitacre's silky blond hair, which fell halfway down her back when it was loose. Like most older people, no matter where they came from, her grandmother seemed to prefer chatting about the past rather than the future, which was certainly more interesting than her talk about the present, which was mostly about her bowel movements. Stroke by stroke, Grandma would tell them all kinds of stories about her life, as she dipped the tips of her manicured fingers into the little jars of cream the girls passed her as part of her morning beauty ritual, and warned them to always keep in mind that frowning caused more wrinkles than smiling. Iris was mesmerized by tales of her life growing up in rural Missouri, the only girl among five brothers, who not only forced her to chop the firewood for the stove, but made her hide behind the barn when she performed the chore, so their friends wouldn't see her and think them lazy.

She spoke of the genealogical connections that made her a distant cousin of President Harry S Truman, surprising them with the information that his middle name was just the letter *S*, and not an initial that stood for something else. She told the girls to remember that like that letter *S*, sometimes things are just what they are, and it didn't do any good to go digging around looking for something that wasn't there. Grandma also shared some of her favorite quotes of cousin Harry, which Iris copied down in the leftover pages at the back of a used composition book for figuring out later, but there were some that struck her right off the bat, like, "Actions are the seeds fate grows into destiny," and "Being too good is apt to be uninteresting." Lily giggled at the quote that said, "If you can't stand the heat, keep out of the kitchen," and ran downstairs to relay it to their mother, who was sweating over the stove.

Hair brushing seemed to stimulate Grandma's mental meanderings, and once she even revealed in a confidential tone that her long-dead daddy, already aging but very much alive when she was born at the turn of the century, had ridden with Frank James, the elder brother of Jesse, in the fearsome Quantrill's Raiders during the Civil War. Iris knew something of Jesse James from the westerns her brothers liked to watch on television, and of course she had heard of the Civil War, but would have to find out about the other stuff. She jotted these facts down in her composition book, too.

Grandma didn't talk much about her other grandchildren down in Missouri, though she did mention marrying a couple of other husbands after her first one died and she scraped by working as a singer in a speakeasy in Kansas City. Iris thought it curious that, unless she counted her husbands wrong, Grandma Whitacre had been widowed three times, yet still she didn't look nearly as sad as Grandma Capotosti's friends who had such a hard time getting over being widowed once. Those Italian widows would probably grieve themselves to death in her shoes, or at very least, would not feel up to wearing orange dresses or dolling up their balding heads in Zsa Zsa Gabor wigs.

One day, smack dab in the dead middle of a hot afternoon, Iris was stretched out on the mattress in the sunroom, clad in denim shorts and a smock top, the grass-stained bare foot of her right leg dangling over the crooked knee of her left, her head propped up on a pillow. "What're you doing?" Lily asked as she walked in, closing behind her the double French doors that led to the living room.

"Reading," Iris said, without looking up from the paperback she was holding in her left hand, as she twirled a lock of hair between the first two fingers of her right.

Lily sat down on the mattress, just as two fat tears detached themselves from the corners of Iris's eyes, rolled across her cheekbones, and slid into her ears. "Hey, are you crying, Iris?" Lily asked. "Whatsa matter?"

Iris rubbed her ears to chase away the tickle from the tears, then removed her glasses, set them down on her tummy, and ran the back of a hand over her eyes and nose to wipe away her sniffles. "It's this book," she said, waving it in the air.

"What is it?" Lily asked, holding Iris's arm still to study the cover, on which the title was printed in green and orange block letters. "*Love Story.* Where'd you get that? It doesn't look like a library book."

"I saw it upstairs, on Marguerite's dresser."

"And you just took it? You know how mad Marguerite gets when you touch her stuff."

"I asked if I could borrow it, silly. She said it was a dumb story, and I was too little for it, but I ran out of stuff to read."

"But if it's a love story, shouldn't it be happy, like in the movies?" Lily asked, leaning on an elbow to face Iris.

"That's what I thought," Iris sniffed. "Oliver, he's the guy, and Jenny, she's the girl, they really love each other. They give up everything to be together. All Jenny needs is Oliver, and all Oliver needs is Jenny."

"That sounds pretty good."

"Sure, until Jenny gets sick!" Iris's lower lip trembled as she spoke. "It's not fair."

"Maybe she'll get better?" Lily suggested.

"No. She dies. I peeked at the ending."

"You peeked?" Lily looked at her with wide eyes. "You always tell me it's against the rules."

"I know, Lily, but this is different. I just *had* to know what was gonna happen."

"So since you already know how the story ends, why don't you just stop reading it?" Lily asked.

"Because I can't. You don't just stop reading a book once you've started it."

"Even if it makes you cry?"

"It's a different kind of crying."

"What's different about it? Your eyes are all red, and snot is dripping out of your nose. It looks like the same kind of crying you do when someone screams at you or Alexander calls you a spoiled brat."

"No, believe me, it's different. It's not a mad sort of crying, it's a suffering sort of crying. Kind of like how I feel on Good Friday, when we have to line up in church to kiss the feet of the crucified Christ."

"But I don't want you to suffer, Iris. Please stop crying. It's only a story, remember. Plus ..." Lily said, with a clap of her hands. "What I have to say is really gonna cheer you up!"

"What?"

"Grandma wants to go to the horse races, and she and Auntie Rosa talked Mom into letting you and me go, too!"

"Cool," Iris replied in a flat voice.

"We're leaving in an hour, so you better put away that book and cheer up. I'm going to help Grandma get ready!" Lily skipped out of the room. Iris's head lolled on the cushion, coming to rest on her shoulder. She stared at the blurry brightness of the windows, at the blurry row of evergreen hedges in the front yard, at the blurry patch of blue sky above. Once in awhile, retreating to the fuzzy vision of her myopic world wasn't so bad. She sighed, put her glasses back on, and began chewing on her bottom lip, as she turned her attention back to the remaining pages of her book.

The fictional woes of Jenny and Oliver were soon lost amid the tangible excitement of the racetrack. The buzz and bustle seemed to have an inebriating effect on everyone, including Iris, who was feeling giddy and reckless. As spectators rushed back and forth to check the odds and place their bets, Iris pulled out the dollar bill she had embezzled from the emergency money in her book bank. The novel she had read made her realize that like Jenny, she could die tomorrow, without ever having fallen in love, or swum in a crystal clear lake, or bet on a horse. To Iris, that seemed like enough of an emergency to warrant busting open her bank. Seeing Iris with a dollar clutched in her fist, Auntie Rosa chuckled nervously, then snapped open her pocketbook, and pulled out the worn old prayer book she always carried with her, where she kept the holy cards of people who had died and a few emergency dollar bills of her own, all bound together with a thick rubber band. She extracted a crisp green note, her voice quivering as she announced she would match Iris's dollar with one of her own, so they could place a bet together. It would be up to Iris to select whatever horse she liked best.

All the horses looked impressively swift and handsome to Iris as they trotted past the grandstand, especially when compared to tired old Jiffy, who wouldn't even walk around the back yard. Lily had picked a horse with a bandaged foreleg right away, saying she felt sorry for it, and hurried off with the adults to place her bet. Though Iris was immediately smitten with the shiny black Beautiful Dreamer, after much debate she finally settled on Flying Fantasy, because she liked the horse's name and number (twelve, like the number of brothers and sisters in her family) and color (purple), disregarding the fact that everyone told her it was a "long shot," whatever that meant.

Iris had taken so long deciding, the betting windows were just about to close when she joined the others, and slipped the two dollar bills under the grate. From the moment the starting bell rang, she could hardly bear the excitement, and as the race drew to a close, Iris stood on her tiptoes, craning her neck to follow the horses, every muscle and tendon in her body taut, her ears straining to understand the words of the commentator in the droning voice blaring over the loudspeaker.

"As they round the final turn, Gambit and Flying Fantasy battle for the lead, with Beautiful Dreamer in a close third. Outrageous is breaking away and closing in fast on the outside! And it's Flying Fantasy taking the lead by a neck! And at the finish line, it's Flying Fantasy, followed by Beautiful Dreamer a close second, and Gambit hanging on for third!" Her heart was pounding so hard she thought it might break away and gallop off with the horses.

"Auntie Rosa! Auntie Rosa!" Iris jumped up and down to jiggle free the words stuck in her throat. "Flying Fantasy is our horse! We won! We won!" Auntie Rosa's jaw dropped, and she made the sign of the cross.

"Well, I'll be a son of a gun! Let me see, honey!" her father said, smiling and shaking his head, as he took the crumbled betting slip from Iris's sweaty hand. "Jeepers Cripes! You did win!" he exclaimed after examining the slip. They all started laughing and clapping their hands.

"How much did we win, Dad?!" Iris asked.

"Let's see, the odds were twenty-five to one, and you bet two dollars..." he began.

"And so?!"

"And so, young lady, that means you and Auntie Rosa have won FIFTY DOLLARS! And that's plus the original two you bet!"

Auntie Rosa shrieked, Iris squealed, Uncle Alfred guffawed, her mother and father congratulated the lucky pair, everyone hugged everyone else. Everyone except for Grandma Whitacre, who watched from her seat, chuckling softly with amusement, her watery blue eyes glistening below her penciled brows, and Lily, who sat next to her, staring dejectedly at her own betting slip.

"I didn't win anything, did I Grandma?" Lily asked. The commentator had not even mentioned her horse, Clueless, which had lagged far behind the others throughout the race.

"No, li'l Lily. Not this time. Y'all picked a loser." Grandma Whitacre replied. She squeezed her granddaughter's shoulder, then hooked a finger under her chin to tilt her head up. "It's like that with lots of things in life," she said, looking into Lily's eyes. "Y'all just have to keep right on betting, even if things don't always turn out right the first time 'round."

"That's OK," replied Lily. "I don't think I like the races anyway."

"C'mon everyone!" Iris cried. "Let's go celebrate!" Seeing the crestfallen look on Lily's face, Iris sat down next to her and took her hand in hers.

"We won, Lily!" she said. "Can you believe how lucky we are?"

"*You* won, Iris," Lily replied. "You and Auntie Rosa and your Flying Fantasy."

"But I'll share with you," she said, not knowing exactly why should she feel so guilty about her good fortune, but realizing that she did.

"It's not the same thing," Lily said.

"I can't help it if I won and you didn't, Lily," Iris said. It wasn't fair for Lily to ruin the festive mood by being a sourpuss. "You should be happy one of us won, and that I want to share."

"Taking something someone gives you is not the same as winning it yourself."

"Well, suit yourself. But Auntie Rosa and I are treating everyone to hot fudge sundaes at Howard Johnson's. I'm sure the ice cream will taste just as good, no matter who pays for it."

With her split of twenty-five dollars already burning a hole in her pocket, (she vowed to return to her bank the original dollar used for the bet), Iris thought of all the ways in which her winnings might change her life. She would buy her very own copy of "Leavin' on a Jet Plane" which she and Lily would spend hours listening to on the record player in the sunroom, imagining all the places they would fly to, and no one could kick them out, at least not until Grandma Whitacre left. And if Iris's mother got her way, and the whole family went on a real vacation to a real lake where Iris could finally swim to her heart's content, she would celebrate by buying everyone cold, frothy root beers, and hot dogs piled high with pickle relish at one of those roadside stands. And when autumn rolled around, she just might turn up at ballet class with a brand new pair of pink slippers on her feet.

This summer was starting to shape up fine indeed.

16. LILY

Now that Iris was taking dance lessons at The Limelight Dance boutique, she would pack her things into the blue valise every Friday, and get on the city bus, disappearing until the next day. Although Lily wondered why she wasn't going along, she never asked about it. You got what you got; asking for extra stuff only made you feel worse if the answer was "no." And it usually was.

Lily would occupy herself in Iris' absence by singing along to the songs on Henry's Beatles albums, practicing playing jacks, and by wandering the vast yard on Chestnut Crest, often spending hours on the swing set, or making up stories like they had on TV in the afternoons and acting out all the parts herself, using the slab of concrete they referred to as "the patio" for a stage.

No one ever really sat on the patio, partly because it was set back so far from the house, but mostly because of its distinct lack of anything remotely resembling patio furniture, unless you counted a stack of three rubber car tires, a deflated basketball, a badminton racket with no strings, and a red and white tricycle with a rusted silver bell at the handlebars. Their patio didn't look anything like the patios on TV, which were filled with people sipping brown drinks out of short glasses and nibbling on tiny hot dogs. Lily's mother never even had one friend over, let alone enough to fill up a whole room. Still, Lily could offer no other name for the pitted and crumbling slab of concrete. It certainly wasn't a patio, but neither was it anything else.

In the winter, Lily's father lined the patio with heavy duty plastic sheeting, which he then anchored down with two-by-fours that were laid to frame the perimeter, creating a curb on all four sides. Using the garden hose, he filled the area with water, and announced that they were now the only children on the block to have their very own private ice skating rink. The children all made clumsy attempts at skating on it, mostly because their father's enthusiastic effort had evoked a sort of grateful pity in them and they couldn't bear to allow the deed to go unappreciated. The ice that formed there was at least as pitted as the concrete that lay beneath, but Iris, Lily, William, Charles, and Ricci all donned whatever ice skates they could find in random boxes in the chicken coop, got on the ice and stumbled and tumbled until it grew too dark and cold, at which point they would haphazardly toss their skates back into the boxes and race to the house for hot chocolate and buttered toast sprinkled with cinnamon and sugar.

Lily's father was ever seeking new ways to devise such amenities - not necessarily to compensate for any shortcomings in his ability to purchase the things other families enjoyed, but to prove that just about anything could be fashioned out of two-by-fours, duct tape, elbow grease, and a little old-fashioned ingenuity.

The summer after they had moved in, their father installed a basketball pole and hoop at the far end of the patio, using the sidewall of the chicken coop as a back stop, which prevented errant balls from rolling off into the woods. This addition made them "the only children on the block to have their very own private basketball court." To hear the children talk about their house - with a patio, ice skating rink, and private basketball court - all wrapped up in an address as stately as 75 Chestnut Crest - it sounded grander than any house could hope to be. Since the children rarely invited friends over, there was little contrary evidence of the run-down, worn-out farmhouse leftover from another era. But no matter how poetically inclined you were, there was simply no elegant way to present the idea of having a chicken coop in your backyard.

The chicken coop looked almost cheery from the street. It was a quaint white building, with a screen door and five windows with red shutters across the front, a proud row of purple irises planted along the foundation, and a red roof that was so low you could pick icicles from the gutter without even jumping. But inside it was dark - stifling hot in summer, freezing in winter.

Even though they called it a chicken coop, the structure was lifeless, save for the occasional Capotosti child who rummaged there for the remnants of a croquet set, a box of Christmas decorations, or for an air pump to inflate a basketball, which – despite her disdain for going inside - was what brought Lily there late one Friday afternoon.

Being in the chicken coop was worse than being in a basement, because at least in a basement you were in the belly of a living place; the sounds and rhythms of life beat all around you, the plumbing flowed and the furnace hummed. In a basement you could hear people walking up above you, and you knew that all you had to do was head for the stairs and in an instant you would be transported back to safety. But in the chicken coop there was no life, no heartbeat; it was empty despite the junk crammed in from floor to ceiling. There was no back door, no telephone; you were alone, a long run away from the house.

The boxes that filled the chicken coop were stacked in rows, forming an aisle from the doorway to the far right corner, and then a second aisle back up from right to left, like a grocery store for ghosts who came to shop for misplaced memories. Every box was clearly marked in Carlo Capotosti's hand with a thick black marker, but the contents rarely corresponded with the labels. The only thing Lily could be sure of was that if she wanted to find the air pump, she should look in every box except the one marked, "air pump."

Inside the box marked "extension cords," Lily found family photo albums - books of baby pictures of Alexander, John, and Jasmine, a few of Violet, one or two of Louis and Henry, and then one small book whose blank pages were punctuated with photos of Marguerite. The box marked "Christmas decorations," was filled with moldy text books that were saved and stored merely because they were books, and not because they might be useful in the future.

Books were the one commodity of plenty in the Capotosti household. They filled every available slot in every available bookcase and curio stand. Some books were permanent fixtures in the house, such as *The Taming of the Shrew, Catcher in the Rye*, and other high school reading assignments that were saved in the hopes that another child might be assigned the same reading list. Some books only visited as Lily's mother opened their home to armfuls of *There's a Wocket in my Pocket, Stuart Little*, and *The Tale of Peter Rabbit* through weekly visits to the Chili library. On winter evenings, Lily's mother would sit in the center of the sofa with a pile of books at her feet, and the children would all scramble to settle around her. Lily always vied for one of the only two spots directly next to her, not to get a good view of the pictures (she had outgrown the picture books that Ricci so loved), but to experience the rare delight of being tucked in among a blanket of little brothers, snugly nestled under their mother's embrace, listening to her voice as it transported them to far-off lands where rabbits talked and children went on fantastic adventures.

"Whadya lookin for?"

There was no lighting inside the chicken coop except for the shafts of sunlight that slipped in through the narrow windows across the southern facing wall, and Lily's eyes had not yet made the adjustment. She could only see a large dark silhouette standing in the doorway.

"Who is it?" said Lily.

"It's just me, silly." Lily recognized the voice, and as he moved away from the door, Lily could discern the features of Henry's face, although the words he used and the sweetness with which he spoke them were foreign.

Henry was the only big brother who never hit Lily or played torture games. In fact, he actually didn't communicate with anyone. All he ever wanted to do was go off by himself and play the guitar, which was kind of silly since the whole point of playing music was for people to hear it. It was almost as though Henry were a visitor instead of a brother.

Henry's withdrawn nature unnerved Lily. When someone was mad at you, you expected them to hit you or scream at you and when someone was your friend, they laughed with you and played with you, but if someone never talked, how could you tell what they were thinking? And if you didn't know what the heck was going on inside their head, how would you know how to behave when they were around? Lily couldn't even remember the last time Henry had spoken directly to her. Now here he was, standing there smiling at her, softly calling her "silly."

"Oh - hi, Henry."

"Are you looking for something?" Henry walked closer, pausing to casually raise the flap of a cardboard box with his fingertips, as though he might be of assistance.

"I'm just looking for the air pump so I can play some basketball." Lily inched away from Henry, toward the end of the aisle.

"I know where it is," said Henry.

"You do?"

"Yeah - it's back there," he said, pointing to the far corner. "C'mon, I'll help you find it."

Henry placed his large hand on Lily's back, and guided her toward the corner. "So you want to play some basketball, huh?"

Something about the situation repulsed Lily, but something about it felt good, too. The strong hand on her back, the offer of help in a dark and scary place, the softness with which Henry spoke to her were all so different from the competition and chaos of the house, from the taunting and teasing of the kids at school, from the loneliness of long afternoons spent in imagination and solo games of basketball. But Lily suddenly didn't want to play basketball anymore. She didn't want to be in this place anymore. Her instinct was to turn and walk back toward the door, but as soon as she slowed down, Henry pressed more firmly on her back, urging her further toward the dark corner.

"It's just back here," he said gently, taking her by her upper arm.

"It's OK, Henry," Lily said. "I don't really want to play basketball anymore." She turned toward the doorway.

"Well, I'm looking for something, too," said Henry. "My old microphone is back here somewhere, and I sure would like to find it and see if it still works. Maybe you can help me look - would you like to help me test it out? I could play a song on my guitar and you could sing..."

In the instant that Lily hesitated, inspired by the fantasy of singing "With a Little Help from my Friends" into a real microphone while Henry strummed along on his Gibson, Henry reached down and swept her legs out from under her, gently laying her on her back on the cool, grimy, concrete floor. He lowered himself onto her, his full weight bearing down upon her, and began sliding his body against hers, up and down, up and down. Lily felt something hard grinding into her belly. It was thicker than a croquet mallet, but shorter... it was like a stick, or maybe the handle of a hammer. She struggled to breathe. It was difficult to get enough air even to speak under the weight of Henry's massive form.

"Henry," she managed to whisper. "Henry, what are you doing?"

Henry just grunted and breathed, rocking his body, grinding the hardness against her. The rafters in the ceiling were dripping with cob webs and spider webs, and a small silken clot with a fly tangled inside was suspended from the ceiling, positioned directly over where Lily lay. She watched the fly intently, looking for movement. If the fly was still alive, she would find a way to get it down from there as soon as she could get up. She hoped she could get to it in time. She wondered, was it looking down at her?

Henry continued rocking and grinding and grunting. Lily saw a man do something like this one time at the drive-in movies. All of the children had been piled into the gold Dodge station wagon and taken to the Starlight Drive-In to see *Chitty-Chitty Bang-Bang*.

At the Starlight they charged three dollars per carload to get in, and they always played a double feature - one for the children and then one for their parents. Lily rarely even made it through the first film before falling asleep, but the idea of a flying car was something so exciting and fanciful that she'd stayed awake, daydreaming of flying over Sacred Family, all of the children in awe, and all clamoring to become her new best friend.

Iris, Charles, William, and Ricci had all fallen asleep, curled up and splayed about in the back of the station wagon. Lily's father had cranked the driver's side window down, and lit a Parliament. Lily loved the smell of a freshly lit cigarette, and she watched as the blue smoke swirled around her father's head, and then followed the trail of his breath out the window and into the warm summer air. Lily's mother sat on the passenger's side of the front seat, her head resting against the window, her auburn waves a pillow; they sat in silence as the second film played. Lily's eyes grew heavy, but she refused to succumb to sleep. She reluctantly drifted in and out of consciousness, catching glimpses of the story unfolding on the big screen, the scenes commingling with her dreams.

In the film, a man and woman were camping in the wilderness, and during the night, the man climbed into the woman's sleeping bag. The woman said, "I have dreamed of this moment ever since we met, but I never dreamed you would love me here, under the stars."

"I do love you," said the man. "With all of the brilliance of that full moon."

The woman smiled, and then the man rocked and breathed just as Henry was doing now. Then, as now, Lily sensed a warm heaviness in her groin, which felt good, but in the way the chocolate covered donut she'd once stolen from The Bungalow tasted good. She enjoyed the sweetness on her tongue but felt nagged by the method of its acquisition. The woman in the film did not seem bothered at all. Iris had recently told Lily that they would become women soon; perhaps this was what she meant. Perhaps being a woman was to be loved like this, and to not really be bothered by it too much.

"Boy," said Lily to Henry. "I guess you must really love me or something... "

"Uh-huh," Henry said between short, quickened breaths. "But it's our secret." It was a command rather than a request. "You can't tell anyone, OK?"

Henry paused for a moment and rested the weight of his body on his left elbow. With his right hand, he unzipped his fly and shimmied his blue jeans and underpants down around his hips. Lily looked down to see a thick strip of black hair leading straight to Henry's belly button - or as Auntie Rosa would call it, his umbilicus. Shocked and frightened at the sight, she squeezed her eyes shut, and in her mind she heard Paul McCartney singing "Do You Want to Know a Secret?".

Henry raised Lily's shirt up, exposing her bare belly. She flinched as he placed his clammy palm against her skin, ran it up along her breast bone, across her smooth chest, and down the length of her left side, coming to rest at the side zipper of her turquoise shorts. He wriggled the zipper down, tooth by tooth, and then fumbled at the waistband, where Lily had secured a safety pin in place of the long lost button, in order to keep the shorts from coming open unexpectedly. Henry gasped, and abandoning the struggle with Lily's shorts, he returned to his rocking and grinding, squeezing Lily's breath out of her again until he let out a cry. It was an enormous groan that was longer than the ones Louis let out from the shower when Lily turned on the hot water in the kitchen, only not as angry. It started out quiet and small, grew loud and big, and then got quiet again, as Henry collapsed on top of her.

Keeping her eyes closed, Lily lay still. Her lungs filled with breath again as she felt the weight of Henry's body lift from her. The sounds of shuffling feet grew distant, and Lily finally opened her eyes at the sound of the chicken coop door slamming shut. The force of the door created a draft in which the fly, suspended in its silken cage, was gently swinging back and forth, but now she knew it was dead for sure. She lay watching as the fly came to rest again. She lay watching, wondering how long it would hang there, rotting. Would she come back in a year, or five, and find it hanging there still?

She lay watching as the light from the windows moved across the back wall, hating the idea of staying, but unsure of what to do next. Finally, the clang of the cowbell rang out across the yard, signaling suppertime. Lily scrambled to her feet, inspired by her fear of being the last one to the table. Being late wasn't as bad as being last. As long as people weren't actually eating yet, you might be able to slip into your seat without consequence. But if you were last, and if dinner was already underway when you walked in the door, the entire clan proclaimed your doom by joining together in an *a capella* performance of the theme song from the *Dragnet* television show. Dum da dum dum... dum dah dum dum DUM. Suppertime was one of only two times of day when Lily's parents could count heads, and you'd better be there. How could your father possibly enjoy his supper if you might be dead in a ditch somewhere?

As Lily pulled her shirt back down over her belly, she stuck her hand into a glob of milky goo that trailed down her stomach, pooling along the waistband of her shorts.

"Ewwwww!" she said out loud to herself. She raised her fingers to her nose and sniffed. It didn't have a particular scent - at least not like that of things which were known for the way they smelled, such as fresh mimeographed paper, or raisin toast - yet it hinted of urine and sweat. She surveyed the ground where she had been lying. She looked up at the ceiling. Nothing but grime and dust and dead fly. She wondered where the goo could possibly have come from and whether Henry had gotten any of it on him. She searched the chicken coop for a rag, but the box that read, "cleaning rags," contained only a rusted saw, a tire iron, and four wrenches.

Lily stepped out into the early evening air, now cooled in the waning light of the retreating sun, letting the front door of the chicken coop slam behind her and latch itself into place. She stripped several leaves from a limb of the peach tree and used them to wipe her belly. She tugged at her shirttail, wishing she were wearing a longer shirt or darker color shorts to better hide the wet spot. She would have to pass through the kitchen to get to the stairway, and now that supper was starting, there was no way she could slip by unnoticed. If anyone asked her about it, she would just say that it happened when she was getting a drink from the garden hose. Bending down, she wiped her hands in the cool grass, then straightened up and ran toward the aroma of meatloaf and broccoli.

All during supper, Lily stole glances at Henry, hoping to catch him glancing at her, too. She didn't know what would happen if their eyes were to meet - if she would smile, if he would wink, how they would acknowledge the secret they shared. She consoled her sense of confusion with the assurance that she was special now, somehow. Henry had chosen her. She imagined him letting her play with his new tape recorder, and maybe singing songs by The Beatles into that microphone of his. Iris sure would be curious to know why Henry was treating Lily so special. Of course, Lily wouldn't be able to tell her, since it was a secret, but if Henry ever gave her any candy or some of his old comic books, Lily would be sure to share.

"Mommy," called Ricci. "Look at my food! Look at my food!"

"Just a second, Ricci." Lily's mother was at the stove, her back to the table, busily shuffling pots and pans, lids and serving spoons and potholders, with the skillful flow of a street hustler playing a shell game.

"Jeepers Cripes, Richard," called Lily's father. "Just eat the gosh darned food, will you?"

"No!" said Ricci, crossing his arms over his chest in defiance. "It doesn't taste good until Mommy looks at it."

Lily's mother climbed over the bench and sat in the empty space next to Ricci. She leaned over his plate, and he watched as she looked at each item. "There." She kissed his thick mat of curls. "Now eat."

Maybe Henry was just waiting for an excuse to talk to Lily. After all, they had never had conversation during supper before.

It would look suspicious if they suddenly got all chummy and started talking and laughing and stuff.

"William, stop touching me!" shouted Charles.

"I'm not touching you - I'm just reaching for the butter."

"No - you're pretending to get the butter, but you're touching me, and you're getting your cooties all over my food."

"William," said Lily's father. "If you want the butter, ask someone to pass it to you - don't reach for it. And Charles, calm down for Cripes sakes. Your brother has the same cooties you have."

"Nuh-huh, poop-face!" said Charles to William.

"Uh-huh, doody-head!" replied William, offering Charles a quick slap on the arm, which started an exchange of slaps and excrement-inspired insults that stopped only when Lily's father slammed the palm of his thick hairy hand against the surface of the table, snapping everyone into terrified silence.

Supper tonight was just like every other night, but it was like no other night. The noise and conversation swirled around Lily, but she didn't feel a part of it. She just wished everyone would be quiet for a minute, so she could think. Her food remained untouched as she waited to catch Henry's eye, to have his reassurance, to be loved by him again from across the table.

Noticing that he had just about finished eating, and fearful of missing her chance, Lily blurted, "Henry, could you please pass the salt?"

"Get it yourself," Henry replied, without raising his eyes from his plate. "It's right in front of you."

Lily's face grew hot, her eyes stung with tears and her gut swelled with a combination of William Nolan and Father Delaney and Alba Ichberg, but those were all bad things and this - well, this was love. It just seemed that at the very least, someone who loved you would be happy to pass the salt. What had she done between then and now to cause Henry to turn cold? Lily reviewed the sequence of events, but could not figure it out. If only she had stayed awake for the entire drive-in movie, then she would've known how to behave and Henry would not be angry with her.

Lily wiped a tear from her cheek with the back of her hand.

Lily's father looked at Lily quizzically, then looked at the salt shaker. Lifting his buttocks off his bench a few inches, he reached for the salt and sprinkled her untouched meatloaf.

"There you go," he said. "Now stop daydreaming and eat your supper. And have a bath before bed tonight, Lily - you look a mess."

17. IRIS

Iris felt miserable. It was unbearably hot and muggy, the most insufferable day she could remember ever, that summer or any summer of her life. The stagnant water of the murky pond repulsed her, but so desperate was she to rid herself of the sweat sticking to her skin and the swarms of mosquitoes feasting on her flesh, that she waded in anyway, and didn't stop walking until the water was neck-deep. Flies buzzed around her head, mud oozed between her toes, gluing her in place and making her lose her balance when the hands startled her, pushing down on her head until she went under, and her mouth filled with muddy water. An eternity later, the hands finally let go, and Iris bobbed to the surface, coughing and sputtering. The water plugging her ears muffled the sound of her brother's sadistic laughter as he swam away, his shape blurred by her myopic eyes. She wanted desperately to get out of the water too, but her feet kept getting stuck in the mud, holding her back though her arms paddled frantically. Finally dragging herself to the water's edge, she fell to her knees in exhaustion, as her lungs coughed up brown liquid. Waves of nausea knocked her down when she tried to stand, and again she became mired in the mud, as a black snake slithered toward her, disappearing, then reappearing, then disappearing into the mud again. She opened her mouth to call for help, but no words would come out. Then the snake was inside her, writhing, twisting, strangling the most hidden parts of her.

Iris tumbled awake, confused and drenched in sweat as she lay on her side. She drew her legs close to her chest and rocked her body to calm the beast tugging at her bowels. She was relieved to be in her bed, but still she felt the snake squirming inside her, still she felt the pain, and the viscous mud sticking to her limbs.

"Lily," Iris moaned.

"Mmmm," Lily groaned.

"Lil-eeey," Iris wailed.

"What's going on, Iris?" Lily rubbed her eyes.

"I feel sick."

"But school hasn't even started yet."

"Please, Lily. Can you just call Mom?"

"Sure," Lily said, hopping out of bed, out the door and down the stairs in her bare feet. Just as quickly as Lily had disappeared, she returned. "She's already gone," she said.

"Great." Just when Iris needed her most, her mother was out training for her new job. It sounded like she would be doing something good, helping poor people find work so they could take care of their families instead of living on government handouts. But did she have to do it now? And while her mother was out helping other people, who was going to help *her*?

"What hurts, Iris?" Lily asked, kneeling on the floor next to the bed. Her touch was gentle as her hand brushed Iris's damp hair from her brow.

"My tummy. Everything. I have to go to the bathroom," Iris replied, pulling herself up. Lily held out a hand to help her, and as Iris gripped it, she also grasped the sense of helplessness Grandma Capotosti must feel when she leaned on Iris for assistance.

"Hold on, you're all tangled up," Lily said, tugging at the crumpled sheet. "Geez, Iris!" she cried. "Did you cut yourself? There's blood all over the place!" Iris turned to look, and to her horror, saw the sheets were soiled with bright red stains. She stared at the bed with a mixture of disbelief and disgust.

"Geez is right, Lily," she said. As she spoke, a warm surge of liquid gushed from somewhere inside her, trickling down the insides of her thighs, down to her knees and ankles. Not knowing what to say or do, Iris shuffled to the bathroom, leaving a trail of blood on the floor, and Lily standing there, wrinkles of worry gathering on her forehead like storm clouds on the horizon.

Iris spent a long time locked in the bathroom, hugging herself and moaning. She had known this was coming ever since that day at Sacred Family when the nuns made the girls go to a separate classroom from the boys, where they were treated to a special lesson on personal hygiene. One of the girls found out from one of the boys that the males were taught about the benefits of underarm deodorants and frequent confessions at their particular stage of development, which seemed pretty simple compared to what the girls were presented with. Using a series of slides with diagrams of internal organs, Sister Brigida mumbled something about the miracle of monthly menstruation, but nothing specific about how it would make you feel and what you should do if you woke up in agony, all drenched in blood, and your mother was off doing training and your big sisters were out trying to make a few bucks at their summer jobs. Not that Iris would have had the guts to come right out and ask any of them what to do; certain topics were never discussed in their house, and what went on in the bathroom was meant to stay private.

Iris couldn't figure out how she could go anywhere without making a mess, and would have sat there on the toilet all day, but for the thought that sooner or later one of her brothers would start banging on the door. By the time the next wave of cramps subsided, she had reached the only possible decision. She left the bathroom, taking the whole roll of toilet paper with her.

Lily was standing across the hall, in the doorway of their room, smiling. "Here, I got you these, Iris," she said, proudly pulling out the box of Band-Aids she was hiding under her pajama tops. "Do you think they'll help?"

Iris felt very weak, but not too weak to smile. "Thanks, Lily, but I don't think they'll do much good. Can you find me some underpants?"

"Sure," Lily said, her expression clouding when her Band-Aid idea was rejected, then clearing again as soon as she was given a new task. She pulled open the underwear drawer, rummaged through it, then did the same with all the other dresser drawers. "I can't find any clean ones in here, but ..." she said, as she began kicking at a pile of clothes on the floor. "Da-da!" She bent over and picked up a pair of white underpants, and waved them in the air. "These don't look too used, but the elastic is kinda stretched out."

"Better than nothing," Iris said, examining the panties before deciding to put them on. "Thanks." She unrolled several lengths of toilet paper, rerolled it around her fingers, then stuffed the wad in the underpants.

"You look like you're wearing diapers, Iris. How are you gonna walk around like that?" Lily said.

"I'm not gonna walk anywhere. I'm gonna take the bus to Auntie Rosa's," Iris said, pulling on a pair of shorts, then a T-shirt. She put all five nickels left from her allowance money in one pocket and another fat wad of toilet paper in the other.

"Good idea. She knows how to give stitches and all that. I bet she'll know how to fix you up," Lily said. "And don't worry about getting found out. I'll wash the sheets while you're gone. They were full of graham cracker crumbs, anyway."

"Thanks," Iris said. "You're as sweet as a real Lily of the Valley."

Pressing her thighs together, Iris hopped down the stairs, waddled out the door and down the driveway to the bus stop on the corner. Auntie Rosa always dashed home from the Medical Center at lunchtime to check in on Grandma, but she was always in such a hurry, that Iris knew she would have to tell her about her predicament right away, before she rushed back to work again. Iris feared she would puke as the bus jostled and bounced its way toward the city over the potholes of Chili Avenue, but by clenching her jaws and swallowing the hot saliva each time it flooded her mouth, she managed to resist until she reached her stop.

She got off the bus at the treeless corner by the gas station, took a deep breath, then waddled past the collision shop where she spotted Al the mechanic and his brother Hal, the body man, in the same identical coveralls they always wore. Together, they looked up from the mangled front end of a Ford Mustang they were inspecting to greet her. Al waved a soiled rag in the air, and Hal shouted, "Hey, Iris! Going to visit your grandma?" This was no time to stop and talk, with the danger of blood rushing down her legs as she stood there, so Iris limited her response to a quick wave and a forced smile. She wondered whether the men could somehow sense what had happened to her, the way the neighborhood dogs could tell when Jasmine's poodle was in heat, and thought with regret that perhaps she should steer clear of them now that she was becoming a woman.

Iris was pervaded with nostalgia for her younger days, when Al and Hal had patronized the Kool-Aid stand she and Rita Esposito set up one summer day, strategically across from the collision shop. With an initial investment of five cents, they had bought a packet of cherry flavored drink mix, added water and ice cubes, a pitcher and glasses, and set everything out on a folding table of Auntie Rosa's, then took turns hawking out their offer, at the price of two cents a glass. When the first pitcher was gone, they counted twenty cents on the table, which was well more than the five they had spent. They went on buying and mixing Kool-Aid all day, and even after drinking a number of glasses themselves, by the end of the day they had each earned enough to buy a big paper bag of penny candy from the corner store. That was the only time Iris had ever set up a Kool-Aid stand, and it was one of the last times she had spent a whole day playing with Rita, who still lived over in the old neighborhood. It all seemed so long ago, Iris thought, as a cramp caused her to double over, and she sat down dejectedly on the curb at the end of Auntie Rosa's driveway, where she waited until the siren at the firehouse wailed the call of high noon.

"Lover-dover! I didn't know you were coming today!" Auntie Rosa called through the open window, as she parked her perfectly polished Ford Fairlane in the driveway less than five minutes later. Hopping out of the car, she wrapped Iris in a hug so tight the nurse's pin on the breast of her uniform dug into Iris's scalp. She still smelled good, but her usual perfume was diluted by the smell of disinfectant. *"Bella della mamma!* That hug really tickled my big toe! Now let's go see how Grandma's doing," Auntie Rosa said cheerfully, leading Iris by the hand.

"Auntie Rosa?" Iris was stuck, like in her dream, except instead of mud bogging her down, it was the simmering blacktop of the driveway that glued her feet in place. She was thankful she had put sneakers on before taking the bus over.

"What is it, Lover-dover?"

"Um ..." Iris thought the embarrassment would choke her, but if she couldn't talk to Auntie Rosa, who else was there? If only she could find the right words to get started. It usually only took a few hints for Auntie Rosa to guess what was on Iris's mind, and being a nurse and all, maybe she could tell what was wrong by looking at her. "I wanted to ask you something."

"Of course, honey. Let's go on inside and see Grandma, and you can ask me whatever you want." Iris knew that once Grandma got her hands on Auntie Rosa, there would be precious little attention left over for her.

"It's about that menstruation thing," she mumbled, staring at the big toe poking through the canvas of her sneaker.

"Menstruation? Why are you worrying about that on a nice summer day?"

"Because it happened to me, Auntie Rosa! That's why!"

"Goodness gracious, honey! You're menstruating? Isn't that wonderful!"

"No! It's gross! There's all this blood, and I feel so sick!" Iris wiggled her toe to make sure it really belonged to her.

Auntie Rosa tilted Iris's face toward hers, and looked her in the eye. "A young lady's menarche is a precious milestone in her life, honey. And dysmenorrhea is only to be expected."

"But what am I supposed to do?" Iris asked, bursting into tears.

"You mean you don't have any supplies?" Auntie Rosa's salt-

and-pepper eyebrows reached over the frames of her glasses to question her.

"Just some toilet paper."

"You poor child! You'd think a woman with a house full of girls would take care of certain things. Of course, now that she's got other things on her mind ...," she said, shaking her head. "You just sit yourself down in the car. I'll run up to check on Grandma, then we'll drive over to the drug store, OK?"

Iris nodded, still far from happy, but overcome with relief that her secret was out, and help was on the way. She pressed her legs together real tight when she sat down in the car, grateful for the clear plastic that covered the seat; she would be mortified if she soiled the powder blue upholstery of the car Auntie Rosa took such good care of. She had always wondered why Auntie Rosa had that plastic on there, even though it made your legs all sweaty, and now realized it must be because she menstruated, too. Funny how you could get up any old day, which might seem like every other day, except out of the blue, something new happened to you, and suddenly it was real easy to understand something you could never figure out before. "Thank you for Auntie Rosa," she whispered to the Blessed Virgin Mary magnet on the dashboard. Twenty minutes later, Iris was reclined on Auntie Rosa's sofa, a thick absorbent pad rigged up to a sanitary belt, a hot water bottle on her tummy, and the most delicious cup of sweet tea clutched in her hands. "You just stay put and rest, Lover-dover. You'll feel better soon."

Auntie Rosa kissed her on the forehead, and turned to Grandma Capotosti as she headed out the door. "*Oggi Iris è diventata signorina!*" she said to her. Iris couldn't understand the words, but she could tell by the funny way Auntie Rosa winked and the expression of pity on both women's faces as they looked at her, that her shameful secret had been shared.

"*Povera bambina.*" Grandma Capotosti shook her head and crossed herself, then turned her attention back to the television set and a rerun of her favorite soap opera.

Iris was only a month into her womanhood when things started to look up again that summer. The excitement at Chestnut Crest was palpable as the corridor between the kitchen and garage filled with bags and boxes of canned goods, dry goods, paper goods and sundry housewares. A battery of army green sleeping bags secured with twine to prevent them from unrolling stood guard alongside the boxes.

"Whose guitar is this?" Iris's father cried, picking up the instrument that rested on the pile of sleeping bags, and waving it in the air as if it were a pagan amulet one of his children had hung on the wall behind the kitchen table in place of the crucifix.

"That's the guitar Alfred gave one of the kids years ago, Carlo," Iris's mother said, her face flustered from the work of selecting and packing the utensils she would need from the kitchen. "I don't play the guitar," Jasmine said, striding past in her work jeans and T-shirt, her thick braid swinging as she went out to feed Jiffy. William and Charles did not even look up from their project of crafting fishing poles from tree branches. "It must be Henry's," Violet said, lugging a garbage bag out the back door. Iris could tell by her lipstick that Violet must be going to steal a goodbye kiss from Todd, whom Iris had spotted lurking by the side of the house from an upstairs window.

"Henry wouldn't just leave his guitar there," Iris said. "That's the family guitar, Dad. I put it there, so we would remember to take it along."

"We can't be bringing house and home with us, Iris."

"But I thought maybe if we lit a campfire at night, we could roast marshmallows, and strum the guitar, and sing some songs. Wouldn't it be fun?" Her father looked at her as if she had suggested that as long as they were vacationing on Conesus Lake, they might like to fly to the moon for an ice cream cone while they were at it.

"One bag each. That's the rule. The guitar will have to stay behind."

Even if she were one to insist, which she wasn't, Iris knew it would be wasted breath. She swallowed her objections, together with her shattered fantasies of sing-alongs and campfires. Disappointment still burning in her throat, Iris opened the kitchen cupboard where the used grocery bags were stashed, ready to be recycled. The thick brown paper was perfect for many uses, such as covering text books, wrapping homemade birthday presents, and soaking up slush from boots left to drip by the door in winter. Most bore the logo of Star Market, which Iris's mother said offered the best value for the dollar, in addition to little green stamps which could be traded in for prizes, but the gifts were not quite enticing enough to make anyone actually go to the trouble of gluing the stamps in the collector's book, so they ended up all stuck together in a drawer. Iris flipped through the bags in search of one she could use to pack her clothes in, one that was still nice and stiff, and did not have any blood stains from leaky packages of ground beef or chicken legs. She was sorry not to take her blue valise on her very first real vacation, but had decided it was a bit too elegant for a rustic lakeside cabin, and besides, there was a question of loyalty and fairness involved. She did not wish to flaunt a luxury item that she alone possessed, and if brown paper bags were good enough for her brothers and sisters, they were good enough for her, too.

Iris could hardly believe they were actually going to go away this time. Every summer, her mother talked about how lovely it would be to take a little family trip, and every year, her father asked whether she preferred to send her kids to school with shoes on their feet, or go lolling about in a place where they would have even fewer comforts than in their own home. But this year when he said that, Iris's mother simply smiled, then showed him her first paycheck, and the brochure of a cabin she had reserved for Labor Day weekend. It may not be a long vacation, but it was a start. And from the pictures Iris had seen, the water in that lake was about as blue as any she had ever dreamed of swimming in. She couldn't wait.

With a crisp paper bag tucked under her arm, Iris bounded up the stairs to pack, but on step number seven (she still counted them every single time she went up or down), she was halted by a pain stabbing her in the side. She had been experiencing similar pains lately, on and off, and figured it must have something to do with that disgusting menstruation business. As usual, it subsided as quickly as it had struck, and she dashed up the last five stairs and into her room. She managed to locate two pairs of clean underpants before the pain gripped her again; a pair of shorts and three T-shirts later it came again, and by the time a nightie and two books were packed, she was sitting on the edge of the bed, sweating profusely and shaking. This was no time to be getting sick, she decided; whatever it was, it would have to wait. Iris forced herself to her feet, took her bag downstairs, wrote the name "IRIS" in block letters across the front, and placed it in the lineup by the door.

"I'm so excited, I don't know how I'll ever get to sleep," Lily said, as they lay in bed that evening. "It's almost as bad as Christmas Eve!"

"Same here," Iris said, hugging her tummy under the sheet. She had decided the best way to get rid of the pains was to ignore them completely. That meant not thinking about them or mentioning them out loud, not even to Lily. The girls chatted about all the fun they would have on the lake, and after a few minutes, Lily said having something real to look forward to and talk about was even better than any fairy story they had ever invented, then promptly fell asleep. Iris counted the cricket chirps for a while, then paced her breathing to fall in sync with Lily's, and eventually drifted off, too.

What seemed like minutes later, pain and nausea roused Iris from her sleep. She crawled out of bed, and made it to the bathroom just in time. She retched with such violence, she was sure her whole stomach would fly out of her mouth and plop into the toilet together with everything else she had brought up. As soon as she felt steady enough to stand, she went down to call her mother, but hesitated in front of her parents' bedroom door.

"Mom?" she whispered, the door creaking as she finally eased it open a crack. The room was enshrouded in a velvety darkness that trembled with the vibrato snoring of her father. She held little hope that her whisper would be heard over the rumble. "*Mom!*" she repeated, in a louder whisper. She peered into the dark room, hoping to see her mother stir, but the moment her eyes grew accustomed to the darkness, the first thing they settled upon was the sight of her father's naked rear end. When the twin beds had appeared in their parents' room, soon after her mother started her job, Iris thought it a leap in status that they now preferred the same sleeping arrangements as all the married couples on television. Iris was as close as she was willing to get to her father's bare butt, and wouldn't budge from the door, or raise her voice to a more audible level. Her mother finally heard her whispering for help, and came to the door.

"What is it, Iris?" she asked. Her mother never yawned or looked sleepy. She was either awake, or asleep.

"I don't feel good, Mom," Iris said. "My side hurts, my head hurts, and I keep throwing up."

Iris's mother placed the back of her hand on her forehead. The gesture seemed to make Iris feel a little better already. "You do feel hot, honey," her mother said. "You must be running a fever. Come with me." She led Iris to the bathroom and slid open the door to the medicine cabinet over the left sink (the one over the right sink was off limits to the rest of the family; it held their father's shaving cream, straight-edge razor, electric razor, Hai Karate cologne, hair comb, Grecian Formula, nail clippers, and some little brown bottles with typewritten labels).

Rummaging through the left cabinet was allowed, but not usually very interesting. You could generally find a couple of tubes of lipstick, a handful of toothbrushes with splayed bristles, a flattened tube of toothpaste waiting for someone to decide whether to squeeze it once more or throw it away, a handful of hairpins that when outfitted with a bonnet of toilet paper were used to remove ear wax. A few medical supplies could be found up on the top shelf, out of reach of the smaller kids: a bottle of red cough syrup that tasted awful; a grape-flavored medicine that wasn't so bad; a blue jar of mentholated goop that you could stick up your nose to help you breathe when you had a cold; a big bottle of aspirin, and a tin of Band-Aids.

Iris's mother unscrewed the cap of the aspirin bottle, shook out a tablet and handed it to Iris. She ran the tap, perfunctorily rinsed out the plastic bathroom glass that always had a film of black crud around the bottom and filled it with cool water, then passed that to her, too. "Here, this should help," she said. "You just lie down on the couch now, where you can call me if you need me. It's probably just a bug. You should be fine in the morning."

"But what if I'm not?" Iris asked. In her current state, the thought of traveling in a crowded car was unbearable, but the thought of being left behind was even worse. Plus, there was no one to be left behind with, unless she was sent off to Auntie Rosa's, and as much as she enjoyed going there, it was nothing like swimming in that blue lake.

"We'll cross that bridge when we come to it," her mother replied, patting her on the head.

Iris curled up on the sofa, where her mother tucked an afghan crocheted by Grandma Capotosti around her shivering body. She looked up at her mother's face, its skin as white as the moon glow that filtered through the living room window. There were no wrinkles to spoil the perfection of its translucent surface, no creases tugging at the corners of her clear aquamarine eyes. Iris searched the eyes for signs of reassurance, but all she saw was calm. Though it wasn't quite the same thing, calm was good, too, Iris thought; if her mother were really worried, she would have called her father, and they would have sat with her and held her hand, and taken her temperature, and put ice cubes wrapped in a washcloth on her forehead. Even after her mother returned to her room, the serene look on her face kept Iris company throughout the night, convincing her as she knelt over the toilet bowl vomiting up a foul green liquid, that she must not be as ill as she felt, and that she would certainly be better in the morning.

Even from her spot curled up on the couch, where she had finally fallen into a fitful sleep, Iris could see this was no ordinary Saturday morning. The house was abuzz with preparations for departure; breakfast was eaten quickly, last-minute checks

264

performed, personal belongings gathered up. Iris witnessed the flurry of activity around her, while fat, hot tears rolled down her feverish cheeks. Lily offered to help, and prodded her to get up from the couch, but her efforts were useless. Try as she may, Iris could not uncurl her knees from her chest, let alone stand erect.

Between trips to load the station wagon, her father ran through her checklist of symptoms, nodding, shaking his head, and mortifying her by asking whether she had already started menstruating. When he asked her that, his eyelids dropped halfway shut, and they made a fluttering movement as he spoke, like they did whenever he was faced with a difficult or embarrassing situation.

Amid the amicable shouts and boisterous laughter of the Capotosti household, a phone call was made to Auntie Rosa, and the departure was delayed long enough for Iris to be seated next to her father in the front seat of the loaded car, and dropped off at Auntie Rosa's. More phone calls were made, surgeons were distracted from Saturday morning rounds of golf until Auntie Rosa located one she trusted, a hospital was driven to, an emergency room was waited in, an examining table was lain upon, flesh was palpated, arms were pricked with needles, blood was drawn, a cup was peed into, opinions were expressed, a diagnosis made, intimate parts shaved with a razor, surgery performed.

Had it not been for the freezing cold ice baths that kept her awake when all she wanted to do was sleep, had it not been for the drainage tube and fetid odors coming from her gut, had it not been for the priest who for some reason always brought Holy Communion at the exact same moment she was on the bedpan, had it not been for the pangs of regret she felt when she thought of the crystal clear lake where Lily and the others were swimming and floating on inner tubes by day, eating hot dogs and hamburgers around bonfires by night, Iris might even have enjoyed her two weeks in the hospital.

She did have the entire ward almost to herself, she did have juice and Jell-O served to her on a tray, she did have nice nurses to talk to, and a handsome young intern that smiled at her and asked her all kinds of questions, and actually listened to the answers. She did get crisp new sheets on her bed each day, she did get to read the entire series of Nancy Drew detective stories that she found on a shelf, she did get to watch Perry Mason every afternoon on TV. Auntie Rosa did come to see her every single day, and after the family vacation was over and he returned to work, so did her father. He timed his visits during lunch hour, which worked out well, because then he got to eat Iris's hospital lunch which would have just gone to waste anyway.

All the doctors and nurses, and Auntie Rosa, and her father, and even the priest said Iris was one heckuva lucky girl (except the priest said "blessed"), because peritonitis had killed lots of people, including cousin Dolores's own father. In the end, Iris was convinced of her miraculous good fortune, but no matter what anyone said, she wished her luck could have waited until after she had swum at least once in that crystal blue lake.

18. LILY

"Show your mother what you learned today at the dance studio, Iris. I'm quite sure she would be very interested to see how graceful you are."

Their mother was extracting a set of coffee cups and saucers from the cupboard, shuttling them two at a time to the massive kitchen table, stopping to turn off the flame from under the whistling tea kettle as she passed.

"Is the coffee ready yet?" their father called from the garage.

She poured the boiling water into the top compartment of the coffee pot. "It's coming, Carlo!" Lily watched with anticipation as she opened the package of black and white sandwich cookies that Auntie Rosa had bought from the Chili Superette, and poured them out onto a melamine plate that once bore what may have been a colorful floral pattern, which had become faded from countless attacks by hungry forks and rigorous trips through the dishwasher. She placed the dish in the center of the table, and Lily counted the cookies. Luckily, it was Saturday night and most of the older kids were out. If she stayed put and waited until the coffee was poured, she was a shoe-in to get at least one.

"Betty - Betty... " said Auntie Rosa, beckoning their mother to pay attention. "Watch - watch this." Turning to Iris she said, "Go ahead, sunshine, show Mother what you learned today at dance."

Iris struck a pose, and with an intent look on her face she

straightened her tall body, brought the insides of her long legs together, feet flat, the toes of each foot pointed in opposite directions, with the outside heel of her right foot touching the toes of her left. She held her arms down in front of her body, elbows slightly bent, fingertips touching.

"That's position five, right, Lover-dover?"

"This is *lower* fifth position," said Iris.

Elevating herself up onto her toes and raising her arms up over her head, she said. "And this is *upper* fifth position."

"That's very nice, Iris," said their mother. She turned the flame off from under the coffee pot. "Carlo!" she called. "Your coffee is ready!"

"Now show her that other dance you showed me - the dainty one where you stand on one foot."

"Oh, that's an arabesque," said Iris proudly. With that, she separated her hands, reaching and stretching her left hand forward in front of her and her right hand back behind, forming a line with her arms, as she raised her right leg off the ground and straight behind her, toes pointed, bringing her torso perpendicular to her standing leg.

Auntie Rosa gestured toward Iris. "Look! Look how graceful!" With her eyes glued to Iris, Auntie Rosa bit her bottom lip with her upper front teeth, and shook her head back and forth slightly, almost imperceptibly, as if she never imagined that she would ever have the opportunity to see anything quite so beautiful as Iris performing an arabesque in the middle of the kitchen. Or perhaps she was imagining all of the arabesques she herself never had the opportunity to strike. "So graceful," she whispered to herself. "So graceful."

"That's very nice, Iris." said their mother, placing a cookie on the table in front of Lily. Even though it wasn't a real Oreo, Lily unscrewed the cookie halves - the way they did on the commercial - and licked the white crème from the center.

"C'mon, Lily," said Iris. "Let's go play jacks!" Iris grabbed the blue valise and headed up the stairs. Lily snatched a second cookie from the plate, and followed.

Iris opened the valise and carefully removed her black leotard and pink tights. It was clear that they had been folded with extreme care, as neatly as they had been in their original package. Iris transported them from the valise to her underwear drawer, holding them gently with both hands, as if they were made out of butterflies. Lily could see why Auntie Rosa loved Iris' gracefulness. Even when she wasn't dancing, she moved like a swan on a pond, slowly and quietly.

Sometimes when Iris wasn't around Lily would go into the closet and take out the blue valise and hold it by the handle and look at herself in the mirror. She imagined climbing the winding staircase up to the second floor at Auntie Rosa's, passing by the lower apartment that had long since been outgrown by the Capotosti clan, and which had been rented by Auntie Rosa to Peggy, Arvella, and their two German schnauzers.

"Good afternoon, Lily!" they would call, as she passed.

"Hello, Peggy! Hello Arvella!" Lily would cheerfully call and wave.

"I'm quite sure your Auntie Rosa will be so happy to see you today!"

"Oh, I'm sure of it!" Lily would chime. "Why, she even gave me this special blue valise for my things!"

"How lovely," Peggy would say.

"Yes, Lily," Arvella would say. "Just lovely."

Even though Lily didn't completely understand what grace was, she knew she didn't have any. That's why she was always dropping things and hitting her head, and why she performed horribly in volleyball during gym class. Competitive sports made her nervous, with so much riding on what you did or how you reacted in the span of a second or two - actions and reactions that you really had very little control over, anyway. Lily discovered that no matter how well she understood the various ways to hit a volleyball, whenever one came flying at her head, she would be more inclined to cover her face and duck than to devise a strategy for hitting it back.

Iris gently closed the dresser drawer and placed the blue valise in the closet. Lily panicked at the thought that she might discover the striped top and soiled turquoise shorts that she had bundled up and stuffed into the corner of the closet after her secret encounter with Henry. When Iris closed the closet without saying anything, Lily was both relieved and disappointed that she did not notice them. Lily knew it was supposed to be a special secret, but it didn't seem right not to tell Iris about something so important as becoming a woman. After all, she knew Iris' secret about that menses thing that happened to her. Plus, Iris was reading books about love and Lily was sure that she would be able to tell her what she was doing wrong, since Henry didn't really act like he loved her at all. Over the past several days, he had lain on top of her two more times, but still he did not become more kind toward her, or do special favors for her, or even act like he remembered anything about it.

"Iris," Lily whispered. "I have something to tell you, but you have to promise you won't tell anyone, ever."

"Oooo, a secret!" Iris climbed onto the bed and crossed her legs in front of her, resting her elbows on her knees. "I promise! Tell me, tell me!"

Lily closed the bedroom door and then climbed up next to Iris. She related the story of encountering Henry in the chicken coop and how he lay on top of her and rocked and groaned and told her he loved her. Iris must have been impressed, because her eyes widened and her jaw dropped open. Lily expected Iris to throw her arms around her and rejoice in celebration that now they were both women, just in different ways. But the timbre of Iris' voice hinted not at joy, but horror.

"Oh no, Lily!" she exclaimed. "Did he take off your pants?"

"No," replied Lily, not sure if that was good or bad. "He tried once."

"You have to tell Mom."

"I do? Why?"

"Because he's not supposed to do that, Lily. It's not right."

Lily picked up the bed pillow and clutched it to her chest. "It's not right? Why not?"

"I dunno," said Iris. "It's just not. It sounds like a sin, too, so you should probably go to confession."

"Why do I have to go to confession?" asked Lily. "I didn't do anything wrong!"

"Father Delaney says that just because we don't know we're doing something wrong, that doesn't make us innocent," said Iris. "Maybe you did something wrong but you don't know it yet. I'm just saying that I would confess it, just to be safe. What if you committed a mortal sin?"

"But what would I say?" said Lily, her throat burning with restrained tears. "How can I confess if I don't know what commandment I broke?"

"Hmm," said Iris, leaning forward to rest her chin in the palm of her hand. "I'm not sure - but I could find out - I could ask Auntie Rosa."

"Noooooo!" cried Lily. "You promised you wouldn't tell!"

"I could just ask her without telling her it was you - I could tell her it was Alba or someone from school..."

"Please don't, Iris! She will know it was me, I just know it."

"Then you have to tell Mom. She'll know whether it's a mortal sin."

The thought of repeating the whole story to their mother scared Lily, made her want to run downstairs, out the door, and into the woods where telling secrets never got you in trouble. Maybe Iris just didn't like that Lily was so special - maybe she wished Henry had lain on top of her the way that Lily wished she were taking dance lessons. Maybe Lily didn't have to tell at all.

"Let's just forget it, OK?" said Lily. "I don't want to talk about this anymore." Lily hopped down from the bed, and started leaping around the room. "What I really want is for you to show me how to do that thing you were doing in the kitchen - you know, when you looked like you were flying? It was so pretty!"

"An arabesque?"

"Yeah - that."

"Well, do you promise me you're going to tell Mom about that thing with Henry?"

271

"Do I hafta?" Lily's ballet improvisation came to a halt with a stomp. "Maybe he'll just stop - you know, like when the toilet gets clogged and the water gets higher and higher and you think it's going to overflow, but then at the last second it stops?"

"It's not the same thing, Lily." Iris crossed her arms over her chest. "I won't teach you any ballet until you promise me you'll tell Mom."

"OK," said Lily, crossing her fingers behind her back. "I promise."

"Let me see both your hands," said Iris.

Lily uncrossed her fingers and showed them to Iris.

"Say it again."

"I promise," Lily reluctantly repeated. "Geez Louise - why don't you believe me?"

"I'm just making sure," said Iris. She turned toward the dressing mirror and began her instructions. "Well, first of all, you can't just start out with an arabesque. You have to learn all the ballet positions first." Iris demonstrated as she moved through each one, with Lily following her reflection. "This is first position... this is second position... this is third position... and this is fourth position." Iris' body flowed from one stance to the next, her long arms moving through the air propelled by a force that was something between a gentle sweep and a flail, as though the slightest lapse in concentration would cause her arms to get away from her, and she would lift off the ground and fly away.

"How do you remember all of them?" asked Lily with admiration.

"Well, you have to practice every day. For like twenty minutes or something like that." Iris tucked her long hair behind her right ear. "Will you practice every day?"

"Yes! Show me, show me!"

"OK, well, first you stand like this." Iris demonstrated first position, with her legs and heels together, toes of each foot pointing out at opposite forty-five degree angles. Lily mimicked her. "Shoulders down," said Iris, placing her hands on Lily's shoulders and making the necessary adjustments. "Chin up!

That's the thing about ballet - you have to look kind of fancy while you're doing it." Lily wasn't sure how to look fancy, but she had seen the ballerinas on PBS, and they always looked as though they were trying to see something that was just off in the distance, over a hill.

"That's good!" said Iris. "You just did first position! Hey - if you want," said Iris, "I can teach you what I learn every Saturday - that way it will be like you're taking lessons, too!"

Lily vowed to herself that she would practice the five positions every day so that she would be ready when Iris came home with new lessons to share.

The next Saturday, while Iris was at her dance lesson, Lily closed herself in the sunroom. She carefully removed the tiara that Jasmine won in the Harvest Queen pageant from its special display in the bookcase, and balanced it tentatively on her head. She selected *The Nutcracker Suite* from the library of classical music and placed it on the turntable. She repeated the five ballet positions for an hour, accompanied by "Dance of the Sugarplum Fairies" and "Waltz of the Flowers." She imagined herself as a grand ballerina on stage, dancing in a spotlight, twirling and leaping and soaring, lighter than air, tall and graceful and beautiful. Like Iris.

Lily's mother burst into the sunroom, pushing the door open with her foot.

"Oh, Mommy!" cried Lily. "You scared me!"

Lily's mother was carrying a watering can in her right hand, and had a red plastic laundry basket full of dirty clothes tucked under her left arm. She looked at the turntable spinning, looked at Lily's tiara sitting lopsided on her head, and asked, "What are you doing in here?"

"Nothing," said Lily. "Just practicing."

"Practicing? Practicing what?"

"My ballet positions. Iris said she is going to teach me all of her ballet moves. I just have to promise to practice twenty minutes every day so I can be sure to remember them all. Mom, did you know that ballerinas have to talk French?"

273

"They do, huh?"

"Yes - and they are very tall and they are soooo beautiful. I was thinking of becoming a ballerina one day."

"Well," said her mother, "Until then, hold this for me." She passed the laundry basket to Lily, pulled a dust rag from the pocket of her apron, and began to dust the record cabinet. Lily held the basket against her chest with both arms. The familiar odor of sweat and dirt filled her nostrils. Looking down into the basket, she noticed the turquoise shorts, still bunched up as she had left them in the back of her bedroom closet.

Lily was reminded of the kinda-sorta promise she'd made to Iris about telling their mother about what had happened. The only thing worse than her fear of telling was her fear of dying with an unconfessed sin on her soul. It would probably be better to spit it out now than to spend eternity in Purgatory. If she told her mother, then at least then she would know for sure, and she could just focus on practicing her ballet. Lily opened her mouth, but the words got balled up inside her throat - the way puke does just before it comes out - making the skin of her face cool and clammy.

"Lily - what is it?" said her mother. "You look like you've just seen Tchaikovsky's ghost."

Strains of "The Arabian Dance" filled the room, and with her eyes fixed on the crumpled shorts, layered among play clothes and church clothes and bath towels, Lily steeled herself to say the words, the way she did in school when she was called upon but was not entirely sure she knew the answer.

She blurted, "Henry lays on top of me sometimes."

Speaking the words was like letting the air out of an overinflated balloon, and a wave of relief passed through her.

"What?" said her mother, the smile wilting on her lips. "What do you mean?"

Lily wished she could grab the words out of the air and shove them back into her mouth. She found herself fighting tears, wishing only for her mother to take her into her arms, tell her it was OK. Maybe even make some chocolate milk, sit at the kitchen table, and talk about it.

"He lays on top of me." She sought another way to say it, but could find none. "He lays on top of me, in the chicken coop. Then he rocks and he yells a little bit, too."

Lily's mother just stared. Lily stared back, searching her memory to find a time when she'd seen this expression of shock and fear on her mother's face, yet unable to remember ever having seen it before. Lily's heart pounded. "Iris said I should tell you."

Reaching over, Lily's mother straightened the tiara on her daughter's head, and said, "Don't allow yourself to be alone with him anymore."

She then went from the zebra plant to the philodendron, to the ficus tree, pouring water into each pot. She tossed the empty watering can into the laundry basket, and took it from Lily's arms.

"Do you hear me?" she said.

"Yes, Mommy," Lily replied.

Before Lily had a chance to ask her what to say in confession, Lily's mother walked out into the living room, leaving Lily standing alone, her tiara glittering in the afternoon sun.

Friday afternoons at school seemed to drag on forever. All Lily could ever think about was how lovely the wall clock looked when it finally struck three. The walk home on Friday was extra nice, because she had Iris all to herself. Iris would tell her the inside scoop on what was going on with the older kids, and who liked whom and who got in trouble doing what. Iris also knew lots of interesting things about the neighbors on Chestnut Crest, because while Lily's interest in Auntie Rosa's coffee visits was purely a matter of confection, holding her interest as long as there were still treats on the table, Iris preferred to linger while the grown-ups talked. Her ability to sit for long periods without speaking or moving enabled her to go largely unnoticed, which caused the grownups to say things in front of her that they normally would never say in front of a child. Lily's walk with Iris helped her to not think too much about how she would spend the afternoon, or whether Henry might be home, and where she could go and what she could do until suppertime to avoid allowing herself to be alone with him.

The Kinley family lived five doors down and had moved into their home the previous week. Mrs. Kinley was on the front steps, shaking the dust out of a small multicolored braided rug. She paused to wave to the girls.

Iris said to Lily, "That's Mrs. Kinley. She has a retarded son."

"What's wrong with him?" Lily asked, waving back.

"He can't talk right and he walks all funny. His head has extra water in it or something. His name is Willy."

"How old is he? Will he be in my class?" asked Lily.

"No, he won't be in your class. Retards have to go to a special school because they can't read and write and stuff."

Lily jumped up, hoping to catch a glimpse of Willy through the front window. "How did he get like that, anyway?" Lily asked.

"Auntie Rosa says that retards have something wrong with their brains. Sometimes they got hurt when they were being born, but sometimes God just makes them like that. Auntie Rosa says that maybe their parents did bad stuff and God is punishing them."

"If the parents did bad stuff," said Lily, "then why didn't God put extra water in *their* heads?"

"I dunno. God can make people whatever way He wants to, I guess. Anyway, you shouldn't question God like that, Lily."

"Why not?"

"Cuz. He's God."

Lily looked over her shoulder at Mrs. Kinley as she disappeared back into the house. It didn't quite seem fair, really, that God could just do whatever He wanted, making people like Willy suffer with things like extra water in their heads, or having buck teeth and not being graceful, like Lily. People should have something to say about being poor, or retarded, or ugly, or clumsy. After all, God wasn't the one who had to listen to people call him "beaver," and He never had to try to nonchalantly give stupid Mrs. Fish a free lunch slip.

When the girls entered the house, they were surprised to find their mother in the kitchen, with her head buried in the refrigerator, as she engaged in her ritual cleaning out of the leftovers. Methodically, she would peel the blue lid back from each plastic container, sniff it, and then either toss the contents into the garbage, put it back into the refrigerator, or eat it.

Peeking over the top of the refrigerator door, she said, "Lily - go pack some clothes. You're going with Iris to Auntie Rosa's tonight."

"I am?" Lily looked at Iris. Iris shrugged.

"Yes. You've been signed up for dance lessons in the morning, so now you'll be taking the bus into the city with Iris on Fridays." She reached into the pocket of her apron and handed Lily a quarter. "That's for your bus fare. Auntie Rosa will bring you both back here tomorrow afternoon."

The girls looked at each other for a moment, and then they both burst into smiles.

"C'mon!" said Iris. "We have to get ready - the bus comes in forty-five minutes!"

Lily grabbed a brown grocery bag out of the kitchen cupboard and ran up to her room to pack, taking the stairs two at a time.

Spending the night at Auntie Rosa's had always been a bit of a mystery to Lily. Whenever Iris came home, she seemed different somehow, and she often had small gifts in her valise such as a new comb, a compact, or a white cotton handkerchief with lace and roses around the edges. Lily imagined that Auntie Rosa had a treasure chest of surprises, like they do at the dentist. Lily would choose a hanky.

"What's it like there?" Lily asked, rifling through the top drawer of her dresser, looking for her best underpants.

"Oh, the teachers are sooo nice!" said Iris. "There's this one teacher - her name is Harmony DiBella - isn't that the most beautiful name you ever heard? She's my tap dance teacher."

Lily was more curious about what it was like at Auntie Rosa's; she hadn't even yet considered all the questions she had about The Limelight Dance Boutique. It occurred to her that she had no idea what to do, where to go, how to act.

"Will I be in your class?"

"I dunno... prob'ly not - you'll prob'ly be in the class with other girls who are new."

"What are they like?"

"Silly - I don't know them 'cuz they're new like you and they've never been there before, either. Here," said Iris, handing Lily a rubber band. "Put this in your bag. You have to put your hair in a ponytail for class."

"Oh. OK." Lily dropped the rubber band into her bag, which now contained one pair of white cotton underpants, one flannel nightgown, and one rubber band. Satisfied, she closed the bag and rolled the end of it up into a makeshift handle.

The girls stood at the bus stop, Iris with her blue valise at her side and Lily clutching her brown paper bag against her chest. Lily had never been on the city bus before, and she was excited and nervous. Iris gave her instructions about how to put the quarter into the slot as you climbed up the little steps, and how you had to find a seat quickly. "It's not like being on the school bus," said Iris. "They don't wait for you to sit down before they go."

"Here it comes," said Iris, pointing to the bus as it rose up over the hill. It looked so small from a distance.

The bus passed their house, and lurched to a stop in front of the girls. Iris climbed the steps, and put her quarter into the slot.

"Good afternoon," said the bus driver.

"Good afternoon," said Iris. "This is my little sister. Her name is Lily."

"Well, hello there, Lily," said the bus driver. His broad smile revealed a neat row of yellow teeth, minus one slot in front, which had been replaced by gold. The brass buttons of his navy blue uniform strained over his belly, which butted up against the huge steering wheel.

"Hi." Lily stood frozen at the top of the steps, her quarter firmly pinched between her index finger and thumb.

"Put your quarter in," Iris nudged Lily with her elbow.

Lily looked at Iris, puzzled. Iris reached over, took the quarter from Lily's hand, and deposited it into the slot. She took Lily's hand and led her back to an empty bench. The engine belched as the bus lurched forward. The driver glanced up at the girls in the large rear view mirror that hung from the ceiling, the whites of his eyes seeming to jump out from his dark skin.

With every house they passed, Lily sank deeper into fear - afraid of the unknowns of Auntie Rosa's, and of The Limelight Dance Boutique, all of which made her want to jump up, to tell the driver, "Stop!" so she could get off the bus and run back down the street, back up the long asphalt driveway, back to where her mother was eating leftover applesauce out of the Frigidaire, back to the sunroom where she could listen to Tchaikovsky and practice her ballet positions safely behind closed doors. She watched out the back window as the house on Chestnut Crest grew smaller and smaller, finally disappearing behind the horizon, and she understood that home could not offer her the refuge she sought. Not anymore.

The first night at Auntie Rosa's, Lily was kept awake initially by the whispers and giggling that came from the bedroom where Auntie Rosa and Iris slept, and then by the street sounds of the city. She was used to the crickets and train whistles of Chili, not the honking, screeching, and shouting that took place in front of Murphy & Nally's, the bar one block over where Grandpa used to sneak out for a nip before he fell asleep in his armchair and never woke up. Lily sure would not be sitting in *that* chair. But at least in the back room it wasn't dark at night like it was at home; the street lights cast a comforting glow across Lily's makeshift bed, and she passed the sleepless hours by reading the prayer books and old copies of *Guidepost* magazine that were neatly filed in the wicker magazine rack.

Even after she had leafed through all the magazines, the travel alarm clock that ticked off the passing hours on the table next to her only read 12:15. Lily tiptoed from the back room through the living room and then as quietly as she could, she snuck down the hall to Auntie Rosa's room, hoping to find Iris awake, to cajole her into raiding the refrigerator, or into playing a game of rock-paper-

279

scissors.

Auntie Rosa's bedroom was dark, except for the glow-in-the-dark rosary that hung from the bedpost, and the sliver of streetlight that slipped in under the window shade. Lily could hear the rhythm of breath - Iris and Auntie Rosa inhaling and exhaling, almost in perfect unison, with a slight rattle differentiating Auntie Rosa's, which was probably due to the fact that she always worked so hard. As her eyes adjusted to the darkness, Lily could see that Auntie Rosa was spooning Iris, and had her snugly wrapped in an embrace, their heads resting on white pillow cases trimmed in lace. Iris' clothes were neatly folded and stacked on the rocking chair, with the blue valise stowed at her bedside.

Lily returned to the davenport in the back room and pretended to be asleep when Uncle Alfred came in from playing at The Luau restaurant. She heard him pass and close the door to his bedroom. For the next hour, she practiced reciting the names of all fifty states in alphabetical order over and over, until she finally fell asleep. She was awakened at seven o'clock the next morning by gentle conversation, clinking silverware, and the aroma of percolating coffee as it all wafted from the kitchen. It took her a few moments to remember where she was, and when she realized that everyone was up but her, she scurried up off of the couch, folded the blankets into rectangles as she'd found them the night before, and tucked herself into a corner of the room where she could change out of her pajamas without being seen. When she entered the kitchen, Lily found the table set with blue china coffee cups and saucers and matching breakfast dishes. Various varieties of jelly, jams, and preserves were displayed on a small lazy Susan in the center of the table, and thick slices of Italian bread sat behind the window of the toaster oven, turning golden brown under the red hot coils, filling the house with their warm, cozy aroma.

Around the table were four chairs, all occupied - one by Grandma Capotosti, one by Auntie Rosa, one by Uncle Alfred, and one by Iris. Lily stood in the kitchen, feeling conspicuous and uneasy.

"Well, look who's up!" called Uncle Alfred.

"If it isn't our little sleepy head," said Auntie Rosa. A deep chuckle escaped from her throat, but she didn't smile. "Have a seat."

Lily looked to Iris.

"I'll get you a chair," said Iris, jumping up. She left the room and returned with a small round wooden tray table and placed the it at the corner, between her chair and Auntie Rosa's. When Lily sat down, her chin just barely cleared the tabletop. She had to place one foot on each side of the leg of the kitchen table and draw her elbows in close to her body in order to fit in without getting in the way.

"You want some toast?" said Iris. "It's the best toast in the world - they make the bread every day, right at the bakery down the street." She plucked a fresh slice of toast from the oven and dropped it onto a small dish in front of Lily. "And here's some butter, and you can choose any kind of jam you want - here!" Iris pushed the butter dish and the lazy Susan in front of Lily's place.

Lily was struck with how easily Iris sat at the table, how comfortably she fit there. It was as though Iris had been living a secret, separate life all this time. A bubble of anger rose from Lily's belly, as she recognized that for all those Saturday mornings when she was home alone eating puffed rice, Iris was here, enjoying the best toast in the world and choosing from ten different kinds of jam.

"You certainly are a very lucky little girl, Lily," said Auntie Rosa, her voice dripping with sweetness. "After all, it's because you have such a wonderful sister who loves you so much - the way I loved my own little sister Teresa - that you will be taking dance lessons now. Isn't that wonderful?" Auntie Rosa beamed at Iris, who cheerily wiped a dollop of half-melted butter from her lips.

Lily's body grew hot and a lump of Italian toast stuck in her throat. She wasn't sure why, but she wanted to run. Run away and never come back. But here is where Iris was, and here is where dance lessons were. She should probably just learn to feel lucky about it, like Auntie Rosa said.

"Just look at those eyes!" said Miss Nancy, Lily's ballet teacher. "You are going to be so beautiful when you grow up!"

"You did a wonderful job for your first day, Lily," Miss Harmony told her. "Practice your tap lessons every day, and you'll be ready for recital in the spring."

This world of encouragement and appreciation, together with the sense of joy that the act of dancing gave Lily made the indignities of Auntie Rosa's house seem inconsequential. For the joy of leaping and flying and panting and sweating, and for the warmth of compliments and encouragement, Lily knew she would gladly pay the price of being fifth at the table. And whenever she felt bad about it, she would occupy her mind with a task such as repeating the twelve times table, or reciting the Joys and Sorrows of our Blessed Mother, until the bad thoughts went away.

The weekends passed and autumn became winter. Lily found the street sounds of Auntie Rosa's back room comforting as she learned to easily drift off to sleep. The familiarity of the routine eased Lily's sense of being an outsider and the dejection she sensed when offered a bowl of Iris' favorite cereal for breakfast, or when taking a bubble bath - which for Lily meant sitting in the back of the tub, behind Iris, where the bubbles were sparse and the water was cold. The small wooden tray became her chair, and the corner spot became her place at the table. Even if it wasn't a real chair. Even if she did have to squeeze in and try not to take up too much space. It was better than not being there, and after a while, you almost forgot that you didn't really belong.

It was at the first dance recital the following spring that Lily discovered her passion for being on stage. Everything about recital was magical - from the sequined costumes, to the lighted vanity mirrors in the dressing rooms. She was enchanted by the way all the girls arrived early in the morning, with their hair in rollers, brown bag lunch in hand, ready to set up and spend the day getting primped, having dress rehearsals, and then gathering in jittery, giggling, nervous groups as each one took their turn on stage. Iris danced with the older girls; Lily was glad to have something that she could call her own, but comforted to know that Iris was close by.

Each year after, Lily counted down the months, weeks, and days until recital, and each year she sobbed uncontrollably when it was over. By her third year of dance, Lily was performing solos and was placed by herself in the front line of the performance group, just in case any of the other girls forgot the steps. It was also the year when Lily first met Kiki Greiner.

Kiki had two older brothers, but she was the youngest by several years, and her parents both doted on her as their precious baby girl. Kiki always dressed in pink, and usually wore a pink barrette in her short blond hair, more for style than function. Kiki lived just a few miles from Lily, but went to public school and attended a Protestant church. The excess thirty pounds that Kiki carried around with her was both the reason why she'd been signed up for dance lessons, and why she didn't do well and hated it so much.

"I'm actually an actress and a singer," she told Lily. Kiki walked over from the dressing area, her pink tights straining under the girth of her thighs, not quite making the trip all the way up to her crotch. Kiki sat down at the vanity and began to empty the contents of her enormous stage makeup kit onto the table.

"I do this dancing thing just for the experience. It's good to be well rounded when you're in the theatre." She handed Lily a container of pancake makeup. "Here, use this for your base."

Lily looked up at Kiki's reflection in the vanity mirror, and then looked back down at the makeup. Aside from the half-used tube of pink lipstick that Jasmine had given her for the purpose, Lily didn't have any stage makeup. She felt lucky to find a way to buy her costumes - the request for which always caused angst and short outbursts of complaint from her mother. ("Honestly," she would say, "Twelve dollars for a costume you'll wear one time?

Do they think we're made of money?") Yet somehow, the costumes always arrived, and the thrill of trying them on fresh out of the package was better than opening presents on Christmas morning.

"Here - lemme show you." Kiki dipped her fingers in a small dish of water, then used them to scoop out a blob of beige crème, smearing it on Lily's face.

"Now use this sponge to blend that all over."

"So where do you sing?" Lily asked, swiping the sponge across her cheek.

"Oh, around. We have a band at our church, and I get the lead in the school play every year."

One of the only plays they ever had at Sacred Family was the Christmas play, *The Gift of the Magi,* in which Lily had been cast as the slave girl. They performed it in the cafeteria and her only line was, "Save me, sir - save me from slavery, from a fate worse than death!" It was at that point that Mike Dylan - who played the slave dealer - was supposed to push Lily, causing her to fall to the ground. Mike performed his role with gusto; he flung Lily so forcefully that she went sliding across the floor, causing all of the parents to break out into laughter.

Lily liked performing, and she didn't even really mind getting laughed at; it was better than going unnoticed. However, the only other play was the May Day pageant, and the only role was Mary, Mother of God. Once the entire school saw you play the slave girl, you could never hope to be cast as the Virgin Mother.

"I also belong to the choir at school," Kiki continued. "Don't you have a choir at your school?"

"No," replied Lily. "Just music class." Even that was an exaggeration. Sing-alongs with Sister Michael Mary didn't exactly constitute musical instruction, unless your goal was to sing the Erie Canal song so many times that it would lodge itself into your mind's ear and pop up at the slightest provocation. *I got a mule her name is Sal...*

"Well, next year when we go to high school they'll have three different choirs - one that does Broadway show tunes, one that performs jazz numbers, and one just for the holidays. You simply *have* to join. We'll have loads of fun!" Kiki delivered the invitation with the polish of a well-rehearsed script. Lily could imagine her sitting in front of her mirror at home, speaking to her own reflection, "You simply *have* to join. We'll have loads of fun!"

Kiki took Lily through the routine of applying the rest of her stage makeup, including red rouge and lipstick. Lily was struck with how different she looked - grown up and sophisticated. Almost like a movie star.

From: Iris Capotosti <iris.capotosti@gmail.com>
To: Lily Capotosti <lilycapotosti@gmail.com>
Sent: Mon, Jun 28, 2010 at 3:45 PM
Subject: Summer and Cicadas

Dear Lily,

Funny how certain details of the past can spring to mind, and whisk you back to a precise time, place and state of mind in an instant, with no forewarning. Whether you want to be there or not.

The same thing happens to me when I hear a cicada. All it takes is one, and it's summer. Yesterday, a lone strident voice announced it was time, and when I went out to the garden to pick some lavender for a bouquet, I found an abandoned shell clinging to a sprig. It's amazing to think that while I was sleeping, hundreds or thousands of cicadas must have been busy molting, because today the air is completely abuzz.

And a hot summer day it is, believe me. The light is so blinding, I had to pull the shutters closed, even though that means depriving myself of what little breeze might find its way from the sea, over the hill, across the valley to my little stone house, and through the window to my makeshift studio. It's still better than air conditioning, though. I remember last time I visited the U.S. in the summer, I nearly came down with pneumonia because it was in the 90s for a whole week, and I kept forgetting to bring a sweater along when I went anywhere. It's not that I don't realize air conditioning is boon to the local economy. People work better in air-conditioned cubicles, and spend more time (and money) in air-conditioned shopping centers. What could be finer on a hot summer day than strolling the halls of a mall so chilly that it makes people want to try on the new fall fashions already for sale in July? What better place to dine than at a restaurant so cold, the already overweight people feel comfortable stoking their blubbery bellies with way more calories than they need, making them swoon at the impact when they walk out the door, and wobble as fast as they can to their air-conditioned cars.

How many people can you think of right now, who know what to do with a hot summer day? Who are happy to sweat a little, pack a picnic, set out on a bike or a hike, spread a blanket under a leafy tree and eat homemade potato salad and watermelon and watch ants lug away the crumbs, then lie on their backs to pick out animal shapes in the clouds? I'll bet you can name a lot more who know where to go to see a 3-D movie and grab a supersize burger with supersize fries and supersize soft drink and supersize ice cream cone without ever going outside.

But I'm digressing from my digression. Between the staggering heat, the incessant chanting of the cicadas, and all the thoughts spinning around in my mind, I'm feeling totally confused. I can't even separate what really went on all those years ago from what didn't, let alone understand why. Which is why I've just been sitting here, wondering.

I started asking myself how much I knew about cicadas, apart from the noise they make, and realized it was next to nothing. So of course, sitting in front of a computer, and not being in the mood to browse through thoughts of my own, not to mention concentrate on the work I should be doing, I started clicking on a site here, which led to a link there, and before I knew it, I had dug up all kinds of information about cicadas, probably some stuff not even Louis would have been able to tell us. The most incredible thing I discovered is that cicada nymphs live most of their lives burrowed underground. For some, that can be as long as 17 years. They go from being buried alive, to invading your life virtually overnight, to obsessing you with their chanting. Then they just disappear again. Incidentally, it's the males that make all that racket, by humping tree trunks to attract the females, who find the behavior irresistible, submit themselves to mating, and are dead within a week. Have any of your mates ever been *that* good? Those females get the job done before they die, though. For cicadas, survival is not only a question of reproducing in great numbers, it's about so many of them appearing on the scene all at once, that their predators can't handle them all. Survival by synchronicity. Capotosti style.

I wasn't planning on writing to you about cicadas, Lily, but since I guess that's what I'm doing, I was wondering whether you've ever seen one of those discarded shells. They are actually pretty creepy looking. You can even see the holes where the eyes once were. During my clicking, I came across a picture of a girl on the Internet with a bunch of them pinned in her hair. Can you imagine? Oh, and guess what? The Chinese have been using cicada shells in traditional medicine for centuries. Apparently, they're good for treating all kinds of ailments, from skin rashes to fever to eye diseases. You should talk to the herbalist who sold you that bee embryo cream you wrote me about, together with that facial treatment you said smelled like alpaca shit, remember? I bet she'd know all about it.

There was something else I wanted to tell you, lots of things, actually, but I wasted almost an hour Googling cicadas, and now it's already Webinar time in LA and I'm sitting here in a sarong. I'd better put a blouse on at least, maybe even some lipstick, but I think I can get away without underwear. There's no webcam under my desk, at least not that I know of.

Love,
Iris

Dear Iris:

Either you're stoned, or you're in love. For your sake, I hope it is the former.

I have to admit that I'm a bit baffled by this note. After these stories we've just shared - you nearly dying from appendicitis and me getting sexually molested by Henry - you want to talk about cicadas and bouquets of lavender? I was so agitated by our latest stories that I haven't been able to sleep, and now I find you prancing through the woods, conversing with nature like a scene from Snow White with birds bringing you ribbons of daisies for your hair.

If I were a Disney character I know who'd I'd be: Cinderella. I remember how they used to play that movie once a year, back in the day when we only had three television stations and there was no such thing as home video. I would ache with anticipation for that movie. To tell you the truth, I didn't care so much about the prince. What I loved - what I related to - was that the one sister who was left to tend to the cinders was eventually given her due. I'm still waiting for my vindication. That's what kept me going, you know? The promise that those who suffer greatly can expect a great reward. (Did I learn that from fairy tales, or from the Church? Is there a difference?)

Still, if only I could get to that fucking ball I know it would all work out OK. I actually thought I saw my fairy godmother once, but when I got closer, she was face down in a ditch, suffocated in her own drug-induced vomit. Good-bye white horses, good-bye fancy-schmancy dress. Good-bye hope.

I often wonder why my life has been marked by hardship. I just looked my birthday up on a perpetual calendar. I could have told you without looking - I was born on a Saturday. "Saturday's child works hard for a living." And you, my dear, were born on a Friday. "Friday's child is loving and giving." Makes me wish Mom had pushed me out a day earlier.

And Iris, I hate to tell you this, but I'm one of those cubicle dwellers who doesn't really know what to do with a summer's day. Well, I do know what to do - but when am I supposed to fit all of that romanticism in, anyway? Not during the week; I have to save my vacation time for personal emergencies. And weekends? I'm running to Mom's, or running to the store for Mom, or doing my own grocery shopping. Sundays I spend cooking so I can catch my breath between work and dinner and bed during the week. I suppose I could figure out a way to have a picnic or do some cloud gazing. But with my luck, it would be raining that day.

It's really too much to bear, on a summer's day, to think about shade trees and red-and-white checkered tablecloths spread out on the cool grass. It's almost easier to convince yourself that you don't hate your life, that your job is fine, and that you love air conditioning. Because for most of us, we need to find a way to survive in our windowless cubicles with their florescent lighting; most of us don't have a choice. We don't have the energy for trivia about cicadas, unless we need it for the report that our boss has been demanding all week. If we knew that sunshine and lavender filled the air on the other side of the concrete, we could never bear to enter those cubicles. But we must, so we learn to cope with the fact that we are trading our freedom in, just to keep from starving. So we shop, we eat, we numb. The full realization of the beauty of a summer's day would break our hearts, sear our souls, make us scream like the cicada.

Love,
Lily

From: Iris Capotosti <iris.capotosti@gmail.com>
To: Lily Capotosti <lilycapotosti@gmailcom>
Sent: Sat, July 3, 2010 at 8:30 AM
Subject: Cinderella and Cicadas

Dear Lily,

I haven't been sleeping so well, either. I've been thinking about what you wrote to me, and I was just going to let it slide, as usual. But I can't.

Do you honestly think I spend my days gazing at clouds and romping through fields to contemplate the wildflowers and cicadas? All you would have to do is look up, or down, or around you for a minute and you just might enjoy the world more, too. But that would imply tearing your eyes away from the miserable image you have of your life and focusing on the beauty at hand. If that's too painful, well, maybe you should do some serious thinking. And maybe I shouldn't even try to share my happy moments with you, if all it does is make you feel bad. I guess you'll always see me as the lucky one who never had to work for anything. I know you haven't always had it easy, but I've been working my whole life too, you know. I just chose a different place in which to do it.

Of course, it's easier for you to think that Auntie Rosa and Uncle Alfred and Grandma wanted me around because I was born on the right day of the week. The fact is, I would have done anything to stay overnight in a quiet house where someone actually paid attention to me. For example, keeping an eye on Grandma, saying the rosary with her, helping her with the mending, helping her dress, helping her to the bathroom, massaging her feet. After the first few times you came, you started getting bored within an hour, and if it hadn't been for the dancing lessons and the coffee with toast, you probably would have come down with one of your stomachaches so you would have the excuse to go back home.

Which brings me back to the reason I became so engrossed in the cicada story. It just took the grating sound of that one chirp to instantly resuscitate a swarm of memories and sensations associated with summer. Just like the words "Russian olive tree" and "chicken coop" and "Limelight Dance Boutique" catapulted me smack dab into those episodes of childhood I hadn't thought about for years. Like cicada nymphs, those memories have been buried deep underground, but I guess they weren't dead. Far from it, otherwise they wouldn't be making all this racket.

When I read page after page of what we've written, it makes my head throb like the insistent, screeching song of the cicadas. I cringe at the thought of how many millions more must be buried, waiting to pounce out and start screaming at me. I thought we'd have fun exchanging memories, but it seems like half the things I write make you mad, and half the things you write either make me sad, or make me wonder which one of us is telling the real story.

Tomorrow is Independence Day. If we were cicadas, it would be a perfect day to molt. We could shed our scarred, wrinkling skins, leave behind the slackening flesh and greying hair and all the other parts we don't want anymore, and emerge, fresh and new. Then spread a pair of gossamer wings, and flit away on a summer song. But that sounds too much like a fairy tale. That's how this whole thing started, but that's sure not how it's turning out.

Love,
Iris

From: Lily Capotosti <lilycapotosti@gmail.com>
To: Iris Capotosti <iris.capotosti@gmail.com>
Sent: Sat, July 03, 2010 at 7:55 PM
Subject: Oh, Toreador-a

Dear Iris:

Regarding who's telling the real story... maybe we both are. Or maybe neither one of us is. All I can tell you is that my stories feel like memories, but when I read yours - I don't know - it's almost like reading a novel or something.

I'm not sure what you want me to say about how or why things transpired so differently for us. I guess what it comes down to is this line from your note: "I just chose a different place in which to do it."

You're right - it comes down to choices. And you had some - just one more difference between us.

Let's just get back to high school. Seems like things were simpler back then. But I know they probably weren't.

Lily

PS: I would have brushed Grandma's hair. I also would have emptied Grandpa's spittoon. In fact, I tried a few times, but he always asked for you. Do you have any idea what it feels like to offer to empty someone's spittoon and get turned down?

PPS: Do you remember that song?: "Oh, Toreador-a don't spit on the floor-a, use the cuspadora, that's what it's for-a."

19. IRIS

"Iris Capotosti and Veronica Rizzo. Step up to my desk before leaving class." Miss Timpani did not have a strong speaking voice, and the extra effort she had to exert to make herself heard over the dismissal bell infused a deeper shade of pink into a face already flustered by the forty-five minute lecture during which she had attempted to explain the human digestive tract to a room full of squirming high school sophomores. Iris seethed with annoyance as the other students hustled one another out of the classroom and into the hallway, eager to make the most of the few minutes between periods during which they would sneak smokes and kisses, slip notes and raid lockers. Not that Iris was ever involved in any of those activities, but she had never been asked to stay after class, and had a bad feeling she knew the reason behind the teacher's order.

"I told you so," Iris hissed, as the girls rose and walked to the front of the deserted classroom, and Veronica lowered her eyes under twin veils of charcoal lashes thickened and lengthened to improbable dimensions by gobs of clumpy mascara. As they approached Miss Timpani, she tossed her head in the scornful gesture Iris had witnessed many times, along with the reactions it provoked. When Veronica's stylishly feathered hair fell over her face in a thick, silky curtain, shielding her expression from scrutiny, the teachers always looked like they would love to slap her, but any boys in the vicinity always looked like they would love to do something else to her.

Iris had met the girl on the first day of geometry class, when Veronica threw open the classroom door and sauntered in, books pressed against her tummy, her precocious forms stretching her skintight Levis and low-cut tank top to the limits of their elasticity. She snapped gum between a set of straight white teeth, her eyes darting around the room in search of a suitable accommodation for her curvaceous, petite frame, apparently oblivious to the fact that Mr. Briggs, surrounded by the cloud of chalk dust generated by his furious scribbling and erasing, was already deep into his explanation of the Pythagorean theorem. Either he was not a stickler for punctuality, or so taken with the notions spewing from his mouth with such unbridled intensity as to cause bubbles of spittle to accumulate at its corners, that he failed to reprimand the tardy student. Though Iris did not think she looked like a front-row kind of girl, Veronica had no other alternatives in the full classroom, other than the vacant spot next to Iris. She sighed audibly as she dumped her load of books onto the desk and slid into the seat.

After fifteen minutes of trying to stir up enthusiasm for what Mr. Briggs was saying about right angles and hypotenuses, Iris had determined that geometry was probably not as interesting as the algebra she had studied as a freshman, but possibly a bit more useful on a practical level, for instance if she ever wanted to help her parents figure out how many square feet of carpeting to buy in the unlikely event they should consider redecorating the living room. Nonetheless, Iris just couldn't get excited about math in general; plus, it was pretty difficult to concentrate with her neighbor snapping gum practically in her ear, while squirming constantly in her seat, and looking around at everyone in the class except the teacher.

"This class sucks," she mouthed to Iris as soon as she caught her glancing at her. Iris shrugged. Granted, Mr. Briggs did not seem to be very communicative on a personal level, but at least he was passionate about the subject he taught. Iris figured he deserved a chance.

"In case you don't know," the girl said. "I'm Veronica." Of course Iris knew who Veronica was. She had seen her flitting and flirting her way through the corridors on countless occasions. Who hadn't?

"I'm Iris," she whispered, figuring there was a fat chance Veronica had any idea who she was.

As soon as Mr. Briggs turned to draw another series of triangles and squares on the blackboard, Veronica nodded to a boy across the room. "See that kid over there?" she said. "The cute one with the puppy dog eyes, sitting by the window?"

Iris nodded.

"His brother was in my brother's class. He woulda been a senior this year. Except for the fact he OD'd over the summer. The parents go around saying he committed suicide. Same thing I guess. I suppose it sounds better, though."

Iris's eyes widened. You couldn't even have a Church funeral if you committed suicide. But if the kid was lucky, maybe he wasn't Catholic.

"See that girl two rows over, in the first seat? The dopey looking one with the glasses and stringy hair?"

Iris nodded. She had actually talked to the girl, whose name was Joanna, one day during Study Hall. She was on the quiet side, like Iris, but seemed nice.

"Her sister got knocked up and had to drop out. Can't see that happening to her, that's for sure." Iris wondered whether that was good or bad, in Veronica's book.

"Briggs is not only boring as hell, he's a faggot."

Iris wondered how she could pass judgment on their teacher without having shut up long enough to listen to him. "Why do you say that?" she asked, ready to leap to his defense. She had a tendency to want to defend people, even those to whom she was indifferent or possibly averse, the moment they fell victim to what Iris considered unjustifiable attack.

"You have any classes with that dyke, Ms. Shue?" Veronica pushed the air out of her mouth to make a hissing sound when she pronounced the word "Ms." Iris wondered what point she was trying to make.

"I'm taking Women in Contemporary Society," Iris said. The English elective was turning out to be one of her favorite courses, and Ms. Shue her favorite teacher.

Veronica rolled her eyes. "Well, just for your information, I've seen Briggs and Miz together in the parking lot more than once. They drive to school together."

"Maybe they're carpooling."

"Duh. Wake up. You just don't get it, do you?" Veronica said, as Mr. Briggs turned toward the class, grinning with satisfaction at the drawings on the blackboard, and clapping his hands to shake off the chalk dust. In fact, Iris didn't get it. If Veronica said Mr. Briggs was a faggot, and Ms. Shue a dyke, what could they possibly be doing together in a car besides driving to school?

Although both Veronica and Iris had Italian surnames, like eighty percent of the Gates-Chili High School student body, the similarities stopped there, and had it not been for their seating arrangements in both geometry and biology classes, they might have made it through high school without ever having spoken to each other. It was obvious which of the two was a Gates girl and which came from the neighboring town of Chili, which the inhabitants of Gates referred to as "the sticks" because of the predominance of old farmhouses and wooded land over neat, new tracts with matching houses, and evenly spaced lawns with statues and fountains, and shopping centers at major intersections.

Gates girls had fathers who drove white Cadillacs or black Lincoln Continentals with tinted glass and air conditioning instead of station wagons you could stretch out in while dangling your feet from the open back window. Gates girls had refrigerators whose pungent smells of pecorino romano and spicy salamis and fat juicy olives from the Italian import store by the railroad tracks made you want to do the tarantella when you opened the door, instead of boring plastic packets of odorless chipped turkey and ham and American cheese that were euthanasia to any taste buds worthy of the name. Gates girls feasted on manicotti stuffed with ricotta or thick squares of baked lasagna for Sunday dinner, followed by fragrant cannolis filled with sweet cream and candied fruit, instead of plain old spaghetti with meatballs, and a dessert of bread pudding made with stale crusts and a handful of raisins. Gates girls' living rooms floated on clouds of plush, wall-to-wall carpeting as immaculate as the freshly fallen snow, whose spotlessness was exalted by the glittering light dripping from sparkling chandeliers, and preserved by unconditional respect of the rule that no one should tread upon it in shoes, not even the fathers. The walls of Gates living rooms were embellished with gilded mirrors and murals of Mount Vesuvius standing watch over fringed velvet sofas with plastic covers, which were reserved exclusively for the well-behaved bottoms of grown-ups. The privileged guests of Gates living rooms were offered strong coffee in tiny china cups, and sweet liqueurs in crystal glasses poured from dusty bottles of Strega and Amaretto di Saronno which sat upon silver trays with lace doilies on faux marble coffee tables.

The unlived-in living rooms of Gates girls had little in common with the living room of 75 Chestnut Crest in Chili. There the couch, crumb-filled and stained, despite the protection afforded by the flimsy throw which tended to slip from the cushions, was the center of relaxation which Capotostis of all ages, shapes, and degrees of cleanliness shared with whatever four-legged companions roamed the premises in search of affection. Fighting for a place on the room's only sofa was prone to cause the toppling of wobbly end tables and the consequent spilling of brimming ashtrays and glasses of milk onto the downtrodden carpeting of an indeterminable color and odor achieved through the blending of sundry organic substances including but not limited to the lingering residue of cat pee, dog poop and puke of both animal and human origin.

Gates girls got their hair cut by real hairdressers, not by their mothers; they had professional manicures and wore makeup to cover their pimples. Gates girls with flat chests (though they were rare) had mothers who bought them padded bras. Some Gates girls were cheerleaders whose boyfriends were on the football team and whose families went to all the games and then to Pizza Hut together, where they actually sat at a table to eat the pizza instead of taking it away. Others had boyfriends who gave them hickeys, and wore leather jackets no matter how hot or cold it was and drove to school on motorcycles or in souped-up Chevys.

Iris had been to the homes of a few Gates girls since her high school debut the previous year, but was somewhat put off by the overpowering degree of Italo in their Americanism; after all, Iris was also half Whitacre, the descendant of a mysterious blend of Celts, which infused her bloodline with a good dose of contradiction. As for her Italian side, her resentment of generalizations spurred Iris to speculate as to the possible differences between the Abruzzo region her Capotosti grandparents had come from, whose descendants attended the annual Scurcolanese picnic way over in Irondequoit Park with the extended families of all the *paesans*, and the places where the majority of the Gates families had originated. Consulting the world atlas at the school library, she was surprised to find that Abruzzo was smack dab in the center of Italy, close to Rome on its western border, and reaching to the Adriatic sea on the east. And it had lots of mountains, including the highest in the Appenine chain.

Although Grandma Capotosti had worn black ever since the death of her daughter Teresa, and had wailed like a banshee at the funeral of her husband Anselmo, (which Iris thought odd, having never witnessed a real conversation between the two, let alone any gestures of affection), she seemed different from the Italian grandmothers of Gates, who spent their days making tomato sauce and Italian cookies, and moaned uncontrollably whenever there was a chance to suffer, whether it be caused by the death of a distant relative, or the lack of appetite of a child (including those who were now grown men, whom the mammas continued calling *"figlio mio"*). Grandma Capotosti had never seemed to attach such importance to food, and although Iris could see how much pain she was in by the way she bit her lip and clenched the hand rests of her rocking chair, she always bore her suffering with dignity until it was taken away from her, together with her gangrenous limbs, in the operating room of a hospital, where she died one Fourth of July, right on the eighty-eighth anniversary of her birth on an Abruzzese hilltop.

When Iris asked acquaintances about their families' origins, they all responded *"Napoletano"* or *"Siciliano."* Her childhood companion Rita Esposito was a mixture of both; she, too, lived in Gates now. But Rita had grown up a city girl, and was possibly too old and definitely too uninterested to be transformed into a Gates girl. In fact, she despised Gates and was as much of a loner at the high school as Iris, but sadly, she and Iris had different schedules and lived miles apart, so they rarely saw each other. During Study Hall period, Iris often found herself the unwitting center of a spontaneously formed cluster which included a few other girls who were not considered stylish enough to be "in," or smart enough to be "brains," or athletic enough to be "jockettes," or sexy enough to be "sluts," or pretty enough to be "cock-teasers." (Iris was not one hundred percent sure what that meant, but had a fairly good idea).

One day, looking around at the girls seated at her study table, she was disconcerted by the realization that she seemed to attract only the physical misfits. One girl suffered from a form of stuttering so severe that the entire right side of her face contorted with spasms whenever she opened her mouth to speak, though that certainly did not dissuade her from jumping enthusiastically into any conversation, which exasperated Iris, who did not have the heart to interrupt her. Another was devastated by a chronic skin disease that covered her doughy, shapeless body with angry pustules and flaky scales; she had taken to sitting across from Iris in the cafeteria, and Iris could tell by the resigned way in which she gazed at her from rheumy, red-rimmed eyes, that she was monitoring Iris's level of disgust, biding her time until Iris moved away from her, which of course she didn't. Iris withered under the disapproving stares she got from some of the people she may have hoped to be friends with, but who would not venture into the territory inhabited by these castaways.

Veronica Rizzo was far from being a misfit. She smoked. She had a boyfriend. One day she even gave Iris a half-used tube of frosted pink lipstick when Iris admired the way her lips shimmered, as if they were just begging to be kissed. She was cool and self-confident; she was popular and pretty, in a Gates sort of way. She talked to Iris. But one thing Veronica Rizzo was not was intelligent. And one thing she did not do was study.

"Now girls. I think you both know why I wanted to talk to you," began Miss Timpani. She looked from one to the other. "Iris? Veronica?"

All the bags of ice cubes in the freezer at Star Market would not be enough to alleviate the burning Iris felt in her cheeks. She was too embarrassed to speak, but seconds later found herself fighting off an urge to laugh. Iris had never really looked at Miss Timpani, and had certainly never seen her this close up. She was struck by how much her face resembled a pig's: the dark beady eyes, the little black breathing holes at the end of her upturned snout, the fleshy pink cheeks and smooth, pointed ears (didn't some people eat sows' ears?). She imagined a pineapple stuffed in her mouth, like the suckling pig she had seen the waiters serve on a huge platter at The Luau where Iris had finally been taken by Auntie Rosa to celebrate her sixteenth birthday.

"Here I have two test papers," Miss Timpani began, waving one in each hand. "Both have been graded with a score of one hundred percent. Which would be praiseworthy, were it not for the uncanny coincidence that the wording of the answers is one hundred percent identical. One of these papers will receive an A and the other will receive an F. This time I will allow you two girls decide who gets the A. Next time you both get an F. You are dismissed."

Out in the hallway, Veronica's boyfriend Al was hovering impatiently, his black leather jacket slung over his shoulder, a pack of cigarettes rolled up in the short sleeve of his T-shirt.

"Shit. If I get an F, I'll never be able to bring my average up," Veronica said to Iris, as Al placed an arm possessively around her shoulders. "For you, it would be a breeze." Veronica batted her caked eyelashes at Iris, then turned them on Al, who tightened his vise-like hold around her neck, looking more like he wanted to strangle or wrestle with Veronica than hug her.

"Are you crazy?" Iris asked, the embarrassment of being confronted by Miss Timpani turning to anger. "I can't have an F on my record! I've never gotten anything below a B. I'm going to college, you know, not beauty school! I knew I shouldn't have let you talk me into it. You're not even smart enough to know how to copy!"

"Don't be such a drag, Iris! If you take the heat for this, we'll get you invited to the party at the Mancusos' on Saturday. Gino's parents are gonna be out of town. Or are you gonna be too busy with your freak-show girlfriends?"

Gino was a dark, curly-haired senior whom Iris thought extremely handsome, and so obviously did the string of shapely girlfriends with whom she saw him parade down the corridors. She knew he was out of her league, but she instantly imagined him pumping her a beer from a keg, offering it to her with a mischievous smile, she pretending to like its taste just to please him. The fantasy fled in a flash as she remembered that she and Lily were planning to spend the evening with Frank and Salvatore Domino, the two brothers whose ages corresponded precisely with their own, whom they had met at Uncle Alfred's new guitar studio, in the new basement of Auntie Rosa's new suburban townhouse. The Dominos had a basement in their Gates house, too, and a very nice one it was, furnished and complete with anything a teenager could desire: a TV, a stereo, a couple of electric guitars hooked up to an amp, a drum set, a pool table, and a wet bar with a fridge full of soda pop. And that most rare commodity of all, privacy. Their parents felt the boys should have a space of their own in which to entertain friends, and never barged in with the excuse of looking for a tool or checking the furnace, which left the boys free to make out in comfort of their own home – too free, for Iris's taste. The two couples of siblings had been officially going out with each other since one Saturday afternoon, when the brothers had arranged to have Mrs. Domino drop the four of them off to hang out at the new shopping center. Rolling Ridge was the first plaza of its kind in the area, only they didn't call it a plaza - they called it a mall. All the best department stores were there, together with restaurants, and places to buy ice cream and soft pretzels, and an amusement arcade with pinball machines and air hockey tables. A beautiful fountain sat at one end of the mall, and a full-fledged merry-go-round at the other. The best feature of the mall was that it was all enclosed under one big roof, so you could go hang out there even when it snowed or rained or was really hot. You could forget about the weather; it didn't make any difference at all.

Perhaps it was because she had gotten herself so worked up about the date, or perhaps it was the overpowering scents of Brut cologne coming from the boys and Sweet Honesty from the girls that were to blame. But as soon as Mrs. Domino pulled the Cadillac over to the curb to let them out, Lily dashed off behind the bushes to puke. Sal had been nice about it, he had wanted to hold her hand anyway as they strolled through the mall, and kiss her goodbye when they parted. That had been a month ago, and Lily told her he had already progressed as far as feeling up her boobs, but only from the outside, and that was plenty far enough for her.

Iris liked Frank, and the fact that he played the guitar, but had been immediately disappointed by the sloppiness of their first kiss, though she would no more admit it to Lily, than she would to herself at first. Iris was certainly no expert on the matter, but knew what felt good and what didn't. Hoping Frank's skills would improve over time as he became more comfortable with her, she always made an effort to wipe off the spittle and force an encouraging smile at the end of a kiss. That had been her tactic until the day she finally realized that Frank's oral secretions seemed to increase in direct proportion with his self-confidence, which increased each time she smiled. Buoyed by what he must have perceived as Iris's expressions of approval, or worse yet, desire, Frank's spongy lips spread open even more greedily, his wet tongue dripped even more copiously as he slathered her face with saliva. Iris grew increasingly annoyed with the way Frank's effusions left her face all chafed and red, the way his wire-rimmed glasses butted frames with her own when he thrust himself at her, the way the sickening scent of Brut lingered on her skin. Despite this unpleasant sensation that was swiftly degenerating into revulsion, she did not have the nerve to break up with Frank for one reason: she did not want to be responsible for ruining the foursome. It just did not seem loyal to Lily.

The sense of entrapment that assailed her every time she thought about the Domino brothers situation, combined with irritation at Veronica's derogatory comments about her friends, aroused in Iris the dormant anger that gripped her so strongly she thought she would choke whenever she was party to an injustice. She would not, under any circumstances, take an F she did not deserve; not for Veronica, not for anyone.

"You know what I think, Veronica?" she blurted out with such uncharacteristic vehemence that Veronica abruptly stopped snapping her gum, backed away a few paces, and stood with her mouth agape. "I think I don't care about going to that party. And I think Gino doesn't even know you exist. And I think I don't even care whether you pass or flunk. Find yourself somebody else to copy from!"

"Hey, cool it, Iris!" Al said, sticking his face in front of hers.

"And those girls are not freaks, they're my friends!"

"You'll be sorry!" Veronica hissed, clawing at the air with blood red nails, as Al gripped her wrists.

"Tight-ass," he said to Iris, then tugged at Veronica's arm. "Come on, babe, let's go for a toke." Dragging Veronica away, he flipped Iris the bird over his shoulder. Veronica's head spun around, accusations of betrayal glinting in her eyes like shards of steel, as she called out, "Bitch!"

Telling herself she couldn't care less about Veronica, but still shaken by the embarrassing incident, Iris glanced at the Timex she had received from Auntie Rosa and Uncle Alfred for her confirmation. Her Women in Contemporary Society class was due to start in exactly three minutes; she would have to hurry if she wanted to pick up her books first. As she approached her locker, she spotted a red flower hanging from the grey metal door. It was one of those carnations that were being sold to raise money for the school play.

"A flower for my flower!" Frank Domino pounced upon her as soon as the carnation was in her hands, slathering her face with saliva, promising to drown her with kisses on the coming Saturday, before running off. Iris shuddered at the thought, and rushed to her class, arriving just as the bell rang, hoping Ms. Shue would take her mind off how much she hated high school.

20. LILY

During freshman year of high school, Lily and Kiki were inseparable, and Kiki helped Lily make the leap from Sacred Family where she shared a single classroom with twenty other children, to Gates-Chili High School, where hundreds of underclassmen fought to make it through the maze of hallways, each one rushing, pushing, and shoving as they were herded from room to room, sometimes having to run from one end of the school to the other in the ten minutes that were allocated for changing classes. Stopping at your locker to get books, and visiting the Girls' Room had to be carefully planned.

Lily had heard the stories of high school from Iris, but since Iris worked at McDonald's in the mornings, Lily had to find another way to learn the ropes. Sal was more than willing to walk her to her classes, but he also wanted to share her locker, citing that was what boyfriends and girlfriends did in high school. Thrilled at the idea that she finally had this little corner of the world all to herself, Lily was not about to share it with anyone. She opted to end the relationship rather than let him keep his Brut-infused biology book on her beautiful empty shelf. Sal was her first "real" boyfriend, and she was thrilled to have someone to spend her Saturday nights with, and happy to have a reason to dash to the ringing phone in the evenings. But after endless phone conversations and countless weekends making out in his

basement, Lily had grown bored of Sal. He was nice enough, a
he was a really good kisser, but he wanted to spend all of his fre
time with Lily and it irritated her than he never seemed to have
anything better to do.

Kiki had spent a good portion of her summer taking private
voice and drama classes from Mr. Howell, the drama coach and
musical program director. Kiki knew her way around, and she
helped Lily by teaching her about the shortcut through the
courtyard, and giving her tips on which bathrooms had the best
mirrors. Kiki also took Lily to her first musical. The Gates-Chili
production of *Hello Dolly* captured Lily's imagination so
completely that when she got home, she rifled through the record
cabinet and discovered a jacketless scratched up copy of the
Timeless Show Tunes album which was buried beneath *Whipped
Cream and Other Favorites* by Herb Alpert and His Tijuana Brass
Band. Lily played the album incessantly until she knew every
song by heart. When auditions for *Oklahoma!* were announced, she
was the first one to sign up. Her afternoons were spent in the
sunroom singing along with the soundtrack, which she borrowed
from the library and renewed so many times that the librarian
made her leave it on the shelf for a week in case someone else was
waiting for the chance to check it out.

Lily took to the theatre with a naturalness and an unconscious
talent that made Mr. Howell giddy with excitement. She was
fearless, and at his slightest direction would leap higher, sing
louder, gesticulate more outrageously - without ever questioning
him, balking, or being concerned about looking stupid - a disease
that plagued most every other fifteen-year-old on the planet.

Before long, Lily was nipping at Kiki's heels for the leading
roles in choir and drama. When parts for the musical were
assigned, Kiki immediately set out counting her lines to confirm
that her leading romantic role was technically a bigger one, while
Lily was engrossed in practicing her comedic timing and playfully
experimenting with her role of Ado Annie, the town flirt. And
while the other kids were making out in the band room and
planning cast parties, Lily was rehearsing and researching

...leges of the performing arts. It was the only way she could ever imagine herself going to college - should she be lucky enough to survive the mind-numbing inanities of high school and get a student loan. She loved drama class, English, and Ms. Shue's Women in Contemporary Society class, but otherwise school was completely unbearable.

Lily's high school experience may have been different if she had become socially engaged, but she found the girls her own age to be silly and shallow, with nothing more holding them together than cheerleader tryouts (Lily couldn't do the necessary cartwheel) and an adoration of the boys on the football team (none of whom would ever want to date a drama geek).

To complicate matters, once Lily's mother went back to work, she had become exposed to the women's movement and abandoned herself to it wholeheartedly. Lily had never seen such fire in her mother - it was a passion that fueled her mother's dedication to a full-time job during the day and classes at the local college in the evenings to earn her master's degree. Lily was perplexed by why anyone - especially someone as old as her mother who was married, had twelve children, and already had a job - would voluntarily go back to school.

"Women have been held back far too long, Lily," her mother told her. "I owe it to myself and to all women to develop my potential to the best of my ability." Lily's mother dropped three chicken drumsticks into a bag that contained a combination of bread crumbs, spices, and "home cooked goodness." She vigorously shook the bag, then retrieved the pieces of meat and placed them on a cookie sheet. "Our options as women have been limited to the kitchen and the Miss America pageant and we have all suffered because of it. We will be silent no more." She slid the cookie sheet onto the center rack and as she turned to wash her hands, she kicked up her heel and tipped the oven door closed.

"If you ask me," Lily's father chimed in, "this women's lib baloney is lousy with gals who can't put a decent meal together and aren't much to look at. Real women are content to stay home and care for their families."

"So Carlo, when I finish my degree I'll be eligible for a job grade promotion and a new pay level. Are you saying you'd rather have me here, baking cookies and sitting under the hairdryer?"

Lily's father raised his cigarette to his lips, and took a long slow drag, peering at her mother through narrowed eyes as he attempted to protect himself from the sting of his own smoke.

"No," said Lily's mother, placing a bowl of salad on the table. "I didn't think so."

While Lily related the conversation with great pride to Ms. Shue - who considered her mother a role model - having a feminist for a mother was not without its price; after all, someone still had to stay home to clean up after dinner and watch the younger children. Thanks to the women's movement, those tasks fell to Lily and Iris, leaving Lily precious little time for much else besides homework and play practice.

The debate over whether women's lib was bad because it depreciated the family dinner to a shake-and-bake experience, or good because at least it made a decent dinner possible, continued over the weeks and months that followed. Each night, the debate grew a little less friendly, the opinions a little more fixed, the language less eloquent and more vulgar as Lily's parents became polarized and ardently pitted against one another. Lily suspected that they weren't arguing about this movement in society as much as they were fighting over something much more immediate and personal. She often wished they would have their "discussions" behind closed doors; she did not want to have a front row seat to their anger and bitterness. Even more than that, the questions they raised confused Lily and it was clear they could not help her understand the issues with which they themselves were so desperately grappling. As she stood on the cusp of womanhood, the way seemed increasingly muddied.

Part girl and part woman, partially liberated but mostly bound, Lily kept one foot in each world, balancing herself on stage and escaping into dreams of her future as an actress - a vision fueled by the rumors that Lily was to be awarded the annual school achievement trophy for drama. Every previous year, the award had gone to the leading lady - and with the most lines, Kiki was clearly the lead. By the time the rumor had made its way around, Kiki was barely speaking to Lily.

"But Kiki," Lily asked, "Why are you mad at me? I don't choose the winner."

"Well, then," said Kiki. "Don't accept the award. Just tell them you don't think it's right you should get it, since you're not the leading lady. Then they'll have to give it to me. It's rightfully mine anyway."

"Don't you dare!" shouted Iris, when Lily told her she was considering Kiki's request.

"It's just a trophy," said Lily. "It doesn't really mean anything."

"Yes it does!" said Iris. "It means that you're the best, and that's worth something. You earned that. She's such a spoiled brat. I even heard that her father called the school to complain. She's just jealous because you're better than she is."

"No I'm not!" protested Lily. "Did you know that she can hit a high A note? I'm lucky if I can make a C! I could never sing her part."

"But yours is more fun; you get all the laughs. And anyway - she's fat."

"Iris!"

"That was mean, I know - sorry." Then she added, "But it's true."

"What is? That I'm better than she is, or that she's spoiled, or that she's fat?"

"All of it!" said Iris, and they both laughed.

Opening night of *Oklahoma!* was especially exciting for Lily, because her family was coming to watch. They had only known her as Lily - non-descript, number nine, youngest girl. Tonight, she was something else, something more. She peeked out into the audience from behind the curtain, and there in the tenth row sat her parents, Iris, Jasmine, Violet and Todd, and Auntie Rosa - all just to see her. Cousin Dolores was there, too - she was sick in some sort of way that no one wanted to talk about and was staying with Auntie Rosa "until she gets back on her feet."

Dolores was forty-one years old, the younger daughter of Bastiana Nuccetelli, sister of Grandma Capotosti, making Dolores Lily's first cousin, once removed. Dolores was known as the family beauty, with thick black hair, a voluptuous figure, a slight overbite that gave her an air of childlike innocence, and deep brown eyes that, when you looked straight into them, caused you to get lost in your own reflection. She was a painter who had also worked as a kindergarten teacher before her marriage to Dr. Julius Corvo, or "the creep" as Iris called him. Dolores' paintings had taken up residence with her in the basement at Auntie Rosa's. Except for her clothes, they were all she brought with her when she came to stay.

Dolores' work was beautiful, yet haunted: a majestic forest scene depicting a path that led into the darkness of thick trees; a dilapidated barn caught in a blizzard, disappearing into an icy grave; a vase of wilted irises. When she showed them to Lily, she had the sense that she could feel what Dolores had felt when she painted them - a grown-up version of the stomachaches she'd had as a child. The paintings had an eerie quality to them. Lily liked looking at them, but she was also relieved to turn away.

As the pit orchestra began its cacophonic tuning and warm-ups, Lily scanned the audience one last time, noticing some of the boys she'd dated over the past couple of years - Salvatore Domino, Kenneth Carpino, Pierre Beauchamp - boys who she'd gone out with simply because she couldn't bear to say no to anyone who asked, even though experience taught her that refusing had to be easier than going out on a date or two and then breaking up with them. Either way, you were bound to do something that would make them feel bad eventually. It all depended on whether you thought it was better to go on a date you didn't want, or not go on a date at all.

Lily scanned the audience twice, but she couldn't find the one face she looked for; she couldn't find the one face she longed to see, the one that belonged to a boy named James. Maybe he was just sitting too far back to be seen, or maybe he hadn't arrived yet. She closed the curtain. It was just as well. She might be a little less nervous if she pretended he wasn't watching.

Lily and James had met at Kiki's house the previous year. Kiki's parents were regular hosts of the weekly Living Youth meetings, sponsored by a regional Christian youth organization. Every Tuesday, a group of teens would meet at someone's house to have a sing-along, play games, and socialize. The evening would be topped off with a talk from one of the youth counselors, intended to help teach young adults how to deal with drugs, sex, and peer pressure in a way that "Honors self and Honors Christ". The irony was that after the meetings, the group would disband and then reorganize itself into various sub-groups that would go find somewhere to have sex or get stoned - except for the clique that Lily and James found themselves in. They ended up at Spangles ice cream parlor every week, where they played music on the jukebox and collectively scraped together enough money from pockets, backpacks, and purses to buy the minimum amount of ice cream required to keep from being kicked out for loitering. And since James was a year older, and the only one in the group with his own car - an Oldsmobile Delta 88 that could fit eight teenagers - at the end of the evening he would make the rounds and drop everyone back off at home.

Lily noticed after a few weeks that James would order the drop-offs so that she was the last one left. Initially, she was suspicious and defensive. Whenever a boy tried to work it out so that you were alone somewhere, it was inevitably because he wanted to try and get his hand up your shirt, or down your pants.

The first time she found herself alone with James in the car, Lily sat as far over into the passenger's side as she could. She kept her hand on the door handle and then as soon as the car stopped, she released the door and hopped out before saying a quick "thanks" and running into the house. But as the weeks passed, she relaxed into the thoughtful conversations they began to have along the way. She moved in closer, and let go of the door handle. Sometimes they would sit in Lily's driveway and talk for hours.

They talked about school, about faith, and about who they thought Jesus really was as opposed to who the counselors said He was.

"I think Jesus would hate Living Youth," said Lily. "He wouldn't waste his time sitting around singing 'Kumbayah.' He'd probably pack us up into an old Volkswagen bus and take us into the inner city to pass out ham and cheese sandwiches to the poor."

"Jesus would never eat a ham and cheese sandwich, Lily - he's Jewish! Anyway, you make him sound like a flower child," said James. "I think he would be more radical than that. Not in a violent way, but I think he'd get his own TV show - like *60 Minutes* - and he would expose those TV preachers and give all their money back to the people."

"So he's not a hippie, but he's a Robin Hood?" Lily giggled. "I wonder how he would feel about women's lib? I wonder if he would attend those bra-burning rallies."

"He'd be the one with the matches."

James spoke of the way he felt confined by the expectations of his father, who had planned his life out for him.

"He wants me to graduate from high school, take over the family auto shop, find a nice girl, get married, have babies," said James. "Every time I look at my dad, and I see the bags under his eyes, and the stiff way he walks... I just don't see any joy in him. It scares me to think I will end up living a joyless life, covered in motor oil."

"What do you want to do?" Lily asked.

"Math."

"Math?"

"Yea - I know it sounds sort of funny, but ever since I was a kid, I've had this thing for numbers. I love them. I love math problems - they're like puzzles to me. Puzzles that reveal a mystery when you solve them." With an air of decision, he added. "I want to teach Math."

"So teach Math." said Lily.

"It's not so easy," said James, rolling down the driver's side window, letting in a gush of cool autumn air. "No one in my family has ever been to college, and my father just doesn't see the point in it. He says, 'Why spend all that money on an education when you already have a decent, honest living waiting for you at the shop?' If I go away to school, he'll be really hurt, and I'm sure he won't help pay for it."

"All of my brothers and sisters have gone to college so far," said Lily. "And I know my father didn't help pay for any of them. Anyway, your decisions about your life can't be based on what your father wants. He'll get over it, you know?" It was difficult for Lily to imagine having a father who took enough interest in your life plans that he would even care if you stayed or if you went.

"He just seems so sad," said James. "I'd hate knowing that I'm responsible for that defeated look on his face."

"My dad has that look too," said Lily.

"Why, do you think?"

"Probably too many bills, too many children... too much work. And now with my mother going to school at night, his sacred dinner is always a crazy production, with her running out in the middle of it to get to class and him screaming at her about how women's lib is destroying our family." Lily paused. "The best thing I can do for them is get out of their way. Move out, become one less burden. And honestly? I can't wait to get away from them, away from the fighting. At least when I'm at college, I'll only have to take care of myself, which has got to be easier than this. I'll have enough credits to graduate next January, and I can't wait to get on with my life."

They sat quietly. James reached over and took Lily's hand. "I think you're a special person," he said.

Lily looked up at him. "Special in a short bus sort of a way?"

"Don't do that," he said.

"What? I was making a joke."

"No you weren't," he said. "You were refusing a compliment. Let's try that again."

James shifted his body so that he was directly facing Lily. Taking her chin in his fingertips, and tilting her head up so that her gaze met his, he repeated, "I think you're a special person."

314

Lily felt a burning in the back of her throat, as her eyes welled with tears.

"You're smart, a good listener, and by the way, you're very pretty."

Lily blushed, and cast her gaze downward.

"Now," continued James. "What do you say?"

Lily looked up at him again, finding sincerity and kindness in his warm brown eyes. Unlike any of the other boys she'd gone out with, James was her friend, someone with whom she had shared secrets and ice cream cones, and now they were sharing this moment, this quickened heartbeat, this space in which there was no auto shop, no dinner to cook, no shouting, no women's lib, no squelched dreams or horrifying memories. There was just the hand of a friend, and a longing to know what it would be like to kiss him.

"Thank you," she whispered.

They leaned in toward one another, and their first kiss unfolded as naturally and effortlessly as their conversation. Lily sighed and collapsed into his arms, all of her defenses down, all of her fears dissolving as James' lips parted hers, mingling breath and tongues and passion. James placed his palm on Lily's cheek, and slid it down the side of her neck. Lily's body ignited with desire and a soft groan escaped her throat.

At that moment, the flood lights outside the garage flashed on and off, on and off, which was Lily's father's code for, "You've been out there long enough. Stop whatever it is you're doing and come inside." *Great*, thought Lily. *Now they decide to start paying attention.*

The opening night of *Oklahoma!* marked the anniversary of that first kiss, but James had never asked Lily to go steady, and they had never exchanged the words, "I love you," even though the proclamation had been on the tip of Lily's tongue countless times. Maybe one of these days, she would find the courage to speak it.

The performance passed in a whirr of entrances and exits, songs and dances, cues, miscues, and last minute technical emergencies that are scripted into every high school production - like the corn field set piece that toppled over in the middle of a chorus number, making one of the dancers yelp and jump into the orchestra pit to avoid being hit, which caused the audience to break out into spontaneous laughter.

After the final curtain call, Mr. Howell took the stage, thanked the audience for their support and then announced the winner of the school achievement award for drama. "Please join me in congratulating Miss Lily Capotosti." The audience erupted into applause and came to their feet, led by a hooting and cheering Capotosti section. As Lily entered stage to accept her trophy, she became aware that this success would come with a price, and she watched the wings out of the corner of her eye as Kiki spun around and stomped away.

When Lily retreated to the hallway to greet her family after the show, she was met with cheers and hugs that were sweeter and more validating to her than any trophy. It seemed that a lifetime of familial obscurity had melted amid this outpouring of affection and congratulations, and for the first time in her life Lily felt that her family caught a glimpse of who she truly was, and they loved her for it. She could tell they were proud of her. She had finally found a way to be special.

Dolores took Lily by the hand and led her off to the side, away from the thick of the crowd of laughing and chatting performers and their families. She had a tissue wadded in her left fist, and dabbed at teary eyes.

"I had no idea you had such talent." said Dolores. "What are you doing about it?"

"What do you mean?" asked Lily. "I thought being in the play was 'doing something' about it."

"I mean, what are you *doing*?" said Dolores. "How are you developing your singing and acting? Are you entering pageants and taking private coaching? Are you out there getting some experience for your resume?"

"Um... no," said Lily, suddenly becoming self-conscious over the absence of a resume or anything resembling one. "I'm just doing the plays and stuff. I'm looking at colleges, but I haven't thought about where to apply yet." Between babysitting all summer and her hefty list of household tasks during the school year, there really hadn't been much time to think about or pursue such things, let alone figure out how to navigate or pay for them.

"Well, we're going to remedy that." Dolores was emphatic, and her voice cracked as a tear slipped down her cheek. "We're not going to let you go slip through the cracks. I would love to take you under my wing, Lily - and I know some people who can really help. How would that be? Would that be alright with you?" A timid smile crept across Dolores' lips, but it wasn't enough to cover over the sadness lurking behind her eyes.

Lily hardly knew Dolores, having seen her only on New Year's Eve and at the family reunions they used to have on the Fourth of July when Grandma Capotosti was still alive. She had always liked Dolores, and admired the graceful way she spoke and moved, yet she rarely saw her now when she wasn't either crying or on the verge of tears. Lily couldn't imagine how this weeping beauty with a storage closet filled with unsold paintings could help her in her performance career, but it was the best offer Lily had received. The only offer. Anyway, there was no way Lily could or would deny Dolores her hope, and she could not deny her own, regardless of how fantastic the idea seemed at that moment. Even this rickety bridge might be sufficient to carry Lily to her future. Perhaps it could bear the weight of their collective hopes and dreams.

So despite her skepticism, Lily's heart leapt at the prospect of having someone in her corner who cared about her, appreciated her, and claimed to have the means to help her - someone who could perhaps be for her what Auntie Rosa had been for Iris - a benefactor, a champion.

"Oh, Dolores," Lily replied, tears coming to her own eyes. "That'd be so great."

"Fabulous!" Dolores gave Lily an enthusiastic hug, and from the view over her shoulder, Lily saw James leaning up against the wall, one ankle crossed over the other, a single carnation in his hand and a smile on his face. It was a smile that never failed to melt Lily's heart.

Dolores released her embrace, and traced Lily's fixed gaze. "What in the world are you doing standing here with me?" She adjusted Lily's hair and pinched the flesh of her cheeks. "We'll talk soon - you go now."

"Thanks, Dolores," said Lily, already halfway across the hall.

As she approached him, James extended his arm and presented the flower to Lily.

"You were amazing," he said. "I mean *really* amazing." He didn't hug her or kiss her. She didn't expect him to - not with all those people standing around.

"Thanks," said Lily. She raised the flower toward her face, and recognized that in order to really smell a carnation, you had to stick your nose way down into it, almost like forcing the blossom to yield its beauty. The joy she felt in that moment, with the exhilaration of the performance, of her family's praise, of Dolores' offer of help, her long-stemmed carnation in her hand - made her want to shout her feelings out to him. Maybe she would. Soon.

They stood there, looking at each other, looking around the vestibule. Lily was hoping he would ask her to go out for a drive, or for a hot chocolate or something. She would have suggested it, except that he was the one with the car. And after all, he was the boy.

"So," he said. "You probably have a cast party or something to go to."

Lily couldn't tell if he was trying to discern whether she was available to go out, or if he was trying to avoid asking.

"Well, there is a party, but I don't think I want to go," said Lily. The drama crowd had divided itself into Lily supporters and Kiki supporters, and Lily didn't want anything to do with it. It was pointless and juvenile, and she didn't want to spoil the way she was feeling tonight by exposing herself to it.

"Wanna go grab something to eat?"

"I'd love to," she replied.

The fact that James was not committed in any way to take Lily places actually made the time they spent together a little sweeter. He could be anywhere, with any girl, and he chose to be here, with her.

Lily and James sat in their booth at Burger King, where she had a Whopper Jr. and a diet cola, and he had two double cheeseburgers, a chocolate milkshake, and an order of fries.

"Can I have a fry?" Lily asked, reaching toward the paper envelope on his tray.

"No!" said James, pulling the tray out of reach, and covering the fries protectively with his arm. "I offered to buy you some, but you said you didn't want any."

"C'mon -" Lily pleaded. "Let me have one. I didn't know I wanted them until I saw yours."

"Nope," said James, pointing his index finger at Lily. "You have to learn how to know what you want, and then say what you want."

"OK," said Lily. "I want to go for a drive." It wasn't *exactly* what she wanted, but the subtext was clear.

The good thing about having a family auto shop was that it was easy to park your car in the lot after hours without being discovered. Whenever they had tried to park in back of the school or along the fence by the airport, either some other couple would park next to them, or a policeman would drive by, roll down his window and shout out, "Let's move it along, kids." But parking behind the auto shop was quiet and private, and so isolated that Lily would never dare go there with any boy but James.

"Wanna go in the back seat?" said James, in between kisses. So far, Lily and James had only necked - nothing more; she was always afraid of getting caught. But as the months went on, the desire to go further with James was bolder than her fear and less tolerant than her patience.

They took turns climbing into the back, and lay down together on the bench seat. Lily felt James' mouth on her lips, on her neck, his hands first against the skin of her back and then against the skin of her breasts. She slid her fingers down his back, and over his firm behind which had been chiseled from the rigors of three

319

years of Varsity soccer. She glided her hand over his hip, bringing it to rest over his zipper. She could feel his erection, and his body flinched at her touch. Her desire ignited, but she didn't know what to do next. She hesitated.

James took her hand from the front of his pants, raised it to his mouth, and kissed it. "Maybe I should take you home now."

No, no NO, Lily thought. *I don't want to go home. I don't want to stop yet.* What would he think of her if she said those words out loud? What would he do? Like so many others, Lily's desire for James remained tucked safely inside, invulnerable to rejection and disappointment.

James drove Lily home and they sat in her driveway, talking until the flood lights flashed. Just as Lily was about to enter the house, James rolled down the car window and called her name. She walked over to him, expecting one last kiss. Instead, he reached into his jacket pocket, and handed her a French fry.

"Good night." He smiled.

Lily placed her carnation into a bud vase, and put it in the refrigerator. She wanted to keep it alive as long as possible, to keep this night alive as long as possible. She climbed the stairs to bed, exhausted from the day, still warm with arousal, still soaring from the admiration of her family, and newly excited about Dolores' proposition and where it might take her. She pulled the French fry from her pocket and slipped it under her pillow.

This must have been the way Cinderella felt when she slipped her foot into that glass slipper. Only this was better because it was real.

21. IRIS

"Ha!" Frances Jejune exclaimed, as she cool-handedly dunked the eight ball into the corner pocket, winning her third straight game.

"You rat!" Lily wailed, throwing her cue stick down on the pool table. "I stink at this, I'm going to have a sauna."

"Let's go swimming first," Iris suggested.

"Better not," Frances said. "My father has been coming to the pool every Friday afternoon." Mr. Jejune, a methodical man of French-Canadian descent, was an insurance broker, and had adopted the annoying habit of wrapping up work early on Fridays. "All I need is for him to catch me here. Especially since I'm still grounded. In theory. And we *are* supposed to be in school. In theory. Now that I think of it, check out the hallway, would you, Lily?"

Lily cracked the door open, sticking her head out just enough to scan the reception area and the corridor that led to the men's locker room. "*Oast-cay* is *ear-clay*!" she pronounced, in perfect Pig Latin. The three teenagers dashed across the hall to the ladies' locker room, where they changed into their bathing suits. Iris cranked up the thermostat in the sauna and they all stepped inside. She couldn't wait to soak up the heat that would obliterate, at least momentarily, the dismal climate she was growing to despise more with each passing year. The calendar said it was spring, convincing Iris to shed her winter coat and boots, but judging from the snow flurries that had been poking fun at her all afternoon, western New York had its own agenda.

Ever since Auntie Rosa and Uncle Alfred had moved into their townhouse at Valley Ranch, Iris had been coming to the clubhouse on free guest passes as frequently as possible, often bringing Lily along. Never before had the girls had access to such luxurious facilities: tennis courts, billiards and ping-pong, an exercise room, and a heated indoor pool and sauna which helped them through the long, cold winter. There was even a lounge to hang out in, and a fireplace to warm up the atmosphere around the conversation corner furnished with black couches upholstered in vinyl every bit as soft as real leather. Iris and Lily and their few friends whose families had membership to the Valley Manor Club sat there talking and flirting, until the bridge-playing blue-hairs arrived and chased them and their giggles away with dirty looks. The clubhouse lounge was a much more desirable place to hang out than Frank Domino's basement, especially because it came without Frank. Iris had finally found the courage to break up with him after he insisted on taking a walk in the snow one night, and had slobbered all over her despite Iris's resistance, leaving her with a face so chapped Lily asked her whether she and Frank had fallen asleep in a snow bank. An even more desirable feature than the absence of Frank, was the presence of Michael Jejune, Frances's older brother, who restored Iris's interest in the art of kissing. Michael was cute, made her laugh with his ironic sense of humor, and definitely knew how to put to good use the muscles and moves honed during his rigorous training as a member of the high school wrestling team. All in all, he was a good boyfriend. But sometimes he really ticked her off.

Like the previous Friday, when they had all been hanging out having a good time in the lounge, and Michael had said he was going to the bathroom, but Iris was sure he had sent some secret signal to his two buddies to follow him outside. In fact, as soon as he walked away, he was trailed by "Mouse," a slight boy with scrawny whiskers and beady eyes, and "Rat," a grubbier, tubbier version of Mouse, who wore tent-like T-shirts over his burgeoning beer belly, complemented by low-slung jeans that revealed his butt crack whenever he bent over, and sometimes even when he stood up straight. Or rather, slouched up straight. The belt loop of Rat's jeans sported a thick metal chain that disappeared into his front pocket; Iris sometimes wondered what was clipped to the other end, but she was afraid to ask, and focusing her attention on his pocket for the purpose of deeper speculation forced her into a territory that was too disagreeably intimate for comfort.

"Why do they do that?" Iris asked herself out loud, her temper stoked by the heat of the sauna, her blood boiling with resentment at Michael when she thought of the episode. It wasn't the first time he had made her feel excluded.

"Why does who do what?" Lily asked. She sat up on her bench, panting. Lily was always dying to go in the sauna, but always wanted to leave after two minutes. Iris wondered why she was always so restless, and could never just lie back and enjoy what few pleasures they could grab for themselves.

"Why do Michael and the boys exclude us when they sneak out back behind the clubhouse?" Iris said. She took a long, slow breath through her nose, enjoying the scent of redwood in her nostrils, and the searing sensation in her lungs each time she inhaled.

"They leave us out because we're girls," Frances said.

"As if we didn't know what they were doing out there," Iris said, her words floating out on a long, slow exhale.

"It pisses me off," Frances said.

"Me too," Iris agreed.

"So what's the *an-play*?" Lily asked. "We should do something about it."

"There's only one logical way to handle this," Iris said slowly. "I say we get some stuff of our own and see how it is. Who needs them?"

"Awesome. But where are we gonna get it?" asked Frances.

Iris sat up slowly; she and Lily exchanged glances.

"I *ink-thay* our *other-bray* has some *arajuana-may in his edroom-bay! Ots-lay of it!*" Lily said, giggling.

323

"Really? How do you know?" Frances said.

"Lily's right. Someone is definitely doing a lot of smoking in that room. And I'm not talking about cigarettes. We can even smell it from our room, but my parents never even notice the stink. Or at least, they pretend not to," said Iris. "There's only one way to find out what the guys like so much about pot, and that's by smoking it ourselves. And there's only one way to find out whether Henry's got a little to spare in his bedroom, and that's by going in for a look. *Ut's-whay the orst-way that can appen-hay?*"

"You can't be serious, Iris! You want to sneak into Henry's room?" Lily said.

Iris looked at Lily; worry clouded her sister's eyes, sweat streamed freely down her flushed face. "Don't' worry, Lily. He'll never catch us," she said. "Tomorrow's Saturday. He'll be playing guitar somewhere until late like he always does. I have to stick around and keep an eye on the boys so Mom and Dad can go see the usual movie neither one of them will like because neither one of them will let the other one pick. Everyone else will be out. Come and stay overnight, Frances. We'll organize a blitz!"

Iris was slightly shocked to hear herself devising a strategy to get her hands on some pot. But she had shocked herself with a lot of things lately. Like cutting chemistry class and hiking across the slushy field and through the supermarket parking lot to the clubhouse. Like the fantasies she had about Michael taking things one step further every time they made out. Like the way she had no desire to push him away when he did. Like the way she suddenly wanted more of everything new she tasted, and less of what she already had.

"I dunno, Iris. I don't like the idea." Lily stood too quickly, and seemed she would lose her balance as she walked out of the sauna, but Frances grabbed her arm as she followed her out, leaving the door ajar. Iris was disturbed by the damp, confused air of the locker room that insinuated itself into the sauna, shattering its warm, woody atmosphere with the smell of chlorine from the adjacent pool, the clanging of locker doors, and the voices of ladies discussing dinner menus and visits from grandchildren planned for the weekend, as they shouted to be heard over the high-pitched whirring of blow-dryers and the incessant running of water in the showers. Iris sat on the bench, her head hanging between her knees. She would slam the door shut and stay there until summer, if it wasn't for the prospect of meeting Michael in the lounge.

The following Saturday evening in the Capotosti kitchen started out as usual, with the smell of oil heating in the kettle, followed by the rat-a-tat-tatting and mouth-watering aroma of freshly made popcorn. Iris tipped the pot over a serving bowl, and the piping hot kernels tumbled down, piling up in a fluffy mound. Setting aside a bowl for herself and Lily and Frances, she sprinkled the popcorn generously with salt, while Lily mixed up two quarts of orange juice from frozen concentrate. She could hear the TV blaring in the living room; it was set on Channel 10, and there it would stay, no questions asked. Their mother and father had left the house for their Saturday evening date, the pitifully thin "On the Town" section of the evening newspaper tucked under their father's arm, as the two continued their debate over which movie to see. When their parents didn't go out, the kids' Saturday evening viewing, which kicked off with the series *All in the Family*, was sadly compromised, due to the fact that their father simply could not tolerate Archie Bunker. Iris suspected that he might recognize some of his own negative traits in Archie, and see in his TV son-in-law the nightmare of his precious Jasmine taking for a husband a man who did not meet his standards. That nightmare now had a name, an unpronounceable, Swedish name, and a ruddy Nordic face to go along with it, because Jasmine had recently married a veterinary student from Minnesota whom she had met at college, while volunteering at the local animal shelter. He worried that Jasmine might end up living way the hell over in Minnesota, though he had hardly batted an eye when the nineteen-year-old Violet, the first to marry just a year before Jasmine, had moved all the way down to Portsmouth, Virginia, where her husband Todd was stationed in the Coast Guard. Both weddings had taken place with little ado and even less budget; the same gowns were worn by both brides, the same Father Delaney performed the same quick ceremony at Sacred Family, and the same relatives on the Capotosti side (plus, of course, the groom's relatives) convened at the same Party House to fill their bellies with baked ziti and a choice of chicken or roast, and indulge in tiered wedding cakes topped with thick white icing and a statuette of a smiling couple. Iris and Lily clapped and cried at both receptions, when they saw their sisters dance with their father for the first time.

Frances opened the refrigerator and said "Can I have some milk?" to no one in particular, as she grabbed a plastic gallon jug from the top shelf, took a glass from the cupboard, and hoisted her big-boned frame onto the kitchen table. She filled the glass unceremoniously, downed its contents in a series of uninterrupted gulps that made her rather pronounced Adam's apple bob up and down vigorously, helped herself to two more refills, then used the back of her hand to wipe her mouth. "Man, you guys have the best milk," she said.

Until Iris had started spending time at her friend's house, she couldn't quite understand why Frances would get so excited about something as commonplace as milk. But Frances was right; a glass of fresh, cold milk could taste like the most delicious drink in the world, once you took a sip of the powdered milk the Jejunes drank at their house. Mrs. Jejune seemed uninspired to figure out a way to make the drink palatable. It was stirred up as needed, so as not to go to waste, and rarely chilled in the fridge. Clumps of the undissolved powder were encapsulated in bubbles which remained suspended in the solution, and burst in the mouth on contact, coating tongue and teeth in a chalky grit.

When the Capotostis ran out of fresh milk, their mother mixed up a batch of powdered milk in the blender, using cold tap water and ice cubes, and whipping it up until it was nice and frothy, adding a few drops of vanilla extract to enhance the aroma. She had a knack for baptizing the most commonplace foods with enticing names, thus her version of powdered milk was transformed into an exotic beverage dubbed "vanilla frappé," which was such a hit, it was often requested even when there was fresh milk in the refrigerator. Having been to the Jejune's house frequently to hang out with Frances and Michael, Iris couldn't help drawing a correlation between the lukewarm lumpiness of their powdered milk and other aspects of the household. With their calm mannerisms and unemotional tones of voice, Mr. and Mrs. Jejune themselves struck her as lukewarm and lumpy. Their recently built house, unlike the Capotosti homestead, was insulated with aluminum siding that didn't peel or fade; the interiors were tasteless but neat, and efficiently maintained. Furniture was dusted, rugs were vacuumed, lawns were mowed, leaves were raked and snow was shoveled, all according to the chore chart attached to the refrigerator with a magnet. Omissions of duty or improvisations in schedule were not tolerated under any circumstances, and infractions, however minor, did not cause shouting, only immediate grounding. All basic needs for food, shelter, and attention seemed to be met automatically, rendering unnecessary the butting of heads that occurred at Iris's house, but at the same time depriving Michael and Frances of the satisfaction of fighting for and obtaining one's just due, of the giddiness that comes with grabbing a bit more than one's share, and of the indescribable thrill that presages each onslaught of guilt.

"William!" Iris called out in the direction of the living room, "Popcorn's ready! Come and get it!" Fresh from their showers, William, Charles and Ricci appeared immediately to grab a bowlful of popcorn and a glass of juice, then disappeared just as quickly back into the living room. Earlier, she had been forced to order Ricci back to the bathroom after he had emerged, his head of curls still matted and wild, his body still reeking of baby B.O., a sign that he had adopted his old trick of running the shower full blast for a good five minutes while standing off to the side, fully clothed, doing God only knew what to pass the time, while clouds of steam filled the bathroom and fogged the mirrors.

Iris looked at Lily. Lily swallowed nervously, and looked at Frances. Frances grinned, and looked at Iris. "Now's the time,

327

ladies. It's just us and the boys, and they won't budge for awhile," Iris said. "Lily, grab a few sandwich bags from the cupboard, wouldya?"

Thus armed, Iris led the way up the stairs, closely followed by Frances, and Lily, several steps behind. They regrouped at the top, in front of the closed door that led to the bedroom Henry shared with Louis, and occasionally Alexander or John, when they were at loose ends between graduate programs, jobs, and girlfriends. Absolutely no one else was allowed in the room, save when it was necessary to retrieve something from the attic, a crawlspace under the eaves accessed by a small door on the far side of the room. Iris placed her hand on the doorknob, but withdrew it immediately, as if she had received an electrical shock. She rubbed her hands together, then tried again. She turned the knob and eased the door open, and a shaft of light from the stairway illuminated the chest of drawers standing against the opposite wall. She took a step forward, craning her neck to look around her in the semi-darkness to verify that no one had miraculously materialized in the empty room, that no silent body lay unpredictably in any of the three single beds that stood, deceptively monk-like, in a row against the wall.

"*O-say ar-fay, o-say ood-gay!*" she whispered to her two accomplices standing immobile at the doorway. "Frances, you watch our backs," she croaked, motioning for Lily to come into the room. Lily didn't budge. "Unless you prefer to stand guard, Lily," she said. Lily said nothing, just shook her head and walked toward Iris. An assortment of odd-looking pipes and a little metal scale cluttered the dresser-top; Iris pointed at the dresser drawers, indicating that their search should begin there. Each grabbing a knob, they slid open the first drawer; Lily kept turning to watch the door as Iris patted the stack of sloppily folded T-shirts, a jumble of unpaired socks, and a pile of frazzled cotton briefs. After easing the drawer back into place, they proceeded to open the second, which was crammed with winter sweaters. Iris probed the folds of scratchy wool with her fingers, but came up empty-handed. She signaled to Lily that they could close the drawer and move on to the bottom one, which refused to budge when they first tried to open it. When they tugged a bit harder, the drawer to grumbled and squeaked, then suddenly yielded to their efforts, causing them both to fall on their butts.

"Shhh!" Frances hissed from the doorway, as the two girls scrambled to their knees in front of the open drawer.

"Wow!" Iris said, her eyes widening at the sight of two black garbage bags. She pressed on them with her fingers, her heart beating quickly. "Either he's really into collecting autumn leaves for his scrapbook, or we just hit pay dirt!"

"What is it?" Frances called from her post.

"Keep it down!" Iris ordered. "But come and take a look!"

"Holy shit!" said Frances, peering into the drawer.

"Okay, girls, let's just fill up those little bags and *am-scray*!" Iris said.

"Maybe we should just get out of here, Iris! He'll find out for sure!" Lily said.

"We've already talked about this, Lily. What's he gonna do? Tell Dad?" Iris whispered. "Besides, no one will ever think it was me." Iris had recently begun to appreciate some of the fringe benefits of always sticking to the rules and doing what was expected of her.

"Exactly. Which is why they'll pin it on me," Lily said. "Even if it doesn't get to Dad, Henry could blame me! Then what?"

"I hardly think Henry would have the nerve to accuse you, of all people." Iris and Lily locked eyes for an instant, then Lily dropped hers to the floor. "Now let's get the job done and split," Iris said, carefully untying the knot in the garbage bag. "Get a whiff of this stuff!" she exclaimed, feigning expertise she did not have, unless you could count French kissing a guy who had just smoked a joint. She took a plastic bag from Lily's hand and stuffed it with the grass, ordering Lily to do the same. When they had filled six little bags, Iris tied a new knot in the black bag, fluffed it up so that its contents would not look depleted, though they had hardly made a dent in the stash, and closed the drawer. The girls backed out of the room silently, shut the door, and sprinted across to the room where Lily and Iris had first gone to bed as little girls, and between one fairy tale and another, somehow woken up as teenagers.

"What a killing!" Frances said. "What is your brother doing with so much pot?"

"Good question," Iris said.

"Maybe he's keeping it for someone," Lily said.

"Yeah, right. But that's none of our beeswax. What we don't know can't hurt us." Iris stared at the chubby little bags lined up on the bed. "You girls ready to give it a try?"

"I guess so, but how?" Lily asked.

"You have to roll it up in really thin paper," Frances said.

"Let me see what I can find," Iris said. She rummaged through her dresser drawers, rustled through the items crammed in the closet, and emerged with a smile, triumphantly waving a shoebox in the air. "Eureka!" she said. "Tissue paper!"

The threesome sat cross-legged on the bed and set to work. Lily cut the tissue paper into strips with pinking shears, the only scissors she could find in the sewing box, which gave the papers a fancy edging. Frances sprinkled the marijuana into the strips, which Iris rolled up into thick, sausage-like cigarettes, then carefully sealed them with tabs of Scotch tape. Lily stashed the leftover bags in a corner of the closet under a pile of dirty laundry, as Iris brushed wayward bits of grass and seeds off the blanket, then they filed out of the room and headed downstairs, each girl concealing a big fat joint in the palm of her hand.

Fingering the illicit substance gave Iris a thrill as she peeked into the living room to check on the boys, remembering not to neglect her babysitting duties. William was stretched out on the sofa with Ricci, Charles lay on the floor, belly down, chin resting on his clenched fists, the cat kneading the small of his back, preparing to settle in for a snooze. Their freshly scrubbed faces were bathed in cathode ray blue, their eyes glued to the TV screen, their popcorn bowls empty and juice glasses drained. Iris snatched a box of stick matches from the cabinet above the stove, and led the group across the back yard, and behind the chicken coop.

"I wonder if there's a trick to lighting them," Iris said.

"Let me try. I spied on Michael once from my bedroom window when he snuck out the back door," Frances said. "Give them to me, but I'll just light one for starters." Iris brought one lit match after another to Frances's cupped hands, but they were all snuffed out by the wind before the joint could catch. Finally, a plume of acrid smoke rose in the night air. Frances puffed on the joint several times to get it going, then inhaled once, long and deep, and held her breath.

"Why isn't she breathing?" Lily asked, a look of concern clouding her face.

Frances burst out laughing, exhaling the smoke. "Duh, that's how you're supposed to do it! You have to hold it in." Frances passed the joint to Iris.

"Shit, this stuff burns!" Iris gagged at the first puff.

"You have to hold it in, I said!" Frances repeated, as she took possession of the joint again. "Like this." She squinted her eyes as she sucked at the slow-burning tissue paper, for what seemed like endless minutes. She closed her eyes and held her breath for several seconds, before slowly exhaling the smoke. "Oh, man," she said, rolling her eyes.

"Geez, I thought you were never gonna come up for air!" Lily said.

"Now it's your turn," Frances said to her. "Remember, it's not a cigarette, Lily. You gotta hold it like this. You too, Iris." She held the joint up, clasped between her thumb and index finger for the other girls to see.

"Am I puffing right, Frances?" Lily asked.

"You're a natural, Lil. But you don't say 'puffing'. You 'toke' on a joint, or 'take a hit'. Remember that, or you'll sound so incredibly uncool."

"Thank you for your divine instruction, O Venerable Master of Future Potheads!" Iris said, giggling, as the joint completed another round. "I can't wait to see the look on Michael's face when he hears about this."

"I wonder what James would say if he knew. I don't think I'll tell him. Not yet, anyway."

"We gotta find a better solution than tissue paper, though," Frances said. "This tape stinks when it melts."

Lily swayed on her feet, and Iris put her arm around her, as they both slid to the cold, damp ground, their backs coming to rest against the wall of the chicken coop.

"Ah, the good old kitchen poop!" Lily laughed, blowing smoke into the air. "Always there when you need it."

"Hee-hee!" Iris shook with laughter. "Whaddya mean 'kitchen poop'? Are you stoned or something? This here's a chicken coop!"

"I never got a chicken from there. But I do seem to recall getting some poop." Lily took another deep draw on her joint and held her breath. Iris poked her in the ribs, causing her to exhale abruptly. "Ow, my throat! It burns! It burns!" Lily sputtered. "This shit can't be good for singers." Iris continued tickling her until the girls rolled to the ground, laughing until tears sprang to the corners of their eyes. Frances looked on, toking away until the joint was gone.

"How the hell did those apples trees get to be so goddamn tall?" Iris said, lying on her back, hugging her tummy to quell the spasms.

"Damn if I know!" Lily said. "They look so beautiful when they're naked like this, just branches with tiny leaves, with none of that wormy fruit falling all over the place."

"We should tell them." Iris rose to a squat, then pulled herself to her feet. She danced over to an apple tree and caressed its trunk. "You're freakin' beautiful!" she said.

"You are amazingly beautiful, too!" Lily sang, skipping across the lawn in the dark, stopping to hug each of the cherry trees.

Iris jetéed over to the peach tree, and pressed her lips against its dry bark. "Hey, even this tree kisses better than Frankie!" she squealed. Frances shuffled after Iris and Lily as the sisters stopped at each tree between the chicken coop and the garage, hugging and kissing them, stroking their bark with their hands and their egos with compliments, wishing them a good night. They eventually found themselves in the kitchen, gulping down humongous glasses of orange juice with ice to extinguish the burning in their throats, and tossing popcorn into each other's mouths. Canned laughter and pre-recorded applause drifted in from the living room, where the boys slumbered peacefully, exactly where Iris had left them.

Iris stood up and pounded the pedals in an effort to get enough traction on the slushy pavement to pump her way uphill, but the harder she pedaled, the more the bicycle slipped and slid. It was five-thirty in the morning, and she had exactly fifteen minutes before punching in for her shift at the new McDonald's across from Chili Plaza, where she was part of the breakfast crew. By six o'clock the early birds would already be trickling in for their take-away orders of hotcakes and bacon-and-egg sandwiches.

The thin nylon uniform she wore beneath her hooded windbreaker did little to prevent the early morning chill from penetrating her bones, but she was soon sweating from the exertion. Although it took a tremendous effort for Iris to climb out of bed, once she was up and running, she was happy to have a head start on the rest of the world. She always worked the same shift as Lynn, a pale, blond girl who lived with her divorced mother and smoked Kools. In the early morning hours, she and Lynn amused themselves by playing little games with the grim, grey-faced customers they served. Each time one approached the counter to croak out an order in a sleep-encrusted voice, the girls launched a competition to see who would be the first to elicit a smile. They had nicknames for all the regulars, and invented stories about their private lives, such as what they may have done the night before or what was on their agendas for the coming day, based on the way they looked and acted and dressed. Often customers still bore the impression left by the folds of a pillowcase on their faces when they walked in, which made Iris feel sorry for them, having to get up so early on such a nasty morning, even though she herself had gotten up earlier to serve them. Some men in suits and ties looked like they took themselves too seriously when they walked in the door, but when they got closer, and Iris saw the flecks of toothpaste on their ties, or the pieces of toilet paper stuck to razor nicks on their necks, she liked them better.

Iris was more disturbed by the procession of sad-faced women who squinted at the menu board hanging behind the cash registers, their eyelids at half-mast, weighed down by remnants of sleep, hastily applied gobs of eye makeup, and the stagnant air of resignation. Two of the saddest-looking women, regulars that the girls referred to as Morticia and Lucretia, invariably revealed lipstick-smeared incisors when they bared their teeth to order, suggesting that they had just returned from a feeding frenzy on the vampire circuit rather than from a night safely tucked away in their comfy suburban bedrooms. Iris wasn't crazy about her job, yet she considered herself fortunate to be behind the counter, with a future ahead of her, rather than in front of the counter, with her future behind her.

By nine o'clock, the first morning rush usually subsided, and the girls on the breakfast team were famished. No free food allowances were granted employees, but thanks to the strict enforcement of the restaurant's quality control policy, products had to be discarded after sitting under the warming lights for a certain number of minutes. So unless production was calculated perfectly to match the flow of customers who hurried in and out, frazzled by their tight morning schedules, there were always excess products at the end of a rush.

"I need to use the ladies' room," Iris called to the shift manager in the back, as Lynn nodded her agreement to cover for her. Lynn picked up a pen, and added a tally stick in the column on the daily waste sheet that corresponded to the egg-and-bacon sandwiches. Iris stealthily lifted a small Styrofoam box from the food bin and tucked it under her uniform, relishing its warmth against her tummy as she trotted off to the rest room. She didn't really mind having her breakfast in the toilet, except when a customer had just stopped in to take a dump, like today, leaving an unappetizing odor to battle for supremacy with the sickly sweet scent of the deodorant that was sprayed with remarkable zeal by the super-efficient cleaning crew. Iris locked herself in a stall, trying not to breathe through her nose as she sunk her teeth into the toasted English muffin, through the layers of melted cheese, Canadian bacon and fried egg, savoring the commingling of flavors and consistencies, imagining the nourishment rush to her bloodstream, replenishing her energy. It tasted divine.

It would be another long Monday, with school right after work. She had been attending the afternoon session at her overcrowded high school this year, which meant that her academic day started at twelve noon and ended at five. She had been lucky to switch to the morning shift at work, and was more than happy to avoid dinnertime duty at the French fry vat. Plus, Michael worked there too, in the evenings, and although she was crazy about him, she was secretly pleased to have conflicting schedules. As long as he worked at night, she would be spared the problem of always having to find excuses for why she couldn't see him. The truth was, she liked having time to read and study, and was determined to keep her grades up in the hopes of qualifying for a college scholarship. Meanwhile, she put in as many hours as she could, and had already saved up enough to buy the contact lenses that had finally freed her from the glasses she despised but could not see without, and was even able to make a small loan to Violet and Todd who were trying to scrape together a down payment for their first home.

Michael kept complimenting her on how great she looked without glasses, what a turn-on he got from the makeup she had started using to accentuate what he called her "cat eyes," and how much he liked the hot-looking feathered haircut she had splurged on at Sassy Scissors Salon. Although Iris hated spending money on something as useless and short-lived as a haircut, she had to admit the result looked more fashionable than the home-style cuts her mother used to give her back in the days when she had time for things other than writing papers and attending women's lib rallies. There was something else that had changed in Michael's attitude toward her ever since her pot-snatching escapade. He seemed intrigued by the spurt of boldness she had displayed, and judging by the way his petting had become more adventurous, he had evidently decided that Iris was not quite as saintly as she appeared to be. Iris was an avid learner, and she eagerly followed Michael's experienced lead, allowing his tongue to meander as it may, while one last thought was spent on poor Frank Domino, as she marveled at the miracle of a human organ performing so differently when placed in the mouths of different people.

After the girls' maiden trip behind the chicken coop, they had decided to share the remainder of the pilfered pot with the boys, who made enthusiastic pronouncements as to its quality and potency, not to mention the added feature of it having been obtained gratis. Frances was not crazy about sharing; she had gone hog-wild right from the start, puffing greedily on the makeshift reefer with the same intensity as she chugged down milk, and wanted to get high all the time. Lily, who complained of a sore throat and stomachache the next morning, said she couldn't see herself ever wanting to smoke pot again, and Iris only tried it a few more times, just to reinforce her capacity for decadent behavior, both to Michael and herself. She actually preferred the menthol-flavored buzz she got from the Kools she had started bumming from Lynn, which they smoked out by the trash cans at the end of their shift, before Iris pedaled back down the hill toward home, where she would hopefully have the time to shower the fast-food smell from her body before running for the school bus.

22. LILY

Lily flipped the round aluminum cake pan over onto the plate, and tapped the bottom of the pan all around with the butt end of a butter knife. Holding her breath, she lifted the pan off the plate, shimmying it gently, revealing a yellow cake coated with glaze, adorned with three pineapple rings and a large hole where the fourth one was supposed to be.

"Damn!" she said.

"What's wrong?" Iris asked.

"Stupid pineapple-upside down cake. I don't know why I even bother trying."

"I'm sure it will still taste great," said Iris, peeling the errant pineapple ring and accomplice chunk of cake from the bottom of the pan and pressing them into their intended spot.

"But now it looks like crap, and no one wants to eat an ugly cake. It's like that green cake I made on St. Patrick's Day."

"Nothing could look as bad as that cake." Iris laughed.

Iris had always been adventurous in the kitchen, enthusiastically cracking open the family's torn and stained copy of Betty Crocker's cookbook when it was her turn to make dinner - and sometimes even when it wasn't. Sometimes, she would get the urge to bake bread, or hot cross buns, or whip up Chicken à la King, just for fun. It was an urge Lily could not fathom.

"Who's cooking tonight?" was a question loaded with expectation. An answer of "Iris," brought everyone to the table with enthusiasm, while the answer "Lily," was often met with groans and jokes of "Where's the Pepto Bismol?"

Lily simply did not have Iris' artistic flair, nor her dedication for the exactitude required to beat egg whites until they peaked perfectly or roll out pie crust to a one-quarter inch thickness without having it crack or tear. Lily's patience often ran out before boiled corn syrup reached the hard ball stage, and she squirmed while stirring white sauce continuously watching for it to become "smooth and bubbly." Even the terms used to describe the particular stages of a recipe were subjective and vague. What exactly is "golden brown," or what is meant, precisely, by "smooth and bubbly"? Lily reasoned that if she had to measure out the ingredients with precision, then the recipe should at least be required to cooperate in a predictable, objective manner. Consequently, dishes never turned out exactly as they were supposed to and Lily was ever torn at the conflict between wanting to get it right, and wanting to just get it over with. Iris' culinary creations were picture-perfect, while Lily's inspired her to rename almost every dish she attempted, just to discourage judgment and criticism. "It's not Chicken Fricassee," she would say. "It's just chicken and dumplings."

To make matters worse, cooking and homework had to be done concurrently, and switching back and forth between the meat thermometer and the protractor made both tasks confusing and frustrating. It would be better to just do your trigonometry homework or make chicken with white sauce and peas. And actually, it would be best to do neither.

When Lily placed the cake on the table at the end of the meal, her father looked at it, looked at her, laughed, and said, "Well, how bad can it be? Let's serve it up."

Lily nervously watched her father as he shoveled forkfuls of cake into his mouth, washing them down with gulps of steaming hot coffee delivered by her mother, fresh from the drip pot, which was a cross between a coffee pot and a puzzle, its pieces snapping together into a tower so you could pour boiling water directly over a basket of coffee grounds, resulting in the strongest, hottest coffee possible. One word of praise would have eased Lily's anxiety, but in silence her father pushed the empty dish away, and then lit up a Parliament, the precise and predictable signal of the official end of dinner.

"What's the matter, Mom?" Lily asked her mother as they filed the dirty dinner dishes into the dishwasher. "You look sad."

Lily had always been able to tell when something was on her mother's mind. It may have been due to Lily's innate hypersensitivity - a trait that was her greatest asset as well as her greatest liability - rendering her helpless to distinguish between her own pain and that of others. Or it may simply have been Lily's acute awareness of the unrelenting demands of her mother's life, and the painfully solitary manner with which she bore them.

Lily remembered seeing her mother's college photo - the broad warm smile, the flowing waves of auburn hair, the reflection of hope and excitement in her eyes. But now, except for the thick mop of hair that still crowned her head, there was little more than a shadow of that college coed remaining. Her face was wrought with worry, her smile was wan, and the light of hope and excitement had been replaced by the smoke of exhausted resignation, like one of the worn out, threadbare washcloths that hung over the edge of the sink, barely held together by the strands of their fabric, waiting to mop up yet another mess.

Since Lily knew when something was weighing heavily on her mother's mind, she also knew that it was a situation that had been occurring with increasing frequency. For all of the countless times Lily had asked her mother, "What's wrong?" she never received a definitive answer, nor any clue about how she might help her mother find her way back to being happy.

"What?" Her mother's attention slowly returned from the Russian olive tree outside the kitchen window to the dishes she held in her hands.

"What's the matter?" Lily repeated. "You look sad. Are you thinking about something sad?"

Lily's mother looked at her, and shifted her gaze up and to the right, as if to review her most recent thoughts.

"I suppose I was," she said.

"What were you thinking about?" It was one of those questions children asked even though they knew the answer, and the purpose of which was to encourage an adult to admit an uncomfortable truth, such as that Santa Claus wasn't real or that babies were brought into the world by a means other than the pouch of a stork. They were the truths that seasoned the innocent and aged the wise.

Lily's mother opened her mouth and inhaled sharply, as if she were going to answer the question, but then she stopped, sighed, and replied dismissively, "I'm just tired."

"Go watch the news, Mom," Lily urged, taking the dishes from her mother's hands. "I'll finish up in here."

Cleaning up the kitchen was a chore from which everyone else ran, but that Lily didn't mind doing, and sometimes even enjoyed. Before dinner the house was chaotic; everyone was hungry and anxious and cranky and rushed. But afterwards, after everyone had eaten their fill and gone their separate ways for the evening, the kitchen was quiet and calm. Lily loved being with the humming refrigerator and the cool stove in their respite, the table cleared of forks and plates and stories and arguments, all the lights turned off except for the small one on the range hood. It was rather like observing a busy street corner in the middle of the night, seeing it stripped of its bustle, realizing that beneath all chaos abide layers of stillness and peace. It comforted Lily to place items back into cupboards, wash the table, sweep the floor, run the dishwasher, as if restoring order to the kitchen could somehow also settle her own restless spirit.

Lily's parents sat in the living room, just as they did every evening, she in the worn avocado-green recliner in the corner, he in his chair. The chair that only he was allowed to sit in. The chair in the center of the room. His place at the center of the universe.

They exchanged sections of the *Times-Union* with an incongruous civility.

"Are you done with the local section?"

"May I see the editorials?"

Lily's mother read the paper to learn about what was going on in the world and stay informed; her father read it to gather ammunition for his nightly rant in which he accused the women's movement of attempting to destroy America and God.

Lily sat listening at the kitchen table, occasionally stealing glances around the corner, frightened by her father's growing capacity for verbal cruelty, and maddened by her mother's refusal to attempt any sort of self-defense.

"Hey - Ms. Steinem," he said, placing special emphasis on the "Ms.", drawing out his "s" in mockery of the new title, the use of which was introduced and promoted by everyone he detested in the world. "Listen to this: 'In the case of General Electric versus Gilbert, the U.S. Supreme Court upheld women's rights to unemployment benefits during the last three months of pregnancy.'"

"Yes," replied Lily's mother, without looking up from her paper. "I read that earlier. It's an indication that they are not insisting on treating pregnancy as a disability. It's very interesting."

"It's very interesting," mocked Lily's father. "I'll tell you what's interesting. What's interesting is that any self-respecting man in his right mind would allow his pregnant wife to work in the first place."

"You don't see housewives laid up in bed every time they have a baby on the way. I always kept on cooking and cleaning and taking care of the other children right up until my water broke. Pregnancy isn't an illness, Carlo."

"You weren't working. You were home cooking and cleaning and taking care of the babies because that's exactly where you belonged - that's where all married women belong: at home, with their children, taking care of the household."

"And taking care of their husbands, who get to go out into the workplace and earn a living - whether they are expecting a new baby or not."

"That's right!" Lily's father shouted, as he crushed the newspaper into his lap. "Because that's the way God intended it." He glared at his wife, as if to challenge her to question the will of God.

341

Not one to pass on a dare, Lily's mother replied, "You mean that's the way men intended it."

Lily's father looked at her in disgusted disbelief, the downturned corners of his mouth contorting his face, as though he were on the verge of vomiting. His lit cigarette dangled from his lips, the long ash teetering precariously.

"You really do have rocks in your head, you know that?" He returned to the paper, snapping it back open in front of him. "Radical feminists. Her husband probably had to put a bag over her head just to get her pregnant." He snickered at his own joke, took a long draw on his Parliament and with the force of his anger held in his fingertips he crushed it out, pounding the butt into the ashtray, with such violence that the entire house seemed to shake.

"Hey, Iris - are you awake?"

"I am now," Iris drowsily replied.

"Sorry," said Lily. "American Woman" by The Guess Who played on the radio. Lily reached over and turned it down.

Iris lifted herself into a half-seated position, and rubbed the blur of new sleep from her eyes. "What's the matter?"

"I just wanted to ask you... what do you think about all the stuff Mom is doing - you know, women's liberation and everything?"

Iris tilted her head to one side and looked up toward the ceiling, as if she had never considered the issue until that moment, or perhaps had, and was retrieving the answer to a question that she had stored away because she never really expected anyone to ask for her opinion. "I dunno. In class Ms. Shue told us that society is going to be unbalanced for a while, until everyone gets used to new ideas about the role of women."

"But what do you think about it?"

"Well, I kind of get it. Ms. Shue says that women don't have equal opportunities and it's pioneers like Mom who are paving the way. I'm glad things are changing, but, well, I kind of wish Mom would stop sometimes. Just be our mother, and not make such a big deal about it."

342

"Yeah. Me too. I guess. I mean, I think it's good, but sometimes I wish someone else's mother could be the one paving the way, you know? I am just so sick of the yelling, and the way Dad picks on her all the time."

"Plus," said Iris, fluffing up her pillow and turning over onto her stomach. "I don't see William or Charles or Ricci taking any turns cooking dinner. We're women, too, me and you, you know?"

"It just seems so hopeless. Mom is never going to go back to the way she was. And Dad is never going to get used to her this way."

"So, they'll keep fighting. The good news is that we won't be here to listen to it much longer."

"I still have almost two years before I can move away to college. I don't think I can take two more years of this, but there is absolutely nothing I can do about it. I just don't have a choice. The thought of that makes me nuts. Makes me feel trapped. I just wish I could run away."

"I know what you mean. Sometimes I close my eyes, and pretend when I open them again, it will be five years from now and this will all be over, a part of my past. But it could be worse," said Iris. "We could be Mom. Or Dad. They have to put up with it for the rest of their lives."

"I am never gonna get stuck like they are." said Lily. "I'm not going to get married until I'm old - like at least twenty-seven. I want to go out and experience life first."

"So, you think you'll go to New York City and become an actress?"

"Maybe." Lily imagined herself striding confidently down Broadway, slipping in through the stage door at two in the afternoon, getting into makeup and costume for an evening performance. "Or Hollywood. I haven't decided if I want to be on stage or in the movies."

"I think you should just sing. Be on the radio."

"I know! I'll be on stage, in the movies *and* on the radio!" she laughed. "Why should I have to choose?"

"If you end up in California, I'll come and visit you every

summer, and you can visit me every Christmas."

"No!" Lily protested. "You have to come with me. We can get a house together, and we'll have wild parties on the weekends, and everyone will want to come over. And we'll have bonfires on the beach, and roast those coconut bread cubes like we used to do in Girls Scouts, remember?"

"Sounds like you've got the whole thing all planned out already."

"I do," replied Lily. "It is going to be so cool..."

"You're going to be very busy," Iris' voice began to drift. "You'd better get some sleep."

As the girls lay in silence, Iris' breath became deep and slow, drawing Lily into its rhythm, leading her to the edge of consciousness as "Dreamweaver" played on the radio.

"Dad, can I borrow the car tonight?" Louis shoved a forkful of potatoes into his mouth, and pushed his glasses back up his nose with a bandaged finger - one of many injuries he brought home from his tool and die apprenticeship. A nearly severed finger, a sliver of metal in an eyeball - he described each new gruesome injury with nonchalance, and with more than a hint of pride.

"Haven't you heard, Louis?" said Lily's father. "Your mother is a big women's libber now. She's got her independence, she's got her own car. Borrow *her* car - unless she needs it go to college and burn her bra." Lily's father looked at her mother, gauging her response, as if hoping to provoke a reaction. She simply speared green beans with her fork, and brought them to her lips with a barely perceptible hesitation. Apparently not satisfied that he had sufficiently agitated her, he added, "And just let her know if you ever want to borrow her penis, too."

Lily's face grew hot. She imagined herself picking up the glass butter dish and smashing it against the wall. She wanted to scream at her mother, "How can you just sit there? Why don't you say something?!"

"He can't use my car," said Lily's mother calmly. "I'm leaving."

"Where are you going?" demanded her father. "To one of your ugly lesbian meetings?"

"I'm leaving." she repeated.

"What do you mean you're leaving?"

"Just like it sounds, Carlo." Lily's mother finally looked up from her dinner plate. "I'm leaving you, Carlo. I can't take it anymore. I can't take your insults, I can't take your abuse. I can't stay here."

"Fuck this shit," said Henry. He shoved the last dinner roll into his mouth, got up from the table and stormed out to the garage, Louis on his heels.

Iris, Lily, William, Charles, and Ricci all froze in place, mouths full of potatoes and green beans and meat loaf, eyes volleying back and forth, carried on their parents' fearsome exchange.

"You're not going anywhere," said Lily's father, with a sneer. "You don't have a place to go, you don't have any money."

"I have a place to go. I'm going to stay with my friend Anita. And I have a job. I'll save up and get my own place soon."

"Save up? You're going to 'save up' for your own place? The money you make is for this house, to help me out - you're supposed to be making a contribution here, for a change. Your paycheck belongs right here, in this family."

Lily could see her mother's veins as they pulsated through the translucent skin of her temple, like tiny purple rivers coursing through a mountainside as viewed from an airplane. The tremor in her voice betrayed the facade of her physical calm.

"My paycheck will be in this family," she said. "But a part of this family will just be elsewhere. Away from you."

Lily's father pounded his fists on the table and raised himself to standing and with such force that his bench toppled over onto the floor with a thud, shaking the room and causing the children to jump in their seats.

"YOU are not going anywhere!" he screamed.

Lily and Iris grasped hands under the table. Ricci began to cry.

"You're scaring the children, Carlo."

"What do you care about the children?" Carlo screamed.

"You're leaving them!"

"I am not leaving them." A tear ran down her face. "I am leaving you."

Without saying another word, their mother got up from the table, strode out through the back door, stopping only to pick up her purse and sweater. Once her car was out of sight, the children all turned to look at their father who stood drop-jawed, his hands shoved into his pockets, jingling loose change.

23. IRIS

The smile withered and died on Iris's lips, as she registered the unequivocal reaction to her attempt at cordiality. After flipping her the bird and mouthing the two-word suggestion that traditionally accompanies the gesture, Michael Jejune turned his attention back to the batch of burgers sizzling on the grill. Iris was more grateful than ever that they rarely worked the same shift.

"Oh, boy. I guess he still really hates me," she muttered to Lily as they walked away, trays in hand. She sat down in the booth across from her sister and sipped soda through a straw, hoping the bubbly beverage would fizz away the lump that obstructed her throat. From where she sat, she could observe Michael's synchronized movements; she couldn't help admiring the way his muscles flexed with each quick gesture, or experiencing a pang of nostalgia for the feel of his well-sculpted arms around her.

"What exactly did you say to him, anyway?" Lily asked Iris. "You never told me."

"I told him that I still loved him, but didn't think we should keep going out."

"I bet he thought that made a lot of sense," Lily said.

"Not exactly," Iris said. "First he got really mad, then he accused me of having a crush on Peter Ponzio."

"Do you?"

"No!" Iris said. "I think Peter's cute, but I've never even really

347

talked to him. Then he wanted to know if I was mad because he wanted to go all the way the night of the junior prom."

Lily's hand stopped midway to her mouth, dangling a ketchup-laden French fry in the air. "*What?* Were you? I mean, *did you?* You never told me that, either!" A splotch of thick red condiment plopped to the table.

"No, on both counts. We were getting along fine in that department, believe me, with all the other tricks in his bag, if you get my drift, but that's all water under the bridge," Iris said. She lowered her eyes as she sipped from her straw, cleared her throat, and continued. "So then he said if I wasn't mad, and I still wanted to break up, I must think there was something wrong with him. I told him there was nothing wrong with him, and if anything, there was something wrong with me. Maybe there really is something wrong with me, Lily. Michael wasn't doing anything differently, he hasn't changed. It must be my fault."

"How could it be your fault?"

"I don't know, sometimes I feel like I'm detached from myself, watching my own body from a distance and wondering why that stranger named Iris is doing what she's doing. Like coming here at six every morning to sell breakfast to people who hate their lives, then attending boring classes all afternoon, then taking the bus back home. Sometimes, just before I walk in through the kitchen door, I catch a glimpse of you while you're setting the table, and I see you aren't putting down a plate at the last place on the left where Mom always sat. But you're still leaving an empty space there. Up until now, each time someone moved out, we were all happy for the extra elbow room, and we spread out the places a little bit more. But Mom's space just sits there during dinner, staring at us while we eat, and we don't know what to do with it. That's when my hand freezes on the knob, and I think about what it would be like to not open that door. To just turn around and run the other way, as fast as my legs can carry me. The impulse only lasts a second, because I see you there, and I hear Dad yelling at one of the boys. So I come in and start cooking like there's nothing else I would rather be doing, then afterwards we clean up as usual, then I do my homework and go to bed. But it's still not enough for anyone."

"It'll never be enough," Lily said. "No matter what we do. Dad's pissed so he yells. Only he can't yell at Mom so he just yells at anyone within range. And as we know, he has quite a range."

"Last night I got up for a glass of water. It was two o'clock, and I found Charles in the kitchen drinking a mug of warm milk. He said he couldn't sleep, poor kid. It broke my heart. That's why I want to keep things going. For them."

Routine, however mundane it may be, provided solace to all members of the Capotosti household, including Iris and Lily who, as the only females left at home, bore the brunt of its upkeep. They were the ones who saw to it that the groceries were bought each Saturday, that the dinners consisting of a meat and a starch and a green vegetable and dessert were prepared and served on time, that the floors were mopped, and the toilet bowls scrubbed. Auntie Rosa couldn't help much, between her nursing job, running her own house, and looking after Uncle Alfred. Plus, Dolores was staying with them again, only this time it didn't seem like a temporary "situation." As she struggled to get back on her feet after the annulment of her marriage to creepy Dr. Julius, who had run off to Toronto with an eyeglass salesman, she was "saved" by Dr. Bob, the psychiatrist who was treating her for depression. According to coffee talk Iris had overheard between her father and Auntie Rosa, Dr. Bob knew just what Dolores needed to blunt the pain, and in the meantime, had no qualms about sinking his talons into her trusting heart and holding on tight until he had squeezed out all the love and generosity she had to give. Then he just released her, and flew away, letting her crash to the ground, broken.

"Don't worry about Michael, Iris. He'll get over it. But it's too bad about our band. I guess it wasn't meant to be," Lily said.

"I know," Iris said. "I think Uncle Alfred was the most disappointed of all."

Despite their added duties, or perhaps because of them, Iris and Lily had thrown themselves into whatever artistic activities for which they could scrape up the time and resources, and under Uncle Alfred's urging and direction had formed what he dubbed a "rock band," though nothing they played seemed nearly rebellious enough to fit the bill. It was around that time when Iris had felt herself withdrawing from Michael, and hoped that by doing something fun together besides making out, her interest in him would be rekindled. It was decided that Michael would play lead guitar, while she played the bass. Rat took a shot at playing rhythm, and Mouse was provided with a tambourine and maracas for percussion. It went without saying that Lily, with her sassy voice that smacked of burnt sugar, would be the lead singer. Things soured one evening during rehearsal at Uncle Alfred's studio, just as they were beginning to master a halfway decent rendition of the first song in their repertoire, "Crocodile Rock." Both Rat and Mouse had developed not-so-secret crushes on Lily, and began battling out their quest for dominance on their instruments. The result was a cacophony of buzzing barré chords (Rat could not for the life of him get his sausage-like fingers to produce a clean sound), and a mad jangling and rattling that drowned out everyone else, including Lily, who was horrified that either could entertain thoughts of ever becoming her boyfriend.

"*BASTA!*" Lily screamed into the microphone, quoting a much-used interjection of Grandma Capotosti's, God rest her soul, that never failed to silence quarreling youngsters. "I've had enough of you two! You're just a couple of big babies!"

At that point, all three guys stormed off in a hormonal huff, no doubt to get high, leading the girls to conclude that the only men who could possibly nurture their talents must be of ambiguous sexuality. Like their own mild-mannered Uncle Alfred; or the effeminate Mr. Howell, the red-headed, freckle-faced high school chorus and drama teacher; or the Parisian-born Monsieur Debonnet, who bourréed across the room to peck Dolores playfully on both cheeks whenever she stopped by to pick the girls up from their advanced level ballet lesson.

Iris scratched the waxy coating of the paper cup with the nail of her index finger, took another sip from the straw, dipped a cold French fry into a pool of ketchup on a hamburger wrapper, and nibbled on it pensively. She looked up at Lily and said, "You were great in *Oklahoma!*"

"What made you think of that now?" Lily asked. "That was eons ago."

"I always think of it," Iris replied. "You should have had the lead. You were the best. You even won the award."

Lily dabbled a cold fry in the pool of ketchup, but did not bring it to her mouth. Instead, she used it doodle different versions of the letter J on the burger wrapper.

"You captivated the audience when you sang, "I Cain't Say No." You turned Annie into the cutest, funniest character of all, and you lit up the whole stage with your presence. It was so magical. Just like when you sang 'Starry Starry Night' at that talent show in Syracuse; it made chills run up and down my spine. You were the best that time, too, but you got robbed of the prize, that's all. What do those hicks know about real talent?"

"It was 'Vincent,'" Lily said.

"Vincent who?" Iris said.

"That song. That's the real title. It's about Vincent van Gogh. He's Dolores's favorite artist. She showed me a book she has about him. Did you know he did a painting called 'Irises'?"

"Really? How cool."

"It's beautiful. But what a troubled life. I wonder if all artists have to suffer so much and die young to be remembered."

"No, not all do, Lily. Plus, he didn't die young. He killed himself. It's not exactly the same thing. You'll be successful. And happy. You have everything going for you."

"You think so, Iris?"

"I know so, Lily."

"Then I can't wait!"

"Me neither! I haven't forgotten about that house you promised to buy us in California!"

Lily tossed her mane of thick hair like a wild mare preparing to break into a gallop, and laughed. Besides Lily's singing voice, there wasn't a sound more beautiful to Iris than her sister's throaty laugh, especially since she heard it so rarely of late. Her heart bubbled over with emotions as she observed Lily: pride for her talent, excitement for the adventures she would soon embark upon, hope for success, admiration for her physical beauty. Iris also felt a slight twitch of envy; from the scrawny, buck-toothed little girl that couldn't kick her thumb-sucking habit, Lily had indeed developed into a very attractive teenager. Unlike herself, who had sprouted only vertically, shooting past a height of five-feet-seven, Lily remained of petite stature, while the rest of her body had budded to perfect proportions. The same halter tops whose cups sagged with disappointment when draped across the flat expanse of Iris's chest were filled with firm, fleshy curves when Lily wore them. Like waves of golden wheat, her thick hair parted to reveal clear, grey-green eyes whose look of misplaced innocence contradicted the unexpectedly proud features bestowed upon her face by her Capotosti ancestry.

At times, Iris sensed she was uncannily attuned to every detail of her surroundings, and stricken with the premonition that a certain precise moment in her life would remain forever etched in her memory. This was one such moment, a sensory snapshot of a fleeting instant when each element was in sharp focus: the jangling of the cash registers, the called orders of the crew, the screeching of children and laughter of teenagers, the clipped conversations of adults between bites of burgers, the anticipatory looks of gratification on neon-lit faces as laden trays were carried to tables; the smell of meat sizzling on grills, and oil bubbling in vats, and coffee simmering on burners; the post-prandial patina of fast-food grease that coated the roof of her mouth, the last sip of watery Coke and ice gurgling to her tongue as she sucked her straw; the feelings of regret and guilt stirred up by Michael's gesture; the multifaceted sparkle in Lily's eyes that bespoke the hope that had been kindled in her soul; her heartfelt wish that Lily's dreams would be made of diamonds, and not glass.

"Let's get going," Iris said, snapping out of her reverie. "We still have to clean the house."

"Let's not and say we did," Lily said, lifting herself unenthusiastically from the booth.

"Come on, we'll make it fun," Iris said. "No one will be around - we can put on *Jesus Christ Superstar*. By the time we're done singing through both albums, the house will be clean."

"Only if I get to sing the part of Mary Magdalene." Lily said. "And Jesus."

"Oh, sure, and I get to ridicule, condemn and betray Jesus Christ. Great."

The most popular fast-food restaurant in the town of Chili remained an important point of reference for Iris, and when school broke for summer that year, she requested to stay on the breakfast crew. She enjoyed riding her bike to work in the cool, early morning hours, and she sometimes took a longer route home at the end of her shift before tackling her daily housework and summer assignments. She was determined to get credit for an extra year of French as part of her plan to graduate early and work full time to earn money for college. She loved the French language, and studying was more pleasure than work. Learning the correct conjugation of verbs and expanding her vocabulary satisfied Iris's desire for order and improvement; training her lips and tongue to deliver properly pronounced phrases gave her such immense joy, she sometimes laughed aloud when she heard herself. She practiced at every opportunity, provided no other ears were within range. *"Je vais nettoyer cette maison!"* she repeated, her voice muffled by the whirr of the vacuum cleaner. *"Ma mère habite à Paris mais ma soeur habite à Lyon!"* she revealed to the washing machine in the basement. *"Quelle merveille! La pluit c'est très fraîche!"* her upturned face exclaimed to the shower. *"Comment vous êtes drôle, Monsieur! Je ne peux pas venir à Cannes avec vous! Je doit me lever à cinq heures!"* she informed the inside of her closet, where she spotted her neglected blue valise gathering dust, as she gathered the dirty laundry.

Iris was already toying with the idea of taking some time off to read that afternoon as she walked to the back parking lot, where she always left her bicycle. She had enjoyed studying Jane Austen in English Literature class, and had decided to read *Sense and Sensibility* on her own. She was quite taken with the Dashwood sisters and imagined herself and Lily in the shoes of Elinor and Marianne. Maybe things hadn't changed much for women in the last two centuries, after all. Maybe what her mother was doing made sense. She just wished she didn't have to pay for it in person.

It was a hot day, and with the sun already high in the sky, Iris decided to ride straight home and change out of the synthetic uniform that made her feel sweaty and sticky as soon as she walked out of the air conditioned restaurant. She hopped on her bike, and began pedaling across the parking lot to the exit.

"Excuse me, miss!" a male voice called out. Iris turned her head, but didn't see anyone. "Yes, you! Over here!" She spun her head around again, nearly losing her balance before turning the bike in the direction of the voice. A guy was standing behind the open door of a blue Plymouth Valiant, waving a hand in the air.

"Can I help you?" Even though she had already punched out, Iris was still in her uniform, and still on McDonald's premises. She felt a duty to go see if the man needed some sort of assistance.

"That's what you said to me ten minutes ago, when you served me this!" The man stepped from behind the car door, hands in the air, one of which gripped a large drink cup. The front of his shirt was dripping with chocolate milkshake.

"Oh, my goodness!" Iris said, backpedaling to a stop as she pulled up next to him. The spill must have been her fault; she was aware of her bad habit of snapping the drink lids hurriedly in place when she was in a rush. She vaguely remembered the blue and white polo shirt standing across from her, while she counted out the guy's change and the minutes until quitting time, anxious to leave before Michael took up his station at the grill and the lunch customers started pouring in.

"I was still thinking about your smile, and the way you said 'Have a nice day!' when I got to my car. I squeezed the cup so hard, the lid popped off, and this is the result!" He looked down at his chest, shaking his head.

"I'm so sorry, maybe it wasn't sealed properly." Iris felt bad, but she didn't know what to do. She hoped he wouldn't report her to the manager. She wondered whether it would sound too weird if she suggested he take his shirt off and give it to her so she could take it home and wash it. "Please forgive me."

"Who am I to withhold forgiveness?" The guy looked up and, fortunately, smiled at her. He looked younger than she had first thought, maybe just out of college. It was probably his neatly groomed, slightly geeky appearance and his unfashionable glasses that aged him beyond his years. "I like to think this was all part of a plan," he said. "Thank you for saying 'have a nice day' like that."

"Sure," Iris said, presuming that meant she was off the hook and free to go.

"I guess I'd better go change," the guy said, smiling as he got into his car.

"I guess." Iris smiled back. Before she could catch herself, she said, "Have a nice day." She said it to everyone.

Five take-out cheeseburgers and chocolate milkshakes later, the same young man extended his hand to shake that of Iris's father. "Rick Rotula, sir!" he said the first time he set foot in the kitchen at Chestnut Crest.

"Nice to meet you," her father replied, pumping Rick's hand enthusiastically. "Nice grip."

"Thanks, sir. Tennis."

Iris had no doubt that her father would approve. For a start, Rick was of Italian extraction, as suggested by his olive complexion and dark hair, and confirmed by his surname. As it transpired between one over-the-counter order and another, together with an invitation to see the new show at the planetarium, Rick was a few years older than Iris, in his junior year at a nearby Christian college, where he majored in sociology, and held a summer job at the eyeglass factory. He lived in their old neighborhood in the city with his mother, a nurse who worked the night shift at the city's insane asylum. When Iris was a child, and the Capotostis drove by the red brick building, they all craned their necks out the car window to look at the barred windows of the "loony bin," fantasizing aloud about wild-eyed inmates chained to the beds, frothing at the mouth, emitting blood-curdling screams as orderlies restrained them and nurses injected them with powerful sedatives through foot-long syringes, before power-saw wielding surgeons with the sadistic grins of serial killers performed lobotomies on them. Iris wondered what kind of woman would want to work in such a place. At night, no less.

The date at the planetarium did not go quite as planned; there were no seats available, so Rick proposed to go bowling instead. Although Iris rarely broke a hundred and was shy about how she would perform, she went along with the idea, and was fairly satisfied at dropping only five gutter balls. Afterwards, they drove to the frozen custard stand by the airport, then went to park by a few other cars in the spot where families sometimes stopped to watch the planes taking off and landing by day, and, with the same pretext, couples parked to neck by night. When they finished their custards, Rick turned to Iris and said, "I'd like to show you something."

"Sure," Iris said, not knowing what to expect, but curious to find out. "What?"

"Something I invented." Rick said, drawing her close, then bending her backwards to place his mouth on hers. His lips were ice cold on contact, and as he pushed his tongue into her mouth, the taste of the chocolate custard he had licked off his cone with remarkable avidity contaminated the purity of the delicate vanilla flavor Iris had been savoring. Rick's tongue darted around the inside of her mouth, slipping and sliding over teeth and gums like a lizard trying to scramble its way out of a glass jar, then came abruptly to a halt. Rick cradled her head in the palm of an open hand, and gripped her jawbone with the other. Pressing his mouth firmly over hers, he inhaled and exhaled through his nose, constraining her to do the same if she wanted to breathe at all. She wouldn't have minded him kissing her, was in fact expecting it, but was disturbed by the forced intimacy of breathing together. His nostrils flared with each deep intake of breath, then flattened as he exhaled through his nose into hers. He thrust his tongue deeper and deeper into her throat, pushing the slippery organ back and forth rhythmically, cutting her lips with his teeth as he battered her mouth with his.

Iris was wondering how to wrestle herself out of the stranglehold, when Rick abruptly detached his mouth from hers, grabbed her by the shoulders and pushed her away.

"Forgive us!" he cried, holding her at an arm's length.

Iris gulped for air. Perhaps it was the lack of oxygen, but she was feeling confused. What was he talking about? Why was he speaking in the plural? Was he schizophrenic, like one of his mother's mental patients?

"Please, please forgive us!" he croaked again in a hoarse voice, as he clasped her hands in his, and raised them to the roof of the car. They were both panting from the exertion of the intense kissing exercise, chests heaving, hearts pounding wildly. Now that she could finally breathe again, all Iris wanted was to extricate herself from his grip, and regain control of all her body parts.

"Thank you!" Rick's words crumbled under the strain of emotion, as he bowed his head, letting their four arms drop to his lap. Iris was moved by his capacity for passion, flattered that he would apologize for being a bit rough, touched that he would thank her for letting him kiss her.

He continued to hold her hands, finally relaxing his grip as he looked into her eyes and said, "Let us both give thanks, Iris. We were led to temptation, but the power of our Lord and Savior has prevailed. He has driven Satan away. And we are forgiven."

Iris looked into Rick's eyes, focusing first on one, then the other. The twin wells of darkness were on the brink of overflowing. The whining engines of a plane coming in for a landing made the car vibrate, as flashing lights reflected in its windows and in Rick's eyes, which flickered eerily in the darkness.

Although her first encounter with Rick Rotula left Iris feeling rather uneasy, the more she thought about it, the more impressed she was by his maturity and flattered by the respect he showed toward her. She had never gone all the way yet, and had been slightly worried that Rick, already a college man, would want too much from her, too soon. She was relieved when, after a few more dates, it became apparent that her virtue would not be tested beyond the limits of the reasonably well-behaved Catholic girl she considered herself to be. Iris still went to Mass every week, as everyone who lived under her father's roof must, and silently recited little prayers whenever she needed a special favor from God or a boost from the Madonna to make it through the day. She could probably learn a lot more about being a good Christian from Rick, who involved Jesus in every single aspect of his life. He prayed frequently when they were together, suddenly bowing his head or raising his arms to praise the Lord for the beautiful day, even if it was raining, or to ask for His guidance when they took a wrong turn while driving through an unfamiliar part of town, or scoured the jammed parking lot by the movie theater for a good spot.

Rick soon developed the habit of stopping off at Chestnut Crest on his way to work at the eyeglass factory, where his shift started at six in the morning, at the same time Iris punched in for her daily tour of duty on the breakfast crew. After letting himself in through the unlocked kitchen door, he would deposit his lunch bag and a freshly cut flower in the fridge, then slip away as quietly as he had entered, to return at exactly twelve noon to consume his lunch and visit with Iris for fifteen minutes before returning to the job.

Knowing Rick would be arriving shortly after she did injected energy into Iris's tired legs as she pedaled home from work. The first thing she did when she walked in the door was open the refrigerator. The sight of a flower waiting for her always made her smile; today it was a yellow rose edged in pink that peeked out from the second shelf. The rose sat atop a brown lunch bag, creased from reuse, whose contents never varied: a slice of American cheese sandwiched between two slices of white bread spread thick with mayonnaise, and a shiny red Macintosh apple. Though she never mentioned it, she found it slightly depressing that a college man would eat the same boring lunch that she had packed for herself every day during grammar school. She picked up the rose and held it to her nose, closing her eyes to fully appreciate the scent of the full bloom, but was disappointed to find it smelled more like leftovers than rose. When she opened them again, she was startled by the sight of a big black bug nestled in the flower. She let out a yelp, and shook the rose by its stem until the bug fell to the floor in a shower of petals. She squashed the bug with her foot then plucked the previous day's already withered white rose from a bud vase on the counter, and replaced it with the fresh rose, yelping again when she pricked her finger on a thorn. *"Non c'è rosa senza spine,"* she heard Grandma Capotosti whisper in her ear, suddenly missing the interjections of Old World wisdom the woman had always been ready to offer on every occasion, as she sucked the droplet of blood from her finger. Grandma was right, all roses had thorns, but wouldn't it be nice, just for once, to find one that didn't?

Glancing at the kitchen clock, Iris realized there was no time to waste on old Italian maxims; Rick would be arriving in exactly five minutes. She wished she had time to jump into the shower to scrub away the odors of the fried bacon and sausages and eggs and coffee in which she had been steeping all morning, but she also wanted to get rid of the pile of laundry which, although washed and tumbled dry, still looked unseemly sitting there on the kitchen table. She contented herself with quickly changing out of her uniform and into a pair of cutoff denim shorts and a smock top. She was folding a pair of her father's faded blue boxer shorts when Rick appeared at the kitchen door. He froze on the threshold when he saw her.

"Oh, my Lord. Thank you for this vision," he said, bowing his head and closing his eyes. After reopening them, he stood still for a few seconds longer, staring at her. "Iris, you look so beautiful like that. So exquisitely feminine. I can already see you, tending to a family of your own." He paused for a second, then grinned. "Of *our* own."

Iris blushed at what she took to be a compliment, and at the rather premature allusion to the future of their budding relationship. "Thanks for the rose," she said. "The one you brought today was just gorgeous." No sense telling him about the bug, it would only make him feel bad.

Rick walked over to her, kissed her on the top of her head and said, "Oh, yummy. You smell like an Egg McMuffin." The changes in his tone of voice and in the curve of his smile were barely perceptible, but Iris was sure they were there, unless of course it was just her, being overly sensitive as usual. She blushed, and was still trying to decide whether to laugh at the remark although it had embarrassed her, when Rick turned away to retrieve his lunch bag from the fridge and sat down at the table. "That's absolutely amazing," he said, between bites of his sandwich, his eyes once again soft with admiration, as he watched Iris continue to hand-press boxer's shorts.

"I picked it up from Auntie Rosa," Iris said, glad the conversation was shifting from how bad she smelled to how well she could do something.

"Now *that's* a woman who knows how to set an example," he said, wiping a gob of mayonnaise from his chin with a finger, then licking it. He and Auntie Rosa had hit if off right away, which was no surprise. Everyone loved Auntie Rosa, and she loved everyone.

Rick was making Iris nervous, sitting there on the bench, watching her every move and chewing his sandwich in slow motion. She was puzzled by the sense of relief that washed over her when he finally left, and wondered how it could be that the fantasy of being with someone you really liked, possibly even loved, could be so much more delightful than actually being together. Even as this thought flitted across her field of reason, she found herself looking forward to that very same evening, when she would be seeing Rick again.

"Great, you're back!" Lily said ten minutes later, as she trudged up from the basement and into the kitchen, where she dumped another load of freshly laundered clothes onto the table for folding. "Ricci is down there talking to himself, or rather I should say, playing with those 'friends' he's been inventing," she said. "William and Charles are out behind the chicken coop with a couple of neighborhood kids horsing around on that slippery slide thing Dad made for them. Either that or trying to set the chicken coop on fire like they did last week."

When Jasmine had gone away to college, her pony had been traded to a local contractor in partial exchange for aluminum siding, which Iris hated, but which put an end to her father constantly cursing the peeling paint. Since then, the chicken coop had been sliding back into its original state of abandonment, and the area behind it cleared of manure. Out in the farthest corner of the yard, Henry had strung a hammock from the limbs of two shady oak trees, a good ten feet off the ground. He sometimes climbed up there at night with his guitar and a joint or two, and occasionally even slept there, despite its height from the ground. During the day, the hammock was usually free, and Iris loved going there to read. Climbing the tree and hopping onto the hammock was tricky, and she had even fallen out once, landing flat on her tailbone, and gotten the wind knocked out of her. But the privacy and solitude of the perch were not to be found anywhere else on the property, indoors or out, making it well worth the risk.

"Looks like there will be nine of us for dinner again, unless someone invites someone else to stay," Lily concluded her report. John was home for a visit, having just finished his third year of medical school; Henry was still drifting between day jobs and girlfriends; Louis spent his evenings tinkering in the basement, working on a secret invention he was sure would make him rich. The only ones who left home and never came back were the girls.

"OK, thanks, you can go. I'll take over from here," Iris said, her hands delving into the pile of laundry, while her mind conjured up dinner ideas. She disliked planning menus in advance, preferring to keep the shelves of the pantry stocked with basic ingredients, and deciding what to cook according to her mood and how much time she had available to spend in the kitchen. A horn honked twice, and Lily headed for the door.

"Don't do anything I wouldn't do!" Iris called after her. It wasn't necessary for Lily to specify who was picking her up; it was obvious by the sparkle in her eye and the spring in her step that the car in the driveway was James Gentile's Oldsmobile. Iris could totally understand Lily's attraction; she and James had been in the same trigonometry class, and Iris knew he was a bright student. On top of that, he had a solid, athletic build, without looking aggressive like most football players, and a lost puppy-dog look in his eyes that would make any girl want to cuddle him and rescue him from the potential dangers of a cold, cruel world.

Lily seemed to think Rick was pretty nice, too, though Iris had never shared with her sister what had happened on their first date. It wasn't that she wanted to hide it from Lily, she just wasn't quite sure how to translate into words the potpourri of sensations she had experienced during that weird kissing session: arousal, disappointment, embarrassment, confusion. At times, she wondered whether she may even have imagined the whole incident. She had figured the best thing to do would be to classify the airport escapade as a trial run, and file it away in the cabinet of experience.

And now that Iris was pretty sure she was falling in love with Rick, she found herself more prone to think of the future, rather than the past. The more time she spent with him, the more she found him attractive. Years of tennis playing had shaped his well-coordinated form, which was lean and strong, as opposed to Michael's block-and-tackle physique. He was also older and more mature than the boys at high school, and took a protective interest in her and her family. He was particularly attuned to the needs of her father and younger brothers, and often engaged in conversations with them. Once, he had come to pick her up for a date, and spontaneously invited the boys along. They had all piled into the car and gone to the County Fair, where he bought everyone cotton candy and paid for rides on the Ferris wheel.

But what delighted Iris most was his romantic side; the flowers he brought her every day were just one example. Not long after they had met, he had even presented her with a cassette tape of a song he had composed and played for her on the piano. Whenever she managed to sneak in a few minutes' quiet time in her room, she would lie on her bed with her eyes closed and the portable cassette player on her tummy. At the sound of the first sweet notes, her imagination swept her away to a grassy meadow filled with wildflowers and butterflies, where she could feel the tepid sunshine kissing her face, a soft breeze tousling her hair. As the song's intensity escalated with a crescendo of passionate chords, Rick burst into her fantasy. He ran toward her in the meadow with outstretched arms, and she flew into his embrace. When the tape ended, she rewound it so it would be ready for her next break from reality, then returned to her duties of cleaning and cooking and breaking up fights with renewed energy.

Iris served the dinner right on time that evening, then sat in silence as she witnessed its unceremonious ingestion by greedy male mouths amid the bumping of elbows and spilling of milk and sharing of bread and banter. No one seemed to appreciate that she had rolled up the meat loaf with a special Swiss cheese and spinach filling, or that the potatoes had been baked not once, but twice, after the pulp had been mashed up with butter and seasonings, and spooned back in the skins again. Lily had called earlier to say that James had invited her to stay out and have a pizza, which meant she would not be home to help clean up after dinner. Iris had told her not to worry and enjoy herself, but that meant she would have to get the dishes done in a jiffy. Thinking about her upcoming date, Iris had been unable to eat a thing, but knowing her father insisted on seeing the whole family gathered at the table for dinner, she did not want draw any attention to herself by asking to be excused. She prayed to God that it would be over with soon, and willed her brothers and father to accelerate their mastication, fill their bellies and get the heck out of the kitchen.

363

At last, her father downed his last sip of coffee and snubbed out his cigarette, and complimented her on the delicious dinner, which buoyed her spirits as she tidied up, and made her feel not all her efforts were in vain. When she finished, she rushed upstairs to the bedroom Iris and Lily had taken over when the older girls moved out of the house. The bedroom was larger than their old one, and faced south, like the sunroom over which it was positioned. The room had three single beds, a more favorable accommodation than one double bed, now that Iris and Lily preferred to fall asleep embracing fantasies of their boyfriends, rather than each other and the fairy stories of their childhood. The extra bed came in handy when Frances or another girlfriend stayed overnight, and the room also offered a more spacious closet, whose fake wood accordion door Iris now slid open on its tracks, and selected a flowered skirt and peasant blouse she had splurged on at SaveMart when she cashed her paycheck just the day before. Nervously glancing at the time on the old clock radio Marguerite had left behind when she went away to college in New York City, she flipped its switch.

"And that was Nazareth, with 'Love Hurts,'" the DeeJay on WBCF announced.

"Ouch! So did that!" Iris cried after poking herself in the eye with the mascara wand. She wet two fingers with saliva to wipe the smudge on her lid as the music faded.

"And if it hurts too much, there are at least fifty ways to leave that lover. Here's Paul Simon, to tell you how!"

Iris switched off the radio, which was only making her more jittery, finished getting ready, and rushed down the stairs, knowing that Rick would probably already be waiting in the driveway. Hearing snatches of an animated discussion filtering in through the screen door that led to the garage, she paused for a moment in the kitchen. She immediately recognized the owners of the two male voices engaged in the conversation: one belonged to her father, the other to Rick.

"… and if the country is going to the dogs, we can thank the women's libbers!" She could visualize the jugular vein pulsating in her father's neck as clearly as she could hear his voice.

"You're absolutely right, Mr. Capotosti! The strength of our nation depends on the strength of our families. The women's libbers, by destroying their homes, are destroying our country! 'The wise woman builds her house, but with her own hands the foolish one tears hers down.' Proverbs, chapter fourteen, verse one."

"What could be more rewarding to a woman than raising a family? Nothing!" Iris's father continued. "I don't care what they say, all this feminist baloney is the result of envy and jealousy. Do you see any normal, attractive women out there burning their bras and blabbing about birth control? No! It's the mean ones, the ugly ones, the ones no man would touch with a ten-foot pole, the frigid intellectuals, the lesbians. The ones that will never have a family because no real man would want them. They're the ones getting the normal women all riled up."

Iris rolled her eyes and sighed. She was sick to death of her father's ranting. So was Auntie Rosa, who had to listen to him over endless cups of coffee in the evenings, though she would never admit it. Ever since her mother had left home and word got out that she was attending rallies to push the passage of the Equal Rights Amendment, there had been an escalation in his outbursts of rage directed at the women's liberation movement in general, and the women from the local NOW chapter that had befriended and sheltered her mother in particular. No one, not even her father, could really believe that men and women weren't entitled to the same rights, could they? Iris was terrified that she might one day be asked to declare her stance, even though she knew the mere fact that she had stuck by her father's side and was running his household would be interpreted by him as proof that she sustained his convictions. Iris didn't really know how she felt about her mother's activities, and was not interested in passing judgement on either of her parents; all she was interested in was keeping the peace at home. But her father needed to vent his anger, and was always eager to blow some steam into a fresh set of ears. Rick, on more than one occasion, had been quick to express his sympathy with a respectful pat on the shoulder accompanied by a Scripture verse or two, nonchalantly extracted from context and adapted to suit the purpose, thus earning her father's instant admiration.

Having heard enough, she called, "Hey, you're here!" and walked out to the garage to greet Rick, letting the screen door slam behind her. Though she would never dream of hugging or kissing him in front of her father, she was bewildered by the realization that she was not so inclined, after hearing him side so openly with her father in her absence. She found herself disturbed by the sight of him standing there in her garage, wearing a pair of plaid shorts, a thick mat of black hair covering his muscular legs, and felt slightly silly in the new skirt and blouse she had put on for their date in the hope that he would take her someplace nice. "Shall we go?" Iris heard her voice suggest.

"We were having a nice chat," Rick said, grinning. "But we'll pick up where we left off next time, right Mr. C.?"

Mister C.? Really? Iris wondered when he had come up with that.

Iris's father stopped working on the bicycle he was repairing, wiped his hand on a grease rag, and shook Rick's. "You kids have a nice evening," he said, more to Rick than to Iris.

"Your daughter is in good hands, Mr. C.!" Rick said.

"I know, son," her father said with a wink, as he returned to his tinkering. "Thank God."

Rick held the door open for Iris as she got into the car, and held her hand in his as he steered the vehicle toward the vestiges of sunlight fading from the multicolored sky. Iris rolled her window down all the way, hoping the breeze would chase away her slight unease and the humidity that was already making her perspire.

"I want to take you somewhere special tonight, Alice," Rick said, as they drove straight down Route 35.

"Great – wait, did you call me Alice?" Iris asked, one ear happy to hear that he had special plans after all, the other ear wondering whether his words had been distorted by the wind.

"I guess I did," Rick said. "Funny."

"Why is it funny? Who is Alice, anyway?"

"Alice. You know. The girl I went out with all during high school? The girl I was planning to marry after college, until she broke up with me?"

Iris knew she could just let it slide, not say anything, and change the subject. She hated discussions of any kind, and really needed to relax this evening, but felt compelled to speak up. "May I ask why are you thinking about Alice?" she blurted out.

"I'm not thinking about Alice. It must have been a slip of the tongue," Rick said.

Iris felt her face flush with anger, but remained silent. Rick was thinking of his ex-girlfriend. Perfect icing on the cake of crap she had caught him feeding her father out in the garage. Her expectations of a romantic evening were fading more swiftly than the daylight they pursued as they continued their wordless drive due west, until Rick turned down the service road that led to the college campus.

"It's so peaceful here in summer. Next week when classes start, it'll be totally different," Rick said in a light, conversational tone, as he pulled into a student parking space and switched off the engine. He reached into the back seat and grabbed a shopping bag, which contained a smaller, brown paper bag and some other unidentifiable objects.

"What's that?" she asked.

"You'll see," Rick replied. The grounds were deserted, the evening was still, the humidity thick. As he led her down a footpath, she was grateful for the crunching sound of the gravel beneath their feet, which muffled the gurgling and growling produced by the waves of hunger and agitation roiling in her empty stomach. They strolled without touching or talking, accompanied by the soft song of crickets and the scents of freshly mowed lawns and sappy pine. By the time Rick stepped onto the wooden gazebo and extended his hand to help her up, she had calmed considerably. Iris. Alice. To be honest, their names *were* rather similar, and anyone could make an innocent slip of the tongue.

"Have a seat," Rick said to her, patting the floor of the gazebo next to where he sat, cross-legged. Iris sat and folded her legs gracefully to one side and arranged her skirt over them, leaving a suitably seductive amount of skin peeking from beneath the flowered fabric, while Rick rustled around in his shopping bag. He took out the brown paper bag, from which he extracted a bottle. Dusk had fallen, but there was enough light for Iris to recognize the label: Thunderbird, the same brand of cheap red wine in which her father indulged on Sundays. Rick was full of surprises tonight. She never would have pegged him for the type who would bring alcohol onto the campus, where it was strictly prohibited, and offer it to a girl under legal drinking age. The evening might turn out to be fun after all.

"Are we celebrating something?" she asked.

"Yes. In fact, we're celebrating something quite extraordinary," Rick said. He rummaged around in the shopping bag and pulled out a linen dishtowel, which he spread out and smoothed with his hands. Next, he produced an object rolled up in newspaper, which he proceeded to unwrap, revealing a beautiful wine goblet. He set the goblet down carefully on the dishtowel. Lastly, he pulled out a loaf of Italian bread, and laid it down next to the glass. Iris was wishing he would pull out a hunk of provolone to go with it before she fainted from hunger. Her stomach performed cartwheels at the thought.

"It's like paradise, just the two of us, here together," Rick said, looking deep into her eyes. "I've been wanting to do this ever since I met you." A swarm of butterflies invaded her stomach, flitting over all the churning and growling.

Rick unscrewed the cap off the bottle of wine, and poured some into the goblet. Iris had never had many opportunities to drink wine, but she liked that tight gurgling sound it made when it was poured from a freshly opened bottle. She hoped a nip would settle her stomach.

"Wait - just one more final touch," Rick said as he produced a candle in a jar, lit it and set it down between them.

Wine and candlelight! She didn't know where all this European romanticism had come from, but it excited her, and inspired her to flaunt her French. *"Mon amour! C'est un reve!"* she whispered.

Rick took her hands in his, kissing each finger gently, one by one; his eyelids made that same fluttering motion as her father's did when he was overcome with emotion or trying to be delicate. After giving her hands a final squeeze, Rick picked up the loaf of Italian bread, tore off a chunk, and held it out to her. A deep, articulate growl issued from her stomach when she noticed from the wrapper that the bread was from Pontillo's, her favorite bakery. She adored Italian bread, with or without cheese, and knew she had better eat some before the sounds coming from her stomach really embarrassed her.

"Eat, Iris," Rick said.

She brought the bread to her lips, inhaled its yeasty scent, sank her teeth into the crispy crust. The taste was nothing short of divine.

"Eat of my body, which has been given up for you," Rick said, as Iris began to chew.

"What?" she asked, in a voice muffled by the chunk of bread crammed in her mouth.

Instead of answering, Rick tore off another piece of bread and ate it. When he had finished chewing, he raised the goblet of wine and passed it to her.

"Drink, Iris," he said, proffering the glass, probably real crystal, judging by the way it sparkled in the candlelight. Choking on a chunk of crust that had become lodged in her throat, she reached for the glass, and gulped down a generous swig of wine, which made her gag. She wished she had nibbled more daintily on the bread, instead of biting off such a big piece, but her hunger had made her greedy.

"Drink of my blood, which has been shed for you," Rick said, raising his voice to make himself heard over Iris's coughing.

"Blood? What blood?" she sputtered, struggling to regain control of the voice devastated by the bitter wine and jagged crust as they tore through her esophagus. "What are you talking about? That's Thunderbird!"

"Where two or three are gathered in my name, there I am in the midst of them," Rick said, taking a sip from the goblet.

He was definitely acting weird tonight, even weirder than on their first date. Now he was playing Jesus Christ himself! She wasn't about to let him turn her Friday night into a prayer meeting, or get into a discussion about the Scripture.

"I know that verse," she said. "Catholics do read the gospel, you know, and I do go to Living Youth bible study."

"Then you must know that a woman should learn in quietness and full submission!"

"Aren't you mixing things up a bit, Rick? You can't just go around preaching and giving people fake communion as if you were a priest. Can't we just have a little fun and enjoy our picnic?"

"What could bring more joy than the Savior's love? Don't you feel it, here, with us? Don't you want to celebrate the communion of our souls, and bask in the grace of the Holy Spirit?" Rick grabbed her by the shoulders, with too much force, and stared into her eyes, with too much intensity. "Don't you?" he repeated, in a tight, low voice.

"Of course," she said, softly. She was afraid of making him more upset, but she had to let him know he could not play God with her. "But I think what you're doing is sacrilegious."

The reflection of the flame flickered on the lenses of his glasses, obliterating the twin pools of darkness behind them. A faint breeze heavy with unease stirred the sticky air.

"Rick - " she began, but before she could come up with any other words to dissuade him from whatever mission he was on, with one swift movement, he pushed her to the floor of the gazebo and straddled her hips, knocking over the bottle of Thunderbird with his knee.

"Why are you resisting me, Alice?" he asked, pinning her shoulders to the floorboards. "Why?"

"*I'M NOT ALICE!*" Iris screamed, her heart thumping against her ribcage. "Let me go! You're hurting me!"

"It's the Scripture, Alice! Woman must submit to man. That is how it is meant to be," Rick said in an even voice, as if he were

370

explaining why little girls should brush their teeth before going to bed.

"No! That's not what it means!" Iris channeled all her strength into the muscles of her abdomen and forearms, in an effort to pull herself to her elbows, but Rick grabbed her wrists out from under her, pushed her elbows flat against her sides, and pinned them down with his knees.

"Let me go!" she cried, unable to move. Rick unfastened his belt and unzipped his shorts. "STOP!" she screamed at him. "HELP!" she called out, to anyone, to no one, to the night.

"Silence!" Rick ordered, sliding his hands beneath the elastic band of his underwear to free his penis. The sight of his erection teetering in front of her face repulsed her, but she thrust her head toward it, ordering her mouth to bite it, just as Rick pulled back, leaving her snapping at the thick night air.

"Naughty Alice!" he hissed, pressing one hand over her mouth, waving his penis at her with the other. He stared down at her as he began masturbating. She may not be able to move, but he couldn't make her watch; squeezing her eyes shut, she concentrated on breathing through her nose, on trying to calm down. It could be worse, she reasoned. She doubted he would force himself inside her, or seriously hurt her, or kill her. She sobbed silently as she waited for him to finish, and in the few long minutes it took him to baptize her with the seed of man, she focused on the feel of the splintered wood jabbing her arms and shoulders, on the dampness of the spilled wine seeping through the fabric of her new skirt, on the persistence of the mosquito feeding on her ankle, on the smell of soap on the hand that silenced her.

The light on the back porch was the only one shining, meaning her father had gone to bed; he rarely waited up for anyone anymore, especially if he knew his daughters were in good hands. Rick waited in the driveway until Iris had let herself in the unlocked door, then backed out and drove away. She crept up the stairs, taking care to place her feet close to the walls where the wood creaked less, and slipped into the bathroom. Despite the heat, she yearned to take a scalding bath, but running the water would make too much noise in the silent house. Averting her eyes from the reflection in the mirror, she ran her fingers through her hair, but they got stuck in the curls clumped together with caked semen. She filled the sink with water as hot as she could stand it, and dunked her head repeatedly, then changed the water, and sponge-washed the rest of her body. She brushed her teeth and flossed, like she did every night, then tiptoed into her dark room, where Lily was sound asleep; she stirred only slightly when Iris slid the closet door open to toss her soiled clothes inside.

Iris had no desire to talk about what had happened, but as she sat there on the edge of the mattress, Lily comforted her. The physical nearness of her sister, the regular sound of her breathing, the outline of her form in the dark, told her that nothing had happened, really. Nothing had changed. After several minutes, she lay down, and though the night was still uncomfortably warm, she pulled the sheet up over her head, and tucked it tight all around herself. Her stomach growled, Lily snored, the freight train wailed, she slept.

She awoke early and fuzzy-headed, but as soon as she moved, the aches in her arms and legs forced her to recall the previous night's events, while pangs of hunger reminded her that she had not eaten anything since the grilled cheese sandwich she had lunched on with her little brothers the previous day. She looked over at the bed next to hers, where Lily still slumbered. She was thankful to have the morning off, and that she would be out of bed before Lily could notice anything, in case there was anything to notice.

She dressed in baggy jeans and a long-sleeved shirt, and went down to the kitchen, where all was still, except for the noise of the lawn mower running in the back yard. Her father liked to get an early start on hot days. Iris opened the refrigerator, and nearly dropped the milk when she spotted the thorny stem of a pink rose poking out from the second shelf. Instead of the usual sandwich bag, next to the flower there was a small manila envelope, the kind bank tellers put cash in at drive-up windows, with the name "IRIS" scrawled across the front. At least he remembered her name today. Nausea surged in her stomach, filling her mouth with hot saliva as she picked up the envelope and the rose, and sat down at the table. Inside the envelope was a sheet of ruled paper folded several times to make it fit. She opened the note and read:

"Today is my last day at the factory, praise Jesus. College starts next week. Senior year! Which means a heavy class load plus field work for me. As for you, it's time to focus on finishing high school and taking care of your family. Your dad needs you. Don't disappoint him.
PTL Rick"

"You hypocritical freak!" Iris spat, beating the rose against the table until all the petals fell off. "You weirdo!"

Her father walked in the back door, his blue boxer shorts peeking out from beneath the hems of his grey work shorts, his white sleeveless undershirt sticking to his torso. "Jeepers Cripes! I'm already sweatin' like a pig!" he said. Iris would have liked to smile and say good morning, yes, it's a scorcher, and can I make you some of that iced coffee you like so much? But she just sat on the bench, staring at the decapitated rose she held in her hand.

"Is something the matter, honey?" her father asked her. She shrugged.

Even if she could have found the words to express the feelings of shame and anger and injustice and betrayal churning inside her, she knew she would never be able to speak them out loud: not to her father, not to Lily, and certainly not to Rick. She would not validate such feelings by granting them form, she would not permit their passage through her mind or mouth, or allow them to dwell in her memory. As her father looked on, her shrug was swallowed by a shudder, then a series of shudders that rattled her until the tears broke loose. Her father sat down beside her on the bench, drew her close, and heaved a sigh deep enough to hold both their pain. He cradled her head to his chest, swaddling her in his humanity, as she bathed his sweat with her tears. She cried at the familiar smell of his body odor intermingled with tobacco, she cried at the strength of his sinewy muscles wrapped around her, she cried at all the silent forms of consolation that still inhabited this old house.

Though she surely must have done so countless times as an infant, it was the first time Iris could recall crying in one of her parents' arms.

Iris:

I am horrified by this! Why didn't you ever tell me about what happened with Rick?!! I can't believe, that after all these years, I find out that you were molested, too. I wish I had known - not only because I could have comforted you, but we could have talked, you know? It's really hard to explain to someone who hasn't been through it what it feels like to be violated that way.

Why didn't you tell me?

Love,
Lily

From: Iris Capotosti <iris.capotosti@gmail.com>
To: Lily Capotosti <lilycapotosti@gmail.com>
Sent: Sat, July 17, 2010 at 5:18 PM
Subject: Because

Dear Lily,

I didn't tell you any of those things about Rick because I was ashamed. Not only about what had happened, but about my poor judgment. I should have known there was something wrong with him, and in fact I guess I did know, but I chose to ignore the warning bells. Which made me stupid, as well as molested. Though back then, I never would have thought of myself in those terms. (Molested, I mean. Not stupid.)

Besides, would you have really wanted to dig up what had happened to you all those years ago in the chicken coop? After you talked to Mom that time, you never complained about Henry again, so I figured the situation had been taken care of, and that you would rather just forget about it. And that was what I wanted to do about Rick. Forget about him.

Didn't we already have enough crap to deal with?

Love,
Iris

24. LILY

"Merry Christmas, Lily," James reached into the back seat of his Oldsmobile and retrieved a box about the size a pair of shoes would come in.

"Oh, you got me a new pair of sneakers - just want I wanted!" Lily laughed to cover up her disappointment. Nothing exciting ever came in a shoe box. She knew she couldn't expect James to give her the opal ring that she had seen in the Present Company catalog, but she would have been happy enough with a little gold heart locket or even an ID bracelet.

"Open it up," said James.

"I hate to rip the paper," said Lily. "The wrapping is so beautiful."

"I have to confess that my Mom helped me with that. In fact, she helped me a lot with this gift."

Lily couldn't imagine what sort of a present James would need his mother's help with, but any vestiges of hope for something romantic or sexy flew out the crack in the driver's side window. Lily gently tore at the taped corners, one by one, wanting to savor the experience of at least having been given a gift by James, and hoping to save the paper, which she would put into her scrapbook along with the dried carnation, an assortment of movie ticket stubs, and the spattering of store-bought greeting cards he had given her over the past year. She released the main seam in the wrapping, lifted the lid from the box and pushed the white tissue paper aside to reveal a brown stuffed kangaroo with a white belly and pink ears.

"A stuffed animal?" she said. Afraid that her response sounded ungrateful, and worried about discouraging future gift-giving, she lifted it out of the box and added, "It's so cute!"

"Look," said James. He took the kangaroo from her and showed her the tiny joey, which he removed from the kangaroo's pouch and placed in the palm of her hand. "It comes with a baby!"

"Aw," said Lily. As chagrined as she was on one level, a revelation presented itself to her. "Do you know," she said, looking up at James somberly, "that this is the only stuffed animal I've ever owned?"

"Get *out*," said James.

"I'm serious."

"You never had a teddy bear or anything like that?"

"Not that I can remember," said Lily. "There were old stinky stuffed animals around, but none of them were mine. No one ever gave one to me as my own."

"That's a shame," said James.

"I do remember getting a baby doll once - the kind that closes its eyes automatically when you lay it down, and then when you stand it up the eyes open again. My mother gave her to me for my tenth birthday. I felt that I was way too old for a baby doll by then, but she was so pretty - and she was mine."

"There you go," said James. "That counts."

"Except that she went missing the next day," said Lily. "I tore the entire house apart looking for her. I finally found her in the basement. Her hair had been all cut off, she was stripped naked, and her body was covered with blue ink."

"Oh, God - that's awful," said James. "Who would do that?"

"One of my little brothers, I'm sure," said Lily. "Or all of them, more likely."

"That's one of the saddest things I've ever heard."

"I'm sorry!" said Lily. "Talk about being a downer..."

"I'll have you know," said James, "that this is a very special kangaroo."

"I know it is," said Lily. "It's from you."

"Ah, but that's not all," said James. He turned the kangaroo over and showed Lily the tag attached to its tail. It read, "Merry Xmas Lily! Love, James."

"Oh, my God!" said Lily. "How did you do that?"

"I made it," said James.

"I know, but how did you get it on the kangaroo? It looks like it's sewn right in there."

"It is," said James, with a laugh. "I made it, Lily - I made the whole kangaroo. That's why I needed some help from my Mom... I didn't understand some of the instructions for the pattern."

"You made it?" Tears sprang to Lily's eyes. James had sewn her a stuffed kangaroo. With a baby in its pouch. She snatched it from James, returned the joey to its home, and hugged them both to her chest. "Thank you, James. I love it." *I love you.*

"Oh - I almost forgot *your* presents!" Lily reached into the bag at her feet, pulled out two packages, and handed them to James.

"I get two?"

"Well, I didn't make them myself," said Lily. "Yours is better!"

"It's not a competition," said James. He opened the larger shirt box first and pulled out a brown and tan plaid flannel shirt. "I love it!"

"I chose it to match your brown eyes," said Lily. "Try it on."

"Right now?"

"Yes, right now, silly," she teased. "I want to make sure it fits OK."

James extracted his arms from his jacket and pulled his sweater off over his head, tossing both garments into the back seat. The sight of his bare chest, his smooth hairless skin stretched taut over chiseled muscles made Lily's hands tingle. James slipped into the flannel shirt, but left it unbuttoned. He fully extended both his arms out in front of him, measuring the length of the sleeves. "Perfect!"

He leaned over and kissed Lily. He quickly broke away, but

she reached out, cupped the back of his head in her hand and pulled him toward her again. The kiss continued as she slipped her hand under his shirt, slowly running her palm over his erect nipple, down the length of his exposed belly, finally coming to rest on his belt buckle. He didn't object.

"Want to get in back?" he said.

"Yes," said Lily breathlessly. "I do."

They climbed over the front seat and lay down in back, on a mattress of shed coats and sweaters. Lily relished the way James' skin felt against her own. Judging from the way his hands eagerly explored her neck, her back, and then her breasts, he liked it too.

"Oh my God!" said James. "I didn't open my other present - I'm so sorry!"

"That's OK," said Lily. "You can open it later."

"Just a sec," said James. "I can see it from here. I can get it without even getting up." He reached into the front seat and retrieved the smaller gift. "Let's see what we have here," he said, planting a kiss on Lily's forehead.

James ripped the paper off and threw it on the floor. He flipped the book over so that it was right-side-up. "*The Prophet!*" he said.

"Khalil Gibran - remember we were talking about that a few weeks ago?"

"I do!"

"You haven't read it yet, have you?"

"No - but I've really been wanting to," he said. "Thank you!" James opened the cover and flipped through the pages. He began reading aloud. How ironic that he chose Lily's favorite poem. She had memorized it before wrapping the gift and as James read the admonition to follow love - even though it may shatter your dreams - Lily knew it was fate that he had turned to that page in this precise moment, a moment when Lily felt as Gibran had so beautifully expressed - enfolded in the wings of love. Tonight simply could not get any more perfect.

In the middle of the poem, James closed the book and let it drop to the floor. Lily rested her cheek against his chest and listened to the beat of his heart.

"I could stay here forever," said Lily.

James abruptly sat up, causing Lily to do the same. "Speaking of forever," he said, "what time is it? I should really get you home; it's late."

"It's OK," said Lily, confused. "No one even really notices if I'm there or not anyway. We can stay."

But James was already trying out the buttons on his new shirt.

"Dolores!" called Lily, as she dropped her purse onto the floor and ran over to embrace her cousin.

"Your hair is gorgeous, Lily." Dolores ran her hand over the crown of Lily's head and down her back. "As shiny as satin."

"That's because I put that stuff on that you got me from the salon. The girls at school all call me Farrah now, after Farrah Fawcett from *Charlie's Angels.*"

"You're much more beautiful than any of those TV angels - you're a real angel - a cherub," said Dolores. "Have you been rehearsing your song?"

"Every day," said Lily. "I've started taking voice lessons as one of my electives, and Mr. Howell said that we could work on it in class."

"Fabulous," said Dolores, tapping the end of Lily's nose with her index finger. "They will be begging you to come to that college - but there's a lot to do to get ready; we have no time to lose! Now let's talk about the next step."

Dolores took Lily's hand and led her over to the love seat by the window, upon which sat two small pillows with hand-crocheted covers and a box of loose photographs. Dolores removed the box and slid it under the love seat. Lily picked up the single photo that had been left behind on the cushion. It was a worn and cracked black and white photo of two little girls standing, holding hands. They each wore a drop waist dress with a large floppy collar, dark stockings, and black lace-up boots that came to mid-calf. The little girl on the right had a serious look on her face - almost a scowl - the look that people in old photographs always seemed to have, as if having your photo taken was some form of punishment.

"Who are these people?" asked Lily.

Leaning over to see the photo in Lily's hand, Dolores let out a heavy sigh. "That's your Auntie Rosa and her sister Teresa - would have been your Auntie Teresa if she had lived long enough to grow up."

"She's the one who drowned, right? In the canal?"

"She's the one."

"Which one is she?"

"This one," said Dolores, pointing to the little girl on the left.

"Geez - what's with the look on Auntie Rosa's face?"

"Who knows?" said Dolores. "Your Grandma Capotosti was known to be a hard woman. She laid a lot on your Auntie Rosa. In fact, I think she even blamed her for Teresa's death." Dolores kissed the photo. "Can you even imagine, Lily? Your Auntie Rosa and Teresa were like you and Iris - or like me and Felicia. They did everything together. They were best friends. Then one day, Teresa was just gone. Forever."

"How awful," said Lily. She couldn't even imagine what it would be like to get up one day and find that Iris was gone.

Dolores placed the photo into the box, slid it back under the love seat, pulled a tissue from the cuff of her sleeve and dabbed at the end of her nose.

"Let's move on to happier thoughts, shall we?" She closed her eyes, inhaled deeply, and shook her head as if to scatter the sadness, as though she were tuning into a new station in her mind. "I almost forgot - I have something for you!"

Dolores grabbed her purse from the floor and pulled out a five-by-seven-inch book, which she handed to Lily.

"*Jonathan Livingston Seagull*?"

"That's my copy of my favorite book. I want you to have it," said Dolores. "I want you to read it and I want you keep it with you always, and whenever you start to think that something's not possible, I want you to open that book and read it again."

"It's about a bird?" Lily asked.

"Kind of. You'll see. Promise me you'll read it?"

Lily opened the cover. On the inside page was a note, written in Dolores' hand. "Lily, Don't ever be afraid to soar above the rest. With love, Dolores."

"I promise," answered Lily, holding the book to her chest.

"Well, now - you and I have some shopping to do today, young lady. We need to buy you two outfits – one for your audition and one for your interview. And then we have to book you some time at the recording studio to lay down the tracks for your song. How does that sound?"

"Sounds expensive," said Lily, wincing.

"Now stop that," said Dolores. "I'm taking care of everything. It's an investment in your future. "

"But that's going to be a lot of money," Lily protested.

"Not compared to what you're going to have one day, my little star," said Dolores. "If you want, you can pay me back when you're rich and famous."

"It's a deal!"

Lily and Dolores spent that afternoon strolling through Rolling Ridge Mall, with Lily trying on dresses and shoes along the way. They chatted and laughed, and stopped to share a soft pretzel and a Coke. Lily loved the way Dolores made her feel; she was a cross between a mother, a best friend, and a favorite teacher. Lily knew too well how a single person's thoughtlessness or cruelty could make life seem hard and sad, but being with Dolores was like looking through a kaleidoscope and seeing a completely different arrangement of crystals with just a touch, filling your view with light and color and wonder.

"This is fun, isn't it?" said Dolores.

"Yes - and I usually can't stand shopping," replied Lily.

"Why don't you like to shop?"

"I don't know. I guess it's because I don't even know what I would buy. All of my clothes have mostly come from Iris - either I got them when she was done with them or I've borrowed clothes from her. Shopping confuses me. And I guess I don't really care too much about it."

"I know exactly what you mean. All of my clothes were hand-me-downs that were bought especially for Felicia by our mother. I never liked very many of them and they never looked right on me. I always felt ill at ease in them, like I was a poor imitation of the 'good' daughter." Dolores was staring off into the distance. "Dressing me up like Felicia didn't help much. It was still just me underneath."

Eager to change the subject and to reignite the spark in Dolores' eyes, Lily replied, "But look at you now - you have such lovely things and you always look so beautiful."

"Well, my husband - I mean my ex-husband - made a good living, and he was always being invited to parties and dinners and that sort of thing. It was important for his career that I portray a certain level of style. I learned to dress like a wealthy optometrist's wife. Now I'm stuck with the wardrobe."

Lily took a sip of the Coke, unsure of what to say.

Dolores drew in a quick breath, exhaled, and straightened her body. "But you, my dear, are a beautiful flower and you should learn to dress in a way that expresses your beauty to the world and is true for you, instead of what others want for you." Dolores placed her hand on Lily's thigh, and leaned in closer. "Don't ever lie to yourself in order to be what someone else wants you to be - especially a man. Speaking of which... how are things going with James?"

"OK." Lily tore off a piece of pretzel and popped it into her mouth.

"Just OK?"

"Oh, Dolores," she said with a sigh, "I am *soooo* in love with him - he's so cute and I love the way he kisses, and he's smart and gentle..."

"All good things," said Dolores. "Try this." She held out a small plastic cup of mustard.

"Mustard? I don't like mustard."

"It's great on a pretzel. Just give it a try."

Lily tore off a piece of pretzel and dipped it in.

"But we've been seeing each other for over a year and I still don't know how he feels about me."

"Does he know how you feel about him?"

"He must," said Lily.

"Have you told him?" Dolores asked.

"Well, no..."

"Why not?"

"I always thought the boy was supposed to say it first," said Lily. "Plus, what if I tell him I love him and he doesn't say it back?"

"Lily," said Dolores, taking her hand. "That young man should be thanking his lucky stars that a girl like you would even give him the time of day."

"Oh, Dolores, that's not true," said Lily dipping another piece of pretzel into the mustard with her free hand.

"That's your problem," said Dolores. "You don't realize how wonderful you are. And that's the difference between you and Iris. And between me and Felicia. Iris and Felicia know they're special, and you and I treat ourselves like bargain basement seconds. In order to get what you want in this world, Lily, you have to expect it. If that young man isn't ready to make a commitment to you, then you're better off without him." Dolores took a sip of Coke. "You know what they say: 'Shit or get off the pot'!"

"Dolores!" Lily laughed.

"Sorry to be so crude," said Dolores, "but there's some truth to that. If he can't appreciate you, don't waste any more of your time on him. Tell him how you feel, and if he can't reciprocate, tell him you can't see him anymore. Nothing will change his mind faster about how he feels than thinking he's going to lose you." Dolores absently raised her right hand and touched her left ring finger, as if to make sure it was still bare.

"Just the thought of telling James that I love him gives me a stomach ache." Lily pushed the rest of the pretzel aside.

"I'm telling you," said Dolores. "That's the best way to get what you want from him."

Lily took a long draw on the straw, draining the Coke with a loud slurp. At least the way things now stood, she still had a relationship with James. Even if it was confusing and frustrating.

"It's scary," said Lily, gathering up their trash from the table.

"The best things always are," replied Dolores. She added quietly, as if to herself, "So are the worst things."

"Hey, Iris - Can I wear your blue smock top?"

Iris lay on the bed on her back, with legs bent and feet flat on the mattress. She propped her latest novel up against her long thighs. Without taking her eyes from her reading, she replied, "Promise you'll hang it up when you're done, and not throw it on the floor?"

"Yes," replied Lily, playfully irritated at how well her sister knew her.

"Then OK."

"I like this top because it makes my boobs look bigger." Lily looked into the mirror and with one hand on each breast, she hoisted them.

"That's why I bought it," said Iris. "Not that you need any help." Iris looked at Lily's reflection in the bureau mirror and rolled her eyes. "Don't stretch it out."

As the girls approached womanhood, they'd developed into two distinctly different body types. Iris' tall, slender build was a gift from the Whitacre side, but she seemed ill at ease in her model's figure, an attitude that was evidenced by the slight hunch she kept in her shoulders, a practice that didn't really make her any shorter, but perhaps made her at least feel a little less conspicuous.

Lily's form was Capotosti through and through, complete with broad shoulders, a hint of bow-leggedness due to a family hip defect, and ample breasts that didn't exactly rival Auntie Rosa's, but on Lily's five-foot-three-inch frame were big enough to get noticed.

"Hey, Iris, can I use your - "

"You know where it is... "

"Thank you, thank you, thank you!" Lily opened the top drawer of Iris' side of the dresser and retrieved the American Teen

Beauty makeup kit that Iris had secretly ordered through the mail.

"I'm gonna do it tonight, Iris," Lily announced.

Iris immediately put down the book and looked up at Lily. "Do what, exactly?"

"I'm going to tell James I love him."

"What made you decide to do that, all of the sudden?"

"Dolores says that if I want him to treat me like I'm something special, I have to act like it. And that means not letting him string me along anymore. If he can't make a commitment to me then I'm going to tell him I can't see him anymore."

"No offense, Lily," said Iris. "But I'm not sure Dolores is the best person to be taking relationship advice from."

Lily didn't expect Iris to understand; Auntie Rosa had been telling her she was special her whole life. She couldn't know what it was like to think you were just ordinary.

"Anyway," said Lily. "What did you think I was talking about when I said I was gonna 'do it' tonight?"

"You know..." Iris formed a ring with the index finger and thumb of her left hand and then inserted the index finger of her right hand into the ring, pushing it and out.

"Iris!!" Lily picked up Iris' pink stuffed kitten from the dresser, and pitched it at her. Iris caught it mid-air and pitched it back. The kitten hit the mirror and landed back on the dresser.

"I can't believe you!" said Lily. "I would never do that!" Turning back toward the mirror, she added, "Not until I'm married."

Iris picked her book up again. Under her breath, she replied, "Whatever floats your boat."

"Aren't you going out tonight?" Lily applied mascara first to her right eyelashes, then to her left.

"Yea - later. Debbie is coming to pick me up after she gets out of work."

Iris was always being invited somewhere. She was likable and sweet and kind - traits that had attracted a steady stream of friends into their life - they were usually girls that Lily knew, and she borrowed Iris' friendships the way she borrowed her clothes:

they fit well enough and they filled the need of the moment. But lately Iris was hanging out with girls who Lily didn't know, girls who worked jobs and had paychecks, drove after dark, smoked cigarettes, and could get into R-rated movies. Iris' friends were becoming exclusively hers, and Lily began to notice that her own social life had shrunken into near non-existence, especially since Kiki wasn't speaking to her at all these days. But no matter. Dolores kept her busy with coaching and rehearsals and planning for college auditions, which helped keep Lily's mind off of missing her mother. Dolores certainly couldn't replace her mother, but life was a little easier now with something to look forward to. Anyway, she still had Iris and after tonight, maybe she would finally have James.

"Did you like the movie?" James asked.

"Yes, I did," Lily replied. She removed her Styrofoam cup of hot chocolate from the dashboard, and cracked open the sip hole. A ribbon of steam escaped. Lily blew on her drink, and watched out the window as the snow gently fell, floating in the brightness of a single lamp in the auto shop parking lot.

"Are you sure? You didn't say two words the whole time. You seem really distracted tonight."

"I do have something on my mind," she said.

"What is it?"

Lily looked at James, the words roiling in her gut, her fingers playing with the lid of her hot chocolate until it popped off and splashed the scalding liquid onto her coat. James reached across her lap, opened the glove box, removed a paper napkin, and dabbed at the spill. With his face inches from hers, he looked into her eyes, and said, "I won't bite; I promise." He smiled.

Lily closed her eyes and pushed the words out from her heart and into her throat.

"James, I love you."

Lily's nerves instantly settled, closely followed by the dreaded realization that the car had grown completely silent. She was sure that when she opened her eyes again she would find the snowflakes all suspended, frozen in place, along with the breath she was holding in her chest. When she finally did open them, she discovered that it was no longer snowing at all. The hot chocolate had caused a spot of condensation to form on the inside of the windshield, and James had returned to his place behind the wheel, with his left elbow on the arm rest and his left thumbnail clenched in his front teeth. He reminded Lily of that *Thinker* sculpture they'd learned about in Art Appreciation class.

James finally broke the silence. "The thing is, I'm just not going to be around next year, you know?"

"What does that mean?" Lily choked back tears.

"It means that I'm going to college. You know that."

"I'm not asking you about your plans," said Lily. *Just tell me you love me. Please. Just say it.*

"What do you see when you look at that building right there?" asked James.

"What? The auto shop?"

"Right. You see an auto shop. I see a prison. A prison where you pound out dents and change air filters in order to pay the mortgage and the dentist and buy groceries."

"I don't really understand what you're talking about," said Lily. "I'm just saying that I love you. Are you saying that you don't love me?"

"I just can't end up inside that building for the rest of my life," said James. "I'm saying that it doesn't matter how I feel."

"It matters to me."

James reached over and unbuttoned Lily's coat, slipping it from her shoulders. He leaned over and kissed her. If he couldn't commit to her, she was going to tell him she couldn't see him anymore. That was the plan. James pulled Lily towards him, and kissed her deeply. She wanted to object, to pull back. She deserved better, that's what Dolores said. Lily forgot what she was supposed to say next and she couldn't find the sense of indignation that Dolores had so readily aroused in her earlier. They were not done talking yet, and he had not answered her question. Lily and James tangled themselves into a knot of breath and hands and feet, fogging up the windows, but never moving to the back seat. They wrangled with their passion, with their youth, and with the steering wheel, abandoning conversation. She wanted to want to stop, but this felt an awful lot like love.

Lily arrived home before Iris, who regularly came in hours after curfew and miraculously never got caught doing it. The scent of James' Pierre Cardin cologne was still on Lily's hands. She raised them to her face, and inhaled deeply. James hadn't said he loved her, but he hadn't said he didn't either. Maybe now, though, he'll really think about it. Maybe he would tell Lily he loved her when they went to his Senior Ball. He'd give her a corsage of miniature roses, apologize for making her wait, and tell her he loved her. Loves her. *He loves me. I know he does. I can wait enough for both of us.*

Lily looked out the window, anxiously waiting for Iris to get dropped off. She wondered what her mother was doing now, and wished she were downstairs in bed, wished she were home again. She tried to pretend that she was there, sleeping, but Lily's imagination was no match for the emptiness that hung heavy in the house, which felt spoiled now. It smelled spoiled. It was spoiled. Lily longed for something to feel right, for something to be normal tonight. She went out to the hallway, picked up the phone and dialed Dolores' number.

"Hullo?"

"Dolores?" Lily hardly recognized the raspy, weak voice on the other end of the line.

"Lily!" shouted Dolores. "Whatre you doin' Lily of the Valley? Dijou have a good time shoppin yesserday? I had a good time shoppin wi' you. You're great!"

"Are you OK Dolores? Why are you talking like that?"

Lily heard a loud thud on the other end of the line.

"Oh, shit!" cried Dolores. "Dijou see that, Rosa?! I fell off the bed - izznt that crazy?!" Dolores burst into laughter. Lily couldn't hear what Auntie Rosa was saying, but she recognized the restrained anger in her voice - she'd heard it many times as a child whenever Auntie Rosa had tried to get an uncooperative Grandma Capotosti to use the commode in the middle of the night, in the hopes she might be spared the chore of changing soiled sheets the next morning.

"But iz my beoo-ful Tiger Lily!" called Dolores.

"Lily?" said Auntie Rosa into the receiver.

"Hi, Auntie Rosa."

"Lily, it's late. Dolores will call you back tomorrow, OK?"

"What's going on?"

Without reply, Auntie Rosa hung up the phone.

Lily returned to her room, turned off the light, and crawled into bed, covered with the vague sense of uneasiness in her life created by words left unspoken.

The following Monday, Lily stepped off the school bus, walked through the diesel fumes, and headed straight for James' locker, fighting to banish the memory of the weekend, hoping that James would also be willing to just forget about the whole embarrassing thing, and that they could just go back to the way things were. So what if he couldn't tell her how he really felt? She knew, and he knew, deep inside. She could be patient. With time, she would help him overcome his fears about love and when he did finally admit to her his true feelings, he would be so grateful to her for her patience, and for showing him what it really meant to love someone. In the meantime, she decided, it was better to have half his heart than not have him at all.

As Lily approached James, she noticed two girls standing with him, chatting. One of them - a chubby blonde - handed him a small piece of paper, which he tucked into his shirt pocket. The girls turned and walked away, heading in Lily's direction.

"Better luck next time," said the chubby blonde to Lily as they passed. She and her friend smirked at Lily, assaulting her with their heavy cloud of Tabu cologne.

Lily turned to look at them as they continued down the hall, with a sense of just having been insulted in a way she didn't quite understand. In unison, the girls looked back over their shoulders at Lily, and the chubby one leaned over to whisper something to her friend. They both burst out laughing as they disappeared into the sea of students pouring into the school.

"What was that all about?" Lily asked James.

"What was what all about?"

"That girl you were just talking to... she said to me, 'Better luck next time,' and then they laughed."

"Well, that wasn't very nice." said James, selecting a book from the top shelf of his locker.

"Who is she?"

"Her name is Paula. Paula Wilson." James shut his locker door, and spun the wheel on his combination lock.

Lily paused, waiting for further explanation. "What was she talking about?"

"Well, she's a senior this year. And she doesn't have a date to the Ball. So I asked her."

"What do you mean?" asked Lily. "You asked her what?"

"To go with me. To the Ball." James looked at the floor. He looked up at the stream of faces passing, waving and nodding to his friends as they went by.

Lily wanted to scream, as the truth of what he was saying dawned on her, but all that came out was, "Oh."

"If I don't take her, she probably won't get to go at all. Everyone should get the chance to go to their Senior Ball. I knew you would understand."

"I guess..." she said, trying to determine if the searing pain she felt was in her heart or in her gut. "Do you like her?"

"She's OK. She's nice. Usually."

Lily wanted to know if they were going to the Ball as friends or as dates, but she didn't know how to ask without sounding jealous, and James abhorred jealousy, saying it was the mark of insecurity. Anyway, Lily wasn't sure she even wanted to know the answer. She pictured James and Paula going out to a fancy dinner before the dance, having their photo taken in their formal wear, parking behind the auto shop afterwards.

"After all," said James, "You'll have your Senior Ball next year, but this is it for her."

Why is that my problem? Lily held back the words. She imagined slapping James, right there in the hallway in front of everyone, which is what she wanted to do, and which would have felt incredibly good. But she doubted she could ever haul off and hit another person, especially James. Anyway, if she got mad it would prove that she wasn't independent or mature enough for him, after all - above all he wanted someone who wouldn't tie him down; the worst thing to do now was to act petty and jealous. The only course of action was to play it cool, pretend like it was OK. Show him how advanced and sophisticated she was, how unconventional. Make him want her more by making him think she didn't need him so much.

"Sure," Lily choked on the words. "I understand."

"You're the best. Well, I gotta go - I'm late for calc class."

Lily watched James' head bob down the hallway, then she ducked into the girls room, and cried right through her Women in Contemporary Society class.

25. IRIS

"Coffee," the waitress said, in the voice devoid of inflection used by those who are forced to ask questions to which they already know the answers. Without waiting for a response, she banged two heavy ceramic mugs down on the table. Iris and Lily jumped in their seats.

"Yes, thanks," Iris said, smiling. "We'll order too, please. I'll have the ninety-nine cent special." The grumpier people were, the more prone Iris was to be cheerful; it was her natural way of protecting herself against contamination, and of trying to obliterate any negativity she encountered.

"Howduyawantureggs," the waitress said, pouring out the coffee, then setting the pot on the table.

"Scrambled, please." The waitress scribbled on her pad without looking up.

"Toast."

"Whole wheat, please."

"Bacon or sausage."

"Bacon. Crispy, please."

"Ditto for me, please," Lily said. The crepe soles of the woman's shoes squeaked as she turned and walked away.

Iris poured a splash of cream into her cup and took a sip of the steaming hot beverage before reaching into her purse. She extracted a stack of coupons bound together by a red rubber band

and placed on them table.

"Whad'ya got for us today?" Lily asked, unfolding a piece of note paper and setting it on the table with a pen, before wrapping her hands around her own mug and lifting it to her lips.

"Let's start with the standard stock items," Iris said, picking up the stack of coupons she had clipped out of the newspaper during the course of the week. The bottom slip stuck to the table, and was ripped in half when Iris tugged at it. "Darn maple syrup!" she said, carefully peeling the stuck piece from the table. "That was a good one, too: fifteen cents off Dad's evaporated milk. I hope they'll take it anyway." She shook her head with irritation, and began flipping through the remaining coupons. "Toilet paper, milk, orange juice, bread, butter, bologna, cereal …"

"What kind of cereal?" Lily asked, raising her eyes from the shopping list on which she was ticking off the items Iris mentioned.

"Puffed rice," Iris said. "Or wheat. It's valid for both."

"Geez, Iris. The boys don't want to eat that anymore, and we still have a huge bag in the cupboard."

"Puffed rice isn't that bad. It was good enough for us all these years. And it's dirt cheap."

"That's because it's all air. I get depressed just looking at the way it bobs around on top of the milk."

"I can't argue with you on that." Iris drummed her fingers on the tabletop, then looked at Lily and sighed. Maybe you're right, maybe it is time to break some of the old patterns and try something new. Any suggestions?"

"How about Wheaties, the 'breakfast of champions'? It's nutritious, and the boys are bound to find the pictures of athletes on that bright orange box more inspiring than those plastic feed bags."

"We don't have a coupon for it, but let's leave our options open. Maybe we'll get lucky and there will be a non-advertised special."

Service at the diner might not always be friendly, but it was swift, and within minutes, the arrival of two piping hot plates, each bearing a steaming mound of scrambled eggs, two pieces of crisp bacon and two slices of buttery toast caused the girls to suspend their strategy session. Less than half an hour later, they had stoked up on enough caffeine and calories to face their Saturday morning task of grocery shopping at the same supermarket where their mother used to shop, located in the plaza across the from the diner. Everyone knew that a hungry shopper was not a thrifty shopper, and Iris had decided that the household budget, as well as she and Lily, would benefit from this little perk. For breakfast, they allowed themselves five of the fifty dollars of grocery money their father gave them, every cent of which was abundantly recouped through the money they saved with the coupons.

Whether it was the buzz they got from the free coffee refills, or their determination to tackle the chore with the same enthusiasm as if they were treating themselves to a Saturday morning at the hairdresser's or shopping at a fancy department store, Iris and Lily always had a spring in their step when they burst through the automated doors of the supermarket. They discussed their purchase options animatedly as they cruised the aisles, casting looks of disdain at the expensive prepared foods they shunned in favor of more economical, basic products that would satisfy the needs of their family, though Iris often paused for a moment or two in front of the spices, wondering what recipes could possibly call for curry or cardamom, until Lily told her she was getting that faraway look in her eyes again, and that it was time to come back to earth.

"One ninety-nine," Iris would say, or "seventy-five cents," dropping into the cart a dented jumbo tin of peach halves on special, or a bunch of overripe bananas, which beckoned her to bake some banana bread. Iris scoured the shelves and made the selections, as Lily steered the shopping cart with her left hand, while in the palm of her right she held a small red plastic device, her index, middle and ring fingers poised on the three white keys that corresponded to dollars, dimes and cents. Each time Iris called out a price, Lily clicked in the amount by depressing the keys, as if she were playing a tune on a trumpet. Keeping a running total of the items in the cart spared the girls the mortification of not having enough money to pay the cashier, and also helped curtail costs considerably as they went along, to the point where they were often able to bring their father back change, sometimes as much as five, or even seven dollars.

"Hey, those cookies are marked down," Iris said, pointing to a bin brimming with slightly crushed red and green boxes.

"But they're Christmas cookies, Iris," Lily said.

"I know, but now that Christmas is over, someone might finally be in the mood to eat them." Iris had dutifully rolled, molded and frosted several batches of Capotosti favorites, in a campaign to convince her family that traditions should be maintained no matter how circumstances changed, but she had the impression people were shoving the cookies down their throats just to be rid of them and the thoughts of previous holidays with their mother, who was not allowed access to the house.

"Give it up, Iris. Everyone would rather eat your banana bread," Lily said.

Iris knew Lily was right. No amount of baking could put happiness back into the holidays, but thank God that horrible Christmas was over and done with, and this was a new year. Things could only get better from here on, especially since she had satisfied all the prerequisites for early graduation, and in another week, would be liberated from high school life for good. There were no courses so interesting, no friendships so binding, no prospects for romance so alluring, to outweigh the advantages of working full time to save for college. Springtime would mean senior portraits and senior balls, and other frivolous expenses she could do without.

"Did you see the way he looked at you?" Lily asked her sister as they struggled to push their laden grocery cart through the ice and slush of the parking lot, passing a tall, handsome youth who was rounding up abandoned carts and returning them to the store entrance.

"Peter Ponzio has been looking at me like that for the past two years," Iris said, popping the trunk of a sporty red coupé. "Exactly the same amount of time I've been looking at him."

"So why don't you guys do something about it?" Lily said, placing a bag in the trunk.

"Bad timing. He started noticing me right after I started going out with Michael. Isn't it weird the way when you have a boyfriend, all the other guys start buzzing around you, and when you don't, they treat you like you have the plague? "

"I guess that's how they can tell," Lily said.

"Tell what?"

"Whether you're worth it. If you already have a boyfriend, you must have something going for you. Plus, seeing what kind of guy a girl goes out with, tips them off as to whether they stand a chance with her. Guys hate rejection."

"Well, goodness gracious, don't you know it all? Did Dolores teach you that, too?"

"We were talking about Peter Ponzio, Iris."

"Well, if he likes me, he had all last semester to do something about it. He just kept looking and smiling, but never approached me, and now high school is virtually a thing of the past. "

"Maybe he'll ask you to the senior ball," Lily said, shoving the last brown bag into the small trunk a bit too violently, and slamming the door shut. Iris hoped it wasn't the bag with the eggs.

"Where would he approach me?" Iris asked. "In the frozen foods section?"

"You never know."

Head down to the biting wind, Iris wheeled the empty shopping cart to the return area, knowing it would spare Peter a minute of work in the miserable cold, then slid into the passenger seat next to Lily.

"I feel weird driving this car," Lily said, as she drove through the parking lot to the exit.

"I bet," Iris said. "It is a pretty hot set of wheels. Leather interiors. Bucket seats. AM-FM Stereo. Tape deck. I wonder why

Dolores doesn't want to drive it. I mean, after all the pain that Dr. Bob put her through, she could at least enjoy the car he gave her. She should run it right into the ground."

"It must make her sick just to look at it. When she dropped it off, she said Dad could keep it, as long as he let me drive it on Saturday mornings. To boost up our morale. That's what she said, those exact words. She sounded just like Auntie Rosa."

"I wonder how long she'll stay at Auntie Rosa's," Iris said. "How long it will take her to get back on her feet."

"I don't know. I just wish she had a place of her own so we could talk and hang out there, with no one else around, you know? But I wonder if Auntie Rosa will ever let her go. It's as if she wants to keep her for herself."

"I don't think that's the way it is, Lily. They have always been so close. Dolores has always gone to Auntie Rosa for help rather than to her own mother or sister."

"I just hope she forgets about men this time, and stays single. Single and independent," Lily said. "Maybe she should talk to Mom or something. She knows lots of independent women. Maybe they can help her, like they helped Mom."

"I somehow don't think they would be her type. Anyway, I just don't get this independence thing. On one hand, there's Mom, who just gets up from the dinner table and walks out one day, leaving us to fend for ourselves. Sure, she got her independence, but that doesn't really seem right if someone else, like us, has to pay the price. Then there's Auntie Rosa's who is also independent. She's always worked, never got married or had a family of her own. But she took care of Grandma and Grandpa all those years, and she still has Uncle Alfred to worry about, and now there's Dolores, too. If that's what you get for being independent, it's kind of a rip-off."

"Uncle Alfred works, though. He teaches guitar, and he still plays at The Luau," Lily said.

"I know. He gets to do what he loves to do because Auntie Rosa is the main breadwinner. I used to see what he made and what he spent on guitars. I'm sure he didn't have much left over to contribute toward the household expenses."

"Well, I'm sure Dolores will get another teaching job as soon as she feels better. And her own place with good light, where she can paint. She can't do that in Auntie Rosa's basement. Maybe I could even stay over sometimes and practice my singing while she paints. She says hearing me sing inspires her."

"It inspires me, too. You're so good!"

"Thanks. I really want to put everything into my singing and acting. That's the one thing I'm sure of. Of course, I won't turn down fame and fortune, but that's not what it's about for me. Maybe I won't make it, but at least I'll be happy, doing something I love. All I need is Dolores to believe in me. And James to love me." Lily said. She stopped at a red light and turned to face her sister. "Is that too much to ask?"

"That's the other snag," Iris said. "I'm not talking about James in particular, but if a man loves you, he should know and want what's best for you, right? But knowing that and acting on it are two different things. Look at Dolores. She's always been so full of love and joy and creativity, but the men she met up with sucked it all out of her like vampires. That's not loving, that's not even caring."

"How about Mom?" Lily said. "She was so smart, she was out of college by nineteen, but as soon as she got married, we kids came along and took up all her time and energy. She depended on Dad to take care of her and us. If he really loved her, he should have loved her intelligence, too, and encouraged her when she wanted to go back to school for her master's degree and get a job instead of complaining that she wasn't taking care of him or us anymore."

"Right. Somehow it gets turned around. Sometimes the independent one becomes dependent on the dependent person's dependence. Does that make sense?"

"To tell the truth: not really. I just … oh wait, I love this song," Lily said, turning up the volume and joining voices with Diana Ross as she sang "Mahogany."

Iris looked out the window as she listened to the beautiful

voices asking each other if they knew where they were going to. It had started snowing again, and Iris was glad she would be going nowhere that day except to the kitchen to bake banana bread.

26. LILY

"So, how are things going for you at school?" Lily's mother gently swirled cream into her coffee, turning it from dark brown to caramel. She smiled, but the puffy circles under her eyes told a story of sleepless, tearful nights.

"OK," said Lily. "I'm getting ready for my SATs. They're coming up pretty soon."

"Are you finding that you have enough time to study? I know you have an awful lot going on, between your drama club activities, and everything you're doing for your father."

"It's fine," said Lily. It felt strange to visit with her mother. Conversations between them had always occurred while they were doing the dishes in the evening, or while canning the cherries, or preparing Thanksgiving dinner. Talking was an ancillary, accidental part of daily life. They'd never actually sat down alone together with the sole purpose of having a chat. She wanted to tell her mother about what had happened with James, and how hurt she felt, but she sensed that her mother just had too many of her own sorrows to deal with.

"Lily, I'm really sorry about all of this," her mother dabbed at the end of her nose with her napkin. "I never meant to hurt you kids."

"Mom, don't worry about it, really," said Lily, fighting to squelch the lump rising in her throat, a lump formed by all the uncried tears for herself and for her mother. But her mother didn't need to see her falling apart right now. Lily had to be strong; crying would only make her mother feel guiltier than she already did. Lily reached across the table to take her mother's hand.

"We're fine, Mom. It's not your fault. At least there's no more fighting. That's good, right?" Lily looked at her mother for some sign of agreement - a nod, a smile - but she seemed lost in her own pain. "I want you to be happy, Mom. Are you happy?"

Short bursts of sobs erupted from her mother as she held the napkin over her face, as though trying to keep her sorrow from spilling out onto the table, ruining their pie. "I'm afraid I won't be happy for a very long time, Lily."

Lily searched for a memory of a happy time, her sadness amplified by the truth that it took awhile to find one.

"Hey Mom - remember last year when you took us camping out at Darien Lake?"

"Oh, God," her mother smiled. "What a disaster that was! It poured rain and that sorry old pop-up camper that we borrowed started leaking, and everyone got soaked while they were sleeping."

"But we had that great little campsite and we roasted marshmallows every night, and I played the guitar and we sang songs. And Dad came up that one night and sat around the fire with us."

"That was really the straw that broke the camel's back," Lily's mother's voice grew dark. "I went through hell and high water to arrange for that trip, and your father refused to come with us. I thought if we could just get away, spend some time as a family... "

"But we got to go on vacation, and we spent an entire day on the rides and everything - remember how Ricci sunk those baskets at the arcade and won that big panda bear? And remember those people we met, who had us over to their campsite for a cook-out one night?"

Her mother was staring out the window, as though watching a film of her life playing on a screen in the parking lot, having rewound it far beyond the previous summer, waves of anger and sadness passing silently across her face.

"Remember them?" Lily's voice trailed off in resignation, as she traced her mother's gaze out the window. "They were nice..."

Lily considered telling her all about the preparations for her college audition, about how Dolores was helping her get ready, about how she got to go to a real recording studio to lay down an accompaniment track with real musicians. But then she decided it would just make her mother feel bad that she wasn't a part of that, that Dolores had stepped in and was doing things a mother might want to do, might insist upon doing.

Instead, she held her mother's hands, noticing how delicate they were, how her fingers tapered off at the tips, how the cuticles of her thumbs were always cracked and peeling, from the way she constantly picked at them. Lily remembered the countless hours of sitting next to her mother, listening to stories from the books they'd brought home from the library, watching her hands as they turned the pages. She found herself wondering how many diapers her mother had changed, how much vomit she had cleaned up, how many scrapes and cuts she had bandaged and soothed, how many bologna sandwiches she had constructed with those hands. It didn't seem fair that she couldn't even imagine using them to build her own happiness, after all of that.

"It'll be OK, Mom," said Lily. "Everything will be OK."

City kids would walk or ride their bikes to take guitar lessons, but out in the suburbs, the children were softer; they needed cars or rides. The soundproofed studio in the basement of Auntie Rosa and Uncle Alfred's new condo was frequented by a dwindling parade of spoiled pimply-faced teen-aged boys wanting to learn to play "Smoke on the Water," or "Stairway to Heaven," requests that Uncle Alfred would not oblige until they first learned to read music, and had some basic theory behind them. It was a delay in gratification for which children from the suburbs were increasingly losing patience, as was evidenced by the blank time slots in Uncle Alfred's teaching schedule. But the studio made a great place for Saturday band practice, and every week a potpourri of musicians would gather there to play, mostly because Uncle Alfred coerced them with his promises of fun, future gigs, and the chance to get a taste of rock star fame.

In spite of the fact that the rock band Lily and Iris put together had fallen apart, Uncle Alfred continuously urged Lily to sing whenever she could, but she was unenthused by the gigs he got for them - local Rotary Club dinners, a retirement party here and there, private cocktail receptions where wealthy middle-aged women in kaftans stumbled drunkenly around built-in swimming pools decorated with Chinese lanterns. Singing "I Left my Heart in San Francisco" for the members of the Moose Lodge wasn't exactly what Lily had in mind for herself as a performer, but she went along with it. It was a chance to practice, to hang out with Iris, and maybe even make an extra twenty bucks.

Since Dolores had come to stay, their rehearsal space also doubled as her sleeping quarters. The couch in the corner pulled out into a bed, and Dolores was more than happy to host the band, as long as she was allowed to watch and listen.

"Dolores, do you mind if I borrow that music stand?" Lily asked.

"Will you sing my song for me?"

"Yes," said Lily, with a laugh. "I'll sing you whatever you want." James and Paula were likely getting ready for the Ball at that very moment. Today, James belonged to Paula and Lily had missed her chance to be the one at his side. But at least she had this, her band and her audience of one. At least Dolores wanted her.

Dolores swiped her array of small brown prescription bottles from the ledge of the stand and dumped them into her large purse, leaving one bottle behind which she opened, shaking a pill out into her mouth and washing it down with the glass of water she always seemed to have in her hand lately.

The basement was well finished, with wall-to-wall carpeting and gently used furniture, but the only windows were two small transoms at the top edge of the wall, and Auntie Rosa had placed white plastic flower boxes with plastic red geraniums on the sills, which were intended to brighten up the room but actually blocked what little sunlight might find its way in.

"Why are you wearing sunglasses?" Lily asked Dolores. "It's so dark in here already."

"I'm going for this whole Greta Garbo thing," Dolores replied. "Don't you think I appear glamorous and mysterious this way?" A smile broke out across Dolores' face, but the edges of her lips trembled. Lily didn't know who Greta Garbo was, but she had a sense that it was better not to push the matter.

The rest of the hodgepodge band assembled, including Iris on rhythm guitar, some weird girl named Kathy that Uncle Alfred had recruited to play percussion, Uncle Alfred's friend Janine who had one leg shorter than the other and carried an accordion that seemed to be permanently plastered to her chest, and of course Uncle Alfred himself on lead and steel string guitars. They fumbled their way through a set of Hawaiian music including "Blue Hawaii," "Pearly Shells," and "Tiny Bubbles" - the one song Uncle Alfred insisted on singing himself, much to Iris and Lily's embarrassment. With his eyes closed, he would tap his foot, strum his guitar, bob his body and slur and stumble his way through the lyrics like a preacher at a revival meeting, overcome with the Spirit and babbling in tongues.

"OK - it's time for my song now," announced Dolores in between numbers. She got up from the bed and sat in a folding chair facing the band. Lily took her place behind the microphone stand, and Uncle Alfred counted off the beat.

"Nice and slow, now," he instructed. "Nice and slow. 1, 2, and– a 1, 2, 3..."

Lily closed her eyes and sang.

"Every day I face the world at large
What lies ahead is yet uncharted
Reflections of the life I've seen
The dreams I've dreamed but never started
But what's done is done and what was
Just doesn't matter anymore

So every day I pray I'll find a way
To let my spirit soar... "

When Lily opened her eyes she found Dolores with her hands in her lap, tears streaming freely down her cheeks from behind her sunglasses, not a tissue in sight. Lily wanted to go to Dolores, but she didn't want to make it worse by calling everyone's attention to her. Dolores didn't seem to be particularly bothered by her semi-public display of emotion. She engaged in her tears with the same detached consciousness as if she were reading a book, or knitting a scarf. Sorrow was one thing the women in Lily's family seemed to come by naturally, and possess in abundance.

"My heart is strong, my soul is free
The weight of the world doesn't bother me
And everything is beautiful if you just choose to believe
I'm where I belong, where I need to be
I walk in synchronicity
And every step just leads me closer
To my destiny
As I walk the path of peace and harmony"

Uncle Alfred ended rehearsal after the song, even though they hadn't run through all of their material yet. Weird Kathy packed up her stuff and left. Uncle Alfred helped Janine haul her accordion up the stairs, and Iris went up into the kitchen to visit with Auntie Rosa. Lily stayed to break down the equipment, and pick up the sheet music that was scattered about. Dolores stumbled back over to her bed. Lily collapsed the folding chair. Dolores shook another pill out of the small brown bottle and popped it into her mouth.

"Didn't you just take one of those?" Lily asked, offhandedly.

"Don't you mind about that," Dolores snapped, draining her glass in a single gulp. She considered the empty glass, and then she considered Lily. "I certainly don't need your help to keep

407

track of my medications."

Shocked at Dolores' response, Lily just stood and looked at her.

"What are you looking at? Why don't you go on and get out of here and leave me alone, so I can take my nap?"

"I'm sorry, Dolores, I was only trying to -"

"Go on," said Dolores, lying on the bed and pulling the covers up over her shoulder. "Leave me be."

"OK," said Lily, fighting back tears of her own. "I'll talk to you soon, then." She switched off the light, and shut the studio door behind her.

Lily tossed and turned half the night, the task of falling asleep made more difficult by the taunting of Iris' empty bed. Typical. Lily had been counting on going to the Ball for months and she was the one home alone while Iris - who'd had no interest in going at all – had reluctantly accepted a desperate invitation from a friend at the last minute. Her absence accentuated the silence and solitude and caused the night to drag slowly on.

The next morning, Lily stepped out onto the back porch and, realizing she was barefoot, stepped into the gold sandals that Iris must have abandoned in her attempt to slink in undetected during the wee hours. As Lily meandered down the long driveway, she let her robe fall open. Even though it was still cold and the landscape was littered with remnants of crusty snow blackened by the exhaust of passing cars, the air hinted at spring, and Lily longed to feel it against her skin. The Senior Ball had hung over the weekend like a black storm cloud, but the rising sun and burgeoning spring were reminders that time does pass, and Lily was grateful to have last night behind her. Soon, life would file the Ball away as a memory, and then she could also file the pain away and move on.

Purple crocuses peeked their heads up through the spongy earth, whispering tales of the Easters of Lily's childhood. She recalled the colorful wicker baskets filled with chocolate rabbits, jelly beans, malted milk eggs, and sugar-coated marshmallow chicks that only Violet liked. Lily laughed to herself, remembering how Violet used to collect the chicks from everyone else and save them until they were stale and hard before eating them. She could almost smell the braided bread that her mother baked only at Easter, with whole hard-boiled eggs cooked right into the sweet dough. Lily loved to slice it and toast it until it was slightly burnt before slathering it with butter and dunking it in her Easter morning coffee.

Without her mother at home, Easter would be sad this year, as so many things were now. She wondered if they would still have a big ham dinner, and if Iris knew how to make the Easter bread, and where her mother would go to celebrate. The thought of her sitting home alone - or with her Jewish friend Anita as though it were just another Sunday - was an unbearable one.

The clicking of the heels of Iris' sandals against the asphalt resurrected the sense of excitement that Lily used to feel at wearing shiny patent leather shoes to Easter Mass, and the yellow bonnet with white lace ruffles that had always been stowed on the top shelf of the closet, retrieved once a year, expressly for the occasion.

The lawn was still mostly brown and desolate, but Lily knew that in a few weeks it would explode with color as the fuchsia hyacinths, yellow daffodils, and crimson tulips her mother had planted over the years would all arise from their slumber, joyfully proclaiming the end of another winter. Lily took comfort in her mother's presence - a presence that could not be lifted out or scrubbed away. She was still here, and she always would be, regardless of where she lived, just as the memories of Easters past and the flowers that announced them would remain long after Lily had moved away to college, onto her new life.

Lily retrieved the rolled up newspaper from the ground, and as she rose again she inhaled deeply, savoring the cold, sweet air as it passed through her nostrils and into her lungs. She loved being the first one awake, and adored watching the sun rise and witnessing the calm, quiet break of day. Her whole body swelled with the contagious optimism of spring, excited that all she dreamed of was just around the corner, beyond the Senior Ball and past her parents' divorce. By this time next year, she would practically be on her way. One short dance of the earth.

A lone car approached and slowed down as it turned into the driveway. Lily stepped aside onto the cool damp grass, as James pulled in and parked. Lily's heart jumped first at his presence and then at the realization that she was in her nightgown and without makeup. Concerns about her own appearance quickly retreated as James emerged and walked toward her, still dressed in a powder blue tuxedo. The top three buttons of his white shirt were open, and his bow tie hung limp, likely exhausted from a night of partying. The cummerbund accentuated his slender waist and broad shoulders. Lily froze in place as he approached.

"Good morning," he said.

"What are you doing here?"

"I wanted to talk to you."

"Have you even been home yet?"

"No," James replied. "I came straight here. I had to see you."

Lily walked over and sat on the chaise under the apple tree, crossing her legs under her and pulling her nightgown over her knees. James took a seat at the opposite end of the chaise. His gaze fell to the neckline of her open robe, and as Lily glanced down she could see that her breasts were visible through the thin pink cotton, the cool morning breeze making her dark nipples erect. She resisted the urge to close the robe, and instead watched James looking at them.

"So what's up?" All she wanted to do was get started on the housework and the shopping, with the intent of putting as much space and activity between her and last night as possible. And now here was last night, come looking for her, sitting under her apple tree.

"I made a mistake."

"What do you mean?" Lily knew what he meant, but she wanted him to say it.

"Not taking you to the Ball. It was a mistake. We should have been there together."

"You didn't have a good time?"

"It was alright. Paula's kind of a princess, though. She didn't like the corsage I bought her - she wanted a wrist corsage of those little roses, and I got her a regular one. And she refused to get out of the car until I went around and opened the door for her."

Lily inhaled deeply and grit her teeth. To think that while she struggled to get through the night, he was pinning on corsages and opening doors only served to retroactively feed her rage. *Play it cool. Don't let him see. Hold it in.* Showing him her anger would mean that he won, and then she would cry and it would ease the guilt he was feeling. He wasn't going to get off that easy.

"Have you eaten anything?" Lily asked.

"No, some kids went out to breakfast, but Paula was too tired so I took her home a couple hours ago. I've been driving around, thinking."

"Want some eggs?"

James sat at the kitchen table as Lily moved about the kitchen, trying to make as little noise as possible. She was pretty sure how her father would feel about finding a boy sitting on his bench, and about Lily entertaining one in her nightgown.

She placed a plate in front of James, then a fork and a knife, a napkin, a small glass of orange juice. With every act of service, James seemed to wince; with every wince, Lily was soothed. She watched him eat his scrambled eggs, using the last triangle of toast and scoop of eggs to make a tiny sandwich, which he ate in one bite.

Lily cleared the dishes from the table and as she passed by the stove, she grabbed the coffee pot, and began to fill the cup in front of James' place.

"I don't drink coffee," he said, with a chuckle. Lily froze, confused by his declaration. She looked at the empty cup, she looked at James, and then she set the coffee pot back onto the stove.

"Do you want to do something later?" James asked Lily, when she walked him out to his car.

You mean like pin a corsage on me, take me out to dinner, and then go dancing? Did he really think he could make it up to her so

411

easily? She wanted him to sit home tonight, feeling sorry for himself and sorry for what he did to her, wondering what she was doing and who she was with.

"I can't," said Lily. The wind blew her robe open. She turned toward James. "I already have plans."

James stepped forward and drew Lily's body to his. She allowed him to hold her close, to press up and feel her skin through the paper thin nightie. She felt him get hard against her as he ran his hand down her back, resting it on her buttocks. She wanted him. She knew she could have him.

"Lily," said James, breathlessly. "I - I-"

Lily broke away and pulled her robe around herself.

"Talk to you soon," she said.

Lily watched as James backed down the driveway and disappeared down the street, leaving her with the scent of his cologne in her nostrils, an ache in her groin, and a searing pain in her belly.

27. IRIS

"Mi-iss! Yoo-hoo!" called the balding, frog-faced man seated at table twelve with a woman half his age and bulk, waving his empty highball glass in the air. Iris wanted to scream back, tell the guy she was neither deaf nor blind, just busy. Instead, biting her tongue and holding his stare, she responded by raising her eyebrows, a signal that indicated she would attend to him as soon as possible.

Since freed by the unceremonious completion of her high school obligations, Iris reported for double shifts, Monday through Friday, at the Sizzling Skillet. Each day afforded her countless opportunities to hone the skills she had learned in the fast-food business, and forced her to develop many others. She was amazed at the level of non-verbal communication she managed to achieve using facial expressions and body language as she buzzed around the dining room dispensing food and drink, clearing away enough leftovers to feed entire families, scooping up loose change left on soiled tablecloths and tossing it into the pouch of her apron. As the day wore on, she took consolation in the growing weight of the quarters and nickels and dimes and pennies, jingling against her thighs, as the tide of chattering customers flowed and ebbed until the last rush was finally over and a spent silence settled over the dining room.

The clientele at the Sizzling Skillet was comprised mostly of the office workers from the factories on the west side of the city, whose meal times were as predictable as the orders they placed. In the short time Iris had been waiting on tables, she had developed a knack for identifying people by the food they ate, and entertained herself by anticipating their requests: would the man in Prince of Wales polyester order New England or Manhattan clam chowder? Meatloaf or beef stroganoff? Lemon meringue pie or apple à la mode? But Friday dinner rush was no time to play games, not with a pile of dirty dishes precariously perched on her forearm, and a battery of cutlery rattling in the first dish anchored on her open palm by her left thumb. Her pace was hurried but steady, as she pushed toward her goal: the swinging doors at the back of the room. Seconds later, she was there, and a swift kick with the rubber sole of her right shoe landed her on the other side, in waitress hell. The kitchen.

"Hey, watch where you're goin'!" Raul the bus boy hissed at her, hopping out of her way to avoid a collision. During the last few yards of the dash, Iris's attention had been focused exclusively on the plates balanced on her arm, willing them to not crash to the floor, rather on than checking for oncoming traffic through the portholes in the doors.

"Sorry!" Iris said, before she could stop herself from apologizing. She would have been quite happy to smash the door into Raul's ugly nose. Since her first day on the job, the guy had started pestering her, popping up out of nowhere when she was setting up the dining room in the interval between lunch and dinner, while he was supposed to be tending to his own chores in the kitchen. She was immensely irritated by the vulgar remarks he half-whispered as he walked by her, in a voice muffled just enough to make Iris doubt whether she had heard right, and allow her to pretend she had not heard at all. That very afternoon, while she was filling salt shakers at the work station, he had passed behind her, gyrating and singing the words "*voulez-vous couchez avec moi,*" while his hand happened to brush against her butt. Never one hundred percent sure about what exactly Raul said or did, she hesitated mentioning it to anyone out of fear that verbalizing her impressions would transform them into accusations, and accusations were bound to lead to unpleasant confrontations. One day, when she had gone home particularly tired and upset, she confided in Lily, who suggested that the best strategy was to avoid being alone with Raul, and continue to ignore him, in the hope that he would stop. These situations usually had a way of resolving themselves.

Depositing her tottering load on the stainless steel counter that was the domain of Walt, who as a young man had worked in a fine hotel in the Poconos and had introduced himself to Iris as the plongeur, Iris heaved a sigh of relief, and ran the back of her hand over her damp brow. Resisting the temptation to rub her burning eyes for fear of popping her contact lenses and losing them forever in the grime of the kitchen, she blinked at Walt in the bug-eyed manner typical of contact lens wearers. Walt encircled the dirty dishes with hairy forearms, sliding them toward him as if they were stacks of chips won at a gaming table. "Not bad for a rookie, sweetheart!" he grunted almost cheerfully, squinting through the blue haze formed by the smoke from the cigarette hanging from the corner of his mouth mingled with the clouds of steam rising from the sink.

"Thanks," Iris said, smiling weakly. "I've had lots of practice." The sound of running water was torture to Iris's bursting bladder. She extracted her order pad from her pocket, studied her scribbling in an effort to decipher what she had written with hurried hand mere minutes ago, and hastened over to the cook.

"Two tenderloin specials medium well with baked, please!" she called out to the cook, but her words were diced and sautéed before they could find their way to his ears.

"Speak up, sweetheart!" the cook yelled back over the din of pans banging and pots clattering and meat searing and knives chopping.

Iris cleared her throat. "I said, two tenderloin specials medium well with baked!" she repeated, in the loudest voice she could muster, feeling the heat in her face cranking up a notch. She hated blushing almost as much as she hated shouting.

"That's more like it! Now move it, sweetheart!" he ordered. "Your fish fries for table ten have been sitting here for over five minutes!"

Iris hopped in place as she reached for the two hot dishes; she was sure to wet her pants any minute. She rushed away, pausing to scoop a serving of coleslaw onto each plate from a metal canister, before heading back out the swinging doors.

"Capotosti!"

She froze in her tracks at the sound of Mr. Henderson's voice, her rubber soles screeching on the tiles as she pivoted to face the owner of the Sizzling Skillet.

"Yes, Mr. Henderson?" she asked.

"Monkey dish!" he said.

"I beg your pardon?" Iris asked.

"Where's the monkey dish?"

"Um. I don't know, Mr. Henderson," Iris replied, not having the slightest idea of where the monkey dish was, nor what it was, though she was certain that was not the response he wanted to hear. The hot dishes were starting to scald the tender underside of her forearm. She wondered if the customers at table ten would notice if her skin came away from her arm with the plates when she served them.

"Coleslaw is cold and runny," Mr. Henderson continued as she squirmed, knees pressed tightly together. "Deep-fried haddock and fries are hot and crispy. If these elements collide, as they are bound to do, the way you are serving them, they all get ruined. Ruined!"

"I'm sorry Mr. Henderson," Iris said.

"We don't serve sorry here, young lady, we serve quality! Now get a move on while those dinners are still edible! You've been lolling around too long. And don't let me catch you without a monkey dish again!" Mr. Henderson admonished.

"I won't," Iris assured him, making a mental note to talk to Gloria, the matronly waitress with varicose veins and dyed red hair who looked like she had stepped out of a TV sitcom. She even called everyone "honey." Gloria had been working at the Sizzling

Skillet since before Iris was born, and was always ready to share her opinions with anyone who asked, especially when it came to gossip about the regulars. Iris was certain she would welcome the opportunity to reveal everything Iris needed to know about the world of monkey dishes, at least enough to help her survive this jungle until it was time for her to go away to college, where hopefully she could aspire to learning experiences of a more stimulating nature.

Iris had bluffed about a few things to land this job, including her age, (she was still shy of eighteen, and serving alcoholic beverages illegally), and her previous work experience, figuring that waiting on tables could not be any harder than serving up meals for a large family or placating the cravings of fast-food junkies. Her rock-solid reference had been Auntie Rosa, who occasionally treated herself to breakfast at the Sizzling Skillet on her way to work, after attending six o'clock Mass. She loved the toasted hard rolls, and the assorted jellies that came in little plastic tubs with a peel-back foil cover, of which she had a stash of "leftovers" crowding the butter compartment of her refrigerator door. Always warm and outgoing, Auntie Rosa made friends easily, and had become well acquainted with Mr. Henderson and his wife, a stately woman with excellent posture who had the habit of fingering her string of matched pearls with her left hand while ringing up bills on the cash register with her right.

Auntie Rosa said the Hendersons were upstanding people, and devout Methodists. It was possible, according to Auntie Rosa, to occasionally come across fine people that were not Catholics, like the surgeon she worked for at the medical center. "He would put any Catholic to shame," Auntie Rosa could be heard declaring in his defense whenever anyone attempted to criticize Dr. Andrews, her case resting on the fact that he was a good family man, and, like Auntie Rosa, had refused to consign his infirm mother to a "home." Auntie Rosa prided herself on her sense of duty and self-sacrifice, and any nagging symptoms that might make her feel underpaid or overworked were alleviated by the expertly dosed compliments administered by the honorable doctor, and soothed by the affectionate hugs of her grateful patients. Auntie Rosa positively beamed when she told the family about the time Dr. Andrews had taken her aside and said, "There's not a selfish hair on your head!" or the Christmas he had given her a bottle of port wine as her bonus, and told her to "put your feet up and tell everyone to go to hell." Everyone but him, of course.

Six weeks into her waitressing career, Iris was dead tired. Each morning she performed a number of chores at home before catching the bus that would take her to the Sizzling Skillet, but was sorry to stick Lily with the cooking, for which she knew her sister had neither the passion nor the patience. She missed cooking and the sense of gratification it gave her to provide her family with nourishment and pleasure; it was the only balm she could offer to soothe their scars of abandonment. However, she did not miss the loud conversations or the bickering or the bad table manners. And she did not miss sitting across the table from that unwanted dinner guest: the empty space left by her mother.

When Iris kicked off her sweaty shoes at the end of the day and collapsed on her bed, she imagined what it must feel like to be a soldier behind enemy lines in a foreign country, struggling to survive in a hostile environment. It was not the challenge of the unfamiliar language and customs that wore her down, it was the sense of being so utterly out of her element. Since her first day on the job, she knew that she did not belong there, in the company of unshaven short-order cooks and disillusioned middle-aged waitresses and vulgar busboys and rude customers. Just as she had not belonged in high school, where the work was too simple and the social life too much of a struggle for either to be worthwhile. Just as she had never felt like she belonged in her own home. Oh sure, they noticed when she was not there to fill the house with the comforting smells of food cooking and furniture polish that made it still seem a home. But did they notice anything else about her? She wanted them to need her, but not as a surrogate housewife or mother. Her, the daughter; her, the sister, the eighth of twelve Capotostis, whose name was Iris.

Salvation from the Sizzling Skillet came one day in the form of a phone call from the head office of Kodak: Iris was being offered a temporary job. Nearly every family in Rochester had a member who at one time or another had worked for the company, and that had been her aspiration since the day after graduation, when she had put on her best dress and taken the bus downtown to apply for a position. She had been trudging down State Street in the dirty city snow, imagining herself passing her days in the sinister looking tower of the tall brick building crowned with five red block letters that stood out against the steely winter sky, when a delivery van sped by, spattering her coat with slush. She was still thinking about her rotten luck and Rochester's crappy climate as she queued up outside the employment office, when the slope-shouldered gentleman handing out applications forms leaned close to her and said in her ear, "You'll get it."

"Excuse me?" Iris asked.

"The job. You'll get it. I've been doing this for over thirty years now. I can tell. You're a Kodak girl." He winked and smiled at her; Iris thanked him, and smiled back, while debating silently over whether his comment should reassure or depress her. Still smiling, the man adjusted his already straight navy blue tie and ran a hand over his impeccably groomed grey hair. Iris could spot patches of a splotched pink scalp peeking through the comb tracks, and wondered what he must have looked like his first day on the job. She imagined the nostrils at the end of his hooked nose, out of which protruded a small army of renegade hairs, sniffing the air of security mixed with the smell of industrial carpeting and half-drunk cups of stale coffee. The complexion of his youthful face, now grey and lined, would have been suffused with sufficient optimism to appear rosy under the greenish hue of the caged neon lights that crawled across over the maze of cubicles as if searching for a way out.

Yet the gentleman seemed satisfied with his career. Thirty years, working in the same office in the same company, in the same city, in the same rotten climate. She wondered what he had dreamed of as a young man; could it have been this? Could reality pose as a dream come true, an understudy filling in for the protagonist who abandoned the scene because no one had set the stage and none of the other players had learned their lines? What good was a dream, anyway, if it could only exist within the confines of fantasy? If by miracle it should come to fruition, it would no longer exist as such. And why was the same word used to describe your highest aspirations, and something that messed with your brain at night as you slept, arbitrarily barraging you with the most pleasant or frightening scenarios, then abandoning you as it stole away in the groggy vagueness of the first waking instant?

"Wow! This place is huge, Iris!" Lily said, making a sweeping motion in the air with her arm. Her long hair fluttered in the breeze as she leaned out the open window of the Chevy station wagon that bounced along lopsidedly on shot springs.

"Let's see, I think it's that way," Iris said, her attention focused on following signs for the Registrar's Office. The leafy trees that lined the road through the University of Buffalo's Main Street campus whispered reassurances of more warm days to come, but the scent and the sound of the leaves had changed since Iris's first tour of the college the previous spring in the company of her mother, who had insisted on offering her guidance when she realized that Iris was already selecting a college. Iris had been disturbed by the flicker of pleasure she felt as she watched a look of surprise, then dismay, disrupt the placid features of her mother's face, when Iris told her that she had already been accepted at three different universities, without her assistance.

For the most part, the drive to Buffalo and back had been pleasant, if a bit awkward, like on the other rare occasions Iris had found herself alone with her mother. They had briefly discussed possible careers which might suit Iris, who was still undecided about a major, and who spent the remainder of the time trying to feign interest in what her mother was saying about the cases she was researching in her free time to help provide legal assistance to women who had been abandoned by their husbands and left with no funds and less recourse under the archaic, discriminatory laws of the State of New York.

During that first visit, Iris had been filled with a sense of promise by the budding branches waving in the frisky spring winds that jumped the Canadian border to play hopscotch between lakes Erie and Ontario. Now, there was a rustling of parched leaves as they clung to the branches, exhausted by the summer's heat, but determined to not relinquish their grip until they could salute the student body with a flourish of fall colors. Whenever autumn approached, Iris could hear Grandma Capotosti's failing voice in the ear of her memory. *"Non si muove una foglia che Dio non voglia,"* she would say as she gazed out the upstairs window, tossing stale bread to the birds from the chair where she rocked away her life sentence to life. "Not a leaf may move, unless God wills it," Auntie Rosa had translated for Iris one day, making Iris regret she had asked. The Italian words sounded poetic, but their meaning had made Iris feel sorry for her grandmother, and angry at God for condemning her to that rocking chair.

"Did you hear me, Iris?" Lily asked.

Iris turned to look at her sister. "What?"

"Sometimes when I talk to you, you look like you're on another continent," Lily continued. "I said, this is an amazing campus! It's huge!"

"You're right," Iris said, bobbing her head in agreement, as she pulled into a deserted parking lot. Indeed, it was an amazing campus, and indeed, Iris knew she had a tendency toward distraction. One minute, she would be washing the dishes or cooking, and the branches of the Russian olive tree outside the kitchen window would tap on the pane, and she would look out at it, and instantly begin fantasizing about the groves of olive trees that dotted the countryside in Italy or Spain or Greece. She could almost taste the delectable flavors of the Mediterranean foods she had never eaten exploding on her tongue, the same way she could perceive the stimulating discussions of the classes for which she had not yet registered enriching her mind.

"Why are you parking here? We must be a mile away!" Lily

said.

Iris proceeded to park the car their father kept for the family's licensed drivers to share, and whose gas gauge somehow always pointed to the desolate area below "E" whenever Iris needed to use it. With a turn of the key, she cut the engine, and closed her eyes briefly, welcoming the silence conceded by the ceasefire from the muffler that had survived another Rochester winter by the rusty skin of its tailpipe. "That's why," Iris said. "I don't want to make my grand entrance with this jalopy."

"So you mean we have to walk?" Lily asked.

"C'mon, it won't kill you," Iris said. She could never figure out why her sister sometimes seemed to have so little energy. Lily's grey-green eyes shone brighter than all the stars in the universe combined when she sang or talked about James Gentile, but at other times, they had the glassy, distant look of a much older person, hardened by a lifetime of hardship and disappointments.

"I'll have plenty of walking to do around here," Iris said, as they slammed their car doors simultaneously. "I'll be living on the other campus, and taking classes on both. I guess there's a bus that goes back and forth." She wondered whether she had made a mistake choosing such a huge, sprawled-out university, after detesting her overpopulated high school. She knew the school enjoyed a good reputation: even her brother John, who knew everything about colleges, having already attended three different ones himself, had said so. And since it was in New York State, she could take advantage of the Regents scholarship she had been awarded to cover part of the tuition costs. But she knew the real justification for her choice lay in the distance, a mere sixty miles, that separated the campus from her family's home on Chestnut Crest, where she would be leaving Lily to fend for herself and their father and younger brothers. Buffalo was just a short ride on a Greyhound bus from home.

"It'll be weird, won't it, Lily?" Iris said as she alternated walking with clipped, rapid steps in the direction of the impressive brick building that stood in the distance, and slowing her pace to match Lily's. Lily seemed determined it should take them as long as possible to cover the distance from the car to the building.

"You probably can't wait to have the room all to yourself," Iris said. Her words sounded as empty as the feeling in her stomach.

Lily stopped walking altogether. "I don't want the room all to myself. I especially don't want the family all to myself. I want to go away, too."

"You will, Lily," Iris said. "You'll be going to that great school for the performing arts, next year. You can do it. You'll have a great time with Dolores preparing for your audition. In the meantime, you're a shoe-in for the lead in the school play this year."

"I wish I could just fly away, right now," Lily said, looking up into the sky. The clouds and humidity had been building up all day. Iris hoped they wouldn't get caught in a thunderstorm on the drive home.

"Sometimes I have this dream, where I can fly," Iris said, tugging on Lily's elbow to prod her along. "I start out walking, then I'm running, and flapping my arms. Suddenly, I just lift off the ground. It's so simple, so natural. I fly real low, so it's not scary, and I can see everything, but in a more detached way. Everything looks so much better from a distance."

"Sometimes I have this dream, where I really have to go to the bathroom," Lily said. "So bad, I feel like I'm going to burst. I'm running around, looking for a place to go, and I finally find these public restrooms. There are rows and rows of toilets, but the doors are either missing from the stalls, or hanging on broken hinges, and as soon as I sit down, someone barges in on me. So I go somewhere else, but all the toilets are overflowing, and the toilet seats and floors are all wet."

"Oh my God!" Iris said. "I have a toilet dream, too! Just like yours!"

"Get out!" Lily said.

"No, really!" Iris said. "Sometimes I can't stand it anymore, and I decide to go ahead and sit on one of the toilets. The seats are all broken and dirty, but I pick the least gross one I can find. I line the seat with little squares of toilet paper, like Auntie Rosa taught me to do when I was little, but the paper keeps flying away."

"In your dream, do you have to go number one or number two?" Lily asked.

"Number two, definitely," Iris said. "And sometimes I have my period, too. It's an awful feeling. I feel so gross when I wake up."

"Me too!" Lily said. "Totally gross."

"Weird." After a few moments of walking in silence, Iris said, "I've always hated sharing the bathroom with so many people. Not that it will be any better at my dorm, but at least there won't be any boys. When I used to go to Auntie Rosa's as a kid, I used to sit on the toilet and look around at how neat and clean everything was. Sometimes, I would sit there so long my feet would fall asleep. Just because I could; just because no one banged on the door and made me come out. Hopefully we'll both have a house with a bathroom of our own, sooner or later."

"Talk about shooting for the stars," Lily said.

Two hours later they were on their way back home, each holding a Wendy's frosty Iris had bought for them to celebrate her official registration as a UB freshman. They cranked the radio up all the way, so they could hear it over the noise from the muffler and the roaring of the tractor trailer engines on Interstate 90 East rolling through the open windows together with the muggy afternoon air. Lily and Iris sucked hard on their straws, but the drink was impossibly thick, and the effort was giving Iris a headache. She placed the frosty between her bare thighs, to help it melt, and at the same time, cool her off. Her short denim skirt had hitched up to her crotch when she scooted in behind the wheel, causing the truckers to blow their horns whenever they passed, which made the girls giggle as they sang along to Fleetwood Mac's "Don't Stop Thinking About Tomorrow."

"I love this song!" Iris shouted, the impact of what she had just done in Buffalo making her giddy with excitement. Paying for her first semester of tuition and room and board with the money she had earned selling Egg McMuffins and Sizzling Skillet fish fries and rolling her mail cart down the corridors of Kodak headquarters with blistered feet and an all-American smile; imagining herself living in a dorm and going to class in those old brick buildings and studying whatever subjects she was interested in (they even taught Swahili!); meeting people from other cities and maybe even other countries, elated her spirit with a sense of independence that only hard-earned money can buy.

"Looks like Dad's already home," Iris said, spotting his car in the garage as they parked in the driveway at Chestnut Crest an hour later.

"I hope he doesn't want to eat early," Lily said. "He's always in such a rush, we never even have the time to catch our breath."

"I threw some beef stew in the crock pot before we left. It's probably ready by now, if he does," Iris said. "Uncle Alfred's car is here, too. What on earth is he doing here, I wonder?"

"That's strange. I doubt he'll be staying for dinner, though," Lily said. "He plays on Friday nights."

The girls walked through the back door into the kitchen. The smell of slowly simmering stew filled the air. "You'd think someone could have at least set out the dishes," Iris said, rolling her eyes at the sight of the bare table.

"God forbid," Lily said.

Through the doorway that led to the living room, Iris could see her father bent forward in his armchair, elbows resting on his knees, looking down at the shabby carpet, smoking a cigarette. It was odd to see him home early, and even more unusual to see him relaxing before dinner on a Friday; he usually used that time to get a head start on the weekend and tend to a few odd jobs. Henry was smoking too, but he was standing, his back pressed against the door jamb, looking at the ceiling. She spotted Uncle Alfred sitting on the sofa, air-washing his hands, his slight frame poised on the very edge of the seat cushion, as if fearful of picking up germs. William, Charles and Ricci all sat cross-legged on the floor. The scene reminded Iris of those brainteasers at the back of the TV guide, where you have to study the scene and figure out what was wrong with it.

"Where is Auntie Rosa?" Iris said, immediately honing in on the missing detail.

"Iris, Lily," their father said, in a flat voice.

"What's going on, Dad?" Iris said. Never had she been in a room with more than two Capotostis and witnessed such silence. A chill of fear shot up her spine.

"There's been an accident," he said, his eyelids fluttering.

His words were a vice, clamping down on Iris's heart. Something had happened to Auntie Rosa! Iris looked at Lily, at their father, at the faces in the living room that were turned on them expectantly, gauging their reactions.

"What do you mean? Tell us what happened!" Iris said, torn between wanting to know, and wanting to run away. Her head was spinning, her knees were weak.

"It's Dolores," he said.

"What about Dolores?" Lily said, her words interrupting the flash of relief that allowed Iris to breath again.

"She's gone," he said.

"She's not gone, Dad," Henry said, squinting at their father through the smoke of his cigarette. "She's dead."

Iris wanted to know more, but could not make her tongue ask any questions. No further details could be discerned from her father's grim face; no hope of some gross misunderstanding was kindled by Henry's hard stare. Dumb and numb, filled with relief, guilt, pity, sorrow, she looked at Lily. Her sister's eyes darted around the room, frantically searching for a way out of the moment; a cry of visceral panic, like the spine-chilling whiny of a mare trapped in a burning barn, rose from deep inside her, piercing the eerie silence of the room. Iris saw the whites of her eyes flash, as Lily threw back her head and began laughing uncontrollably.

28. LILY

Green carpeting, juice stain. Uncle Alfred's hands, one gliding over the other, again and again. Is he cold? Cigarette smoke everywhere. Can't see. Can't think. Iris. Her green eyes crying. The kitchen clock. Tick tock, tick tock. Dad, over there, sitting in his chair two feet away, on the other side of the world. He looks so small. Henry leaning up against the sunroom door jamb. Stop staring at me. Legs like jelly. Can't breathe. What is that awful sound? Is that me? Am I laughing? Why am I laughing? What's happening? What is everyone doing here? Shut UP - it isn't funny!

Iris wrapped her arms around Lily, pulling her in close, holding her tight. "Shhh..." she whispered into Lily's ear. "It's OK. It's OK, Lily. Calm down."

The convulsions of Lily's body slowed and her wailing subsided to a whimper.

"What happened?" asked Iris, looking over Lily's shoulder.

Their father and Uncle Alfred exchanged a glance, and then Uncle Alfred looked back down at his hands.

"It was an accidental overdose," said their father. "Dolores was on some anti-anxiety medication and she took too much."

"Oh my God!" shouted Lily, breaking away from Iris' embrace. "I saw her do that - I asked her about it and she got mad so I didn't say anything to anyone." Lily turned toward Iris. "I should have said something... I should have told somebody..." Tears flowed freely down Lily's cheeks. "If I had told Auntie Rosa that Dolores was taking too much medicine, she could have watched her, could have made sure. I didn't want to make Dolores mad..."

"It wasn't your fault, Lily." said Henry. "It wouldn't have mattered. Why don't you tell her the truth, Dad? Tell her what really happened."

Don't you dare try to comfort me.

"Henry - that's enough." said their father. "We don't know."

Henry looked at Lily. "Dolores killed herself, Lily. She checked out. She couldn't take it anymore."

Shut up, Henry.

"We don't know, Henry," repeated their father, louder this time. "She didn't leave a note. There's no way to tell for sure."

"Wake up, Dad - she did leave a note," said Henry. "An empty bottle of pills and a fifth of vodka, drained one glass at a time into that tumbler she always had in her hand. Translation: Dear Family, Adios - I'm outta here. Love, Dolores."

Vodka? It was vodka, not water? Dolores killed herself? Didn't want to be here anymore?

"Jesus, Mary, and Joseph," mumbled Uncle Alfred. He continued to wring his hands, while rocking back and forth on the edge of the loveseat.

Something was really wrong here. This couldn't be true. Dolores could not be dead, could not have killed herself. She would never do that. Not to herself. Not to Lily. Why would she? There was so much to look forward to. So many dreams. Dolores would not leave her this way.

Mechanically, Lily walked over and sat down on the ottoman at her father's side. "All of my audition clothes are on layaway," she said to no one.

"What?" asked their father.

Iris sat by Lily's side and Lily rested her head on her sister's shoulder. "Iris," Lily said. "She's gone."

"I know, Lily. I'm so sorry. She loved you so much, you know that, don't you?" Iris pulled the cuff of her cotton blouse down over her hand and used it to wipe the tears from Lily's face.

"I knew she was sad," said Lily between sobs. "But I didn't know she was that sad. I wish I knew. I could have tried to make her happy."

"Oh, you did, Lily," said Iris, tucking a stray tuft of hair behind Lily's ear. "She so loved being with you - you were the light of her life. She bragged about you all the time, she believed in you with her whole heart."

That meant something. Once.

"The song - I didn't finish recording the song for my portfolio. We were supposed to go next week. And then we - " with a sigh, Lily stopped speaking.

"I want you to sing at the service, Lily," said Uncle Alfred. "I want to play that song she loved so much."

"Yeah, sure," Lily answered absently. "When is the funeral?"

Uncle Alfred and Lily's father exchanged glances again.

"What is it?" Lily asked, sitting upright.

Henry jumped forward into the silence of his father's hesitation. "There isn't going to be a funeral, Lily."

Shut up, Henry, I'm not talking to you. You don't belong here, you don't want to comfort me; you just want to shock me, watch me suffer. Go get your thrills someplace else.

"Dolores wanted to be cremated," Henry continued, "and the Catholic Church doesn't allow cremated remains to, well, to attend service, so to speak."

"What do you mean?" Lily asked their father. "They won't let her ashes into church?"

"More or less," Henry replied.

"That is such bullshit!" Lily shouted. "Doesn't the Church know what a beautiful soul she is? Don't they realize how completely anti-Christian it is of them to exclude her, to tell people who loved her that they can't say good-bye to her properly?!"

"Now Lily," their father said. "I realize that you're upset, but let's not go around accusing the Church of being anti-Christian."

"What would you call it when they say that a person who suffered so much her whole life and was in so much pain that she couldn't even stand to be alive doesn't deserve a funeral?"

"There have to be rules, Lily. The Church needs its rules."

Lily shot up out of her chair. "Screw the rules, Dad!" she screamed. "And screw the Church, and the vodka and the sleeping pills! And screw Dolores!"

"Lily Elizabeth Capotosti!" Her father's exclamation was lost in the din of her mind, her rage, the stomping of her feet as she bolted from the living room, and out the back door.

Lily ran down the street to the duck pond, with Iris following close behind. She found a place under a willow tree, and let her body collapse to the ground, without even checking for duck droppings. Iris sat down next to her. The sisters sat in silence, holding hands.

"Would you rather be alone?" Iris finally asked.

"Apparently," said Lily.

Iris drew in a breath a few times, as if she were going to speak, but each time she opened her mouth, a sob escaped, followed by a rush of tears.

Finally, Iris said, "You know Lily, there is a chance that she didn't kill herself. It really could have been an accident."

"Yeah. Sure. I know." Lily knew that was what everyone would tell themselves.

"She did love you - she thought the world of you."

"I loved her too. And I know this is going to sound awful and selfish, but - so what... she loved me. So did Mom. It doesn't mean anything. Just because people love you doesn't mean they want to stay with you. In fact, if you ask me, it almost seems the opposite. Seems like everyone who loves me ends up leaving."

Just as Lily began to wonder whether Iris felt accused by the statement, Iris let go of her hand. Iris would be leaving for the university in two weeks; the idea of it was suddenly terrifying to Lily. She had been so distracted by the activity and excitement that Dolores brought into her life that she hadn't truly considered it before. Iris was leaving. And so was James. For the first time, Lily was glad that he didn't love her. At least that would make it easier to watch him go. Lily began to sob.

"What is it?" Iris asked, placing her arm around Lily's shoulder.

Don't go, Lily wanted to tell her. *Please, Iris, please don't leave me here alone. Not now.* However, Lily had learned all too well that when the time came for a Capotosti to cut free, there wasn't anything that could be done but to watch them go, and hope your time would arrive soon. As much as Lily was afraid to be alone, to live in a world that she couldn't even yet fathom, she still longed for Iris get out and live her own dreams, whatever they were.

"I'm going to miss her, that's all," said Lily.

"I know. Me too."

"I'm OK, Iris," said Lily. "You can go back to the house now. I just want to sit here for a bit."

"Are you sure?"

"Yep," said Lily, forcing a smile. "I'm sure."

"OK." Iris stood and brushed off the back of her skirt with her hands. "I should go see what else I can scrounge up to add to that stew I made. I imagine the house is going to fill up with people pretty fast."

Lily scanned the duck pond - the swans and geese, the calm surface of the water, the graceful willow trees, and of course the ducks. It looked like a photograph, and Lily wished she had suggested that Dolores come here and set up her easel. Everything about it seemed so gentle and beautiful, but the scene was tainted with Lily's own sense of sorrow, the way all of Dolores' paintings seemed to be tainted with the darkness inside her.

Lily's vision became blurred as her eyes filled with tears that ran down the sides of her face, dripped into her ears, trailed down her neck, her sadness draining into the cool soft earth. Her eyelids grew heavy and, weary from the effort of sobbing, she drifted off to sleep.

Lily opened her eyes to find James draping his navy blue Varsity jacket across her chest.

"Hi," he said softly. "Iris said I would find you here."

"Hi." Lily sat up, pulled the jacket around her shoulders, and swiped her palms across her face, embarrassed, knowing that her eyes were probably puffy and red. "I must be a mess."

James sat down next to Lily and plucked a leaf from her hair. "I'm so sorry to hear about Dolores, Lily. I know how much she meant to you."

In the moment before full consciousness, Lily had forgotten and was reawakened to the miserable truth yet again.

Dolores. Dolores is dead. Dolores killed herself.

Lily dissolved into tears.

James took Lily's face between his hands. He placed a kiss on her forehead, allowing his lips to linger there, before pulling away to look into Lily's eyes.

"Lily" he said. "I love you."

Lily collapsed, toppling sideways, her head landing in James' lap. He stroked her hair and let her cry.

Bastard.

Dolores' memorial service was short and sparsely attended. The few local family members who were there rattled around in the vacuous sanctuary. Monsieur Debonnet the ballet teacher came late and sat in the back row between Lily's mother and James.

Lily made a mental note to get remembered in a smaller church when she died. Either that, or find a way to make a friend or two along the way. That Dolores had none to come and honor her life was tragic. Lily hoped she could at least hold it together long enough to give Dolores this memento, her one final gift.

Lily climbed the set of stairs to the dais and adjusted the microphone. She turned and nodded to Uncle Alfred, who began strumming his guitar. Auntie Rosa let out a yelp, and leaned on a weeping Iris. Lily closed her eyes to block out all the images that would crumble her composure. She pictured Dolores sitting there in the front row, the way she always had during band practice, clutching her tissues, struggling to smile despite her pain.

"Every day I face the world at large
What lies ahead is yet uncharted

Reflections of the life I've seen
The dreams I've dreamed
But never started
But now what's done is done
And what was just doesn't matter anymore
Every day I pray I'll find a way
To let my spirit soar"

Lily stopped to clear the lump that formed in her throat. Uncle Alfred played two extra measures of transition, to give her time to regain her poise. She nodded to him, drew in a breath, and continued.

"My heart is strong, my soul is free
The weight of the world doesn't bother me
And everything is beautiful if you just choose to believe
I'm where I belong, where I need to be
I walk in synchronicity
And every step just brings me closer to my destiny
As I walk the path of peace and harmony
I want to walk the path of peace and harmony
I always walk the path of peace....
... and harmony."

As Lily stepped down, the only sound - except for a sniff here and there - was the final echo of Dolores' life as it reverberated from stained glass window, to altar, to baptistry, to Christ on the Cross, finally coming to rest on the heads of those who had come to mourn and say goodbye to a cousin, a niece, a friend, a dream.

29. IRIS

Iris blew into her cupped hands, hoping the heat of her breath would thaw her frozen fingers. When the numbness began to subside, she unzipped the pocket of her hooded sweatshirt with stiff fingers, and found three pieces of icy metal on a ring. The cadenced jingling of the keys in her pocket as she jogged was annoying, but she was grateful for this concrete reminder of her passage into the world of people with something to lock. Back home the door was always open, and she owned no car; unless you counted the key to a pair of roller skates Auntie Rosa had bought her when she recovered from peritonitis, and the miniature key to the little blue valise that remained tucked away in the corner of her bedroom closet, the keys to her college dorm were the first she had ever possessed.

Making a beeline for the row of aluminum mailboxes that lined the far wall of the dormitory foyer, she grasped the smallest key on the ring, wriggled it into the slot beneath the label "L301D," and flipped open the hatch with the same sense of cautious expectancy with which she approached even the most minor events which might mark her daily life with unexpected spurts of joy or stabs of disappointment. Two envelopes huddled together in the cold metal cubbyhole: one was small and pink, with an embossed crown on the flap, and before even glancing at the flowery handwriting on the front, Iris knew it was a greeting card from Auntie Rosa; the other bore the postmark ELGIN USAF Pensacola FL. Her heart, still pounding from her run, fluttered with excitement.

Iris slammed the mailbox shut and sprinted up the stairs to the third floor. She hoped to find her roommate absent for once, instead of glued to her chair studying. Emma Zeiss had been recommended by a mutual friend who knew both girls were looking for someone with whom to share a room; she was from Rochester, and like Iris, was studying to become a physical therapist (after admitting to herself that she had never really been interested in her father's profession, Iris was already considering a deviation from that course to become a dance therapist). Contrary to Iris's expectations, their common provenance and freshman curriculum contributed little to creating a sense of collegiate conviviality between the two young women. Iris had envisioned a dorm life of animated, intellectually stimulating discussions crammed between intense study sessions, concluding late at night with junk food binges; she had thought they would chat in bed after lights out, like she had always done with Lily, only their conversations would be about the latest news from home, or the guys that begged them for a date, or their dreams for the future. However, Emma's lack of academic brilliance coupled with her unflagging ambition to succeed in her course of studies exacerbated her bookish nature, and had it not been for Iris, who occasionally rattled her cage, she would hardly have ventured from her room except to go to classes and the student cafeteria.

Iris studied hard, too, but after the anemic social life that had characterized her high school years, she was eager to explore the opportunities offered by life on campus. She thought they should try and make some friends, but each time she convinced Emma to accompany her to a dorm party (Iris seemed an extrovert when compared to Emma, but never would have gone to a party alone), she found herself wishing there were some redeeming quality in the girl's appearance or personality that would facilitate their acceptance into some circle of friends. Iris's wishes could do little to remedy the fact that Emma's most striking traits created an image that would appeal to few: a moon face whose surface was disseminated with the volcanoes and craters of chronic acne, a limpid gaze whose absolute lack of underlying currents was magnified by the thick lenses of her granny glasses; a cow's tail of lank brown hair rounded up in a rubber band at the nape of the thick neck which joined her potato head to her beanbag body. Emma's propensity to blush severely when spoken to and to stammer when asked any question coupled with her intolerance of alcoholic beverages and visceral terror of the opposite sex, made parties about as enjoyable as chemistry lab.

"Hi, Emma," Iris said as she opened the door, swallowing her irritation at the sight of her roommate bent over an open book, her lap cradling a half-empty bag of chips which looked suspiciously like the sour cream and onion variety Iris had stashed away in her closet, in anticipation of a late night study session of her own.

"Hi," Emma mumbled, while her eyes and the highlighter she clenched in her pudgy fist remained firmly planted on the page. Iris recognized the textbook from their Psychology 101 course. Save for a few lines here and there, the text was awash with yellow ink.

Emma finally looked up, her eyes indiscernable behind the light of the reading lamp that ricocheted off her glasses. "You got a letter from Peter?" she asked.

"How did you guess?"

"You got that look in your eyes." Emma held out the bags of chips. "Want some?" Iris shook her head; Emma helped herself to more. "You went running in this weather? You must be nuts."

"I couldn't sit on that chair one more minute. My legs were stiff and my brain was shutting down due to lack of oxygen," Iris said. "But you're right, it's freezing! Colder than a witch's tit, as my sister Violet used to say."

Emma stared at her with a blank look, and Iris braced herself for a forthcoming request that she explain the method for measuring the temperature of a witch's tit, but Emma just reverted to her studies. Iris had been poring over those same chapters for an upcoming test, when the twitching in her limbs and the crick in her neck and the ringing in her ears and the pounding in her head made her spring from her chair, lace up her sneakers and rush out the door. She loved the way her cheeks burned when she ran in the cold, and the way each greedy gulp of air stabbed her lungs, and shocked her system. She preferred running alone, at her own swift pace, along whatever walkways or roads were sufficiently plowed, though sometimes she was joined by Mary Ann, a curvaceous premed student from Westchester who, in order to restrain her bouncing boobs, jogged with her forearms folded across her chest like a straight-jacketed escapee from an insane asylum. Once in a while, Mary Ann would drag along her roommate Nancy, a red-headed, freckle-faced Jewish girl from some town on Long Island with an Indian name, who adored Billy Joel. Nancy was slow, and easily winded, more from chatting than exertion. Iris had only met a couple of Jewish girls before coming to Buffalo, but none with red hair, nor had she ever met anyone who loved Billy Joel.

Iris stripped down to her panties and wrapped her fleece robe around her body, clammy with sweat and pink with cold. Auntie Rosa had given her the robe as a going away present; it was snuggly and warm, and its striking shade of turquoise reminded Iris of the tropical sea depicted in a mural at The Luau, bringing a note of cheer into the long Buffalo winter. The gift box had also contained seven pairs of silky undies in as many colors, embellished with lace trim along the waistband and legs. Iris had opened the package and thanked Auntie Rosa, while bracing herself to hear the oft-repeated story of how as a young woman in nursing school, her aunt had been so ashamed of her coarse cotton drawers that she would slink away into the closet to change, while the other girls puffed on cigarettes and pranced around in their fine lingerie. Safely out of sight but still within earshot, she would listen to them chatter flippantly about the schoolwork for which they professed little interest, deeming much more beneficial for their present happiness and future prospects the art of flirtation and the science of obtaining dates with the medical students and interns they encountered in the hospital wards. She pictured her aunt as a young student, around Iris's age, crouching shamefully in a closet. She felt pity for that girl, still hiding inside the withering body of an aging woman who could finally buy her own fancy panties, but had no one around to admire them.

In that moment, Iris was so overwhelmed with empathy for the young Rosa Capotosti, she could taste on her own tongue the bitter flavor of missed opportunities macerated in regret, swallowed down one bite at a time. She felt the deep ache of her aunt's deprivation; she was fraught with frustration and anger at the insensitive minds and tight purse strings which determined what was essential and what was frivolous for a girl. Things like dainty underwear. Or long-distance phone calls, like the ones her floor mates received from their parents for no special reason, other than to tell them they were missed, and check whether they needed anything.

Iris thought it best to file away this unannounced rush of melancholy under the generic classification of homesickness: at least that malady was familiar to her, and might be remedied by the letters she clutched in her hand. She would read them right away. Placing one foot on the edge of the bottom bunk, even though she knew it irritated Emma, who always chided her for not using the ladder, she hopped to her bed above. Settling in with her back against the cinder block wall, she picked up the small pink envelope, slipped her index finger under the flap, and extracted the card it contained. A fluffy white kitty peeked out from a wicker basket brimming with spring flowers; Iris opened the card, and found two crisp dollar bills and the verse "With each little mew, I'm thinking of you!" The words "thinking" and "you" were underscored twice in the same red ink used to add the note: "Lover-dover! Have a Coke on me! You're in my prayers. Love, Auntie Rosa." Beneath the signature there was a "P.S.: How does the second half of May sound, *Bella della mamma*?"

It sounded *perfetto* to Iris, who was thrilled that she might actually succeed in executing her plan. Auntie Rosa had been devastated by Dolores's "accident," which she insisted was caused by a broken heart. In a way, she was right; Dolores had opted for the expediency of putting her shattered heart to rest for good, over the painful endeavor of trying to patch it back together again. After finding out that Auntie Rosa had been the one to discover her adored cousin dead in her basement room, Iris had been tormented by the macabre scene replaying in her imagination: Auntie Rosa panicking when she saw Dolores's inert figure lying in the bed, her mouth agape, her shocks of thick, black hair strewn across the embroidered white pillowcase; Auntie Rosa recoiling in horror when she touched the pale skin, and found it suited in the cold armor of death; Auntie Rosa immobilized by disbelief, her heart impaled by the pain; Auntie Rosa crumbling in grief, her soul seared by sorrow.

Iris had been the one to hatch the idea of a trip to Italy, suggesting it might assuage Auntie Rosa's pain and guilt for not being able to save Dolores from herself, just like she had not been able to save her sister Teresa from the canal. Between her student loan and the money she had earned the previous year, Iris would have sufficient funds left over at the end of the semester to pay her own way, and then she'd earn good money at Kodak, where she had been offered a summer job. A trip to Italy would be a sound investment in her education, and a welcome opportunity to make some memories of her own, before spending another summer locked up in a place that thrived on reproducing the memories of others.

A shiver of excitement ran through her, as she set aside Auntie Rosa's card, then crossed her ankles and buried her cold feet under her thighs to warm them. She studied the handwriting on the second envelope with the USAF postmark, and imagined Peter Ponzio taking a pen in hand to write her name on it. If she opened the thin envelope and found it empty, she would have been content to simply sit and stare at her name written in his peculiar, elongated scrawl. She eased the envelope open slowly, deliberately, to denude the letter that lay within. She fondled it with her fingertips for a moment before spreading it open, savoring the fact that she did not yet know what perceptions and emotions its words would convey to her. Peter was not a gifted writer; the unrefined thoughts he presented in his unpolished style would have sunk under the burden of spelling and grammar errors, had they not been buoyed by Iris's enthusiasm; his rough-hewn letters would have made her cringe, had Iris not convinced herself that they were utterly endearing, and denoted the writer's spontaneity and sincerity.

One Saturday morning the previous August, when she and Lily were grocery shopping, Peter had finally approached Iris and asked her if she would like to see *The Spy Who Loved Me*, and Iris had said yes. They had held hands and kissed all through the show, and decided on the spot that "Nobody Does It Better" would be their song. They had spent almost every evening together since then, until it was time for them both to depart on their separate adventures: Iris to Buffalo, and Peter to Air Force boot camp. A Polaroid of him in his uniform and combat boots genuflecting by a sign on a lawn, coupled with a burgeoning bunch of letters in a shoebox, was all it took for Iris to fancy herself in love. None of the boys she met on campus could inspire the same level of romanticism she derived from writing and reading letters. She felt free, as she roamed the realm of the written word, dipping her pen into the thoughts and feelings and reactions and provocations that eluded her tongue, and indulged in the delicacies of an idealized love rendered perfect by the lack of foreseeable opportunities for its concrete expression.

In his letter, Peter wrote of a possible tour of duty in England. Overseas! She imagined the foreign stamps and postmarks on the letters he would mail her, and wondered what captivating notes she might write on the postcards she would send him from Italy. She must be sure to post one from each place she visited, which would make the trip almost as romantic as if he were there with her, perhaps even more so. This was the stuff of the novels she kept by her bedside, in her backpack, in her purse, whose narrative swept her off to eighteenth-century England, nineteenth-century Russia, twentieth-century France, any time or place she could find a heroine who captured her attention and aroused her sympathy. She tucked her letters under her pillow, slid down from the bed and gathered her shower supplies.

She no longer felt homesick. Except for Lily. She would have to tell her about the Italy plan soon. She felt guilty going without her, but what could she do? Thriftiness had never been Lily's forte, and what money she might have scraped together this year would have to go toward paying for her first year of college, certainly not squandered on a vacation abroad. If only Dolores were still around. Maybe she would have helped Lily, and all four of them could have gone together. The beauty that abounded in Italy's art and countryside, the warmth of its climate and people might have soothed Dolores's aching soul. Then again, maybe not. Maybe Dolores was born to be sad, and destined to be broken. Iris sighed; there was nothing she could do for Dolores now, just like there was nothing she could do about the fact that she would have to leave Lily behind.

They'd spend the rest of the summer together, anyway. They would have their jobs, and they'd be busy running things at Chestnut Crest, but there would be ample time for late night heart-to-heart talks, for catching up on the things that had happened in each other's lives during their time apart, for playing the guitar and singing, for drinking iced tea under the apple tree and dreaming about their futures. It struck Iris that just maybe the time for dreaming was at last turning into a time for deciding. This was the year in which they would both finally be in a position to begin shaping their own lives and forging their independence. They would have three full months to talk about all the exciting possibilities that were opening up before them, before they would both finally be on their way, separated, but never far apart.

30. LILY

Unlike her sisters who had dreamed of the day when they could have their own rooms, Lily had always taken comfort knowing that someone was sleeping in the bed next to hers. The snoring of another was a lullaby you could never enjoy if you slept alone. Thoughts of her mother, now gone, living another life; of Dolores, simply gone; of Iris, in college; of the last time she had seen James - the tearful, passionate goodbye they'd shared with no acknowledgement of the future and no resolution of the past - they all hung in the silence, swinging menacingly overhead. Lily had to push them aside to find sleep. In the corners of the silence crouched the sights and smells of the chicken coop, the faces of her childhood, the back room at Auntie Rosa's. Lily's lifelong quest had been to avoid thinking about those things, to block them out, drown them, obliterate them. The noise and commotion of home had always been the perfect antidote for reflection, but life's dwindling chatter was stripping Lily of her hiding place.

The proliferation of silence was the least of it. Since Iris had moved away, keeping up with the household chores took more effort and had become joyless. The grocery budget had been cut due to her father's mounting legal fees, making it increasingly difficult for Lily to bring any change home, let alone pay for eggs and bacon. Anyway, it was too sad to go out to breakfast alone.

With each item selected from the shelves at Star Market, Lily saw the reflection of what her life had become. Lemon scented furniture polish was Saturday afternoon. Frozen chicken pot pies were for Saturday evening, after Mass. Pasta and sauce, Sunday. Laundry soap, day after day after day. As she filled the shopping cart, she scripted her week, and all she saw there was cooking, cleaning, and tampons for one.

As her father and the boys grew more and more dependent on Lily to care for them, the idea of moving away to college had grown distant. Dolores had been the visionary, the planner, the one who truly believed, the one who fed the fantasies that Lily and Iris had conjured as they'd lain in bed at night. Dolores' act of self-destruction - which Lily's father and Auntie Rosa continued to refer to as an "accident" - caused Lily's clarity for the future to become blurred and faded. How would she ever pick up and go on without Dolores? She certainly couldn't ask her father to help her with her audition; he was consumed with lawyers and bills and rage. What could she expect him to do for her, when he couldn't even manage to cook his own dinner?

"For crying out loud," Lily's father said. "This cube steak is like shoe leather."

"Sorry, Dad," said Lily. "That's how it comes... I don't know how to make it more tender. I cooked it slow and let it simmer and everything."

"Jeepers Cripes, I can't eat this. Pass me the mashed potatoes."

He scooped a heap of potatoes onto his plate, shoved a forkful into his mouth, and then doused the mound in salt, pepper, and butter, and mixed it all together.

"Damn your mother," he said, furiously jabbing at the potatoes with his fork.

Sometimes Charles and William came home for dinner, but often they did not. Ricci spent his afternoons sitting motionless in front of the television, tearing himself from his programs just long enough to eat, before retreating to a cable-induced semi-catatonic state that would take him far into the night. The camaraderie and tenderness that Lily had shared with the boys when their mother had first left had gradually ossified under the pressure of their father's desperation and hate. Where they had once looked to Lily for hugs and comfort, all they wanted now was to stay disengaged. Whether due to their own bitterness, or as a by-product of their father's effusive wrath for his wife in particular, and for all women in general, their demeanor toward Lily had become marked with disrespect and cruelty.

Bedtimes and curfews were initially relaxed and then abandoned in the turmoil, as the boys - who were now all in high school - learned that their father had neither the emotional capacity to argue with them, nor the courage to risk alienating them by enforcing rules. Their mother had recently moved into a duplex located in the local school district, which meant that any of the children could simply take the bus to her house after school any time they were so inclined - which Lily would do on occasion, partly to spend time with her mother, but mostly to avoid being at the center of the chaos, like the burned out matron in a home for wayward boys.

"You got anything to eat, Mom?" Lily asked.

"I haven't been to the store," Lily's mother replied. "But let's see what we can come up with."

After rifling through the pantry, Lily's mother emerged with a can of cream of broccoli soup, and the remnants of a box of rotini. She shook the contents of the can into a small saucepan. She sniffed the open milk spout once, then paused and looked up at the ceiling - as if trying to remember what fresh milk should smell like - then sniffed it again before adding it to the soup. Lighting the flame under a second saucepan filled with water, she joined Lily at the small dinette set, wedged into the corner of what she called the "eat-in kitchen."

The house was built into the side of a hill, so the living room was cool and quiet, decorated with variegated green shag carpeting, macramé plant hangers, and a brown bean bag chair in the corner. Every table top and surface was blanketed with newspapers, magazines, flyers from the National Organization for Women, the battered women's shelter, the League of Women Voters, and weekly programs from the First Unitarian Church. A half-eaten package of oatmeal cookies sat on the coffee table next to a copy of *The Feminine Mystique*. As Lily looked around, she felt that she was getting a sense of who her mother was for the first time. Lily herself was the only evidence there of Carlo Capotosti, or of her mother's life on Chestnut Crest.

As the women sat and ate their pasta with creamy broccoli, Lily noticed a calm creeping upon her, like a peace egg that had been gently broken over her head and was running down her face, dripping onto her shoulders. Unlike the silences at home, which were stretched taut between fits of rage, the silence at her mother's house was open, though tinged with sadness. Being there was like sitting in an empty church alone, observing Jesus on the cross, feeling both safe and sorrowful at the same time.

"I don't want to go back there, Mom," Lily blurted.

"Back where?"

"Home," said Lily. "I don't want to go back home." The words themselves were simple, but the ideas that trailed behind them were terrifying.

"You could always come and live here," the words shot like projectiles from her mother's mouth. "I have an extra bedroom. I moved back out this way to give you kids that option."

"Dad would kill me." Lily's heart pounded at the thought of confronting him, of telling him she was going to live with the enemy.

"The fact that you would say that is all the more reason why you should, Lily. He's your father, not your husband, not your jailer. He's supposed to be taking care of you - not the other way around."

Lily raised a spoonful of pasta to her lips, but found that what she had already eaten was threatening an encore.

"Money is tight, I won't lie to you," continued her mother. "You'll have to get a job, and we'll have to share the car. Why don't you just go on up and take a look at your room, see how it feels to you?"

"I have a room?"

"Someone does," said her mother. "Might as well be you."

Lily sat on the floor of the empty bedroom, listening to the gentle hum of the traffic that flowed along Buffalo Road, a road that - if you followed it for a couple hours - would eventually lead you all the way to the University, a straight line to Iris. The room was austere. No curtains, no carpeting, no clothes hanging in the closet, no shelf for fear, no memories, no loneliness, no fantasies about the future, no more comparing life to what it once was, or to what she had hoped it would be some day. She still grieved Dolores and the dreams they had conjured together, but maybe it would be better to find a way to be happy with an ordinary life. Maybe she could start over here. Begin again.

Lily and her mother stood in the driveway at Chestnut Crest, preparing to confront her father and tell him that Lily would be moving out.

"When dealing with violent men like your father," Lily's mother told her, "it's important to have a plan, and then follow through with conviction. If you hesitate, he will take that for weakness and he will do absolutely anything to coerce you to stay."

Lily thought her mother may have been over-dramatizing the matter, but even though her mother now stood beside her there in the kitchen - or perhaps because she did - her father's behavior was as she predicted. The force of his response frightened Lily viscerally, as though his rage and his stare could vaporize her, and she would simply cease to exist the moment she stepped out the door.

Lily's father marched to the phone and furiously pounded out a series of numbers. "My ex-wife is here, and she is trying to take my daughter away, and we need her," Lily's father shouted. He glared at Lily in the pause, before screaming into the receiver, "This *is* an emergency!"

Lily's body was shaking, and had been ever since the words, "I'm going to go live with Mom," were birthed from her throat. The tension inside her had been building ever since she'd made the decision, and the past few days had seemed surreal: secretly collecting and packing her clothes; taking a clandestine trip to the market to make sure the cupboards and freezer were stocked with easy-to-prepare meals; the way she'd squirmed and watched the clock all day; the image of she and her mother trying to get the keys out of their locked car with a coat hanger in the school parking lot that afternoon; the planning, the timing and the details, like two prisoners of war plotting their escape.

Lily's father slammed the phone down and turned to her. "I should have known that you would abandon us too. You're just like your mother."

"Dad - I'm seventeen years old... I can't handle all of this... I -I-" Lily's composure headed out the door before she did.

"Go ahead and go," he snarled. Lily's father walked toward her, and she took a reactionary step back. He stopped in his tracks and let out a derisive giggle. Lily couldn't tell if he was dismayed or pleased that her reaction to his approach was to recoil.

"There's one thing you should know before you go." He picked up the paper grocery bag stuffed with the remnants of Lily's belongings. "You know that twenty dollars I paid you each and every week for helping out around here? Well, you weren't worth it." Shoving the bag into her arms, he added, "Get out - both of you."

Lily burst into tears with such force that she was sure she would open her eyes and find her guts lying on the yellowed linoleum.

"Fuck you, Carlo!" Lily's mother shouted, encircling Lily's shoulder with a trembling arm.

"I bet you could, with that big dick you have hanging between your legs, you dyke!" Carlo slammed the kitchen door, and the last thing Lily heard as they started down the driveway was the shattering of glass.

I hope he knows where we keep the broom.

"Can you work weekends?" Cory, the assistant manager at Burger King, was just a few years older than Lily, but she imagined that he must be very good at his job to be a boss already.

Perhaps she could become assistant manager some day, too. But first she had to get the job.

"Yes, I can work weekends," Lily replied. Remembering the coaching her mother gave her, she added a smile and made eye contact with Cory. "I'm done with school already, so I can also work during the day."

"That's great." Cory made a note on Lily's job application. "We have a hard time keeping the register staffed during the day, but it gets pretty hectic at lunch time. Do you think you can handle it?"

"Sir, I've spent the last three years cooking and cleaning for a houseful of boys. I can do hectic."

Cory looked at Lily for a few seconds. She smiled.

"C'mon back to the office and get your uniform. You're hired."

Lily was struck with how easily and quickly the job materialized, like it was meant to be. The entire last few weeks had unfolded that way. With a simple graduation ceremony at the end of January, she had gleefully left high school behind. Once settled in her new home, all the pieces had started to fall into place.

"Don't you have a college audition coming up soon?" her mother asked one evening.

"What do you mean?" Lily asked.

"College - you know, college? That place you go to learn more after high school?"

"Well, I did have an audition appointment, but I don't know what's going on with it - Dolores had all that stuff. I didn't bother keeping up with it."

"SUNY Purchase, right?" her mother asked.

"Yeah. Why?"

"I'll give them a call and see what I can find out. I'll have to get time off of work, if we're going to drive down there. But you'd better start making some money, because you'll need to make a contribution toward the expenses - and you'll need to have some savings for your first year away. I don't have much to spare, and I think we can safely say we can't depend on your father to help."

"Wait - are you saying you're going to take me?"

"Well, I don't expect you to drive to New York City by yourself."

Lily felt torn between the recycled excitement of possibilities and the need to protect herself from the disappointment she feared awaited at the end of this path. Giving up her dreams once was bad enough; the pain was just beginning to become rounder and smoother than it was at first. Now it was less like cutting yourself with a knife and more like hitting your leg on the corner of the coffee table. If she tried again and failed, she would have to go back to the rawness of the fresh wound. Yet as much as she tried to talk herself out of it, Lily knew she ultimately had no choice. To turn away from this opportunity was to give in to fear, to disrespect what Dolores had tried to do for her, and to deny her mother the chance to make up for lost time. Maybe it wasn't too late after all.

The days passed quickly, crammed with activity. Lily took as many hours as they would give her at Burger King, saving her spare time to rehearse for the audition. She and Dolores had done a lot of what they called "vision shopping," just to get ideas, but the closest they had come to actually buying anything was when they placed a few dresses on layaway at the mall. Surely they had found their way back to the racks by now. The application fees and the money needed to get to New York City were just about all Lily could manage to save for anyway. She sorted through her closet and selected a pair of black palazzo pants, then rummaged through her mother's clothes until she found a blue and green paisley print rayon blouse with ruffled cuffs that fit her just right. The only thing missing was a pair of shoes; she would just have to find something on sale at SaveMart.

The old Plymouth Duster made the trip to New York sputtering and coughing. Lily acted as navigator, and they got lost twice on the way, making the trip ten hours long instead of seven.

"Let me see the map," her mother had said with irritation, as they pulled into a gas station seriously north of Albany.

They laid the map out on the trunk of the car, and Lily traced the route she had instructed her mother to follow. "See, we got off of I-90 here, and then we went left here - "

"Lily Elizabeth Capotosti! You're looking at this upside down, for goodness sake!"

With the map in its upright position, they had finally reached New York City, discovering that arriving in Manhattan wasn't nearly the same thing as finding a particular address among the millions stamped on countless doors of countless buildings. Lily rolled down the car window and stuck her head out into the cool evening air, gazing up in wonder at the buildings that stretched imploringly toward the moon as if they knew it was not just the city and not just the moonlight but the combination of the two that lent magic to nights such as this. She wished Iris could see this, and hoped that one day, she might see something at least as beautiful.

The first time they passed their hotel, they were in the wrong lane and couldn't move over in time to make the turn. The second attempt put them in the right lane, but the hotel traffic was backed up into the street and when they stopped to wait for it to clear, the cab driver behind them laid on his horn and shouted, "Move that goddamned piece of shit!", so they abandoned the line and circled the block again instead. The third time around they finally rumbled into the hotel parking garage, Lily's mother exhaling in short puffs like air escaping from an over-inflated beach ball - the only sign of stress or worry that she ever exhibited. Their plans of spending the evening exploring were thwarted by sheer exhaustion. They grabbed a burger and fries from the Burger King across the street before collapsing into bed.

Still, she could hardly believe that they were there, just one day and thirty miles away from the dream she and Dolores had designed together. Her heart swelled with gratitude for the time she had spent with Dolores, and for the efforts her mother was making to help her see it through.

Lily woke the next morning to a grinding in her gut and an icy-blue radiance that filled the room. Pushing the sheers open, she found the city buried in snow.

"Oh, shit!" she cried. "We got hit last night!"

"It's just a little snow," said her mother.

"Oh shit," Lily cried again, placing her hand over her belly. "I think I just got my period." She and her mother rarely discussed such things; too irritated by the snow and the badly timed cramps, Lily forgot to be embarrassed. Even when Lily had gotten her first period, her mother had simply handed her four Kotex pads and a sanitary belt, and then returned to the conversation she was having with John, who had just returned from a semester of college, full of ideas and of himself. Lily had learned most of what she knew from Iris, from her friends, and from Health Education classes at school. She had little concept that most mothers and daughters had open conversations about puberty, sex, and womanhood, but Lily didn't find her mother's silence strange. In the Capotosti home, conversations were practical - who used the last of the gas in the car, what's for dinner, whose turn is it to set the table - there was never any discussion of sex or money or spirituality - unless someone was getting yelled at for having a *Playboy* magazine, skipping Mass, or getting a hickey.

Within the hour, Lily was back in bed, buried under blankets, cupping a mug of hot tea in her hands and writhing in pain. A half-eaten English muffin and a bottle of aspirin sat on the end table.

"Welcome to New York," she mumbled, watching news coverage of the storm on TV.

"They say it's supposed to let up by lunch time." Her mother was doing her best to be cheerful, but Lily could hear the little puffs of air. "We'll still have a few hours to do some sightseeing before we have to head for White Plains."

"What channel has the report about when these cramps will let up?"

"Maybe it will help if you get up and walk around a bit. We'll find a nice salon, get you that new cut we talked about, then we'll go see St. Patrick's, buy ourselves a treat at Macy's. It'll be fun!"

Lily groaned as she grabbed the garbage can from the floor, and threw up half an English muffin into it.

By midday the storm subsided into gentle flurries. Lily's

451

cramps refused to follow suit. The streets below were busy with cabs and buses and snow plows, and even a bicycle or two. Pedestrians crammed the sidewalks, all frantically making their way to somewhere. It would take more than an early spring blizzard to slow down New Yorkers.

Lily dragged herself into the shower and let the hot water run on her lower back, groaning as she struggled to stand upright. She knew from experience that she would have to endure the cramps for a few hours longer, but she couldn't bear to deprive her mother of showing her around the city.

Even through the snow and the pain, Lily loved Manhattan. More than the shops and the restaurants and the impressive office buildings, it was the way it felt. There was an energy in the air that lifted her spirits, even if it couldn't ease her pain. Street vendors offered an array of delights; on one corner you could get a fresh bagel, roasted nuts on the next, a hot dog down the street. Everyone Lily passed seemed doggedly determined about every building they entered, every corner around which they buzzed. Lily was enchanted, despite the homeless blind selling pencils and the stench that rose up from the sewer grates. None of the sights and sounds were familiar, but the experience of them felt natural, comforting even.

"This looks like a good place for a haircut," said Lily's mother, stopping in front of Starz Salon.

"I don't know, Mom..."

"Lily, you are in New York City! You can't come here and not visit a salon."

Distracted by her cramps and the hum of activity around her, Lily agreed. At least it would be an opportunity to sit down for a while. An hour and a half later she found herself looking at her image in a mirror, a sob lodged in her throat, as she managed to say to the stylist, "Yes, it's great - thank you."

Road salt had turned the fluffy white snow into brown slush. Their excursion through the streets of the city brought them past countless plate glass windows, each one reminding Lily of how terribly they had botched up her hair, of how she had wanted to

452

say something when she realized how much they were cutting off, watching her thick brown locks falling into a pile on the floor. But by then it was too late, and she could see her mother behind her in the mirror, glowing with pride at having given Lily this experience. *It'll grow back*, Lily told herself. *By this time next spring, it will all be grown back.*

"How are the cramps?" her mother asked.

"I really just wish I could reach in and pull my uterus out," Lily replied. "I don't plan on using it anyway."

By the time they spun through Macy's revolving door, Lily's feet were soaked and freezing, leaving watery footprints as they made their way to the escalator.

"Let's go get you a pair of fresh socks," said her mother. "And maybe a new blouse, for a treat."

Lily browsed through the juniors section, reading the price tags on every piece of clothing.

"Mom, this stuff is expensive."

"No, it's not. Not really. You're just used to shopping at SaveMart and Two Guys. This is quality stuff. Here - try this on." She handed Lily a beautiful white blouse, covered in a print of tiny pink rosebuds. It was sheer and light and delicate, with lace around the cuffs.

"Mom - this is the most beautiful blouse in the whole world." Lily said, admiring herself in the dressing room mirror.

"Good. Hand it over." Lily's mother stuck her hand through the curtain. Lily reluctantly took the blouse off. Except for the audition clothes Dolores had almost bought her, she couldn't even remember the last time someone had bought something new to wear, selected just for her. She couldn't wait to put it on again.

They allowed two-and-a-half hours to get from the city to the college, but Lily's relief at having arrived in time was supplanted by panic as they walked around the campus for thirty minutes, searching for the auditorium. The campus map was more confusing than the entire road map of New York State. When they passed the Student Union a second time, Lily broke into a sweat.

"I don't think we're headed in the right direction, Lily."

"No kidding, Mom." Lily snapped. "Why am I the one leading, anyway? You should be reading the map and I should be following you."

They arrived at the auditorium five minutes before Lily's audition appointment. She dashed into the bathroom to pee, check for leaks, and try to make sense out of her hair, which proved futile.

"Number four hundred and thirty-five," announced a faceless voice from the seating area. Lily grabbed her audition bag and walked up onto the stage. "Please state your name, and then tell us the name of the song you're performing for us today."

"I'm Lily Capotosti," stated Lily, in her best stage voice. "And for my musical number I'll be singing 'Many a New Day' from *Oklahoma!*" The song itself was a bit of stretch for Lily in terms of vocal range, but she had been working with the recording Dolores had made for her at the studio, which had been transposed to take the tune down one whole step, making it possible for Lily to demonstrate the full range of her voice without screeching.

Just as she reached down into her bag to get the transposed sheet music, the pianist on stage began playing the introduction to the song. Lily looked over in terror. The pianist nodded at her to come in with the vocals, and as Lily scrambled to gain her composure, she realized that the pianist was playing the song in its original key. "If you screw up, screw up big." That's what Mr. Howell always used to say, so Lily took a big breath and jumped in, hoping she could get out of her head long enough to forget about the key, forget about the sweat running down her back and dousing her pink rosebuds, forget about the blood that gushed from her each time she hit a high note, forget about the bad haircut and the fact that Dolores was sitting in an urn on cousin Felicia's mantle.

Months of rehearsal, days of preparation, hours of hand-wringing anxiety, and in less than fifteen minutes, it was over. Lily could barely remember the song, or the monologues she performed. The experience passed by as though it was someone else standing on stage.

"Very nice," said the voice. "Thank you for coming in. We'll be in touch."

The rest of the Friday night crew at Burger King included Cecelia Iacovangelo, a former classmate from Sacred Family, and Danny Harris, who was one year behind Lily and on the Junior Varsity swim team. Working the drive-thru window at night was Lily's favorite assignment - you got to talk over the headset, and basically work alone, taking orders, making change, pouring drinks, packing food. Lily liked Cecelia and Danny well enough, but she simply didn't find that she had much in common with them beyond the fact that they all worked together and would slip botched up burger orders to each other instead of throwing them into the garbage like they were supposed to.

"Welcome to Burger King, may I take your order?" she said into the microphone.

"Yea, I'll absolutely take a hamburger, plain - no ketchup, no mustard, nothing - just plain, and an order of onion rings."

The car pulled up and the driver rolled down the window, releasing a gush of cigarette smoke and disco music into the night air. He gunned the engine of his metallic blue sports car, and then turned down the volume on his eight-track player. He was about Lily's age, maybe a year or two older. His dark hair was blown dry, and sprayed into a carefully constructed windswept look.

"Hey, cutie." He flashed a smile at Lily, his mouth framed by a shadow that was either the result of a lack of hygiene or the inability to grow enough facial hair to constitute an entire moustache.

"Hi," Lily replied. *Did he just call me cutie?* Her heart quickened. She handed him his bag of food and his change, then slid the window closed. He pulled away and Lily opened the window again, watching the tail lights and the word, "Barracuda" as they disappeared into the night. "Nice car," she said out loud to herself.

Lily's job kept her busy and intermittently distracted, but she couldn't help thinking about the fact that the next day was

Saturday, marking two weeks since her audition. The waiting had become excruciating; her decision letter from Purchase would have to arrive soon.

The drive-thru bell chimed again. "Welcome to Burger King. May I take your order?"

"Yeah - I'll absolutely take a chocolate milkshake."

Lily smiled as the engine rumbled over the speaker.

"That's fifty-nine cents," said Lily, sliding the window open again.

"What? You don't even say 'hi' - after all we've been through together?"

"Hi." Lily extended her palm. "That's fifty-nine cents, please."

He gave Lily two quarters and a dime. She handed him back a penny, which he tossed into the air.

"It's only money," he said. "And there's a lot more where that came from."

Lily laughed.

"Now there we go," he said. "A pretty girl like you should be laughing all the time."

"Thank you for dining at Burger King," said Lily coyly, sliding the window closed.

"Whoa, whoa - wait a minute!" He reached out and stuck his hand through the window, pushing against it, forcing it back open. "I'm Joe. Joe Diotallevi. What's your name?"

"Please let go of the window." She hoped he wouldn't.

"Not until you tell me your name."

They both kept their hands on the window frame, she pretending to try and force it closed, he half-heartedly trying to pry it open, both perhaps hoping to prolong the contest a bit longer.

"I promise I won't bite," he said. "Unless you want me to. I'm going to keep ordering food until you tell me your name. I just got paid, so this could go on all night. How many orders of French fries can I buy with a hundred and eighty-five bucks?"

"A lot." Lily laughed. "Lily. My name is Lily, OK?"

"Like Mrs. Munster? From *The Munsters*?" he asked.

"Yes, exactly like that. Now please let go of the window, so I can get back to work."

Two minutes later the drive-thru bell chimed yet again.

"Welcome to Burger King. May I take your order?"

"Marry me." said the voice.

"Go home," said Lily into the speaker, laughing. "It's late and I have to close up. And I'm pretty sure you need to go do the Hustle somewhere."

Cory rarely scheduled Lily to close the restaurant two nights in a row, and even though she wasn't thrilled about working on a Friday night, she was glad for the slightly fatter paycheck she knew she'd get - she sure would need the money for college. Besides, it wasn't like she had anywhere else to go. She swept the floor in the cashier's area and wiped down the counters before turning out the house lights for the night.

"Hey Lily," called Cecelia from the kitchen. "We're going to check out that new club that just opened across the street. Wanna come?"

"I can't get in - they serve alcohol."

"It's your lucky day," Danny said. "My brother is working the door tonight so no pro-blem-o."

Lily's only other prospect was to go home and try unsuccessfully to fall asleep so tomorrow would arrive faster, and hopefully the waiting would finally be over. Going out for a while might help pass the time.

"I just need to run home and change. I'll meet you there in forty-five minutes."

When Lily walked out to her car, she caught a glimpse of a blue Barracuda in the parking lot of the pizza place next door. The headlights flashed off and on twice and the faint strains of The Bee Gees singing "More Than a Woman" swirled in the night air.

31. IRIS

Iris nudged aside the two trophies that presided over the uninhabited room, and set down the potted plant she hugged in her arms; it was a spider plant, a farewell gift from Peter Ponzio, and had traveled with her to Buffalo and back. Iris doted on the plant and the numerous plantlets it had propagated in the asexual confinement of her college dorm, and fancied its fertility was a good omen for their relationship. Brushing crumbs of potting soil from her hands, she walked to the window and tugged on a cord to tip open the venetian blinds. Stripes of late afternoon sunshine slipped through the slats, spotlighting the dust dozing on the painted black dresser and fashioning puffy powder wigs for the heads of the statuettes, one of a ballerina in fifth position relevé, the other of a winged goddess, which attested to the once noteworthy artistic achievements of Iris and Lily Capotosti.

Six cardboard boxes bearing the logos of laundry detergent brands stood by the door. Iris had departed for Buffalo with only two boxes shortly before Labor Day, and vowed that this rate of accumulation would not be a constant in her future transfers, of which she hoped there would be many. For all her sighing and swallowing, the tightness in her chest and the lumps in her throat persisted as she set about unpacking clothes, text books, bulging binders, dog-eared paperbacks, and a leather-bound edition of *The Living Bible*, the only relic of her relationship with Rick Rotula. He had sent it to her as a Christmas gift the year they broke up, together with the announcement of his marriage to his ex-girlfriend Alice. She couldn't very well toss a bible into the garbage bin, so she had torn out the page on which he had written the dedication that made her want to throw up, and toted the fancy Tyndale edition to her weekly youth group meetings on campus. That is, until she stopped attending, after one of the leaders had incensed her by insisting that even the most devout Catholics like Auntie Rosa could not aspire to Eternal Life unless they pronounced, verbatim, the words, "I accept Jesus Christ as my Personal Savior."

She left the Bible in the box, together with a tea-stained ceramic mug, an immersion heater, a half-empty box of the blueberry Pop-Tarts and one of the chicken noodle Cup-a-Soups that had filled the gaps left in her tummy by the cheapest meal plan available. Traces of the habits, experiences and knowledge acquired during her first year of college surrounded Iris. So much had happened in the past nine months, yet none of the changes affecting the most intimate spheres of her life could be construed from the hodgepodge of items she had secured to ensure her academic and physical survival. She opened the top drawer of the dresser, and her stomach sank at the sight of its utter emptiness; not one pair of Lily's underpants remained, not one unmatched sock. She threw into the drawer the bundles of letters and cards of various shapes and sizes she had accrued over recent months, together with packs of color prints and negatives in photo lab envelopes, and slammed it shut. There was no sign of Lily in any of them, either.

The room in which Iris now stood had seemed so spacious when inhabited by Jasmine, Marguerite and Violet, the butterflies on the gold-speckled wallpaper so exquisitely ethereal. She recalled how she and Lily had listened to their sisters' conversations through the heating vents, and defied all interdicts by peeking in their dresser drawers when they were out on dates, sometimes being bold enough to even try on their bras, and how excited they had been when they had finally inherited the southerly windows, the closet of left-behind hand-me-downs, the four walls that would protect them and bear silent witness to their fears, tears and dreams.

As Iris looked around her, she was dispirited by how unsubstantial and close the walls now appeared; she grieved for the faded butterflies on their peeling, yellowed backdrop, forever entrapped in a dimension from which there was no escape. Perhaps it was because of the butterfly wallpaper, or the legacy of feminine scents and secrets lingering in the air, but none of the now teenage Little Boys coveted this room, and there were no other Capotosti girls in line. It had remained vacant, exactly as Iris and Lily had left it, uncertain of its future.

Iris was dismayed that she could not recollect where Lily had been, what they may have said to each other the day she went away, or why she had never seen the room in this light before, despite the fact that she had visited often on weekends. That was until recently, when a weariness of nausea-inducing Greyhound buses, an avalanche of assignments, and a battery of final exams to be studied for had conspired to keep her on campus. These, at least, were the reasons she cited to the inner voice pestering her to explain how it could be that she did not notice Lily slipping away.

Only a few months earlier, Iris had entertained fantasies of her homecoming, of how she and Lily would talk long into the night about her experiences. Iris would give her tips about life as a college freshman, and reassure her that she had the talent to make it as a performer. Iris was sure she would get into Purchase, and even if she didn't, there were plenty of other good schools that would want her. That place was full of cutthroat New Yorkers, anyway, who at best would be ruthless in their quest to outshine her, and at worst be openly hostile. Lily would confide in her about what had been going on with James in the meantime, and Iris would read her excerpts from Peter's letters. She would smile when Lily complained about the complaints about her cooking, and Iris would tell her that she had missed the kitchen and would be happy to cook all the dinners, if their father would adapt his mealtime to her summer work schedule. They would reminisce about the high school they had never been fond of, and of their cliquey classmates who had never allowed them access to their social circles. There might be some cautious talk about their mother, some tentative expression of concern, some half-hearted, humorous speculation about her latest escapades with her women's libber friends. There would be little talk of Dolores; she was gone, and whatever feelings they harbored about her wasted life and tragically premature death were better off left unsaid.

The scenario had played out perfectly in Iris's mind, over and over again, its conversations becoming the mantra that gave her the strength to stick it out for the rest of the semester with Emma Zeiss studying in the chair beside her by day and snoring in the bunk beneath her by night. She had no doubt Lily would be as excited as she was, although neither of the girls had actually verbalized such thoughts. These were just things sisters knew, without having to come right out and say them. Just like Iris knew that if Lily didn't keep in touch, it was because there was no allowance for long phone distance calls in the household budget, and that Lily must find writing a bit of a chore. At least that was what she figured, since she had never answered the letters Iris had written her.

Even if Lily had made the effort to write, or call, or hop on a bus to Buffalo herself to explain her motives, she would not have been able to prepare Iris for the desolation she felt, standing there alone in the room with three beds, in a house with three brothers and a father. Of course, she had heard about the "when" of Lily's decision to move out; her father, deciding that this bit of news was worth the buck it would cost for the call, had phoned Iris himself, and speaking in the controlled, stoic tone of Catholicism's most revered martyrs, informed her of this latest test of faith. She could also understand the "why" behind Lily's impromptu defection: she was all too aware of how unrewarding it could be for a seventeen-year-old girl to devote her time and energy to cleaning and cooking for a household that offered little joy and less serenity in return. What eluded Iris was the "how": how she could turn her back on her distraught father and abandoned little brothers; how she could put Iris in the position of returning here alone, knowing she may never have the courage to leave again. Had she persevered just a bit longer, they could have spent the summer together, using the time to prepare the all-male menagerie to manage without them. They would have devised a strategy, perfected a plan, led the boys and their father down the road to self-sufficiency. In the meantime, they would have cleaned the house, top to bottom; they would have stocked up on Hamburger Helper and Rice-a-Roni; they would have filled the freezer with gallons of chicken soup, and dozens of meatballs in spaghetti sauce. Then, at the end of the summer, they would have both gone off to college, their consciences appeased. But no: Lily couldn't wait. Now it would all be up to Iris.

She slid open the accordion door to the closet with such force that it derailed from its track. "Cheap crap!" she cursed, as she reached in to grab a handful of hangers, but could not disentangle them from the rod from which they dangled, because some faced one way, some the other. She scowled at the hangers, silently accusing them of rebelling against the order she had always imposed upon them, cursing the flimsy wire they were made of, so pathetically bent of out shape from years of sustaining the clothes of growing girls, and the dreams stitched to their hems.

Kicking the disjointed closet door out of her way, her foot encountered the object that was blocking it. She reached down to move it, and found herself holding her little blue valise. She shoved it into the back corner of the closet before more memories could assail her. This was not the time. Today she was just passing through; the rest could wait until her return.

"Now that's what I call meatloaf!" Iris's father said, stabbing a piece with his fork and shoving it in his mouth. "How the heck did you do that?"

"It's no big deal," Iris said, pushing around on her plate the half slice she had served herself. It was the same meatloaf she had made countless times before, and no one had noticed. "Just regular old meat loaf, except I spread it out on wax paper, sprinkled some chopped spinach and Swiss cheese over it, then rolled it up and put it in the pan. Oh, I also put some bacon strips on top, to give it extra flavor."

"Well, I'll be! Aren't you clever!" Auntie Rosa said. Fixing her eyes on Iris, she wagged her head from left to right and back again, tsk-tsking in wonder, as if her niece had just disclosed one of The Three Secrets of Fatima delivered by the Madonna herself. "Isn't she clever, Alfred?" she said, turning to her brother.

"Mmm-hmm," Uncle Alfred said, adding another heaping spoonful of topping to his baked potato as he chewed. "I've never had sour cream like this, either. Nice and light. Where did you get it?"

"Actually, it's just plain yogurt. We didn't have any sour cream. I just doctored it up, added some herbs, you know, some chives," Iris said, observing the concentrated pleasure on the faces gathered around the table.

"Can I have some more meatloaf, Iris?" Ricci said.

"Sure, here you go, honey," Iris said, serving him a slice from the nearly empty platter. "How about you guys?" William and Charles nodded their heads and lifted their plates to be served.

"Don't forget to eat some bread with that, boys," their father said. Some things never changed.

Her brothers had been exceptionally quiet during dinner, and Iris wondered whether their silence was simply due to their absorption with their food, or if they refrained from expressing their appreciation of the meal out of fear of being disloyal to their father, who had been wrestling with the task of cooking in the interim, or to the absent Lily who had, for what it was worth, done her best. Although she was in no mood to sit at the table, watching them eat infused Iris with warmth, as if the eggs and bread crumbs she had worked into the ground meat to hold it together could do the same for them, and for what was left of their family.

"Jeepers Cripes, Iris. Now I remember why we missed you so much around here," her father said with a smile, wiping his plate with a piece of bread. "That sister of yours says she felt 'oppressed' in the kitchen. She's turning out to be just like her mother. Last time the boys saw Ms. Libber you know what she fed them? Kentucky Fried Chicken. What kind of a mother is that? One with bats in her belfry, that's what. Good riddance to the both of them." He patted the breast pocket of his shirt, pulled out a

463

pack of Parliaments, and lit one. As Iris watched him blow the smoke high into the air, she found herself craving a cigarette, although she had given up her occasional smoking way back when she had given up Michael Jejune. She had never smoked in the house, had never even been suspected of smoking, and could imagine the shocked look on the faces of her father and aunt and uncle and brothers if she were to reach over and grab a Parliament for herself.

"Let's wait a few minutes for dessert and coffee," her father said. We won't be having a dinner like this for another couple of weeks. You two ladies pulled a fast one on me, running off to It-ly like that." Her father always pronounced the name of the country in two syllables: It-ly. So did Auntie Rosa, and Uncle Alfred, but for some reason, it only irritated her when her father did it.

"*Mamma mia*, I can hardly believe it, Lover-dover!" Auntie Rosa said. "Tomorrow at this time, we'll be on that plane."

Iris smiled. Between the fantasizing and planning, the upcoming trip had been vying for an increasing share of her daydreaming time. Images of piazzas with fountains, pigeons perched on marble statues, and cappuccinos sipped under the striped awnings of sidewalk cafés encroached on the territory once populated exclusively by Peter, blurring his features, rubbing out the select passages of his letters she had committed to memory. Now that the trip was about to become reality, she almost wished she could prolong the wait, for the same reason she had been secretly relieved when Peter's leave to visit from England in August had been postponed until Christmas.

"If only poor Dolores were here," Auntie Rosa said, crossing herself and sighing. "She could have come with us. She would have loved It-ly." So would Lily, Iris thought.

"Now don't start with that again, Rosa," Iris's father said. "You did all you could for Dolores. We all did. Just go and have fun, and forget about everything. But don't forget to come back. And remember to bring Iris back with you."

"I may never get to leave, if I don't pack," Iris said. "In fact, if you don't mind, I'll skip dessert. I can't eat anyway, with all these butterflies in my stomach." The feeling was actually more a gnawing than a fluttering, but the result was the same.

"You go ahead, *Bella della mamma*!" Auntie Rosa said. "I'll take care of the dishes."

"Thanks," Iris said, sliding out from her place on the bench, and heading for the stairs. A black telephone sat on the landing, a desktop model with a rotary dial her father had brought home from the office when the new push-button phones were installed. There was no desk or table here, but the phone had a cord long enough to allow its use in the boys' bedrooms, and in the bathroom. Iris went to her room, and looked at the clothes she had stacked on the spare bed. She had been unable to select anything from the pile. Nothing looked right. Nothing felt right. She couldn't pack with that gnawing in her gut, and she knew the feeling wouldn't subside until she talked to Lily. Fishing through her shoulder bag for her address book, she flipped it open to the letter M. She memorized the number next to the entry MOM, walked back to the landing, picked up the phone and took it into the bathroom, shutting the door behind her.

"Hello?" Lily's voice sounded small, and faraway, though they were barely three miles from each other.

"Hi, Lily! It's me, Iris," Iris said.

"Iris! Where are you?"

"I'm home. Just got here today. I've got a million things to do, but I want to see you. Can you pick me up? We can go to the diner for a cup of coffee. My treat."

"I guess so. Let me ask Mom if I can borrow the car." Iris studied her face in the mirror above the sink as she tried to discern words from the distant female voices ringing like wind chimes out on a porch. She was contemplating whether she should be more daring with her eyebrow plucking, when Lily's voice came back on the line.

"Um, Iris?"

"I'm here."

"Mom thinks you should borrow Dad's car and come over here. She says I would be facilitating him if I used her car to pick you up."

"Facilitating?" Iris said, watching the medicine cabinet reflection of her face turn crimson. "What's that supposed to mean?"

"You know, making it easier for him."

"I know what the word means, Lily. I just don't see how Dad has anything to gain if you pick me up and we go for coffee."

"Please. It's no use. Just come."

"Give me ten minutes," Iris said.

The front door and Lily's arms were opened wide before Iris's finger touched the bell.

"Hey!" Lily said.

"Hey!" Iris said, embracing her. "Your hair looks great like that."

"You think so? Don't tell Mom, but I hate it. Thank God it's growing back fast," Lily said, brushing back her bangs from her eyes. "Come on in."

Iris stepped past the entrance and into the living room; her eyes roamed over the shapes she assumed belonged to a sofa and an armchair, a desk and a coffee table, cowering under the burden of self-help books and *Ms.* magazines, back issues of newspapers and outdated newsletters, open notebooks and scribbled upon legal pads, spread over every horizontal surface. "Thank God no one smokes around here," she said.

"Yeah, it could get pretty hazardous," Lily said. "Hey, Mom? It's Iris!" she called out in the direction of the kitchen.

Their mother walked into the room carrying a half-empty plastic package of fudge stripe cookies. "Oh! Iris!" she said, as if she had no recollection whatsoever of having discussed with Lily who should go to whose house and why, less than half an hour earlier. "We haven't seen you around in a while." Setting the cookies on top of the papers that risked sliding off the coffee table, she gave Iris a hug, then pulled back suddenly, crinkling her nose and coughing. "Oooh, you smell like Estée Lauder. You're not dipping into Rosa's Youth Dew, I hope."

"God, no! It must have rubbed off when I hugged her," Iris said. "She and Uncle Alfred came over for dinner."

"I see. Special occasion?"

"Well, you know, I just got back from college."

"How did it get to be May already? I can't believe how time flies. How did it go there in ... where were you again?"

"Buffalo, Mom," Lily interjected. "You even went once with Iris to see the campus, remember?"

"That's right," their mother said. "You kids are all in so many places these days, I lose track." She let out a little puff of air. "Ithaca and New York and Boston, and what was it? Portsmouth, where Violet went? Up in New Hampshire?"

"It was another Portsmouth, the one in Virginia, but she's been back for a while now," Iris said.

"Of course she has," said their mother, nodding her head. "I'm sure you got your usual good grades at Buffalo?"

"I guess. Chemistry was pretty hard, but I'm still hoping to make the Dean's List. I'll know when I get back."

"Get back from where?" Lily asked, looking Iris in the eye.

"I'm going on a trip," Iris said, dropping her gaze to the floor, noticing it was in sore need of vacuuming. This wasn't how she had wanted to start the conversation.

"Oh," Lily said, removing the foil wrapper from a stick of Juicy Fruit she had taken from the pocket of her jeans. "You mean, as in a vacation?" she asked. She rapidly folded the stick in four and placed it in her mouth. The movement of her jaw was quick and tight, as her teeth clamped down on the gum.

"Well, yes. I guess you could call it that," Iris said, struggling to find an alternate word. Her eyes wandered to the window, where an angel with a trumpet dangled from the sash lock, perennially poised to herald the arrival of Christmas. "To see some relatives. With Auntie Rosa."

"Oh. Those people from Scurcola? Those paesans that live down in Yonkers?" Lily said, snapping her gum as she spoke.

"Actually, we *are* going to see some people from Scurcola," Iris said. "But, well, we're going to see them there. In Scurcola."

"The real one? In Italy?"

"Yes, that's the plan." It was the truth, that was their plan, if they had time left over, after touring Rome and Genoa and Bellagio and Portofino.

"So Auntie Rosa is taking you on a vacation to Italy?"

"She's not really taking me. We're going together. It was actually my idea. To help her get over the whole Dolores thing, you know? She took it awfully hard."

"Yeah, tell me about it."

"Come on, Lily. Don't do that."

"Do what?"

"Act like you're the only one who suffered when Dolores died."

"Dolores's death was a tragedy," their mother said. "Her whole life was a tragedy. It was generous of her to step in and sponsor you, Lily. She did more for you than your own father did. But she was not exactly what I would call an exemplary role model. Just look at the way she allowed herself to be victimized, the way she got enmeshed in one abusive relationship after another. And while we're on the subject, Lily, I'm not so sure getting into that college would be the best thing for your future. I brought you there because I thought it was important for you to follow through with what you started. But really, why would a bright young woman like you want to be an actress or a singer, prancing around half-naked on some stage, just begging to be exploited?"

Iris looked at Lily; now it was her turn to stare at the floor. "That's not what Lily wants!" she said.

"Well, this is real life. Where you don't always get what you want, no matter how worthy your intentions at the outset. You either get empowered, or you suck up and swallow. By coming to live here with me, Lily showed everyone she is not sucking up to your father, or your aunt or anyone else."

"I didn't want to show anyone anything, Mom," Lily said.

"And now of course, when it's time for a trip to Italy, who goes with Auntie Rosa? Certainly not Lily. You should not allow your aunt to play favorites like that, Iris. It's just not right."

"She's not playing favorites. I just told you, it was my idea. I've been working hard, too. I want a break. Is that so bad? I'll be spending the rest of the summer working and taking care of the house."

"That's another thing, Iris. That house is your father's responsibility. He wouldn't let me have it, just like he wouldn't let me have my kids. Now you are being used. Just like Lily was being used. You're playing right into his hand, Iris."

"What's so wrong with trying to make other people happy?" Iris said. "Is there some kind of law against it? Isn't that what families are for? To help each other out?"

Frustration at her motives being misinterpreted, resentment at being unjustly persecuted for something she did not consider a crime, made Iris feel powerless, as if she were standing defenseless before a tribunal in a country whose language she neither spoke nor understood.

"I come over to see my mother and my sister, and I'm faced with a firing squad! I thought you would be happy to see me. But I guess that's just me being silly Iris, living in my little dream world." She was shocked by her own outburst, mortified by her mother's opinion of her, frustrated at not being able to explain things to Lily. Tears streamed down her cheeks as she ran out the door to the car and slid behind the wheel. Her hands were shaking as she rummaged through her purse for her keys, but could not find them. She dumped its entire contents on the seat next to her: no keys. She heard a tapping on the window, and looked up to see Lily standing there, the car keys dangling from her hand. Iris rolled down the window.

"You dropped them on your way out," Lily said.

"Thanks," Iris said, wiping her eyes with the back of her hand. They were burning so badly, she wished she could pop out her contact lenses right then and there.

"Don't let her get to you, Iris. She doesn't mean anything by it."

"No one ever means anything, do they? But they all still manage to make me feel guilty."

"I know, same here." Lily looked over her shoulder, then back at Iris. She reached a hand under her shirt, and pulled out a piece of rolled up clothing. "Here, take this," she said, laying it on Iris's lap.

Iris ran her fingers over the fine rosebud fabric, fingered the tiny buttons, the dainty ruffles and cuffs. "It's your favorite blouse," she said. "The one you wore for your audition."

"With my luck, it won't be getting out of here any time soon on my back, so I figure maybe it would like to go to Italy with you."

Iris wished her insides would stop quivering. "Thanks, Lily."

"What is it they say? *Bon voyage*?" Lily tugged at the gum in her mouth with her thumb and forefinger, stretched it out is if she were pulling taffy, then twirled it around her finger, like a ribbon around a maypole.

"I'll see you when I get back." Iris started the engine, threw it into reverse, and backed out, too blinded by the tears fogging up her contacts to notice the aluminum garbage can, which the car crashed into and sent rolling noisily down the driveway.

"Don't worry," Lily shouted, waving her away. "I'll get it."

Iris shrugged apologetically, and waved back. As she approached the main road, she looked in her rear view mirror, and saw Lily dragging the trash can back up the driveway.

From: Iris Capotosti <iris.capotosti@gmail.com>
To: Lily Capotosti <lilycapotosti@gmail.com>
Sent: Fri, August 13, 2010 at 7:12 AM
Subject: Before you say anything

Good morning, Lily,

Every time we exchange chapters, I am always so anxious to read what you send me, but last night I forced myself to go to bed without reading your next chapter. I learned pretty early on in this experiment of ours that going to bed on a full brain has the same effect on me as drinking a pot of Dad's drip coffee used to. But even though I didn't read, I kept waking up and wondering whether you had read my chapter, and what kind of memories it must have brought back to you.

Before you say anything, I want to tell you that the day I came home from Buffalo was one of the worst I can remember from that entire year – and there were plenty to choose from. You didn't have the monopoly on those, believe me. I still remember how excited I was about completing that first year of college. It gave me a feeling of accomplishment I had never experienced before – definitely a notch or two up from baking a lemon pie piled high with a meringue that doesn't weep or crack. But just like with the pie, no one really even notices unless you botch it.

I had been hoping to celebrate with you, in some little way. You know me and my imagination. But reality slammed into me the moment I walked into that empty bedroom. I had never slept alone in my entire life. After rooming with that bore Emma, I'd really been looking forward to some late night chats in bed with you. The disappointment and loneliness I felt were crushing - and that was before I was treated to Mom's welcome home speech.

But what upset me most were the feelings of guilt. Guilt for having left you to run things in that house. Guilt for having successfully completed my year of college, when you still didn't know where you would be going. Guilt for spending money on a trip to Italy, while you worked at Burger King.

How I wish it could have been you and me getting ready for that trip, instead of Auntie Rosa and me. Every summer I see college kids traipsing all over the country, and they don't even seem interested in half the places they visit. As if they'd already seen and done it all. Ah, we would have had the time of our lives, you and I.

But I had to go, Lily, even without you. Buffalo was never far enough away. I needed to burst through those clouds on a 747.

Still, I carried that image of you lugging that garbage can up the driveway with me the whole time. And the rosebud blouse, too. Thanks for that.

I hope you are sleeping better than I did last night.

Love,
Iris

From: Lily Capotosti lilycapotosti@gmail.com
To: Iris Capotosti <iris.capotosti@gmail.com>
Sent: Fri, August 13, 2010 at 10:00 AM
Subject: I don't want to hurt you, but...

Iris:

I'm so glad that things worked out so that you could have a good night's sleep, but now I am left here to face a day full of work and responsibilities, and with the added pleasure of processing not only your chapter, but this email as well.

All my life, I've heard that from people, you know? "I don't want to hurt you but...", "I don't want to leave you, but..." "I don't want to burden you, but..." but - but - BUT - they always do.

Do people think that by telling me how much they don't want to hurt, burden, or abandon me before they actually DO hurt, burden, or abandon me that they are then somehow absolved? Adding that little disclaimer BEFORE following through on it with action only makes it worse, because then I become stripped of my delusion that they were just being thoughtless, or ignorant, and that they weren't knowingly offending me.

So please don't tell me how sorry you are for me, or how much you wished you hadn't hurt or abandoned me, because that only enrages me, really. I would much rather hear that you knew exactly what you were doing and you chose to do it anyway. You did what was best for you, regardless of what the effect was on me. Don't we all do that, despite the pains we take to cloak ourselves in sensitivity and consideration? We do - we all do. Mom did, Dad did, Auntie Rosa did. James did. Dolores did. You did. I did. I do, you do.

Just once back then, I would have liked to hear someone say, "But I just can't do that to Lily," and then come knock on my door, and sit down

473

with me and talk to me and set me on a different trajectory. Stop me from making the choices whose ramifications have rippled out farther than even my imagination could fly.

I am sorry you came home to an empty house that summer, but at least you didn't have to stay. Besides, even if I had been there, I wouldn't have been there.

Love,
Lily

32. LILY

The 2001 Club was named after the discotheque in the film, *Saturday Night Fever*. Lily had asked James to take her to see the film when he was home at Christmas but he claimed that it wasn't the kind of movie a boy should take a girl to see. He went with his friends, and Lily could think of few things more pathetic than going to the movies alone, so she decided to wait until she and Iris could go together. Lily hoped it would be soon.

James would be coming home for the summer too, but Lily didn't expect to see him. She resolved that he would have to call her if he wanted to see her, and she was fairly certain he wasn't about to make such an ambitious commitment as calling her on the phone. When he went away to Houghton College - just a week before Iris had left for Buffalo - Lily had given him ten envelopes stuffed with blank note paper. Each envelope was stamped and pre-addressed to her. All he had to do was jot down a few lines and drop the note into the mailbox. He hadn't written once. He never told her that he loved her again, he never invited her up to see his dorm. Lily entertained the idea of breaking up with him when he returned to school after Christmas break, but then realized that they had never officially been going steady in the first place, so breaking up was sort of beside the point. Her New Year's resolution had been to resist the temptation to initiate contact with him, in favor of maintaining what little dignity she had left.

Lily dropped her Burger King uniform into the laundry basket. There was no time for a shower, so she spritzed her hair with White Shoulders cologne, which Grandma Whitacre had sent her, pulled on a pair of jeans, and grabbed the paisley blouse she'd worn to her audition from its hanger. Not exactly disco-wear, but it was the best she could do on such short notice. If she got into Purchase, it would surely be dubbed her favorite blouse. If she didn't get in, she would certainly never wear it again after tonight.

Cecelia and Danny were standing outside the club waiting for her.

"C'mon, c'mon!" Danny cried. "The dance contest is just getting started!"

He escorted her past the guy at the door who winked at Lily as they slipped by.

"What do you want to drink?" Cecelia shouted, trying to be heard above the music.

"I don't know," said Lily. "Just a Coke, I guess."

"No way!" said Cecelia. "You gotta learn to relax a little, Lily. Loosen up!"

"What are you having?"

"Whiskey sours," said Cecelia, extending her glass to Lily. Lily took a sip and winced.

"It's too bitter!" Lily turned toward the bartender. "Really, just a Coke for me."

Cecelia placed two dollars on the bar. "And add a little rum to that," she said to the bartender.

"This is really good," said Lily, sipping the beverage through the tiny red straw.

Cecelia grabbed her by the hand. "Let's find a place upfront to watch. I've heard some of these guys are pretty amazing - like John Travolta!"

The cold glass in Lily's hand offered relief from the hot smoke-filled room, with people pressing in on all sides, and music playing so loud you could hardly hear yourself think. But the Coke was helping.

A wall of people surrounded the dance floor. Cecelia

masterfully weaved her way through the crowd, with Lily in tow. "Scuse me - Scuse me!" Cecelia shouted until finally they arrived at a spot right at the front. The house music stopped, leaving only the deafening buzz of conversation and anticipation. Translucent floor tiles marked the dance floor, which was lit up from below, sending shafts of red, blue, purple, and green light onto the first couple as they struck a pose center stage.

"OK, everyone," announced the DJ. "Please give a warm Club 2001 welcome to our next couple, Joseph and Monica!"

The crowd cheered as strains of "Staying Alive" filled the room. Monica wore a red and white satin dress and Joseph was dressed in high-waisted white pants, a red satin shirt, and a white vest.

"Check out that coolie!" shouted Cecelia, adding a "Whooo!" as Joseph pulsated his hips back and forth in time with his partner's own gyrations. The couple moved in perfect synchronization, twirling and gliding from one end of the dance floor to the other, drawing cheers from the crowd each time they executed a spin or a lift. Lily sipped on her drink, mesmerized by the sensual movements and shocked at the way her own body responded in watching. Her arousal intensified each time the dancers passed by. The draft created in their wake brushed up against Lily, penetrating the thin layer of paisley, caressing her breasts, causing her to inhale sharply, anxiously awaiting their next passage. She would love to be able to dance like that girl. With that guy. To have a boy like that lead her and guide her and tease her and hold her. Yet they were from another world. They were from this disco world of rayon wrap-around skirts and glitter eye shadow and high heels. They were sexy and sophisticated and Lily felt silly standing there in her Hush Puppies, drinking a Coke through a straw.

As the song neared its end, Joseph and Monica each took a place at opposite diagonal corners of the dance floor. With a deep breath, Monica ran across the floor, and launched into a swan dive in the air, landing against her partner's body, his arms catching and encircling her at her knees. With her body pressed firmly against his, he lowered her to the floor, inch by inch by inch. Lily watched as first her navel was at his eye level, then her breasts, her chest heaving and beaded with sweat. Finally, they came face to face, their lips parted, but not touching the other's. She wrapped her arms around his neck, and he placed his hand on the back of her head. As her feet touched lightly down onto the floor, she raised her arms overhead and came into a backbend. He bent forward, releasing her head toward the ground as the music ended.

"Let's have a big hand for Joseph and Monica!" called the DJ. "And join us right back here in fifteen minutes as Tony and Tina try to top *that*!"

The crowd erupted into applause. With nowhere to place her drink, Lily stood and stared, breathless, as Joseph and Monica joined hands at the center of the dance floor and took a deep bow together. When they raised themselves back up, Lily's eyes locked with Joseph's as they shared in the stunned recognition that just a couple hours earlier, she had absolutely sold him a hamburger, an order of onion rings, and a chocolate milkshake.

This Joseph - whose every move for the past five minutes had sent shocks of electricity through her, whose tight pants and loose hips had inspired the sexual fantasies that were still suspended in Lily's mind - was the same Joe that she had so cavalierly dismissed at Burger King. This charismatic and beloved king of the dance floor had called her "cutie" and flirted with her. For reasons that she didn't quite understand but that felt somewhat like embarrassment, Lily turned, fought her way through the crowd, and headed for the door, stopping by the bar on her way out to return her glass and place a dollar bill on the counter.

Before she could lift her hand from the bar, another one - thicker and broader than her own, a hand with short burly fingers, a hand wrapped in skin that was reddened and chapped, the way Lily's father's would become after a Rochester winter spent shoveling snow and spreading salt along the long driveway on Chestnut Crest - came to rest upon hers.

"Mrs. Munster!" he called. "You sure do move fast for a

zombie."

"Oh - hi," said Lily, trying to feign surprise at finding him standing there, his breath still heavy from the *grande finale* and his satin shirt soaked through with perspiration.

Joe grabbed a cocktail napkin from the bar and wiped his brow. "So - what did you think?"

"What did I think?" Lily knew what he was asking, but she could find neither the language nor the nerve to reply. Anything she could say would only make her seem more childish and naïve than she was sure she already did.

"Yeah - about my performance there... you saw me, right?"

"Yes," said Lily. "How could I miss you? You were great. Really great."

"I will take that as a big compliment, coming from a nice girl like you."

"What makes you so sure I'm nice?"

"Cause. I never seen you in here before." Joe raised his hand to summon the bartender. "And that means one of two things - either you're too young to be here and somebody snuck you in, or you're old enough to be here, but you got better things to do on Friday night besides standin' around, gettin' wasted and watchin' the same people compete in the same dance contest every week."

The bartender nodded toward Joe. "Hey - Mike!" Joe called. "Gimme a seven-n-seven, wouldja? Oh - and a -" he turned to Lily. "What are you drinking?"

"Oh, nothing," she said. "I don't really drink... I just had a Coke. At least that's what I think it was."

"Let's get you something fancier than that, huh?" Turning back to the bartender, Joe said, "How about a Kahlua and cream for Lily Munster here?" Joe pulled up a barstool and offered it to Lily. "Uh-oh," he said, "I have the feeling you're not crazy about that new nickname, am I right?"

"Not really," replied Lily with a smile. "But I can't stay anyway, I really have to get going." She stepped her foot onto the crossbar of the stool and raised herself up into it.

"OK, OK," said Joe. "You're right - you are way too pretty for a nickname like that. You're more like a Lily of the Valley."

Lily giggled. "That's what my family calls me."

"Well then, it's settled, Miss Lily of the Valley. And what, may I ask, is your last name?"

"Capotosti."

"Capotosti?! Madonna - you're a paesan?"

"Yes, actually," said Lily. "My grandparents came here from Italy."

"I think I've died and gone to heaven." Joe winked and handed her what looked like a small glass of milk. He raised his glass and Lily followed suit. "To Italia!"

"To Italia!" echoed Lily. She took a sip of the drink and said, "Wow - this is really good - what's in it?'

"Magic," said Joe.

Lily blushed and cast her eyes down at her lap. Joe was soon surrounded by an assortment of young men slapping him on the back and young women hugging and kissing him, offering their congratulations. Lily nervously sipped on her drink, trying to cover over her sense of self-consciousness, which she was certain was evident to everyone who passed. By the time the small crowd around Joe dissipated, Lily was sucking on the ice cubes from the bottom of her glass, intent on getting every last drop.

"Whoa - slow down, there," Joe said with a chuckle.

Lily raised her eyebrows and put her hand to her lips, aware that she had drained her glass too quickly, knowing she should care, but didn't.

"Now," said Joe. "We dance." He stood up and took Lily by the hand.

A rush of panic shot through Lily's body. "Oh, no!" she shouted, pulling her hand back. "I don't know how to dance."

"Sure you do," said Joe. "Everyone knows how to dance."

"Not like you do," said Lily, gesturing with a flourish toward the dance floor, which was quickly filling up with couples as Andy Gibbs' "I Just Want to Be your Everything" began to play.

"That?" Joe said, waving his own hand in the air dismissively. "That's performance, that's all. C'mon, I promise I won't do anything crazy... just one little dance... Look," he said, gesturing to the crowded dance floor. "It's almost half over already. You'll be out of here before you know it." He held his hand out to her.

Warm from the liqueur, swooning from the attention Joe had been giving her, she wanted to tell him, *Try just a little bit harder... Please convince me.*

"And after all," he said, "You did practically kick me out of Burger King."

With a laugh, Lily rose to her feet, took Joe's hand, and followed him out onto the dance floor.

Joe took Lily's right hand in his left, and gently placed his right arm around her waist. "That's it -" he said, as they began to sway back and forth to the rhythm. "You got it."

Lily couldn't help but notice the irony - the guy she had shunned at her drive-up window was the one she had been fantasizing about dancing with when she arrived, and the one who held her now, who steadily and confidently led her around the floor, as the mirrored globe that spun overhead cast stars all around. Almost like fairy dust.

As the music subsided, the crowd broke into applause, and Cecelia ran out onto the dance floor. "There you are!" she called. She was nearly frantic. "What the heck happened to you? I've been looking all over for you!" When Cecelia noticed who Lily was with, her eyes widened. "Hi," she said to Joe. She stood staring.

"So where's the fire?" asked Lily.

"Oh, right – shit! We gotta get outta here. Danny's brother said that the club owners are here and they are proofing everyone in the place. So unless you have an ID that says you're eighteen, we hafta make like a coupla hockey players and get the puck outta here!" Cecelia turned to Joe, "It's been lovely, I'm sure, but she has to go now. If they see you with an under-aged girl, you'll get busted, too." Cecelia grabbed Lily by the wrist as they erupted into laughter and headed for the door.

The return address on the envelope announced that Lily's

future would begin the moment she extracted the letter and read the first sentence. She slid her finger under the flap, giving herself a paper cut.

"Ouch!" she brought her finger to her mouth, and sucked on the cut, noticing the metallic taste of her own blood. Each step through the thick cool grass and back toward the house felt long and heavy as she unfolded the paper, assaulted by the words, "Thank you for your recent audition with SUNY Purchase. We regret to inform you that we are unable to extend admission to you at this time..." The letter went on to expound on all the great and famous people who had been rejected from great and famous schools, but Lily didn't care about any of them. All she cared about was that she had spent the last two years dreaming of her life as a student at SUNY Purchase and all she had to show for it was a form apology and a paper cut.

She handed the letter to her mother. Tears came to her eyes, but she didn't cry. Tears rolled down her face, but she didn't weep. Her body was having the experience, but somewhere deep inside, Lily felt shut down, as though a vault had been slammed closed and the wheel had been spun, with her still inside.

"I'm so sorry about this," her mother said. "What rotten luck."

Is there any other kind? Lily thought.

"But they said you did a great job, right?"

But not great enough to get in.

"Look," said Lily's mother, holding the letter up to Lily's view and pointing at the copy on the page, "It says right here that they only have room for about a thousand new students - out of the whole country. The chances were pretty slim in the first place."

Not for the thousand who were accepted.

"What about the other schools?" her mother asked. "You received five acceptance letters this week. What about Geneseo, or Cortland? Fredonia is lovely..."

Lily left her mother rattling off attempts at comfort, as she mechanically walked up the stairs to her room and lay on the bed. She woke up two hours later to the sound of the ringing telephone, and despite her wish that the day had been a dream, reality came rushing back with consciousness.

"Lily -" called her mother from downstairs. "Telephone."

Lily flopped over onto her stomach, and reached for the phone. "Hello?"

"I'll absolutely take one Lily of the Valley," said the voice. "And I won't take no for an answer."

33. IRIS

"Alla faccia di chi ci vuol male!" Auntie Rosa said, lifting the glass of red wine Iris had poured for her from a miniature bottle. An eruption of laughter forced her aunt's head to jerk back and her mouth to fly open. Iris was partly amused at her spontaneous expression of pure joy, partly disgusted by the view of her mouth it afforded her: the plastic and metal of crowns and bridges, the bits of masticated peanuts, the bumpy pink tongue. Had it not been for the testimony of her dental work and the wispy cloud of white hair that topped her head, Auntie Rosa might have seemed a giddy girl, buckled into the seat of the Boeing 747, airborne and soaring its way toward its destination of Rome, Italy.

"Now you have to tell me what that means," Iris said, touching her glass to her aunt's before taking a sip of wine, then setting it down in the round indentation on the tray table. She picked up the pen and spiral notebook she had brought along for the purpose of jotting down all the expressions and impressions she would encounter on her very first trip to another country. That is, if you excluded the Canadian side of Niagara Falls.

"Doesn't *faccia* mean face?" Iris asked. She remembered that word from some slang term she had heard from some of the Gates Italians, though no one seemed to know exactly what the rest of the expression meant.

"Yes, it does!" Auntie Rosa said. *"Brava!* Let me see, I guess you could translate it, 'in the face of those who wish us evil.'"

"It sounds better in Italian," Iris said, intent on transcribing the words. She had never studied Italian, but had gotten straight A's in high school French. One of the things she loved about Italian was that it was written exactly like it was pronounced. "Is it f-a-c-i-a?"

"Oh, gosh darn it, honey, I'm not really good at the spelling, but I think it has two c's. I never wrote in Italian, I only spoke it to Ma and Pa, God rest their souls," she said, making the sign of the cross.

"That's OK, I have my pocket dictionary," Iris said, enthusiastic to be learning something she could actually put to use right away, unlike chemistry formulas or logarithms, which she was more than happy to leave on the other side of the Atlantic.

"*Carne o pesce?*" the dark-haired stewardess in a green apron with a lopsided "A" emblazoned over her heart inquired of Auntie Rosa. Iris looked at her name tag: Lucrezia.

"*Io carne, per favore,*" Auntie Rosa said. She turned to Iris and said, "You can choose between meat and fish. I'm having the meat."

Lucrezia handed Auntie Rosa a plastic tray divided into compartments; in one, a rubbery-looking slice of hard-boiled egg with a fluorescent yellow yolk sat atop a chunk of iceberg lettuce. In another, a multicolored dessert substance jiggled with the vibration of the plane. Iris wished she could have a peek at the main course, concealed under a thick foil cover, before making a decision. Lucrezia's scowl suggested that was not an option.

"*Carne* for me, too, *per favore,*" Iris said. She knew her r's didn't roll quite the way they should; she would have to keep practicing.

The emotional and physical upheaval of the previous days had exhausted Iris. She vowed to put all thoughts of Lily, their mother, and Chestnut Crest out of her head as she sipped appreciatively on free wine. She discovered she was ravenous, and dug into her meal of airplane food with gusto. As they ate, Iris asked Auntie Rosa about the people they would meet, and how they were related; Auntie Rosa's descriptions were more confusing that clarifying, but they helped her to stop worrying about those she had left behind and start wondering about those she would soon encounter. Oblivious to the look Lucrezia gave Auntie Rosa the second time she asked for an extra roll for the *scarpetta* (Iris jotted down the word for the Italian rite of mopping your plate with bread), her aunt finally wiped her mouth with a napkin, looked with astonishment at her empty tray and remarked, "Goodness, I must have been hungrier than I thought!" a phrase Iris had her heard pronounce whenever a heaping plate sitting in front of her miraculously found itself empty; in other words, every time she had a meal.

By the time the cabin crew had finally finished pushing and pulling their carts up and down the aisles, all Iris could see from her window was the reflection of her face against a black background of nothingness. Not a quarter of an hour had passed since the cabin lights were dimmed and the movie projector set in action, when Auntie Rosa's jaw dropped, and she began snoring. Iris reached under the seat for her carry-on bag, and extracted a hardcover copy of *The Agony and the Ecstasy* she had purchased for seventy-five cents at the used book store; even though it was a novel, she thought she might glean some information about the life of Michelangelo Buonarotti. Performing the ritual by which she became acquainted with any new volume, she put the book to her nose as she fanned its pages and sniffed, read the back cover and jacket flaps, then closed her eyes for a moment, and hugged it to her chest. She could hardly grasp the fact that she, Iris Capotosti from Rochester, would be granted the opportunity to behold masterpieces like the *David* and the *Pietà* with her very own eyes. That she would stroll through grandiose piazzas, light candles in cathedrals built hundreds of years ago. That she might see the Pope, walk through the ruins of the Roman Forum, swim in the Mediterranean sea, admire the peaks of the Alps, throw coins in fountains, float down canals in a gondola, ride on a train.

The steady, high-pitched whirring of the jet engines reminded her that her body was being propelled over the ocean at an altitude of thirty-three thousand feet. She tried to divert her thoughts from the black void above and below and all around her, and hoped that the mechanical miracle that kept the jumbo jet high in the sky would prevail for the duration of the trip. She was not interested in sleeping, and when she closed her eyes, her imagination painted colorful scenes of Grandma Capotosti's steamship crossing of the Atlantic decades earlier. How different it must have been for her, back then, sailing in the opposite direction, in steerage. How elemental, frightening, life-changing.

Her thoughts traveled back to the year of college she had just completed; she was pleased with her academic results, but disconcerted by her lack of conviction and direction. She was fairly certain she wouldn't become a physical therapist after all. That had been her plan, but nothing was etched in stone, was it? If she had the time and money to waste, she would just keep taking courses that interested her, like last semester's Body Movement class that made her briefly consider a career in dance therapy. Or more English electives; the effusive praise from her Creative Writing teacher made her wonder whether she might become a journalist, maybe even a novelist. Then she thought of the three college graduates who had worked with her at McDonald's; they all held degrees in English. Iris could hardly afford to run up four years' worth of student loans and find herself back there selling Egg McMuffins. But summer had yet to begin. She would decide about next fall when the time came. She would cross that bridge when she came to it.

Iris leaned back in her seat as her thoughts wandered back to the young Irene Capotosti and her transoceanic voyage. Did she and Anselmo have a plan of their own back then, or were they looking for the fastest, most definitive way out? Were they pursuing a dream when they boarded that ship, or running away from a nightmare?

As she opened her book, she wondered whether this trip would leave her with more than a mouthful of phrases she would soon forget, an album full of snapshots that would soon fade, a notebook full of scribbling that would gather dust on a shelf. She hoped so.

Six hours later, Auntie Rosa had bantered their way through customs procedures, infecting with her laughter the officers of *polizia, guardia di finanza* and *carabinieri* alike, without distinction of uniform or rank, who chuckled at her quirky pre-World War II Abruzzese colloquialisms, and congratulated her on the loveliness of her niece. At least that was the gist of the comments she translated for Iris.

Just outside the Customs area, Iris was greeted by a blur of incomprehensible salutations and double-cheek kisses by the chattering crew loosely defined as "relatives," who were waving in the air a black-and-white photograph of Auntie Rosa taken at Dolores's wedding in 1958. The effusions were finally interrupted long enough for the group to herd out the door of Rome's Leonardo da Vinci airport the mismatched battery of bulging luggage, while Iris considered how cool it was for a country to have a native like Leonardo to name an airport after, instead of just presidents. Her first kiss of Italian sun stirred Iris from her airplane-induced stupor, welcoming her to a fresh new day on the old continent. She blinked slowly in the bright light, her eyes as unfocused as her thoughts as they took in her surroundings. She felt detached, displaced, as if she were in a trance, or a dream. She figured that must be what they meant by jet lag, and that she would recover after a good night's sleep.

Her sense of dreamy displacement ballooned after indulging in the heaping dish of pasta placed before her at the table of cackling relatives. She could not recall a single phrase in Italian, so absorbed was she in savoring the fresh plum tomatoes and basil and olives and capers and all the Mediterranean flavors she had always craved, and she found herself slipping more deeply into a dreamlike state as people refilled her tumbler with table wine poured from a big bottle labeled "Castelli Romani." The wine went down much better than her father's Thunderbird, which had made her gag the only time she tried it (if you didn't count the time in the gazebo with Rick Rotula), or the overpriced Lambrusco she sometimes drank with her friends at the 2001

Club, which turned everyone's teeth and tongue purple under the strobe lights, like those tablets dentists used to detect tartar buildup.

As lunches overflowed into dinners, she looked on from the sidelines while a parade of smiling faces belonging to people whose names she could not remember were introduced to the American girl called Iris. Iris? *Come il fiore?* Yes, Iris, like the flower. Tantalizing tastes, inebriating smells and breathtaking sights rushed at her senses from all directions, jolting her from one dimension to another, where the peals of church bells were alternated with those of laughter. Roaring, liberating, laughter, the kind that made you "wet your pants," as Auntie Rosa howled, squeezing her legs together under the table and dabbing at her eyes with a linen dinner napkin. Never had Iris seen her aunt laugh so much. Or eat so much. And never had she herself felt so free and unencumbered, despite her total dependence on others for her survival. Stripped of responsibility, constricted to dependency, she felt as if she were on the outside looking in, and was delighted by the vision of herself as a lucky little girl in wonderland.

"*Vieni, Iris!*" Fabrizio said to her after dinner the third day, motioning with his arm for her to join him. "Come for a ride. Rome by night!" Fabrizio was the oldest son of the family, relatives of relatives from Scurcola, who were hosting Iris and her aunt in Rome. Barely a year younger than Iris, he liked to practice his English with her; he was tall and lanky, with chestnut eyes and a square jaw that might have made him look like the type that played hard-to-get, had it not been for the smile that never abandoned his face for longer than it took to say "*mamma mia.*" Iris thought he must have plenty of girlfriends.

"Where?" she asked.

"You will see," he replied. "*Ciao, Mamma, ciao Zia, ciao tutti!*" he called as he waved to his mother and Auntie Rosa and the rest of the family and neighbors who were still gathered around the table, having coffee and thimbles of Sambuca, the *digestivo* selected for its purported powers to neutralize the after effects of the mounds of spicy tomato and bacon sauce of the *bucatini all'amatriciana* they had devoured. Everyone they had met so far, regardless of age or connection, referred to Auntie Rosa as "*Zia*." Their aunt. Just like back in Rochester, where she was everyone's "Auntie Rosa."

"*Ciao tutti!*" Iris mimicked, waving to the group as she turned and walked out the door which Fabrizio held open for her.

"*Divertitevi, ragazzi, voi che siete giovani!*" Fabrizio's mother called after them.

"Oh, they'll have fun all right!" said Auntie Rosa. "At their age!"

The elevator touched down on the garage level of the condominium with a jolt. Fabrizio slid back the grate and pushed open the doors; as they stepped out onto the concrete floor, he said, "You remain here. I come back."

"Okay," Iris replied. After standing in the semidarkness for a moment, she jumped at the sound of reverberating machine gun fire. *Ba-ba-ba-bam! Ba-ba-ba-ba-bam!* "What the heck?!" she cried, her eyes darting around, searching for signs of movement in the shadows. Over dinner one of neighbors who spoke English had been talking to Iris about the recent kidnapping of Italy's ex Prime Minister Aldo Moro. Just weeks earlier his body had been found in the trunk of a car, murdered by the Red Brigade terrorists. What if …

A moped rounded the corner and screeched to a halt in front of her.

"*Vieni!*" Fabrizio said, gunning the engine before scooting forward on the seat, in order to make room for her. With each flick of his right wrist on the accelerator, a new round of machine gun fire exploded and ricocheted off the concrete walls and ceiling of the garage. "*Stai comoda?* You OK?" he asked her, as she settled into the most secure perch she could find on a saddle made for one.

"Um, I guess. What about helmets?" she asked.

"Helmets?" he repeated. It wasn't clear whether it was the word or the concept that he was unfamiliar with.

"Helmets. You know," Iris repeated, placing both hands on her head as he glanced over his shoulder to look at her. "Those hard hats you wear so you don't get killed?"

Ba-ba-ba-bam! Fabrizio gunned the engine again and laughed. "You don't need in Rome!"

"Oh," Iris said, wondering what was the worst that could happen. Hoping he wasn't ticklish, she clasped her arms around Fabrizio's waist, as the moped shot forward like a bucking bronco, down the wide avenue with too few trees and too many apartment buildings, accelerating and braking its way through the city's coughing traffic that didn't seem to know the difference between night and day.

"The ancient wall of Aurelius!" Fabrizio shouted after some minutes, pointing to an old stone wall that flanked the road.

Iris stole a quick look, then shut her eyes again.

"Over there we cross the Tevere, see? By Castel Sant'Angelo, there is a bridge," Fabrizio continued, using his left hand, which Iris didn't think he could spare, to point. As Iris peeked out of one eye, she recognized the monumental cylindrical-shaped construction adorned with statues she had seen the previous day when Fabrizio's mother had accompanied her and Auntie Rosa to St. Peter's, where they lit candles for special intentions (what better place to beg forgiveness for skipping months of Sunday Mass?) and bought rosaries blessed by Pope Paul VI himself. Had she known about this little excursion, she would have added it to the list of things to pray for, but at the sight, her fear was supplanted by awe.

"Wow! It's even more beautiful at night!" she said. The orange glow of the lighted monument filled the May night with magic, the waters of the Tiber with shimmering reflections, her heart with joy.

"Bellissimo!" Fabrizio concurred, as he jerked and maneuvered his Ciao through the jammed traffic. Horns blared, Vespas and mopeds zigzagged, their passengers balanced precariously behind the drivers, holding their arms high in the air, bearing huge flags that unfurled in a blur of red and orange.

"What's going on, Fabrizio? Is it a holiday or something?" Iris shot the question directly in his ear to be heard over the din.

"Yes! A holiday! Today is the day Roma won!" Fabrizio called over his shoulder.

"Won what? Its independence? Like the fourth of July?"

"Yes, the historic battle of Roma against Atalanta! Our team won the football match!"

"You mean the Atlanta football team came over here?"

"Not Atlanta, Atalanta. The soccer team from Bergamo, that's up north."

"You mean they're all driving around with flags because Roma won the soccer game?"

"It's tradition! Me, I don't care much about soccer," Fabrizio said with a shrug of his shoulders. "But we have fun driving around, no?"

Iris laughed. "Sure!" She took a deep breath, wrinkling her nose at the exhaust fumes, and vowed to keep her eyes open, focused, alert. From now on, she wasn't going to miss a thing.

And she didn't. Not all that night, as she clung to Fabrizio, hopping on and off the moped on a whirlwind tour of the center, starting with Piazza Navona, where the cacophony of Roman voices was accompanied by the languages and laughter of foreigners, and where she licked the creamiest vanilla ice cream she had tasted in her entire life from a fragrant wafer cone, thinking if she were the mayor, she would outlaw the little cardboard cups and plastic spoons that littered the cobblestone streets. Fabrizio showed her an authentic Egyptian obelisk, and a fountain more beautiful than any she had ever dreamed of, which he told her was by Bernini, and called *La Fontana dei Quattro Fiumi*. Then he scooted her off to Piazza Venezia, to show her the colossal *Altare della Patria*, built in honor of Vittorio Emanuele II, and home to tomb of the unknown soldier, but derisively dubbed *"la macchina da scrivere,"* or typewriter, by the Romans, who had many more splendid monuments than this in their backyard. Taking his role as tour guide seriously, Fabrizio pointed out the balcony from which Mussolini delivered his spirited speeches, and the area where once stood the house in which Michelangelo died. He would not rest if Iris did not elbow her way to the Trevi Fountain and toss in three coins, before he whisked her off for a cruise past the Forum and the Colosseum, the sight of which filled her with the desire to take a course in Ancient Roman History, and sparked the fantasy of throwing to the lions anyone caught defiling the scene with discarded Coke cans and cigarette butts. She wondered how anyone living in such a city, seeped in such a glorious past, could stay focused on the present or worry about the future.

Sleep was slow in coming that night, as the sounds of her tour of the Roman night reverberated in Iris's ears, drowning out the snores of a slumbering Auntie Rosa: the screeching and honking of the knotted traffic, the animalistic shouting of the Roma supporters, the raucous laughter and shrieking voices of the silly girls whose dark beauty Iris would have admired more in a painting. From her bed, she could hear the grinding whir of traffic still clogging the thoroughfares several floors below; she closed her eyes, wondering how she could possibly sleep, wondering where she could possibly find the words to describe the spectacular sights that danced behind her closed lids, unwilling to end a day that would never be forgotten.

Iris awoke early, her spirits floating on the magnificence which a night of fitful sleep had cleansed of impurities, but which were soon dampened by the pitter-patter of rain against the closed shutters, and the realization that their time in Rome was drawing to a close. *"Roma piange,"* Fabrizio said, holding an umbrella over her head as they dashed from the car to the train station, as quickly as their cargo of suitcases would allow.

"Rome cries?" Iris said, taking a stab at the translation after recognizing the verb *piangere,* and mentally reviewing its conjugation.

"Yes, Roma cries because you leave!" he said. Iris was sad to say the first goodbyes of her trip at the Termini station, where she and Auntie Rosa prepared to board their train. She wished they could stay longer, instead of going up north to Genoa, to visit the widowed cousin of a cousin of Auntie Rosa's, whose father was also from Abruzzo. Iris wondered if the lady would have fat ankles like Grandma Capotosti's *paesan* friends in Rochester. Despite the chaos and crowds that left her exhausted at the end of each day, she regretted leaving Rome, and Fabrizio, whom she might even have ended up kissing, if it weren't for the thoughts of Peter Ponzio that kept her fantasies in check.

Despite her reluctance to leave, Iris had been looking forward to her first train ride, and to the eight hours of travel it would take to get to Genoa. She planned to enjoy the time reliving her recent experiences and committing them to her journal, reading her book, writing postcards, flipping through an Italian magazine, thinking. Once settled in their seats, she was relieved to see Auntie Rosa take out her prayer book and cross herself, meaning she was content to talk to God instead of Iris for a little while.

As the train rumbled through the densely constructed outskirts of Rome, Iris decided that although she adapted easily to different environments, she was essentially uncomfortable in big cities. They seemed to sap the energy from her, confuse her, alienate her. A sense of peace began to pervade her as the ugly high rise buildings and unsightly industrial areas were left behind, and the view switched to poppy fields and herds of sheep grazing as they soaked up the morning sun that had broken through the clouds. Iris had first glimpsed the Mediterranean from the plane, and now she was thrilled to get a closer look from the train window. Checking her map as they headed north, she learned that the portion of sea flashing by to her left was referred to as the Tyrrhenean, while the mountains she admired off in the distance to her right were the Apennines.

A few hours into the journey, she was delighted by views of the Tuscan shore, with its groves of umbrella pines clustered near the sea, and marveled at how precisely the neat rows of cypresses standing guard on the inland hills corresponded to her idea of a typical Italian landscape. She was perplexed at the sight of snow on the slopes of the chunky Apuan Alps, until it dawned on her that she was looking at marble quarries. This was the very spot where Michelangelo had toiled to obtain the stone into which he chiseled life through his art. She was reading these very stories in the book that rested face down on her lap, open for the past two hours to page two hundred and twelve. Her mind had been too occupied to concentrate during the train ride, but as other passengers came and went from their compartment, she soon realized the English title was an effective deterrent to unsolicited chatter.

She looked at Auntie Rosa, who sat directly across from her. Her head lolled and her eyes were closed, her lips slightly parted. It was odd to see her so completely devoid of animation and purpose, so utterly relaxed and peaceful. Her hands rested in her lap, still clutching her frayed prayer book and her spanking new rosary that had not yet logged in its first hundred Hail Marys. Sunlight streamed in the window, bathing her in gold, conferring upon her a saintly aura. Iris imagined her aunt laid out in a casket, just like this, and was certain the gates of Heaven would fly open at the mere sight of her, no matter what those born-agains in Buffalo said. She would probably joke with St. Peter as he waved her in, just like she had done with the customs and immigration officers at the airport.

Iris opened her bag, deciding this would be an ideal time to write the postcards she had bought for another Peter, Peter Ponzio. It vexed her that his letters had been less frequent since she had written to him of her plans to visit Italy. Instead of being excited for her, he had said something about it being her life, and she being free to do what she wanted. She didn't know exactly what he meant by that, but she had promised to send postcards, and she would keep her word, even if so far, she had only gotten as far as buying them. She arranged the cards in chronological order according to when she had visited the places depicted, accurately backdated them, and addressed them to his APO address in England. Even though she knew it wasn't completely honest to put different dates on the cards to give the impression she had written them day by day, as she had intended, she didn't really think it could be considered lying.

"Ciao from Roma! Arrived safe & sound after a long trip. Auntie Rosa's cousins are super nice and hospitable. There is so much history and art everywhere you look! The Colosseum is spectacu-"

Her writing was interrupted by the total darkness that suddenly invaded the compartment. Through the window Iris had opened one more time than the other passengers had closed it, came a deafening rattle as the train lurched through a tunnel. Just seconds after reemerging in the daylight, the train was swallowed up again, and again, as the *rapido* bolted through the bowels of the Ligurian coastal cliffs, each tunnel eclipsing the sun and sky and sea, echoing the screeching and rumbling of the train on its tracks. Tiny harbors and storybook hamlets flashed in and out of view, as Iris struggled to read the blurred signs that hung at each station: she made out the name Monterosso on one, Levanto on another. Each time the train burst through the end of a tunnel, her eyes were astonished by the saturated colors in the slide-show of exotic palms and cacti and multicolored blossoms. There were olive trees, too. Scores of them.

At last the train decelerated and ground to a halt, metal screeching against metal. Iris stood and looked out the window; a sign said they were in Rapallo. Auntie Rosa's eyes popped open and quickly surveyed her surroundings. It made Iris happy to witness her features gradually register the fact that she was on vacation somewhere in Italy, instead of in the midst of some medical emergency.

"Oh, honey!" she said. "I guess I must have drifted off. Last thing I remember I was saying my prayers, but I don't think I finished. Son of a gun!"

"Shame, shame, shame, the devil knows your name, Auntie Rosa!" Iris said, running the index finger of her right hand over the index finger of her left. "First you start drinking wine with dinner, then I catch you having a glass at lunch, and the next thing you know, you're falling asleep in the middle of prayers!" Iris laughed at the look of astonishment in her aunt's eyes, as she bit her lower lip and shook her head, reflecting on her rapid moral degeneration. "Don't worry, God understands. And we did receive the Pope's blessing, which must be worth something. By the way, you drifted off about three hours ago!"

"Son of a gun!" Auntie Rosa repeated. "Can you believe that? Where are we?"

"Some place called Rapallo." She could see rows of apartment buildings towering over the tracks, but the station only had two platforms; it must be a small town, but densely populated. Thinking back on the sense of suffocation she had sometimes felt in her dorm room, Iris wondered how people managed to live in such close quarters, with no space to cushion contact with the outside world, or with each another. Even when all fourteen people in her family had lived under the same roof, at least they didn't have to share it with strangers. It was their haven, for however imperfect it might have been, and for all the chaos and all the infighting, the Capotosti household put up a formidable common front against the outside world.

"Rapallo? Already? The ticket man said it was the stop before Genoa."

"Then we'd better get ready," Iris said, packing up her belongings. She was grateful they had more trust in Italian train passengers than did the authors of the tour guide she had read, and left their suitcases in the corridor. They would never have been able to get them down from the overhead racks without assistance, and Iris hated asking others for help.

Half an hour later, Iris helped Auntie Rosa down the steep stairs that folded out from the door of the train, which seemed to have been designed with young athletes in mind, and certainly not for older women with short legs and ailing knees, nor for any woman in high heels or a tight skirt. Iris was glad she had stuck with jeans and sneakers, which she dressed up with Lily's rosebud blouse. It was light, and feminine, and wearing the blouse made her feel she was somehow sharing her experiences with her sister. After assisting Auntie Rosa, she hopped down to the crowded platform, where she was greeted by a malodorous bouquet of abandoned cigarette butts still smoking on the concrete, urine, engine grease, and other train station smells still unidentifiable to her inexperienced nose.

"You just stay here," she said to Auntie Rosa, as she deposited the first two suitcases next to her on the platform, and climbed back up the stairs to retrieve the heavier ones. She was still pushing and pulling and dragging and kicking them down the narrow corridor when the train whistle tooted, signaling its imminent departure. What would happen if it left while she was still on board? Perspiration sprang from her pores, making her frantic hands slippery, her brow glisten, her armpits dampen the rosebud blouse, whose tight shoulders and cuffed sleeves hindered her movements. She would have no idea how to contact Auntie Rosa, or her distant relative whose name she couldn't remember, who was supposed to pick them up.

A second series of whistled warnings prodded her to make one final, Herculean heave to the door. She climbed over the suitcases, jumped down to the platform, and began tugging at the first one, which came crashing down the steps, until she managed to block it with a bent knee. She was unsure of how to disentangle herself from this position without ending up under the suitcase, or under the train, but knew she must act fast. While her muscles trembled with exertion, her ears registered the whooping of Auntie Rosa's unrestrained laughter somewhere behind her. Iris was starting to panic, knowing she couldn't resist much longer, when she felt a hand on her right shoulder, firmly but gently nudging her aside. Another hand reached in front of her, grabbed the suitcase by its handle and lowered it to the ground. Shaking and sweaty, she pivoted on her heels to thank the owner of the arms. Her face was level with his neck, where she noticed the perfectly formed knot of a regimental tie held in place by the button-down collar of a light blue Oxford cloth shirt beneath a navy blue blazer with gold buttons. Iris raised her eyes a few inches and encountered a polite smile nestled between a sandy moustache and matching goatee; a few inches above the smile, a pair of amused blue eyes gazed down at her.

"Thank you so much," Iris said.

The man rescued the second piece of luggage from the train just before the door slammed shut and it began to move.

"*Grazie,*" she added, to make sure he understood. The next time she traveled to Europe, she swore she would only carry what would fit in her little blue valise.

"*Prego.*"

One softly spoken word, one silent gesture of kindness was enough to set this man in a world apart from the loud, showy types in Rome who had begun flirting with Iris as soon as a friendly word or innocent smile of hers somehow led them to believe she was up for grabs.

"I'm Gregorio," the man introduced himself, in English. "Gregorio Leale, Isabella's son. I just met Rosa. The picture Mamma gave me was very old, but I recognized her right away."

Iris quickly processed each new bit of information, each firsthand observation, and within seconds was forced to discard the unappealing images she had conjured up in her mind to prepare herself for inevitable disappointment of the Ligurian leg of their trip. Whether or not his mother was an old lady with fat ankles who spoke an incomprehensible dialect, this Gregorio was a handsome man, probably around the same age as her oldest brother, who knew enough English to make himself understood. "Auntie Rosa has looked the same ever since I can remember," she said. "My name's Iris."

"Yes, I know. But Mamma had no picture of you." Gregorio smiled apologetically. No big deal, Iris thought. Her own mother probably didn't have a picture of her, either.

"*Piacere,*" she said, extending her hand, as she had seen the Romans do. She couldn't say much in Italian, but it only seemed polite to use what few words she knew instead of making him do all the work.

"*Il piacere è tutto mio,*" Gregorio replied, extending his hand; it was warm, but dry, unlike hers, which was embarrassingly clammy. His grip was neither limp nor overpowering; it seemed the handshake of an honest man.

"We must save your aunt," Gregorio said, nodding his head in the direction of the spot where Iris had left her, from which she had vanished. A familiar laugh rose over the sounds of crowd, and Iris followed it with her eyes to the source: Auntie Rosa standing by the opposite track, helping an elderly gentleman with a cane as he boarded his train.

"And save our suitcases, too," she said. From where she stood, the hunched little man on her aunt's arm looked enough like Grandpa Capotosti to have inspired Auntie Rosa's abandonment of the baggage she was supposed to be guarding.

Auntie Rosa waved to the smiling old man, then caught sight of Iris and Gregorio. "*Andiamo, ragazzi!*" she called, with another burst of merry laughter as she wobbled toward them. "Let's go! I'm starving!"

The condominium Gregorio shared with his mother was reached by a maze of winding roads which took them high above the city, and made Iris want to vomit. The traffic was heavy, but drivers seemed to accept it as something they must deal with on a daily basis, unlike the Romans, who aggravated themselves and everyone around them by honking, cussing and screaming at every blocked intersection and illegally parked vehicle, as if they were all victims of an unsolvable problem, rather than part of its cause.

Iris's stomach had settled by dinner, and she enjoyed trying *risotto agli asparagi*, a rice dish made with asparagus grown in the area of Albenga, a town west of Genoa, followed by a second course of *cima*, a local specialty which was the Genoese interpretation of how to make a little bit of meat go a long way, by stuffing a pocket of veal with eggs and cheese and vegetables, sewing it up and boiling it. Isabella explained that the process was time-consuming and annoying, and confessed to buying her *cima* from her trusted *rosticceria*, which Iris had learned in Rome was similar to a delicatessen, only better, because it was filled with Italian food.

During dinner, Auntie Rosa and Isabella made perfunctory and largely futile attempts at catching up on news regarding distant relatives and ancient acquaintances whom each assumed the other knew, but in most cases didn't. Iris couldn't scrape up enough interest in the conversation to try and follow it, but Isabella kept scanning the table with quick eyes, as if she were a schoolteacher purposely trying to bore her students so she could catch them daydreaming. Iris had a hard time trying to appear alert, when her eyes were constantly drawn through the French doors of the dining room to the spacious balcony. She wished they could have eaten out there, where she would have been able to observe more closely the passenger ferries and cargo ships come and go, and admire the lights of the coast flicker to life. Each time she began wondering to which faraway destination one ship or another was sailing, her attention was called back to the dining room by Auntie Rosa's voice asking whether she understood the question Isabella had asked her, which of course, she hadn't even heard.

After a few such incidences, Gregorio came to her rescue. "I see your eyes are somewhere else," he said to her, as the older women turned back to their conversation.

"I'm sorry," she said. "It's just all so new, so beautiful."

"And so are your faraway eyes, if you don't mind my saying so," he said.

Blushing, Iris lowered her eyes, smiled. "When I was a little girl, my teachers always scolded me for looking absent, even when I was paying attention. As it turned out, I was just myopic."

Gregorio chuckled, then went on to ask her questions about her life in America, what she was studying, what plans she had.

"Physical therapy?" Isabella interjected, pricking her ears at one of Iris's responses. Though the woman had immediately demonstrated an excellent command of English grammar, she pronounced the word "terapy."

Iris looked at Isabella, trying not to stare at her eyebrows. They were the first thing she had noticed about the compact woman who had presented herself at the door so coiled with tension, Iris thought she might have sprung to the ceiling, had it not been for Auntie Rosa's energetic hug anchoring her to the ground. The brows had been plucked and penciled, until they were perfectly

501

arched, like two little frowns indicating their tacit disapproval of whatever passed under the gaze of the stainless steel eyes below. A mound of carefully coiffed and lacquered waves added a few inches to her birdlike stature, making her about the same height as Auntie Rosa, but the similarities stopped there.

"Yes. I think so, anyway," Iris said, flustered by the woman's unwavering stare, embarrassed about not yet knowing the details of her future. Iris had an inkling that Isabella did not live by her mother's "cross that bridge when you come to it" philosophy. "I want to do something useful, help other people," she added, instantly regretting the beauty queen contestant response.

"Gregorio is a doctor, you know?" Isabella said, pronouncing it k-now, with a total lack of respect for the silent *k*.

"A doctor? Isn't that wonderful!" Auntie Rosa said, looking at Gregorio's hands. "I'll bet you are a surgeon, I can tell by the way you hold your knife."

"Not quite. I work in the operating room, but I put patients to sleep," Gregorio said. "*Anestesista*. It is difficult to pronounce in the English language."

"Oh! An anesthesiologist! Now that's exciting, isn't it Iris?" Auntie Rosa said, beaming at her.

"Of course," Iris said, smiling and nodding her head politely.

"He works at the Policlinico, the biggest hospital in Genoa," Isabella said, dropping the *h* of hospital. She held her fork, tines facing downward, in her left hand, and her knife in her right, and cut a piece of *cima*; using her knife, she assisted the morsel onto the fork, and placed it in her mouth, without switching the cutlery from one hand to the other like they did back home. She chewed slowly, swallowed, took a sip of water, dabbed at the corners of her mouth with her linen napkin before continuing. "After he received his degree, he worked in Germany, but when my husband died, he returned to stay with me. He is a good son. His sister Cinzia is married, so the house was empty. No husband. No children."

Isabella was probably not yet sixty, and it sounded like her husband had been dead for a while now; Iris wondered whether she ever dated, but something in her proud, sad demeanor, and her elegant way of combining tones of grey with black suggested she was content with the respectable state of widowhood. Turning to Gregorio, Iris asked, "How was it in Germany?"

"A very good place to work. I like the German respect for order, and for the rules. But family is family, and you only have one Mamma."

"Your Mamma is lucky, Iris. She has so many children to keep her company," Isabella said.

"Well, we don't all live together," Iris said, looking down at her plate, upon which she struggled to make her knife and fork imitate Isabella's movements. "The older ones have moved out. And my mother lives by herself. With my sister Lily."

"So your father is dead, too?" Isabella asked, resting her knife and fork against the edge of her plate without creating so much as a *clink!*; she bowed her head, and crossed herself. "*Poverino*, I did not know." She picked up her cutlery and resumed eating.

"No, he's not dead," Iris said. "My parents are getting a divorce."

"Divorce?" Isabella repeated. "*I genitori sono divorziati?*" She looked to Gregorio and Auntie Rosa for further confirmation.

"*Sì, Mamma.*" Gregorio said to his mother, then glanced at Iris.

"Well, actually, they're still just separated," Iris said.

"The fact of the matter is, she abandoned us," Auntie Rosa said, shaking her head. "My poor baby brother."

"Mamma did not accept the idea of divorce when it was made legal," Gregorio said to Iris. "She was working in the *tribunale* every day then, she is a *giudice*. How you say that in English?"

"A judge!" Auntie Rosa said. "My, oh my! A judge. Can you imagine that, Iris?"

"A judge," Iris repeated, nodding her head.

"*Divorziati!*" Isabella said, shaking hers.

Thanks to Gregorio, who led the conversation to the more amicable territory of sightseeing, Iris was spared further questions about her family, which may have forced her to either lie or reveal that her oldest sister was already divorced, too. By the end of dinner, Gregorio had determined he would use a few of his accumulated vacation days to accompany Iris and Auntie Rosa to the lakes. In fact, he would go the very next morning to his travel agency to plan an itinerary and book rooms for them. It was better to plan ahead, he said, to avoid unpleasant surprises. Iris might like to come along, and then he could show her around a bit, while the ladies enjoyed a relaxing visit at home.

After admiring Piazza De Ferrari, which boasted a beautiful fountain, but nothing like the ones she had seen in Rome, Iris was impressed by the cathedral of San Lorenzo, where Gregorio took a snapshot of Iris next to one the marble lions that guarded its entrance, and showed her the shell of an unexploded bomb from WWII on display inside, a testimony to the church's miraculous survival. It was odd to think that Italy and her country had been on opposite sides of the war, and she wondered what effect it must have had upon her immigrated grandparents.

As Gregorio guided Iris through the maze of narrow alleys flanked by ancient buildings several stories tall that huddled around the historic center of Genoa, he took her elbow now and then to escort her up or down stone stairs worn by the passage of centuries' worth of feet, or across a patch of pavement in disrepair. When they approached Via Prè, he showed her the safest way to hold her purse to avoid snatching, and even led her away by the hand when a man tried to sell her a contraband carton of Marlboros. She was thrilled by the undercurrent of possible dangers and petty crimes, and reassured by Gregorio's protective presence. The street was in the heart of the bustling area right across from the port, and lively with the sounds and sights and scents of people and products from all over the world. The burlap sacks of dried beans and rice and grains, the bags and jars of exotic spices, catapulted Iris's imagination back to the time, centuries earlier, when vessels sailed from this very port in search of new worlds. She smiled to herself, knowing that from now on, she would recall these scents whenever she browsed the meager spice section of Star Market. One of the things that most amazed

Iris, was the fact that unlike Rome, where most of the ancient buildings she had seen were impressive monuments to a glorious but remote past, Genoa seemed to be a one huge monument in which people lived, worked, ate and prayed.

After trying some slices of *farinata*, straight from the wood oven, where the chick pea flour and water batter was cooked in the biggest copper pizza pan Iris had ever seen, Gregorio suggested a drive down the coast to Portofino. Iris was delighted by the picture-perfect colorful buildings that framed the half-moon harbor, and flabbergasted by the amount of painstaking work required by their finely detailed trompe l'oeil decorations. They sat at a café in the *piazzetta* for a while, watching tourists amble back and forth, while Iris was served a frothy cappuccino, eliciting an amused smile from Gregorio, who informed her that only foreigners would drink a cappuccino in the afternoon. He just ordered a glass of water, but Iris didn't feel too guilty about enjoying the beverage leisurely, especially after noticing it cost him several thousand liras; she made sure Gregorio got his money's worth, sipping slowly while taking in the view of the enchanting harbor, and the parade of passersby. Gregorio used the time to fill a pipe (he said it was a Savinelli, and showed her how to recognize the quality of the briar) with tobacco he picked in little pinches from a leather pouch, and laughed when Iris asked if she could sniff it. Iris could not help but note how sophisticated he looked in his blazer, puffing on his pipe in Portofino; how the sound of his laugh rang warm with indulgence for her curiosity.

They strolled along the wharf to admire the luxury yachts and Gregorio asked her to pick out which one she would choose, if she were to set off on a honeymoon cruise right then and there, which made her blush, as she pointed out the sailing yacht which struck her fancy right away, and which Gregorio informed her was called a schooner. As they climbed the steps to the church of San Giorgio, the scent in the air made Iris swoon with pleasure; she wondered whether the shrubs with the tiny white flowers responsible for the inebriating perfume (Gregorio said the plant was called *pitosforo* in Italian) would grow in Rochester, but she doubted they would survive the harsh winters. Iris lit a candle in the little church, which though charming, she didn't think nearly as beautiful as the striped marble-and-slate church of San Matteo in Genoa, which dated back to the twelfth century; Gregorio agreed, and informed her that was because Portofino's original church had been destroyed by a bomber during the war. As they sat on the stone ledge overlooking the sea, watching the gulls soaring and circling and diving, Iris could not imagine such horribly devastating acts taking place in such an idyllic corner of the world.

On the way back to Genoa, they stopped at the emerald cove of Paraggi, where Iris took off her shoes and squealed with joy as she waded up to her knees in the fizzing sea foam. She was glad they had not brought bathing suits, as she would have been too intimidated by the waves for her first swim in the sea, and too embarrassed to show herself to Gregorio. She blushed when he told her he was happy she couldn't swim, so she would be forced to come back another time. As if flying over to Italy were something she did on a regular basis.

They stopped for an ice cream in Camogli, which reminded Iris of the little seaside hamlets she had seen flashing by from the train, and walked along the breakwater, where she could feel the sea spray on her face, and taste its salt on her vanilla ice cream, and wondered how each ice cream cone in the country could taste like the best she had ever eaten. Before heading back to Genoa, they stopped in Recco at a special little shop Gregorio knew his mother liked, where he bought handmade *trofie* and pesto to have for dinner, which would save Isabella the fuss of cooking. Gregorio said Iris could not come to Recco without trying the *focaccia,* so he bought a whole tray of different varieties, some plain, some made with sage or rosemary or onions or olives, to have with dinner, and insisted she immediately taste the *focaccia al formaggio,* just out of the oven, which she decided on the spot was absolutely the most delicious thing that had ever touched her lips, or dripped down her chin. Gregorio chuckled, as she reached for a paper napkin, but he was quicker; he carefully dabbed the stracchino from her chin, wiped the crumbs from the corners of her lips, and smiled. The tenderness in his movements, the sparkle in his eyes as they searched hers for a reaction, made her insides as runny as the melted cheese.

Isabella disliked sleeping in strange beds, so she remained behind when the trio set off to explore the lakes north of Milan. They visited Como and Bellagio, and even crossed the border to Lugano, in Switzerland, before swinging back down to Stresa, on Lago Maggiore. Iris continued to buy postcards every place they stopped so she could share her experiences with Peter, who ironically seemed even farther away than ever, though he was just a hop across the English Channel. She never seemed to find the words or time to write them, and wondered vaguely where she would buy postage stamps and mail them if she did. She had even picked out a card for Lily, one with a beautiful view of the Borromean islands, and the peaks of the Alps in the background, but couldn't remember the address of the house where she and her mother lived.

On the last day of their excursion, after a lunch of pizza and *paciugo*, Auntie Rosa opted to rest at their hotel while Gregorio and Iris took a boat tour. "Isola Bella," Gregorio said, pointing to the island with terraced gardens leading up to an immense villa. "Named after Countess Isabella."

"Like your mother," Iris said.

"That's right. Or just Bella. Like you," he said, removing his aviator sunglasses. His clear eyes deepened to a darker shade of blue, the exact color of the glacial lake on which they floated. He pushed her Foster Grants to the top of her head and peered into her eyes. Iris tried to hold his gaze, but ever since she had started wearing contact lenses, she had become hypersensitive to the sunlight; she kept blinking, and turning her head away. He caressed her cheek lightly with the back of his hand, then took her chin between his thumb and forefinger to hold it still. His lips were so close to hers that the roof of her mouth tingled, the same way it used to do when she rubbed heads with the cat. Her eyes began tearing profusely and she worried that her lenses might pop out of her eyes and drift away on Lago Maggiore, but the look on Gregorio's face suggested it would spoil the moment if she were to explain; better to let him believe her tears were a sign of uncontainable emotion.

"*Posso?*" Gregorio said. She did not know what the word meant, or what exactly he wanted to do, but she had an inkling it would be something romantic, like everything else they had done together. She looked up at him, and nodded her consent, whatever the question. His lips touched hers, softly, gently. She had never experienced such warmth in the form a kiss.

The boat shook as it maneuvered into its slip, sending vibrations from the soles of her feet up her legs. When they came to a standstill, she held up her Kodak Pocket Instamatic camera and said, "*Posso?*" The voice was hers, but it sounded just as foreign as the word it mimicked. Though he had been reluctant to have his picture taken earlier, he now smiled and leaned back on the railing as she snapped a shot. She had already gone through two rolls of the film she had brought with her, and couldn't wait to show everyone the pictures when she got home. She would get the film developed as soon as she started her job, and could take advantage of her employee discount.

Gregorio had a boyish grin on his face when he joined Auntie Rosa and Iris for breakfast the next morning. He announced he had decided to take two more days off in order to accompany Iris and Auntie Rosa back to Rome to catch their return flight. He said he had never taken days off like this, on the spur of the moment, but he had called in favors from his colleagues who owed him for the numerous Sundays and holidays and summer vacations he offered to work so they could be with their families or girlfriends.

They chatted and taught each other expressions in Italian and English as they drove south, each laughing at the other's mistakes. Gregorio said they could not even consider leaving Italy without seeing the leaning tower, so he made a stop in Pisa, where he borrowed Iris's camera to take a picture of her and Auntie Rosa standing on the lawn of the Piazza dei Miracoli, posed so that it would look like they were holding up the tower with their arms. Then they went on to Florence, where she stood speechless in front of the copy of Michelangelo's *David*, in Piazza della Signoria, which was even more impressive than she had imagined, and strolled over the Arno river on the Ponte Vecchio. She fell in love with the brightly dyed kid gloves displayed in a shop window, and couldn't resist buying a red pair for herself, and a purple pair for Lily. The gloves were stunning, though Iris realized they would offer little insulation against the frigid winter temperatures of upstate New York. Frivolous accessories were not something to which Iris or Lily were accustomed, but maybe the time had come for them to learn to enjoy something for its useless beauty.

Gregorio, who refused to let the women pay for any of their meals or accommodations, treated them to pizzas for dinner and one last gelato in Santa Marinella where they would spend their last night, to be close to the airport. They strolled back to their *pensione* slowly, arms locked in a threesome, with Auntie Rosa in the middle. As they were walking, Iris felt a nudge in her ribs, as Auntie Rosa said in a perfectly audible whisper, "Let me tell you, if I had met a doctor like Gregorio back when I was in nursing school, I certainly might have considered settling down! *Mamma mia!*"

Gregorio smiled and said, "I'm sure those surgeons had a hard time concentrating on what they were doing, with your big brown eyes watching them over your mask!"

"Ha! They did used to compliment me, but I was always too busy to listen. And now it's too late. Remember, kids, it's later than you think." She sighed, then added, "We Capotostis all have the *occhi dell'amore!* Iris has them, too, only green. Look at Gregorio, Iris. Show him those Capotosti eyes!"

Iris looked at the ground, then over Auntie Rosa's head at Gregorio.

"It's true," he said. She blushed, and glanced away. "The eyes of love."

They entered the *pensione*, and Auntie Rosa kissed Gregorio on both cheeks. "Thank you for the dinner, Gregorio," she said, still grasping Iris's arm. "*Grazie.* For everything. *Buona notte e buon riposo.*"

"You sleep well, too," he replied.

"Good night, Gregorio," Iris said. "*Grazie!*"

"The pleasure is mine, Iris. *Sogni d'oro, fiorellino mio,*" he replied, kissing her on both cheeks.

Iris blushed an even deeper shade of red, as Auntie Rosa ushered her down the corridor to the room they were sharing. "Did you hear that? 'My little flower,' that's what he called you!" she said, giggling like a teenager.

"How sweet," said Iris, looking over her shoulder. Gregorio still stood where they had left him. He blew her a kiss on two fingers and nodded.

"When you will arrive home, perhaps you will find a letter waiting for you," Gregorio whispered in her ear after she and Auntie Rosa had checked in for their flight.

"A letter? From you?" Iris said. How did he know she loved letters? "What will the letter say?"

"You will see. And you will write to me what you will think, *va bene?*"

Instead of waiting for an answer, he bent to kiss her on her cheeks. Iris could never remember if it was the left cheek first, or the right, and what with all her false moves, first in one direction, then the other, her lips ended up directly in front of his, touched by his, kissed by his. She shied, embarrassed by her clumsiness, her cheeks burning and her lips tingling from the tickle of his whiskers, then glanced at Auntie Rosa, who was pretending to be preoccupied with checking their boarding passes and passports. Gregorio smiled, then opened his arms for a farewell hug. She stepped toward him, and let him cradle her for a moment in a gentle embrace. His body felt solid and reassuring against hers; there was none of that horny pressing she loathed in guys her age. She liked his clean, masculine scent, which reminded her of the last espresso they had just shared and the pipe he had puffed on earlier. She stood still but stiff, with her ear resting against his chest, and thought that if she didn't have a plane to catch, she might very well have enjoyed standing like that for a bit, feeling the steady beating of his heart which both provoked and soothed the agitation coursing through her body.

Then she was doing as she was told: proceeding to her gate and boarding her plane and stowing her belongings and buckling her seat belt and studying the instructions on a plastic card she had extracted from between an airsick bag and a glossy magazine in the seat pocket in front of her. The JFK-bound jumbo jet lumbered down the runway, gaining momentum until it finally hoisted itself into the air. Auntie Rosa, sitting next to her, made the sign of the cross. Iris followed her example, then pressed her forehead against the window, hoping the vibrations would go straight to her brain, and rattle her jumbled thoughts into place. Puffy clouds teased her with a game of peek-a-boo, alternately confiscating and surrendering the views of the contours and colors of the land and sea that receded into the distance as the plane banked and climbed, banked and climbed.

She reflected on how things which just days ago had seemed so foreign to her had already acquired a flavor of familiarity, and how the previously familiar now seemed part of another, remote world. She could hardly bring into focus the last image she had of Lily from the rearview mirror of her father's car, lugging the garbage can she had sent rolling down the driveway as she drove away with her heart in her throat. Or of her mother's face flushed with misplaced zealotry as she criticized Iris for the way she let her father and Auntie Rosa treat her, without ever sparing a word to thank her for looking after her youngest boys. Or of herself standing at the kitchen sink, staring at the Russian olive tree as she washed the supper dishes. Now she was going back there, she had no choice, but she knew the next time she looked out the window at that tree, its silvery leaves would remind her of the olive groves that dappled the hillsides of Tuscany and Liguria. She would tell the tree to bend closer, and she would whisper to it that she had found confirmation of what she had suspected all along: that they were both from the wrong family, both planted in the wrong place.

Iris was lugging her suitcases through the door, wondering how people who traveled adjusted to the reality of homecoming, when her jet lagged eyes were flagged down by an air mail envelope waving at her from the mail holder nailed to the kitchen wall. After all she had experienced abroad on the first real vacation of her life, the hope of finding a letter from Peter was one of the few things that made her want to walk into the house at all. The last time she had heard from him, she was still in Buffalo, and when she spotted the envelope, she was impressed that despite his chronic distraction, he had remembered to send the letter to Chestnut Crest, and not to her college dorm. He must have received some of her postcards already, and must be dying to know more about her trip. Maybe he would want to go to Italy someday, too. Maybe together, who could tell? She dropped her suitcases with a thud, shook the tension from her fingers, and reached for the envelope. She was intrigued to see that the handwriting was not Peter's at all, and when she saw the *Via Aerea* stamp and the *Genova Centrale* postmark, she realized the letter must be from Gregorio. He had written, just as promised. She wondered how the heck the letter had beat her home.

Iris was anxious to read what he had been in such a rush to write her about, but resisted tearing the letter open on the spot. She wanted to settle in first, get her bearings, savor the fluttering feeling of curiosity mixed with anticipation. Lord knew there wouldn't be much of that around here in the coming weeks. She sighed as she glanced around the kitchen where she would spend the summer evenings after work making dinner and cleaning up after her father and brothers. She realized how much she had enjoyed Gregorio's chivalrous pampering: not once did he allow her to open a door, pay for an ice cream, or lift luggage. Maybe it was time her family started treating her like a lady, too, now that she had been to college and to Europe. Let one of them carry her suitcases to her room, she thought, leaving the bags by the door, and rushing upstairs before the unfamiliar feeling of expecting something from someone could abandon her.

The bed springs squeaked a tired welcome in the empty room, as Iris plopped down on the mattress, exhausted from twenty-four hours of travel, between flights and layovers. She ran her fingers over the Italian envelope in her hands, turning it over to examine it more closely, and found another thin air mail envelope stuck to the back flap; this one bore the unmistakable handwriting and overseas address of Peter Ponzio. Uplifted by the prospect of reading not one, but two letters, both from men overseas, Iris pulled herself up in the bed, scrunched up the pillow behind her back, and decided to open the letter from Peter first. She was surprised by the unusual amount of flattery directed toward her as she read through the run-on sentences of the first three poorly defined paragraphs whose sole purpose appeared to be the extolment of her beauty and virtues. The page was filled with so many compliments, that by the time Iris flipped it over to read the back (while nonetheless being irritated by his deplorable habit of scribbling on both sides of the cheap air mail paper he used), she was instinctively steeling herself for a "but." She was not disappointed.

Peter (he wrote), was only human, and a pretty dumb one at that. He didn't deserve someone as nice and pretty and smart and etc. etc. as Iris, who was obviously moving on, going to college, traveling to Italy, and who was he to hold her back? That realization had made him feel sad, and lonely, just like the girl from Liverpool he had met in a local pub, whose boyfriend had dumped her just two months after taking a job in London. He was confused (he wrote) and Iris's letters only made it harder on him. He thought it best if she stopped writing for now, and maybe he would be more clear-headed when he came home for Christmas.

In his illiterate, incoherent way, Peter was breaking up with her. As her eyes automatically filled with tears, her father called up the stairs, inviting her to come down and have a cup of coffee with him and tell him all about her trip, but all Iris wanted was to be left alone to sort out her head and unpack the suitcases no one had brought up yet, then take a long, hot bath. The thought of her father catching her sniveling over a guy again and trying to console her, like he had when Rick Rotula dumped her, was enough to dry her tears, at least for now. She went downstairs to get the chat and coffee over with, feeling bad that she was not more excited to talk to her father.

"This here came in the mail," he said, pointing to an envelope sitting next to the coffee cup he was filling for her. "I set it aside for you."

"Thanks." Iris took a sip of the steaming coffee, deciding that after developing a taste for espresso, she would start drinking it black. She picked up the letter, her hands shaking slightly when she saw it came from her university. "Must be my grades." She looked at her father, as she sat on his bench and stirred evaporated milk into his coffee. Ripping the envelope open, she scanned the slip of paper inside.

"3.75!" she gasped. She had not botched her Chemistry final as badly as she had feared. With grades like that, she'd be able to get into any department, provided she ever managed to decide what course of study to follow.

""I'm not surprised," her father said. "You always were smart." He took a sip of coffee, lit a cigarette. "Now tell me about your trip."

"That means I made the Dean's List, Dad!" A surge of pride made Iris's hands tremble. She placed the slip on the table, for her father to see.

"Can't see much without my reading glasses," he said. "So what did you see over in the Old Country? Who did your Auntie Rosa introduce you to?"

Iris wasn't ready to talk about her trip yet. Her college life had seemed so far away, her relationship with Peter Ponzio so childish, while she was in Italy, being whisked here and there by Gregorio. All these letters were encroaching on the fresh thoughts and impressions she still had to metabolize before she could put them into words. She needed to catch up with herself, before she could update anyone else.

"I'm really beat, Dad," she said. "And tomorrow is my first day of work." But as soon she saw the disappointed look in her father's eyes, she felt guilty for not wanting to sit and talk. Without her or Auntie Rosa around, he had probably been starving for a friendly ear at the end of the day. "Listen," she said. "I learned a few fantastic recipes while I was over there. How about we invite Auntie Rosa and Uncle Alfred over for dinner tomorrow? I can make us a nice spaghetti dinner. Who cares if it's not Sunday. In Italy, they eat pasta every day. Even twice a day."

"All right, then. It's a deal," her father said. He took a long drag on his cigarette, exhaling the smoke in rings that floated to the ceiling.

Iris stood, poured the rest of her coffee down the drain, and rinsed out her cup, pausing a moment to stare at the Russian olive tree. She went to pick up the suitcases that still stood by the door.

"Let me give you a hand with those," her father said, stubbing out his cigarette in the ashtray, and grabbing one of the suitcases.

"Thanks," Iris said.

When they reached her bedroom and set the suitcases down, she pecked her father on the cheek. He wished her a good night, but when she closed the door, there was something in the way he looked at her that made her feel sorry for him. His anger seemed to have abandoned him, leaving him alone with his hurt and loss. She wondered how long it would last.

Finally alone, she retrieved the pack of letters from Peter which she had stashed in Lily's ex underwear drawer, and proceeded with the farewell ceremony she knew she must perform. Sitting cross-legged on her bed, she opened the letters one by one, in the order in which they had been written. Tears trickled down her cheeks as she recalled exactly where and when she had been the first time she had read each letter, and how it had made her feel. Though she had indulged in the habit of picking out some of her favorites and rereading them from time to time, she had never read through so many letters at one sitting, and her pangs of hurt were gradually blunted by page after page of uninteresting, barely legible script. By the twenty-forth letter, she had grown utterly annoyed with Peter's sloppy handwriting and total disrespect for the most basic rules of grammar and punctuation. But it was another revelation which came to her for the first time that made her stop reading. Iris realized that the unarticulated feelings she had freely extrapolated from Peter's words, and coaxed from between the lines he wrote were, for the most part, absent. Confused and angry with herself, she blew her nose, and picked up the letter from Gregorio.

Sniffing the envelope with her eyelids half-closed, Iris could swear she detected the same scent of tobacco mixed with espresso mixed with floor wax mixed with sea breeze she recalled from Gregorio's house. She slid her finger under the flap, opened the envelope, and extracted three neatly creased sheets of white onionskin paper of the highest quality texture and cockle finish. She checked the date at the upper right-hand corner of the letter; the month and day were inverted, continental style, and she noted with surprise that it had been written the very day Gregorio had come to meet her and Auntie Rosa at the train station. Iris scanned the pages in her hand for a clue, an impression, a premonition, before reading the words. The irregular thickness of the elongated, upright letters suggested that Gregorio had probably used the antique gold fountain pen that had belonged to his father. Iris loved pens, and had spotted it right away, in its fancy holder on the writing desk in the study, when Isabella had shown her and Auntie Rosa around the apartment. The scene had made Iris fantasize about how lovely it would be to have a room just for study, and a writing desk, or at least a table and chair of her own.

Fingering the letter, she pictured Gregorio the evening they had first met, after dinner, after everyone else had gone to bed, stroking his goatee as he paced back and forth in the balcony. Waving the sheets of translucent paper in front of her nose, she could smell the tobacco in the little leather pouch she had sniffed for the first time that day in Portofino; she could see him pluck tiny pinches of it using his thumb and first two fingers, and sprinkle them into the bowl of his pipe; she could observe the precision in his movements as he pressed down the tobacco with a little silver tool made specifically for the purpose; she could see the little clouds of smoke billowing from the pipe as he held a wooden match to the bowl. She wondered what musings might have been meandering through his mind as he puffed and paced and stroked, perhaps glancing down at the ships in the harbor, or across to the lights along the coast, or up at the stars and moon in the patch of velvety sky left unencumbered by the elegant palazzos of the respectable Genoese neighborhood perched above the city. She imagined those thoughts, whatever they might have been, prompting him to shuffle silently to the study, careful not to disturb the ladies' sleep, in the padded felt slippers he and his mother wore around the house to polish the marble floors as they walked. She imagined him sitting, with a burgeoning sense of purpose, at the mahogany desk, taking a sheet of paper from its drawer, carefully setting his pipe in the brass nautical style ashtray so as not to spill its contents, unscrewing the lid from a bottle of India ink, dipping in the tip of the antique pen.

His cursive was fascinating to Iris's eyes, but not simple to decipher. She did not attribute this to sloppiness, but to a European method of penmanship, as well as to Gregorio's profession: illegible handwriting was quite possibly a trademark of physicians all across the globe. Iris did not mind the challenge, reasoning that it would prolong the joy of reading.

After the Italian greeting "*Cara Iris*," Gregorio switched to English. The introductory paragraph informed her of his surprise and delight at having such a lovely young woman as a house guest, making Iris smile while impressing her with the impeccable structure of his sentences and the exactitude of his spelling and punctuation. She wondered how long it must have taken him to fill three full pages (front side only), how many times he must have stopped writing to search his vocabulary or consult a dictionary for the proper words with which to convey his thoughts. Not one word was crossed out in confusion, smudged with hesitation, or smeared with haste.

Gregorio's measured compliments and keen observations of her behavior made it evident that the mind which had so swiftly formed opinions of her character, and guided the hand that set them in writing, was that of a mature, perceptive man, and not of a befuddled fledgling. He outlined in a logical, comprehensive manner the reasons for his desire to become more deeply acquainted with her, though they had just met, and hoped she would pardon his urgency. In addition to the kindness and generosity Gregorio had demonstrated in person, he was now projecting the image of a man who had a clear idea of what he wanted, and, as such, backed his words with actions. He informed Iris that his friend at the travel agency had put on hold an airline reservation in his name, and if she consented, he would like to visit her and meet her father and family in December. He suggested the Christmas holidays as a suitable time, considering his mother would accompany Cinzia, her husband Franco, and their three little boys and to their usual hotel at a ski resort in Limone, in the Piedmont region, which they enjoyed because of its convenient location just a couple of hours from Genoa, and its wholesome, family-oriented atmosphere.

Gregorio concluded his letter in a crescendo of admiration for her person, followed by a touch of Italian romanticism, culminating in the unexpected declaration that the moment he had laid eyes upon her, he realized he was looking at the first woman he had ever visualized as the future mother of his children. Gregorio's words made her blush, even though she was all alone in her room; they flattered her, intrigued her, perplexed her. After reading the letter a second time, Iris folded it neatly and placed it back in its envelope, then set it on the nightstand, next to her freshly blessed rosary.

She picked up Peter's last tear-stained letter, which still sat on the bed. She folded it into a paper airplane, and flung it from her hand with a snap of the wrist. It glided across the room, then crashed quietly against the faded butterflies of the peeling wallpaper, and fell to the floor.

She would write Gregorio in the morning, and tell him she would be happy to see him at Christmas. What was the worst that could happen?

34. LILY

"Well, you've probably seen *Saturday Night Fever* a hundred times by now..." said Lily.

"You haven't seen it yet?!" Joe cried. "Then that's the one we have to go see. It's the best movie ever made."

Lily was excited about her first date with Joe, but a little afraid of dating someone who was so sophisticated and worldly. He smoked and drank and danced and she doubted if any of the other girls he'd dated were virgins. What would she say if he asked, what would she do if he tried?

"We'll cross that bridge when we come to it," Lily said to her reflection in the mirror as she swept her eyelashes with black mascara.

"Lily!" her mother called from kitchen. "I think your date is here."

Lily ran downstairs pulling her sweater coat on. "See you later, Mom!"

"Honking the horn in the driveway is not a proper way to pick up a girl for date, Lily," said her mother.

Looking around the apartment Lily was relieved that Joe hadn't come inside. It was bad enough that he would see that the lawn chairs had all but disappeared into the overgrown brush, having slipped down the ever-growing list of causes to uphold. The more difficult Lily's parents' divorce had grown, the more absorbed her mother had become in her various civic and political groups. If she wasn't at work, she was at a meeting or a rally, or scanning newspapers and magazines, looking for nuggets of information that could be filed into one of the swelling, towering piles she'd built around the house. Lily knew that in some way, each clipping had relevance for her mother, but to an outsider, the place would just look like the nest of a crazy person.

"It's OK, Mom," said Lily, placing a peck on her cheek. "We're just late for the movies. He'll come in next time, OK?"

Lily could see why Joe loved the movie. The disco dancing was phenomenal and she had to admit that some of the sex scenes were pretty steamy. No wonder James hadn't want to see it with her; he might have been inspired to take her behind the auto shop and just let himself go. She hoped Joe didn't notice that the palm of her hand was clammy.

After the movie, they went to the local diner where they had burgers and fries and lingered over a cup of coffee for two hours. Lily shared her disappointment at not having been admitted to Purchase, and she told Joe all about Dolores. She filled him in on her parents' divorce, and the dramas that had since become a part of her daily life, including the awful scene between Iris and their mother, the memory of which Lily couldn't seem to shake.

"Wow - she's in It-ly?" asked Joe.

"Yeah," said Lily, pushing down the lump that formed in her throat. "We have family there. She went with my aunt."

"How come you didn't go? I would absolutely go to It-ly if I had the chance."

"So would I," said Lily. "But it seems like I have trouble getting out of Rochester."

"Lucky me," said Joe with a wink.

"But I did make it from Chili to Gates when I moved in with my mother, so that's something." Lily hoped her smile didn't look too forced.

"How did that go over with your old man?" Joe asked.

"Not great," said Lily. "But I couldn't help it, you know? I stayed as long as I could. My father - he is always so angry, always yelling about my mother, calling her names, complaining about the house and the meals and everything. Once Iris went away to college, it just got too hard. Plus, you know, my mother was all alone." Lily's eyes began to tear up. "It's just the two of us now," said Lily. "We're not so good at keeping up with the yard work, or fixing the car, but we manage." Anxious to change the subject, she added, "What about you? Tell me about your family."

Joe spoke of the tightly knit clan of five Diotallevi brothers - and of two parents who'd been together since they were teenagers. Joe still lived at home, but had a good job on the shipping dock at La Casa Bella, his Uncle Frankie's furniture business where all the Diotallevi brothers had gotten their first real job. Each week, after giving his mother money toward his board, Joe would spend the rest of his paycheck on clothes, clubs, and eight-track tapes. And Burger King, of course.

"We don't have a lot of money either," said Joe. "But we have family, and when you have family, you have everything."

Lily winced.

When Joe brought Lily home, he leaned across the front seat, casually kissed her goodnight, and let her out in the driveway. She was relieved that she did not have to fend off his advances, yet disappointed not to have had the opportunity to do so.

"Can I call you tomorrow?" he asked.

"Sure," said Lily. "Thanks for the movie and everything."

"A girl like you?" said Joe. "Deserves a lot more than that."

Lily wanted to ask him what he meant. *What is a girl like me? What do I deserve?* She stood at the back door as his Barracuda peeled out down the street.

The next morning, Lily was awakened by the roar of an engine. She looked out her bedroom window to find Joe laboriously forcing a lawn mower back and forth through the thick lawn in the early morning sunshine.

"What's going on?" Lily asked her mother, as she ran down the stairs, cinching the belt of her robe.

Lily's mother had the Sunday paper spread open over the entire surface of the kitchen table, a cup of coffee in one hand and a pair of scissors in the other. "Your young man knocked on the door at eight o'clock, introduced himself, and offered to cut the lawn."

"You're kidding!" Lily pushed the sheers aside and looked out the living room picture window. Joe saw her, smiled, and blew her a kiss.

"Does he shovel snow?" Lily's mother asked, turning the page. "If so, please don't let him go."

"No problem, Mom," said Lily. "Glad to help." *How very liberated of you*, she wanted to add.

"Hey, Lily - it's me!" said the voice at the other end of the phone.

"Iris! When did you get back?"

"Day before yesterday," Iris replied. "But I was so tired from the jet lag, and then I had to start my new job, and of course there's so much to be done around here all the time... I'm just exhausted!"

"Yeah, I bet," said Lily, wondering what jet lag was.

"What are you doing tonight?"

"Nothing - I was supposed to work but I guess they scheduled too many people so they called me and told me not to come in.

"Perfect!" said Iris. "Let's meet for coffee. I want to tell you all about my trip!"

"Yes - I can't wait to hear about it."

Lily's throat tightened at the prospect of sitting and listening to Iris' stories of Italy, but Lily had missed her, and they hadn't had a chance to really talk since before she'd left. Since that awful night when she had stopped by the house. There was so much Lily had wanted to say to her then. She'd wanted to tell her how desperately she had tried to endure her role at Chestnut Crest, and about the nights she'd lain in bed, praying, crying, searching for a way to hang on. She'd wanted to tell her how disturbing it was, listening to their father tearfully and brutally cursing and insulting their mother with his every breath - in front of Lily, in front of the boys, in front of anyone who would listen. If only Iris knew how Lily had fantasized about running away, how she'd dreamed of just stuffing a few things into a duffle bag, standing on the shoulder of the highway and sticking her thumb out for anyone who would take her anywhere. It seemed that there had to be a way out, but no matter where Lily turned, there was suffocating sadness and anger. Moving in with their mother was like opening a window, just a crack, and all Lily knew was that she had to have some air.

Lily wanted to tell Iris how much she'd missed her when she was at college, and how much she'd wanted to visit her in her dorm, but there never seemed to be enough time, or enough money, or an available car. Mostly she wanted to tell her that she was sorry for the things their mother had said and how much Lily had regretted not giving Iris a hug when she left that night. Maybe they could talk about that, too. Maybe they would have a chance to patch things up. Yes, that would be wonderful. They could share secrets and laughter and the knowing glances that they had spent a lifetime encoding and decoding, learning to speak in a silent language only they shared. It would be like old times. The only thing that would make it perfect would be if they could lie in bed in their old room with the windows open, the distant wail of the freight train rumbling through the Coldwater Road crossing. But Lily knew she was no longer welcome at Chestnut Crest, and there wasn't a room at Lily's that held sweet memories for them. Where did they belong now?

"Let's meet at the diner, OK?" said Iris.

"Sure," said Lily. "What time?"

"Well, I already talked to Frances, and she gets out of work at seven o'clock. I haven't seen Rita in ages, and I promised her I would get in touch as soon as I got back, so I'm picking her up at seven-thirty. How's quarter to eight?"

"Oh," said Lily.

"Lily? Are you there? Is seven-forty-five OK?"

"Yeah - uh, sure." So much for that.

"Great! Ciao!"

Lily tried to shake the sense of uneasiness that draped itself over her as she hung up the phone. Was it because Iris had been home for two days before she even bothered to call? Or maybe it was because she had clumped Lily together with Frances and Rita - as though they were all equal, as though Iris had missed them just as much and was equally as excited to see them. Or maybe it was the way she said, "Ciao!" Or that she said it at all. Maybe it was all of it.

Lily picked up the phone and punched in a series of numbers.

"Hey Cory - it's Lily - how's it going over there?... Oh, it is?... Yeah, I was just calling to see if you needed me to come in tonight, you know, in case it got busy or whatever... because I can come in if you need me... OK... sure, no problem... See you tomorrow then."

When Lily arrived at the diner, she found Iris, Rita, and Frances huddled together in a horseshoe booth. Iris was firmly wedged into the center spot between them, flipping through the photos she had taken on her trip. Lily used her best plaster smile to fend off threatening tears.

"Here's my cousin Fabrizio!" said Iris, pointing to a young man on a scooter. Iris laughed at the photo. "Oh, what fun we had!"

"What a hunk!" said Rita. "I want to go to Italy!"

"Lily!" cried Iris, stretching her arms over Rita's head.

"Hey!" called Lily. She stretched across the table top, three coffee cups, and a maple syrup caddy to try and accept Iris' hug, but was unable to quite reach.

"Oh - here -" said Iris, taking her purse off the bench and placing it under the table. "Scooch in so you can see!" Iris quickly returned her attention to the photos in her hand.

"Aw..." Iris let out a sigh. "Here's me, throwing coins into the Trevi Fountain." She turned to Rita and added, "That's what you do to make sure you return to Roma!"

Lily immediately noticed the changes in Iris. The adolescent slouch in her shoulders had straightened itself up into a stance of confidence. Her laugh was louder, more free. She was drinking her coffee black. Lily feigned interest as she craned her neck to see the photos over Frances' shoulder, and she smiled and nodded whenever Iris looked at her to gauge her response. With each story of adventure Iris told, Lily's heart sank, and her image of Iris grew softer around the edges. In Italy, Iris had eaten things that Lily had never even heard of. She'd swum in the Mediterranean Sea. Been to the Vatican. Eaten a real pizza. Seen Michelangelo's *David*. Met a man.

"What's his name?" Rita asked, staring at the photo. "And how old is he, anyway?"

"His name is Gregorio," said Iris, blushing. "Gregorio Leale. It's spelled L-E-A-L-E. At first I thought it was pronounced 'Leele' - thank God that Auntie Rosa told me it was pronounced 'Lay-ah-lay' before I made a complete fool of myself! It means 'loyal' - isn't that cool? He's thirty-one and he's even more handsome in person - and he's sophisticated and kind and gentle - so intelligent." With a grin, Iris scanned the faces around the table and added, "And very romantic." She offered the photo to Rita.

"What does he do?" asked Frances. "For a job, I mean?"

"He's a doctor," said Iris proudly. "An anesthesiologist."

"Oh, Gregorio," Rita said to the photograph as she kissed it.

"Geez, Rita, you want a napkin for that drool?" said Frances, snatching the photo from her. "Hey Iris, this guy has blond hair and blue eyes and is at least as tall as you are - are you sure he's Italian?"

"His father was Sicilian," Iris said.

"Since when are Sicilians blond?" Rita said.

"Since the eleventh century. The coloring comes from Norman ancestors that invaded the island. Not all of them are blond, of course. But some. This one." Iris took the photo from Frances. "You want to see it, Lily?" Iris offered the photo to her.

"That's OK," Lily replied. "I can see it from here." The smile temporarily vacated Iris' face - until she looked back at the man in the photo who was smoking a pipe and looking lovingly at Iris, who stood at his side laughing. There was something familiar to Lily about the way the man beamed at her sister, but it was strange to see how Iris beamed back; she was glowing. Lily bristled.

Iris carefully wiped the surface of the photo with a napkin before sliding it back into the yellow and white paper envelope with the others. Lily was relieved that they were finally tucked away. Maybe now they could talk about something else. Someone else.

"You know," said Iris, "Gregorio's grandfather was actually our grandmother's cousin by marriage."

"Doesn't that make him our cousin?" said Lily. "You can't just go around falling in love with your cousins."

"Everyone is related to everyone else in those little towns," explained Iris. "He's not a first cousin, or even a second one. Besides, it's OK to even have children with your cousin as long as they're not your first."

"Have children?!" cried Frances. "Did you guys do it?"

"No!" cried Iris. The flush in her cheeks hinted at the desire her giggle tried to conceal.

"Here's what I want to know," said Rita in a whisper, "Is he blond all over?"

Frances and Rita burst out laughing.

"Stop it you guys," said Iris. "It wasn't like that. It was just, well, it was nice." She closed her eyes and heaved a gentle sigh. "Very nice," she added softly.

"What about Peter?" said Lily. "You can't just go off and get a better boyfriend when you have a perfectly good one already."

Iris opened her mouth, but no words came out.

"Oh, it doesn't matter," said Lily, with a wave of her hand. "It's not like you're going to be seeing Gregorio again anyway."

"Actually, I am," said Iris. "When I arrived home, I found a letter from him waiting for me. He'd written right after we met! He's planning a trip to America for the holidays. He's coming on December twelfth and staying until New Year's!"

"Oh, my gawd!" shouted Rita.

"He must really like you to come all that way," said Frances. "Very cool."

"OK - let me see those pictures again," said Rita, extending her hand. "I didn't know this was so serious!"

Iris pulled the yellow and white envelope back out of her purse, as the three of them flipped through the photos again, this time passing them down the line to Lily one at a time, forcing her to come face-to-face with the images of Iris by the Trevi Fountain. Iris in front of the Leaning Tower of Pisa. Iris on a scooter looking happier than Lily had ever seen her. In that moment, Lily realized that while Iris was touring the Italian countryside and meeting new and exciting people, Lily had been spending her days flipping hamburgers and her nights holding ice packs on her mother's latest migraine, inevitably brought on by her father's latest litigation. How was that fair? Lily could have gone, too. She could have worked more hours and saved up the money if she'd known ahead of time. If Iris had bothered to ask. And why didn't she? How did Iris just so easily take off like that and not even invite Lily to come along? The answer was evident. Iris didn't ask Lily to come along because she didn't want her there, probably didn't want to carry along the excess baggage. Lily slipped the blurry photos back into the envelope. One thing was suddenly sure: if Iris' big deal Italian doctor boyfriend was going to be hanging around at Christmas, Lily was not going to be here to watch.

"Gee, Iris," said Lily, pouring herself a refill from the coffee carafe on the table. "It's too bad I'll probably be in college when Gregorio comes. I won't even get to meet him."

"Oh, after a semester of college," said Iris, "You'll be coming home for Christmas, believe me."

Rita nodded in agreement.

Lily couldn't imagine that. Especially not now. "We'll see," she said. "We'll see."

"Oh - I almost forgot!" said Iris. "I have presents for everyone!"

Iris reached under the table and retrieved a bag with handles and a word in Italian printed across the front. She stuck her hand in and pulled out a small gold foil box, and placed it in front of Rita.

"One for you..." said Iris.

"Wow!" said Rita. "What is it?"

"Open it up!" said Iris. She reached into the bag again, and pulled out an identical box and placed it in front of Frances. "And one for you!"

"Yum-MY!" said Rita, opening the box to reveal four artfully crafted pieces of chocolate.

"They are beautiful!" said Frances.

"It's from Perugia," said Iris. "Gregorio says it's the finest chocolate in the world!"

By the time Iris reached into the bag a third time, Lily's mouth was already watering.

"And for you, my *sorellina*," said Iris, beaming, "we have something special." Iris placed a small leather pouch and a package wrapped in white tissue on the table in front of Lily. Pointing to the leather pouch she said, "Open that one first."

Lily loosened the drawstring, reached her fingers down inside, and drew out a rosary made of blue crystal beads and sterling silver.

"A rosary," said Lily, puzzled. She did her best to sound impressed and excited, although she couldn't remember the last time she'd said the rosary - probably not since the last time she stayed over Auntie Rosa's for dance class. Had to be at least five years by now.

"That's not just any rosary," said Iris, leaning in toward Lily. "That rosary has been personally blessed by His Holiness the Pope."

"THE Pope?" asked Frances. "The guy in the Vatican who wears the cool hat?"

"That'd be him," said Iris.

Even though she hadn't seen the Pope herself, Lily knew she should probably be impressed by the fact that the Pope had at least looked at her rosary. It reminded Lily of the way Ricci refused to eat dinner when he was small until their mother looked at each and every mound of food on his plate. Lily smiled.

"Thank you, Iris." Lily dangled the rosary over the open pouch and lowered it down, the beads *click-click-clicking* against each other as they coiled themselves back inside.

"Now open the other one!" said Iris.

Lily carefully tore at the seam of the tissue, which was held in place by a single square of transparent tape. She unfolded the paper to reveal a pair of purple gloves.

"Gloves!" said Lily.

"They're kid gloves," said Iris. "Feel how soft they are."

Lily picked up one of the gloves and held it against her cheek. "Oh, it *is* soft!"

"Lemme see," said Frances. She grabbed the other glove and started to slip her hand inside.

Rita snatched it and gave it back to Lily. "Don't you dare, Frances! With those mitts of yours, you will stretch them out and ruin them."

Lily slipped both gloves on and held them to her face. "I would be afraid to wear these in the snow, though," said Lily. "They are so delicate."

Rita and Frances laughed.

"Well, you don't wear them for shoveling snow, silly," said Iris. "They're dress gloves. You'd wear them when you get all dressed up for a nice dinner or when you go to a garden party or something like that."

"Well, I know they're not show-shoveling gloves," said Lily, with a burning in her throat. "I just never heard of gloves that you wear just for parties." Lily had never been to a garden party. In fact, she was pretty sure that Iris had ever been to one either, so it was curious that she suddenly knew so much about the proper attire. And Burger King was the only place she ever went to dinner besides the diner. However, even if she ever did have any occasion to wear the gloves, she would pull them on and would remember the way Rita and Frances laughed at her, and how Iris thought she intended to wear them to shovel the driveway, and she would probably just put them back in the drawer.

"They're your favorite color," said Iris, as if she were trying to supply Lily with additional reasons why she should appreciate her gift.

"They're beautiful, Iris. Thank you." Lily pulled the gloves off one at a time and wrapped them back up in the tissue. She imagined herself sitting at home, wearing her new kid gloves, rattling off a series of "Hail Marys" as she ticked her way through the crystal beads of her sacred new rosary, trying to convince herself that it was better to be pious and proper than it was to indulge in the sin and mess that can only be achieved with a box of fine chocolates.

Two weeks after their first date, Joe brought Lily home for Sunday dinner. As they pulled into the driveway, he warned her, "They're kinda loud. And they don't put on false airs and shit. With my family, what you see is what you get."

Lily assured him that his family could not be crazier than hers. She would be right at home.

Inside, she found herself steeped amid the familiar and comforting chaos of a clan gathered for pasta, surrounded by new faces with whom she bore no burden of history or of expectation except perhaps for a smile and a passing of the Parmesan. Joe's father - who everyone called "Big Tony," was a massive figure, an ex-cop with a commanding voice and who - according to the stories - could get a confession out of a punk just by staring at him. His intimidating presence was offset by his disarming laugh, which he vocalized distinctly as "Hee-hee-hee." Lily was amused that someone would have such a literal giggle, much as she would have been if a rooster had opened his mouth and actually uttered "Cock-a-doodle-doo."

Once everyone had finished their pasta and the salad began making its way around the table, Joe's brother Anthony said, "OK, everyone - lissen up. I have an announcement to make."

"Hurry up and make it then," said Big Tony. "Tip off is in ten minutes."

"I've decided to ask Nancy to marry me."

Joe and his brothers cheered, and slapped Anthony "high fives" across the table.

"Jesus Christ, Ant'ny!" cried Joe's mother, Lucy. "She's

divorced, for Chrissake. You can't marry a divorced woman."

"Says who?" said Anthony, shoving a chunk of heavily buttered Italian bread into his mouth.

"Says the Pope, that's who." Lucy shook a Winston out of the pack and lit it. "Is that good enough for you, Mr. Smarty Pants?"

"Ma - " Anthony laughed. "She had the marriage annulled. Don't worry - I'm not gonna go to hell."

"I still don't see why you can't marry someone who's fresh."

Anthony was looking down at his lap, absentmindedly wiping butter from his fingers with a napkin. Without looking up, he said, "You mean like you were?"

The entire family froze in place. Forks suspended in midair, jaws dropped open. Anthony slowly raised his head, wearing a look of alarm on his face, as if suddenly aware that he'd made the comment aloud.

Lucy took a deep drag on her cigarette, and blew the smoke up toward the ceiling, without breaking the gaze she had fixed upon her son. She crushed the butt out in the ashtray, stood up in her chair, leaned over the table, and slapped him squarely across the face. Lily jumped in her seat. Alfonso, Blaise, and Stefano burst out into laughter.

"Oh, nice -" shouted Joe. "Hey - Mohammad Ali," he said to his mother. "We got company."

"It was a love tap," said Lucy, sitting back down. She pointed a finger at Anthony. "You watch your mouth - and just remember - I've made my mistakes, but I accepted responsibility for them, too. You kids should be thanking your lucky stars that me and your father have stayed together all these years instead of giving up and walking out like people do these days."

Joe shot a glance at his mother. She looked at Lily, and then returned to her salad.

"We stick together, is all I'm saying," said Lucy, spearing a tuft of lettuce with her fork. "That's what families do - they stick together."

"OK," said Big Tony, "Enough of this touchy-feely crap." He raised his glass of Chianti. "Let's make a toast. To Anthony and

Nancy: May they have many happy years together. And let's welcome little Lily to our table, because if she hasn't run away yet, maybe we will see her again."

"*Salud!*" they all shouted, raising their glasses.

"Sorry about that business with my mother and Anthony," said Joe, as he opened the car door for Lily.

"That's OK," said Lily, recalling the countless times she had made a similar apology to any one of her friends who may have had the misfortune to be hanging around during one of the fights her parents used to have. "But I feel bad for Nancy - it would be hard to have a mother-in-law who doesn't like you."

"Don't let my mother fool you. She likes Nancy just fine. She just has to stick her nose in. That's how we know she cares. I can tell my parents like you, too - and when you're in with them, you're in. They'll look after you like one of their own."

Lily continued to join Joe and his family for Sunday dinners, feeling less like a guest with each passing week. She discovered that being a Diotallevi was something between being in an exclusive club and a cult. Being a Diotallevi meant that life's questions were answered for you simply; clad in the armor of validation by ever-present family, you were protected from your own senselessness, and from the scrutiny of the outside world. The rules were simple: women cooked and cleaned and had babies, with men helping out in times of childbirth or other illness; men worked as much as possible, even if it meant they had to put in twelve-hour days, which could be a combination of earning wages at a job and going to the racetrack to try and turn a paycheck into enough to keep the lights on. On Sundays and holidays, the family gathered together to eat, after which the men watched sports on television while the women watched children and chatted about the comings and going of their households. The suggestion that such a life left any need unfulfilled was met with resistance and suspicion. What more could anyone want than good food, a roof over their head, and family they could count on? What more could Lily want?

The Diotallevis were everything the Capotostis were not: Big

Tony used real swear words instead of making up replacements so as to avoid the need for confession; the brothers used poor grammar and shared a crass sense of humor; Betty Capotosti and Lucy Diotallevi were as different as two women could be, with Lucy often offering unsolicited advice to Lily on cooking, cleaning, hair coloring, and the art of being a good wife. Lily's mother would be incensed if she knew. Lily sometimes found herself admiring Lucy for the way she'd managed to keep her family together, and felt guilty at the swelling affection she felt for her.

"Your pasta is always so good, Mrs. Diotallevi," said Lily as they cleared the table one Sunday. "What brand of sauce do you use?"

"What brand?" Lucy let out a sound that was something between a laugh and a cough, bringing up a chunk of phlegm. She turned and spit it into the garbage can. "I don't use store bought sauce. I make it from scratch. That's genuine Diotallevi sauce - you can't get that sauce in any restaurant or grocery store, I'll tell you that. We are full-blooded Italians, after all. That Ragu shit is for *medigans*. Maybe someday, if things work out with you and my Joey, I'll be passing the recipe along to you." Lily didn't know what a "medigan" was, but she didn't ask, for fear of revealing her ignorance and *ipso facto* branding herself as something other than a "real" Italian.

Grandma Capotosti had been born and raised in Italy, and she always used sauce from a jar, but Lily didn't dare tell. It was bad enough that her mother was divorced *and* Irish - facts that Joe and his family never failed to recall whenever Lily revealed her ignorance of the secret Italian code of behavior, such as the proper order in which to dispense kisses when you entered a gathering, or the point during a meal at which one should eat dinner salad. "That's the way Italians do it," they would say, and they seemed quite sure of it. Lily was ashamed that she had been raised in an Italian-American household yet knew so little about the ways in which things should be done.

Lily and Joe saw each other at every opportunity. He made it part of his routine to cut the lawn at Lily's house, as well as change the oil in the car, replace blown fuses, and fix leaky faucets.

Their late night love play moved from the back seat of the Barracuda to the couch in Lily's living room, and from simple necking to heavy petting. While she adored the fact that Joe craved her, she was still intent on saving herself for her future husband. It was way too early to tell who that might be. However, setting boundaries wasn't something at which Lily felt competent. Growing up, there simply hadn't been enough room to afford them, and with James, she had been too painfully aware that they weren't necessary. If anything, she had to goad him into the urges that other boys were dying to express. James would initiate intimacy and then withhold his passion, always acting as though he might get up and leave at any moment. It had confused Lily and put her in a constant state of tension when they were together, wondering if the wrong move or the wrong word might snap James out of his desire, leaving her alone with her arousal and her guilt. Lily mused that being with James had been like sitting down to dinner with someone who was finicky and allergic, but being with Joe was like going to a buffet with a starving man who had recently been rescued from a deserted island.

Joe's sheer need for physical contact evoked Lily's desire to care for him. And she wanted him, too. His lean, firm dancer's body was flexible and beautiful to look at, reawakening the desire in Lily that she had become so adept at subjugating. He moved with ease, always decidedly going in the direction of his desire. There were no guessing games. Making out with Joe was simple; a kiss was just a kiss, a caress was a caress, and they exchanged them with each other because they were young and alive and falling in love.

"I think we need to talk," Lily told him one night, as they lay tangled on the couch together.

"I don't like the sound of that." Fear registered in Joe's eyes.

"Oh - no, no," said Lily, giving him a gentle kiss. "It's nothing bad, really. It's just that, well, I - I - don't think we should go all the way. I kind of decided that I wanted to be a virgin when I get married, and I thought I should just let you know that."

Joe kissed her. "I knew you were a nice girl," he said. "There aren't many like you around these days - you're beautiful, sexy, and you have good morals. But - I am a guy, after all, so you're prob'ly gonna hafta remind me a bunch of times. You know, keep me in line. I'm not as strong as you."

"I can do that," said Lily. She loved hearing that her virtue was rare, and that Joe appreciated that in her. She would be the voice of reason and conscience for them both.

"I got another letter from SUNY Geneseo today," she said, buttoning her blouse. "I'm thinking of going there in the fall."

"What? You mean college?"

"Yeah. Geneseo's not my first choice, but I might be able to get a student loan, and they do have a pretty good musical theatre department."

"I thought you were done with all of that. What about us?"

"This doesn't affect us that much, Joe. Geneseo is only forty-five miles from here."

"Where are you gonna live?"

"I don't know yet. On campus. In a dorm."

"So you won't be living in town?" Joe sat up, and grabbed a pack of Winston's from the pocket of his leather jacket.

"Well, no, but I can come home some weekends. Or you can come and visit me."

Joe turned and looked at Lily and stated, "I am *not* going to go and 'visit' my girlfriend," he said. "And what am I supposed to do the whole time you're at school?" He stood up, walked out the back door, and took a seat on one of the rusted white wrought iron chairs that flanked the entrance. Lily followed.

"I don't understand what you're getting so upset about," she said, taking the cigarette he offered.

"Look," said Joe. "None of the women in my family have ever gone to college, and they are all perfectly happy with their lives. Why would you want to spend all that time and money studying acting? It's not like you can get a job with it or anything."

"I don't know," Lily a took a drag on the cigarette. "I just always wanted to, that's all."

"Well, you can go ahead - we're not married or anything so I can't stop you, but-"

"But?"

"Lily, I care about you - you know that. And you can do whatever you want, but four years is a long time. I can't guarantee that I'll still be here when you're ready. I thought we were starting a life here. Maybe you're not the girl I thought you were, after all."

"Joe, you're only twenty - and I'm only eighteen. What's the rush?"

"Hey - my mother was fifteen when she had Alfonso, sixteen when she had Anthony, and seventeen when she had me - and my parents have been together for thirty years. Hell, my mother didn't even finish high school. It didn't hurt her one bit."

"Things are different now, Joe. It's not like it was back then."

"And people were happier." Joe took another cigarette out of the pack and lit up. "Look at your family, Lil - two of your brothers are divorced, your sister Jasmine is divorced, your parents are like a train wreck. Why do you think that is? It's because people don't care about the basics anymore. They don't care about family, and traditions. Do you want to end up like them?"

"I absolutely do not," said Lily.

"Well, it's up to you," Joe said, blowing smoke into the cool night air. "Go ahead and go to college if you want. But I need to get on with my life, too." Joe flicked his cigarette butt onto the driveway and it landed in a puddle with a hiss.

"I'll call you tomorrow," he said, kissing Lily on the forehead.

Joe pulled the Barracuda out into the street and disappeared into the night. Lily took another drag on her cigarette, noticing the dented garbage can toppled over, no longer possessing the sound frame necessary to keep it upright. She exhaled, looking to the stars, scrutinizing the mysterious forms they sketched in the vast black sky, as if they could somehow help her weigh the hope for a home against the fear of the unknown, the company of friends over the solitude of strangers, the sting of rejection and abandonment against the comfort of the familiar.

35. IRIS

Christmas seemed so far away when summer had barely begun, but never a letter was exchanged between Iris and Gregorio without a mention of the holiday, which drew closer with the arrival of each colorfully stamped airmail envelope. No longer was Iris forced to scrounge the lines of the letters she received for signs of affection, as she had been forced to do with Peter Ponzio. Quite to the contrary, each carefully composed sentence on each sheet of onionskin paper she fondled expressed Gregorio's appreciation of the impressions Iris had made upon him, and confirmed his desire to delve more deeply into the numerous other hidden qualities he was certain she possessed. On her part, Iris wrote little about how she spent her time; what could she possibly say about wheeling around a messenger cart at Kodak eight hours a day, or about cooking and cleaning house, or about the latest level of litigation between her parents, that could possibly interest a sophisticated man like Gregorio? Her letters opened with the usual polite inquiries into his well-being and that of his mother and sister, followed by the types of questions that would confirm her interest in Gregorio's professional life, without revealing her ignorance as to what it actually entailed. In closing, she never failed to reiterate her gratitude for the wonderful time he had shown her and Auntie Rosa in Italy, hinting that there was nothing she would enjoy more than the opportunity to travel there again in the future. One Sunday afternoon, Gregorio even called her on the telephone, saying he simply could not go to sleep unless he heard her voice, the musical sound of which was fading all too quickly from his memory, despite his constant efforts to keep it alive. The thought that Gregorio would go to the trouble and expense of placing an overseas phone call just to hear her voice flattered Iris immensely.

Two weeks later, on returning home from the afternoon matinee of *Grease* with Rita Esposito, the chorus of "You're The One That I Want" still playing in her head, she was disappointed to hear that Gregorio had phoned in her absence. The following Sunday, she elected to stay home just in case he tried calling again, and he did not disappoint her. From then on, she opted to stay home to read on Sunday afternoons, instead of wasting her money on the movies and a hamburger. After all, Gregorio would still have to pay for the call if she were out with friends, and it might send him the wrong message if she weren't around, even though she knew he might call. Her consideration was rewarded, and Gregorio soon developed the habit of calling every Sunday afternoon. Iris watched the clock anxiously whenever they spoke, though their conversations, stilted by frequent misunderstandings and poor connections, never lasted more than a few minutes. When at the end of his sixth call, just before hanging up, Gregorio told her that he loved her, Iris remained seated in silence, the dead receiver in her lap, for several minutes. At the end of his seventh call, Iris told him that she loved him, too.

Living her life between letters and phone calls and fantasies, the weeks passed quickly for Iris; by midsummer, it had become apparent that it would probably make more sense for her to bide her time and see how things developed, rather than rush back to Buffalo. Her reasoning was validated by the flicker of relief she detected in her father's eyes when she expressed her thoughts to him; though he would never come right out and ask her to stay, he reminded her that the were a number of good colleges within driving distance. By the time the falling leaves had spread their blanket of crimson and gold over the grass, she had convinced herself that university could wait. She would stay on at home through the autumn, see what happened at Christmas, and still have plenty of time to register for the spring semester. The money she was earning now would come in handy later, whether it be to pursue her studies here, or in Buffalo, or elsewhere. Who could say what the future might hold in store?

Thanksgiving came and went, marking the official beginning of the Christmas season. Iris began sleeping poorly, waking in the middle of the night to stare at the dark ceiling of her empty room, wondering what would happen when she and Gregorio were finally reunited. Every morning and every evening, she studied the few snapshots he had allowed her to take of him, trying to recall the kind look in his eyes and the amused turn of his smile, trying to conjure up that feeling that had fluttered inside her when they were together. Regardless of how her memories may have faded, regardless of whatever difficulties she may have encountered trying to decipher the handwriting in Gregorio's letters or his heavily accented words over the phone, one thing was very clear to Iris: Gregorio Leale was a serious man, with serious intentions.

She hoped and prayed to God that everything would go smoothly during his visit, then rolled up her sleeves and did her part to make that happen. She cleaned the house from top to bottom, although for the sake of propriety, arrangements had been made for Gregorio to sleep at Auntie Rosa's, whose condominium was also more orderly and quiet, and more suited to a man of his professional standing and refined upbringing. Iris busied herself baking tray upon tray of Christmas cookies, and decking the halls with the most beautiful decorations that had ever graced the Capotosti residence. Iris vowed that the holiday would be celebrated in great style, with joy and serenity. No one would rob her of what promised to be a very special Christmas. No one.

The anticipation that had been building up over the months of their long-distance courtship reached its peak when Gregorio finally stepped off the plane, walked purposefully toward her, and wrapped his arms around her. The scent of tobacco that tickled her nostrils when he kissed her on both cheeks was remarkably familiar, but the scratchy woolen overcoat he pressed her head against was not; it had no place in her memories of that marvelous Italian May, and smelled slightly of mothballs. It was odd to see the object of her romantic Riviera fantasies bundled up in this winter version, embodied in this foreign man with the blond goatee, standing on her icy North American turf.

A series of snowstorms thwarted any plans Iris might have made for sightseeing, had there been any sights to see in western New York in the dead of winter, with ten-foot snow drifts and a wind chill factor of minus twenty degrees – and that was Fahrenheit, she pointed out to Gregorio, who thought being snowed in rather adventurous. The main roads were plowed regularly, making it possible to drive back and forth to Auntie Rosa's, and each evening Iris cooked hearty meals for the extended family. Gregorio never failed to compliment her on her culinary skills, and seemed to enjoy conversing amicably with her father and anyone else who hung around afterwards, eating Christmas cookies (one per evening was all Gregorio would allow himself) and drinking coffee (Gregorio preferred the chamomile tea he was in the habit of drinking, of which he had brought a supply). Iris had tried to arrange an evening out with Lily, but she declined, saying she was fighting off the flu, and did not want to spread her germs; maybe after Christmas, when her symptoms and the snow subsided.

Shortly before it was time to leave for Midnight Mass on Christmas Eve, Gregorio invited Iris's father to step outside with him, the former with his loaded pipe, the latter armed with cigarettes. Iris was quite certain the purpose of Gregorio's invitation was not the contemplation of the freshly fallen snow, though neither man revealed the subject of their conversation to her, and she did not ask. On Christmas morning, when Gregorio presented Iris with a little velvet box and a very big question, she knew what her answer must be. Her voice trapped by a lump in her throat, she nodded her head vigorously in assent as he slipped the ring on her finger. The prospect of becoming the wife of Dr. Gregorio Leale and moving to Italy left her speechless.

"Hey, Lily!" Iris honked the horn and waved as she turned down the side street to the house where her mother and sister lived. Lily must not have seen her, otherwise she would have stopped, or at least waved. Instead, her car pulled out into the traffic on to the main road, muffler belching, radio blaring, cigarette smoke billowing out the open window.

As she pulled into her mother's driveway, Iris was pleased to notice how neat the lawn always looked since Joe had started hanging around. It occurred to her that he had already put in an entire season of maintenance; the leaves had been raked in the fall when Iris came to say hello at Thanksgiving, and the driveway had been shoveled when she brought Gregorio over to meet her mother and Lily at Christmas. She thought it a bit of a pity Joe had decided to tame the side yard, though. The last time she had stopped over, the patch had been filled with wildflowers, and now it was just another rectangle of cropped grass.

Iris wondered where Lily was off to in such a rush. She hadn't seen much of her lately, what with working up until the day Gregorio and Isabella had arrived, and all the last-minute preparations to attend to, but since her mother had insisted Iris drop everything and come right over, she was hoping she would at least be able to kill two birds with one stone and catch Lily, too. There had been an urgency bordering on frantic in her mother's voice when she called to say she wanted to see her in private. Maybe she had been the one to ask Lily to leave; she probably wanted to talk to Iris one-on-one before the wedding, give her a reassuring squeeze of the hand, tell her she was sorry she had found herself saddled with so many responsibilities at such a young age. Maybe she wanted to assure Iris that the sacrifices they had all been called upon to make had been worth it, that the sociopolitical causes she had worked so arduously to sustain had made the world a better place for all women.

Iris would tell her mother that she had never judged her, that she understood her choices a little more now that she herself was a grown woman, that she was proud to have a mother who stood up for her beliefs. Then they would embrace, and Iris would try not to cry, though just about everything made her cry these days. Everyone said it was normal. Pre-nuptial jitters. In a way, she was glad her mother had insisted she come; soon she would be far away, but Iris would have the wisdom of her mother's words to bear in mind, and the warmth of her embrace to carry in heart.

"Hi, Mom." Iris said with a smile as her mother opened the door.

"Hello, Iris. You look pretty today. Come right in." Her mother turned and led the way to the kitchen. "Coffee?"

"Thanks," Iris accepted the mug her mother held out to her, hoping the coffee wouldn't aggravate the roiling in her stomach that had been making it a challenge for her to keep food down since the arrival of the Leales.

"Cream? Sugar?" her mother asked.

"No, thanks. Black is fine," Iris said. She wondered how many other things her mother did not know about her, how many things she had known but forgotten, like whether she had liked Babar books as a child, or preferred Dr. Seuss.

"I'm in the middle of some research here, trying to make some sense out of New York State divorce laws, as if that is even possible. Here we are, in twentieth century America, and a woman getting divorced in this state doesn't have a snowball's chance in hell of fair treatment." They both looked at the table strewn with open books and legal notepads, as if expecting some answer, some explanation, some suggestion. "Why don't we go sit in the living room?" her mother said, leading the way to the sofa, from which she rounded up a stack of papers she then dumped on the already cluttered coffee table.

"How are the boys?" her mother began, as they both sat. "It's hard for me to pin them down for a visit these days."

"They're fine, and all three of them are so smart and handsome! I'm sure they'll be breaking hearts right and left.

Maybe they already are. I hardly see them myself, except at suppertime."

"They've been lucky to have a big sister like you." Her mother took a sip of coffee, cleared her throat. "You've grown up into a lovely young woman, Iris. And you have some truly remarkable qualities."

Iris felt her cheeks grow hot. She wondered whether it was normal to blush at a compliment from your own mother. Auntie Rosa was so openly biased and paid her so many that she didn't even take them seriously anymore. "Thank you."

"Your generous spirit and smiling face draw people to you."

"Really?" Iris said. The wounds left by her mother's abandonment had long since crusted over; her unexpected words of praise were a salve that soothed the scabs and smoothed the scars.

"However, those very same qualities can bring about your demise. There are forces at play here that you are not aware of."

"There are?" Iris hugged her mug tight, took a gulp of the liquid. Bitter, lukewarm. Her father was right about one thing anyway: her mother did not know how to make a decent cup of coffee.

"Rosa. Your aunt," she said, little puffs of air escaping her lips as she set down her mug. She folded her arms across the breasts that still looked weary after serving twelve consecutive terms of lactation. "She's lured you into her trap!" Her mother's thin voice rose with the vehemence of the whistle-blower into which she had morphed, but its timber remained that of the harried mother struggling to regain dominion over a situation that was spinning out of control.

"What trap, Mom?" Iris asked, putting down her mug. She was irritated at the cookie crumbs sprinkled across the dusty table and stained carpet; at Lily and her mother for their sloppy housekeeping; at the fact that such details should claim her attention at a time like this.

"The trap she set for you when she hauled you over to the Old Country last year!"

544

"What are you talking about?" Iris was starting to feel confused and frustrated, as if she had walked into a candy shop with a craving for bonbons, only to find the shelves lined with jars full of nuts and bolts.

"It's too late for Rosa to go find herself an Italian husband or marry one of those demigod doctors she worships. She spent her life taking care of your crippled grandmother as penance for letting Teresa drown, but she was never forgiven. She was denied her chance, so now she's coerced you into living her life for her. She has set you up with just the right man – Italian, and a doctor to boot. What more could she want? It's despicable, the way she's using you!"

"How can you say those things?" She wasn't used to challenging her mother; it had always been easier to simply ignore her. But she had never heard anyone speak of Auntie Rosa in a negative way. Auntie Rosa was the most generous, loving woman Iris knew; if anything, *she* was the one who had been used her whole life. "I'm the one who wanted to go to Italy last year," she said, her voice tight. "I'm the one who convinced Auntie Rosa."

"Why you went doesn't matter now. What matters is why you would go over there again. And why you would want to live in such a backward country. You think women here have it bad? Wait till you see what you'll have to deal with over there! Oppression! Discrimination! Exploitation!"

"You don't know what you're talking about, Mom! It's way more modern than you think over there! Look at Isabella! She's a judge! Women don't sit around rolling meatballs and reciting the rosary all day like people here think!"

"And this Gregorio! He's far too old for you! He gets the best of both worlds by snatching you up so young and fresh yet already so well-trained to clean the house and cook meals and look after children."

"I have you to thank for that experience, Mom! You left the job vacant, in case you don't remember!" Iris spit out the words before she could stop herself.

"That's irrelevant. You're a bright girl. Your intelligence could take you anywhere. You need to get back to college, before you find yourself stuck in a house full of bawling bambinos."

"Look who's talking!" Iris felt dizzy, short of breath. She placed a clammy hand on her forehead to stop the banging inside. For once, her mother had finally decided to talk to her, and all Iris wanted was for her to shut up.

"I have a right to talk. I've earned that right. Because I know. If I could go back, I would do things differently."

"Thank you very much, Mom!" Iris jumped to her feet, determined to have her say before her anger turned to tears. "You probably wish we were never born. Well, now you'll have one less daughter to worry about!" She ran to the door, turned, and added, "As if you ever did!"

She made it outside just as the bitterness churning in her belly spewed onto the freshly mowed lawn.

All in all, thirteen months of air mail correspondence and overseas telephone conversations, plus three transatlantic crossings (only one of which was made by her) were all it had taken to ease Iris's slender feet into the pair of bargain basement sandals that separated her white-stockinged soles from the downtrodden carpet of the living room at Chestnut Crest. She wondered why the rough nylon stitching cutting into the skin of her toes now hadn't bothered her when she tried the shoes on at the store. Probably because they were miraculously both her size *and* on the $7.99 clearance rack. There was nothing she could do about it now but bear the discomfort, and be thankful for the sensible square heels that would guide her feet through the steps she was about to take.

Iris was tired of standing, but dared not sit for fear of wrinkling the skirts of the frothy white gown cascading around her legs; she stooped to lift the ruffled hem and remove the scraps of toilet tissue stuck to her ankles, hoping that the razor nicks had stopped bleeding. The gown had been a bargain, too, on sale at Best Brides downtown store for ninety-nine dollars, basic veil and alterations included. Rita Esposito had helped her pick it out. Though Lily had seemed a bit cold that evening she and Rita and Frances had met at the diner upon Iris's return from Italy, the years of separation from Rita had melted like April snow, and they had resumed their childhood friendship with amazing ease. Rita would be waiting now, in the vestibule of Sacred Family, together with Lily and Frances. All three would be decked out in mismatched gowns which, like the girls who wore them, had survived the test of high school proms. Having the bridesmaids wear perfectly good gowns that were already hanging in their closets had seemed the sensible thing to do when there were corners to be cut. With its shortened hem and form-fitting bodice, Iris's Senior Ball gown actually looked quite lovely on Lily, and flattered her shapely bust nicely, something it had been unable to do for Iris.

"Less is more," she had heard or read somewhere. Though she wasn't sure whether that was true when it came to breasts, the philosophy had fit her strategy perfectly as she ticked off the items subject to budget cuts. Recalling how Gregorio had shied from her camera clicking during their first encounter, she decided to do without an official photographer, which had saved her at least a hundred bucks. Deciding what to do about the music had been tougher. Months earlier, on New Year's Eve, when she had suggested that they celebrate their engagement and at the same time surprise Lily by joining her and Joe at the 2001 Club, the horrified look on Greogio's face left no doubt that he abhorred disco music. And when, with only two days left in the old year and no plans to ring in the new, she had suggested they might go to dinner at a hotel in the city, where a local band would be playing oldies, he had again indicated a certain reluctance. When she had finally asked him what kind of music he liked to dance to, Gregorio had informed his young fiancée that participating in any form of human aggregation on any dance floor made him feel ridiculous. Keeping in mind that this was Gregorio's wedding just as much as it was hers, Iris felt she should respect his wishes. What mattered was the ceremony, certainly not the dancing, and doing without a band or disc jockey for the reception translated into further savings. But since music was too important to Iris for her to give it up entirely, she took the liberty of accepting Uncle Alfred's offer to provide some entertainment during the buffet, in addition to accompanying Lily, who had agreed to sing in church. The Hawaiian melodies would be a novelty to Gregorio and Isabella, and Uncle Alfred also wanted to play some Italian tunes in their honor. She wanted this to be a classy wedding, one that would impress her family-to-be with its simplicity.

As Iris thought back on all the arrangements made in a few short months, she felt proud of the fact that she had been able to pay for everything herself. Not that people were lining up to help; in fact, the only offer had come from Gregorio, but she would have died rather than accept. She had no doubt he would take care of her once they were man and wife, but everyone knew that the wedding was the responsibility of the bride's family. Once they had become officially engaged, she simply changed her other plans accordingly. Instead of going back to Buffalo, she enrolled in a few night courses at the community college, and stayed on at Kodak, where her commendable punctuality and performance earned her a position as a permanent employee. So what if the job was boring; the money was good, and enabled her to pay off her college loan, with enough left over to buy some new clothes, order a spare pair of contact lenses, get checked out by Violet's gynecologist (whose recommendations regarding birth control were politely disregarded), and have all four wisdom teeth extracted by the dentist for whom Rita worked, so that she could present herself in marriage debt-free and with no foreseeable extraordinary maintenance expenses.

Everything that needed doing had been done. Now she just wanted to get the waiting over with and celebrate her special day. One of the things she had been looking forward to most was seeing all of her brothers and sisters gathered in the same place one last time before she moved away. And one of the things that worried her most was seeing her forever feuding parents together in the same place; she prayed to God they wouldn't embarrass her in front of Gregorio and Isabella. She ran a hand over her cheek as she recalled her mother's words to her the previous day, wishing she could rub away their sting.

As she stood in the empty living room of the empty house, her agitation swelled and receded in waves. She had been so busy planning the wedding that she hadn't given much thought to how her new life in Italy would really be, on a daily basis. But it was both too late and too early to worry about that now; she was already on her way to finding out, and she would cross that bridge when she came to it. First, she had the wedding, and then the honeymoon to look forward to.

She couldn't wait to see the house Gregorio had rented for them; from the pictures, it looked small, but incredibly romantic, with a view of the sea, and a spare room for guests. Auntie Rosa would surely come to visit, at least once a year. Maybe her father could come, too. Lily might even make it over sometime; Iris would convince her to make the trip soon, before a little one came along to claim the guest room, together with all of her time and attention. Thoughts of Lily brought tears to her eyes, but she blinked them back; it would be a disaster if she started crying before she even set foot in church. Dabbing at the corners of her eyes with a knuckle, she reflected that maybe it had worked out for the best that Lily had moved in with their mother. If they had continued sharing their room and their lives, it might have been impossible for Iris to leave her sister now. But Lily had chosen to leave, and now it was Iris's turn.

Inspired to say a prayer for all those she loved and was leaving behind, Iris raised her eyes to the ceiling, but was distracted by five dark specks she spotted through the milky glass of the overhead light. "How could you be so stupid, getting yourselves trapped like that?" she said to the dead flies. "If you flew in, you should have been able to fly back out." It was so quiet, she could have sworn she heard the dead flies buzz back a reply. So quiet, she started when the floorboards stretched and groaned their relief at this moment of rare respite from stomping feet. So quiet, she flinched with each tick of the kitchen clock as its hands advanced implacably toward the hour of seven, heedless of the consequences of their actions. She stood in the fading light, as the vestiges of an anemic sun were put to rest under a blanket of somber grey, squelching any hope that the drizzle would let up.

Iris closed her eyes, preferring to look at the insides of her eyelids rather than at the walls and floors that held so many memories. Dropping her chin to her lace-covered chest, she lowered her bridal veil over her face. "Dear God," she prayed. "Please give Dad the strength to manage without me. I already asked you to bring Mom back many times, but you obviously didn't think that was a good idea. So all I ask of you now is to release them from their fighting, for everyone's sake. Please keep him and the boys under your wing. And please, please send someone to protect Lily, and make her happy. Joe seems like a good guy, and he makes her laugh. If he's the right one, please give her a sign. And never let her forget me like I know I will never forget her. And please look after Auntie Rosa and remind her every day of how much I love her, even though I'll be far away. Maybe she and Lily can get together sometimes, too. They need each other. Maybe you could help them see that. Amen."

Earlier in the day, when the clouds had started breezing into town from across Lake Ontario, Auntie Rosa had tried to put on a cheerful front, though the look in her eyes belied her heartbreak over losing Iris to the love story she herself had fostered. She drilled Iris on her Italian vocabulary as she coaxed her to eat a ham sandwich, and taught her a saying meant to console brides cursed by bad weather: *sposa bagnata, sposa fortunata.* A wet bride is a lucky bride. When Iris had shared the new phrase with the bridesmaids who had come over to dress in her room, they had giggled over another possible interpretation. She had laughed, too, though the whole sex thing made her nervous. She had never felt comfortable discussing intimate details with anyone, not even Lily, who just looked at her sister and shared her silent smile when Frances and Rita teased her about the fact that she and Gregorio hadn't done it yet.

How could those girls understand that waiting was precisely what made their love story so romantic? Those girls had never

550

been kissed in a boat on Lago Maggiore. They had never received love letters from abroad, or been courted by a real man. They had never been proposed to by a doctor already in his thirties who offered more love and security than a girl could dream of. And they had never believed in fairy tales, like she had. There was no way they could understand.

Standing there in her gown, Iris felt grateful that Gregorio had been such a perfect gentleman, and that he had shown such respect for her. Within hours, their marriage would be consummated the way it should be, in a proper room, on their wedding night. It hadn't been too much of a sacrifice for them to restrain themselves, and there had been little opportunity to do more than steal a few kisses on the rare occasions they had been alone together; all told, they had only been on the same continent for a couple dozen days since they had met. If her attraction to Gregorio was any indication, she had no doubt that theirs would be an extremely satisfying union, and attracted to him she was. Otherwise, why would she have spent all those nights lying in bed rereading his letters and gazing at his picture and kissing it good night before switching off the light? Why would she have fantasized incessantly all this time about their upcoming honeymoon in Sardinia, dreaming of the clear blue water they would swim in, of how he would chase her playfully on one of those deserted beaches, of how she would pretend to trip and fall on the hot white sand, of how he would stand over her, his tanned body blocking the blinding sun, of how her giggling would subside when he lowered himself onto the sand next to her, of how he would slowly undo the top of her bathing suit, of how her chest would rise when she sucked in her breath, of how he would lick the saltwater from her nipples and of how his finger would trace a line from her dripping breasts down to the tiny puddle in her belly button and then slip inside her bikini bottoms? If she weren't attracted to him, why would those thoughts make her hand wander beneath her nightie and fondle her breasts until her nipples grew hard, and why would they make her reach for the wetness between her legs and coax out the desire trapped inside her with a hot surge of pleasure that made her blood rush and her ears pound?

All of this waiting was starting to make her nervous, and she wondered what was taking her father so long to come back and get her. He had been shuttling people to the church for the past forty-five minutes, and the bride was the only one left. Walking into the sunroom to get a better view of the road, she was overwhelmed with memories of all the afternoons spent there with Lily: practicing ballet moves to Tchaikovsky, acting out the entire *Jesus Christ Superstar* rock opera during Holy Week, talking and giggling and sobbing over boys. They had been there for each other, helping each other figure out the boys they were interested in - up until James Gentile, who had been impossible to figure out, and Rick Rotula, who wasn't worth figuring out. The more she thought about it, the more relieved Iris was that Lily had Joe now. That she finally had someone who could show her a good time, someone who didn't play games with her, someone who knew how to treat a girl.

It looked like things might work out for them both after all. Lily could still become a performer, even if her original plans had been thwarted. Maybe she could sing with a band, or act in one of those community theatres. It might not be Broadway, but it was better than letting her talent dry up and wither. And she could go on to college any time. Just like Iris could, once she settled in and learned enough Italian. Maybe she would pursue the study of languages; she could become a translator, or an interpreter. Or a mother, if that happened first. She'd see what worked out best, then take it from there. She'd cross that bridge when she came to it.

The honking of a horn and the flashing of headlights snapped her out of her reverie as her father pulled into the driveway. He had come to pick up the prize for today's lucky winner of the great Capotosti Giveaway.

36. LILY

Joe continued to whisk Lily away for Sunday dinners, holiday celebrations, and countless Diotallevi family birthday parties, where she was enthusiastically welcomed as a displaced child from a broken home, even being awarded her own place at the dinner table. They fed her with home-cooked meals and compassion seasoned ever so delicately with pity. The flavor was sweet on Lily's tongue. She quickly became accustomed to the routines of her adopted family, spending more time with them and less time at home, where supper often meant a peanut butter and jelly sandwich, or a can of soup warmed on the stove. At home, Lily felt like a boarder; at the Diotallevi's she felt like one of the family.

Lily hadn't been able to make a definitive decision when Joe asked her to choose between him and college, so she just never brought the issue up again and put off taking any action. She quit her job at Burger King and took a full time position in customer service at SaveMart. Instead of assembling Whoppers, she spent her days assembling toys and small pieces of furniture for customers who preferred to pay a fee rather than wrestle with cryptic instructions that had probably been translated from Japanese. The job offered her more hours, and even included paid health insurance. Maybe she could try to put some money away toward tuition while she thought about what to do next.

Lily couldn't imagine losing Joe and all that he had brought into her life - the security, the fun, the passion, the sense of belonging. Yet she hadn't been ready to close the door on college forever, either. The deadline to start classes for this year had passed months ago. But she could still go next year. Or in two years, or whenever her relationship with Joe came to its inevitable end.

If there was one thing Lily had learned definitively it was that no one stayed, no matter how much you loved them or needed them. It seemed like years since Iris had married Gregorio and shipped her things and her self to her new home across the Atlantic. Lily could remember singing "The Hawaiian Wedding Song" at her ceremony. She remembered the delicate crown of baby's breath Iris gave her to wear in her hair. She remembered Iris walking down the aisle, arm-in-arm with their father, slowly marching toward Gregorio. She remembered, too, watching them drive away after the reception to make their flight to New York. But for some reason, Lily could not remember saying goodbye. She must have cried; it must have been devastating for her. Wasn't it? Perhaps Lily had become so accustomed to watching people leave that it didn't hurt as much anymore, sort of like plucking your eyebrows. It really hurts at first, but if you keep doing it, the hairs just slide right out no matter how deeply rooted they are, and you hardly even feel it.

Joe would soon fade out of her life as everyone eventually did. So what was the big rush? Anyway, he was right - what would she do with a degree in theatre? If she really did have any talent, she would've been in class at that very moment. Or maybe already done with her first year, even. Someone else was living that dream now, and since Lily couldn't think of anything else for which she would be willing to conform her life - not to mention her restless behind – enough to take on the desks and demands of school for the next four years, she decided not to decide.

On Saturdays, the Diotallevis would meet at Batavia Downs for an evening of horse racing, and then animatedly regale each other over Sunday pasta with the repeated stories of four-figure trifectas lost "by the hair on a horse's ass", a defeat which meant that the mortgage, car payment, or dentist bill would have to be put off for another week, at least. The brother who had the worst night at the track was the one who went home with the greatest portion of leftover pasta, accompanied by a fistful of crumpled bills for gas and groceries, donated to him by his slightly less unlucky siblings. If you bet and you won, you had money. If you bet and you lost, you still had money. Those with good fortune bore responsibility for those who had none. They looked out for each other. They depended on one another. As Lucy would always say, "There's nothing like family."

Observing them made Lily think of Iris and of the ways she used to look out for Lily - like writing "From Iris and Lily" on all of the Christmas gifts, even though Iris had purchased them by herself with the money she earned as Uncle Alfred's secretary, or paying Lily's way at the movies, or leaving her make-up and Gee-Your-Hair-Smells-Terrific shampoo where Lily could have access whenever she wanted. The ache in her belly made her wonder what Iris was doing now.

"Do you know which horse you want to bet on?" Joe asked Lily one Saturday night. They sat together with Anthony and Big Tony around a wobbling table at The Home Stretch Cafe where racing spectators hung out, washing down dried-out turkey sandwiches with bitter coffee as they killed time between races.

"I don't know," said Lily. "Hollow Rabbit is a funny name. Maybe I'll bet on him." Lily hadn't been to the horse races since the last time Grandma Whitacre had come to visit many years ago, and she knew nothing about the track except that she'd lost the only wager she'd ever made.

"How do I know if I'm picking a good horse?"

"You gotta read the racing form," said Joe. He unfurled the booklet that was rolled up in his hand, opened it to the page that listed horses in the upcoming race, and set it down in front of Lily, flattening the curled corners with his thick hands.

"See this here?" he asked. He retrieved a short, green, eraser-less pencil from behind his ear and underlined a section of the form. "This is a previous race that Hollow Rabbit ran in. This little number means that's the position that Hollow Rabbit was in at that stage of the race."

"It says one, then two, then four, then six, then seven," said Lily. "What does that mean?"

"It means that Hollow Rabbit started out in the lead, but as the race went on, he fell behind, and then finished second last."

"Well then we don't want to bet on him!"

Joe laughed. "Not so fast," he said. "A horse has to qualify at each level, so if your horse has no business in this race he wouldn't be allowed to run it. We have to look and see who else was in that other race, and try to figure out why your horse hit a wall."

"How do you do that?"

"See this here?" Joe circled a section of the form and sidled his chair closer. The hairs on Lily's arm stood at attention as she admired his bow-shaped lips, his brown eyes intently trained on the paper in front of him. Joe continued, oblivious that she was watching him. "This tells you the finishing order of the horses in that other race. We need to see if any of those horses are also in this one - ah, see? Here's one - Triumphant. So now we have to find Triumphant and see what he did in that race." Joe scanned the form. "Here he is. See this mark?"

"What?" Lily tore her eyes from his face, and squinted at the paper. "That little x?"

"Yeah. That means that Triumphant broke in that race."

"He broke?"

"He broke stride - but it's just 'broke' for short. It means the horse lost the rhythm of his gait. Like if you're dancing, there's a rhythm, right?"

Lily nodded. Her heart swelled with pride to hear Joe speak so knowledgeably on a subject that so few people knew anything about; she could sit there all night listening to him. It was interesting how much there was to a person that you could never tell from the outside. Lily found herself wondering what other

556

surprises he held in store for her.

"And if you lose your rhythm when you're dancing, you absolutely might mess up the whole routine. Same thing happens here. If a horse breaks, it's really hard for him to get the rhythm back. They usually fall way behind the pack."

"What does that have to do with Hollow Rabbit?"

"You tell me," said Joe, placing a kiss on Lily's forehead. "Look at Triumphant's position when he broke in that race against Hollow Rabbit."

"It says that Triumphant started out second and then he was first, and then he broke."

"Good!" said Joe. "And where was Hollow Rabbit?"

"In second place!" said Lily, excited at having figured out the puzzle. "So when Triumphant broke, Hollow Rabbit was right behind him!"

"Right! And when the horse in front of you breaks, you're in big trouble. That's why when there is a horse in a particular race that tends to break, it's really important to find a horse that can get out in front of him and stay in front of him - if you're behind him and he goes down, he'll take you down with him. So now tell me - is Hollow Rabbit still a bad bet in this race?"

Lily wrinkled her nose. "It depends?"

Joe smiled. "On what?"

"On whether or not Triumphant breaks and whether Hollow Rabbit is behind him?"

"She's a friggin' genius," said Anthony, shoving a limp ketchup-soaked French fry into his mouth but not taking his eyes from the form.

"Hee-hee-hee," laughed Big Tony.

"Now," Joe told Lily, "you have to do that with all of the horses in the race and try to figure out who has the best chance of winning, according to the form. That's how you handicap a race."

"For all the good it'll do ya," said Big Tony. He slowly dragged the fingertips of his left hand back and forth along the length of his jawbone as he looked up at the tote board that displayed the odds for the race and then looked back at his form. "These jockeys are all so crooked, you might as well just close your eyes and point."

"The worst thing to do," Joe continued, "is split your money. Whether you handicap or not, you gotta commit to a horse, and don't second guess yourself - you'll go crazy. If you can't commit, you're better off sitting out until you find a race you can get excited about. 'Cause in the end, you gotta know it in here." Joe tapped on his chest with a closed fist.

"OK, here you go." Joe handed the pencil to Lily. "You have fifteen minutes till post time - but if you wait too long to choose, the teller windows will close and you'll get shut out, so you should decide within the next ten minutes. Don't over-analyze it."

Lily nervously studied the form until her mind swooned with its tiny notations and numbers as they danced on the page through her haze of concentration. She finally settled on a roan named Abracadabra.

"Abracadabra to win," said Lily, handing Joe four dollars.

"Hee-hee-hee."

"What's so funny?" Lily asked.

"Nothing," said Joe. "It's just that he's the three-to-two favorite. Lots of people think he's going to win."

"Then I did a good job, right?" Lily smiled.

"But you won't make no money," said Anthony. "A three-to-two only pays five bucks on a two-dollar bet. If you bet four bucks and he wins, you'll collect a sawbuck."

"A sawbuck?" asked Lily.

"Ten dollars," said Big Tony. "It's a waste of time to bet on him."

"But if he's the best one," said Lily, "then at least I won't lose. Gaining ten dollars is better than losing four. Isn't it?"

"You won't never strike it big with that attitude," said Anthony. "The trick is to find a long shot that has the best chance to surprise everyone."

"Even if he has the worst chance of winning, and you lose your money? That doesn't make much sense."

"That's why they call it gambling," said Anthony.

"Hee-hee-hee."

Anthony stood up and put his hand out to Joe. "Lemme have a coupla bucks," he said. "I only got five minutes."

Joe handed his brother a five-dollar bill and a single.

"If you bet that on Abracadbra," Lily said. "At least you'll get fifteen dollars."

"She's got a point," said Joe to Anthony. "I'm tapped out after this, so I hope you got toll money for the ride home."

"Let's just all pound Abracadbra to win," said Big Tony. "Maybe Lily will be our good luck charm. Lucky Lily. Hee-hee-hee."

Triumphant broke, Abracabadra won, and Hollow Rabbit came in fourth.

"How much did you have on him?" Joe asked his father.

"A lot," said Big Tony. "It's a good thing for your girl here that he won. Hee-hee-hee." He counted twenty-dollar bills out onto the table. "Twenty, forty, sixty, eighty, a hundred. Twenty, forty, sixty, eighty, two hundred." He pushed the two piles over to Anthony, and then shoved the remainder of the wad into his pocket. "That's what I owe you," he said. "And this is for you." Big Tony slid a twenty-dollar bill over to Lily.

"What's this for?"

"For picking me a winner."

Lily looked up at Joe. "Go bet it right away," he told her, laughing. "Before his luck turns bad and he comes looking for that twenty."

Between her own winnings and what Big Tony had given her, Lily had earned thirty dollars in five minutes - and she didn't have to do a thing except pick a horse. That was more than she'd earned in a week cooking and cleaning for her father, and almost as much as an entire day at SaveMart.

Lily was still buzzing with excitement as she and Joe entered the dark apartment. Lily's mother was out for the evening and she often failed to anticipate that it would get dark later on and that it might be nice to leave some lights on. Not surprising from someone who claimed to have used the rhythm birth control method yet still ended up with twelve children. Lily felt her way through the living room, and clicked on the lamp next to the couch.

"That was so much fun!" she cried.

"You were quite the star tonight, picking not one, but two winners - you sent everyone home happy." Joe took Lily in his arms. "You were just like one of us. It made me love you even more." Joe kissed Lily and then led her over to the couch. "It made me more sure than ever about something I wanna ask you." Joe sat down and motioned for Lily to sit next to him.

"What is it?"

"Lily," he began. "Ever since I first saw you, I knew you were a special girl. And now that my family has been spending time with you these past few months, they know it, too." He reached into his jacket pocket and pulled out a small red velvet box, which he handed to her.

"What is it?" Her heart pounded.

"Open the box, silly," said Joe. "And see."

Lily raised the lid to find a small ring with a tiny diamond displayed inside.

"What is it?" It couldn't be an engagement ring. She was still trying to decide about college. She was still trying to figure her life out. She scoured her mind for something appropriate to say. Something about how much she loved him, but how young they were and how she was still confused about her future. Or maybe she would say something about how much she loved him and how wonderful it would be to dismiss all those annoying questions about her future and just start living a life. She didn't feel ready to say "yes," to dismiss the vague yet persistent ideas about her dreams. Still, if she said "no," he would surely leave her right then and there. There would be no turning back.

"Lily," Joe said. "I know you had a hard time of it when you were a kid. So did I. Neither one of us had much and both of us still live in crazy houses with crazy people. I want to take care of you. Don't you want to take care of me?"

"Yes," said Lily, without hesitation.

"We can get away together." His voice cracked as he added, "I know that's not the biggest diamond in the world, and I know we will have to work really hard to build the kind of life we want - a house in Gates, a family of our own - but I will do whatever it takes. I will work night and day to make you happy." Joe's eyes filled with tears. "Please make me the happiest guy on earth. Please marry me."

Lily's heart swelled at the image - a little house with a fenced-in yard and dark-haired olive-skinned children running through the sprinkler. She saw Christmas trees surrounded by piles of gifts and Sunday mornings reading the paper in bed with Joe at her side and a cooing baby in a crib. She felt the angst and fear of an uncertain future lift from her, easing the burden she'd carried since Dolores' death. She looked at Joe and she saw the hope in his eyes as he awaited her reply. She saw how much he wanted this, how desperately he wanted her to say she would stay with him and be his wife. What she couldn't see, could not imagine, was breaking his heart. Or watching someone else leave her. In that moment, she could not imagine saying "no".

"Yes," she said. "I will marry you." A wave of joy erupted within her and she threw her arms around his neck.

"Woo-hoo!" shouted Joe. He took her face between his hands and kissed her passionately. "Let's get this thing on your finger before you change your mind!"

Joe removed the ring from the box and placed it on Lily's finger. He took Lily in his arms and kissed her with a voraciousness that reminded her of the way the bull calf from Cousin Bill's farm used to suck on the nipple of his feeding bucket - as if his life depended on it.

"Can we go upstairs?" said Joe, breathlessly. "To your room?"

"I guess," said Lily. Since her mother wasn't home, it wouldn't make much difference where they were, and it would be nice not to have the sharp zippers from the couch cushions to contend with while they made out.

Lily cleared her bed of her guitar and sheet music to make room for them and their new excitement. Joe was especially enthusiastic, charming each article of Lily's clothing until it yielded to him, one at a time ending up on the floor. Her blouse, her bra, her socks, her Calvin Klein jeans.

Lily placed her hand over Joe's as he started to slip her panties down over her buttocks.

"Let me," he said. "I want to."

"I thought you were looking forward to marrying a virgin." Lily was not prepared for this tonight. She had spent her entire life protecting her virginity, its surrender always suspended in some nebulous future. This was not the future. It was still today.

"C'mon, Lil - we're engaged now. What's the difference if we do it now or wait a few months?"

There was no difference as far as she could tell. Except that you can give a ring back. And except that she just didn't want to do this right now. Shouldn't she want to? Joe was sexy and handsome - sweet and worldly. And they were engaged. Why didn't she want to?

"I don't want to risk getting pregnant." That was a great reason. He would have to agree.

"Would that be the worst thing that could happen?"

"No," Lily said. *Yes,* she thought. "But your mother would have a fit."

"I'll pull out before I finish," said Joe. You can't get pregnant if I pull out first."

"I've heard that takes all the fun out of it for guys," she said. Someone had told her that. Was it Iris? She wished she could talk to Iris now.

"I don't care," said Joe.

"Besides," she said. "I promised myself I would save myself."

"For your husband," Joe said, covering her neck with kisses. "That's me. You did save yourself - and that's why I want you so bad right now."

While Lily was trying to convince Joe to agree that they shouldn't have sex, he had come up with his own compelling reason why he thought they should: because he wanted her so bad.

Joe lowered his Jordache jeans and lay on top of her. Maybe she was just conditioned like that dog they'd learned about in school... what was his name again? Maybe she was so used to saying "no" that saying "yes" seemed wrong, even when it wasn't.

Joe kept the steady rhythm of his body as he worked himself in-between her clamped knees, prying them apart.

"Pavlov!" blurted Lily.

"What? What are you talking about?"

"I'm sorry, I was just... thinking..." She wished she'd had more warning, more time to decide. The prospect of losing her virginity right at that moment caused her heart to race. Was it fear, or excitement? As a girl she had been charged with doing whatever she could to avoid this very experience. She was a woman now. Perhaps her virginity was an obsolete amenity, the contents of a hope chest whose musty linens needed to be aired on the line.

While Lily avoided taking a definitive stand, Joe decided for them both.

Lily's head swirled in an eddy of emotion and desire. Actually, it would be a relief to finally have the choice behind her. She was glad that Joe insisted, that he convinced her to allow him to discharge her of the dull duty of guarding her honor, yet oddly sad and disappointed that her first time would not be as she had imagined: in a fancy hotel bed, with a bottle of champagne on the nightstand, wearing a sexy negligee and a sense of wild exhaustion.

Joe's breath quickened. He thrust himself into her with such vigor that she had to squelch the cry of shock that shot up into her throat. She struggled to catch her breath as he raised his upper body onto his hands and drove himself into her with a force that lifted her buttocks from the mattress.

She panicked. "Joe!" she cried, "Don't forget to pull out."

"Shit!" Joe scrambled from the bed and bolted toward the hallway. Lily first heard the bathroom door close, then the toilet lid hitting the tank. She lay still, her heart pounding in her chest.

"Uhhh," groaned Joe. "Uhhh.... uhhh..."

The moans grew louder and closer together, then suddenly

stopped. The toilet flushed, the faucet ran, and Joe reappeared in the doorway. He put his pants on and sat on the edge of the bed.

"Now I'm going to ask you this question once," he said, "and I want you to absolutely be honest with me, OK? I promise I'm not going to get mad, just don't lie to me."

"I promise."

"Are you really a virgin?"

"Yes!" Lily cried. "Of course I am! Well, I was. I don't think I am anymore. Am I?"

"Cuz I didn't notice you bleed or anything and it absolutely didn't seem like I even hurt you just now. Did you bleed?"

"No," she said, pulling the bedspread up to her chin, covering herself. "But that doesn't mean anything, you know - I've read that sometimes when girls use tampons, they don't bleed the first time."

"Did it hurt?"

"Yeah," said Lily, wishing she had let out the cry that she now found was still lodged in her throat. "It still does."

Joe stood up, fastened his belt, and pulled his sweater on.

"What are you doing?"

"I gotta take off. I told Anthony I would meet him at OTB to listen to the last few races from Hollywood Park."

"You do believe me, don't you?" Lily asked.

"Yeah, I guess," Joe replied.

"What do you mean, you guess?" Lily asked. Her heart sank to think that she had saved herself for him, like a precious gift, only to have him cast it aside like she did whenever she came across an extra part for a crib or a stroller.

"Joe - you were my first, I swear." Her eyes stung with tears.

"That's just not how I thought it was going to be, is all."

"What did you expect?"

"I dunno," said Joe. "But it don't seem normal, is all."

They sat in silence for a few minutes, Lily berating herself for worrying about getting pregnant. They would be married soon anyway. She shouldn't have made him pull out. Now she would always remember that their first time was with her, Joe, and the toilet. If only she had just let him go, he would have enjoyed it, and who knows - maybe she would have, too. And maybe now he would be holding her in his arms instead of standing there with one foot out the door. She hoped Joe would tell her what to do next, searching for a way to make him stay, to let her have another chance at it.

"My mother won't be back until late," said Lily finally. "I thought we could put a pizza in the oven, maybe watch some TV... "

"I'm not really hungry," he said. "And like I said, Anthony is waiting for me, and I don't have any way to get a hold of him now. I'll call you tomorrow."

After he left, Lily went into the bathroom and checked herself for signs of bleeding, for some evidence to help determine whether or not her virtue had recently been surrendered, but found nothing there.

"We're only having a hundred-and-fifty people at the wedding," Lily protested. "We don't need six bridesmaids and six ushers."

"You can't ask some of the wives and not the others," insisted Lucy. Turning to Joe she said, "What's the matter with you? You can't ask some of them and not the others." Lucy rarely bothered arguing with any of the women in the family; it was much more effective for her to employ the leverage she had with her sons. But at least Lucy was interested in their plans, which was more than Lily could say for her own mother, who was too distracted to spend time on such mundane matters as buffet fare and wedding bands. If it hadn't been for Lucy and Anthony's new wife Nancy, Lily wouldn't even have known where to buy favors or what kind of flowers to order for the church.

"OK, Ma, OK - don't worry about it," said Joe. "We'll figure it out."

"And you know your brother Anthony has been out of work for three months now, so make sure the tuxedos are simple. Go with something simple. Just have plain black tuxedos."

Simple and plain. They were the colors of Lily's wedding.

"What do you think, Nancy?" Lily asked, turning her back to the mirror and looking over her shoulder to see what the dress looked like from behind. Victorian in style, the ivory dress boasted a long line of fabric covered buttons from the nape of her neck to the small of her back, accentuating Lily's slender waist and shapely behind, a feature that Joe considered one of her best. "Your eyes might be Irish, but your coolie is Italian," he'd said. Through long lace sleeves and a high lace collar, the dress both protected and revealed the promise of bare skin.

"I think it looks OK," said Nancy.

Lily turned and looked over the opposite shoulder.

"It fits," said Lily. Better to have a nice expensive wedding dress that was borrowed, than a crappy cheap one you owned. After all, it was just for the one day.

Lily felt more comfortable wearing an ivory gown; it was perfect for a woman of ambiguous virtue. Joe hadn't asked for sex again since the night of their engagement, and Lily sometimes wondered if he had asked her to do it just to make sure she was telling the truth about being a virgin, which of course didn't make much sense since that method of proof would make her virtue a moot point. She hoped that wasn't why he'd asked. She hoped that he'd wanted to make love because he loved her, and that he hadn't asked since so they would still have something to look forward to on their wedding night. She was sure the lovemaking would be better once they were married, once she wasn't worried about getting pregnant or getting caught, or about changing her mind about marrying him. She couldn't wait to have the ceremony behind her.

A week before the wedding, Joe and Lily picked up the keys to their new apartment at LaMont Manor behind the Gates Bowling Center. Joe had stayed in the apartment all week, moving small items in a carload at a time.

"Make sure I get those back," Lucy shouted after them as they maneuvered a card table and four folding chairs into the Chevy Monte Carlo, which he got on even trade for his ailing Barracuda.

Lucy stood on the front steps with a towel around her shoulders and a Winston at its permanent spot between the yellowed first and second fingers of her left hand. Lucy fancied herself a flaming redhead, and spent every other Saturday morning with her hair dripping in drugstore coloring. "No sense paying a hairdresser thirty goddamn dollars when I can do it myself for five bucks," she would say.

Over the years, Lucy's short hair had become thin and frizzed, a situation that was remedied by endless teasing and spraying, making the outline and surface of her scalp visible, as though her hair were a ball of red smoke sitting atop her head. Together with her over-arched, over-plucked eyebrows, the resulting effect was that of a woman in shock upon discovering that her head was on fire.

"Yeah, Ma - I know," called Joe. "As soon as we get some furniture I'll bring back your precious card table." He anchored the trunk lid down to the rear bumper with an old piece of clothesline and flicked his cigarette butt onto the front lawn. "Jesus Christ," he said to Lily. "You'd think the goddamn card table was made out of gold."

Lily laughed at Joe's ridicule, the way only family can get away with. She flicked her cigarette butt out the window, careful that it did not come back in where garbage bags full of Joe's clothes were making the trip to their new apartment, which would be temporary until they could save enough for a down payment on a starter house. Between Lily's position at SaveMart - which included a store discount - and Joe's job at La Casa Bella, they planned to put enough money away to move again in a year or two.

"I absolutely am not going to miss her," said Joe as they drove away, leaving Lucy on the front stoop scratching her left armpit, the cigarette dangling from her lips.

It was an ordinary morning. Ordinary May sunshine nonchalantly announced the day as Lily tumbled from her bed and wandered downstairs to make coffee. It seemed like a pretty good day to get married.

Lily's mother was on the couch, engrossed in the local section of the newspaper, apparently more interested in what was happening in the world than she was in Lily's wedding day. The bridesmaids wouldn't be arriving for a few hours, so Lily settled next to her mother with the Saturday morning comics and two slices of toast with strawberry jam.

"Hey, Mom," said Lily, smacking jam from her fingertips. "I had a really weird dream last night."

"What was it?" said Lily's mother, without looking up from the paper.

"Well, I was a deer, in the woods, running from a hunter."

Lily's mother put the paper down and turned her attention toward Lily.

"And I found this house and there was a lady inside baking cookies," Lily looked off into the distance, as she continued. "And she had this apron tied around her waist. I ran into the house and I hid under her apron. Then the lady said to me, 'Don't worry little one - hunters are not allowed to shoot doe.'"

Her mother laughed.

"Isn't that weird?" Lily asked, turning her attention back to her mother and taking another bite of toast.

"I don't know if it's weird, but it is very interesting."

"Interesting?" asked Lily.

"Let's just say it's a classic," said her mother. She lifted the paper again.

"It seemed so real. I was really scared."

Lily played the dream in her mind again, getting lost in the emotions it evoked – the terror of being chased, the relief of being protected.

"You know what I mean, Mom? It just seemed so real."

"Uh-huh," said her mother, lost again in the newspaper. "Dreams are like that."

After breakfast, Lily returned to her bedroom to collect the things she would need for the ceremony. "Well, my dress is borrowed, so I have that covered," she said to herself. "And this is new," she said, slipping the garter over her toes and sliding it into place just above her knee. "Now for something blue." She rummaged through her underwear drawer and came upon the small leather pouch that Iris had presented her with when she'd returned from that first trip to Italy. Was that really just two summers ago? Lily unknotted the drawstring and lifted out the rosary of blue crystal beads. She held it up in the morning sunlight. It sparkled like a tiny constellation in her hands.

The telephone rang and Lily's mother shouted from the living room, "Lily! Iris is on the phone!"

Lily rushed to picked up the extension in her room. "I got it, Mom! Hi, Iris! I was just thinking about you!" Though it only took a second or two for the telephone line to transport a voice across the ocean and then return its reply, the awareness of the distance between them wedged itself into the minuscule chasm of silence.

"Hello there, little bride - happy wedding day!"

"Thank you!"

"What kind of weather did you get?"

"It's really nice right now - sunny and warm. They say it will rain later, but I don't know - what's that saying again? *Sposa bagnata, sposa fortunata?*"

"*Bravissima*! A wet bride is a lucky bride - it sure has proved true for me!"

"I forgot that it rained on your wedding day," said Lily. *But at least I was there.* "I wish you were here, Iris."

The pause was longer than normal, and Iris' voice cracked when she spoke. "Me too - it's just that since we came for Christmas, you know, it was too hard for Gregorio to get off work and everything."

"Yeah, I know." *But Christmas comes every year,* she wanted to say. *This is my only wedding day.* What did it matter now? What good would it do to tell her that? She knew. She already knew.

"But we'll be there again this Christmas - that's only seven months away!"

"Yeah," said Lily. *That's not exactly the same thing.*

"Lily," shouted her mother. "The photographer is here! Come

on down and let's get you dressed!"

"I gotta go," said Lily. "The photographer is here."

"Well, have a great time today, kiddo! And remember, I love you!"

"I love you too." *But you should be here.*

"Ciao!"

"Good-bye, Iris." Lily slowly set the receiver back into the cradle. "See ya," she said as she grabbed her dress off the back of the door and walked out of her bedroom, leaving the rosary by the telephone.

Lily gathered up the long train in her arms and backed her body out of her mother's rusty old Plymouth Duster. She settled herself into the side vestibule, as the last of the guests filtered into the church. The bridesmaids sorted through the box of flowers, each one selecting a nosegay, only to discover that there was no bridal bouquet in the box.

"Hmm... they must have forgotten it," Lily remarked to her bridesmaids. "If each one of you just gives me a couple flowers, I'll have enough to make a bouquet. No one will even notice."

As Lily stood at the back of the church, the train of her gown lay twisted and crumpled behind her, the job of straightening it into a grand splay having fallen to a disinterested bridesmaid - all of whom were Joe's sisters-in-law, not one of whom Lily could call a real friend.

One by one, the bridesmaids proceeded down the aisle toward the altar. Lily stood arm in arm with her father. It was the first time she had seen him in months - since the last time Iris had been home. He jingled the loose change in his pocket with his free hand. They both faced silently forward. Lily could not wait to get to the other end of the aisle, to be relieved of the discomfort of the facade.

"He's your father," Joe had said. "You have to have him give you away."

"But he doesn't even really like me - or you, for that matter. He isn't giving me a penny for the wedding. He didn't even call me or send a card on my birthday. Why do I have to have him give me away? It's so fake."

"Because - think about how bad he would feel, how embarrassed to be at his youngest daughter's wedding, sitting in a pew with everyone else. You can't do that to him, Lil. Plus, people will ask questions, and then we'll have to tell them that your parents are divorced and everything. This way no one has to know."

Joe had become the voice of reason in their relationship, guiding Lily and protecting her from making decisions clouded by emotion. It was a comfort to have access to such unwavering clarity.

The flower girl reached the top of the aisle, which meant Lily was next. As the organ belted out "The Wedding March", Lily inhaled sharply, automatically tightened her grip on her father's arm, and stepped into the sanctuary. From behind her veil, the pews appeared to be occupied by ghostly figures, some of them snapping photos, some dabbing at their eyes with tissue, many of them staring blankly, most of them strangers. At the front of the church stood Joe, clad in an ivory tuxedo, fidgeting.

If Iris were there, she'd be sitting right in that pew in front of Henry, Louis, Violet, Jasmine, Marguerite, all with children in their arms and spouses at their sides. If Iris were there she would have been Lily's Matron of Honor, and she would have been sure the flower order was right and that Lily had a proper bridal bouquet and that her train was arranged in a perfect display behind her. If Iris were there. Lily blinked back tears.

The organ music drew Lily forward down the aisle. How curious that the instrument used to present brides to their grooms was the same used to escort unsuspecting travelers toward houses of horror in the movies.

Lily's attention was drawn to the crucifix suspended from the ceiling, appearing to hang directly over Joe's smiling face. She was gripped with fear, suddenly feeling that she didn't belong there. *It's just cold feet. Like Jesus had in the Garden of Gethsemane.* Jesus wouldn't allow her to go through with this if it was a mistake, if it wasn't meant to be. Doing the right thing doesn't always feel right. After all, he gave his life for us - saving us from ourselves was kind of his thing, right? *Dear Jesus*, Lily prayed. *If I'm not supposed to do this, please give me a sign.* Yet she couldn't imagine what kind of a sign would have the power to stop a wedding in progress, short of an earthquake or a tornado. Especially a wedding where Lucy Diotallevi was the mother of the groom. Anyway, what about all these people, all the money she and Joe had paid for the reception, all the embarrassment it would cause? Lily repeated to herself, *It's just cold feet. It's just cold feet.*

The Diotallevi side of the church held twice as many people as the Capotosti side. The modern stained glass windows cast gentle geometric patterns over them all: a splash of blue on Auntie Rosa's white head, a veil of green on Lily's mother in her simple pink suit. Lucy stood proudly in the first pew, chin held high, lips pursed and eyebrows raised, in her best effort to look refined and proper, the chatty glitter of her green beaded dress fading to a whisper as the sun slipped behind gathering clouds in the sky.

Halfway down the aisle, Lily was seized with the desire to stop. Stop walking forward. Turn around. Run back outside. Get into the car. Drive home. Go in the house and lock the door. Her gait was interrupted by an instant of hesitation, and her father turned to her. In the split moment that they looked at each other, Lily imagined him asking her, "Are you OK? Are you sure you want to do this? It's not too late to change your mind." She was ready to say, "Daddy, please get me out of here." And then he would encircle her with his arms, and walk her back out into the sunshine, to safety. Instead, he tugged on her arm, leading her forward. He must have lifted her veil, for it was raised. He must have kissed her cheek, for the scent of H'ai Karate cologne lingered on her skin. He must have walked away and left her there, because one moment she was holding his arm, and the next she was holding Joe's.

The music stopped. Someone coughed. The back door of the sanctuary creaked, announcing a latecomer. Thunder rumbled in the distance. The priest's lips started to move. Indiscernible sounds tumbled out into air.

Lily looked at Joe. He smiled and winked. He had been her only friend these past couple years. The acrimony between Lily's parents went endlessly on, her father refusing to divorce his wife on the grounds of abandonment, and her mother - in the absence of documented proof of any sort of abuse - having no legal grounds of her own. They were locked together in separation, even more violently and hopelessly than they had been in marriage. Till death do us part.

"I, Lily Elizabeth Capotosti, take you, Joseph Michael Diotallevi, to be my lawfully wedded husband..." Lily repeated the promise of undying love and fidelity doled out to her by the priest. She wasn't yet twenty; forever seemed like a very long time.

The congregation recited prayers. They stood, sat down, knelt, and raised themselves up again on cue until at last Lily found herself facing them, being announced by the priest as "Mr. and Mrs. Joseph Diotallevi!" As the organ pounded out the recessional, the congregation erupted into applause. Lily heaved a sigh of relief. *It's over.*

Lily and Joe walked arm in arm back down the aisle toward the open doors and out into pounding rain and flashes of lightning.

Hi, Iris:

Reading about our wedding days made me think of those "Fractured Fairy Tales" that they used to have on the Saturday morning cartoons when we were kids. Do you remember them? They started with this little Fairy Godmother trying to open the cover of a book and she wouldn't have the strength to do it, and each time, the book would slam shut on her. The stories were all convoluted, but ironically, they still ended well. So whether you get the real fairy tale like you did or a the fractured one like I did, it all comes down to the ending, I suppose.

It makes me wonder: If we had known what our lives were going to be like today, would we have even believed it? Would we have made different choices back then? Could we have?

I remember your wedding so vividly, but for the life of me, I can't remember saying goodbye to you. It's like I just ripped out that page of the story.

This morning when I was out on my bike ride, I was listening to my iPod and "Your Auntie Grizelda" came on - Peter Tork of The Monkees! I clearly recall having a major crush on him when I was a young girl, but now I see that he wasn't nearly as cute as Davy Jones, and he didn't have a good voice, and I sort of remember that I chose him precisely because I thought he was undesirable. This would mean that he would be more likely to be available and of course, more likely to want me. Who wants to be Davy Jones' girlfriend? Wouldn't you live your life in fear that he would leave you for someone better?

So much of what we thought we knew back then was because, as Peter sang, we "only know the things they want you to know." Makes me wonder what I don't know now.

I hope I pull myself out of this funk soon, though. This story is getting to be a real bummer. Can I skip ahead and see how it turns out?

Love,
Lily

Dear Lily,

I remember certain details about my wedding day so vividly, but the rest is a blur. I suppose I must have been ecstatic, just twenty years old, the leading lady in my own fairy tale, romanced by a dashing Italian man, whisked away from a wacky family, a rotten climate, a lifetime of dressing up in too many responsibilities and having nowhere to go.

I wanted to see what my face looked like on my wedding day, so I dragged out a box of the snapshots friends and family mailed to me back then, which never found their way into anything remotely resembling a wedding album. The colors have faded, but not the smile on the bride's face. *Radiosa,* that's what Gregorio called me. Radiant, as befits a bride. Everyone was smiling in the pictures, except for you and Dad. No one sent me any pictures of Mom.

I wish I had a photograph of me standing alone in the living room, after everyone had gone to the church. I can't imagine how all the emotions, expectations, and doubts I was feeling could have possibly fit into the expression of my eyes, the curve of my lips, the texture of my skin.

I remember just as clearly when I called you on your wedding day. I had tossed and turned all night, wondering what you were doing, how you were feeling, whether you needed anything. I was so mad that day. Mad at myself for not realizing in time how badly I wanted to be there. Mad at Gregorio for not reading my mind or knowing me well enough to insist that I go. Mad at you for not adding a note when you sent the invitation, begging me to come. Then the anger turned to sadness, the sadness to tears, the tears to silence, and life went on.

I think we both already knew that a wedding wouldn't make a marriage, any more that being born gave us a life. But we had to start somewhere, didn't we?

Love,
Iris

More from authors Angela and Julie Scipioni

The story continues...

How do the decisions that Iris and Lily have made impact their lives? What challenges will they face as they respectively navigate marriage and adulthood? What are the ramifications for them, and what happens to their relationship now that they are separated by an ocean?

For the complete story of *Iris & Lily*, read Book Two and Book Three

Iris & Lily is also available in ebook form.

Visit IrisandLilytheNovel.com

Made in the USA
San Bernardino, CA
25 March 2017